ANASTASIA

SOPHIE LARK

INTERIOR ART: LINE MARIA ERIKSEN
INSTAGRAM: @LINEMERIKSEN

COVER & INTERIOR DESIGN: EMILY WITTIG
INSTAGRAM: @EMILY_WITTIG_DESIGNS

COVER DESIGN: NATHAN MELO
INSTAGRAM: @WHITEDOG_STUDIOS

SOPHIE LARK
WHERE TO START

romantic suspense

BRUTAL BIRTHRIGHT
1. BRUTAL PRINCE
2. STOLEN HEIR

dark romance

SINNERS DUET
1. THERE ARE NO SAINTS
2. THERE IS NO DEVIL

My Website   Amazon   Patreon

ANASTASIA

Sophie Lark

DEDICATION

For D.A.C., who knew it was time for Anastasia to get her happy ending.

For my muse Line, who inspired me every single day with her art.

And for Ry, my other half. I've never felt more powerful than when you charge me up. All the things I've done that matter most, you were right there beside me, giving me everything you have.

Xoxo

Sophie Lark

ANASTASIA SOUNDTRACK

1. 10,000 Emerald Pools - BØRNS
2. The Tradition - Halsey
3. Dreams - The Cranberries
4. Retrograde - James Blake
5. Sunlight - Hozier
6. I'm Ready - Niykee Heaton
7. Where's My Love (Acoustic) - SYML
8. NFWMB - Hozier
9. Infinity - Niykee Heaton
10. The Chain - Fleetwood Mac
11. Once Upon a December (from Anastasia) - Emile Pandolfi
12. Imagine - Jack Johnson
13. Better Days - NEIKED, Mae Muller, Polo G
14. Make You Mine - PUBLIC
15. Unstoppable - Sia
16. Rasputin - Boney M.
17. Problématique - Lenovie
18. Kwaak (mazurka) - Andoorn

Spotify   Apple Music

PREFACE

I think what captivates us about Anastasia is our dream of what could have been. Anastasia's death was so tragic, I wanted to give her another life.

This book is not a retelling of any other Anastasia story. It's set in 1919 in a world similar to ours, but with magic.

This is my fantasy of the happy ending Anastasia deserved. Not because she was a Romanov, but because she was a human.

I want all of you to have the happy ending you deserve—it's why I love writing romance.

–Sophie

ST. PETERBURG
TSARISKAYA SELO
RIGA
RUSYA
GUMBINNEN
LORNE MOUNTAIN
FROST FOREST
COSSACK VILLAGE
EPPES

PART ONE

prologue

FIRST BLOOD

Gezirah Palace Hotel
Cairo, Egypt

Husani sat in the lounge of the Gezirah Palace Hotel in his favorite seat at the end of the bar. The bartender kept him stocked with free seltzer and mango juice because Husani was hard at work, though from the outside it looked as if he were doing nothing more than leaning on his elbow, watching the queues of Albion tourists waiting to take the steamer up the Nile to view the pharaonic remains.

The guides wore loose white tunics and turbans, while the tourists, ignorant of the blazing desert sun and sand, dressed in layers of dark wool, the men in bowler hats, the women in petticoats that reminded Husani of layered cakes. They looked pink and sweaty and miserable.

Inside the hotel was cool as the breeze from a tomb. The airy archways and marble fountains attracted aristocrats from all over Europe. They ignored Husani, having no idea how much of their comfort they owed to him.

Husani was a little shorter than average, slightly built, with shaggy hair and a deep brown tan. The hotel paid him enough that he was remarkably spruce for someone born in a brothel and raised in an orphanage. The Serene Sisters had been quick with the switch but they'd taught him to read, which he viewed as the greatest gift he'd ever receive.

He wiled away the long hours at the hotel burning his way through any book he could get his hands on. He'd made a deal with the housemaids where they passed along novels abandoned by departed guests and he provided unlimited ice for their water.

Currently, he was nearing the end of *The Scarlet Pimpernel*. Husani was lost in a world of ruffly French frocks and false-bottomed picnic baskets when a woman entered the lounge.

All sorts of beautiful and stylish people frequented the Gezirah, yet this girl yanked his head around like she'd hooked a finger in his mouth and pulled. It was something in the way she moved, gliding above the corner of his page like she was underwater and everyone else in dry air.

Husani wondered if she was a dancer. She wore embroidered slippers and silk trousers with a head wrap of the same material. Her glossy dark hair hung loose underneath, black as an Egyptian's though her skin was fair.

She took a seat at the bar, just three down from Husani. With all the empty chairs, she could easily have taken a seat by the window overlooking the fountains. Her eyes met his as she slipped onto the stool. She tucked a strand of hair behind her ear. Her hands looked smooth and soft as cream. Husani could imagine her making shapes with them like a belly dancer.

She asked the bartender for a gin and tonic. Her voice was lower than he expected and sounded close, right in his ear almost. The little hairs on the back of his neck stood up. He could feel every shift in the air.

Even Monto, who'd been serving drinks at the hotel for thirty years, couldn't help staring.

"On the house," he muttered.

Husani wanted to tell the woman she'd gotten the only free drink he'd ever heard of out of Monto. He'd love to tell her just about anything but never would have had the guts if she hadn't turned and looked right at him. Her velvety eyes slid over the spine of his book.

"I've read that one."

She said it like a secret, like they might be the only two who'd ever read it. Husani was dying to reply with something brilliant but his brain had emptied out like a sieve. He hadn't realized he was even holding a book anymore.

"Did you like it?" he blurted. His voice cracked like a kid's.

The girl only smiled.

"Immensely. I love a good disguise."

"Are you an actress?"

That voice ... it'd be wasted on a dancer.

"A writer, actually."

She might as well have said she was the goddess Isis. Writers were the source of everything he loved best.

"What do you write?"

"Poetry, mostly."

"I'd love to hear some."

Now her smile was both warm and approving.

"I'm glad you know that poetry ought to be heard, not read."

Husani felt tipsy, as if he'd been drinking much more than mango juice.

Rashly, he said, "I might like to be a writer. Someday."

"The man who waits for 'someday' waits all his life ..." She swirled her straw lazily, her nails lacquered red.

"I've written a few things. Just scribbles, really. But sometimes, once in a while, there's a line I think could turn into something ..."

"And what do you do when you're not writing?" she said in that lilting, teasing voice. He found himself leaning closer to her, the way a plant will grow toward a window.

"You're looking at it right now."

She raised an eyebrow.

"Drinking mango juice?"

"No." He flushed, wishing he were allowed to have a proper drink. He'd have ordered a gin and tonic himself, and then they'd have had all the more in common. "I'm ... well, let me show you."

He took his chance to slide off his stool and slip onto the one directly next to hers.

"May I?"

He put his hand close to her glass.

"Go ahead."

She leaned in, lips parting slightly.

He pressed his palm against the side of the tumbler. The drink frosted over in an instant, so cold that a curl of condensation rose in the air like a ghost of a breath.

"So beautiful. Like lace ..." She trailed one dark red nail against the side of the glass where the frost had formed shapes. She raised the glass to her lips and sipped gin so cold it must feel like a thousand tiny blades down her throat.

"Incredible," she said, almost in a growl.

A shiver ran down Husani's spine. Something else happened in his trousers that forced him to press his knees together and turn toward the bar. He was sweating, and he turned up the cold automatically.

The girl let out a sigh, her shoulders relaxing.

"Much better. Is that you?" Her eyes closed with pleasure.

"Yeah." His voice was steady now, confident. "The ice, the frozen sherbet, and all of this ..."

He swept his hand around to indicate the entire hotel at a perfect seventy-two degrees at all times, a literal oasis in the desert no matter the temperature outside.

"Remarkable," the girl murmured. "I've never seen that kind of range."

Husani thought he might just jump off a bridge to keep impressing this woman. The way she looked at him made him feel ten feet tall.

"What's that accent?" he said. "Are you ... Italian?"

"Further away than that."

Her smile showed only the edges of her teeth. Husani couldn't stop looking at her mouth.

He'd never been in love but he was starting to think he'd like to try it. Surely it was destiny how this girl appeared all alone just as the sun was going down. Husani was only allowed to leave when the heat of the day had all bled away.

He saw a vision of the two of them walking hand in hand down the plaza with strings of colored flags overhead, bathed in sweet hookah smoke and the music seeping from the doorways of the tea shops. She could recite one of her poems to him in that voice that felt like fingers stroking through his hair, and he might possibly have the courage to read her a few lines of a story in return.

"Have you seen much of the city yet?" he asked her. "The spice bazaar or the hanging gardens? I could show you, I've lived here all my life ..."

"Could you really? I haven't seen anything yet."

Her smile was like fireworks in his head.

His mind leaped far ahead of any reasonable reality and ran straight through a kiss or even a night together, all the way to them curled up in a little flat on the north side of the city, writing all day long while eating sun-warmed figs and laying on cushions with their bare feet entwined.

He saw this vision so clearly that it almost seemed to float in the air before his eyes. When he snapped back, the woman hadn't seemed to notice.

4

He scrambled off the stool.

The sky had gone completely dark by the time they exited the hotel. Husani was too used to the stunning desert sky to even look up, but the girl stood still and gazed upward, the starlight turning her cheeks silvery.

When she turned to him, she seemed to have come alive in a whole new way.

"Anything lovely by daylight is even better by night."

"*You* are," Husani breathed.

She smiled all the way now, teeth glinting.

"I want to see the moon over the river."

She led him down toward the water. Husani thought he should call out to her not to get too close—the river was thick with crocodiles. But he felt a strange and dreamy warmth that didn't allow him to believe there could actually be any crocodiles tonight.

"Come on." She held out her pale hand.

He seemed to fall rather than walk to her.

Her face drew closer to his. He drowned in eyes so dark they seemed all pupil.

Even in that delirium, he held onto a shred of the old caution he'd learned in the orphanage. He only closed his eyes partway. As their lips touched he saw, for a fraction of a second, the way her eyes seemed to flicker and her face changed in some incomprehensible way, as if someone had gripped the crown of her hair and pulled tight, yanking the skin back.

Ice blasted from his palms, smashing into her chest.

The ice didn't come from him exactly, but from the air directly in front of his hands. It rocketed outward, half-formed, viciously cold, hitting her with a force that should have frosted her heart.

She staggered, making some inhuman sound. Hair stood up all down his arms. She rushed at him and he tried to hit her again and again, throwing ice with both hands, pouring out every ounce of the extraordinary power he possessed. She slipped and darted like an eel, a flash in the dark he could hardly follow.

Her nails slashed out, catching him across the face, the throat, the belly. It was white-hot heat and instant agony. The torn flesh bled heavily, especially at his neck. He clamped his hand over the wound, warmth leaking through his fingers.

"Stop!"

A male voice rang in his ears.

Husani felt himself freeze in place as if he were the one encased in ice. He couldn't move. Couldn't speak. Couldn't even breathe. His chest was stiff as iron, unyielding against the automatic hitching of his lungs.

"I told you to wait for me," the man said quietly.

His voice had the same quality as the woman's, his words like a physical touch on the skin. But his anger chilled Husani to the bone.

Not the woman. Low and furious, she said, "I've *been* waiting."

He could feel their fury like a storm behind him, two forces clashing silently in the air, but couldn't so much as turn to look. The moon shimmered on the river. Husani's head swam. He'd been more than a minute without air.

A slight rustle and the tall, spare figure appeared before him.

"Careful." The girl came around his other side. "He's stronger than he looks. He cools the entire hotel."

The pleased fisherman, displaying what she caught.

"It won't matter," the man said. As he exhaled, his breath shimmered a moment, violet in the air. Power sparked at his fingertips. Husani had thought he was like the girl, some sort of creature, but no ... this one was a sorcerer.

His pale blue eyes were blind like a mask, intently staring but empty all the same. He wore a monk's robes.

He seized Husani by the throat and lifted. Black sparks burst before Husani's eyes. He still hadn't taken a single breath. Claustrophobia overwhelmed him—trapped in his own body, his own mind.

Still, he struggled and fought in the only way he could—blasting all the cold left in him outward into the hand clutched round his throat.

The sorcerer ripped back his arm, too late—black spots already bloomed like mold on his palm. Husani dropped to the ground. The woman leaped on him as the man snarled, "*No!*"

Too late. She'd already hit Husani so hard it felt like his head spun 'round. He lay on the ground, crumpled, twisted.

"You killed him," the sorcerer said, cold with fury.

"Not yet," she panted.

It was only then Husani realized he'd never learned her name. She'd never said it, and somehow he'd never thought to ask.

"He's no use to me dead."

The sorcerer's displeasure was rough against the skin. Something that scraped you open and laid you bare.

His anger was directed at the girl, but even Husani shook beneath it.

The girl lost her grace and went rigid, curling into herself. She turned her face away, showing nothing.

She looked down at Husani. All the connection he'd felt, from her eyes to his, had vanished. He could have been meat on a plate.

"He's still breathing."

The sorcerer swept past her. He lifted Husani easily. Husani's body was a rictus of pain, twisted, broken, screaming at him. Strangled noise leaked from his lips, the sorcerer's bone-white fingers cutting off anything more.

He peered into Husani's face. There was nothing human at all in that gaze—it was the look of a cold kind of god, examining something of interest.

Low and approving, he said, "Well done, Katya."

She lifted her head, a flush of color in her pale cheeks.

"You can get it?"

The sorcerer smiled.

White-hot pain ripped down the side of Husani's neck, an agony that made all that had come before seem trivial. This was a level unreached, undreamed of, signals screaming along every inch of his nerves, maxed-out, continuous, cranked up to full voltage.

Without knowing what he said, he begged, pleaded, babbled like a baby. He had no plan, no control, no dignity—only pure desperation to stop the pain pulling apart his brain.

"Please, stop, I beg you! Stop, please, please! I never harmed you—why are you doing this? You don't have to! I'll help you, please, I'll help you! Whatever you need, I'll do it, please I beg you, have mercy ..."

The sorcerer paused long enough to answer, his soft voice filling the break in the pain.

"I'm sorry, my friend, I truly am ... But this is necessary."

Husani's body whipped backward with a crack of spine. Something inside him was being ripped out—something wound tight round muscle, nerve, and bone. All came apart as it tore free.

The sorcerer tossed aside the empty corpse. It rolled away amongst the reeds.

He walked to the river's edge without a glance for anything else that might be lurking near. Stooping on the muddy bank, he thrust his hand into the water.

The wide, flat Nile, dark as the sky overhead, went white in an instant, ice racing outward from the sorcerer's hand. Crocodiles reared upward, frost forming in drifts around their leathery heads, glazed over, mouths open, teeth crusted with ice.

The sorcerer and the girl looked at each other, too electric to speak.

She opened her mouth but he was already standing, wiping his hand on his robe.

"Let's go. I want to get out of this godsforsaken heat."

The girl walked past Husani's body without a glance, hurrying to follow the sorcerer.

chapter 1

UNCLE COMES HOME

ANASTASIA

There was a new mystic in St. Petersburg. People said he could tell your future in a cloud of smoke and read the whole of your past in a drop of blood from your finger.

He was a healer. He cured Madame Dubois of pneumonia and vanished the scar on Liza Taneeva's cheek. Some whispered that he even raised a peasant child from the grave.

Ollie laughed at me and said I was a gullible prat.

"Once you're dead, you're dead. It's an irrevocable law of magic."

"I know that." I ripped up a dandelion in fury. "Liza says he's like nothing she's ever seen. He's a holy man from Siberia."

"Liza is easily impressed."

Ollie swung the stick she was holding, decapitating a row of Mama's peonies.

We were tramping through the gardens on the south side of the palace. Margaretta hollered at us to play outside after Alexei rode his bicycle into the urn in the semi-circular hall.

The urn was large enough that Alexei could have hidden inside it if the neck were a little wider. It toppled over, shattering so aggressively that pottery fragments scattered across the whole of the hall and all the servants came running. Even Alexei was too surprised to hide. He only stood there wide-eyed, straddling his bike, until Margaretta seized him by the ear.

"That was a gift from the Emperor of Japan!" she scolded.

"Nobody cares about some musty old urn," Alexei said. "He ought to have sent us a suit of samurai armor!"

Margaretta tossed us all outside, including Maria and Tatiana.

Tatiana was furious at being included in the eviction when she'd only been reading quietly in the library. She wouldn't speak to any of us, stalking over to the maple tree and sinking down on the swing to continue her book.

Alexei rode his bicycle through the colonnades so he could zip past the palace guards and make them all salute him in turn.

Maria followed along after Ollie and me, much slower because she kept stopping to cut flowers. She laid the blooms carefully in her basket so she could arrange them on the dinner table later.

"I want to know my future," I said to Ollie, stubbornly.

"What for? He's probably not a real oracle."

The gift of second sight was rare. Much more common were the charlatans who traveled with fairs or set up tea shops in St. Petersburg, charging two coppers to read your palm, or a silver coin to tell your tea leaves.

"Even if he is a real oracle," Ollie continued in her practical way, "everything they see is so vague it's not much use anyway. Papa says second sight is the joke of the gods. People have ruined their lives trying to avoid some dire prediction that turned out to mean something completely different."

"I wouldn't want to see my future," Maria said from where she knelt in the sunny soil. She'd stopped to cut the early spring roses, Mama's favorites. They only lasted a week. As Maria snipped the stems, fingertips perched between the thorns, petals fell from the soft, drooping heads.

"I can already tell you exactly what will happen to you," Ollie laughed. "You're going to marry a handsome soldier and have a dozen babies. You'll throw the prettiest dinner parties and your servants will steal the silverware but you'll never punish them."

Maria blushed and looked pleased. I could tell she liked the soldier part—she'd had crushes on at least a dozen officers since they started training on the parade ground at the back of the palace.

"She can't marry a commoner," I snorted.

"Uncle Michael did."

"And look at him—exiled to France."

"I don't care who I marry as long as they're Rusyan." Maria snipped the last rose and placed it atop the others. "I don't want to move away."

Ollie glanced back at Maria but kept her mouth shut.

If it was me, she would have said our parents would marry us off to whoever they liked, probably some bald cousin in Germany or Albion. There was almost no chance of Maria staying in Rusya.

Ollie was gentler to Maria. We all were, even Alexei.

I could hear him whooping and hollering. The sound came up to us in loops, which meant he was probably riding his bicycle around the fountain in the courtyard.

For a long time Alexei wasn't allowed to ride a bike or even sit on his old donkey. But he got downright depraved all cooped up in the house, so ungovernable that Margaretta threatened to turn in her notice and Papa said Alexei had to play at least.

It was no small concession. For Alexei, a bloody nose turned into a week-long ordeal and a broken arm could kill him. He had the bleeding disease, what Dr. Atticus called "haemorrhaphilia," and Margaretta called "the royal disease" because only the noble houses seemed to catch it.

Alexei had it from the day he was born. The moment the midwife cut his umbilical cord, the stump began to bleed and kept on for two weeks. Alexei got so thin and pale, he almost died right then.

He'd been trying his best to finish the job ever since. He got in more trouble than the rest of us combined and was almost never punished because what could you do to him? You couldn't whip him, and if you took away anything he liked, he went into a rage that could kill him.

He was Alexei the Terrible and all of us had to keep him alive.

Tatiana sat up on the swing, back straight, eyes unfocused.

"Uncle Nikolasha is here."

"How do you know?"

"The dogs are barking."

I had to strain my ears to hear the chorus of yips coming from the kennels, faint and distant.

"I'm surprised you didn't hear his horse coming up the road," Ollie teased her.

"I probably would have if you two weren't talking so loud."

Tatiana rose from the swing, silky dark hair slipping off her shoulder. Her muslin dress was spotless, and so were her stockings. As often happened when I stood next to Tatiana, I became aware of my own grubbiness. I'd begun playing outside by rolling down the uncut grass on the hill, and finished by kicking clods of dirt around the garden.

Ollie saw me glance between Tatiana's snowy stockings and my beat-up shins. She grinned. "You better wash up, Anastasia."

Instead I bolted for the house, knowing damn well she only wanted to beat me to Uncle Nikolasha.

Ollie sprinted after me, taking advantage of her longer legs to vault the hedges.

Smaller, stockier, and highly motivated, I put my head down and pelted past her into the house.

I dashed through the Marble Drawing Room and the Portrait Hall, Ollie's shoes clattering behind me on the polished floor.

I'd almost reached the grand entryway when Margaretta intervened, blocking the hallway with her bulk.

"Don't you dare tell me you're planning to meet your uncle looking like that!"

She seized me by the elbow and hauled me off to the closest sink while Ollie sailed past, all smiles. I kicked and hissed like a captured housecat.

Margaretta made me wash my face and hands, then she scrubbed them all over again with a rough cloth. She brushed my hair, bound it with a blue ribbon, re-tied my sash, and forced me to change socks before she'd let me go to my uncle.

By the time she released me, I was clean and stinging and utterly furious, planning all kinds of revenge.

"You can wipe that look off your face while you're at it," Margaretta said, tartly. "The Grand Duke expects a Grand Duchess, not a *Fomhoire*."

"I don't know what that is!" I shouted, though I did.

Margaretta and I had long been at odds. Our goals were diametrically opposed—she wanted me to dress and behave as a lady, while I believed that I could have been captain of my own pirate ship if only she'd stop interfering.

I hadn't seen Nikolasha in months. He'd been off in the steppes, fighting the Cossacks.

If he was back, it might mean Papa would be coming home soon, too.

Released from my torture, I dashed down to the grand entryway.

Ollie, Tatiana, Maria, and Alexei had already received their hugs. Alexei was hunting through Nikolasha's saddlebags looking for gifts. My mother crossed the foyer with hands outstretched to greet my uncle.

Liza Taneeva followed after her, hanging back because Nikolasha didn't like her and might just say it.

Nikolasha lifted my mother's hands and kissed them, saying, "Another princess? I thought there were only four ..."

"The gods will punish you for lying." My mother was so happy to see him she did look like one of us, all the worry lines smoothed away, her hair loose and soft because she hadn't been expecting anyone, wearing one of her nice cotton morning dresses and not one of the stiff gowns she would have put on to receive him.

She searched Nikolasha's face for news of Papa, or just for the pleasure of seeing features that could have been my father's.

Papa and Nikolasha were only first cousins once removed, but so alike that my uncle had been addressed as "Your Imperial Majesty" by more than one dignitary.

Both mammoth and broad-shouldered, they could best be told apart by the length of Nikolasha's beard, never trimmed and bound with gold rings on formal occasions. Because Nikolasha was precisely one inch taller than my father, he was sometimes called Big Nicholas, while Papa, still taller than every other man in the room, was known as Little Nicholas. It was their favorite joke.

I waited for Mama to finish greeting Nikolasha, then darted forward and threw myself into his arms. He swung me around twice before setting me down, saying, "This can't be my little Stassie! You've grown so big! Or you've got rocks in your pockets."

In that moment I remembered that I'd found a toad under a rhubarb leaf and slipped him into my pocket for safekeeping. He must have hopped free, because he was nowhere to be found when I thrust my hands in to check.

"Is this for me?" Alexei pulled a dagger from our uncle's saddlebag, wrenching the blade free of its sheath and swinging it around.

"Alexei!" That was as sharp as Mama got and it wasn't that sharp.

"Of course it's for you," Nikolasha laughed. "I brought shawls for the girls."

I tried not to show what I felt as my uncle took the gifts from his bag and removed the paper wrappings. He handed the red shawl to Ollie, the green to Tatiana, and the yellow to Maria.

Alexei was always getting the best gifts—swords and guns and tiny military uniforms. Meanwhile my relatives had given me an entire collection of dolls I'd never touched, itchy frocks, yards of lace, and at least two copies of *A Young Girl's Guide to Social Etiquette*.

I'd hoped for better from my uncle.

He turned to me empty-handed, the edges of his mouth twitching.

"I could give you a new shawl, little mischief, but I thought you might prefer something I found along my journey ..."

My heart rebounded. I whooped so loud that Mama gave me the look that meant three more like that, and she might actually do something.

Nikolasha retrieved a wooden box from inside his traveling coat. The box was long, with holes drilled in the side.

I took it carefully, already intuiting that it contained something alive.

The soft weight shifted as I lifted the lid.

A pair of dark eyes fixed on me, black as jet. The bird lay still in its nest of cotton, wing splinted and body wrapped in gauze to keep it immobile. Yet I had no doubt it would spear me with that wicked beak if I dared put a finger near.

"A gyrfalcon," I breathed.

"I found her in the Frost Forest. She had an arrow through her wing."

"Will she fly again?"

My uncle shrugged. "She should. It went between the bones."

"She's small."

"She's not grown yet. There was a storm, she might have blown away from her nest. You'll have to feed her and care for her until she heals."

Liza Taneeva wrinkled her nose. Mama pressed her lips together. We'd had many conversations about bringing animals in the house.

Ignoring them both, I asked, "If she can fly again, will you help me train her to hunt?"

"It's difficult," Nikolasha warned me. "A falcon's not a kitten. Especially not a gyrfalcon. It can break a dog's back when it strikes. I've seen them drive bears away from their nesting grounds."

This was too much for Alexei.

"How come Anastasia gets a falcon and Maria got a dog?"

"Because people keep gifting us animals," Mama said, exasperated. "We've kept Nikolasha standing too long. Let him clean up while I call for tea."

I HAD HOPED Liza Taneeva would leave us alone with my uncle, but of course there was no way she would miss hearing a single piece of news she could spread around the court.

Worse, she made Maria change places with her, declaring that her sciatica wouldn't permit her to sit anywhere but on the chaise, which happened to be the most comfortable chair in the room, as well as closest to the tea cakes.

She made a show of settling herself in place, smoothing her skirts, wincing dramatically.

"I never complain. Few people can endure such pain in silence, but I would never distress my friends with the truth of how horribly I suffer."

"Is it a bad day?" Mama asked, low and gentle.

Liza closed her eyes, nodding as if even speaking would be too much.

Liza often had "bad days" when visitors appeared, or an engagement was announced, or anything occurred to draw attention onto someone else.

"You should go lie down," Ollie said.

Liza's eyes snapped open, narrowing in on Ollie's face.

Ollie smiled back at her innocently.

"Maybe after tea," Liza said. "I'd never leave the empress to entertain on her own."

"It's only Uncle," Alexei said. "He's family."

Now it was Alexei's turn to receive Liza's glare because he put a little too much emphasis on the word "*he.*"

Liza was not family, and barely even noble. Tatiana told me other women at court were offended that Mama made such a friend of her when she was nobody, really.

The truth was Mama was shy. She hated all the visiting and receiving, all the balls she was supposed to host but didn't. She was friends with Liza over anybody else because Liza pursued her so hard and made loving her so easy. She demanded it really, and that was Mama's weakness, though only a few people had discovered it—she tried to be hard, but she was soft when you pushed. Alexei never had to push. I only could if Papa wasn't around.

I disliked Liza much more than Margaretta. Margaretta was strict and bossy, but never cruel. She'd tell you to your face if she was going to get you in trouble. Liza would smile at you and two weeks later you'd get a slap for something you didn't even know about. She was a sneaky little snake and every one of us children hated her, even Tatiana who got praised like an angel by every adult alive.

Mama, busy with the tea things, missed the filthy glare Liza shot at Alexei. She was arranging the samovar and the eight china cups, ringing the bell for more sandwiches because Uncle Nikolasha was sure to be starving after such a long journey.

I set the wooden box containing the gyrfalcon underneath my chair for safekeeping, wondering what I should feed her.

Nikolasha strode into the room, hands and face freshly washed, beard combed. He'd removed his traveling coat but hadn't changed his clothes, so he still smelled of campfires, which was not only the best smell, but one you couldn't be calm around.

Mama heaped his plate with cake and sandwiches. She poured out the tea, then clasped her hands on her lap, saying, "And how is Nicky?"

"Miserable," Nikolasha said. "He misses you terribly."

Papa was so lovesick over Mama that everybody talked about it. A huge portrait of her hung right next to his desk and he hated going anywhere without her. He'd give her anything he even thought she wanted, which drove his family crazy.

I'm sure they wished they never let him marry her. Grandma Minnie didn't stay at the palace long after the wedding. Mama said it was all their pride—she was a minor German princess and they only let it happen in the first place because she was Queen Victoria's favorite.

My great-grandmother Victoria didn't like the plan one bit, but couldn't say so publicly. She told Mama she'd be mad to run off to a country of scheming nobles and violent peasants and a million miles of outlands stuffed with gods know what. Mama just smiled and said, "Nicky will protect me."

Mama loved being Queen of Rusya. She immediately started calling herself Rusyan, not German. The people still called her the foreign empress.

The courtiers were nice to her face but sniped behind her back. Tatiana heard all their complaints. They loved the parties and balls; they hated having to attend church every week and being told if their gowns were too low cut.

Papa let Mama do whatever she liked. He even moved us away from the grand old Winter Palace in the center of St. Petersburg to little Alexander Palace out in Tsarskoe Selo.

It was only supposed to be a summer home, but it was much prettier, hidden away in Alexander Park, with acres of woods, rivers, an island, and a menagerie. "No people peering in your windows," Mama said, which they really could from the streets that ran directly below her old rooms.

Grandma Minnie said, "Nicky would lie down on hot coals for that woman."

"Yes," Aunt Xenia murmured. "And she'd walk right over him."

"A stack of petitions the size of a small child piles up on his desk while he's planning a holiday for her in Nice. Though what she's resting from, I couldn't say ..."

They didn't know I could hear them, because I happened to be hiding behind their sofa.

Mama was delicate and frail. She got tired easily, while Grandma Minnie could open a hospital, build a road, and visit a factory all before lunchtime. Grandma was adored by the people. I'm sure it bothered my mother when they cheered so loudly for Minnie's carriage, and only hers.

All of this is to say, Mama only had a few close friends, so Liza was lodged in tighter than a limpet.

Nikolasha was the exception—he'd fight a bear for her.

"I have a long letter for you to take back to Nicky," Mama said. "Almost a novel, really."

"It'll be the last, I hope," Uncle said, smiling under his beard. "We've routed the Cossacks. Their Ataman's agreed to terms."

Mama gave a squeak of relief, sinking into her chair. "Thank the gods."

"You won't like this next bit as much ... Nicholas wants Alexei brought to the steppes to witness the surrender."

"It's too far," Mama protested. "And too dangerous."

Her hands covered her mouth. Liza Taneeva pulled them back down to her lap and patted them under her own swollen, many-ringed fingers.

"He'll be safe with the Grand Duke," she soothed Mama. "It's time for Alexei to take responsibility, to see how these things are done ..."

There was a nasty glint in her eye.

"I want to go!" I cried.

I desperately wanted to see my father and couldn't bear the thought of Alexei going on an adventure while I was stuck at home.

I could tell Ollie felt the same, though her sense of dignity wouldn't allow her to shout *Me too!* in front of Uncle Nikolasha.

"A war camp is no place for a girl." Mama shut me down. "It's bad enough for Alexei."

"And you're wild enough already." Liza rapped me sharply on the knee with her unopened fan. "Sit up straight and close your legs."

That was insult on injury. I had to swallow down what I'd like to say to Liza Taneeva, or risk being sent to my room and miss everything else Uncle was sure to tell us.

At that moment, I noticed a small brown toad perched on a stack of leather-bound books next to the chaise. He was so still that he might have been an ornament, if not for the flick of a lid passing over one beady little eye like a transparent shade. I recognized him at once.

Hastily, I gulped down the rest of my tea and caught him under my cup, holding him trapped against the saucer. Ollie saw and grinned.

"How did you defeat the Cossacks?" Tatiana asked our uncle.

"It was damned difficult," Nikolasha said. "I've never seen such horsemen. They ride like demons, and I swear their horses can understand them."

"Can they?" Maria asked.

"Maybe." Nikolasha shrugged. "Powers are always more common where they're needed. That's why you see so many pyromancers here—what's a Rusyan need more than fire, eh?"

"Sandwiches," Ollie said, taking two more for herself.

Nikolasha scooped up the last of the spice cake and ate it in a bite. "If my horse could talk, he'd never stop asking for oats."

"And if Hans and Boris could speak, they'd always be arguing," I laughed.

Hans and Boris were Nikolasha's twin borzois. They traveled everywhere with him and were likely gorging themselves out in the kennels. I planned to visit them after tea.

"We weren't fighting only the Cossacks," Nikolasha told us. "At night the wolves would come. They harried our lines, picked off our men. When we weren't fighting the Cossacks, we had to hunt the wolves."

"How did you hunt them?" Alexei was half out of his chair with excitement.

"A wolf close to the city might only be the size of a dog, but the ones in the Frost Forest are twice as large. Cunning, too. They hide their tracks, they circle around. But they can't disguise their scent. When Hans and Boris catch a trail, they run the wolf down. Trap it between them so it can't turn and bite. They hold it there while I jump down and cut its throat."

Maria let out a squeak of terror, wide-eyed and shivering.

Liza's mouth turned puckered and sour. She pointedly set down the last bite of her cake. This was precisely the sort of talk she didn't like.

"What a life you lead, Nicholas Nikolaevich. It must be so difficult for you to readjust to the demands of polite society when you return to civilization."

My uncle held out his cup so my mother could refill it.

"Indeed, Liza Taneeva. I am often discomfited when I leave the savagery of the outlands and return to the *politeness* of St. Petersburg."

Liza gave Nikolasha a thin smile.

While her head was turned, I plucked the cup off the saucer balanced on her lap and replaced it with my own.

Still holding my uncle's eye, Liza delicately gripped the thin china handle and lifted the cup to her lips. The toad, sensing that his moment had come, leaped upward with all his might, landing in an ungainly sprawl on the bridge of Liza's nose.

Sciatica forgotten, Liza Taneeva leaped from the chaise, shrieking and flailing. Unable to bring herself to touch the toad, she spun in circles while the toad clung on for dear life.

Ollie roared with laughter. Maria rang for the servants. Alexei chased after Liza, trying to bat the toad off her nose. Calmly and coolly, Tatiana suggested, "If you'd hold still, Liza Taneeva ..."

It was Uncle Nikolasha who caught hold of Liza and held her so my mother could pluck the toad off her face. She cupped it gently in her hands, walked to the window, and released it out into the garden.

Then she turned to face us, stern as I'd ever seen her.

I'd stayed quiet in my chair through all the madness, willing myself not to laugh.

That was my mistake. Mama's blue eyes zeroed in.

"Apologize at once."

Hanging my head, I mumbled, "I'm sorry, Liza Taneeva."

"Go to your room," Mama said. "You'll have no pudding for a week."

Gathering the little wooden box from beneath my chair, and careful not to make eye contact with Ollie or Alexei, I scurried away.

I knew I'd gotten off light—Liza was still in hysterics. Mama would have to coddle her for an hour at least.

The prize was worth the punishment.

chapter 2

AN UNEXPECTED GIFT

Mama let me rejoin the others for dinner, though she held firm on the punishment of no pudding.

Because Uncle Nikolasha was there, Aunt Xenia and Princess Irina joined us, along with Grand Duke Dimitri Pavlovich.

Princess Irina was seventeen, same as Ollie. They'd been best friends all their lives.

That evening they were whispering about some gorgeous man who reined in his horse to stare at Irina.

That was probably as common as hiccups for Irina, who was all the best bits of my father's family in one person. All the colors on her seemed to go together just right—black hair with a hint of blue in it, eyes that were blue with a bit of black, marble skin and a body like a statue. No wonder a famous artist begged to paint the picture of her that now hung in St. Isaac's Cathedral.

Her being so beautiful was useful because it balanced Ollie being so famous. Neither of them had to be jealous.

Aunt Xenia had plenty to be jealous about. She had the kind of looks people called "handsome" and she was smarter than her brothers, which put her in a terrible mood most of the time. They only listened when she made them.

Right now she was telling Nikolasha all the things he did wrong fighting the Cossacks. Nikolasha said he would love it if Xenia handled the next campaign.

Dimitri Pavlovich sat next to Alexei, trying to amuse him so he wouldn't torment Ollie. Ollie hated when Mama forced her to mind Alexei during dinners. She was barely behaved herself and not at all maternal.

Alexei was never at his best with company. He was especially intolerable that night because he wanted to sit at the head of the table in Father's place. When Mama put him at the foot instead, he kicked the table legs until the plates rattled.

Dimitri distracted him by snuffing and re-lighting the candles without touching them. That only goaded Alexei into begging for other things to be set afire, starting with the napkins and the drapes.

Dimitri Pavlovich was the next thing to an orphan. He practically lived at the palace with us.

Before this he stayed with Uncle Sergei, until an anarchist chucked a bomb under Sergei's carriage and blew it up in the street right in front of the house. Poor Dimitri had to run out and pick up pieces of our uncle from the gutter before they were trampled and dragged away.

Dimitri had been sleeping in the east wing ever since, playing tennis and dominos and drinking Papa's favorite Madeira until he fell asleep in the sun. In the fall he'd return to cavalry school.

He was a magnificent rider but too gentle for the military. He had a soft face that looked like it might cry and a full mouth like a girl's.

His crush on Ollie was so established we didn't even tease him about it anymore.

Ollie said he was like a brother, and anyway she was too young for lovers.

That didn't stop a fleet of ambitious young princes from coming to visit us. Ollie was the prize as the eldest—she'd been receiving proposals since her ninth birthday.

When Prince Carol of Romania came to examine her, Ollie dressed as ugly as possible and deliberately didn't bathe for three days beforehand. Tatiana overheard Carol complaining to his mother on the phone that he had "no idea why so much had been made of the Romanov beauty. He could see nothing of it."

Ollie howled and said she'd do the same to anyone else who came calling.

Tatiana said books were ten times more interesting than any boy.

Maria would frankly admit to crushes on anyone who smiled at her, which was everybody.

She was sitting on Dimitri's other side, giggling over his tomfoolery with the candles almost as much as Alexei. Dimitri held his hand above the flame, fluttering his first three fingers as if he were sprinkling salt in a stew. The flame twisted beneath his fingertips, forming shapes: a stag with antlers, then a hare.

"Do a dragon!" Alexei commanded, eyes fixed on the fire.

Dimitri stretched his palm flat. The flame died down to barely a glow. Then, as Dimitri snatched his hand into a fist, the fire leaped upward in the shape of a dragon, wings outstretched, before blowing out a ball of fire that singed the ceiling.

"*Dimitri!*" Xenia gasped.

Dimitri only cared if Ollie had seen. She gave him an approving look.

"Not bad, m'boy," said Uncle Nikolasha. "You should have joined the pyromancers, not the cavalry."

"I like horses."

"The Japanese pyromancers gave us a hell of a time in Port Arthur," Nikolasha speared a piece of venison on his fork. "Wiped out most of our fleet. Flung fireballs so hot even the steel ships caught ablaze."

He popped the meat in his mouth and chewed with gusto.

"Sandro said half their army can manipulate fire," Aunt Xenia said. Sandro was her husband, Grand Duke Alexander Mikhailovich.

"I don't know about half, but a hell of a lot of them. They don't call it the Kingdom of the Rising Sun for nothing. They burned us like dry grass."

I shivered. Nikolasha had a soldier's callousness in describing the loss of three-quarters of our navy. Papa came home with burns all down his left arm and an agreement with the Japanese that satisfied neither country.

"I hope we'll have peace for a while," Papa had said.

Less than a year later, the Cossacks rebelled and he had to leave again.

I couldn't remember the last time we'd truly had peace. Maybe I'd never experienced it.

Even here in St. Petersburg, barely a month went by without a riot or a strike. Only the week before, a hundred thousand factory workers put up barricades in the garment district, until the city guard broke them all down and dispersed the crowd with whips.

"Can we talk about something else?" Mama asked.

"Of course," Nikolasha said easily.

He took a large swig of wine before settling on a new subject, giving Xenia time to cast around her beetle-black eyes and fix upon me.

"Has Anastasia begun to manifest yet?"

That was a question I loathed. I squirmed in my seat, not wanting to admit that I hadn't yet shown a shred of ability.

"She's only eleven," Mama said calmly. "She has plenty of time yet."

Thirteen was the commonly accepted cutoff by which a child would show evidence of their magical abilities.

Nobles commemorated that event with a public display. Ollie and Tatiana had performed theirs with all the elegance and skill one would expect from Romanov princesses.

Ollie set up a network of a hundred hanging lamps and illuminated them with a touch of her finger, to the delighted applause of the court.

Tatiana stood in a field and named the composition playing on the gramophone over a mile away inside the palace. That alone would have impressed the spectators, but ever the showman, she performed the encore of hanging Mama's wedding ring from the topmost bough of the old oak tree and bringing it down with an arrow through the band.

Mama and Papa were pleased. The courtiers showered Tatiana with praise. She only scowled. I knew she was angry that she hadn't yet shown any of Papa's ability. None of us had.

That was another thing Mama was blamed for. She wasn't particularly powerful. She could move objects without touching them, but nothing very heavy—only what she could have moved with her hands. People said she diluted the Romanov blood, failing to pass along the gift that had kept us in power for three hundred years.

Maria held my hand under the table, squeezing my fingers.

"Never mind," she whispered. "Something will come."

Maria was nervous about her own demonstration in a few months.

At least she had a power—she could make a flower bloom if she cradled it in her hand and whispered to it. She liked to lay out amongst the living things. Sometimes I thought they made her live, too. When she came back inside, her skin was soft as a petal, her cheeks pink as roses.

Most people had at least a little magic. But sometimes a person developed no powers at all, and there was nothing that could be done to fix it.

Even Alexei, ill as he was, had shown bursts of ability. Just last week he knocked Margaretta's tea into her lap without touching it.

I was the only one who had never exhibited even a spark of magic.

"Are you practicing?" Aunt Xenia demanded, pinning me in place with her dark eyes.

"Yes," I lied. "Every day."

I had no idea how to practice something I couldn't do.

Mama dismissed me from the table early. Uncle Nikolasha followed me upstairs a few minutes later, pretending he wanted to check on my bird. He pressed a slice of lemon cake into my hand, only a little squashed from his pocket. I devoured it in seconds.

"Now what about this falcon?" he said. "What are you going to name her?"

"Artemis," I said at once. "Because she's a hunter."

Nikolasha nodded his approval.

I opened her box carefully, noting that she was instantly alert and watching us.

"She must be hungry, Uncle. And thirsty."

"I'll show you how to feed her."

Nikolasha departed for about ten minutes, returning with two day-old chicks wrapped in an old rag. Down in the park we had a farm with several coops so we could eat fresh eggs every day.

I couldn't help letting out a whimper at the sight of the chicks. I loved animals and had not entirely considered the implications of my new pet.

"Can't we feed her grubs or something?"

"She's not a chicken," Nikolasha said severely. "You'll have to feed her chicks and rabbits until she can hunt for herself. Mind you give her a fresh rabbit each time—gyrfalcons will break through the ribcage and eat the organs. If you force her to eat the whole of the rabbit, she won't get what she needs."

He threw the live chicks into the box. Artemis dispatched them with a ruthlessness that left me wishing I hadn't eaten so much cake. I had to admire how ferocious she was, even injured and splinted.

"Glad to see she got her appetite back," Nikolasha said. "She didn't eat much on the way here."

He showed me how to bring droplets of water to Artemis on my fingertip, one at a time so I didn't drown her.

I was nervous to bring my finger anywhere close to that still-bloodied beak. Artemis must have been thirsty, or else we earned a little trust by feeding her. She accepted the water and didn't bite.

When Maria came upstairs she said, "Are you keeping that in here?"

"Of course."

She frowned. "Ortipo won't like that."

Ortipo was her French bulldog, gifted to her by one of the palace guards.

27

"Ortipo better leave Artemis alone," I said darkly. "In fact, he better stay out of here altogether while she's healing."

"It's his room, too!" Maria protested.

"He likes sleeping with Ollie better."

That made Maria furious because it was true. She went to sleep with her back to me.

We slept in little camp beds, woke at six in the morning, cleaned our own rooms, and washed our faces with cold water, just as Papa and his siblings had all done as children. The servants were instructed to call us by our names and not our titles. Mama and Papa were determined that we wouldn't grow up spoiled, except perhaps for Alexei. With him, they couldn't seem to help themselves—they'd waited so long for a boy, and he was so fragile.

Though none of us would say it aloud, and we prayed every day for a miracle, boys with haemorrhaphilia didn't live long. Mama's brother Friedrich died of it before he turned two.

Alexei's childish pleasures might be the only ones he would ever have.

IN THE EARLY light of dawn, I woke to someone shrieking in my ear:

HUNGRY!

The cry was sharp and piercing, stabbing into my head.

I sat up in bed, covers pooling around my waist, staring around the room.

Maria was still sleeping, sprawled on her belly with her bedding piled on her head. Soft snores emanated from the cavern under her pillow.

Our window was closed, and our door too. I didn't have Tatiana's ability to hear people speaking in distant rooms.

For a moment I thought I might have dreamed it. But the sound was too loud and much too direct. Something real had woken me.

I slipped out of bed, only to stand foolishly in the middle of the rug.

HUNGRY!

This time I heard it with my ears as well as in my head—a cry that was part screech, part speech.

I dropped to my knees and pulled Artemis' box out from under my bed.

She was already awake as I knew she would be, staring at me with those savage black eyes. She was angry. And indeed ... hungry.

Feeling very stupid, I whispered, "You want more food?"

She only stared back at me in that apt way birds have, with tiny abrupt movements of her head.

Then she opened her beak and made a sound. With my ears, I heard the same sharp cry, a little quieter now that I was looking at her eye-to-eye. In my mind, I heard the word again, in lower volume, but just as demanding:

Hungry!

"I'll get you food," I said aloud. "Just a minute—but don't keep screaming, you'll wake Maria."

Artemis only stared at me.

I pulled on my galoshes and dressing gown so I could race down to the coops.

The palace was quiet. Almost everyone was still asleep, except for the guards on duty and a few of the servants.

My heart was racing, and not from running.

Was it really possible I'd heard Artemis speak?

I'd never known anyone who could talk to animals, not in real life—only in stories.

Was I half asleep and dreaming, or did I truly understand her? And could she understand me?

I plucked two more chicks from the coop and carried them back upstairs, trying not to feel them wriggling around inside the rag.

Artemis waited quietly. She tilted her head at the sight of me, still silent.

I threw the chicks into the box. She ripped them apart and swallowed them down as I interested myself in the empty stretch of lawn outside my window.

When she finished, I gave her a little more water.

I desperately wanted her to speak so I could know for certain if I'd only imagined it.

She picked at the gauze around her wing with her beak, her eyes as black and wild as ever.

"Was that enough?" I whispered. "Do you want more?"

No response.

I chewed on the edge of my lip, cramped from crouching but barely daring to breathe, let alone move.

The rest of the palace began to wake up around me, Tatiana and Ollie speaking quietly on the other side of the wall, the servants hurrying up and down the hallway, Alexei arguing with whoever was supposed to be getting him dressed. Even Maria stirred under her covers.

As the mundane world came alive, my excitement faded. Artemis cleaned her feathers like a normal bird.

I was as likely to be crazy as magical.

chapter 3
THE IMP EMERGES

Uncle Nikolasha stayed with us only two days before he had to return to the steppes with Alexei.

The long journey southwest from St. Petersburg would begin on Uncle's private train. His magnificent steam locomotive puffed on the tracks like a live thing, lacquered in navy and gold, with a double engine so Uncle could run at a blistering seventy-eight mph down open track.

Hans and Boris had their own private carriage, as did my uncle's horse Caviar. Nikolasha himself slept in the Pullman Palace Car, which contained an observation deck, a parlor, and a stateroom.

Uncle boasted that his rooms on the train were just as luxurious as his country estate. Even his favorite French chef rode along with him.

Though I'd seen the train before, I'd never actually ridden on it, which made me insanely jealous of Alexei.

The platform was a hive of confusion as we gathered to see them off. Porters loaded supplies and soldiers milled about. Uncle was taking an entire regiment back with him, to keep Alexei safe and to refresh Papa's exhausted men.

Mama and my sisters had come along, as well as Liza Taneeva and my mother's favorite lady-in-waiting, Baroness Sylvie Buxhoeveden. Liza and

Sylvie had played together as children, hunting mushrooms in the countryside. You wouldn't know it to see them stand beside each other—they only spoke to Mama, barely sharing a glance between them.

I stayed back from the smokestack because I had Artemis in her box under my arm. Though she hadn't spoken again, I wanted her with me every minute in case she might.

Mama was pelting Uncle Nikolasha with dozens of last-minute instructions. Alexei's sailor-nanny Andrei Derevenko would be coming along, but Mama behaved as if Nikolasha would be the nursemaid.

"If he gets a bruise, you've got to massage the limb and elevate it!" She clasped her hands until the fingers were white. "He mustn't sit in any place where the motion of the train could jostle him ..."

Nikolasha listened with infinite patience.

"I'll care for him like his own father," he promised.

"Even a little more, if you don't mind." Mama smiled.

Nikolasha kissed each of us girls on the forehead. My sisters ran down to the end of the platform so they could call one last goodbye to Alexei, hanging as far out the window as he could manage while anchored by Andrei Derevenko's iron grip on his legs.

"One moment!" Mama cried. "I have to tell the chef that Alexei can't have heavy gravy on his meat!"

She rushed off to confirm the dietary instructions that had surely already been given to the chef. The list of foods my parents believed would help Alexei's condition was long and ever-changing. Alexei's good and bad days were as mercurial as the weather. Whether or not what he ate actually had an effect, I could never tell.

Liza Taneeva pulled me aside, saying, "You'll be riding home in the other carriage—there isn't room enough in ours."

Though we had dozens of cars in the Imperial Garage, Mama preferred to travel through the town in closed carriages so no one could stare at us. The carriages were cramped and stuffy, especially with the curtains drawn. I had no desire to crowd in with Ollie, Tatiana, Maria, and Margaretta. Nor did I believe this was Mama's wish—I suspected Liza would present it to her as my own idea once I was safely squashed in the other vehicle.

Liza was holding a grudge over the toad. Or the fact that I'd sat on her shawl on the way here.

I opened my mouth to argue. Then an idea came into my head.

This idea was so devilishly tempting and yet so extraordinarily naughty that for once I actually stopped to think about it.

It was well known that I was the worst-behaved Grand Duchess. If not for Alexei occasionally outshining me, I might be the worst child ever to cross the threshold of the Alexander Palace.

It's not that I wanted to misbehave, but the most interesting things were always forbidden.

My curiosity was a demon that lurked inside me, awake and watching.

When something caught its attention, the demon took hold. I became what my mother called *shvibzik*—the imp.

The imp was fully alive in that moment. It had sprung inside my skin, taking complete control of me. It looked left and right down the platform, hunting for its chance.

Uncle was hustling the last of the soldiers onto the train. Mama stood down by the dining car, distracting the chef while he tried to oversee the loading of the heavy ice-filled chests containing the meat and perishables. Sylvie Buxhoeveden flirted with a handsome officer. Only Liza Taneeva watched me.

I began walking toward the end of the platform where my sisters stood as if I planned to join them. I walked slowly, aimlessly, trailing my fingers along the gilt scrolling above the train's wheels.

The moment Liza's back was turned, I jumped up into the carriage containing Hans and Boris.

If a stranger dared step foot inside their private home, the twin borzois would rip off his arms. They loved me almost as much as chicken cutlets. They attacked me with their long red tongues, licking all over my face and hands until I begged them to stop.

The dogs had a palace on wheels complete with bedding, food and water, even toys. They were ferocious as lions but squabbled and played like children when their work was done.

The stationmaster shouted the last call. I heard the thuds of soldiers jumping aboard and my mother's faint voice begging Nikolasha to *Please, please take care!*

I didn't actually think I was going to get away with it. Any moment, Margaretta would notice I was missing from the platform and a hue and cry would raise. I was already planning how I'd tell Mama I only wanted to hug the dogs one last time.

Then, to my delight, the doors rolled shut, closing me inside. The chugging of the engine increased. With a jolt, the wheels began to roll.

Still, I couldn't believe it. I sank down between the dogs, arms around their necks, Artemis safely stowed beneath my skirts.

The train picked up speed. The slow chug became a steady roll. I longed to peek out the window but couldn't risk it.

I could picture my family climbing back into the carriages, Margaretta and my sisters having no idea I was supposed to join them.

The tricky part would come when Liza Taneeva informed my mother that I was riding with the others. Would she check the carriage to confirm?

I supposed it would depend on how smoothly and convincingly Liza relayed the new plan. For the one and only time in my life, I blessed her powers of persuasion.

The train continued to barrel down the tracks. In short time we'd pass beyond the edges of St. Petersburg. Once we were on open track, not a horse alive could catch us.

I counted the seconds, and then the minutes. I didn't dare slide open the window shade to check how far we'd gone.

Hans and Boris settled down in the clean straw padding the wooden floor of their carriage. They didn't seem to think there was anything unusual in me joining them. In fact, they were pleased to have company. Hans curled around me like a backrest, Boris laying his long, elegant snout across my lap.

Artemis stirred in the box pressed against my thigh, not liking the scent of the dogs so close. Lulled by the motion of the train, she eventually stilled.

The train went on and on.

An hour passed, then two. I had no watch, so I could only guess how the time slid by. The gentle rocking of the train and the friendly heat of the dogs soon worked its magic on me as well. My head nodded, and I slept.

A LONG TIME LATER, I woke to the sound of the latch on the door turning. I dove under a pile of blankets, barely covering my head before my uncle came into the carriage.

The borzois leapt up. I heard Nikolasha roughly rubbing their heads, saying, "There's my good boys! Glad to be back on the road, are you? Get down, Hans, you great oaf! What is it? You're full of tricks today. Don't bark, Boris, you'll deafen me."

The dogs' heavy feet scrambled about, nails scratching at the wooden floor. I was lucky they couldn't speak because they surely would have blurted out how happy they were that I'd come along.

I was afraid they'd run over to me and pull the blanket off my body. I needn't have worried—Uncle brought food. The borzois were too hungry to pay attention to anything else. I heard the wet sounds of Hans and Boris demolishing whatever Nikolasha set down in their bowls.

My own stomach growled. If I had thought this plan out ahead of time, I would have packed a snack.

Woken by the noise, and probably equally as hungry, Artemis let out a chirp.

"*Shh,*" I whispered into the holes in the side of her box.

The dog's slobbering drowned out the noise. My uncle gave the twin borzois one last pat and departed the carriage, leaving us alone once more.

I crept out.

Boris looked up from his bowl, giving me a pleased snort when he saw I was still close by, then sinking his face back in his food.

I wished they were eating something I could share instead of raw meat. What I wouldn't give for a lemon cake right now, or even a crust of bread.

My stomach clenched and gurgled, my head spinning as the motion of the train bumped me against the wall.

Artemis screeched again. This time I heard it:

Hungry!

I snatched up the box and opened the lid, lifting her out so we were eye-to-eye.

"I hear you. I'll get you some food."

My own hunger was forgotten in the thrill of knowing that I wasn't imagining it.

I set Artemis back down, carefully approaching the dogs. I knew better than to put my hand near their bowls while they were eating. I sidled up to Hans, who was slightly the calmer of the two, waiting until he'd satiated the worst of his hunger. When he paused, I scratched his favorite place behind his ears.

"Could I take a little of this?" Slowly I reached for a chicken cutlet.

Hans made a rumbling sound that wasn't quite a growl. He let me take the food.

I carried it back to Artemis, wondering if she'd eat something that wasn't alive.

"It's food," I said, laying it in the box next to her head.

She eyed the cutlet, displeased.

Hunger won and she gulped it down.

I brought her a little water from the dog's bowls.

When she seemed reasonably content, I reached out a finger to stroke the soft, silvery plumage where her head met her back.

Faster than I could blink, she nipped me with her fierce little beak. Blood welled from my finger, bright and glistening as a jewel.

"Ouch!" I cried.

Artemis glared at me with those glittering black eyes, her chest feathers puffing up beneath the gauze wrap.

"Alright, I'm sorry," I said. "I didn't mean to offend you."

I sucked at the wound. It hurt, but I guessed she could have cut me deeper if she wanted to.

"Why can I hear you?" I asked. "Is '*hungry*' the only thing you can say?"

I could imagine myself displaying this particular power to a crowd of observers. I'd bring Artemis out, she'd screech at top volume, and I'd inform everyone that she was hungry. They'd laugh in my face.

Besides being a useless ability, it was basically unprovable. No one would believe me.

I sighed, leaning back against the wall of the carriage, Artemis nestled in her box in my lap.

Well, even if it wouldn't help with my demonstration, at least *I* knew I was no longer Maladroit.

The train chugged along. Certain we were long out of the city, I walked to the window and slid open the shutter. Thick forest whipped past the tracks, the sky soaked in deep purple twilight. With no glass in the frame, I could smell the scent of cold soil and pinesap.

I'd been on trips to Rhineland and Denmark and cruised all the way to Finland in the imperial yacht, but never crossed the wilds of my own country.

I knew Rusya was vast. Seeing the scale of it with my own eyes was something different. Mile after mile streamed by, the sky darkening and the moon rising. All this time and distance, and if we were looking at the map on Papa's study wall, we'd only have traveled as far as my pinky.

The train passed over a trestle bridge. The woods dropped away. For a moment all I could see outside the window was a perfect square of black night sky, studded with stars.

As we entered the forest once more, I heard the long howl of a wolf. The howl followed the train as if the wolf were running alongside us.

I shrank back from the window.

I'd never been away from home without my parents.

Mama must have long since realized I was missing. Did she assume I jumped on the train, or did she think I'd been kidnapped?

Guilt seeped into me like cold water soaking through my clothes.

I hadn't thought this through. All I'd been picturing was the marvelous spectacle of Papa's army spread across the steppes.

I could go and find Uncle Nikolasha now, but what if he turned back? It would all be for nothing.

I shivered in the chilly carriage. Spring in Rusya is no gentle time. I wished I had a fur coat like the borzois.

I huddled down with the dogs, wrapping their blankets around us, Artemis' box tucked under my arm. Hungry as I was, the train soon lulled me back to sleep.

THE SLOWING of the train woke me. I sat up in the tangled nest of blankets, straw in my hair.

Nikolasha came striding in from the next car, letting out a shout at the sight of me.

"By the bones of the gods, what are you doing here?"

The idiocy of my plan was beginning to settle on me like snow, heavier by the minute.

"I ... wanted to come along," I said lamely.

"What were you—how could you—your mother will be tearing the country apart looking for you!"

He filled the small carriage with his bulk, so red-faced that even his eyes were bloodshot, beard bristling outward, fists clenched like hammers. The twin borzois stumbled backward, toenails scrabbling on the boards.

"I'm sorry," I whispered, cringing like a puppy.

I wanted to cry but knew I had no right. I'd brought this on myself.

My uncle's teeth ground together, his shoulders shaking. He opened his mouth to shout some more, but the whimpering of the dogs pressing against me seemed to remind him that he was a terrifying giant and the three creatures before him were all quite stupid.

He heaved a sigh.

"I can't take you back—your father is expecting us.." Ever the pragmatist, he added, "Let's get you some food."

I'd imagined a whipping, and perhaps being tied to the roof of the train as punishment, so that perked me up immensely.

Uncle led me through the train to the dining car, Artemis tucked under my arm. Alexei was enjoying a plate of cold ham and pickles with Andrei Derevenko. He leaped up from his chair, whooping at the sight of me.

"Stassie! How'd you get here?"

"She stowed away," Uncle said curtly. "Get her some meat, I'm sure she's hungry."

The gratitude I felt for that ham far surpassed any of the fine meals I'd ever eaten at home. I gobbled it down, messier than Boris and Hans put together.

Andrei Derevenko eyed me with a horrified expression. He knew Mama's protectiveness and the maelstrom of trouble that must be raging back home.

Andrei was about forty years old, stocky and mustached. I suppose he never planned to be a nanny when he crewed our yacht, the *Standart*. He was always friendly to us children, particularly Alexei, who had his own tiny sailor suit made in imitation of the ones worn by the crew. When the ship hit a rock in the Gulf of Finland, Andrei rushed to catch Alexei, saving him from a tumble on the deck. Mama hired him on the spot.

Andrei had two sons of his own, the only boys Mama trusted to play gently with Alexei. His big, rough hands brought some measure of relief when Alexei's joints swelled or a bruise blocked off blood flow.

Andrei didn't believe he possessed any special healing powers, but no one else seemed to have his touch. The sailor would patiently massage Alexei late into the night while Alexei cried and howled and begged for mercy from the heavens. I'd seen Andrei leave Alexei's room in tears, though he pretended it was only a sneeze.

In Alexei, at least, I had an ally who was not at all angry that I'd tagged along. We crowded together on the bench seat attached directly to the wall of the carriage. I regaled him with the particulars of my journey, adding in a little spice about how many wolves I'd seen in the woods, and how close they got to my window.

"They were bigger than normal wolves, just like Uncle said," I recounted, to Alexei's wide-eyed admiration. "Probably near as big as a horse. I wasn't afraid. I had a knife with me, and Hans and Boris, if they tried to jump in the window."

Andrei Derevenko let out a soft snort from under his mustache.

"Big as horses?"

"Well ..." I grinned. "*Nearly* as big."

"Perhaps they were *oboroten*," Andrei said, with that menacing hush Alexei and I had come to know so well.

We perked up like bloodhounds. Andrei's sailor's yarns could curdle your blood and give you nightmares for a month. They always came with the solemn vow that he'd witnessed it all with his own eyes when he sailed to distant northern ports with the navy.

"What's an *oboroten*?" Alexei demanded.

"I don't want to frighten you ..."

"Tell us! Tell us!" we begged.

Andrei leaned forward, eyes pale and haunted in his sun-battered face.

"It's a shapeshifter," he rasped. "A wolf that's not really a wolf at all, but a man prowling around in an animal skin."

Alexei gaped. I tried to pretend like I'd heard this sort of thing before.

"Can they *fully* change their form?" I asked, all skepticism.

Andrei nodded gravely.

"It's rare ... you have to be incredibly powerful. A real sorcerer. They use talismans to help them ..."

"How do they do it?" I whispered.

"Well ... the sorcerer has a set of silver knives, seven of them. When the moon is at its peak, he goes deep, deep into the forest where no human foot has walked before. He finds an ash stump that's been struck by lightning and split down the middle. Then he lays out his knives across the lightning strike, and he turns them over, one by one ..."

Andrei's voice dropped low, rasping down my spine. All the little hairs stood up straight on my arms.

"He leaps over the stump. And in the pale moonlight, his flesh begins to change ... Hair grows first. Then teeth and nails. The bones bend and crack and he screams, but it turns to a HOWL!"

Alexei shrieked. Maybe I did too. Even Artemis chirped in her box.

"What does he do then?" Alexei begged.

"It depends ... what was his dark purpose that night? Perhaps he intends to snatch a baby from its cradle and raise it as a demon ... or maybe he plans to stalk an enemy and rip out his throat ..."

"How long does he stay a wolf?" I asked.

"Well that's the danger," Andrei warned. "To break the spell, the sorcerer performs the incantation all over again, backward this time. But he's left his knives behind on that lightning-blasted stump. If someone comes along and steals them, he'll be trapped as a wolf forever. Or until he hunts down the thief and recovers his knives ..."

That was deliciously horrifying. I could imagine myself either as the raging sorcerer trapped in the body of the wolf, or as the thief fleeing from a vengeful monster.

"Some say Karol Volk is shapeshifter," Andrei growled.

"Who's Karol Volk?"

"The king wolf. A wolf far larger than a horse, Anastasia. White as frost, cruel, and wickedly clever. Some say he's a sorcerer who has been living as wolf so long he's forgotten that he was ever a man at all—"

Uncle Nikolasha came back into the carriage. Andrei shoved an enormous bite of bread in his mouth. Alexei and I were too bright-eyed and flushed for that to work.

"What are you all jabbering about?" Nikolasha said, dropping down in his chair. He rang for more food.

"*Oboroten!*" Alexei cried. "And Korol Vok!"

I couldn't kick him under the table and risk giving him a bruise.

Nikolasha raised an eyebrow.

"Tales for children," Andrei said sheepishly.

"Perhaps not," Uncle said, surprising us all.

"Andrei says sorcerers can turn themselves into wolves." I wondered if my uncle would confirm or deny it.

"My old nanny told me it was a curse," Uncle said. "Once a farmer built a new barn. Afraid of thieves, he struck his axe three times on the threshold of the door, saying, 'Anyone who crosses this line becomes a wolf.' Pleased with his cleverness, he set down his ax, stepped over the threshold, and was forever transformed."

"That's only a fairytale," Alexei scoffed.

We'd heard a similar legend from Margaretta, though in her version it was an Irish farmer who turned into a mouse.

"Is it?" Nikolasha said, scowling down at us with terrible gravity. "Hunting wolves this winter, I cut the throats of a hundred at least. One night at twilight, Hans and Boris ran a wolf down. I dismounted and drew my blade across its neck—but it caught upon something. The beast fell. There in the bloody snow lay a gold chain with a medallion of St. Alypius. As the wolf died, I saw human tears on its face. What do you think is more likely? That someone put a necklace on a wolf ... or that the animal once wore human clothes?"

"You killed him," Alexei said in a slightly accusing tone.

Uncle shrugged. "If he wasn't a wolf, he was a Cossack."

Nikolasha's meal arrived on several plates from the kitchen: smoked herring, a handful of sausages as fat as his fingers, thick slices of buttered bread covered in an inch of black caviar, a hunk of Dutch cheese, and several apple fritters.

"Eat up," he said to Alexei and me. "You're both too skinny."

At home, I was often told I was getting too plump, but Mama assured me I'd grow out of it like Ollie and Maria had done.

All of my sisters were growing into beauties, even Ollie who at first had only been a little pretty, too much like Papa with her broad face and the upturned nose that she liked to call her "humble snub." At seventeen, she was now considered quite lovely. She'd grown taller, her hair had turned a brilliant red-gold, and her eyes were a brighter blue than ever, as wide and laughing as her mouth.

Tatiana had always been acknowledged as a great beauty. She was dark-haired, silvery-eyed, and already taller than Ollie, though so elegantly shaped no one ever criticized her height. She was like Mama in temperament—calm, even grave. Like Papa in ambition.

Maria was the fairest and sweetest of us all. She was soft and smiling, with round blue eyes and golden lights in her hair. When Mama had to cut Maria's braids off during an illness, her blonde hair curled all around her head until she looked like a cherub peeking out from her cloudy pillows.

There was no chance of me matching my sisters in looks. Short and stocky as a boy, with carrot-colored hair and a smatter of freckles, I wasn't even as pretty as Alexei.

While I hated hearing the ladies-in-waiting discuss me as if I were a piebald horse standing in the yard, I didn't entirely mind being ugly. Nobody expected me to dress up as nice as Tatiana, and I certainly didn't attract any unwanted admirers like Ollie.

A soldier poked his head into the dining car to tell Nikolasha they'd loaded all the wagons.

"Up, then," Nikolasha said, hustling us along. "Did you bring clothes, Anastasia?"

"I didn't bring anything but Artemis," I admitted.

"Probably for the best—you can wear some of Alexei's."

Though he was three years younger, Alexei and I were nearly the same height. I felt a thrill at the idea of wearing boys' clothes in public, when I wasn't even allowed to wear them around the palace. The superiority of trousers to skirts was obvious, and I suspected there was a great deal of value in being taken for a boy.

Alexei was in a phase where he dressed almost exclusively in sailor suits. We chortled at the sight of each other. I'd been forced to match Maria a hundred times, but never Alexei. With my hair tucked up in the cap, I could have been a young Tsarevich, too.

"God's beard," Andrei grumbled. "This is just what I need. Two little devils."

Alexei grinned. "I always wanted a brother."

I didn't believe him for a second. "Then you wouldn't get all the attention."

"I still would," Alexei assured me. "That's the only good that comes of being sick."

Andrei made a rumbling sound to remind Alexei not to speak about his illness where the soldiers might hear.

My parents concealed my brother's illness whenever they could. Even the servants who waited on Alexei were forbidden to mingle in St. Petersburg.

Members of the court suspected, especially those familiar with the affliction.

Once the German Kaiser came to visit us. Mama had done everything she could to keep Alexei's milky skin free of the huge black bruises that bloomed so easily. Right before the retinue arrived, Alexei snuck away from the servants and ran his head against a doorknob. A great blue goose egg swelled on his forehead—there was no hiding it. The Kaiser only shook his head sadly, whispering to Mama that his brother's three sons suffered the same disease.

We climbed down from the train. It was fully night already. The mountains blocking out the sky were a deeper black, inky and endless like a void in the stars.

The wagons waited. I was pleased to see all the horses coming along with us—I loved horses almost as much as dogs.

Recognizing a few of the soldiers from the palace, I waved.

"Stop that," Andrei knocked down my hand. "If you don't draw attention to yourself, they'll think you're one of my sons."

Alexei's perch in the wagon had to be padded with dozens of blankets and mats. Nikolasha checked the seat several times before he'd allow Alexei to settle in.

"I sent a telegraph home to your mother," Nikolasha informed me, all his severity returned. "And a message ahead to your father."

Half the reason I'd come was my desperate desire to see Papa. Now I wished I could hide under Alexei's mound of blankets until the end of eternity.

My father would not be amused. The one lesson he drilled into us again and again, above any other, was duty. Duty to our country and to our family. He'd be furious when he learned what I'd done to my mother.

I had a long time to sit and stew. The wagons lurched along far slower than the train. I leaned out the back, trying to follow the zig-zag track cut up the side of the mountain. The small settlement at its base was stuffed with soldiers.

"What are they all doing up there?" I asked Andrei Derevenko.

"What do you think?"

It took me a minute to figure it out, then I said, "Ohh," softly.

"What?" Alexei demanded. "What are they mining?"

"Charoite."

"That's right," Andrei grunted.

Charoite was the treasure of the Romanovs—the prize we alone possessed.

It explained why my father had battled the Cossacks so aggressively. We couldn't afford to lose control of this land.

Alexei glanced back at the mine, uninterested. His face was pale and sweating. I thought the motion of the wagon was probably hurting him, though he was trying not to show it.

"We'll be there soon," I murmured to him, patting his leg.

Even that made him wince, so I stopped.

chapter 4

A NEW AGREEMENT

I'd seriously underestimated the size of Papa's army. We smelled them long before we saw them—camp smoke twisting through the air, mixed with manure and gunpowder. We heard them next—shouts and bustle, horses stamping, and more cheer than we likely would have heard a week ago in the same place.

The Cossacks were waiting to sign terms with my father. The rebellion was over—they'd been forced to concede.

It had been a long and bloody fight, I knew that much from my mother. Papa wrote that the Cossacks fought like devils. All their life was war—they trained for battle from boyhood. They lived in the borderlands, raiding the surrounding territories and selling their services as mercenaries.

Each Cossack was supposed to give ten years of service to Rusya. That's why they were always rebelling.

This time several hosts banded together under an Ataman called Taras Kaledin. He'd already completed his ten years, but fought anyway. Papa sent three different armies to subdue them under three different generals. Finally he'd been forced to come himself. Papa and Nikolasha rained blood and fury on the field until Kaledin threw down his flag.

Kaledin would be signing a new agreement on behalf of all the Cossack hosts. Papa wanted Alexei to witness it because someday Alexei would have to rule the Cossacks, and they'd probably be just as stubborn then as they were now.

I didn't know if I was more terrified or excited to meet one.

Who was I kidding—wild, vicious bandits that galloped around murdering people? I couldn't wait.

But first, I had to pay the devil his due.

My father was waiting to speak to me.

Uncle Nikolasha took us on foot to the center of the camp, Hans and Boris sentinels at our heels. Soldiers stared at us. A few whispered, *the Tsarevich!* as Alexei passed.

Nobody said the word *princess.*

I smiled to myself. It was nice to feel anonymous for once.

Papa's tent was the largest save for the long, low dining hall made of tan canvas the same color as the dry prairie grass. The two guards at the entrance saluted my uncle, making way for us to pass through.

I stepped into the gloom, heart in my throat.

My father stood up from his desk, nearly as tall as Nikolasha and infinitely more terrible. I saw the broad shoulders draped in full military regalia, the perfectly trimmed beard and the stern mouth. I met his gaze, shivering under that cold, clear stare.

"Anastasia."

The four syllables fell like hammer strokes on the gong of doom. I let out a squeak, falling to my knees on the rough carpet and clasping my hands in front of me. There was no hope of dignity here, I could only show my complete and utter penance.

"Forgive me, Papa! I knew it was wrong, but I didn't think how wrong when I jumped on the train. I was bad but I didn't mean to be so bad ..."

I chanced the tiniest glance up at my father.

There was no pity to be found. I might have been staring up at a stone idol.

"You made your mother wretched. You're thoughtless. Careless. You should be ashamed of yourself."

"I am. Truly, I am, Papa."

I cast my eyes back down to the carpet. I was a limp, pathetic teabag steeped in shame.

"We'll discuss your punishment when we return home."

I squirmed in place, suppressing a groan. The axe hanging over my head was so much worse than any actual punishment.

"Yes, Father."

The next thing I felt was a hand on top of my head, heavy and warm.

I stood, slowly. Papa pulled me against his chest along with Alexei.

"You're here now, safe at least."

As he drew back, I saw how tired he looked, wrung out like a sponge. For the first time, I noticed bits of gray at his temples and in his beard.

"Send them to bed," he said to Nikolasha. "We meet Kaledin in the morning."

Nikolasha bustled Alexei and me off to a small tent that smelled of mildew. Andrei Derevenko brought us a bag of dusky apples and a slightly squashed mouse for Artemis.

"Where'd you get him?" I said, lifting the dead mouse by the tail.

"Storage tent. Lifted up a bag of oats and a dozen of the buggers went running."

"You want to feed Artemis?" I said to Alexei.

He didn't reply—he'd already fallen asleep.

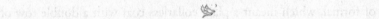

WE WOKE WITH THE SUN, the camp already noisier than it had been the night before.

Nikolasha wasted no time ordering us about, washing our faces and hands, making us change clothes all over again. He stuffed us into a pair of military jackets with gold braid on the shoulders and the sashes of officers across our breasts.

Both uniforms had been made for Alexei, one in black and gold and the other in silver and white. The latter was a dress uniform. Uncle put it on Alexei anyway, because the Tsarevich could not be less fine than his companion. I snickered at Alexei, pleased to wear the more appropriate day uniform. I looked dark and dashing, even with the trousers too short. Alexei scowled, knowing *he* looked a bit of a peacock.

I peered into the cloudy mirror, sucking in my cheeks and narrowing my eyes, trying to picture myself with a mustache.

I could hear the soldiers outside, dressed in the same uniform, laughing amongst themselves. They got to gallop around the country, fighting and drinking and doing whatever they pleased. I didn't have crushes on the soldiers like Maria—I wanted to be one.

Father came in to inspect us. He nodded his approval.

"You'll stand with Andrei Derevenko while the oaths are spoken and the treaty's signed. You won't move and you most certainly will not speak."

I nodded, lips already clamped together. The demons of hell couldn't drag a word out of my mouth.

"Watch everything that passes."

"Wait, father," Alexei said. Papa paused to listen. "Why not just kill the Cossacks? Why make a treaty at all?"

"The Cossacks are Rusyan, too."

"But they rebelled!"

"They've fought with us before and they'll fight with us again. I want to beat them, not break them."

It was true—they'd fought with us against Japan only a year earlier, and many times before. After Napoleon got a taste of them, he said he could conquer the globe with an army of Cossacks.

Uncle led us out to the open field where Papa's men already gathered. Alexei and I stood on a little dais with a wooden writing table where Papa and the Ataman would sign the treaty. Andrei Derevenko joined us, dressed in his version of formal, which meant a plain collarless coat with a double row of brass buttons.

The soldiers formed long, straight lines. They faced south, looking out over the hills where I was certain the Cossacks would come.

I felt proud of our army. Rusya was the greatest nation on earth to my mind—vast and beautiful, with the kind of magic that only exists in places that have never been entirely tamed. I believed Andrei's stories of monsters still roaming in the wild north. I hoped they were true.

And I believed what I'd been taught all my life: that the gods chose the Romanovs to rule. It was our sacred duty to keep the country strong.

Father had never looked more imposing. He wore his splendid scarlet uniform, as did Uncle Nikolasha. The two giants stood side by side, impressive at rest, unbeatable in battle.

Crows circled overhead, calling their harsh cries. They were smart enough to see the soldiers assembled and hope they might have a battlefield to pick over later.

I glared upward, wishing Artemis could scatter them all in terror. Maybe in a few more weeks.

Nikolasha had checked her wing and said it was healing well.

I was still annoyed at him for making me leave Artemis in Papa's tent. I hated abandoning her in a strange place, even if she was well supplied with food.

A hush fell over the waiting army. Tension ran down the ranks like a current. The crows stopped wheeling, dropping to perch on tents and flagpoles.

A long cry floated up from the valley, as lonely and inhuman as the wolves at night. The ground vibrated beneath my feet—a thousand hooves thundering like a river toward us.

The Cossacks crested the hill in one black wave.

I'd never seen such riders—bent low over their horses' necks as the beasts surged at full gallop, curved sabers at their sides and rifles on their backs.

Alexei and I drew close together, barely breathing.

The Cossacks formed a line opposite our men, pulling up their horses and swinging down in their flat, unpolished boots.

They were wild, there was no other word for it—as wild as the wind and the grass and the horses they rode. Their heads were shaved on the sides, long shocks of hair swept back or braided. They wore Rusyan military uniforms modified with skins and badges and braids of their own making, and loose trousers in the Eastern style, double belts of ammunition across their breasts. Narrow eyed and dark featured, they could have been Mongols but for the thick black mustaches, curved upward at the corners.

When they leaped down from their horses, they landed silently on the turf, no jingle of weapons or creak of boots. Eerie like ghosts.

The Ataman Taras Kaledin rode at the head of his host, out in the open, no one protecting him. He had a shock of black hair shaved down one side, and the thickest mustache of all running from his hook-like nose down to his hatchet jaw. His black brows nearly met in the middle, his face etched in deep, determined lines. A wolfskin cloak slung over one shoulder, his blue and scarlet vest open over his bare chest. His flag was a firebird.

He was a barbarian king, unbowed and unbroken, as he strode boldly between the double ranks of soldiers.

The rest of his host stood fearless before us. These were not the battered and humbled nomads I expected to see—they looked ready to rebel again after an hour's rest. Alexei was going to have his work cut out for him.

The Ataman paused in the center of the line, waiting for my father.

Papa began to walk down the ranks of soldiers to meet him.

Papa's crimson-colored coat looked as if it had been tailored that morning, gold buttons gleaming. His hair and beard were freshly trimmed, ceremonial cutlass glinting at his side.

He was the picture of civility and urbanity. But it was the Ataman who looked at home in the wild, open steppes.

Our men stood at attention as Papa passed. The Cossacks merely watched, faces dark and closed.

One of the Cossack soldiers was only a boy—fourteen at most, tall and reedy. He had no mustache yet, his long black hair tied back.

I noticed him because he was so young. Also, while the other Cossacks were barehanded, he wore a pair of black leather gloves.

There was something sinister about those gloves, so thin it looked as if his hands were dipped in ink.

I saw his fingers move, twitching by his sword. That little flinch seemed to jolt the ground beneath my feet.

I stumbled in place. Andrei Derevenko grabbed my shoulder.

"Did you feel that?"

"Feel what?" Alexei said.

I looked at the boy. His feet were planted far apart, eyes narrowed to slits, like he'd felt it too.

Papa was coming up the line, only a dozen yards from the Ataman now. When they met in the middle the Ataman would have to kneel and swear his oath.

The boy watched my father. His chest rose and fell, his shoulders tense.

My father's eyes were locked on the Ataman, just a few steps ahead.

He passed the boy.

The boy's black-gloved hand seized the handle of his cutlass and ripped it free in one graceful pull, swinging through its arc toward the back of my father's neck. The blade bit down, whistling through the air.

I leaped off the dais, screaming, "FATHER, LOOK OUT!"

My shriek startled the crows that had settled along the tops of the tents, and the horses standing behind the line of Cossacks. The Ataman's great gray stallion reared. The crows exploded upward in a burst of wings.

Then the whole world froze in place.

I was falling through the air from the dais to the grass, but I was the only thing moving. The gray stallion paused, hooves wheeling through space. The crows pulsed their wings with aching slowness, then stilled, hanging suspended in the air. The flags stopped flapping, the fabric an arrested wave. Even the ripples of dry grass halted as the wind held its breath.

I'd never felt such stillness. The whole world paused around me. The young Cossack's teeth were bared, his blade an inch from my father's neck. The soldiers on both sides of the line stared open mouthed, some having heard the first part of my scream, some still oblivious when time stopped.

The air felt thick as syrup against my skin. I ran forward, shoving my way through the soldiers to my father. It was easy to push them out of the way—the men tilted and hung in space, weightless and floating. The grass dented beneath my boots and failed to spring up again, leaving footprints in my wake.

I ran to my father and touched him on the arm, looking up into his frozen face.

As I touched him, we swapped. I was flung back into the current of time while Papa was released from it.

Now I saw my father as everyone else saw him. I watched as he unleashed his power.

The gray stallion reared, whinnying, pawing the air with its front hooves. The crows continued to barrel upward, screaming. The boy's curved saber swung down, but my father's neck was no longer beneath the blade.

Faster than the eye could follow he slipped out of the way, grabbing the boy's wrist and twisting it with a snap of bone, striking him in the face with the heel of his hand, sending the boy flying backward.

It all happened in less than a second, my father a streak of scarlet, a blur so fast that it was all over before the last echo of my shriek died in the air.

The boy tumbled to the ground, cradling his broken wrist, blood streaming from his eye. His cutlass lay on the grass between the two lines of soldiers. My father stood safe and untouched, except for a thin cut on the side of his neck where the blade of the sword had bit.

Uncle Nikolasha rushed forward with a dozen men. Before they could lay hands on the boy, the Ataman threw himself on his knees in front of my father, hands outstretched.

"I take responsibility! I take responsibility."

Nikolasha already had his sword drawn. The soldiers pointed their pistols at the boy's face.

A firing squad *would* be a mercy—the emperors of old would have cut the boy's limbs from his body with an axe, then broke his back on the wheel.

The boy snarled like an animal, his left eye split across the brow, his gloved hand twisted in his lap.

"*Please.*" Kaledin's hands shook as he raised them to my father, palms upward. "Don't kill my son."

Silence stretched down the line of soldiers.

I didn't think my father knew the Ataman had a son. His face was difficult to read as he studied the boy on the ground.

At last he said, "Stand."

The Ataman stood, and so did the boy. Though he didn't touch his son, I thought Kaledin would throw himself in front of the boy if he had to.

"What's your name?"

The boy lifted his chin. The whole side of his face had swollen, blood running down from the closed eye.

"Damien Kaledin, son of Taras Kaledin, leader of the Free Men."

My father stared down at Damien, his face closed and cold. He was the Tsar now, not Papa.

"Do you know who I am?"

The boy breathed through his teeth, the bones of his wrist visible through the skin. The angle of his hand was awful, his left eye swollen shut. He stared up at my father like he'd still love to kill him. His hate was metal in the air, I could taste it.

"You're Nicholas Time-Walker." His lips twisted in a sneer. "Nicholas the Bloodstained."

Uncle Nikolasha made a sound in his throat. Several soldiers cocked their guns.

My father loathed that epitaph. It was forbidden to speak it aloud in the dead of the night in one's own home, let alone in his presence.

He towered over the boy, magic thick in the air. Everyone knew if my father drew his sword and cut Damien's throat, the strike would come so fast no one would even see it. The wound would open as if cut by the hand of a god.

"I'm your Emperor," Papa said quietly. "You will kneel before me."

The Ataman dropped to his knees. All the other Cossacks did the same. Only the boy stayed standing. He shook with anger, not with fear.

If Damien refused to kneel, my father would cut him down.

Every second felt like a scream. Damien's fingertip touched the wrist of his glove. Then, all at once, he dropped to his knees.

My father said, "Do you serve your Ataman faithfully?"

Damien nodded, jaw tight. "I do."

"When your father swears his oath to me, will you serve him still?"

Damien's good hand twitched in its black leather glove. He glanced at his father, who remained stone faced and kneeling, like he could see and hear nothing. Actually, I think he was feeling everything, ten times as much.

"*Yes,*" Damien hissed. "I'll serve him still."

My father extended his hand to the Ataman, palm down.

Nikolasha said, "Do you swear your allegiance and the allegiance of your people to protect Rusya with all your strength, under the command of his Imperial Highness, Nicholas the Second?"

"I swear," the Ataman promised. He took my father's hand and kissed his gold ring.

53

Nikolasha turned to the ranks of kneeling Cossacks.

"You all bear witness. Your leader has sworn his fealty. You will continue to serve your Ataman as he serves the Emperor."

Father's soldiers raised their rifles, shouting, "TO THE EMPEROR!"

The Cossacks were forced to do the same.

Even Damien raised his uninjured fist and saluted my father, though hatred burned on his face.

"Bring him to the dais," Papa said.

The Ataman helped his son to stand. Damien couldn't hide the pain of his wrist. His face was pale and sweating beneath the half mask of blood.

The pair approached the dais, Uncle Nikolasha taking care to stand between my father and his would-be murderer.

Papa hardly paid the boy any attention. Face to face, my father was as invincible as ever. He wouldn't be caught by surprise again.

I was much less comfortable, wearing the same military coat as Papa with none of his authority. The boy turned his wolf eyes on me. He knew it was me who screamed. I shrunk behind the tattooed mermaid on Andrei Derevenko's arm.

Papa lifted the heavy gilt pen from the table and scratched out one part of the contract, writing over the line.

"Each of your men will provide ten years' military service to the empire," he said to the Ataman. "Including you."

"I gave my years."

"And now you'll give more. 'I take responsibility'—that's what you said." Damien looked like he'd lost all his air. Kaledin signed the contract.

Papa looked down at Damien, arms crossed in front of him.

"I remember you from the field ..." His eyes held that strange purplish light that lingered a week or so after he returned from a battleground. "Death spreads his gifts among the Cossacks. It would be a shame to waste yours. You'll attend the military academy in St. Petersburg so you can learn to be of use to me."

Damien blanched. Kaledin's mouth went thin beneath the heavy mustache, but his shoulders sagged with relief.

"As you say, Imperial Majesty."

I could tell Nikolasha didn't think much of the idea. He looked at Damien as if one of his borzoi had just given birth to a wolf pup—as if he'd like to drown him in a river and be done with him.

"The Grand Duke will take charge of your son," Papa said. "He'll provide him with everything he needs to enter the academy."

Damien and Nikolasha stared at my father in horror.

Nikolasha had withstood decades of maternal nagging to remain unmarried and childless. He loved roaming between his various estates with only his dogs and his horses for company.

He looked remarkably like a Cossack as he muttered, "As you say, Majesty."

Damien swayed on his feet. His wrist was still bent at that sickening angle, blood running down from the gash in his eyebrow, disappearing on the breast of his dark coat. He gazed out at the wide-open hills of the steppes as if they were already disappearing before his eyes.

"Clean him up," Papa ordered. "He'll take the train back with the rest of us."

chapter 5

THE BOY ON THE TRAIN

The two armies parted, the Cossacks remounting their horses and galloping back the way they came. The Ataman and a few of his men remained to accompany Damien to the infirmary tent.

I was bustled back to my father's tent, where I found myself alone in the dim, cool space, a headache pounding behind my eyes. I flopped down on the carpeted divan that matched one Papa had in his office at home.

Papa joined me a moment later. His weight made the cushion sink. I rolled partway onto his lap, horribly nauseated.

Papa stroked my hair with his heavy hand.

"You feel sick, little mischief?"

"Yes," I groaned.

"That happened to me, the first time."

I lifted my head a few inches. Even that small motion made the room spin.

"What happened, Papa?"

"You slowed time."

The words hit me like a blow. That was the gift of the Romanovs—the greatest power anyone possessed. It made us gods among men.

Alexei was supposed to have it, not me.

I looked up at my father.

"Are you sure, Papa?"

He smiled beneath his beard. "You saved my life."

I let out the breath I'd been holding. The floral pattern of the divan seemed to pulse before my eyes with each thud pressing against my temples.

"I didn't mean to. I saw the boy—Damien—I saw him grab his sword and it just ... happened."

Papa nodded.

"It was the same for me. My brother Michael climbed up on the windowsill at Anichkov when he was maybe two or three. He leaned against the glass and the latch gave way. Everything slowed. I ran faster and faster, while all the world stilled. I snatched him by the arm and saved him from the fall, though a doctor had to come to put his shoulder right. I didn't know then how speed increases force."

I realized why I'd been able to push the soldiers out of the way so easily, and why Damien's injuries had been so severe. As dull as our Swiss tutor could be, I did occasionally remember our physics lessons.

"When did you manifest?" Papa asked me.

"I ... I don't know. When Uncle came home, he gave me Artemis, and I thought I heard her speak ... but then she went silent again ..."

"Let me see her."

I got up from the divan and retrieved Artemis, the room still tilting around me.

When Papa opened the box, she screeched. I lifted her out and she calmed in my hands, nestled against the warmth of my body.

Papa looked at Artemis without touching her. She watched my father in return, tracking every movement with those beady black eyes that showed that her mind moved as fast as the rest of her.

"Beautiful creature," he said.

I stroked Artemis' head with the ball of my thumb. This time she let me.

Papa laid his heavy hand on my head in much the same way.

"I always knew you had power in you."

"I can't control it."

"You'll learn."

I'd seen my father slip in and out of time as graceful as a diver in deep water. To wield that type of power would be ... intoxicating.

Nikolasha came into the tent. He was a time-walker too, though no one could do it as long or as well as Papa. In the battle of Mukden, my father stopped time for two straight minutes, slaughtering General Nori and a hundred of his host while they stood frozen on the field.

There was no defense against it. No counterspell. Even the Cossacks on their horses couldn't outrun my father.

Nikolasha approached as if I were a stranger, peering into my face.

"Little Stassie," he murmured. "How you love to surprise us."

"You think I'll be able to do it again?"

He nodded. "It's in you—we know that now."

Papa sighed. "Nothing ever goes as you think it will, does it, cousin?"

Nikolasha grunted. "I didn't expect to end the day with a ward."

My father made a sound that was almost an apology.

"It'll be good for you, Nikolasha—another wild animal for you to tame."

"I've never been partial to *wild* animals." He frowned. "Anastasia should add him to her collection."

"Why did you spare Damien?" I looked sideways at my father. "Because he's so young?"

"To ensure his father's loyalty. If Kaledin retains control of his host, it buys me ten years of peace."

"*If,*" Nikolasha scoffed. "That's the trouble with democracy—it's damned fickle."

The Cossacks elected their own Atamans. Their leader's authority was subject to the whims of the people.

I saw the way the Cossacks followed Kaledin. Even Damien knelt when his father knelt.

"They trust him," I said.

"They do." My father gave me an approving look. "And Kaledin must be attached to his son—I never thought I'd see him beg. The boy's valuable. Keep him alive, Nikolasha."

Nikolasha sighed. He was Papa's closest friend, but even he bowed to the Emperor.

"The academy will put his head on straight," Nikolasha said. "Or knock it off his shoulders."

WE STAYED the night at the camp, taking the wagons back to the station in the morning.

59

Damien rode in the back of an emptied supply wagon like a prisoner of war. His wrist was freshly splinted, hands unbound, but he sat like a captive, head bowed.

He still wore those black leather gloves, even on his injured hand.

The night before, I saw the medic stumble from the infirmary tent, gray and reeling, to vomit in the grass outside. I knew it must have something to do with Damien, though I couldn't guess what. His wounds weren't severe enough to make a man sick—especially not a medic used to battlefield injuries.

Damien eyed the locomotive with suspicion, only boarding after a soldier nudged him in the back with the barrel of his rifle. I wondered if he'd ever ridden a train before.

Alexei climbed the steps quietly, sweating and pale. The long journey was taking its toll on him. He walked stiffly, Andrei Derevenko holding his arm.

Papa was returning home with us, along with Uncle Nikolasha. They disappeared into the smoking car together, maybe to discuss matters of state, but more likely to catch a nap.

Alexei likewise retired to his cabin.

I was too keyed up to sleep. I roamed up and down the length of the train, Artemis cradled in my arms like an infant. She was always most docile in motion, though "docile" was a relative term.

I wished we'd seen more of the steppes. We hadn't visited the Cossack camp, or the mine, or ridden in the Frost Forest ...

I walked down to the caboose, which was a large, open observation deck with a view of everything you were leaving.

I blundered inside before I realized Damien sat facing the open windows, monitored by two of my father's guards.

The guards stood and saluted, gripping Damien by the arms so they could hustle him out.

"Stop!" I said. "He can stay."

I couldn't rob him of his last glimpse of the steppes—even if he tried to kill my father.

It didn't earn me any gratitude. The boy turned one furious look on me, then faced the window again.

He was lean and wiry, deeply tanned though it was only early spring. I supposed he spent all his hours outdoors.

He was supposed to be my enemy, but I wanted to know all about him. I wanted to ask where he lived, what he ate, whether he had a mother.

Slipping onto the opposite bench, I set Artemis on the cushioned seat. Her injured wing was still splinted and wrapped, but Uncle had removed the gauze bands that bound her wings to her body so she could extend them for balance as she hopped about.

Artemis took a few experimental steps, acclimatizing herself to the motion of the train. She didn't stumble even when the car lurched. I couldn't wait to see her fly.

Her feathers glimmered like metal, rich black speckles all down her back. Her face and breast were pure as fresh-fallen snow.

Even Damien had to admire her.

"She's a gyrfalcon," I said.

"I know that." He paused, frowning. "*You're* a girl. "

I was unreasonably annoyed that he'd noticed.

"So what?"

"Why are you wearing boy's clothes?"

"Why are you wearing those gloves?"

Low and soft he said, "Come here and I'll show you."

I stayed right where I was. The guards wouldn't allow it, and I wasn't a complete idiot.

"I'm Anastasia Nikolaevna."

"The *princess*," he sneered.

Technically I was a Grand Duchess, but I didn't think Damien was interested in the nuances of imperial court titles. He'd already turned back to the windows.

I'd lived all my life in cities. The scale of the steppes awed me. The sky shimmered like silk, the grass like dry gold. The air ran into my lungs, cold and clean as water. Wild horses raced over the downs.

"Do you capture the horses?" I asked Damien.

He looked at me without answering. I had thought his eyes were brown, but now I realized they were dark green, like a pine bough in the part of the forest where the light never shines.

"All Cossacks capture their first horse," he said at last. "It took me three days to run down Mercury."

"Mercury's the filly you were riding?"

It had been a magnificent creature—a pale frost color with a jet mane and tail and a dark nose.

Damien's face twisted before he could hide it.

He'd had to leave his horse behind, along with everything he owned.

Pity bit at me again.

I'd never be a proper princess if I couldn't learn to control my emotions. My father warned me, "A court is no place for kindness." Kindness could get you killed.

Even now, the guards watched Damien's every move in case, having failed with my father, he decided to attack a more vulnerable target.

"It's beautiful here," I said carefully. "But St. Petersburg is beautiful, too. In the summer we have fairs and boating parties, in the winters ice skating and dancing bears. There's balls and parties—"

"You think I care about *parties?*" Damien hissed.

Artemis made a low chirping sound that was almost a growl.

One of the guards raised his hand to strike Damien, barking, "Watch your tongue, you dog."

"*Don't!*" I cried. "He's my uncle's ward."

The guard lowered his hand, frowning.

"As you wish, Imperial Highness. But if I might say—"

"You may not. Don't interrupt again."

I wasn't usually such a tyrant. Wearing Alexei's clothes was rubbing off on me—I felt as imperious as a Tsarevich. Nothing was going to stop me talking to Damien. He annoyed and intrigued me in equal measure.

"I was only trying to cheer you up," I snapped back at him. "You're lucky my father didn't kill you."

"He's lucky I didn't kill *him.*"

The guards rumbled but didn't dare move.

Low and disdainful I said, "You never would have had a chance if you didn't attack from behind like a coward."

"A coward!" he seethed. "You think it's bravery when your father slaughters us before we can move or blink? You think that's a fight?"

"You use whatever powers you have, everyone does! Just because yours aren't as effective—"

"You use more than your powers," Damien snarled. "What's it like to fight fair, princess? I'd love to see how you'd fare on the battlefield without your precious rock."

We were almost past the long black mountain range with the mining town at its base. Irresistibly, we turned and gazed upon the rocky slopes, barren and dark, with streaks of unmelted snow at the peaks.

"You don't care that this land is *beautiful*," Damien said. "You only want it for one thing."

"We found Charoite. We discovered how to use it. It's how we united Rusya!"

"United," Damien jeered. "Conquered, you mean."

"You wish Siberia was still overrun with monsters and demons?"

"The victors write the history," Damien said coldly. "You think the Romanovs were the first to discover Charoite?" He laughed in my face. "The Free People knew it. We didn't dig it from the mountain because we knew it was dangerous."

"Dangerous to *you* when we use it, maybe."

"You know what we say about you? Ruskies think they painted the sky blue."

I flushed. "Maybe we did."

"I'm sure *you* think so."

I couldn't let it go.

"We use Charoite to protect the people."

"You enslave the people. Have you ever set foot in that mine?"

Of course I hadn't. Angry as I was, I'd never admit it.

"The miners are paid for their work."

"What price do you pay to smother on dirt? To break your back? To be crushed under a mountain of fallen rock? What price would I have to pay *you* to do it?"

"All jobs have their disadvantages," I said lamely.

"How would you know? You've never worked a day in your life, *princess.*"

That infuriated me more than anything. My mother was a great believer that hands should never be idle. I was constantly kept busy, unless I was outside in the garden.

"I work and study all day long!" I cried. "I speak Albion, German, French, Rusyan, I know algebra and geometry, I can calculate the path of the planets, I know the history of every European nation, the rise and fall of the noble houses, the principal wars and achievements. And *besides* that, I do needlepoint for charity!"

"*Needlepoint!*" Damien scoffed. "How kind of you to share your *needlepoint.*"

I flushed red.

Damien leaned forward so we were eye to eye, separated only by the narrow aisle between benches. The guards shifted, hands close to their swords, but didn't intervene.

"What did you do to me?" he demanded, voice pitched low so the guards wouldn't hear over the chug of the train and the wind passing the open windows. "What did you do when we stood across from each other on the field?"

"I didn't do anything."

"Don't lie, I felt it."

"Maybe *you* did it!" I cried, outraged. "Why are you blaming me?"

As we glared at each other, I could feel it again—a loss of balance that had nothing to do with the motion of the train. The air crackled with potential magic.

Damien touched his eyebrow with his fingertips.

Spitefully I said, "You'll have a scar."

"Good," he retorted, just as bitter.

"They're going to eat you alive at the academy."

He snorted. "I've fought grown men. I'm not scared of aristocrats."

Now it was my turn to be contemptuous.

"You've never been a noble. Every day is war for us. Enemies all around—spies in your own court, your own family, even. My great-grandfather survived a dozen assassination attempts. He survived a bomb under his dining room table! I doubt you could do the same."

"I could if I had your power."

"It's a gift from the gods. The gods keep us alive because it's our divine destiny to rule."

"Isn't that convenient?" Damien tossed his head. "The gods' wishes line up so well with yours."

"That's blasphemy."

"I keep the Old Beliefs."

"And that's why you live like a savage."

Damien snorted.

"You think your stinking cities are progress? You've probably never tasted air so clear."

He took a deep breath as if he'd fill his lungs with it and hold it there for all the time he was captive in St. Petersburg.

I almost wished I'd let the guard slap him.

"You'd better learn to like it," I hissed. "You're not going home anytime soon."

Damien's gloved hands clenched in his lap.

"The treaty won't last. It's a disgrace."

"Your father signed it. Unlike you, he strikes me as a man of honor."

Damien looked so murderous that I pulled Artemis onto my lap, out of his reach.

"I'd never surrender," he hissed. "When I'm Ataman, you'll see."

"And what a great Ataman you'll be," I mocked him. "You'll be king for a day before your whole host is killed."

"We'll see." His eyes burned. "No dynasty lasts forever. Where I failed ... someone else will succeed."

I gathered Artemis against my chest and stood, trembling with anger and wishing I'd never spoken to Damien at all.

I said, "Talk like that around my uncle and he'll cut out your tongue."

PART TWO

chapter 6

THE MYSTIC

2 YEARS LATER

The night before my exhibition, Liza Taneeva threw a party. As a general rule, my sisters and I would do anything to avoid Liza's evening parties, which were stingy on both food and entertainment. That night, however, we dressed with actual excitement because we were finally meeting the mystic who'd been the talk of St. Petersburg for the past two years.

We ran back and forth between Ollie and Tatiana's room and Maria's and mine, swapping sashes and necklaces, ribbons and broaches.

Our favorite maid Nina Ivanova came in to help us lace up our stays.

I'd started wearing a corset after weeks of arguments with Mama. Mama had never been as cruel as the noblewomen who started their toddlers in corsets and forced their daughters to tightlace day and night. But she could no longer ignore that my waist was a horrifying twenty-nine inches.

Tatiana measured a perfect eighteen, though she was taller than Mama now. She hardly flinched as Nina pulled her laces tight.

"I don't mind it. In fact, it feels stranger when it's off."

"It feels like I'm being swallowed by an anaconda!"

"You can loosen it after the party," Ollie said. "That's what I do."

I planned to burn my corset after the party but didn't say so.

All the pain and trouble to beautify myself was pointless. I'd finally sprouted a few inches—it only made me more awkward. And no amount of rice powder was going to cover how tanned I'd become boating and picnicking all summer long.

"You're brown as a peasant!" Nina lamented. "Don't you own a parasol?"

"I like being brown! And I like sunshine even more."

Nina sighed. "It doesn't matter what you like. It matters what your husband will like."

"I don't want any husband."

"Don't be a twit. Of course you're going to have a husband."

Nina was clever with her hands. She could fix anything, even complicated toys or fragile bits of jewelry. She made her own tools and had built an entire sewing machine out of spare parts. Neat and dark haired, she was barely older than Ollie and saved every penny she could to marry a handsome officer named Armand who visited her whenever he was on leave.

"Everyone marries eventually." Ollie slid a glittering dragonfly hairpin into her curls.

"*Et tu, Brute?*" I shook my head at her.

Ollie should have been my strongest ally, but even she'd been beaten into shocking conventionality since turning nineteen.

It was the balls that did it. Athletic as ever, Ollie was becoming known as one of the finest dancers in St. Petersburg. She was in higher demand than Tatiana even.

My sisters had gone so mad for balls that Mama had been forced to throw several. Apparently balls were like mushrooms, because now they were popping up everywhere.

My sisters hauled the gramophone all over the palace to practice. You couldn't cross the billiards hall or the parlor without someone sweeping you into a waltz.

I felt a little betrayed, especially by Maria. We were the "Little Pair." I'd been the leader of our duo when the agenda was hunting for snakes in the garden or playing Marlinspike with the guards. Now I could only tag along while my sisters walked the endless length of Nevsky Prospect looking for the most elegant ostrich feathers or a choice trimming of lace.

I knew I was supposed to be growing up, too, but I didn't want to. I liked our family just the way it was, when we were all together all the time. I didn't want anything to change.

Once we were all dressed, we went downstairs to meet Mama in the Mountain Hall.

Rusyans call slides "mountains". That hall used to contain an enormous mountain built for my great-grandfather Alexander II. We'd spent endless rainy days skidding down it at reckless speeds on bits of old carpet, while the servants desperately tried to prevent Alexei tumbling into the porcelain ornaments perched all around the room.

The slide had been removed in the spring when Alexei informed Mama he was too old for such things. At ten, he decided he was a young man. I thought he'd be back to his toy soldiers and miniature Mercedes soon enough, but he maintained his newfound dignity all through the summer.

Papa was pleased. At last Alexei was coming into his study voluntarily, and he'd even begun to show a modicum of consideration to people other than himself.

I sighed. If Alexei was no longer spoiled, and Ollie was resigned to the concept of marriage, what would come next? Would Maria lose her shyness? Would Tatiana cease to be vain? What a horrible thought.

Mama came into the Mountain Hall, looking utterly elegant. Her champagne gown was draped with lace and pleated all down the skirt. She lined us up in front of the largest mirror so she could examine us.

We resembled a flock of butterflies in our fluttery frocks. Ollie wore lilac, Tatiana frothy waves of seafoam green, Maria pink, me my favorite shade of blue. I looked like I fit with my sisters, the way objects seem to go together if you arrange them right.

"What angels you are!" Mama kissed us each in turn. "I've never seen such loveliness."

I smelled roses in her hair. All the lamps in her room burned pure rose oil. It lingered in her clothes and even her handkerchiefs.

Mama was escorting us to the party. Usually she'd have sent one of our aunts, but Liza made such a fuss about how she'd ordered in all Mama's favorite cheeses that Mama knew Liza was ready to be good and pouty if she didn't attend herself.

Both my aunts were joining us anyway because that's how famous this mystic was getting—even Xenia wanted to meet him, though she pretended Irina dragged her along.

Aunt Olga was such a favorite with all of us that Papa gifted her a palace on Sergievskaya Street. She was the baby of Papa's family and felt more like an older sister than an aunt. She'd been married eight years without any children, so she lavished all her attention on us.

We picked her up on the way to the party. She crowded into the second carriage with Maria and me, putting her arm around my waist and kissing me on the cheek. She was the only relative that liked me best; she smuggled me books I wasn't supposed to read and told me secrets no one else knew.

"I never thought I'd be so excited to visit Liza Taneeva's house! Have you met this mystic?"

Maria shook her head. "Mama wouldn't let us."

"Even though Liza never shuts up about him," I laughed.

Liza Taneeva became the mystic's most ardent admirer after he predicted she would meet her future husband within the year. Liza married Alexander Vasilievich Vyrubov ten months later, despite the fact that the mystic also warned her the marriage would be an unhappy one.

"I suppose she had to take who she could get," Aunt Olga said. "The beaus weren't exactly beating down her door."

"*Are* they unhappy?" Maria asked.

I shrugged. "See for yourself—he'll be there tonight."

Aunt Olga picked at the lace on her sleeve.

Her marriage wasn't happy, either. Her husband lived in the opposite wing of their palace.

"Why wouldn't Alix let you see the mystic?" Olga asked.

"Mama doesn't like sorcerers," Maria said. "She says it's all dark arts—trying to enhance your power through supernatural means. She says people ought to be satisfied with what the gods gave them."

"Alix brings religion into everything," said Aunt Olga with distaste.

Papa's family wasn't devout, or no more than they needed to be. Mama was a true believer and thought everyone else should be, too. She was like a nun who doesn't notice she's the only one wearing a habit.

We arrived at Liza's lemon-yellow house in Tsarskoye Selo. A dozen carriages lined up on the curb, excited partygoers hurrying up the walk.

The mystic was the talk of the city. There was no end to the miracles he was said to have produced.

As soon as we entered the house, I looked around for my first glimpse of this supposed sorcerer. All I saw were the same old courtiers and aristocrats.

Princess Irina ran up to us, pink-cheeked with excitement.

"He's already here!" she cried. "Liza Taneeva says he's upstairs getting ready."

"Getting ready for what?"

"I don't know! I hope he puts on a show. I heard a mystic in Moscow can make indoor fireworks that don't even singe the drapes!"

Irina was looking particularly lovely with her black curls pinned up, diamond pins glittering here and there like stars. Her white dress revealed the luscious figure for which she was famous, a black velvet band around her creamy throat.

Across the room, a young man gaped at her. That was too common for me to even point it out.

Ollie and Tatiana joined us a moment later. Ollie had already drunk a full glass of champagne and was in high spirits, snickering at some bit of gossip.

"You shouldn't eavesdrop," Irina said.

Tatiana shrugged. "I can't help it if people whisper their secrets where I can hear them. What am I supposed to do, wear earplugs?"

Ollie hid her second drink behind her back while Mama passed us.

"Did you see, Mama?" She grinned. "Liza brought in all your favorite cheeses!"

"She's the kindest of friends." Mama was oblivious to how hard we were trying not to laugh.

"She only mentioned it a *hundred* times," Ollie muttered, once Mama passed. Tatiana and I dissolved in giggles.

Ollie gulped down the rest of her champagne. "Liza really did put on the Ritz. I've never seen her tables so heavy."

I laughed. "She must like this mystic more than us."

The last time we'd come, Liza only offered us cold mutton with pickled cucumbers, promising it was wonderful for the constitution. Ollie said Liza must be hung over, because that was the only time anybody wanted cold mutton.

Now the tables groaned with sturgeon and salmon, piles of caviar, sweet braided breads, and dozens of imported cheeses, all sitting on mounds of ice that must have cost more than the food at this time of year. I followed Ollie's example and gulped down a glass of champagne before Mama could notice.

Aunt Olga didn't care. Aunt Xenia was another thing—Irina reached for her own glass, then drew back her hand as if she'd been stung as her mother snapped her fan at her from the other side of the room.

Olga said, "Xenia's against a glass of champagne now, is she?"

"Mama told me she never touched a drink until she was married."

Aunt Olga snorted. "That could be true ... if she was always wearing gloves."

Liza Taneeva approached, greeting us as loudly as possible.

"Welcome, welcome! I'm so glad you could all come to meet my very special friend! Have you helped yourselves to all this excellent food?"

Her new husband followed close behind her, stiff and upright and unsmiling. He had a pencil-thin mustache and hair parted to a razor's edge, slicked tight to the skull, gleaming with Brillo cream. He looked as dour as an undertaker and old enough to be her grandfather.

I almost felt sorry for Liza. Until she leaned in close to Ollie and sniffed.

"I certainly hope that's not champagne on your breath."

"Mouthwash," Ollie lied, too tipsy to bother trying to sound convincing.

"You know how your mother feels about drinking."

"Oh yes," Ollie smiled. "I'm intimately acquainted with her, you know."

Liza drew her mouth in until it almost disappeared. It was hard to remember that she hadn't even celebrated her thirtieth birthday—she was primmer than Grandma Minnie.

"Is this your husband?" Aunt Olga interjected.

"Alexander Vasilievich Vyrubov," Liza's voice went extra soft and breathy. "Allow me to introduce you to the Grand Duchess Olga Alexandrovna, youngest sister of Tsar Nicholas the Second."

Vyrubov bowed at the waist. "Charmed."

"Thank you for hosting us." Aunt Olga curtseyed in return.

Vyrubov's face was sour. "I don't think much of fortune-tellers. But women must have their entertainments."

Liza forced a laugh. "Yes, we must. You'll see that my friend is much more than a fortune teller—even you, my love, will be impressed."

"I doubt it." In the tone of someone who knows it's impossible, Vyrubov said, "Enjoy the party," and carried on his way, his wife trailing in his wake.

"What a delightful man," Aunt Olga said, making the rest of us snort.

"Who's delightful?" Dimitri Pavlovich said. "Other than me."

He carried a flute of champagne in each hand. Seeing nowhere to set them down, he tossed them back one after another. "I think Liza watered it down..."

"We're talking about Vyrubov," Aunt Olga clarified.

"Oh, him." Dimitri ditched his empty glasses behind one of Liza's potted plants. "He's a cold fish. They like him in the cavalry, though—he's got quite an unusual ability."

"What?" Tatiana asked.

"He can make you fall asleep," Dimitri said. "Just by laying his hand on your arm. Comes in handy in the field when nobody can nod off."

"I bet he uses it on Liza all the time." Ollie grinned. "She starts going on about how they need new rugs and next thing she knows she's waking up from a nice, refreshing nap ..."

We hadn't seen much of Dimitri Pavlovich over the summer because he'd fallen in with a new group of friends. Mama said she was glad he'd stopped moping around so much, but now we heard rumors of wild parties and scandalous pranks pulled by his pack of hooligans.

"I want to introduce you to my best mate," Dimitri said to Ollie and Irina.

"You're not talking about *Felix*, are you?" Tatiana made a face.

"What's wrong with Felix?"

Tatiana listed his crimes on her fingers. "He's flunked out of every school he's attended, he's been arrested three times, plus Aunt Xenia hates him."

Irina cast a nervous look at her mother, deep in conversation with Viceroy Uvarov.

"Never mind all that." Dimitri seized Irina by the wrist. "He's hilarious, you'll love him."

I hadn't been invited to the introduction, but after Tatiana's recommendation, there was no way I was going to miss out on meeting this Felix person.

Dimitri pulled us through the press of party guests, weaving in and out until we stopped behind a young man in a stylish cream-colored suit, a straw boater perched rakishly on his head.

Dimitri tapped him on the shoulder.

The young man spun around, hands stuffed in his pockets, already smiling.

"There you are, old sod! I've been looking for—" He broke off, catching sight of Irina. Staggering back a step, he clapped his hand to his chest and cried, "It *is* you, I knew it!"

Irina blushed to the roots of her hair. "Hello again."

"I saw this gorgeous creature two years ago in Alexandria Park." Felix was smiling and shaking his head at the same time. "I've been kicking myself ever since that I didn't stop to speak with you. You were with the most dour-looking woman—"

"My mother."

"The loveliest-looking woman, I meant to say." Felix grinned. "I plucked up my courage and rode back a minute later, but you were gone. I asked everyone who you might be, but no one seemed to know. The mystery was driving me mad! And now I find out all I had to do was ask Dimitri!"

He turned on Dimitri, delighted and accusing.

"These are my cousins, Princess Irina Alexandrovna and the Grand Duchess Olga Nikolaevna. Oh, and Anastasia," Dimitri added.

"Dimitri's told me all about you." Felix shook hands with us as fast as he could so he could go back to staring at Irina.

Irina was blushing like a sunset, which only made her prettier.

"He told us about you, too," Ollie warned. "Didn't you attend the governor's ball dressed in your mother's gown?"

Felix laughed, unabashed.

"You heard about that?"

"I heard the governor threw you out."

"He was only mad because he didn't realize until *after* he asked me to dance."

Irina glanced up from under her lashes.

"Are you fond of dancing?"

"I'm mad about it." Felix took Irina's hand and lifted it lightly to his lips. "If you come to the officer's hall next week—"

Aunt Xenia inserted herself between the pair. Tall and broad as she was, this was no small barrier.

"Irina!" she said severely. "Come with me. I wish to introduce you to the Duke of Montebello."

"Yes, Mama."

Irina tried to smile at Felix before her mother hustled her away.

"I remember *her*, too," Felix muttered, once Xenia was out of earshot.

"Better watch out," Ollie said cheerfully. "Aunt Xenia will skin you alive if she catches you skulking around Irina."

"I don't *skulk*." Felix winked at Ollie. "I'm so much sneakier than that."

Ollie and I caught up with Irina just in time to hear the end of the chewing-out Xenia was giving her.

"—reckless, irresponsible, drunk half the time, an utter disgrace to his family! I don't know why Liza Taneeva invited him."

"Probably because he's the richest man in St. Petersburg," Sylvie Buxhoeveden remarked.

"Not yet he isn't," Xenia snapped. "And he's not likely to live to inherit, the way he carries on."

"Dimitri was only introducing us," Irina said softly.

"I'll have a word with *him* later," Xenia seethed. "I'll introduce you to the devil before I see you acquainted with Felix Yusupov."

Aunt Xenia seemed determined to keep an eagle eye on Irina the rest of the night, but only twenty minutes passed before Archpriest Belyaev and the Minister of Culture sucked her into some political debate.

"The proletariat need a voice in government—"

"They can bring their petitions to the Tsar."

"But petitions aren't always heard. In a parliamentary system—"

"Rusya will *never* have a parliament," Xenia cut in.

"Albion has one. France, too."

"We're not *French*," Xenia said with utmost disdain. "Much as you might admire their cooking, Belyaev. Look at how it emboldened their people— Marie Antoinette's head on the chopping block. Is that how you want to end up? Remember that they executed the priests and the politicians too, not just the royals. Give the people autonomy and they only want more. And what will they do with it? They'll write laws to benefit the farmers and the trades-men, while the army weakens, the roads fall apart, the taxes dry up, and the country collapses. They have no idea how to run a nation, how could they?"

Ollie and I grabbed Irina by the elbows, sneaking her away while her mother was distracted.

We were just in time. Liza Taneeva rang a gong, inviting everyone to proceed into the next room.

Liza's parties had never been so well attended. There was a scramble to fill the seats, leaving many people standing against the wall.

Mama was given a place of honor in the front row with Sylvie Buxho-eveden on one side, Tatiana and Maria on the other. Aunt Olga sat next to Sylvie, and Aunt Xenia next to Olga, close enough to my mother to appear friendly without actually having to speak to her.

Ollie, Irina, and I deliberately took positions along the side wall where we'd have a good view of the proceedings without falling under the watchful eye of our chaperones.

Ollie took out her fan, flapping it in her own face.

"What does Liza mean, stuffing us all in here? The least she could do is open a window."

The room was abominably hot, packed with heavy drapes, layers of carpets, and dozens upon dozens of pouffes in Liza's favorite shades of sunshine yellow and salmon pink.

Ollie wasn't the only one shifting mutinously. The Archpriest wiped his sweating face with a handkerchief, and the Minister of Culture muttered that this mystic better be worth a night away from his dinner club.

Liza Taneeva didn't seem to notice. She faced her guests, hands clasped girlishly in front of her, face alight with excitement. I could see how carefully she'd dressed for the evening in a velvet jacket with puffed sleeves, lace spilling out the cuffs, her gold eyeglasses perched on her breast at the end of a long chain.

"I'm so glad you could all come here tonight to witness something truly spectacular. I want you all to relax ... and open your minds ..."

Her dark eyes glittered as the lights began to dim.

I couldn't see who was lowering the lights, only that the lamps were fading, long shadows falling over Liza's face.

Felix Yusupov took the opportunity to slip in next to Irina. He leaned against the wallpaper, partially concealed by a Japanese screen and fully out of view of Xenia.

Liza continued, "You've heard of this holy man, who walked thousands of miles on his journey to our great city. Everywhere he goes, magic and miracles follow. Since he came to St. Petersburg, some of you have born witness to the great blessings he's bestowed upon us! He healed Madame Dubois of a pneumonia so severe that the priest had already come to bestow final rites."

A tiny woman in the front row, gray haired and bespectacled, nodded vigorously, confirming this story—Madame Dubois, I supposed. My mother turned her head and gazed at her a moment before facing forward again.

"He told Baron Razumovsky where to find the body of his son that had lain lost in the Frost Forest for many years."

Another small disruption as several people turned to look at the stern, black-haired baron. Razumovsky didn't acknowledge the attention. He remained stiff and unsmiling, his eyes burning with zealous light as he waited for Liza to continue.

"He stopped the bleeding when Charlotte Golovina began to miscarry her child."

"Indeed, he did!" Charlotte cried aloud, waving her handkerchief in the air, then dabbing at her eyes. "My baby lives today, because of him!"

Now my mother turned all the way around. She stared at Charlotte, her face pinched and pale as paper.

I was beginning to feel uncomfortable. This was not what I expected. I thought we were here to see a magic show.

There was something worshipful in the way Madame Dubois, the Baron, and Charlotte Golovina waited, as if on pilgrimage to see this mystic again.

No one moved, even Ollie stopped fanning. The light had all faded away. Felix shifted a little closer to Irina.

Liza Taneeva stood in front of us, shawl around her shoulders, head bowed like an acolyte. I could no longer see her face.

Her voice sounded unlike her own, deep and resonant:

"He's a man who understands great mysteries and reveals truth. A seeker of knowledge. A light in the darkness. May I present ... Grigory RASPUTIN!"

I expected a flash and bang, smoke and fire, the usual tricks of mystics who wanted to make an entrance.

Instead, there was nothing but silence.

Then a cold wind blew into the room.

It danced across our sweating faces, lifting the hair off our brows. It caressed my skin, light and sensual and deliciously cool. It whispered in my ear, *Anastasia* ...

All the hair stood up on my arms. I stared in every direction, seeing nothing in the thick, black dark.

Softly, ever so softly, music began to play, as if Tatiana were practicing in some distant corner of the palace, late in the night ...

♪♪ *Problematique—Lenovie*

A pale blue light kindled everywhere and nowhere—just enough to illuminate the edges of Ollie's fan, the buttons on Felix's jacket, and Irina's white-gloved hand resting on the wall. Felix's pinky brushed against Irina's.

Something cold landed on my cheek.

I touched it. A snowflake perched on my fingertip like a tiny frozen star.

More snow fell, drifting down from the ceiling.

The partygoers gazed up in wonder, mouths open like children to catch the snow.

I'd never seen such magic. The snowflake melted on my finger, forming a droplet like a tear.

No one saw him come in.

One moment, Liza was alone. The next, Rasputin stood beside her.

He wore the plain black cloak of a priest, head bowed, hands concealed within the long sleeves of the robe. When he lifted a hand to rest it upon Liza's shoulder, I was surprised how slim and pale it was—almost like a woman's.

Liza took a seat.

Rasputin stood before us, silent, head bowed. The seconds stretched out, no one moving, no one making a sound.

Then he pulled back his hood in one smooth movement, baring his face.

Those who hadn't seen him before gasped. My mouth fell open.

He was so young.

His long, pale face was clean shaven, no beard or mustache. His hair fell in waves to his shoulders, thick and dark, no threads of gray.

He wasn't handsome, not really—his features were too bold, too large for his face. His eyes were disturbing, so pale that they seemed to look intently at you and all the way through you at the same time.

But you couldn't help staring at him, and that was more powerful. He captured our attention instantly and fully.

"Hello, my friends."

His voice was soft and rich, deep and gentle. It caressed me like the breeze, sliding over my cheek, through my ears, down my spine. It put pictures in my head.

I saw Artemis alighting on my arm, silvery wings outstretched. I thought of Maria and me lying in the garden, laughing in the sun, the leaves warm and alive all around us.

Without meaning to, I took a step forward off the wall.

"How kind of you all to come here tonight," Rasputin said. "When you've been a wanderer as long as I have, you never take hospitality for granted."

The blue light gathered around him, a vivid corona behind his head.

"Perhaps you've come here tonight to see tricks and illusions ... I'm no performer. Only a holy man, blessed by the gods with a few simple powers. If it is their will, I'll share their gifts with you. The gods decide what may be known and what must remain concealed."

Felix Yusupov gave a disdainful snort.

I could guess what he was thinking—that sounded like exactly the sort of nonsense a charlatan would say to conceal the inadequacy of their abilities.

If Rasputin heard Felix, he didn't show it.

"Who will volunteer?"

A pause fell, thick with tension—many wanted to speak, but no one dared.

"I will," Ollie said.

She strode forward.

The crowd murmured with excitement.

"Excellent," Rasputin said.

He held out his hand as Ollie approached.

I was impressed by my sister's boldness. At the same time, a chill crept into my heart. Ollie placed her hand in Rasputin's. His pale fingers closed around hers.

"Your name, my child?"

"Olga Nikolaevna," she said.

Her voice was steady, but I thought even Ollie looked a little frightened as she gazed into Rasputin's pale eyes.

"I'll have to prick your finger," he said. "Can you stand it?"

"Of course."

I could see Mama in the front row, not liking this at all, but unable to make Ollie sit down again without offending Liza Taneeva.

She could only watch as Rasputin reached into the front of his robes, pulling out a silver raven's skull on the end of a chain. He held the skull in his palm, pressing Ollie's finger against its pointed beak. A drop of blood welled up, black in the low blue light.

Rasputin lifted Ollie's finger to his mouth and closed his lips around it. He closed his eyes, his hand cradled around hers.

"I see ..."

"What do you see?" Ollie's eyes locked on his face.

"I'll show you."

Rasputin lit a long-stemmed pipe. Both pipe and lighter seemed to appear from nowhere. I suspected he had pockets in the loose sleeves of his robe but in the dim light, all I could see were those white hands floating in space. Still, I could swear the fire flamed into being before he touched the lighter.

Rasputin took several long puffs off the pipe, holding the smoke in his lungs before releasing it into the air.

The smoke swirled upward, hanging suspended in a cloud. Blue light crackled like lightning, illuminating the clouds from within, creating shapes and patterns. Images rose and sank again, figures swimming to the surface.

"You're the eldest of five ..." Rasputin said, "born with the fire of an eldest son in a woman's body ..."

The blue light flickered.

"Bold ... intelligent ... an excellent rider ..."

I thought I saw a horse within the mist, a dappled mare like the one Ollie adored before the poor old thing finally passed away.

"You wish to know your future because you think you'll never be satisfied..." Rasputin said. "You believe you must choose between one kind of happiness and another ..."

Ollie wasn't watching the shapes shift within the smoke. She stared into Rasputin's eyes, transfixed.

"Find the one who can beat you where you thought you'd never be beaten ... the one who was lost and then found ..."

The smoke swirled so quickly now, I could hardly make out the images as they flickered and died. I thought I saw a sleigh pulled by reindeer, a scarlet flag, and bowl heaped with some sort of fruit, maybe pomegranates...

"And then I'll be happy?" Ollie asked, eyes shining, hands clasped loosely in front of her. Her voice was soft as a sigh.

"You'll have everything you dreamed," Rasputin promised.

I saw a mass of storm clouds. White flowers bloomed in the smoke. Something dark dripped down onto the petals. Rasputin exhaled one last time, blowing it all away.

Ollie blinked, hands dropping to her sides. She seemed to come awake again, realizing she stood in front of a room full of people, all staring at her.

"Thanks," she stammered, hurrying back to her place against the wall.

The guests murmured to each other, a rumble that swelled to a tide.

"Are you all right?" I asked Ollie, touching her hand.

Her flesh was cold, her cheeks red.

"He knew me ..."

Felix Yusupov scoffed. "You're the Grand Duchess, of course he knows who you are. Liza Taneeva probably filled him in on every person in the room —it's part of the schtick."

"No," Ollie said quietly. "It was more than that."

Rasputin waited patiently.

The whispers of the crowd swelled like wind. He knew how to wait for the right moment, how to turn his sail.

"Who else wants to know their future?"

Emboldened by Ollie, Irina stepped forward.

Felix grabbed her by the wrist and pulled her back against the wall.

"*Don't!*"

Irina blinked those heavy black lashes that made her look like a doll.

"Why not?"

"Because ... I want you here with me," Felix said, linking his fingers through hers.

Irina smiled and stayed where she was.

Sylvie Buxhoeveden had already taken her place at the front of the room. Her hand shook as she held it out to Rasputin, from fear or excitement. Rasputin pricked her fingertip. Sylvie gave a little mew like a cat. Rasputin brought the blood to his tongue, closing his eyes. The smallest of smiles played on his lips.

"Are you ready?"

"I ... I think so ..."

Rasputin lit his pipe with that pale blue flame. He puffed, exhaling a floating cloud of smoke.

This time I saw mushrooms and flowers, and heard children laughing ...

A ghostly taunt: *Frog face, frog face!*

In the front row, Liza Taneeva shifted.

Then the images changed. I saw a pair of silver candlesticks marked with the imperial crest, a gift my mother gave Sylvie one Michaelmas. Gems and ornaments, Faberge eggs, glinting and glittering as they turned within the smoke ...

"You're close with the Empress," Rasputin said, softly. "She trusts your judgment ..."

"I always look out for Alix." Sylvie's voice was dreamy, her blue eyes gazing at the shapes floating before her as if she were a child peering in a shop window at all the things she wished she could buy.

The smoke began to swirl and I saw the mast of a ship—tall like my family's yacht.

Then the shapes of buildings, strange and exotic ...

Rasputin said, "You've traveled far, Baroness. And you'll travel further still. You'll see what you long to see ..."

"Italy?" Sylvie asked. "Japan?"

The images darkened. They swirled around each other, coming together and breaking apart, as if at war amongst themselves. I saw a pale finger pointing up to the sky and heard a crash of thunder that dissolved into a storm of white leaves, papery and thin ...

Sylvie's eyes darted around the smoke. She made a soft moaning sound, her hands pawing the air.

"Courage ..." Rasputin said, in his low, hypnotic voice. "You alone must take the first step on your journey ..."

I saw a set of tracks stretching up into the sky, and then a train. Steam billowed in time to the chugging engine. The train barreled toward me through the smoke, its headlamp like a glaring eye ...

Rasputin exhaled and it all blew away.

"Is that all?" Sylvie asked, disappointed. Like most of the unmarried women here, she might have hoped for a glimpse of her future love.

"All will become clear," Rasputin said, his thumb gliding across the back of her hand.

Sylvie looked at the hand he had touched for a long moment, then walked slowly back to her seat.

Rasputin locked eyes with Mama.

"Perhaps the Empress would like to know her future?"

Mama was stricter on this topic than almost any other. While the mania for mysticism swept the court, she flatly refused to participate in seances or to invite the French healer Philippe Nazier to bless her womb so she might bear more sons, even after he gave one of her ladies-in-waiting an amulet that made her conceive twin boys.

Mama had never consented to so much as a palm reading. Yet she hesitated when Rasputin held out his hand to her.

"You have a question ..." Rasputin said softly. "I know the answer."

Everyone in the room wanted her to rise. Even me.

Mama shook her head.

"I pray to the gods for my answers."

Rasputin showed no disappointment. He only bowed, saying, "As you wish, Imperial Highness. When the time is right, you will send for me."

Every face in the room fixed on him. There was no question that he'd be refused again.

"I'll read one more future. Who wishes to access the infinite knowledge of the spiritual realm?"

"I'll do it."

All the heads turning in my direction made me realize I'd volunteered. I was already walking forward, pulled to Rasputin as if each of us stood at the end of a long rubber band stretched to its furthest limit. Each step I took seemed to ease the tension.

I slipped inside the cocoon of smoke. The rest of the room disappeared, even Mama in the front row. Rasputin and I stood alone.

He was so tall I had to tilt my chin to look into his eyes. They reminded me of a rim of ice over a dark lake—so pale they were nearly transparent, with unknown depths beneath. Though his face was young, those eyes seemed ancient.

"Give me your hand."

I held it out to him.

His fingers were cool and strong. They held my index finger extended while he pressed it with the silvered skull.

The tip of the beak bit deep like a fang. I felt no pain—only a chill as if the silver were ice.

Blood welled, dark as a berry.

Rasputin lifted it to his mouth.

His tongue rasped against my fingertip.

I'd never touched a man's mouth before. I should have been embarrassed, touching the lips of a stranger in public. Instead, warmth spread over me, melting like butter. My body relaxed, my mind opening up like a clamshell.

I heard that distant music again, haunting and melancholy ...

Smoke swirled around us, curling out of Rasputin's pipe, swallowing me whole. Shapes shifted and danced, large as life all around me.

I saw a little brown toad, squat and ugly. My mother's voice said, *No one will ever want to marry you looking like that* ...

I saw four butterflies, lilac, sage, rose, and sapphire ... They fluttered across a bed of flowers until hit with a blast of wind that froze them in the air. Their wings shattered like glass, crumbling away to nothing.

I saw a black mountain and a deep hole in the earth.

I felt sadness and the weight of rock crushing down on me.

I saw a clock with the hands spinning faster and faster.

Then a boy, his face twisted in anger, a sword in his hand ...

The boy's face changed, his jaw wider, neck thicker, shoulders filling out. Now he was a boy no longer, but a hardened warrior, eyes dark as pine, the scars of battle on his face, chest, arms ...

He lifted one hand, stripping off a leather glove. The flesh beneath was just as black, dripping darkness like ink.

Rasputin jolted. For a moment I glimpsed his face, eyes flicking back and forth as he searched the images in the smoke. His hands made rapid motions in the air, fingers jerking like spiders. He wasn't making predictions like he'd done for the others.

The smoke pulled me back in.

I stood in front of a mirror, my own face looking back at me. If I turned my head one way, I looked as young as a baby. When I turned the other way, I became ancient.

The Anastasia in the mirror reached up her hand to touch the glass. I imitated her. When our fingers met, I fell all the way through ...

I floated away on the music, the ice-blue strains carrying me along ...

A silver band twisted and squirmed like a snake. It breathed smoke from its mouth and turned and bit its own tail, becoming a circlet that became a bracelet, dangling with charms.

People danced in frock coats and glittering gowns, a host of aristocrats in their finery, laughing and twirling ...

Damien again, tall and slim, a scar on his brow. He held out his gloved hand to me, unsmiling ...

Then snow, snow drifting down ...

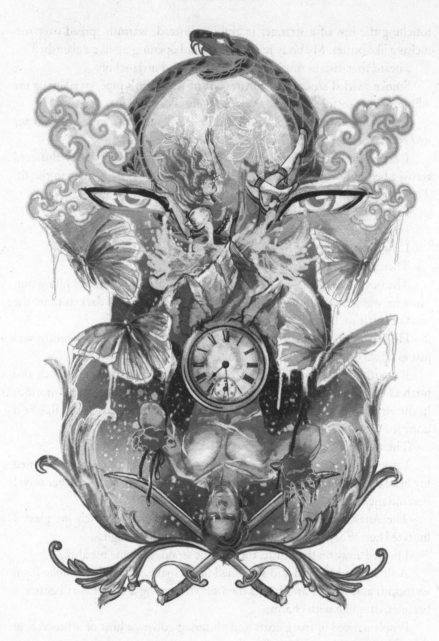

Pain slashed me like a knife and the whole world shattered. I was falling, falling, into the dark and the cold ...

I looked up at a sky that was not a sky at all, flat and hard and pale as Rasputin's pupils, with black water beneath ...

Then it all blew away.

We were back in the room, standing in silence.

Rasputin watched me, eyes narrowed.

"Have you done this before?"

"No. Never."

My voice came out in a croak as if it had been hours since I'd spoken.

The partygoers sat still, no babble of excited chatter like there had been after Ollie and Sylvie.

"What did you see?" a sharp voice demanded. It was Xenia, craning from the front row.

"Second sight is no science," Rasputin's voice was calm and soothing once more, a smile curving his lips. "The gods reveal what they wish. All I know is this young lady has many balls in her future."

A chuckle ran through the crowd.

The lamps began to illuminate, the golden light swelling gradually so no one's eyes were dazzled. The smoke faded away, leaving nothing but the subtle scent of eastern spices.

"I wish I had time for you all," Rasputin said. "Those who wish may visit me for a private session at my rooms on Garden Street."

Liza Taneeva hurried to stand beside him, elbowing me out of the way.

"I hope we'll have many more nights like this! Rasputin blesses us all with his presence. Don't forget what you've seen here tonight! Tell everyone you know, the doubters and the skeptics—Rasputin is gifted by the gods!"

I stumbled back to Ollie and Irina, head pounding.

"What was it like?" Irina asked.

"Confusing. I wasn't sure which images were real ..."

"I didn't see any pictures," Ollie said. "It felt like my head was a library and he was standing in the middle of the stacks, rifling through the books ..."

"You couldn't see anything in the smoke?"

Ollie shook her head.

"I thought I did with Ollie and Sylvie," Irina said. "But when it was your turn, the smoke wrapped around you both and I couldn't see anything at all."

"I think he's a fraud." All Felix's good humor had vanished. He watched as guests swarmed the black-robed monk, eager to speak with Rasputin or even to touch his sleeve.

"Maybe," Ollie shrugged. "He knew all about me, but he didn't seem to see much with Stassie. You hate dancing!"

I forced a smile. "I don't hate it. I'm just awful at it."

Felix lifted Irina's hand to his lips, speaking quickly before Xenia could intervene.

"Can I come see you?"

"Mama won't allow it ..."

"I'll find a way."

He grinned and hustled off as Aunt Xenia came marching over.

"Where were you sitting?" she demanded.

"In the back," Ollie lied so Irina wouldn't have to. "She could hardly see."

"For the best." Xenia sniffed. "What was Liza thinking, telling fortunes for young ladies? You ought to have stayed quiet Ollie, and Anastasia, you shouldn't have come at all! You're much too young to be out this late. The night before your exhibition, too—I hope you don't muff the whole thing. Remember how many people will be watching."

"Anastasia doesn't need sleep." Ollie cuffed me lightly on the arm. "She'll be great!"

I'd completely forgotten that tomorrow was likely to be the best or the worst day of my life. I wished Rasputin had told me which.

"Where's Mama?" I said. "We probably should head back."

"Over there." Ollie pointed.

Our mother was deep in conversation with Charlotte Golovina, the woman who said Rasputin had saved her from miscarriage.

We waited, not wanting to interrupt. Many carriages were called and most of the guests departed before they finished talking.

chapter 7

BRIBES FOR ARTEMIS

I hardly slept that night.

When I drifted off at last, I wandered through dark and twisting dreams that seemed to carry me through the corridors of my own mind. Memory and fantasy twined together, until I was no longer certain what I had seen in Rasputin's smoke and what I'd only imagined.

I woke exhausted, shadows under my eyes.

Maria snored softly in the bed next to mine.

We were outgrowing our room with its stencils of butterflies all around the walls and the tiny dressers that hardly contained our clothes anymore. Neither of us wanted to move.

I slipped out from under the covers and dressed, then went directly down to the grounds. Fog lay heavy over the open fields, the old oak tree with its hanging moss resembling an ancient, shaggy beast rising from the mist.

The grounds of the Alexander Palace were vast, including several ponds and rivers, a cathedral, an armory, follies meant to resemble medieval ruins, the magnificent green and gold Dragon Bridge, and an entire Chinese village.

You could wander through the park all day long without coming to the end of it.

I walked to the northeast corner of the grounds, toward the Llama

House, the Elephant Pavilion, and the Imperial Farm. That was where Papa had built Artemis' mews.

It was a three-story tower, gray brick, all open on the inside. Artemis could fly around inside the freeloft or rest on any number of perches. As our only falcon, she didn't have to share the space.

Once her wing healed, Uncle Nikolasha helped me to train her. The process took several months—not because Artemis was unintelligent, but because she was horribly stubborn.

That made two of us. I worked her day after day, testing my will against hers.

It was a long process, getting her accustomed to the jesses on her legs, teaching her how to step up onto my arm in exchange for lumps of raw meat, then training her to fly to me from a perch.

I kept her on a creance, a long string on a spindle as if Artemis were a kite. That was to prevent her flying away the moment she got full use of her wings.

Artemis began to speak consistently. At first she only shrieked her hunger or annoyance, but eventually she expanded her vocabulary and began to string words into sentences.

Only I could understand her—the words formed in my head, while all anyone else heard was a gyrfalcon. I think that's what kept her coming back once she was flying free. She liked being understood.

What made her love me was hunting.

I taught her to chase lures shaped like rabbits and pheasants. That was when I saw her first sparks of joy—when I'd fling the lure as high as possible so she could swoop in and bear it to the ground, crushing it beneath her talons.

The pleasure of the lure was dwarfed by the thrill of a real kill. Uncle Nikolasha said he'd never seen a falcon take to the hunt so quickly. She almost never missed, and when she did, her fury was so great that she would obliterate the next prey she sighted like a bolt of lightning from the sky.

I learned the things she liked—favorite foods, favorite places to be touched. And I learned not to do the things that infuriated her.

Artemis was far from civilized, but we'd come to an arrangement that suited us both.

When I entered the mews, she flew down to me, landing on my arm. The tips of her feathers brushed my cheek as she closed her wings.

I wasn't wearing my gauntlet. Her talons cut through the sleeve of my dress and dug into the flesh beneath. I had too many welts on my forearms to notice, but Margaretta would bawl me out when the maids had to scrub the blood out of my sleeve.

"'Morning," I said, scratching the back of her neck. "Big day today."

Hunt! she cried, her beak sharp and prehistoric.

"Not hunting. Today's the exhibition, remember?"

Hunt!

She had no eyebrows but you could tell when she was annoyed.

"Please, Artemis," I begged. "Today's important to me."

Artemis was the main feature of my exhibition. All of it, really. I needed her to cooperate or I was going to look like a fool.

Perhaps I shouldn't have staked my entire magical reputation on a consummate murderer who disliked crowds and being told what to do.

Chicks, she commanded.

I groaned.

"Fine. But you better make me look good."

I was pretty sure she only liked eating baby chicks because she knew how much I hated feeding them to her. She was a bit of a sadist.

Maybe all falcons were—she was the only one I could understand. The only animal I could talk to at all. And I'd tried a few, until I felt stupid enough staring at the dumbfounded sheep and goats in the yard to stop.

So much of magic was guesswork. Most people had completely different abilities, and even the same ability could manifest differently. What I knew, I knew from anecdote or experimentation.

Abilities seemed to run in families, but even that wasn't certain. So far, I'd been the only Romanov child to show evidence of time-walking, and I'd really only done it the one time.

I'd tried practicing with Papa. It only seemed to work when he was physically touching me, pulling me along. The moment he let go, I was fighting against a current. I had no control—the smallest thing could knock me back into the normal flow of time.

Any use of magical ability was exhausting, like running at a full sprint. The best practitioners made it look effortless, but plenty of people hardly used their abilities at all because it was too tiring. Mama almost never moved things with her mind, preferring to use her hands. That could have been convenience or decorum—she hated when people flaunted their abilities or tried to increase them.

She despised the use of talismans—ignoring the fact that we possessed the most valuable enhancement of all.

Mama never used Charoite. Papa only did on the battlefield.

Charoite was rarer than gold; the only veins we'd found lay deep in the Lorne Mountain. Once the power in a stone was exhausted, it became as useless as a paste jewel.

The charge was unpredictable. There was no knowing how it would affect the abilities or the mind. Some of my relatives had gone mad from it.

"Charoite corrupts," Papa told me. "It wants to change all of you, not just one part of you. You have to be stronger than the stone."

"You make it sound like it's alive."

"Is rust alive? Is fungus? It wants to take you over, that's what I mean."

I'd never so much as held a piece of Charoite in my hand.

"Will you show it to me, Papa?"

"When you're older," he said, and changed the subject.

He hadn't been keen to practice time-walking any more than he wanted to teach me to shoot a gun or wield a sword. Women's abilities were meant to be ornamental, not practical.

Liza Taneeva explained it to me this way: "You're the cask in which the wine is stored. A good cask is necessary, or the wine will spoil. But *you* are not the wine and never will be."

The most annoying thing about Liza was that she was more right than I wanted to admit.

Papa was never going to show me Charoite.

It would stay locked in the vault under the Alexander Palace unless Papa or Alexei needed it.

Everything interesting was always forbidden.

I wanted to know everything—but not the things Pierre Gillard drilled into my head. He only wanted to drone on about algebra and Latin conjugation, while I was dying to know whether a new ability could ever be learned and how powerful a person could become through practice.

Pierre never wanted to talk about magic, probably because he knew Mama didn't like it.

Nobles were absolute hypocrites about magic. We were as rich in abilities as we were in cold, hard cash, and the link between the two was obvious. The very first Romanov became Tsar because he cleansed Rusya of monsters—he never could have done that without magic. Yet it was as gauche to discuss one's powers as one's banking details.

Hypocrisy isn't complete until it's also inconsistent.

Just as it was unseemly for a young lady to be too powerful, neither could I be completely lacking in magic. Then I'd be a faulty wine barrel, as the charming Liza would say.

It was crucial that I exhibit in a manner that would make my family proud.

Which meant I needed Artemis' cooperation.

I retrieved six chicks from the farm and dropped them off on the fresh grass outside the mews. By that point, I was too used to Artemis' barbarism to even turn away.

Gyrfalcons had to eat meat, preferably alive and kicking. Artemis never felt guilt about her nature.

I wished I could be as free as her.

I felt guilty all the time.

Or at least, I knew I was supposed to.

Really what I most often felt was curiosity, gnawing at me like hunger, like a need to run. I wanted to see everything, know everything, do everything.

I couldn't stop thinking about Rasputin. I'd never met anyone with so many different powers. He'd conjured snow, read the future, and, I suspected, manipulated fire without the use of that lighter.

Maria called him a sorcerer.

Sorcerers were people who tried to amplify their powers.

I remembered Andrei Derevenko's story of the magician who used seven silver knives to turn himself into a wolf.

Now that I was becoming an adult, I was supposed to put aside my belief in childish things like werewolves. But in a world of magic, who decided myth from truth?

Rasputin kept that raven's skull on a chain around his neck. He used it to prick my finger.

Was it a talisman? Would he tell me if I asked?

Perhaps I could visit him in his apartments on Garden Street ...

No, Mama would never allow it.

I crouched on the grass with my arms around my knees, stewing while Artemis devoured the chicks.

When she finished, she flew back to my arm to flaunt her bloodstained beak.

Delicious.

That was as close to a thank you as I was going to get. Probably also as close to a handshake on our agreement. Still, I pressed her:

"Are you going to help me today?"

She preened her feathers, smug with power.

Probably.

As long as I kept on her good side and the task wasn't too annoying.

Seeing my stress, she gave me a friendly nip on the shoulder that was supposed to be comforting.

What did I care what a bunch of strangers thought of me?

I didn't. But I cared what my family thought. I wanted to make them proud.

And I dreaded making a fool of myself in front of Damien Kaledin.

He'd been attending the military academy in St. Petersburg only a few miles away. During the school year he lived on campus. On holidays he stayed with Uncle Nikolasha.

I supposed Nikolasha had kept him apart from us on purpose. Damien was part of his own exhibition today—proving he could be around Romanovs without trying to murder us.

I wondered if he'd wear his school uniform. An image of Damien in the tight black academy jacket swam into my mind. I batted it away, face hot in the sun.

I didn't need any extra pressure.

But I was glad he was coming all the same. If only to satisfy my curiosity.

chapter 8

EXHIBITIONS FOR ALL

A hundred empty seats sat waiting on the open lawn of Alexander Park. The exhibition was meant to be a coming-of-age celebration. Nina Ivanova hung streamers in the lilac trees and festooned the spindly golden chairs with garlands of peonies. Pastel-colored cakes melted next to heaps of crustless sandwiches. Waiters in spotless white uniforms handed round trays of frothy pink drinks adorned with slices of frozen strawberry.

Our cook had the ability to freeze anything she touched, which meant we never had to order in ice like Liza Taneeva. Gria could make ice cream simply by churning cream in a metal bowl frosted against the palm of her hand.

The Crimean regimental band played a spritely tune as the guests began to arrive. Sweat dripped down the musicians' faces beneath the brims of their stiff black caps. The guests gulped down their drinks and begged for more. It was the hottest day of August, though the sun hadn't reached its peak in the sky.

"Are you nervous?" Maria asked me.

She'd completed her own exhibition two summers before. Mama had dressed her in a golden gown with a headdress of wheat as if she were the harvest goddess. She grew a tomato from seed to plant to fruit in the palm of her hand, a short and simple demonstration that pleased everyone.

I wanted to wear my usual hunting clothes, but Mama kiboshed that idea, ruthlessly pointing out every last patch and stain until I agreed I'd wear the new hunting suit Madame Bulbenkova designed.

Madame Bulbenkova owned the fashion house that provided all the imperial gowns, which meant she was the architect of every instrument of torture I'd ever been forced to wear to a formal event. She was Tatiana's favorite friend and my most hated enemy.

The hunting suit was not fit for hunting at all and damned hot for a summer's day—a many-layered monstrosity of cobalt-colored wool with gold braid at the cuffs and collar in military style. The matching tricorn hat included a ridiculous ostrich plume that bobbed whenever I moved my head.

"Don't laugh," I hissed at Ollie.

She tried to turn down the corners of her mouth. "I'm not laughing. I'm not even smiling."

My sisters wore light linen summer dresses. They looked comfortable and cool, all three secure in their successful completion of a task that seemed long ago and childish in their minds.

"I wish I could do mine over again." Tatiana frowned. "I wanted to show how I can see in the dark. Papa said it wasn't appropriate."

"Nor would it be," Mama said primly. "Not every talent should be exhibited."

Mama was pale, shadows like bruises under her eyes. She'd been up in the night with Alexei.

He'd fallen a week earlier trying to leap a stream in Alexander Park. His thigh swelled up horribly. A bruise the size of a fist bulged on his upper leg, but he seemed to be recovering, until a rough carriage ride caused the hematoma to burst. He had to be carried into the palace, white as talc, eyes rolled back in his head.

All through the night I heard his groans and sobs floating down the hallway between our rooms. He finally fell asleep right before breakfast.

He would not be attending my exhibition. Mama said it was because he was too tired, but I knew my parents wouldn't want the guests to see Alexei carried to his seat by Andrei Derevenko, or wheeled in a push-chair. Though it was impossible to quash the rumors that the Tsarevich was ill, we tried our best to starve them.

"Can I please go down?" I said. Margaretta was digging a hatpin into my scalp, locking the cap in place at an angle that made the ostrich plume dangle in my eye. "I want to calm Artemis before we start. And I have to be able to *see*, Margaretta!"

"I thought the bird was going to see for you." Her sarcasm was unmuted by her mouthful of pins.

"She's not going to help me get down the stairs, so unless you plan to carry me on your back ..."

Margaretta snorted. "Not in your lifetime. You're a Grand Duchess, not the Pharaoh of Egypt."

And if the Pharaoh ever came to visit, Margaretta would put him in his place just as quick.

She yanked out the hatpin, shoving it back an inch to the left.

"Happy now?"

"Thrilled."

"Then my life is complete."

She always had to have the last word.

"Is Uncle Nikolasha here yet?" I asked my mother.

"He's waiting for you in the tent down on the lawn."

Heart beating a little too hard for someone who was just going to see their uncle, I ducked my head so the wispy white ostrich plume hid my face from Ollie as I hurried past.

My boots pattered down the steps, stiff and slippery on the polished marble. Everything I was wearing was uncomfortably new. Gods, I wished I could wear what I liked.

My mother changed her clothes six times a day—a peignoir in the morning, then a house dress, a walking dress, dresses for tea, for dinner, then for the ballroom or the theater.

She had to plan her outfits with her three maids at the beginning of the week. Two of those maids were employed almost entirely for the purpose of pressing and maintaining my mother's closets of clothes, protecting the hand embroidery and delicate lace from the relentless damp of Rusya. Mama wasn't even a fancy dresser by the standards of the Imperial Court.

Each year that passed, the torture of what I was expected to wear increased. When I had nightmares of being married off to become a queen of some foreign land, the shackles that wrapped me tight were clothes, clothes, clothes: corsets, petticoats, bustles, gloves, headdresses, collars, hats and heels, and pounds and pounds of gems and jewels and lace, weighing me down until I clanked like Marley's ghost, like a pirate drowned with all his booty.

As soon as I was out of Margaretta's sight, I ripped off half the ostrich plume so it no longer dangled in my face.

I found Nikolasha easily enough—it was never difficult to spot my uncle, head and shoulders above everyone else. He was standing in the shade of a striped summer tent with our gamekeeper Farad. Farad had come to us escorting a pair of Asian elephants that were a gift from the King of Siam. He stayed to care for the elephants and the rest of the exotic animals in our menagerie, including whatever Artemis required that I didn't handle myself.

Artemis liked Farad, as all the animals seemed to—he had a soothing voice and a deliberate way of moving that was never abrupt or surprising. I sometimes wished Farad was in charge of me instead of Margaretta. I was never more peaceful than after we shared a pot of mint tea in his little house next to the mews.

Farad carried Artemis on his arm, her legs already clad in jesses but no hood on her head. While most falcons were calmest with their eyes covered, Artemis had never learned to tolerate a hood. She'd go mad trying to tear it off until she could see again.

Farad was deep in debate with Nikolasha over the sorts of dogs that could be used to hunt tigers in India. He broke off when he saw me, grinning so his teeth flashed white beneath his neatly curled mustache.

"She's in fine form today, Imperial Highness. She'll impress them all."

Artemis puffed her chest feathers, pretending she hadn't heard.

"She better." I threw Artemis a sharp look. "We made a deal."

She preened, refusing to make eye contact.

"You're grown up in that suit." Nikolasha squinted as if he didn't quite know me. "I don't think I've seen you in long skirts before."

"I hate it, I'm boiling already."

Nikolasha caught my quick sweep of the tent that contained only my uncle and Farad, plus the bustle of waiters trading dirty glasses for fresh drinks.

"He's out on the Dragon Bridge."

I didn't pretend not to know who he meant, but ignored Nikolasha's wink as I hurried off across the lawn, passing under the drooping branches of lilac that dropped a carpet of wilted purple petals, sending up a smell like wine when I crushed them underfoot.

The Dragon Bridge was as vivid a green as the summer leaves all around, the water beneath smooth as glass and transparent all the way down to the riverbed.

Nina had woven her garlands of peonies along the bridge, twined through the railings. The breeze tugged away a few loose petals. They floated across the grass like soft pink snow on a wind as warm as the air from an oven.

I crept through an avenue of lime trees, wanting to see Damien before he saw me.

He sat between the gilt pillars of the bridge, a great brass sculpture of a grinning dragon on either side of him. The pagoda-like roof shaded him from the sun. His feet dangled down above the water in brand-new boots, soft and well-fitting. He was slim and dark in his academy uniform, much taller than the last time I'd seen him. Then he was boy—now a young man. I held my breath, the scent of lime in my lungs, watching him.

Damien dropped a pebble down into the river. It broke the surface, disappearing without a trace. Though his face was half hidden by the brim of his cap, the set of his mouth told me he was scowling.

My fingertips tingled, and the points of my ears. My heart grew frantic in my chest.

Blood surged around my body, full of that electric energy that sparked in me the moment I laid eyes on Damien. It was the same as when I saw him in the steppes—even stronger this time. My feet were rooted to the ground, my fingertips welded to the bark of the lime tree, as if I were connected to the earth and the plants and the air going in and out of my lungs.

Damien went still on the bridge. I felt certain that he knew I was there. He was waiting for me to come out.

Before I could step out of the lime bower, a pack of young men came traipsing over the bridge from the Chinese village. They were dressed in the academy uniform, broad in the shoulders, with enough half-grown mustaches to make me think they must be in their last year.

Sighting Damien, they paused at the end of the bridge. Their chatter died and they drew close together, before crossing the bridge with new speed and purpose.

Damien intuited what was about to happen before I did. He rose to his feet, back to the pillars, facing the group that fanned around him, trapping him in place under the awning.

They circled around him, making snarling sounds and yips. Hemming him in from all sides, they feinted and jabbed, trying to get behind him, putting their feet out to trip him. They pulled at his uniform, yanking at his jacket until buttons popped free.

I recognized the leader of the group, tall and handsome, with a black band on his arm. I'd met him once before at Ollie's sixteenth birthday party. His father was a minister and his name was Vasta Vyacheslav.

Vasta took a backhand swipe at Damien's face, knocking his hat off into the water. The river swallowed it up like it had done to the pebble.

"Uh oh," he sneered. "The Khokhol lost his cap."

Khokhol was what Rusyans called the Cossacks because of the way they cut their hair—it meant a sheaf of wheat. When Damien had been forced to cut his hair for the academy, he'd shaved it short on the sides with a longer strip on top, in imitation of how his father wore it. It made his face look leaner and harder, and left no cover for the scar that split his eyebrow.

"Dogs don't need hats," a second boy said, trying to get hold of Damien's arms. Damien fended him off, ripped his arm free, and shoved him back, only for a stocky boy with wire-rimmed glasses to jab his hand into Damien's side, hitting him with a jolt of power that made Damien stiffen up, teeth bared, limbs twitching rigidly as if he'd been electrocuted.

The other boys howled with amusement.

"Hit him again," Vasta ordered.

His friends pinned Damien's arms behind his back. The one with the glasses hit Damien with a punch in the kidney that jolted him until his body snapped back.

"*Stop that!*" I shrieked, running up onto the bridge.

The boys were so intent on their quarry that they didn't hear me coming. While the others held Damien pinned in place, the stocky boy approached. He put out one blunt finger and, with queasy satisfaction, twirled it in the air in front of Damien's face before touching Damien in the center of his chest. Damien's eyes went white, his body shaking so hard that his boots beat a staccato against the flagstones of the bridge.

"STOP!" I screamed.

That time they heard me. Their heads jerked up. The ones holding Damien relaxed their grip on his arms enough that he wrenched free and launched himself on the stocky boy with glasses, knocking him backward onto the bridge, hitting him again and again with his gloved fists until Vasta hauled back his foot and booted Damien in the ribs, sending him rolling against the railing.

"LEAVE HIM ALONE!" I shrieked, flinging myself into the fray.

Damien rose, shoving me off along with the rest of them.

"Get off!" He swiped the blood dripping from his nose. "I don't need your help."

I was back to hating him in an instant.

"Oh, I can see that. You've got it well under control."

"How adorable," Vasta laughed. "The Cossack dog has a bitch."

Though he was handsome, his smile stretched his face in an unpleasant way.

I wasn't surprised he didn't recognize me—we'd never been formally introduced. He'd been busy stalking Tatiana all night long, trying to coerce her into dancing with him again.

"That's Anastasia Nikolaevna," one of his friends muttered in his ear. "The Grand Duchess."

His smile faltered, but only for a moment. Cocking his head, he looked me up and down. "Here to protect your uncle's pet?"

"I'm not the one who needs protecting." Damien stood by the railing, lips dark with blood. He peeled the leather gloves off his hands, tucking them into his pocket.

His hands were paler than the rest of him, the skin ashy because it so rarely saw the sun. The shapely fingers were pristine, as if stored away in preparation for moments just like this.

The other boys shrank back, not nearly as interested in swarming Damien now that his hands were uncovered.

Vasta's eyes flicked to Damien's hands and back to his face. "You think that scares me?"

"If it doesn't, you're stupider than you look."

Damien plucked a peony from the garland wrapped around the railing and held it in the palm of his hand.

The pale pink bloom was the size of a teacup, the petals lush and fragrant, tiny droplets of dew clinging to the anemone-like stamen in the center.

Almost as soon as the fragile bloom touched his skin, it began to wilt. Spots of brown materialized upon the edges of the petals, eating away at the flower like a lattice of rust. The peony blackened and died in his hand, crumbling away to nothing.

Damien let the wilted bits fall to the ground.

The boys exchanged looks with each other, a few drawing back.

Not Vasta. Damien's demonstration only seemed to increase his disgust. He leaned in close, bits of spittle flying off his lips. "You're supposed to keep those gloves on so the rest of us don't catch whatever the *fuck* is wrong with you."

Damien held his eye. "You better hope you don't catch it."

"I'm the son of a minister, you filthy mongrel," Vasta hissed at him. "Lay one finger on me and see what happens."

"Yes," Damien agreed. "Let's see what happens."

And he laid one finger on the garland of peonies that ran all the way down the railing of the Dragon Bridge.

The first flower he touched withered and died, then the next, and the next. The blight ran all the way down the bridge, the rot spreading through the garland until the blackened petals shivered and fell to the river below.

It wasn't only the flowers that felt it. The light seemed to fade and the breeze chilled. The finger of death rested on the bridge, touching us all.

Damien lifted his hand. A weight rose off my chest. I could breathe again.

The boys' faces were pale. A sheen of sweat coated Vasta's upper lip.

"That's not normal. That's dark magic! They should hang you for that. Or better yet, burn you."

"It's his ability!" I snapped. "Did you pick yours?"

I was defending Damien because I loathed boys who operated in packs. But I felt the chill of his power like everyone else. It was disturbing.

Vasta's head whipped around like a snake. "What would *you* know about it? I heard you don't have any power at all."

"Then why would you be here today, idiot?"

One of Vasta's friends snorted, a mistake that drew a look from his leader that stifled the sound in his throat.

"I guess we'll see soon enough," Vasta said softly.

He jerked his head at his friends, telling them it was time to go.

As they gathered to leave, Vasta turned and spat. The glob of spittle landed on the toe of Damien's carefully polished boot, quivering like jelly. Vasta waited to see if Damien would respond, then carried on his way, chuckling.

Damien was so tight with anger I thought he might explode. If this was how his classmates behaved in public, I could only imagine how they tortured him when they caught him alone at school.

He turned away from me.

I thought he was looking down at the water, trying to breathe, maybe even holding back tears. I knew I'd be bawling if I was in his shoes.

Then I realized he was staring at the garland, eyebrows drawn together.

"What is it?"

"It's never spread like that." Damien gazed down the railing at the chain of blackened peonies.

"How does it usually work?"

His eyes met mine. His breath touched my hand, resting on the railing. I felt the warmth of it on the little strip of skin where glove and sleeve didn't meet.

I hadn't realized how close we were standing. Though I hadn't seen Damien in two years, it felt like we were back in the train car together, as if no time had passed at all.

"Anything I touch, I kill," Damien said. "If I hold on long enough."

I licked my lips.

"What if I touch you?"

Damien extended his hand, palm upward, eyes locked on mine.

"Go ahead."

It was a dare. A challenge. He didn't think I'd do it.

I stripped off my own gloves.

Our hands looked naked, unbearably intimate. I could feel myself blushing.

Still, I reached out and laid my hand on his, palm to palm, my fingertips just touching the warmth of his wrist.

The moment our bare skin touched, I felt a sucking sensation, like my body was a bathtub and our linked hands had pulled open the plug so all the water drained out. Whatever was in me began to flow into him. My legs went weak. The color leached from my vision so the summer leaves hardly looked green anymore, cinder colored against an ashy sky.

My knees buckled. I would have fallen if Damien hadn't slipped his arm around my waist to hold me up.

The contact broke between our bare skin.

My dizziness faded and I was able to stand on my own.

Something warm dribbled down my upper lip. I touched my fingers to the wetness and brought them away bright with blood.

"Your nose is bleeding," Damien said.

"So's yours."

Damien touched his own lip and saw that it still was.

Somehow, that made us both smile.

"Were you spying on me?" Damien asked.

"A little."

"I knew you were there. I could feel it."

We both accepted the thing we couldn't understand, that seemed to happen every time we got close to each other. I didn't know what it was or what it meant, but I could feel it even as we stood there on the bridge, even with my head pounding and my nose bleeding. Already the dizziness was gone, the weakness in my limbs washed away by that surging power that seemed to flow back and forth between us on an endless circuit. I might not be able to touch Damien, but standing next to him lit me up like a holiday tree.

"You're brave," Damien said. "Or stupid. Most people won't even touch me through my clothes."

He said it calmly, but sudden shame came into his face, surprising us both.

I thought of how the boys drew back from him, the disgust in Vasta's voice when he hissed, "*That's not normal ...*"

"Is that why they harass you?"

"I think being Cossack annoys them more."

"Don't the teachers do anything to stop it?"

Damien made a rude sound. I blushed harder than ever, knowing how stupid I sounded.

"That's the curriculum," Damien said. "Learning our place in the social order."

"Can't you—"

"It doesn't matter," he barked. "Nothing I do will change it, and I don't care. What they think of me means less than nothing. What they do means nothing."

That's what he said, but his face told the opposite. I saw his misery. And his loneliness.

He was stuck here, away from everything he loved. He was angry because he had no options, no hope of anything but endurance.

I understood it, and my heart hurt for him.

"Vasta's nothing special," I said. "Barely even an aristocrat."

Damien gave me a look that was hard to read. Did I sound like a snob? I only meant Vasta wasn't as high on the social scale as he liked to pretend.

"His father's influential."

"How do you know?"

Damien had only been out of the steppes for a couple of seasons. The idea that he might comprehend the political situation in St. Petersburg better than I did seemed highly unlikely, further evidence of his arrogance.

"I pay attention," Damien said.

"So do I."

"Not to the time ..."

"You don't even wear a watch!"

"Look at the sun ... it's half-past noon."

I looked up and saw he was right. Damien laughed at me—he probably knew how late I was the whole time we were talking, the bastard.

I sprinted back the way I'd come, intercepted by Ollie who was panting almost as hard.

"Stasia! Where have you been? Mama's going mental trying to keep everyone entertained."

"Sorry, sorry!" I shouted my apologies to everyone I passed rushing back to the summer tent. Farad had Artemis ready and waiting. Nikolasha tried to hide his smile as my parents chastised me from both sides.

"What on earth were you—"

"Today of all days, Anastasia!"

"Never mind." Papa shoved me out of the tent. "We've kept them waiting long enough."

The guests on their spindly golden chairs were hot and annoyed, fanning themselves in the stagnant heat. Aunt Xenia cast me a particularly caustic glare from under the shade of a hat the size of a fruit basket.

Vasta had taken a seat in the front row between a woman who would have been beautiful if not for her pinched mouth, and a man who had never been good looking but was imposing nonetheless with his boxer's shoulders and bulldog jaw. Vasta smirked at me, making a subtle gesture with his hand as if to say, *Go ahead. Can't wait to watch you cock it up.*

Nikolasha had saved a seat for Damien, but Damien preferred not to walk up the long aisle of chairs to take it. He found a place in the back row, next to the aisle where I could still see him easily.

My sisters turned their heads to examine him, not at all subtle as they whispered and giggled behind their hands. They'd heard all about Papa's would-be assassin. Saving Papa from a much deeper cut was the only reason my parents hadn't hung me from the rafters after what Ollie called "the Stowaway Incident," and Nikolasha called "the Great Train Debacle."

Damien ignored my sisters and everyone else. His eyes were fixed on me alone. I felt them burning on my skin everywhere I turned.

I began my exhibition flushed and sweating, already off my game.

Artemis was as irritable as the guests. Her feathers stood up on the crest of her head, ruffled and spiky.

I'd struggled how to demonstrate our ability to understand each other.

Pulling on my leather gauntlet, I stood on the open lawn under the blazing sun, trying to ignore the hundred pairs of eyes trained on me and the expectant silence I was supposed to fill.

Artemis alighted on my arm, her weight comforting even when she let her wing cuff my hat, knocking it askew.

I pushed it firmly back in place.

"Ready?"

She gave a noncommittal chirp.

I nodded to Farad. He pulled the strings of the three boxes he'd arranged on the lawn, opening their lids.

Three different animals burst out: a fox, a dove, and a hare.

The hare exploded off across the lawn, dashing for the cover of the trees. The dove flew directly upward into the cloudless sky. The fox hesitated a moment, then ran toward the pond.

"Catch the hare!" I called aloud to Artemis, adding in an undertone, "*Please.*"

Artemis barely waited for the order. She already had her wings open, the impulse to take chase nearly irresistible.

She rose a dozen feet in the air with three muscular pumps of her wings, then pelted after the hare. The hare seemed to sense death swooping in from behind. It raced for the copse of alder trees without even zigging on the grass, so swift that hardly a creature alive could have caught it.

For Artemis, the hare might as well have been standing still. She dropped upon it so precisely that her talons pierced its heart. It gave one last kick and died, already limp as she lifted it from the ground. She dropped its soft corpse in my hand, landing on my arm to receive her praise.

"No one has ever flown faster," I murmured, stroking her head.

Artemis made a low sound in her chest that was almost a chuckle. Compliments never failed to please her.

The audience applauded enthusiastically. I heard their gasps as Artemis rose in the air—she was magnificent in size, her feathers beaten silver. She flew like a blade through the sky, lethal and beautiful.

I'd chosen the hare because it was the most difficult to capture. Artemis could have given it twice the head start. The audience was impressed with her more than me.

The important thing was that they were impressed.

First task successfully completed, my confidence began to rise. I faced my observers, grinning.

"Can I have a volunteer?"

I glanced at Damien without meaning to. His arms were crossed firmly over his chest. I wondered if he wanted me to succeed or if he'd be as pleased as Vasta if I made a fool of myself.

Ollie and Maria put their hands in the air. I couldn't pick a family member for this. I pointed to a stranger instead, a woman in a pale yellow summer dress with a parasol over her shoulder. She looked vaguely familiar, her dress so lavishly trimmed in flax lace that she must be a baroness at least.

"I'll only need you for a moment," I promised.

"Happy to help."

Her eyes were bright, her expression merry as she crossed the lawn to join me. She regarded Artemis with curiosity, not afraid to stand close to her.

Loud enough for everyone to hear, I said, "Three flags stand at the end of the lawn. I want you to choose one and wave it in the air. But don't tell me which one you're going to pick. Can you do that for me?"

"I think so." She smiled.

"Could you blindfold me first?"

I turned and waited while she tied the blindfold over my eyes. It was a silk scarf of Mama's. The scent of her White Rose perfume calmed my heart until it was almost back to its normal tempo.

When the possible-baroness had tied the blindfold tight, I said, "Now go wave one of those flags, then set it down again. Make sure everyone can see you!"

I heard her first few steps across the lawn, then only the rustle and murmur of the crowd as her footsteps faded away on the soft grass.

"Up you go," I said to Artemis, giving a light toss of my arm.

Really, there was no need for her to take to the air—she could see ten times as far as I could from the ground. But I thought it would be more impressive to the audience if she wheeled in the sky, illustrating how useful a skill this might be when spying on enemy armies.

The seconds ticked past. I wondered if the woman in the yellow dress had made it to the end of the field.

I underestimated how disorienting it would be to stand here blind with everyone staring at me. Someone snickered in the front row—probably that garbage bag Vasta. I knew Damien was still watching me because I could feel it, hotter than the summer sun beating on my skin. I threw my shoulders back and thrust my chin in the air.

Artemis landed hard on my arm, making me yelp.

Red, she screeched.

"It was the red flag!" I shouted.

The snort from the front row was unmistakable.

I ripped off the blindfold in time for Vasta to loudly remark, "You could have planned that all out before. Trained her to do it. She doesn't understand you."

Artemis shifted on my arm, tilting her head like she spied a pheasant in the field.

The rest of the audience fell silent, waiting for me to respond.

I stood there disheveled and sweaty, while Vasta looked all-too convincing in his spruce uniform, clean shaven and handsome, the black band on his arm lending an extra air of authority. I assumed it meant he was a captain at the academy.

Ignoring Vasta, I turned to Artemis and said, "Take his band for me, will you?"

She dove from the gauntlet.

You have to be close to Artemis to realize that her talons are as thick as your thumb. Her wings spread as wide as a man's open arms.

It looked as if she meant to embrace Vasta. Or spear his heart.

Vasta gave an almighty shriek.

Artemis snatched the band from his arm, leaving a tiny tear in the material of his sleeve as if he'd passed a raspberry bush.

She did it for herself more than for me. He insulted her.

I laughed at Vasta's scream. So did Damien. Only a chuckle, but it lit me on fire.

I was charged up, bursting at the seams.

"You want to see something impressive?" I looked Vasta dead in the eye, and his snooty mother and rapacious father, too. "I can do what my father can do. I'm a time-walker."

I said it proudly for everyone to hear.

The look on my parents' faces confirmed what I had suspected: they didn't want it announced.

Alexei was supposed to have the gift. Not me. They'd hide it if they could, like his illness.

Now I'd done something that couldn't be taken back. Whatever they said would be remembered and recorded. It froze them in place.

"How wonderful," said Vasta's mother, in a velvet tone that in no way matched the expression on her face. "We're all so eager to see you demonstrate."

I hadn't thought that far ahead. The impulse to show off for Damien, to impress him, was not accompanied by any actual plan.

I turned to my father, wild-eyed.

"I'll do the same demonstration you did, Papa! With the Faberge eggs."

Papa stared at me, blinking too long. I knew exactly what position I was putting him in—an impossible one. He could either shut this down publicly or allow me to proceed, risking a much larger embarrassment.

I hadn't practiced. I didn't know if I could do it. I was swept up in fantasies of fame and glory, outshining my sisters for once in my life. Making my parents proud. And maybe, maybe ... giving Damien something to chew on.

"Get the cabinets," Papa ordered the servants waiting by the buffet tables.

The waiters scurried off to retrieve the pair of glass cabinets that resided in the Mountain Room, stuffed with the fifty Faberge eggs Papa had commissioned for Mama over the years of their marriage.

It was madness, but it wasn't like waiting blindfolded in the field. Power bubbled in my veins. I'd never felt more confident.

I stood a dozen yards from Damien, watching him watch me. The connection between us fueled me—strongest when his eyes were locked on mine. Then the link was so clear I almost thought I could read his face like words spoken aloud. The smile he couldn't quite hide that said, "*Do it. I dare you.*"

I wasn't looking at Vasta. This wasn't for him.

The ten minutes it took for the footmen to haul out the cabinets, and a parade of maids to bring the eggs, each priceless ornament cradled carefully in their hands, flew by in an instant.

The guests fidgeted in their seats, this time with excitement. This was immensely more engaging than what they'd expected when they'd traipsed out to watch the youngest Tsarina exhibit her reputedly meager abilities.

The probable-baroness in her yellow dress had returned to her seat, sweating delicately from her journey across the lawn in high heels. She gave me an encouraging smile.

Mama looked nothing less than completely stressed. She was trying to keep up appearances for the general on her left side, her laughter high and slightly hysterical as she said, "Anastasia is always surprising us! Always full of such an amusing spirit of adventure."

Tatiana shook her head at me slowly. Ollie mouthed, "*You've lost your mind...*"

The transparent cabinets were assembled twenty paces apart from each other. The maids deposited the Faberge eggs on the glass shelves of the leftmost cabinet. The right remained empty.

Papa stood before the crowd, holding a stopwatch.

"Anastasia will be recreating the exhibition I performed as a young man. In the space of three seconds, I moved twenty eggs from one cabinet to another."

Papa gave me a significant stare.

"Of course, I performed my exhibition at the age of fifteen, as was common then, with far more training. I'm sure we'll all be impressed if Anastasia can move any eggs at all."

He was telling me not to bite off more than I could chew. To focus on slipping into the time-stream and laying my hands on even a single egg if I could.

I had no doubt I could do it. I could feel the liquid edges of time flowing against my skin. I longed to lean into it.

But first, I ripped the tricorn hat off my head. It pulled the pins out of my hair, but I didn't care. I'd rather be indecent than incompetent.

"Ready," I said to Papa.

His thumb depressed the stopper.

I twisted, and the whole world slowed around me. An eerie sense of calm closed over my head. I spared a glance for the crowd, frozen mid-gesture like figures in a diorama.

Vasta was right there in the front row, ugly smile plastered in place like the old adage Margaretta used to say: *Don't make that face, the gods point a finger and you'll be stuck with it forever.*

I could walk up and box his ears—he wouldn't even know what had happened, only that his head was ringing.

Instead, I glanced back at Damien. The others resembled lifeless waxworks. Not him. He remained vivid and alive, heart still pumping, all of time flowing around him.

My heart jumped in my chest, shooting me forward. I sprinted to the left cabinet and pulled it open, seizing hold of the Hen Egg, commissioned by Grandfather as an Easter gift. Its gleaming enamel shell enclosed a golden hen on a gilded nest. Inside the hen itself was a tiny diamond crown, hidden in her belly as if she'd swallowed it. Each egg was different. The only rule was that they all contained a surprise.

I grabbed hold of the Hen Egg. Objects could be difficult to manipulate in altered time—the enamel shell felt slippery and frictionless in my hands, as if it had been greased.

I ran across the lawn to the second cabinet, pulled open the doors, and thrust the egg inside, leaving the doors wide so I could move the eggs more quickly.

Dashing back across the lawn to grab a second egg, my feet passed over Artemis' shadow, shaped exactly like herself, motionless on the grass. I looked up and saw that even she was fixed in place in the flat blue sky, as if she'd been drawn there. Looking up disoriented me. I almost tripped and fell.

Steadying myself, I focused on the second cabinet. It was horribly difficult to keep my bearings, like swimming underwater. Gravity didn't work the same. The silence deafened me.

I took hold of the Winter Egg, carved from a block of crystal, clear as ice. My head was pounding, my heart thundering even harder. Sweat poured down my back. Though I felt light enough sliding over the grass, the exertion burned up my magic like pure gasoline.

I sprinted back with the second egg, then another, and another.

Pausing long enough to glance at Papa's watch, I realized that less than half a second had passed. I was certainly going to get five eggs. Maybe even ten.

I put my head down and pelted back and forth between the cabinets. Getting reckless, I grabbed one in each hand so I could move them twice as fast.

Soon the right-hand cabinet bore an impressive dozen eggs on its shelves, with only a single second elapsed.

The crowd had shifted, so slowly it was imperceptible to me. Tatiana's fan pointed down now instead of up. Maria's mouth had opened in a round O of amazement.

I wondered what I looked like to her—probably a smear of navy and red, a woolen comet streaking across the grass.

Laughing madly, I ran back to the stash of eggs.

Maybe I could beat Papa's record. Maybe I could get more than twenty. What would everyone say then?

I wouldn't be the screw-up anymore. The fourth daughter nobody wanted, always underfoot, always in trouble. I'd be impressive for once.

I ran until I thought my heart would burst. Sweat flew off me in droplets. Eighteen eggs, then nineteen ... I was really going to do it.

I carried the twentieth egg to the right cabinet and placed it on the shelf. I'd done it. Only two seconds had passed.

A deeper madness seized me. The imp came alive from whatever hole I'd stuffed him in after the train debacle.

He whispered, *Get them all. You can do it.*

I ran. All the world was a kaleidoscope of color. I could feel Damien watching me from the back row. He'd be more than impressed ... he'd be astonished.

The left cabinet was empty, I had no idea how much remained of the final second on Papa's stopwatch. I sprinted for the finish line, the forty-ninth and fiftieth eggs clutched in my hands.

Only to trip on that goddamned skirt.

It went under my foot with active malice, like it had only been waiting for its moment.

I stepped full on the material, yanking down the front of my dress, sending myself tumbling head over toes. I slammed into the cabinet like a cannonball, sending every last Faberge egg crashing down on my head. The explosion of glass and porcelain blasted me out of the time-stream, back to normal life.

I came to covered in glass and shattered eggs. I thought I'd broken to pieces myself, but was only bleeding from a dozen cat scratches on my hands and one thin slash down my cheek.

Commotion bore me away like a wave. I was carried into the house to be patched up by Dr. Atticus, who had to be called away from Alexei's bedside. I was pawed over by my mother, then roughly examined by my father who couldn't hide his relief when he grunted, "She'll live."

He was fully furious with me.

I'd made a complete spectacle of myself and destroyed a small fortune of my mother's most precious ornaments.

"What were you thinking?" Papa roared when he was certain there was nothing lastingly wrong with me—other than the usual.

"I had to do it." I sat up on the chaise, batting off Dr. Atticus. "You heard them—they didn't believe I had any power."

"One minister's son!" Papa bellowed. "Are you going to be provoked by every idiot with an opinion?"

My face burned but I couldn't back down, not after everything I'd done.

"Did you see how many eggs I moved before I tripped? Almost all of them! I beat your record, Papa!"

My parents exchanged a look. Mama made a flicking motion with her hands that told the servants to leave the room. The silence as they exited was worse than anything.

Papa towered over me. His face was dark, his mouth unsmiling.

"Someday when you're betrothed, your ability will make you a valuable match. But it's not appropriate for you to flaunt your power. You're a young lady, a Grand Duchess, and a future queen. You shame yourself, Anastasia. You shame all of us. And you paint a target on your back when you display ability without skill."

No skill?

I was furious that he wouldn't acknowledge what I'd accomplished. He wouldn't admit that it was spectacular—even if I flamed out at the end.

I turned to Mama, anger blazing in my face. And met nothing but disappointment—not a shred of sympathy or admiration.

I should have known. My mother hated attention. She'd like me to be as elegant and innocuous as the embroidered pillows on the sofa.

"It was badly done, Anastasia. You've embarrassed us dreadfully."

I pressed my lips together hard, raging inside, but never allowed to show it.

"I suppose I'm sent to my room."

"You'd like that, wouldn't you?" Papa pointed a finger at me. "You still have a ball to attend."

chapter 9

FIRST BALL, LAST DANCE

Margaretta laced my corset with spiteful tightness. She hadn't been watching the exhibition, but apparently had heard all about it.

The gown she dropped over my upraised hands was so heavy with silver embroidery that I wobbled like a matryoshka doll, its ermine cape speckled with pounds of glittering black jet.

"Supposed to look like Artemis' feathers," Margaretta said drily. "Guess we should have made it resemble a Faberge egg. What color fabric does one use for a pile of shattered porcelain?"

"Someday when I'm Empress of Rusya, I'm going to invade Ireland," I informed her.

"Empress of Rusya? Plannin' to marry your brother, are ya?"

My face burned.

"I could inherit."

She scoffed. "When pigs fly. Emperor Paul put paid to that—had enough of the lady Empresses. Can't say I blame 'im—worse than the men, the pack of harpies."

"That's my great, great ... great-grandmothers," I said, without much heat.

"Can you imagine Ollie as Empress?" Margaretta was warming to her subject, pink in the cheeks as she buttoned my gown and tied the sash. "She'd offend every head of state in a thousand miles. Tatiana would make Ivan the Terrible look magnanimous. Maria would fall for some hapless shop boy and turn him Tsar. And you!"

She spun me around so I could observe the full measure of her ridicule.

"Every Romanov in Rusya would have to die before we got that desperate. The gods sent you last for a reason. Your job's to keep your head down and stay out of trouble—though you've never done it yet!"

She cut me down like grass. Still I glared up at her, green and alive.

"I'm more than you think I am."

Maria interrupted before I could find out what disdainful response Margaretta would have for that.

"Don't dawdle, Anastasia. You're still in trouble, you know."

Maria took me by the hand, pulling me down the hallway to the spiral staircase that led directly into our mother's room. She linked her fingers in mine.

"You were so fast I couldn't even see you."

It was the only compliment anyone had given me on my performance. I squeezed her hand as hard as I could.

"I was on fire, Maria. I was a comet in the sky. Nothing could stop me."

Maria turned and stared, blue eyes round and innocent as a Siamese kitten.

"That sounds terrifying."

I couldn't explain that it was the opposite: I felt no fear when I was powerful.

My mother's favorite maid waited in her suite of private rooms. I succumbed to an hour of having my hair singed on hot tongs, then arranged all in my eyes smelling of burnt toast.

At last I was acceptable to be presented at my very first ball.

I met my parents at the double doors of the Portrait Hall, pausing while the attendant called out, "Presenting Tsar Nicholas the Second, Her Imperial Highness the Empress Alexandra, and her Imperial Highness Grand Duchess Anastasia Nikolaevna."

My sisters followed after us, alongside our aunts, Uncle Sandro, Princess Irina, and Grandma Minnie.

I stepped forward into the cavernous Portrait Hall, surrounded on all sides by triple the guests who had attended the exhibition. Over their heads, the gargantuan visages of my ancestors stared down at us.

This was not an official "coming out." I would be formally presented to society on my sixteenth birthday, which was really the equivalent of posting me for sale on the royal marriage market. My personality and pedigree, body and fortune, would be scrutinized closer than any cut of choice meat hung in a butcher's window.

At sixteen, I would be old enough for marriage.

Thirteen only allowed for the speculative examination one might give a two-year-old colt not yet quite old enough to race. If the men could run their hands down my legs and look in my mouth, they'd line up to do it.

Instead, they stared from a distance, muttering to their cronies or conspiring with their wives, running through lists of sons that might offer an appropriate match.

Ollie was the most eligible maiden in all of Rusya. I wasn't that far behind her—even if news of my catastrophic showing had already spread from St. Petersburg to Moscow.

The buzz of whispers rising all around me was more chaotic than usual.

What does it mean? Is she powerful or not?

I knew what they were saying behind their fans, behind their hands, because I was wondering the same thing myself.

Aunt Xenia joined us, detaching me from my mother so she could escort me from group to group, ensuring that I personally greeted every person of prominence in the room.

"You'll apologize to Madame Vyachevslav," she hissed in my ear, steering me by an iron grip on my upper arm. "You humiliated her son."

"Isn't he in any trouble for … casting doubt upon the royal performance?" I waved my hand airily.

Aunt Xenia was having none of it.

"Your father ought to have you whipped. He ought to keep you under lock and key."

I was sorely tempted to ask what Grandpa Alexander did to Xenia when he discovered her on the sofa with Uncle Sandro, playing "Mummies and Daddies." But I kept my mouth shut, not reckless enough to lose out on future gossip snatched from the lips of Aunt Olga.

I was frog-marched up to Madame Vyachevslav, thankfully not accompanied by husband or son at that particular moment.

I had to admire her dark beauty as she turned to meet me. There was elegance in every line, like calligraphy. Until you came to the rigid set of her mouth. That was not a mouth for tenderness—or forgiveness.

The cold formality of her bow was anything but deferential.

"What a staggering performance today, Your Highness."

"I'm sorry about that bit with Artemis." I thrust Vasta's black fabric band at her, torn and bedraggled. She made me hold it out a long time before consenting to pinch it between her thumb and index fingers, tucking it away in her bag like evidence. "I got carried away. Meant it all in fun."

"I should hope so. Vasta is a handsome boy. Intelligent, ambitious. I'm sure that's not the sort of attention you want from him."

I didn't know if that was supposed to be a threat or a pitch to consider her son in a more romantic light.

Either way, the disgusted look on my face heaped insult on injury.

"You think he's beneath you?" Madame Vyachevslav's lips almost disappeared. "The Romanovs would do well to remember that merchants can be just as powerful as aristocrats. It's time to build bonds with the people who control this city."

"This city?" Xenia piped up, her cold, clear tones slicing through Madame Vyachevslav's velvet. "What about Moscow? What about the rest of Rusya? What about Georgia, Serbia, Germany, Albion? You think you have friends here? We have friends everywhere—a dozen nations at our call. You're an ant by comparison."

Madame Vyachevslav's face closed up like a fist.

"Of course." She put her hands together and bowed. "I meant no disrespect. We all advocate for our families."

As she slipped off into the crowd, even I felt a little frightened of Xenia.

"Was that a lesson in diplomacy, Aunt?"

Xenia glared down at me, resembling Papa in every line of her face.

"Nothing is more dangerous than showing weakness. Remember that."

The rounds were not over. I didn't have a chance to taste a single speck of the rich spread of cold hors d'oeuvres the rest of the guests were stuffing into their mouths as quickly as they could: dozens of meats, unsteady mountains of caviar, cheese from every nation in Europe. Vodka flowed in a fountain—a literal fountain sculpted of ice, spouting upward crackling cold, clear as air and twice as light.

Of course I wouldn't get any of that. Not with Xenia latched onto my arm.

She continued our punitive tour, introducing me to the most ancient and tedious people, keeping me away from anyone I liked.

The doors leading into the Semi-Circular Hall opened at last, the liveried servants announcing it was time for dinner, as if no one had eaten yet.

Though Alexander Palace was not nearly the grandest palace in Rusya, its three adjoining rooms opened into one long hall that was truly spectacular, fashioned after an ancient Roman bathhouse with walls clad in solid slabs of lustrous Italian marble.

There my parents feasted their guests according to the tyrannical rules of Rusyan Court Etiquette, which decreed that dinner could only last forty-five minutes to one hour, not a moment longer.

Because my parents still served dinner in the French manner, that meant all seven courses of fish, soup, fowl, salad entree, roast, dessert, and sweet must be served at breakneck pace to five hundred guests.

Each guest required two personal servants. No time was accorded to slow eaters. If you set your fork down for a moment, one of your twin sentries would snatch away the whole plate.

I was hungry enough to eat seven courses in seven minutes. I'd burned up every last shred of breakfast in the first moments of the task and had been running on fumes ever since.

Mama sat on my right-hand side, Prince Christopher of Greece on my left. Dimitri was across from me, though he kept twisting around in his seat to shout remarks to Felix Yusupov at the next table. Since Felix's immensely wealthy mother had been accorded a spot at the head table with us, I could only assume Felix had been banished one row over to keep him separated from Irina, who was safely sandwiched between her formidable parents.

I didn't mind Christo at my elbow, even though I suspected his mother had been matchmaking behind the scenes, this being the third time in as many months he'd been thrust into my proximity.

There was no chance of sparks flying, not even if he started turning up in my bathtub. Christo was fifteen years older than me, stoop-shouldered and already balding, with a mournful face and a pensive voice. He'd wanted to be a pianist, but his family made him join the navy instead.

He could easily sit an hour without talking, which gave me plenty of opportunity to stuff food in my mouth. Once I'd gorged myself on poached trout and potato soup, and ripped apart a roast Cornish hen, it was me who broke the silence, saying around a mouthful of food, "Is it true you turned down another throne?"

Christo gave a start, so lost in dreamy thought that he'd apparently forgotten he was sitting amongst a hundred diners who might fire questions at him.

"Why, yes," he said mildly. "I wish they'd stop offering them."

"You'd think you'd be safe as a fifth son."

Christo had four older brothers in line for the Greek throne, but his family owned such a swath of territory that he'd been offered the rulership of Portugal, Lithuania, and Albania at various times. He'd refused them all.

"What's so bad about being a king?"

Christo shuddered. "Nothing under the sun would induce me to accept a kingdom."

"Why not?"

"The gods have a sense of humor when they choose our position in life. How rarely we suit it."

"Can you imagine feeling like you were doing exactly what you were born to do?" I grinned. "And everyone was happy about it and all your family supported you enthusiastically ..."

Christo gave a small smile. "That's difficult to even imagine."

Damien was way back in the fifth row of tables, looking the picture of a fish out of water amongst a pack of Romanov cousins who lived on a country estate near Moscow. Nikolasha probably sat him there hoping he'd find something in common with my rustic relatives.

It might have worked if Damien didn't look as if he'd been attacked by wild dogs. His hair stuck up in a crest without any cap to cover it, ragged threads sprouting where the buttons had been torn off his jacket.

That didn't stop my cousin Ella sneaking glances at him from under her lashes.

Plenty of girls found their eyes drawn to the fierce young officer with the undeniable air of exoticism.

Even Christo noticed him, saying, "Is that the Cossack Nikolasha sent to the academy?"

Dimitri twisted round to gawp at him.

"I've seen him on campus. We're not in the same division."

"You should be," I said. "He's a magnificent rider."

Dimitri's equestrian skills were so advanced that he'd gone all the way to Stockholm to compete in the Olympics. Knowing that I thought even *he* would be impressed piqued his interest.

"Makes sense—Cossacks are born on horseback. He could transfer to my unit—we've got two spots open."

"Would you arrange it, Dimitri? You'd be his commander, wouldn't you? You could request it."

"If Nikolasha agrees. He'll need a horse. Chargers don't come cheap."

I sat back in my chair, pleased and hopeful.

Whatever was going on in Damien's current division, he'd surely be happier under Dimitri, who could be careless at times, but never a tyrant.

The rest of dinner, I amused myself by observing which bits of the dishes placed before him Damien would consent to eat. I wondered what Cossacks liked.

Our last course of candied sweets was whipped away just before the chimes of the hour.

The guests filed through the large glass doors so they could proceed onto the terrace to watch the sunset. The doors along both sides of the palace could be thrown wide open to let in the air, unveiling the endless vista of the park.

The guests sipped their drinks in the cool evening air, blue clouds of smoke drifting up from the men's cigars.

The smoke made me think of Rasputin. I scanned the crowd, wondering if his performance the night before had been enough to secure him an invitation.

It certainly would have in a more frivolous court. Any other society woman would have capitalized upon the Mad Monk's notoriety to enliven her event. Not Mama.

I heard the boom of cannon shot, launching a dozen flaming balls into the sky that exploded in a shower of light. The fireworks rained down on our heads, colored sparks sizzling against our skin with a delicious tickling sensation. Vibrant bits of flaming soot glittered in our hair and on our clothes, burning harmlessly with no heat.

Each explosion was another deluge. The sparks were so gentle that they could fall in your open eyes as you gazed upward at the great blossoms of light. Some of the youngest guests stuck out their tongues to catch the glittering fall, remarking that the orange one tasted of cinnamon spice.

I hadn't known that my parents ordered fireworks. I pushed my way through the crowd to the railing where Papa stood, throwing my arms around his waist.

"Thank you, Papa. They're heavenly."

He touched my hair.

"You're my little firework, Stassie. You go out with a bang, but you light up the sky."

"Fireworks don't go out with a bang, Papa. They start with one."

His smile moved his beard in the way I knew so well.

"Then I'm intrigued to see what happens next."

THE INTERLUDE ALLOWED the army of servants to remove the tables, chairs, and service stations from the grand hall. In their place, twin rows of padded seats bracketed the open expanse of polished floor, offering a resting place for those who wished to watch the dancers or pause between sets.

Ladies scorned of partners would have to sit in shame, pretending to adjust a strap on their shoe or fanning themselves as if they'd been dancing heartily moments before.

At least I didn't have to live in fear of that particular horror. My aunts were too adept at finding partners. I could be twice as ugly and they'd still scrounge up a boy for me.

The real cross to bear was my goddamned corset. Its vice grip on my ribs was bad enough before I ate several plates of dinner. Now I had no room at all for conveniences like internal organs or air in my lungs.

The Master of Ceremonies announced the opening dance, a stately polonaise that would last the entire first hour. My parents took their place at the head of the set, their most distinguished guests forming the line below in order of importance.

Aunt Xenia had agonized over who to pair me with for the first dance. As I wasn't old enough to be formally courted, she didn't think it appropriate to select a suitor. Instead, the ever-useful Dimitri Pavlovich scribbled his name as the very first entry in my ball book. He was so close to an adopted son that nobody should whisper about it, though I knew they still would.

My mother retired after the polonaise—she had no stamina for dancing. Papa asked Sylvie Buxhoeveden to join him for the waltz. Liza Taneeva watched jealously from the padded seats. Her geriatric husband did not care to dance, settling himself amongst the card players with a store of cigars at his elbow that indicated he planned to sit there all night long.

Christo's mother presented herself in the interval between dances. Her son managed to slip away crossing the ballroom, so she had to hunt him down and drag him back again before he could scribble his name down in my book.

Andrei Derevenko's eldest son took me through the waltz. I was gasping tight, tiny breaths by the end, my head spinning and a railroad spike jammed in my side.

"Have you got a pocketknife?" I asked Kolya.

"Of course."

He pulled what looked like a sailor's jackknife from his pocket. I seized it and turned on my heel, stalking off in search of a powder room.

My goal was nothing less than the complete dismemberment of my corset. The problem was getting around to my own back.

My savior materialized in the form of Damien Kaledin, smoking moodily behind a potted palm. I cornered him in the niche when he turned to stub out his cigarette in an amphora of gilded Venetian glass.

"Cut this off for me," I demanded, shoving the knife at him.

"Cut off what—your hair, your head?"

"My corset."

"Not a chance."

"Why not?"

"Because if I get caught cutting the corset off a Grand Duchess, your father will burn me alive."

"He wouldn't do that."

Damien stepped in close, his breath hot on my skin. "Your grandfather did it to my uncle."

I stared at him. "I can't tell if you're joking."

"I'm not."

I tossed my head.

"And what did your uncle do? Nothing, I suppose. Innocent as a newborn lamb."

"He sacked four cities along the Dnieper," Damien said, unashamed. "Would have held them, too, if his brother hadn't betrayed him."

"You're not talking about your father, I hope."

Damien gave me a cold look.

"My father mounted their Judas brother on a pike and split his chest with an axe so the crows could pick him clean. If a bird eats your heart, your soul can never find rest."

"And I thought *my* family was petty."

Damien gripped my shoulder and turned me around roughly, pushing me against the curved walls of the niche.

"It doesn't matter," he hissed in my ear, his breath hot against my neck. "After that, my father took the firebird as his symbol. Burn us again and again...we only come back stronger."

The knife pressed hard against my spine, then slashed upward.

My ribcage expanded like a balloon, all the pressure released. I pulled off the whole damn apparatus and chucked it behind the potted palm.

"That's better."

"You're welcome." Damien tried to push past me.

"Well, do me up again!"

"You have such a charming way of requesting favors ..."

"I just did *you* a favor."

"I don't think I enjoyed that as much as you think I did."

"Not the corset—I asked my cousin Dimitri to transfer you to the cavalry division. He'll be your commander now."

For once, Damien didn't have a retort at the ready. He looked at me, confused and strangely vulnerable.

"Why did you do that?"

"So you'd have a horse again. Don't you want to ride?"

"Of course I do."

"Then why are you complaining?"

"Because!" Damien spat. "I *told* you, I don't need your help!"

"Stop being stubborn."

"That's the thief accusing the robber ..."

"Oh, shut up."

Damien clamped his hand over my mouth. I tried to bite him, but it was impossible through the leather glove.

He held me trapped behind the palm as two people hurried past, whispering and giggling as quietly as they could. It was Irina and Felix, slipping out from under the watchful eye of Aunt Xenia.

I grinned as Damien removed his hand from my mouth.

"We should follow them and see where they're going."

"I'm pretty sure I know where they're going."

That made me blush more than it should. I was still flushed from the feel of Damien's arm pressed hard against my lower back, shoving me against the wall. He was so much stronger than me. Nothing like wrestling with my sisters.

We both became aware that we were hidden away together, as if we'd snuck off on purpose like Felix and Irina.

"You need to get back inside," Damien said.

"I *will* go back inside—but not because you told me to. Because I want to try dancing again now that I can breathe."

"Good luck with that."

Damien escaped the niche, stalking off in the opposite direction.

I returned to a ballroom thick with the humid heat of bodies in motion. The dancers wove through the patterns I'd been taught by my dancing master, far more intimidating at full speed in a crowded ballroom. The women's glittering skirts swirled and the men's heels beat against the polished floor. The tuxedoed aristocrats wore polished dancing shoes, but the Hussar officers in dress uniforms would never remove their boots and spurs.

"Have you seen Irina?" Xenia barked in my ear, making me jump.

"No."

"Here—" She thrust a freckled boy at me. "Prince Ilya wants to dance."

Ilya did not at all want to dance, as far as I could tell. His hands were sweating through his gloves and his voice squeaked every time he tried to ask me a question.

On the plus side, he was a competent if not inspired dancer. He led me through a Hungarian folk song, then a pas-de-quatre.

Dancing without a corset was pure bliss by comparison. I felt light as dandelion puff, twirling and bowing, catching glimpses of my sisters as we passed each other in the set.

Maria was surrounded by a trio of young officers, all begging to write their names in her book. Tatiana glided across the floor in the arms of the fabulously wealthy Duke Biron. Ollie swapped partners each song, in hot demand for the quadrilles, which were fast and intricate, a challenge for even the most talented dancers.

I wished Alexei could come down from his room. He could sit on the side and watch if he were feeling a little better.

Across the dance floor, Vasta Vyachevslav was steering a pretty blonde heiress through a joyless series of steps. He seemed to be regaling her with an anecdote far more interesting to him than to her. I was glad we were separated by a dozen couples and that my apology to Madame Vyachevslav hadn't involved writing her son's name in my ball book.

In the pause between quadrilles, I took a seat to catch my breath. The day had drained me dry. I was tired down to my bones and wished I could go to bed.

At least the mazurka was coming up next—I wanted to see who my sisters would take as partners.

The mazurka was what everyone waited for. Wild and flirtatious, it was the dance you asked of the person you'd really come to see.

Damien returned from wherever he'd been hiding, taking a seat at the very end of the row of chairs, furthest from the action. He looked as if he'd rather exit the party entirely, but that was impossible with Uncle Nikolasha firmly ensconced at the card tables. Unless Nikolasha lost all his bets, it would be another hour at least before he'd order his carriage.

My cousin Ella took a seat two down from Damien, refusing several requests to dance, perhaps in the hopes that a certain sulky Cossack would ask her instead.

Her brother Tom plopped down between them, oblivious to her plans or deliberately barricading.

The Master of Ceremonies announced the mazurka. A flurry of activity commenced, the attendees eagerly finding the partners they'd already engaged or hastily taking a last shot at securing one.

I saw the pretty blonde heiress slip away through a side door moments before Vasta returned with a drink in each hand. He hunted for her, face reddening as he realized he'd been ditched. He slugged down the drinks, then cast a bitter glance around the room for a subject on which to vent his spleen.

He smiled when he spotted Damien.

"Can't find a partner?"

"Looks like you lost yours." Damien raised an eyebrow at the two empty glasses in Vasta's hands.

Vasta's lips went white in the center just like his mother's.

"At least I had one. There's not a girl here who'd be caught dead dancing with a filthy savage. Look at yourself—I'm surprised the Tsar let you through the door. Probably just so he could show you off like a trained monkey."

Bastard.

I longed to shout something down the row of chairs, but I'd already been told off twice by Damien for interfering.

Instead I watched as Vasta wheeled on Ella, his handsome face ugly with spite.

"You wouldn't dance with him, would you Ella? Not if I paid you."

Ella cast a nervous glance at Damien, biting at her lips. She opened her mouth to say something, but her brother cut her off.

"No, she wouldn't."

I saw the twitch of Damien's jaw before he smoothed his expression to stone.

"I don't give a shit about dancing."

"That's lucky," Vasta sneered. "Since you'd look pretty stupid standing up by yourself."

Damien rose from his seat, a dark look on his face. He swept past Vasta, stomping down the row of chairs and coming to a stop in front of me.

"D'you want to dance?" he said ungraciously.

Tom and Vasta watched us.

I knew Damien was only asking because I was a Tsarina. I might be the youngest and least-impressive Grand Duchess, but it was still my exhibition.

I could turn Damien down in revenge for every nasty thing he'd ever said to me. Perhaps I would have, if he seemed sure of his answer. But I saw the flicker of nerves behind those dark eyes. He was afraid I'd humiliate him, like everyone else.

I held out my gloved hand.

We took our place at the end of the set just as the musicians put bow to string.

Felix and Irina slipped in next to us, waiting until the last moment to join the dance so Xenia couldn't interfere.

♪♫ Kwaak (Mazurka)—Andoorn

Damien took my hands in his and immediately stomped on my foot. "Ow!"

"Don't put your feet under my feet."

"Don't lead me, *I'm* the one who knows the dance!"

Through his teeth he said, "I have to lead you, *I'm* the man."

"I thought the point of this was to avoid embarrassment."

"That's why I'm doing it so fucking splendidly."

He swept me around in a huge circle that made my skirt flare out like a bell. It was an impressive twirl, though not at all a part of the mazurka.

Damien imitated the next several steps quite well, inserting his own when he didn't know what to do. He was strong as a horse, and he obviously knew how to swing a girl around.

Though half his moves were invented, admiring eyes turned his way. A flurry of whispers whirled around us.

I started the dance exhausted, but with every minute locked in his arms, my feet grew lighter, my steps quicker. I was charging off him like a battery.

I wondered if there was something symbiotic in our magic. If so, that was another irony of the gods, because in every other way we were oil and water.

Damien wouldn't stop trying to lead me through his mad mix of moves and I wouldn't stop yanking him back in the right direction. We were wrestling as much as dancing.

The floor was packed with couples, hotter than a Swedish sauna. Sweat dripped down our faces.

We swept past Uncle Nikolasha, who had abandoned his cards to take Stana Leuchtenberg for a spin.

Stana and her sister Militza were famous at court. Daughters of the King of Montenegro, it was said they could speak to the spirits of the dead. Tall and dark, Stana had the tight curls, imperious nose, and well-shaped lips of a Roman bust. She was one of the only women who could dance with Nikolasha without looking childlike next to his great size.

"It's too bad Nikolasha never married," I said to Damien. "He ought to have children of his own. I wonder why he never wanted to?"

Damien made a sound partway between a snort and a laugh.

"What?" I demanded.

"He's dancing with the reason right now."

"Stana?" I scoffed. "She's already married."

"You're right. Nobody's ever fallen in love with a married woman."

I took a second look at my uncle, who was gazing into the large, dark eyes of his partner. They might have been alone in an empty room for all the attention they paid to anyone else.

"Papa would never allow it."

He never granted divorces, especially not to his own family. He was just as strict as Grandfather in that way.

"Then I guess your uncle's never getting married."

I fell silent. It annoyed me that Damien was acting like he knew Nikolasha better than I did. On the other hand, he had been living with my uncle for almost two years now, at least when school was out of session. Who knows what he'd seen. Or what Nikolasha had told him.

Men seemed to occupy some secret world to which women were never admitted. It was why they had their clubs and their private parties, why they were always disappearing after dinner to smoke and discuss the matters they'd never speak openly with women present.

I knew the version of my uncle he chose to show me.

That he might have shown more to Damien made me angry and jealous.

"You don't know everything."

Damien merely smiled in his infuriating way, sweeping me through the last few bars of the mazurka without missing a single step. I had to admit, he was a fast learner.

We came to a stop next to Ollie, who was dancing with a handsome young officer I'd never seen before. He must have been a friend of Felix Yusupov, because Felix slapped him on the back as he and Irina joined the group.

"That's showing us how it's done! The two best dancers in St. Petersburg, together at last."

"I don't know," Ollie threw me an amused glance. "I think Stasia and Damien invented a whole new mazurka."

"And why shouldn't they?" Felix said. "Somebody invented the steps in the first place. Are they supposed to stay the same forever?"

"I think that was the idea," Ollie laughed.

"Sounds pretty dull to me."

Foolishly, we'd all gathered together in a bunch with no lookout for Aunt Xenia. She descended upon us like a bunch of baby rabbits asleep in a carrot patch.

"*Get over here this instant,*" she hissed at Irina and me. "You too, Olga."

The last three dances of the ball passed by while Xenia bawled us out for selecting a Cossack with no hat and the most frivolous playboy in all of St. Petersburg as our dancing partners. Even Ollie got a verbal licking—apparently she was engaged to dance the mazurka with the Crown Prince of Serbia but had opted for the dashing officer instead.

"The Crown Prince ate an entire herring at dinner." Ollie sniffed. "I can't dance if I'm suffocating in fish breath."

"It doesn't matter! You were committed!"

"How was I supposed to know that?"

"Can you read?" Xenia brandished Ollie's ball book in her face.

Sure enough, the name *Prince George of Serbia* was inked in a fussy script I recognized as Aunt Xenia's.

"Promising the same dance to two men is the highest vulgarity!"

"*I* didn't promise it to him," Ollie muttered mutinously.

"There will be no more dancing for any of you!" Xenia decreed.

"There's only one song left anyway," Ollie said.

I didn't mind so much. My exhaustion had returned, dragging on my limbs like lead weights. Besides, after the wildness of Damien's mazurka, a polite cotillion with a partner of Xenia's choice would seem tediously tame.

chapter 10

ONE FOOT IN THE GRAVE

That night, Alexei took a turn for the worse. His screams echoed down the narrow corridor between our rooms. My sisters and I haunted the hallway in our nightdresses like four pale ghosts, not allowed to see Alexei, but always hovering in case we were needed to run a message or help the maids with the endless pans of cool water used to sponge his swollen joints.

At three o'clock in the morning, the Archpriest was called. He entered Alexei's room, black cowl flapping behind him and holy book tucked under his arm.

"Why did they call him?" I whispered to Tatiana.

For once, even Tatiana wouldn't speak the truth aloud.

The priest's sonorous voice floated through the closed door, chanting the prayer for untethered souls.

My brother was dying.

Liza Taneeva arrived twenty minutes after the Archpriest, puffing slightly. I noticed she'd taken time to put rouge on her cheeks.

"I couldn't sleep! I had the presentiment of something awful occurring. And then when I saw the doctor's carriage passing the gates—well! I knew I had to run up and see what had happened. Please tell me it isn't Tiny!"

It grated when Liza used my mother's nickname for Alexei. Everything she did annoyed me unreasonably. I hated to see my mother sink against Liza's shoulder, accepting the flood of sympathy and the promises of imminent recovery that seemed as steeped with sickly insincerity as gooey candied fruit.

The doctor gave Alexei something that put him in a fitful sleep. Dr. Atticus was a wizard with chemical tinctures—he could make draughts to cure stomach aches, banish hiccups, or send you away on a floating sleep during a painful tooth extraction. But he'd never managed to make anything that helped Alexei for long.

"Will he wake?" Papa whispered to Dr. Atticus, hollow eyed and stiff in the shoulders.

"He should."

That was no kind of promise at all.

I was determined to see Alexei for myself. I waited until just after four, when silence had fallen in the corridor.

Tatiana sat in the window seat of her bedroom, reading a book with her shoulder pressed against the fogged glass. There was no hope of her sleeping with any sort of noise going on, not even with earplugs stuffed in her ears. Ollie had drifted off next to her, her head nestled on the toe of Tatiana's silk slipper. Maria snored face down on Ollie's bed, one of Alexei's old bears tucked under her arm.

I slipped past the doorway, entering the playroom.

Alexei had a real teepee that had been a gift from an American ambassador. Its back fetched up against a small cherry-painted door with a round brass knob. That door connected with one inside Alexei's bedroom closet.

Grandfather built a warren of passageways through the palace walls for his many children. One came out behind the slide in the Mountain Hall, though it was blocked now by a cabinet. Another led from the ballroom to the kitchens. And one ran all the way from the kitchens to the old horse graveyard. The passageways were deliberately narrow—Ollie had already outgrown them.

I crept through the teepee into Alexei's room, careful not to wake him.

Papa had likewise fallen asleep next to Alexei's bed, slumped over with his head resting on his thick forearm curled across the nightstand. From the position of Alexei's limp hand on the coverlet and Papa's dangling arm, I supposed my father had been holding Alexei's hand before he dozed off.

The palace was so silent, it felt as if all my family had fallen into an enchanted slumber.

My bare feet sunk into the thick carpet. I approached in silence, wanting to check for myself that Alexei's chest still rose and fell beneath the blankets.

It did. Slowly and shallowly, but moving nonetheless.

I let out the breath I was holding.

Alexei's hand was gray against the white sheet.

I glanced up at his face, startled to see his eyes open, watching me. They looked huge in his pinched face, surrounded by purplish shadows. His hair hung over his forehead, dry as straw.

"When I die, I want to be buried in the woods, in the trees," he croaked. "With a stone marker."

"What are you talking about?" I whispered back. "You're not going to die."

"I don't want to." Alexei closed his eyes. Tears ran down toward his ears. "You can have all my swords, Stassie. And my horse."

His lips were purplish too. Alexei was a handsome boy, but in that moment he frightened me. He looked as if he had already died and was speaking to me from a hole in the ground. His eyes had an eerie, far-off look, as if they'd seen beyond this world.

"Where do you think we go?" he rasped.

"I ... I don't know." And then, fiercely, though I didn't know if I believed it, I said, "Someplace beautiful. Someplace better than here."

"I like it here."

I had never heard him so plaintive. So hopeless.

I seized Alexei's hand, cold as a tombstone, and held it as if I could tether him in place.

"You aren't going to die. I won't let you."

"I should have been nicer. Not Alexei the Terrible."

"That was just a joke! You're wonderful."

Alexei hadn't been terrible for a long time. He'd learned kindness in suffering. He thanked the nurses who helped him instead of teasing them, and clung to Andrei Derevenko in a way that broke our hearts, though it was what we'd always asked for.

"It hurts." His face screwed up in pain. "At least I won't hurt anymore."

His face twisted, teeth bared, and he thrashed his legs until his covers kicked off. I saw his thigh, swollen and mottled where his pajamas had been cut away, and the distended bowl of his belly. The bleeding had swollen his abdomen like a monstrous gestation.

The noise woke my father. His head jerked up. He leaped to hold Alexei in his arms, hardly noticing that I was at his elbow.

"My son! My son!"

Alexei turned his head against my father's chest, groaning.

I fled the room, through the door this time, running back to my sisters. Ollie was just lifting her head from Tatiana's slipper, rubbing her eyes. Maria still snored on the bed, oblivious.

"What's happening to Alexei?" Tatiana demanded.

"His stomach," I said, miserably. "It's all swollen."

My sisters stared at each other.

Then Tatiana twisted her head, hearing something out in the park.

A dark figure strode up the lawn, tall and bareheaded. He glided through the fog, his robe swirling around him as if he walked underwater.

"Rasputin," I breathed.

I ran down to the back garden door, sure that's where he would enter.

Mama and Liza Taneeva already waited. Mama wore a wrap over her head, her hands clutching tightly at its folds as if she were freezing. Liza was bright-eyed and anxious.

"Here he is!" she cried, grasping Mama's arm as Rasputin's knock rang out.

All the servants had been ordered away. Even now, Mama didn't want anyone to see Rasputin arrive.

I hung back behind a suit of armor, watching from the shadows.

My mother opened the door.

"Please, come in."

Rasputin's voice was gentle, his expression sorrowful. "Matushka ... did I not tell you we would see each other again soon?"

I'd never heard anyone address my mother so informally.

She only nodded. "Indeed you did."

"Where is the Tsarevich?"

"I'll take you to him."

My mother ascended the staircase, Rasputin beside her and Liza hurrying to keep up with their much longer strides.

Ollie and Tatiana peeked out the doorway of their room. Ortipo, Maria's dog, put his nose out as well, then dove back out of sight.

I hung back on the staircase.

Rasputin strode into Alexei's room without asking which was his. Mama and Liza Taneeva tried to follow, stopped by the command "I'll see the patient alone."

"No one sees him alone," my father said. "I'll hold Alexei while you examine him."

"That's impossible."

I was shocked by the impudence of a Siberian peasant opposing the Tsar. Yet even my father bent to Rasputin, desperate as he was.

"What will you do to him?"

"I'll put him in a hypnotic state. It will relax his body and allow me to coax the blood back where it belongs. I'll need complete silence and utter isolation."

A pause, then my father said, "That's what you'll have."

My parents left Rasputin alone with Alexei, closing and locking the door.

I waited until the hallway was clear, then crept up from the stairs and pressed my ear against Alexei's door. If Rasputin was chanting like the Archpriest, it was too quiet for me to hear.

I slipped inside the gloom of the nursery, lit only by the moonlight streaming through the window. The distorted shadows of toys rose up around me as if I'd shrunk and the rocking horse and Ollie's old dollhouse now dwarfed me in size.

I wanted to creep back into the passageway but feared I might hurt Alexei if I somehow interrupted whatever was going on in there.

Before I could move, someone else entered the nursery.

My mother stooped to hunt through Alexei's toy chest as quietly as she could.

"What do you need, Mama?"

She startled, dropping one of Alexei's toy soldiers on the rug.

"I can't find his old bear. The one missing a leg."

"Maria has it."

Mama picked up a stuffed rabbit instead, one Alexei received for his birthday a year or two past, and pressed it against her chest.

It seemed impossible that the rabbit could still be here when the sun rose, but not Alexei.

I'd always known he was ill, but every time he had an attack and survived, it seemed to prove the opposite: that nothing could actually kill him.

Now I was finally old enough for reality to place a cold finger against the base of my skull.

"I can't stand it, Mama. If he dies I'll—"

"You'll go on," Mama said. "We all will. It seems impossible now, but it happens whether we want it to or not."

My mother was strangely calm. She was pale and wrung out with misery, but less panicked than the rest of us.

She'd already lost her brother, her mother, and two sisters by the time she turned six. Her father died of a heart attack right after her nineteenth birthday, her beloved grandmother Queen Victoria a few years later.

Papa called her Sunny because when she smiled, you could feel it on your skin. But she wasn't happy, not often and not really. She'd known grief all her life.

"I can't stand it," I said again, weakly.

Mama pulled me against her side.

"It hurts because we love him. That's the balance of life, hard as it is to accept. A heart open to joy is a heart vulnerable to sorrow. There's no family without loss, no love without pain."

She clutched me to her chest and rested her chin on my head, her body shaking with silent sobs.

I wanted to cry. The unshed tears burned behind my eyes, hotter by the minute. My sorrow felt like anger, and anger felt dangerous.

"Pray with me," Mama said.

She sank to her knees on the rug, hands clasped in front of her, lips moving as she silently begged.

"The gods made him sick," I said dully. "Why would they save him?"

Mama paused. She took my hand and pulled me down to the rug. Looking in my face, she said, "Whatever else is taken from you, never lose hope. Even if you see how dark the world can be, choose to believe it could be better."

I didn't know if you could choose to believe in something. It seemed to me that you either believed, or you didn't. You couldn't force love or faith into being.

Still, I closed my eyes and prayed harder than I'd ever prayed that the gods would spare my brother. I promised anything if only Alexei could live.

Rasputin stayed locked up with Alexei for the better part of two hours.

The rest of us waited in Ollie and Maria's room. Papa sat by the window with his head in his hands. Mama perched on the edge of the bed, stroking Maria's hair with her hand while she slept. Tatiana set down her book to fetch tea for everyone. Ollie tried to entertain Ortipo on the rug but she was listless, and even Ortipo seemed too dull to play.

Liza Taneeva bustled around the room, insisting on fetching a warmer shawl for Mama, interfering with Tatiana's distribution of the tea, and wondering aloud what Rasputin was doing, so many times and with so little variation, that at last Papa raised his head and said, "Liza, would you be so good as to supervise the servants? Keep them quiet if you can, about ... everything."

I could tell she wanted to be at hand when the door to Alexei's room opened, but unlike Rasputin, she couldn't refuse an order from my father.

"Gladly," she said, with a pained smile. "This is why I'm at hand, to make myself of use to you."

When she was gone, the room was at least quiet.

Too quiet.

The horrible thought occurred to me that Alexei might have passed away on the other side of the wall. Rasputin could be waiting silently by his body, too frightened to tell my parents that he had failed.

At last morning light began to illuminate the gilded edges of the dragonflies on the frieze along the upper wall, the edges of Tatiana's mirror, and the handles of Ollie's silver brush and comb. Fog pressed against the windowpanes, thick as smoke, until it burned away.

"The boy is awake."

Rasputin stood in the doorway. Tatiana's head snapped up—even she hadn't heard him coming.

My parents rushed to Alexei. Ollie, Tatiana, Maria, and I all crowded in the doorway of his room, breathless as my mother dropped to her knees next to Alexei's bed.

She pushed his hair back from his forehead. His eyes fluttered open—clear and blue, no longer gazing blankly into worlds beyond our own.

"Mama," he said. "It stopped hurting."

My mother let out a sob, lifting Alexei's head to press his cheek against her neck.

Papa turned away, hands covering his face.

My sisters were all crying, running to the bed to touch Alexei, to be sure he was really all right.

My parents had brought in countless healers to examine Alexei. None had ever been able to help.

Now his color was the best I'd ever seen it, his cheeks as pink as a china doll, his eyes bright and alert once more. His stomach no longer bulged beneath the bedclothes, and he was already trying to sit upright, asking, "Did I miss tea?"

Rasputin stood by the window, a little to the right of the glass, out of the path of the morning sunlight. He wasn't looking at his patient—only at my mother, a smile playing on his lips.

His confidence was unruffled, his expression serene. As if he'd known all along he could heal him.

How did he do it? *How?*

"You'll be rewarded for this," Papa said hoarsely.

"All that I have and all that I am belongs to the gods." Rasputin's pale eyes flickered in the stillness of his face. "Perhaps you can make a donation to the cathedral in St. Petersburg. A monk should be at home in any heavenly house, but sadly my brothers make distinctions the gods did not intend."

"I'll speak to the Abbott myself," Papa said. "He will receive you."

Rasputin bowed, hands in his sleeves.

"Alexei isn't entirely healed," he warned. "His blood disorder is severe. It will require repeated treatment."

"You'll come and see him?" Mama begged.

"Whenever I'm needed."

"Thank you, thank you."

Mama took Rasputin's hands and kissed them. His skin was pale and smooth, not rough like a peasant's. I reminded myself that he was a monk, not a farmer. But even wandering monks were marked by labor.

Wandering *starets* little resembled the priests in cathedrals with embroidered robes and golden staffs, and jeweled amulets resting on their chests. Rasputin's robes were coarse, his feet bare in their sandals and his head uncovered even in the presence of the Tsar.

His manners were plain as a peasant's, but he didn't sound as if he'd been educated at a country school.

He puzzled me.

When our eyes met, I felt a cool breath against my face, like the soft kiss of snow.

"Anastasia," he said. "You've been dancing."

I was in my nightdress, no trace of the ballgown anymore.

Softly he said, "Who was your partner?"

An image came into my mind: Damien as a boy, an adolescent, and then a man.

I pushed it away.

"I danced with my cousin Dimitri Pavlovich."

"Ah," Rasputin said.

He was still smiling, but I was sure he knew I was lying.

PART THREE

chapter 11

THE ROOTS GO DEEP

3 YEARS LATER

♪♪ *The Tradition—Halsey*

Grandma Minnie asked me to meet her in the Portrait Hall the morning of my sixteenth birthday.

Grandma had moved into her own house in the city after her falling out with Mama over the crown jewels. It was Mama's right to take them, but some were sentimental to Grandma Minnie. As with most of our family drama, nobody was really in the right but everybody took sides so the hurt feelings, public snubs, and passive-aggressive letter writing went on for months.

Grandma Minnie was popular as Empress and even more so as Dowager. She held more dinners and was invited to more parties than both my parents combined.

She was once Princess Dagmar of Denmark, a bold and clever beauty with the same dark curls and button-black eyes as her daughters. She learned such fluent Rusyan within two years of marrying my grandfather that he wrote to her exclusively in his native language.

Grandpa was known as the Colossus, so strong that he could bend iron bars and tear books in half with his bare hands. When the imperial train derailed, Grandpa held up the roof, saving his family from being crushed like peas in a can.

I think neither of my parents quite felt they measured up to the previous Emperor and Empress. It made them prickly to advice.

The Portrait Hall was Grandma's favorite room in the palace, and mine as well. Minnie's magic was her painting. Her portraits captured the spark of the subject, their personality radiating from the canvas until you could almost believe they moved and breathed before you.

She'd painted the portrait of my grandfather and also the one of my father as a boy, tall and skinny in his parade uniform, with his turned-up nose so like Ollie's and the sad and nervous look in his eye that might be the reason Papa said it "wasn't her best work."

Walking down the gallery was like strolling through a history book—the pages written by Romanov hands, sometimes in Romanov blood.

It was a humbling thing to walk beneath the ten-foot-tall visages of your ancestors scowling down at you from horseback. A child of royals is never under the impression that their ancestors were "nice." These were conquerors. The violence of their times meant that they were brutal or they were dead.

Three hundred years of Romanov Emperors lined the walls, starting with the first Romanov Tsar, Mikhail Fyodorovich. He looked like a Turk with his thick black beard and pointed fur hat. Grandma Minnie stood beneath his portrait, staring up into his face. Her eyes flicked across the canvas.

"What are you looking at, Grandma?"

"I'm seeing what the artist saw."

She took my hand and laid it directly on the portrait. The oil paint lay in layers like scales, thick and waxy in places, flaking away in others, its scent sweet and earthy. As Grandma pressed her hand over mine, the color grew richer, swirling beneath my palm as if the paint had turned liquid. Mikhail Fyodorovich's gloved hand tightened around his reins and his horse's ears pricked. I heard the thunder of hooves and smelled torches burning.

"Incredible ..."

"You can see it?" Grandma Minnie smiled, pleased. "Olga can, too, but not Xenia. Funny how that happens."

She pulled back her hand and the painting returned to normal. I could only see more while her hand touched mine.

"Look at his armor," Minnie said.

Mikhail's breastplate was battered and scarred. Fyodorovich was a warrior before he was ever a Tsar, tasked with clearing Rusya of the monsters that kept the people huddled in their towns, unable to spread across the fertile farmlands.

I'd read all about him in one of the most deliciously gruesome books in the Grand Library. He hunted through the wildlands with a band of mercenaries, mostly Cossacks. They bought supplies from tiny villages that had hardly seen men with guns. That's where Mikhail first encountered the crystal that would set our destiny.

The Setos used Charoite in their religious ceremonies, gathering flecks that washed downriver from the mountains. Fyodorovich followed the river to its source, a place the Setos never visited because it was said to be cursed. Long before he reached the caves, Mikhail found chunks of purple jade the size of goose eggs glowing in the riverbed.

He picked up a stone and felt power surge into his arm. The power of a god.

"Have you ever used Charoite?" I asked Grandma Minnie.

She shook her head. "It's not to be used lightly."

"Papa said it's alive."

"All magic's alive. That's why it's so goddamn unpredictable."

I laughed. Grandpa had cursed like a sailor and Grandma Minnie picked up the habit, much to her children's embarrassment.

Mikhail used Charoite to clear Rusya of wolves the size of bears, hungry corpses that rose from the grave, succubi that seduced travelers and birthed demons ... He fell upon them like an avenging angel, clearing the wilds of the west, the steppes, and the Frost Forest. Then he moved on to the frozen north.

There he found creatures of legend, monsters that had no name. The people of the north were primitive and pagan, huddling in their huts, living in terror of the horrors that haunted their nights and snatched their children from their windows. Some practically worshipped the demons that preyed on them.

Mikhail and his army of Cossacks swept through Siberia. With the Charoite in their hands, not even the hosts of hell could stand in their way. They cleansed the frozen wastes, making them safe for habitation.

Settlers moved north. The fur and timber trades swelled. Rusya's fortunes turned at last.

The Cossacks were paid in ropes of gold, the merchants who funded the expedition becoming wealthy beyond measure, their descendants among the most powerful aristocrats to this day. Mikhail was rewarded with rulership of all of Rusya. Who could keep it from him? He consumed the Charoite voraciously, providing smaller portions to his soldiers.

Mikhail forced the Cossacks to sign a treaty of indenture in exchange for the right to govern their own people within their lands. Their Ataman was bitterly angry that the Cossacks were not to be given even a portion of the territory they had won to create a nation of their own. He refused to sign the agreement. The Tsar's scepter struck him in the brow with so much speed and force that it clove the Ataman in two.

It was a schism that had never entirely healed. The Cossacks rebelled again and again each generation, rampaging through the borderlands until they were subdued, the rebels drawn and quartered or burned alive.

I understood why Damien resented my family. The Cossacks longed to be free—truly free. But they wanted to carve off a piece of Rusya for their own, and that could never be. Our sacred duty as Emperors was to keep Rusya unified and whole.

"My friend says Charoite's dangerous."

Calling Damien "my friend" made me blush for some reason. Grandma pretended not to notice.

She said, quietly, "It's been a blight on the Romanov tree for generations."

Grandma Minnie was the beating heart of our family, the gravity that kept us all together. I never thought she'd criticize one of the pillars of our dynasty.

She led me down the gallery, the skirt of her gown whispering against the polished parquet floor. She moved slowly, carefully, her back upright. Xenia had inherited her force of will, Aunt Olga her warmth. Papa was the odd duck, the son who was never meant to be Tsar.

"You know who this is?" Minnie paused before a portrait of Peter the Great.

I gave her a look.

"Grandma. I'm not that hopeless."

She laughed. "Possibly the greatest ruler Rusya ever knew. The reason St. Petersburg exists at all. But he tortured and murdered his own heir."

She lifted my hand and pressed it against the canvas.

I looked into Peter's face, the first in the gallery to be clean shaven, his white ermine cloak flung over full plate-mail armor. He gazed off into the distance, fist on his hip, the proud visionary.

But when Grandma's hand lay over mine and her power flowed through me into the canvas, I heard the sounds of a lash cracking again and again. Peter's painted face flinched as someone screamed, *Please, Papa, I'm innocent!*

I jerked back my hand.

"He crowned his mistress instead," Minnie said. "Made her the first female Empress."

The portrait of Catherine the First stood next to Peter's.

"She only lasted two years," Minnie said. "She went picnicking with her court and began to choke and sputter. She keeled over on the grass, lips blue, eyes full of blood. When the surgeon performed an autopsy, her lungs were filled with seawater."

"Who killed her?"

Grandma touched the moon-pale cheek of the beautiful peasant who'd enchanted an emperor. "When I see an invisible hand at work, I ask myself who benefitted ..."

She passed the portrait of a fourteen-year-old boy.

"They crowned the son of the murdered Tsarevich—he died of a mysterious illness. And then we got Anna ..."

I'd never been able to pass the portrait of Anna Petrovna without shivering. Her dark eyes seemed to follow wherever I moved, the edges of her mouth curved up in a cruel smile.

"Peter the Great's daughter," Minnie said. "Married off at seventeen to the Duke of Courland. Bride and groom entered the carriage, but only one stepped out alive. The Duke suffered a stroke on the road home. Anna traveled on alone and ruled her husband's Duchy for twenty years until she was called back to Rusya to take the throne."

"Tatiana says she was a witch."

"People who offended her sickened and died or suffered horrible accidents. Once she had access to the resources of the crown, her court became as cruel as Caligula's."

Ollie used to terrorize me with stories of Anna Petrovna's barbarism. She was the boogeyman of my nightmares, and yet I'd beg Ollie to tell me my favorite story of all, Anna's Ice Chamber.

Anna Petrovna loved to humiliate her enemies. She forced Prince Mikhail Alekseevich to serve as her jester, then married him to her ugliest maid. She built them a bridal suite carved from solid ice, with frozen beds, tables, chairs, and even a fireplace filled with logs of ice.

The prince and his bride were locked in a cage atop a pair of elephants, paraded through the streets, and pelted with garbage. When they were deposited in their frozen chamber in the dead of winter, Anna sneered for them to make love with vigor if they wanted to stay warm.

"They called her rule 'the Dark Time,'" Grandma Minnie murmured. "Thousands dragged from their beds in the night, never to be seen again ... No one knows who poisoned her tea. She died alone on the floor, foaming at the mouth, while her servants looked on in silence."

She swept past Anna's portrait.

"Elizabeth Petrovna ... locked her nephew in a cell when he was only two months old and left him there until he went mad. Catherine the Second murdered her husband and took his throne."

"She's still my favorite ancestor."

I idolized Catherine the Great because she was clever instead of beautiful, and she ruled Rusya well for thirty-four years, longer than any other Empress.

I also liked that she continued to take handsome young lovers all the way up to her death. When she passed away at sixty-seven, she was in the midst of a passionate affair with the dashing Prince Zubov, forty years her junior.

"Her son Paul was murdered by *his* son Alexander—"

"And you think it's all because of Charoite?"

Grandma said. "There's never just one reason for anything. What I'm trying to illustrate, Anastasia, is that a lust for power will poison your mind. It strengthens you ... but bends your sense of what should be traded. Be careful what you allow to shape you. Ruling is a responsibility, and a heavy one. It's what we owe to the people, not what they owe to us."

My neck felt hot and prickling, and I couldn't quite look Minnie in the eye. I understood the point she was trying to make, but even knowing every nasty thing my relatives had ever done, I still longed to get my hands on a chunk of Charoite.

Magic was intoxicating. I practiced every chance I got, but as Papa wasn't exactly keen on training me after the Faberge incident, my progress was painfully slow.

Charoite would be like strapping a pair of wings on my back. Who could say no to that?

"I'm not going to be ruler of anything," I said, "so it doesn't matter what I do."

"That depends on who you marry," Grandma said. "And you know that's not what I mean, Anastasia. You were born to power, by birth, by position, and by ability. Some are satisfied with their place in nature. And some are hungry for more."

I flushed. I wasn't trying to be Tsar—I just wanted more magic. What was so wrong with that?

We'd come to my great-grandfather Alexander the Liberator, who freed all the serfs. He was a liberal Tsar. On the very day he signed a document that would have allowed the people to form a parliament, a group of revolutionaries threw a bomb at his feet.

My grandfather Alexander III took the throne and immediately repealed every democratic initiative his father had ever signed.

That was why Papa was so opposed to a parliament. Like Aunt Xenia, he'd been raised to believe that the people had no idea how to govern themselves. Handing them power only emboldened their worst impulses.

The portrait of Grandfather was one of the best in the gallery because Minnie had painted it herself. My grandfather was a great bear of a man, barrel chested and barrel bellied, bald headed and bearded. Minnie managed to capture the glint in his eye that showed he also had a sense of humor. He liked to turn the hosepipe on visiting dignitaries and once set a small crocodile loose at a garden party.

Next to Grandfather's portrait was one of his brother. Nicholas Alexandrovich had been painted as a young man of twenty-three, thin faced and curly haired.

Neither my father nor grandfather had been first in line to the throne. They each had an elder brother who'd died unexpectedly.

In fact, Grandma Minnie had been engaged to Nicholas Alexandrovich first.

How different everything would have been if the thin-faced young man had lived. My father never would have been born and neither would I.

Grandma Minnie looked at Nicholas' portrait a long time. I wondered what she was seeing. And even more, what she was thinking.

"I have a gift for you," she said at last. "My grandmother gave it to me on my sixteenth birthday."

She took a little box from her pocket and held it in her hand, looking into my face.

"My grandmother had great ability, Anastasia. There was a time when I also wished to be great. I dreamed of making art that all the world would know. But I lived a very different life than what I planned. We can't know where our talents will take us—the gods decide, not us. Cherish what you have, not what you wish for."

She passed me the music box. Its mechanical innards made it heavier than it looked. The metal lid and sides were perforated with tiny mountains, stars, and moons. I couldn't see how to wind it.

"Like this," Grandma Minnie said.

She lifted the music box to her mouth and exhaled, letting her breath flow inside.

The little box began to glow, golden light spilling through the lid and sides, beaming out in all directions, projecting the shape of the pine trees, stars, clouds, and crescent moon onto the walls and ceiling all around us. The projection rotated slowly, tinkling music playing.

It was beautiful, utterly beautiful. In the dimness of the shuttered portrait hall, the projection was brighter and more real than the oil paintings of my ancestors.

Grandma set the box down on the polished floor.

Now the projection changed. It no longer showed stars and trees. Instead I saw a rocky beach with two figures running along the shore. One was a young man, tall, slim faced, his trousers rolled up on his shins, feet bare and sand caked. The other was a girl, dark haired, tiny, and trim.

He scooped her up in his arms and spun her around. The girl laughed and laughed. Her hat whipped away in the wind and her dark hair streamed free. She clapped her hand to her head, too late, and laughed harder. I recognized Minnie, only nineteen at most, as pretty as a song.

"What is this?"

"A memory." Minnie's voice was soft and far away. "A memory of a perfect day."

I watched the couple walk down the beach, arms around each other's waists, their footsteps consumed by the tide lapping against their ankles.

They lay down together between the dunes. Minnie stooped and lifted the music box, snapping it shut. The projection faded away. There was no sound of laughter or surf anymore, just a few tinkling bars of music, until the box went silent and dark.

She placed it in my palm once more.

"You can record any day you like. One single day. Start in the morning, when the day is full of promise. Press here." She showed me a recessed button on the side—the cut in the metal that looked like a crescent moon. "Keep it in your pocket all day long. It will store all the best memories and play them for you."

"Grandma, this is remarkable magic. I've never seen anything like it."

"Nor have I. It's very old—it wasn't new when my grandmother got it. And remember, it can only hold one day at a time—if you record another, you'll lose the memory."

"You kept this one all these years?"

"It was the only one I ever took of Nixa. He died a week later."

Unconsciously, we both gazed at Nicholas' portrait on the wall, trapped forever as Minnie had last seen him, never aging past their youthful love. And next to him, the man she'd married and had children with. Two very different brothers, one slim and thoughtful with the eyes of a poet, one brash and booming with the hands of a brawler.

"Do you love him still?"

"I grew to love your grandfather in time," Minnie said. "But I loved Nixa desperately. That doesn't go away. It can't."

"Then I can't take this."

I tried to give her back the music box. She shook her head.

"It's time for a new memory, little bear. Pick a day you know will be grand. Cherish it until another comes along."

I threw my arms around her and hugged her tight. Grandmother had shrunk, or I had grown. It was the first time I noticed myself taller than her.

"Who are you dressing as tonight?" she asked me.

I was being formally presented with a costume ball at the Winter Palace.

"I wanted to be Catherine the Great, but Mama said it wasn't appropriate."

She pretended it was because of all the young lovers, but when I said I'd choose a different Empress instead, she gave me a long, silent look. Then suggested "that lovely nurse who discovered how to treat pyromancer burns."

My mother didn't want me going as an Empress, especially not the greatest that had ever ruled.

I was still the only Romanov of my generation who could time-walk. Not even any of my little cousins could do it.

Alexei was thirteen years old now. His telekinesis had grown stronger as his health improved, but he'd developed no other power. He'd inherited only my mother's ability, not my father's.

My parents delayed his exhibition, saying he couldn't perform to capacity when his health was bad. It was difficult to access one's magic when tired, ill, or even in a low mood.

But the truth was, Alexei was stronger than he'd ever been. He'd made a miraculous recovery after Rasputin's visit, walking down to a late lunch on his own two legs and eating a full helping of soup. He'd bloomed for an entire month, full of so much energy that he became bolder and bolder, galloping his horse around the countryside and sliding down the banisters.

His renewal of health had not corresponded with a reemergence of Alexei the Terrible. He joked with the guards instead of trying to steal their swords and even gave his pocket money to a cook's son who had his bicycle stolen. He tried to behave himself.

Still, the inevitable occurred: he tripped sprinting across the park and cut his knee on a stone.

It bled—but only for a few minutes. A clean rag pressed against the spot stopped the flow before it soaked through. The wound clotted. And just like any other person's would have done, it healed.

We checked his knee every hour of the day, closer than we'd ever watched anything in our lives. We cried, we cheered, we celebrated. It seemed Alexei was truly healed.

My father had already secured Rasputin's appointment to the cathedral in St. Petersburg—now he had him promoted to bishop of our private cathedral on the palace grounds. Mama added him to the guest list for imperial events.

We began to see him at parties and balls whether we'd invited him or not. His popularity was exploding amongst the elite of St. Petersburg.

That was without Rasputin breaking his promise not to tell anyone of his visit to the palace or the nature of Alexei's disease.

Even with his lips sealed, no one could fail to observe how often the young Tsarevich was appearing in public. Not only appearing but participating in activities he'd never done before. Alexei became a common sight sailing out in his skiff with Andrei's sons or galloping around on his favorite courser with his spaniel Joy at his heels.

They had suspected that Alexei was ill. Now it seemed clear he was better. The rumors that Rasputin had a hand in the cure soon followed. At minimum, it was known that Rasputin had met the Empress and her daughters at a party at Liza Taneeva's house. The marked difference in my parents' behavior told the rest of the tale.

The wild rumors whirling around the court were much more outlandish than what actually occurred. Tatiana heard whispers of a seance, an exorcism, a battle between Rasputin and the demon that clutched the boy's soul in its claws.

That was always the way, in St. Petersburg. Gossip became fancy, and fancy became madness if the story had enough fuel to feed it.

We only cared that Alexei was healed.

Until the swelling returned to his joints.

We told ourselves it was the weather turning cool in the fall. Then Alexei cut his finger on a pen knife and it bled for over an hour.

My parents called Rasputin back to the palace. He visited Alexei in private and emerged looking grim.

"As I feared, the disease was forced into retreat, not eradicated. I'll need to watch him closely."

Rasputin returned to the palace every day, closeted with Alexei for an hour or two at a time.

When he was finished, he would speak to my parents in private, sometimes for even longer.

I asked Alexei what Rasputin did when they were alone together.

"He sits me somewhere comfortable—usually on the bed. Then he holds his hands over me and chants. The words feel like warmth washing over me. My body relaxes. I can feel my blood flowing backward, and all the poison draining out."

"What does he chant?"

"I don't know." Alexei shrugged. "Just, you know ... words."

"Try to remember them for me."

I was annoyed, as usual, by my brother's practicality. He didn't care what Rasputin was doing as long as it worked.

Under Rasputin's repeated ministrations, Alexei returned to full health. Rasputin had to visit the palace daily, something that could hardly be concealed from the servants.

Papa said it didn't matter. Nothing mattered, as long as Alexei was saved.

So the pattern continued. The disease was contained but never eradicated. Over the winter, Alexei caught a fever that caused all his limbs to swell. Rasputin tended to him night and day until the fever broke. After that, Papa gave Rasputin his own quarters on the grounds, in the White Tower just south of the cathedral. That way Rasputin would always be close at hand when needed, and wouldn't have to return the fifteen miles to St. Petersburg afterward.

Alexei's safety brought a peace to our family it had never known. His illness had haunted us for as long as I could remember. I hardly recognized my father with clear eyes and my mother laughing aloud.

But as always seems to happen in the balance of the universe, the tranquility at home wasn't matched outside its doors.

The riots in the city swelled again and again like a tide, impossible to beat back with any permanence. The people were angry when the crops failed and bread prices rose, they were angry when Papa sent troops to Persia. Each time, the city guard attacked with whips and clubs, smashing the barricades, arresting the organizers, jailing anyone who resisted.

It'd gotten so bad that we'd spent the last six months in Denmark visiting Papa's family. There we could visit the shops and picnic in the park with no bodyguards, no escorts. It made us all realize how much we'd become prisoners at home, barely able to leave the palace grounds.

Papa returned to Rusya with new ferocity, declaring that he'd be at the mercy of the people no longer.

"I'm the Tsar. They'll fall in line or they'll hang."

I knew all this was connected to the reason my mother wouldn't let me dress as an Empress tonight, nor any kind of ruler.

Now that Alexei was in full health, she intended to squash the rumors that had persisted after my exhibition.

Tonight I would be presented as a marriageable young lady, nothing more.

"It's for the best," I said to Grandma Minnie. "I'd drown in a Rococo gown."

"Catherine loved her French fashion." Minnie smiled. "And French men."

My mind had already drifted off in another direction.

Mistaking the look on my face, Minnie patted my hand.

"Don't worry—you'll do wonderfully tonight."

"Thanks, Grandma."

I wasn't actually thinking about my presentation at all. I was remembering that I was about to see Damien for the first time in months.

EVERYONE HAS A SECRET

DAMIEN

I woke with the first bleached light slipping through a crack in the drapes. After a lifetime of rising with the sun back home and another five years getting up at 4:45 for morning drills, it was impossible to sleep in, even if school was over for good.

I washed and shaved at the basin in the corner of my room, brushed my teeth, and pulled on a robe. Nikolasha had hot water delivered to my room every morning and bought the heavy velvet robe and expensive slippers on my feet. He paid for everything I required during my captivity.

Is it strange to come to like your jailor?

I had to at least admire Nikolasha. He was bold and open, generous and fair, devoted to the Tsar, and beloved among his men despite his horrible temper. His booming laugh was impossible to begrudge, even when directed at oneself.

He'd treated me well after the first few months of mutual resentment.

I suppose we realized about the same time that we were stuck with each other.

When I returned from my first semester at the academy, Nikolasha waited for me in the knee-deep snow around his dacha door. By way of greeting, he said, "How well can you shoot?"

"Very well."

"Good. The wolves are bold this winter."

We rode his train into the Frost Forest, the cars filled with packs of dogs, servants and horses, and bins of ammunition.

My heart beat painfully as we passed into country I knew well. I hadn't been so close to home in months. I could feel the steppes calling me like a voice on the wind.

When we disembarked in the rigid cold of the last station, the chill searing our nostrils with every breath, I thought of leaping on one of the horses and galloping off. I doubted any rider could catch me, including Nikolasha himself.

It would be pointless. Even if I could make it to the steppes without freezing, my father would only send me back again. Anastasia was right: he was a man of his word.

Nikolasha watched me. I'm sure he knew what was in my head. Maybe it was a test.

I turned my back on the direction home and said, "Where do we start?"

Nikolasha and I rode deep into the woods, in the eerie silence of winter when all the birds are gone and the animals sleep or slowly starve. To see pines taller than the pillars of any cathedral and deep drifts of sparkling snow—nothing like the filthy piles of slush in the city—reminded me what it was to be in the wild once more, instead of the teeming human chaos of St. Petersburg.

I hated that I was never alone. Always surrounded by the noise and smell of the hundreds of other students at the academy.

I wouldn't have admitted to anyone how much I missed my father and uncles, my horse, and the rest of the hosts, who were family, too, whether or not we were linked by blood.

Hans lolloped along at my ankle. He'd taken an immediate liking to me, something that helped thaw Nikolasha's resentment that I tried to murder his cousin.

Already that blunder seemed so childish that I flushed every time the memory popped into my head. It had been rash in the extreme, not thought out at all.

And I'd been paying a bitter price.

I hated the academy with every fiber of my being. Not only because of the tyranny of the older students, who viciously hazed every new student, but were especially inflamed by the presence of a Cossack amongst the children of generals, aristocrats, and ministers.

No, what I hated most were the rules. Rules for when to wake and how to wash, how to wear your hair and button your jacket, how to stand and when to sit, what to eat, where you could walk ...

And the drills. The endless, tedious, robotic drills. Marching and twirling and posing until I felt like nothing more than one of those German clocks with the figures that pop out and jerk around on a fixed track before zipping back inside their little house.

That was me, every day, over and over.

Galloping through the woods with Nikolasha was more than a break—it was a reminder of freedom.

He taught me how to take the dogs through looping circles until they scented a wolf. Then we split off in opposite directions, the borzois between us, creating a triangular net to trap our quarry.

A massive black timber wolf exploded from cover, sending all the dogs into a howling frenzy.

I'd seen wolves before in the steppes, but never one so large. The beast was brindled as a lion, its winter coat shaggy and soot dark, paw-prints like dinner plates pressed into the snow.

It leaped on one of Nikolasha's borzois and tore out its throat with one tug of its jaws. Before the other dogs could swarm upon it, the wolf dashed through the gap it had created.

I galloped after it, Nikolasha close behind. Hans and Boris closed in from two sides like twin arrows. They crashed their shoulders into the wolf, pinning its head between them so it couldn't turn and bite. Even so, the creature's snapping jaws came within inches of their snouts. The two dogs could hardly hold it. Their back paws dug trenches in the snow deep enough to throw up clods of frozen dirt.

I dropped from my horse and stabbed my hunting knife in the wolf's heaving side, then cut its throat. Its blood ran out on the snow, dark as winter berries, too hot to freeze.

It was dead before Nikolasha's boots hit the ground.

"You've hunted wolves before?"

"A few times. They don't often come near our villages—only in the worst winters. I've never seen one this big ..."

Even dead, the great curved claws and yellowed teeth sent a shiver down my spine. The incisors were as long as my thumb.

"You should see the king wolf." Nikolasha's voice was grim.

"Did you kill it?"

He pulled up the heavy sleeve of his coat. A long purple scar ran from wrist to elbow, twisted as a river.

"It got a taste of me. I'd like to return the favor."

We slaughtered wolves for five days until their corpses were stacked by the train like cordwood. All were enormous, but according to Nikolasha, none were the king.

The servants skinned the carcasses, taking the furs to be made into cloaks. Even the lowliest of Nikolasha's servants possessed a wolfskin cloak fit for a lord.

Nikolasha owned several palaces and dachas. They were all alike in being comfortable and untidy, with furniture that looked like it was hewn out of slabs and proportioned for giants. Nikolasha hated to be cramped on tiny chaises, his feet hanging off the end of spindly beds. His own sleigh bed would have fit a half-dozen women across its breadth, and sometimes did when Nikolasha was lonely and low.

He liked to get drunk in front of the fireplace, downing a quantity of brandy that would have pickled the liver of any lesser man. His must have been trained to it, because he still rose most mornings with barely a headache.

I'd long suspected the source of these morose benders, confirmed the night Nikolasha got drunk enough to admit he'd been in love with a married woman for the better part of a decade.

"I'd give anything—anything!—to have her. And my cousin, that hypocrite, will never grant the divorce. No matter what I've—what I do for him. He was in love with a commoner himself—a little ballerina. His parents had to send him off on a world tour to get his head clear of that madness. And yet he won't—says he'll never ..."

Nikolasha elapsed into sullen silence.

Not knowing what to say, I passed him the nearly empty brandy bottle.

"Thanks." He splashed the rest in his glass. Realizing he'd drunk it all except the shot he'd poured me in the beginning, he grunted, "Didn't want anymore, did you?"

"No." I swirled mine and slugged it down. "This is good."

Even bleary-eyed and slurring, Nikolasha was tactful enough to omit the lady's name. I learned it a year later, over Michaelmas at his estate in Peterhof.

We heard sobbing and hammering at the door. Nikolasha wrenched it open and a woman fell into his arms—tall, slim, and dark, with swelling all down the left side of her face. Her left eye was a slit in the puffy flesh, her nose bleeding onto her teeth.

"WHAT DID HE DO?" Nikolasha roared.

I had seen his temper flare a dozen times before, but in that moment I almost wanted to hide under the couch with Hans and Boris. His face was as red as his beard, his shoulders rising up until he looked like a grizzly rearing on its hind legs before it charges.

"We fought," the woman sobbed. "He went mad. Even the servants couldn't stop him."

"I'LL KILL HIM!"

Nikolasha ripped down the axe that hung by the door, used to split kindling in the yard. He liked to do the job himself, stripping off his shirt and wearing only his trousers and suspenders, until sweat ran down his chest and steam rose off his back into the frigid air.

I had no doubt he could cleave a man's skull much easier than the iron-hard logs.

The woman knew it, too.

"Stop him!" she cried.

Nikolasha had already crossed the yard with his enormous strides, making for the open field, following the set of smaller footprints that had come the opposite way.

I stripped off my gloves and sprinted after him.

It took all I had to match his long legs and blind rage. I leaped on his back, clasping my bare hands on either side of his face.

I might as well have jumped on the back of a rampaging bull. Nikolasha bellowed, twisting and shaking, trying to fling me off.

"Get your hands off me, you little—*arggh*—"

I poured all my strength into holding him pincered between my hands. Still, he would have flung me into the trees if we hadn't been midway through another sad drinking night. The sweet scent of brandy seeped from his skin. He swayed, then fell to one knee, blood spurting from his nose. I held on until he keeled over.

"You didn't hurt him, did you?" the woman hurried to us through the snow. Now that she wasn't crying, her voice was low and musical, with some exotic accent.

"He should be fine." I hoped.

"Drag him into the house then, so he doesn't freeze."

We hauled Nikolasha back across the icy yard.

The woman was strong. There was a stark spareness to her clothes, dark and flowing, that made me think of a priestess. Or perhaps it was the solemness of her expression and the far-off look in her eyes.

It was no easy task to haul Nikolasha up onto the couch. I brought warm water so the woman could wash his face, and her own.

"I'm Stana," she said. "And you're the Ataman's son."

"Damien Kaledin."

She nodded slowly.

"I dreamed of you."

A man might easily take that the wrong way, but I already sensed this woman was more interested in the spirit than the flesh, whatever she might be doing with Nikolasha.

"What did you dream?"

She looked at me without answering, examining every feature of my face as if it meant something to her.

"You should come see me in St. Petersburg. I'll scry for you."

I was familiar with the practice of looking for portents in tea leaves and bones. We had oracles among my people. My own Baba possessed the sight.

"I don't know if I want to know my future."

"Your future is all our futures, boy," she said softly.

That's why I hated mystics—always speaking in riddles.

I was saved from answering by Nikolasha groaning on the couch.

It took him a few minutes to come around, and a few more to express even grudging gratitude at finding himself on his own sofa instead of in a jail cell. He still swore he'd murder Stana's husband, but legally, after challenging him to a duel.

"Don't be an idiot," she said flatly. "He knows better than to accept."

I left the two of them alone by the fire, retiring to bed. By morning Stana had disappeared. I didn't see her again until the night of Anastasia's exhibition, when she danced the Mazurka with Nikolasha.

I assumed they were still seeing each other, because Nikolasha continued to disappear at odd intervals, and the sad drunken evenings proceeded as usual when he was home.

So my last morning at his house in St. Petersburg, I was not entirely surprised to see a woman slipping out the side door, a cloak pulled over her head, but her height unmistakable.

Nikolasha was already in the kitchen. He jumped when he saw me.

"You're up early."

"Looks like you were up late."

Nikolasha had pulled on the crumpled trousers of the night before, his hair and beard wild enough to tell tales, the remains of wine and cheese for two still scattered across the table. Hastily, he scooped up the dishes and threw them in the sink.

"There's porridge." He pointed a thick finger at the bubbling pot on the stovetop.

Nikolasha's cook liked to throw any fruit and nuts she had handy into the grains, then Nikolasha would heap on fresh cream from his own cows and an inch or two of rich brown honey.

The food at Nikolasha's house was ten times better than what they fed us at the academy. Sometimes I dreamed of it in the lengthy interims between holidays.

I used to dream only of the steppes—endless waves of grass like a golden ocean, the flat blue sky that seemed an entirely different shade than smog-tinged St. Petersburg. The sound of Mercury's hooves galloping across the downs. My father's voice and the warmth of his hand on my back through my shirt.

I'd wake to the cold emptiness of my dorm, the walls plain plaster, damp and chill compared to the forgiving fabric of a tent hung with brilliant rugs.

My mind couldn't tolerate such a harsh awakening. Or I was forgetting my home and everyone I loved.

I hardly ever dreamed of the steppes anymore. When I did, I dreamed that I returned home and no one recognized me. Nobody remembered me at all.

It wasn't true, of course—my father wrote me regularly. My uncles too, from time to time.

Papa's letters were short, factual. He was a good leader but no scholar.

I wrote back in much the same way. No complaints, no mention of attacks from older students, my belongings stolen and destroyed, dog shit stuffed between the sheets of my bed. I already knew what my father would say:

You're one of the Free Men. No matter where you are—in chains, in prison, in servitude—you remain free in your mind, in your soul.

I was used to a certain level of isolation. When you can't touch any living thing, when people are afraid of you, you accustom yourself to distance.

But to be hated by everyone you encounter, to have no friends or family or anyone who will even smile in your direction ... that was a new level of loneliness.

Maybe that's why a bond formed between Nikolasha and me. We were both longing for something we couldn't have.

Other friends followed, eventually.

Dimitri Pavlovich was true to his word—he had me transferred to his cavalry division, and Nikolasha paid for a mount. That was when the academy finally became tolerable. Finally I could show what I could do.

The morning drills were infinitely more pleasant on horseback. I was already used to loading and firing from a saddle, even in the dark, even in the rain, so I never received the twenty blows with an iron bar that were the penalty for getting your shot off last. Only a few months passed before I ranked highest in the class.

Though the stallion Nikolasha bought me was no match for Mercury—overbred and touchy, prone to rearing—it was still a magnificent animal. Galloping across the training fields on Hercules' back was the first thing I truly enjoyed since leaving home.

Dimitri was elated to find someone who could keep with up him. He took me hunting in the fall and racing in the spring. He introduced me to his fellow officers and must have told the older students to back off, because the harassment mostly stopped, especially once Vasta Vyachevslav graduated.

I knew I owed the changes to Anastasia. I thanked her the next time I saw her. She laughed and said, "It's weird when you try to be polite."

Though neither of us were in control of our own schedules, our paths crossed every few months when I was with Nikolasha and he was visiting the Romanovs.

Anastasia and I spent one New Year's Eve debating a book we'd both been reading, growing increasingly tipsy on a bottle of Madeira stolen from her father's store. She interrupted my diatribe on *The Magnificent Ambersons*, holding up one finger and saying, "Just one moment, please," in a courtly tone, before turning and vomiting into a vase.

The following summer, Nikolasha took me on a day trip on the imperial yacht. We sailed around the bay in Reval and ate roasted clams on the shore. Anastasia and I got in a row because her father had once again blocked the Duma from forming a parliament. We shouted at each other until we were red in the face, then sulked on opposite sides of the ship the rest of the afternoon.

After that, I told myself I wanted nothing to do with the spoiled princess.

Still, just a few weeks later, I found myself catching her eye across the aisle of the Bolshoi theater. She grinned and plopped herself down beside me during intermission, jabbering away as if nothing had happened between us.

I didn't know what drew me to her over and over. Maybe I only wanted to feel that crackling energy that surged through my body whenever we stood close.

It made no sense—she was just a kid, awkward and freckled, her sash and ribbons always undone, stockings torn. She was stuffed with Romanov arrogance, blindly defending her family, refusing to acknowledge the pressure boiling all throughout the city.

She didn't live in St. Petersburg, not really. Alexander Palace was fifteen miles south in Tsarskoye Selo, and her visits into town were as controlled as a staged pantomime. If she went into a shop, the shop was first cleared of commoners, and she was waited on hand and foot by the proprietor while her guards stood watch outside the door. If she ordered food at a cafe, she ordered whatever she wanted without glancing at the price. She knew nothing of what life was like for normal people.

I knew this because I accompanied the Grand Duchesses on one of those shopping trips my last year at the academy. It was Dimitri who invited me, pretending he wanted to take a walk along the Neva River on a sunny Saturday morning in spring.

The meeting seemed an accident. Once I saw that Anastasia had invited Princess Irina, and Dimitri had brought Felix Yusupov, the real purpose of the expedition became clear. To the girls' escort as much as to me—Aunt Olga had obviously not been warned about this "chance encounter." She wasn't buying it for a second.

"Absolutely not! Xenia will skin me alive."

"How can Xenia be angry that we happened to see our cousin on the street?" asked Ollie, innocently.

"Was this your idea?" Aunt Olga gave Dimitri a sharp look. "Or yours?" She turned her furious gaze on Felix Yusupov.

"Everyone comes down to the Neva on Saturdays," said the smoothly plausible Felix. "The whole city is here."

The street along the riverbank was a riot of candy-colored parasols, children with ice cream cones melting down their hands, little dogs on leashes, and packs of dandies in striped trousers and straw boaters.

Aunt Olga took a look around as if canvassing the sidewalk for spies. A pointless maneuver, since any one of the shoppers gawping at us, or the half-dozen palace guards who trailed the girls everywhere they went, were perfectly capable of reporting to Aunt Xenia. We were hardly subtle, especially with Anastasia's enormous gyrfalcon perched on her arm.

Aunt Olga's affection for her nieces must have defeated her common sense. She sighed and said, "Only for an hour while we visit the shops."

That's how I found myself trailing the four Grand Duchesses down Nevsky Prospect while they fingered bolts of silk and yards of lace.

Anastasia barely glanced at the trimmings. She wanted to visit a filthy animal shop down by the ugliest part of the docks that her sisters flatly refused to enter.

"I'll take her," I said.

The shop was dim and quiet compared to the bright, bustling shopping district. The sweet scent of hay and the must of fur and droppings were thick in the air. I liked those smells. I missed living among animals instead of just people.

The cages were stuffed with all sorts of creatures: monkeys and owls, Komodos and snakes.

Anastasia bought new jesses for Artemis, a process rather like choosing a child's first pair of church shoes, because Anastasia had to hold each option aloft for the bird's approval or disgusted rejection.

"Is she really telling you what she wants?"

"Yes."

The falcon made a sound like a growl, deep in its throat. Anastasia's lips tugged as she smothered some response.

"Did she say something?"

"Mmm ..."

"What? What did she say?"

"She said you smell like a horse."

"So she's an honest bird."

Anastasia smiled. "Let's call it that."

She asked the shopkeeper for a box of white mice that scrabbled and squeaked as the old woman wrapped them up.

"They're Artemis' favorite," Anastasia said regretfully.

Artemis' black eyes were fixed on the holes in the sides of the box with fearful intensity.

"There you are," the proprietress croaked.

She tossed a mouse aloft by its tail. Artemis snapped it out of the air, her beak slicing shut like shears.

Anastasia seemed on familiar terms with the old woman, whose face was as brown and seamed as a crumpled paper bag, her hands so gnarled that I was surprised she could tie the twine around the package of mice.

"Varvara's daughter works at the palace," Anastasia explained. "Her name is Nina Ivanova."

I'd seen the pretty maid at Anastasia's exhibition. The news that this was her mother, not her grandmother, must have put an impolitic expression on my face.

"You can well look surprised, boy. No more than me. I was closer to fifty than forty, my husband even older. We hadn't a dream left in our heads of children. The doctor didn't even consider it—said it was a growth. Said I might die ..." Varvara gave a soft snort. "I almost did when I felt it kick."

That kind of earthy detail didn't bother me. I'd seen both women and animals giving birth.

Anastasia probably hadn't, but she laughed along with the old woman all the same.

"I bet Nina was the prettiest baby."

"Like the fairies left her."

I watched Anastasia pick her way through the crowded shop, touching a few of the animals through the bars, greeting them by name. The turnover of wares was probably slow enough that some of the tenants became pets as much as products. Two or three loose monkeys had the look of shop assistants in their tiny hand-sewn vests.

The large parrot in the back of the shop, gray as stone and longer than my arm, likewise seemed a permanent resident. He shuffled back and forth along his open perch without a cage to contain him, not even a thin chain around his ankle to keep him in place.

"Bird girl," the gray parrot said, in a perfectly intelligible voice that sounded older than Varvara's.

"Hello, Seymour." Anastasia scratched between his wings. "I brought Artemis to see you."

Though the parrot was an impressive creature in his own right—broad backed, long winged, with an intelligent glimmer in his eyes—he was a donkey next to a thoroughbred compared to the sleek metallic sheen of the raptor.

Artemis seemed genuinely pleased to see him and even consented to share space on his perch.

Freed of the weight of her falcon, Anastasia moved lightly around the shop, casting glances back over her shoulder at me.

She'd stripped off her gloves to touch feathers and fur with her bare fingers. Her hands were scuffed across the knuckles, nails plain and short, a scatter of freckles tossed across the back of her hand.

Her dress was simple by the standards of aristocrats, the material that shade of blue Anastasia seemed to love best. It was the color of the flowers that appear all in one day in spring in the steppes, turning the grass into a sea of hazy blue. And it was my mother's favorite color once upon a time—or so Papa said.

Anastasia's eyes flicked up at me, clear and saturated as colored glass, set in her face at an angle, slightly slanted up at the edges so she always seemed to be laughing in mischief or in mockery.

The muggy shop was stuffed with animals. The heat of their bodies made the red curls frizz at the nape of her neck.

I wondered if she was fucking with the flow of time. Everything seemed to pause when our eyes met.

"What are you doing?" I said.

"What do you think I'm doing?"

It was hard to tell if she was slowing time—the dust motes already drifted so lazily through the slats of sunshine, the animals calm, the old woman glacial in her movements.

"Are you curious?" Anastasia grinned as she bit at the edge of her thumbnail. "To see what I can do now?"

"Is your father teaching you?"

"No." Her blue eyes glinted, metal now instead of glass. "Someone else."

The heat in my chest was sudden and unexpected. Who was this *someone?* I licked my lips.

"Who?"

The jingle of bells at the door made us both jump.

"Stasia! Don't make me come in here, it stinks!" Tatiana's furious face stood silhouetted in the doorway.

"See you next week!" Anastasia called to Varvara, holding out her gloved arm for Artemis.

Artemis swooped down, alighting too softly for me to hear. Only the creak of talon against leather gave her away.

We rejoined Anastasia's sisters and cousins and aunt, taking tea in the private back room of the Eliseyev Emporium. Artemis was allowed inside and provided with a dish of clear water and a little raw meat.

We were a noisy group, boisterous and laughing, everyone young and stylish and finely dressed, except for me in my plain school uniform.

I was still growing and hated to ask Nikolasha for more clothes. I didn't want to have my hair cut like Dimitri's or a baggy rah-rah suit made in imitation of Felix's. I didn't want to look like I owned an oil refinery.

Yet there I sat at the table with everyone else, drinking the same expensive tea imported from India, eating the same cakes and sandwiches.

I was laughing like everyone else. Enjoying myself, while the waiters scurried around ferrying heavy samovars of hot water and plates piled high with fresh pastries. Down on the street below, a teenaged skivvy dumped filthy water into the gutter with raw, chapped hands, next to a blind beggar who held out an empty cup for coins that never came.

I didn't belong at that table, but neither did I belong on the street below.

I was like that parrot on the stand—all the appearance of freedom with nowhere to go.

Aunt Olga made a point of sitting next to me, leaving Irina unprotected at the other end of the table with Felix. Though her face was softer than Xenia's, I didn't fool myself into thinking this was a friendly gesture.

"How much longer do you have at the academy?"

"This is my last year."

"What will you do then?"

Anastasia kept her eyes fixed on her cake, her head turning a fraction of an inch. I knew she was listening.

"It's not up to me. I owe the Tsar ten years of service."

"They say war's coming in Europe. A Great War, the biggest the world has ever seen."

"You think Rusya will be drawn in?"

"How could we avoid it? We have agreements with Serbia, Albion, France ... if any of them go to war, so must we."

"Isn't the Empress German?" I said, with another glance at Anastasia.

This time she looked up at me.

"Mama loves Rusya. She's not German anymore."

Aunt Olga raised an eyebrow as if she wasn't quite ready to agree with that statement. "German or not, the Kaiser listens to no one. He's quite mad —thinks it's a game. They all do. They're spoiling to use their tanks and their ships, like a pack of boys playing with toy soldiers."

"Not Papa," Tatiana interjected. She was further away than Irina but had heard every word we said.

Ollie said, "You always defend him."

Ollie had been quieter than usual throughout our excursion. I'd noticed her watching Felix and Irina. At first I'd thought she was jealous—not romantically, but in the way girls often are when their best friend has their head turned by a man. Now I wondered if it was something else.

"Why shouldn't I defend him?" Tatiana tossed her head. She had the darkest hair of any of the sisters and the least blue in her eyes.

"Please don't fight," Maria pleaded.

"I'm not fighting, I'm asking." Tatiana's jaw was set.

"He acts like he's different, but he isn't." Ollie's voice was low and fierce, her hands twisted together in her lap. She hadn't eaten much lunch or touched her tea.

"This isn't talk for the table," Aunt Olga said, with a look pointed at Felix and me.

She meant that Ollie shouldn't criticize her father in front of outsiders. She needn't have worried about Felix—he was whispering with Irina, oblivious to anyone else in the room. She also didn't have to worry about me—I was already in full rebellion.

"Let's talk about something else, then," Dimitri said. "Who's seen KR's latest?"

"I have!" Maria cried.

"Not me," said Aunt Olga. "Is it any good?"

Dimitri, Maria, and Aunt Olga launched into a discussion of the various plays written by their famous cousin Konstantin. Tatiana joined in but Ollie remained silent.

Anastasia waited until their chatter drowned her voice as she muttered, "Would you really go fight in some war in Germany?"

I frowned at her. "What choice do I have?"

She chewed on the edge of her lip. "None, I suppose."

I changed the subject as abruptly as Dimitri. "What's Ollie upset about?"

"Oh ... she just turned twenty-three. Papa says it's past time she marries."

"Marries who?"

"Someone suitable."

Our eyes met, then skittered apart as we looked determinedly in opposite directions.

We both knew what that meant. For Ollie, and for any other Romanov.

Anastasia would be married off to some prince or duke. She'd have a little say in it—her parents might have patience for a rejection or two before she accepted one of their selections. But accept she must.

She could never be with a commoner.

Ironically, that gave us a little more freedom in our interactions. If Anastasia were to sit next to a prince at dinner, it would give rise to rumors of a match in the making. I could sit next to her at a tea table, everyone safe in the knowledge that nothing romantic could ever happen between us.

That was the last time I'd seen Anastasia. She'd been traveling with her family ever since.

I'd completed my last year at the academy and received my first set of orders: placement in the city garrison. I was disappointed, but not surprised. Though I'd hoped to rejoin my father, I knew the Tsar would never send me home. I was a better hostage at a distance. And my brainwashing wasn't complete. The academy was only the beginning—now I had to fight in the Tsar's name.

On the plus side, my new regiment was stuffed with Cossacks. Even my captain was a Cossack, though from Siberia, not the southern steppes like me.

That was the great irony of the Tsar's army—his best soldiers were

Hussars and Cossacks, drawn from the far-flung corners of the empire, from the warrior tribes who learned to fight and shoot and ride and kill almost as soon as we learned to walk. Our powers were lethal, and apparently, our loyalty could be bought.

This was my last night at Nikolasha's house. The next day I was moving into the Peter and Paul fortress on a little island in the Neva.

I wondered if Nikolasha would be sorry to see me go, or only relieved. He'd never wanted a ward—never even fathered a bastard son.

"Thank you," I said to him, across the table. "For getting me Hercules so I could switch to cavalry."

It was a favor three years past, but I knew Nikolasha would understand what I meant. He'd been kinder to me than he needed to be.

"You were young when you came here," Nikolasha grunted. "But you behaved as a man."

I understood what he meant, too.

"I wonder if the Leuchtenbergs will be at the ball," I hid my smile by shuffling over to the pot to scoop out another heaping spoonful of porridge. "I saw their carriage outside their house. They must be back for the season."

After a short pause, Nikolasha said, "If they're in town, they'll be there tonight." He was probably squinting at my back, trying to decide if I'd noticed the extra wineglass.

It hadn't been difficult to observe Stana stepping down from her carriage to take her husband's arm—their house in St. Petersburg stood only a block from Nikolasha's, just as their country estates adjoined.

I wondered if it enraged Prince George Maximilianovich to see his wife followed everywhere she went by a lovesick suitor, or if he got perverse pleasure out of retaining what the Grand Duke so desperately wanted.

"D'you want to come to the Kremlin with me this afternoon?" Nikolasha asked. "I've got to pick out a costume."

"Guess I'd better."

I needed one myself.

It was Anastasia's birthday. I'd heard the cathedral bells ringing, as they did on any royal holiday. No school today and only a half day of work, courtesy of the youngest princess. Then the ball tonight.

I was invited by Nikolasha, not Anastasia.

Would he invite me to anything else once I no longer lived with him?

If not, this might be the last time I'd see her for a very long time.

chapter 13

INSULTS AND WARNINGS

Nikolasha's carriage waited at precisely eight o'clock.

As we wound through the streets, I heard shouting from the direction of the Putilov steel plant. The workers were striking again.

Dozens of strikes had broken out already this summer, but this was the largest so far. The chants and howls were incessant.

Nikolasha turned and looked. He never pretended something wasn't happening.

"Maybe you'll be over there tomorrow," he said.

The thought made my guts churn. If I joined the strikers, I'd want to stand on the other side of the line.

The man whose clothes I was wearing would have done it. I'd taken the armor of Stenka Razin out of the Kremlin. He was a Don Cossack who led a rebellion all along the Volga river, much like my uncle, but with even greater success. Until the Tsar of 1671 had him drawn and quartered.

This armor was the only Cossack clothing kept in the vault amongst the rich robes and jewelry of the Romanov's ancestors. Nikolasha had borrowed a cloak from Peter the Great, the only ruler tall enough to share clothes with him.

I didn't know why I was so adamant on never dressing like a Rusyan. It was my own obstinacy that made me stand out—I could have avoided some of the aggression that came my way.

There was a stubbornness in me that wouldn't die. The Romanovs brought me here. But they could never make me one of them.

We pulled up to the Winter Palace. It was thrice the size of the one Anastasia lived in. And her parents owned many more.

"How come the Tsar doesn't live here?"

"Too dangerous these days," Nikolasha grunted. "Can't keep the family safe. Ministers and clerks going in and out all day long—this is where the actual governing happens." He pointed to the far side of the sprawling building. "Thousands of people come through there. You can't get near Alexander Palace with the park all around."

I didn't know if it was as safe as he thought. Hundreds of servants still worked there. It only took one to plant a bomb under the dining room table, as Anastasia reminded me.

Yet I was glad to know there were many more miles between Anastasia's bedroom and the shouting from the steel factory, so loud that I heard it the moment I stepped from the carriage. I wondered if she'd heard it, too. Did it frighten her?

They were only workers with bricks and clubs and the most menial of powers. The soldiers had the guns. A hundred thousand of us, stationed all over the city. Anastasia would be safe wherever she was.

I told myself that, though in my mind I'd just told Nikolasha the opposite. So it always was with Anastasia. I thought two things at once. I wanted two things at once.

We climbed the steps of the Winter Palace.

The Master of Ceremonies announced us, garbling my name, and we proceeded into the ballroom.

I'd never seen such splendor. The four hundred guests all dressed in ancient Rusyan finery. Pillars of candles cast flickering light across the embroidered gowns of the women, their headdresses adorned with precious stones. The men's caftans were just as brilliant. They wore the tall fur hats of boyars, thick with pungent mink.

I saw the Tsar himself holding a jeweled scepter, his robe stiff with gold brocade. The Empress stood next to him, all the way up to his shoulder from the height of her glittering crown, a veil of white gauze hanging down all around her.

I hated how the Rusyans wore their veils—like a shroud.

The women probably liked not having to smile. Only the Empress' dark eyes peered through the translucent material.

I thought how little Anastasia resembled her parents, except for the red in the Tsar's beard.

I turned and searched for her.

It was as if my eyes moved themselves, as if they already knew where she stood.

I saw her, and my heart stopped.

She looked as if much more than a year had passed. She was taller, her face longer. Her hair was longer, too—I could see it bound up in a mass, heavy and flaming brighter even than the brilliant scarlet robes swirling on the dancers behind her.

Her features had sharpened. They were still strange and oversized for her face—eyes wide apart, tilted up at the outer edges, nose upturned, mouth wide and red. She hadn't covered her freckles with that awful white rice powder that made wealthy women look papery and dull. Her cheeks glowed with exertion, her lips chapped.

She wore blue silk robes, trousers, and tall Moroccan boots. A pair of falcons battled on her breast in silver thread. She'd dressed as a royal falconer.

"Nobody can get mad at this." She grinned, coming to join me. "Farad lent it to me—it's the real thing."

"Mine, too. Straight from the Kremlin."

"One of your ancestors?"

"A spiritual grandfather."

There was no malice when we smiled at each other. So much blood and pain in the annals of history, but it didn't seem real in the candlelight. It was all so long ago.

I hardly remembered that I myself had fought the Romanovs. At fourteen years old, I'd killed for the first time. Nikolasha probably commanded the field—we might have come within a yard of each other, swords raised. I didn't know his name then, or Anastasia's—only the Tsar's.

It was like another life.

Or I was another person.

My stomach clenched. Did my father recognize me when he read my letters? Did he know me still?

"What's wrong?" Anastasia looked in my face.

The Tsar's voice sounded behind me:

"Interesting choice of costume."

I turned to face him. We'd never actually spoken since the time I tried to kill him. He gave his orders through Nikolasha—if he thought of me at all. He was an indifferent god, manipulating my life only when I chanced to cross his mind.

I realized that I was dressed as a rebel and he as the Tsar that signed his death warrant.

"It was the only Cossack costume I could find. Your Imperial Highness." I added the title a little too late.

"What costume will you wear tomorrow?"

"Not a costume, Your Highness. The uniform of the Imperial Guard. I took an oath when they gave it to me—and I hold to that oath."

I promised to protect the Emperor with my life. I promised to obey him. Like a wedding vow, it could never be dissolved.

If you're born on Rusyan soil, that oath is extracted from you at birth. Fail to uphold it, and the sentence is death.

It was never a choice, not really. But I'd never agreed to it until that moment.

I could feel Anastasia standing behind me, tight with tension.

Her father glowered down at me. I'd grown taller but not passed him yet. I still had the shoulders of a boy. He was nearly as broad as Nikolasha.

I could kill a man if I got my hands on him. The Tsar could do it just by pointing a finger.

Did he want to do it?

Did he even care?

"See that you do," said the Tsar, turning away.

I remembered the hatred I'd felt at the sight of that back once before. Cold and blank as a rock face, and just as unfeeling. The impulse had risen inside me and I acted ...

Not this time.

This time I stood and watched him walk away.

Anastasia let out a breath.

"Why do you always antagonize him?"

I rounded on her.

"What should I have worn? A butler's suit?"

"No!"

"Should I have dressed as a boyar?"

"NO! I like your Cossack clothes."

"What, then?" I was seething.

Anastasia's eyes were large in her face, not laughing now.

"Do you hate us still?"

Those blue eyes were water on fire. They put me out in an instant.

I sighed. "I don't hate you. Sometimes I want to ... but I just can't seem to do it."

The rest of them, perhaps. Anastasia was something different. She'd woven her way deep into my fibers. To cut her out would hurt me, too.

"Do you hear them shouting out there?" I asked.

Our eyes turned to the bank of windows. The low murmur of the crowd was distant, but you could hear it below the music like an unsteady heartbeat.

The Tsar motioned to the band to play louder.

I gripped Anastasia's wrist with my gloved hand.

"This is foolish. The people are angry. To parade your wealth in this way ... it's an insult. They see it. They're not as stupid as you think."

"I know that," Anastasia snapped. "Papa is dressed as Aleksey Mikhaylovich."

"So?"

"There were rebellions all through his reign—riots from the people, revolt from the Cossacks. He put them all down, brutally. Papa's costume isn't an insult ... it's a warning."

"You stand by that? You stand by him?"

Our eyes were locked, our faces inches apart.

"Should we allow them to swarm the palace and kill us?" Anastasia said. "Would you stand back and let them do it?"

"They're not trying to kill you. They want a parliament. They want laws to protect them. They don't want to be at the mercy of your whims!"

She shook her head impatiently. "Don't fool yourself that you're hearing the people's voice. They're pawns in the hands of powerful men. Who will head the Duma? Who will be the new Tsar of the people?"

Some motion caught her attention. She grabbed me by the sleeve, dragging me back below the windows between the heavy drapes.

"What are you doing?"

"I don't want Rasputin to see you."

I tried to look but she put her gloved hand against my cheek to stop my head from turning.

"Don't!" she hissed.

"I want to see *him*. Everyone's been talking ..."

"He's behind you, twenty yards back, speaking with Sylvie Buxhoeveden. Take a look, but don't stare."

She let go of my face. I twisted my head and brought it back again, mentally examining the image I'd seen at a glance:

A tall man, younger than I expected. Paler, too. No look of someone who'd spent years wandering out of doors. In a sea of rich brocade, he wore a plain black robe. His hair was down to his shoulders, black as coal. His eyes were paler than Anastasia's, so bleached of color that they hardly looked blue at all. His pupils floated in all that whiteness.

"He's the one who healed your brother?"

I'd noticed Alexei's ill health on that very first train ride back to St. Petersburg. It was impossible to miss for anyone who spent time around the family.

"Alexei isn't healed," Anastasia said. "The disease always comes back."

"Hm." I had my own theories about that. "Why don't you want Rasputin to see me?"

"It's hard to explain ... he saw a vision of you in the smoke, the first time I met him. He wants to know who you are, but I won't tell him. It's like a bargaining chip."

"What are you—" Even as I asked the question, I realized the answer. "He's the one who's been teaching you."

"Yes." Her eyes were bright, her voice an eager whisper. She might have been worried that Tatiana would hear, even with all the space and noise between them. "He can do magic like I've never seen. It's incredible, Damien ..."

The sound of my name on her lips made me shiver. Yet I was hot with something like anger and fear, all mixed up together. It might have been jealousy.

"Do your parents know?"

"Of course not. They'd never allow it."

"What has he taught you?"

"Only a little so far. He doesn't want to, I have to get it out of him—"

I didn't trust the Black Monk, even before I saw him. I'd heard rumors. He was no holy man.

"Don't think you're the one doing the manipulating," I warned Anastasia.

She tossed her head, looking rather like Tatiana.

"Don't think I'm an idiot! I told you, it's a battle of the minds—"

"He's wormed his way into your family. He's not doing this out of the goodness of his heart—"

"Of course not, he's being paid by the boatload, and he's the toast of the town. He deserves it, no one else could help—"

"You don't know if he's helping—"

"Just look at Alexei!"

She pointed at her brother. He stood proudly next to his father in ornate robes of gold brocade, a replica made to his size. The Tsar and his heir, the succession clear for all to see. Alexei was no longer wan and waxy. He'd finally gained the proper height for a young man. His limbs had filled out, and his face shone with health. His hair sprang back from his brow, thick and full, gold as the thread on his robe.

"He *is* better," Anastasia insisted.

I could hardly argue with the proof before my eyes.

Still I felt some unseen danger, like the murmur of the crowd outside the palace walls.

"I have to join the dancing," Anastasia said. "Xenia stuffed my book for every song. But I saved the last for you!"

"How are you going to dance with me without *him* seeing?" I jerked my head in the direction of Rasputin.

Anastasia's mouth opened foolishly.

"Never mind," I said. "I should leave anyway. I start with the city garrison in the morning. Did you know that? I'll be the one holding back the workers, just like you said."

"Don't be like that, Damien ..."

"How else can I be? Besides, your father wouldn't like it."

Or her mother. Or her aunt. Or probably her sisters ...

Nobody wanted us to dance together.

Nobody but me.

chapter 14

AN UNWILLING PROFESSOR

ANASTASIA

I woke early the morning after the ball, head pounding and mouth dry as cotton. After Damien left, I drank too much champagne and danced in a wild frenzy until the room spun like a carousel and my feet throbbed with every heartbeat.

Seeing Damien was always a coin flip. Half the time I found myself telling him things I'd never told anyone, as if he were my best friend in the world. The other half ended with one of us storming out in a rage.

My stomach was still a writhing mess of anger and guilt. When Damien and I fought, it felt as if I were tearing along every seam. The hangover afterward was worse than the one from the champagne.

Sometimes I missed Damien desperately, and sometimes I wished we'd never met. It was too painful and too impossible. We could never be more than we were, and I couldn't bear to be less.

I went to the wash basin, lifted the ceramic jug, and gulped down half the water that was supposed to be for washing my face.

Maria and I no longer shared a room. She kept our old one while I moved into the Crimson Room at the end of the hall. It had been a sitting room formerly, with a piano and a large portrait of my Grandmother Alice, who died long before I was born. She looked very like Mama with her porcelain skin and large, sad eyes. The room had been painted to match the crown of roses on her head, the furniture and drapes likewise a deep shade of red.

I'd asked the servants to take out the piano because I was shit at playing it, and the portrait as well. I was tired of the eyes of my ancestors following me everywhere I went.

Instead, I stuffed the room with books and records and a gramophone, all the rocks and seashells I'd brought back from the cruise to Reval, and pretty colored glass from Denmark.

The topmost shelf above my dresser contained my most precious treasure of all: the memory-keeper from Grandma Minnie. I didn't know when I would use it. She said I could record a new day whenever I wanted, but I knew it would be hard to erase what I'd saved. I should choose wisely in case I only ever saved one day like she had done.

My room was a complete mess at the moment—discarded stockings tossed over the backs of chairs, empty teacups stacked on the windowsill. I was responsible for keeping my own space clean, but I'd been distracted lately.

The source of that distraction occupied the White Tower in Alexander Park. I'd hauled myself out of bed so I could visit him before everyone woke.

I picked a crumpled smock off the floor and pulled it over my head. My hair was still in its nighttime braids, heavy down my back, fuzzy with escaping strands.

I slipped from my room and ran down the dark hallway, the drapes still drawn.

Everyone would sleep in today, even the servants. They'd had their own party down in the kitchens after they finished cleaning up after ours. They'd sleep in their uniforms next to their bells, secure in the knowledge that nobody was likely to ring them until ten o'clock at the earliest.

I ran past Kolya Derevenko, snoozing against a pillar, propped on the butt of his gun. I thought of waking him since he'd surely be punished if his captain caught him, but as I'd seen Captain Cross drunk at the card tables at 3:00 in the morning, I doubted he'd be making early rounds.

The White Tower and our private cathedral were the two buildings closest to the palace. I only had to run across a long stretch of lawn and skirt the moat that went partway around.

The White Tower had been built in imitation of a medieval castle. A set of ruined gates stood on either side of the rectangular tower, crenelated ramparts running all along the upper levels. The first Nicholas built it for his sons to practice their military and gymnastic exercises. Later it was used as the workshop of the court painter. Now it was inhabited by Rasputin.

I should have assumed he'd still be sleeping like everyone else—he stayed at the ball later than Captain Cross. But I'd watched him long enough to know that he often stayed awake until the early hours of the morning, then slept through the heat of the day.

Sure enough, when I tapped lightly on the brass knocker, only a short pause preceded the door swinging open. Rasputin wore a long velvet robe, his hair uncombed. I didn't think he'd been sleeping. His face was pale and smooth, no puffiness or pillow marks. Despite all the wine I'd seen him drink, his eyes were clear and lucid. He smiled at the sight of me.

"The littlest princess."

"Not so little anymore."

"Ah, yes. You're a woman now."

Rasputin spoke politely, but I heard a thread of mockery. What he seemed to be saying and what I felt from him never quite aligned. I was always trying to figure him out, a puzzle that shifted and changed in my hands.

The key to engaging him was to puzzle him in return.

I learned that the first time I visited the White Tower.

My heart had hammered against my ribs when I tapped on his door. I didn't know if he'd let me inside.

The impulse that drove me to the tower was nothing more or less than curiosity. Rasputin intrigued me as nothing had before. He was a cipher, an equation where nothing added up.

I wasn't the only one with suspicions. I'd heard Nikolasha warning my parents that their reception of Rasputin was not well received. Rumors persisted that the Black Monk frequented the bathhouses in St. Petersburg, that he dined with prostitutes, that he engaged in wild orgies, steeping himself in sin so he could feel the full measure of forgiveness from the gods.

Mama dismissed the slander with a wave of her hand.

"The Archbishop's behind it. He's angry that Nicholas promoted Rasputin without his approval."

Papa was quiet through Nikolasha's relation of the rumors. I thought he believed them more than Mama did, but it didn't matter—he'd allow the devil himself into our house if he could heal Alexei.

Still, my parents tried to keep us girls away from Rasputin. A difficult task when he came to see Alexei so often and increasingly attended the same events.

Rasputin was no pencil to be carried around in a pocket and shut away out of sight when he wasn't of use. He was a savvy social operator with his own motivations.

I could see that in the easy way he shook off the patronship of Liza Taneeva. She wanted him to be her pet. After introducing him to Mama, she expected to be the go-between.

Rasputin drove right past her house the night he first visited Alexei. I heard her begging to be brought along, to watch while he tended to Alexei. He shut her down smoothly and firmly.

Liza was furious that her protégé threw her over the moment he no longer needed her. She still trailed after him like a lovesick puppy, begging to bring anything he needed to Alexei's room and asking when she could host another party in his honor.

"Soon," Rasputin told her, with zero sincerity.

He had more important people throwing parties for him now.

I watched as Rasputin built friendships all throughout the palace—I saw him joking with Nina Ivanova outside the maids' quarters and eating honey-cakes with the cooks in the kitchen. He remembered the names of even the lowliest stewards and brought gifts like holy icons from Constantinople and sweet sage for burning that he picked and dried himself. He gave nicknames to the courtiers and also to us. He called Papa "Batushka" and Maria "his little pearl."

He had an easy informality that won over the reserve of even someone as shy as my mother. He called her "Matushka" and made her kiss him on his cheeks three times in peasant style.

Aunt Olga couldn't resist him. On their very first meeting in my mother's Mauve Boudoir, Rasputin took her hands in his and stared into her face. Gently stroking his thumb across the back of her hand he said, "I see how you dote on the Grand Duchesses. Why don't you have any children of your own?"

Aunt Olga's eyes filled with tears. I thought she'd pull back her hands or refuse to answer. Instead, she whispered, "I want them desperately."

Rasputin's voice was low and gentle. Caressing.

"Do you love your husband?"

Aunt Olga hesitated.

So quietly I could barely hear her, she said, "He doesn't visit my bedroom. He never has. Not even on our wedding night."

Tatiana and I exchanged glances from opposite sofas. That was a rumor long suspected but never confirmed. People said that Peter of Oldenburg didn't care for women at all, not even one as pretty as Aunt Olga.

Rasputin's hands tightened around Aunt Olga's until his knuckles went white. "I can help you conceive."

Aunt Olga's breath fluttered in her chest. Her lips parted. "I'd give anything."

"Come see me in the tower."

He extended the invitation to her, not to me. But I was the one who knocked on his door.

I don't think he was happy to see me that first time. He didn't court my affection like he did Maria's or Ollie's. There was a wariness between us since that first night when he read my future.

Still, he let me into the entryway and shut the door behind me so we were alone together in the gloom. That was how I knew I had a chance of success.

He towered over me, seeming taller than he was because he was so thin. His cheeks were hollow, blue with shadow, his lips almost the same color as his skin.

"What can I do for you, little one?"

"I want to know how you see things in the smoke."

He spread his hands like a shrug. "It's a gift."

"I don't think it is. That's not your only power."

His smile wasn't entirely friendly.

"What do you know of my powers?"

"I think you have many. Pyromancy. Clairvoyance. Manipulation of weather. And"—this one I was just guessing—"I think you can read minds."

He had zeroed in on Aunt Olga's marital issues without ever even meeting Peter or seeing the two of them together. Perhaps Rasputin simply had his ear to the ground, but there was something in the way he led conversations and anticipated people's answers ...

Rasputin wasn't smiling anymore, or replying.

I pressed on.

"I think you have more powers than that. The most I've ever seen."

"Is that a crime, little one?" The teasing tone returned to his voice. "You sound accusing."

"I know you didn't tell everything you saw in the smoke. You picked and chose what to relay."

There was a slight change to the angle of his head.

"You could see the images."

"Some of them. That's how I know you were lying."

"Reading the smoke is an art—interpretation a guess."

"You lied about mine."

Something flickered into being in his face. It was like he came alive for the first time, like he'd only been sleeping through our encounter up to that moment. His hand whipped out from his robe, seizing my wrist. I couldn't have pulled away with my hand still attached.

"What did you see?"

The grip wasn't to intimidate me—it was to create contact between us. Everywhere his fingers touched my bare arm, it felt as if a burning liquid seeped through my skin. Then a crawling sensation, wriggling up my arm, jolting up my neck, scattering across the underside of my skull. Tickling and jerking, writhing and climbing, like a thousand spiders scrambling around in my head.

I wanted to shriek, to thrash, to tear off my own face.

I knew—some distant part of me knew—it wasn't real. I could still see Rasputin standing before me, his eyes fixed on mine, fingers locked around my wrist. The rest of my view was overrun with thousands of squirming black legs.

They dug at my brain, tugging, burrowing, searching for an opening. An assault of not one pair of hands, but ten thousand.

He was trying to get in. He was looking for something.

What?

We were talking about the vision in the smoke. My vision, the one he wouldn't say aloud.

He wanted to know what I saw ...

Before the answer could appear in my mind, I snuffed it out. Only it wouldn't stay snuffed. It was like a rocket in a box. Though I'd clasped a lid on it, it kept exploding upward again and again as my brain struggled to perform the paradox of forgetting the very thing I was thinking about.

Meanwhile I was drowning in spiders, a flood, a deluge, scrambling up my nostrils, burrowing in my ears, digging at my eyes ...

Use them. Use the spiders.

I can't! I hate them!

They're not spiders. You don't hate them. They're beautiful. Look at them ... black as the black widow you saw in its web on the wall of Artemis' mews, hard and glittering, like a piece of jewelry hung in cotton, ruby on the belly ...

The spiders stiffened, glinting like beads.

Instead of squirming away from them, I turned *into* the spiders. I turned into them like I turned into the time-stream—letting them flow all around me and over me, not something to be feared or fought against, but something I controlled, something I could use.

The spiders rolled down my body like midnight rain, black and glittering. I let them pour down my skin until they were gone, shaking the last few off my fingertips.

Rasputin released my wrist.

We were back in his entryway, no spiders, no beads, just the two of us.

I was breathing hard. He was as calm as glass.

"How dare you," I hissed.

He had attacked me out of nowhere, rummaging his fingers through my brain.

But I hadn't given him what he was looking for. I wouldn't let myself think of it even then.

Rasputin ignored my anger. He was smiling to himself, as if many things at last made sense.

"You have an affinity for magic."

"What does that mean?"

Rasputin's hands steepled together between the sleeves of his velvet robe. His fingers moved through the gloom as he spoke, as if he were drawing invisible shapes.

"People are keys, Anastasia. Sometimes they're a common key to a common lock, sometimes the only key of their type in existence. A few unlucky, misshapen keys can open nothing at all. And then ..." His pale fingers moved lightly through the air, inscribing a circle that contained him and me. "There are skeleton keys ..."

I knew it.

I could hardly breathe I was so excited.

"You *can* learn magic."

"Some people can."

"How much? How much could I learn?"

He gave a faint shrug of his shoulders. "It's affinity, not universal ability."

"But I could practice. I could get better."

I'd already seen that to be true. Practicing magic in incremental steps, like how I'd trained with Artemis, allowed me to improve. But with Artemis, Nikolasha had shown me what to do.

"Teach me," I said to Rasputin.

"No."

"Why not?"

"You know very well why not."

He meant my parents.

"No one has to know."

189

I saw that flicker in his eyes, the part of him that was interested.

"The world is made of ears and eyes."

"No one knows I'm here right now."

"Still no." He seized my wrist once more, this time to drag me toward the door. "Because I don't want to."

"You owe it to me!" I cried. "After what you just did. I could barely fight you off—"

He snorted.

"You think you fought me off?" His fingers tightened on my wrist, digging into the flesh. "If I wanted to take something from your mind, I would take it. That was me being polite."

He was angry, and more angry because he'd allowed me to see it. His hand was on the doorknob, he was about to throw me out.

"I just want to learn!" I cried. "No one will teach me!"

I was desperate, he could hear the longing in my voice. He hesitated, and for the first time I saw indecision in his face—two impulses battling for control.

Then his expression smoothed. He sighed, hands dropping to his sides.

"I remember what it felt like when I realized I could do more."

I let out my breath, too.

"No one will tell me anything. And even if they would ... I don't think they know."

Rasputin slowly shook his head. "It's not only finding the information that's difficult. It's knowing what's actually true ..."

He trailed off and was silent.

I stood very still, hardly daring to breathe.

"Come inside." Rasputin drew deeper into the tower.

I followed, heart leaping.

The White Tower contained six floors stacked on each other with a spiral staircase running up the center. The kitchen occupied the lowest level. I could hardly make out the sink from the iron stove in the gloom. Rasputin had all the drapes drawn and none of the lanterns lit. A few candles guttered on spindly stands.

He'd stripped out the belongings of the painter who preceded him. The kitchen was spartan, plaster walls, no dishes in the sink. From the upper levels I caught the tantalizing scents of fresh-growing herbs, dried spices, and old paper and beeswax, in place of oil paint and varnish.

Rasputin lit a fire in the iron stove. This time, he didn't bother to pretend to use a lighter or match. He simply made a motion with his long, pale fingers, as if drawing up smoke from the wood, and the flame burst into being. Though I'd seen Dimitri light a candle in the same way, it was much more impressive in the darkness of the room, kindled by Rasputin's graceful movements.

Within a few minutes he had a kettle boiling. He filled a tray with cups and saucers, arranging biscuits from an unopened packet. All his dishes were simple and heavy, the color of stone. The teapot was slightly misshapen as if he'd made it himself.

He made a motion with his head for me to follow and carried the tray. I trailed him up the stairs, wildly pleased that I'd be getting a look at another level.

The parlor looked nothing as it had before. The chintz sofas and chaises, pillows and end tables, had all been removed.

In their place stood shelves of supplies. This was the source of the alluring scents—row upon row of beakers and jars, boxes and canisters. I saw a fully articulated skeleton of a lizard with wings, and another of a toad with two heads. An entire wall was given over to mineral samples: geodes and crystals, rocks studded with spikes.

The herbs I'd been smelling grew in pots by the window, some on shelves and some in hanging baskets that dangled from the rafters. The reedy look of the plants indicated that they rarely received enough light.

Brass cages were scattered around the room. The first two were empty; squeaking from the third drew me close. I thought I'd find mice—instead I saw an albino bat dangling upside down by one claw.

A mobile swung lazily without any breeze. Its thin golden spindles carried amulets with queer symbols, nothing like the holy icons I'd seen Rasputin give to the servants. Likewise, I couldn't read a word of the massive book that lay open on one table; it was written in a language I didn't know, in an alphabet I'd never seen.

I couldn't resist walking all around the room, examining the contents of the jars, peering into the glass-fronted cabinets. I hardly recognized anything, and nothing was labeled.

"What do you do with all this?"

"I experiment."

A thrill ran down my spine. What I would give for all the objects in that room ... for all the knowledge in those books ...

"Teach me," I said, more urgently this time. My mouth was practically watering. My skin tingled.

Rasputin was pouring the tea, slowly, methodically. He took his plain and dropped two sugar cubes in mine without having to ask. He stirred the spoon three times around my cup, considering.

"No one could know," he said at last. "Not even your sisters. It would have to be a secret between us. Are you good at keeping secrets, Anastasia?"

His eyes met mine.

"I know things that no one knows."

"Good." He held out the cup of tea. "Come and join me."

I'd been to visit him twice since then. It was difficult to find blocks of time when I could sneak away unnoticed. This would be my fourth lesson.

I rapped the knocker three times, which was our signal. Rasputin let me inside.

Today he had nothing on beneath his velvet robe but a pair of loose trousers. The silver raven's skull lay against his bare chest. His flesh was hairless, hard and pale like marble.

"Tea?" he said. "Kvass?"

"Kvass." My head still pounded from all the champagne.

Rasputin poured us each a mug. The kvass was warm and foaming, cloudy as lake water. I gulped it down.

"Did you enjoy the ball?"

"Well enough."

While Rasputin's pale eyes rested on me, I forced myself to think only of the whirlwind of partners I passed through, working my way down the entirety of my ball book. Only once he looked away did I allow the image of Damien to flash into my mind.

It was a game we were playing, unspoken, but known to both of us.

I didn't know why it mattered to him, but it must be part of the reason he'd agreed to teach me. He wouldn't risk angering my parents out of sympathy alone.

I followed him up the spiral staircase to his parlor. His little bat was awake for the first time, stretching its leathery wings outward from its inverted position. The bleached membranes were transparent enough to show each fragile bone.

"What's his name?"

Rasputin threw a swift glance over one shoulder as he took something down from his shelf. "He has no name. His name is Bat."

The bat made its high-pitched squeak, so shrill I could hardly hear it, revealing a mouthful of needlepoint teeth.

Rasputin unscrewed one of his innumerable jars and withdrew a few sprigs of dried plant. Papery purple blossoms studded the stems, fragile as tissue.

He laid them out on the low table in the center of the room. The table was circular, marked with scars and grooves, only a couple of feet higher than the floor. We sat on large cushions instead of on chairs.

"*Dictamnus albus,*" Rasputin said. "In the heat of the summer it exudes an oil that smells of lemon—so incendiary that it can burst into flame if a warm breeze passes by."

I thought I knew where this was going.

Rasputin gestured to the sprigs, palm upraised.

"Set it alight."

I looked at the plant. Stared at it. Imagined it bursting into flame.

Nothing happened.

"Try again."

This time, I made the same motion Rasputin had made over the kindling in the stove—or at least, I tried to imitate him. I trailed my fingers above the sprigs as if I were drawing up a thread.

Still nothing.

For over an hour I tried while Rasputin sat silent, watching. He gave no suggestions, no hints.

At last I sat back on my heels, red faced and sweating.

"I can't do it!"

"You're not creating fire," Rasputin said. "You're altering the state of what's already there."

"Like when you made the snow."

"That's right. I froze the water already in the air."

"How, though?" I cried.

"That's what affinity is. It's seeing what others can't."

I wondered if he was being vague on purpose. If he had no intention of actually teaching me.

Our previous lessons had been similarly infuriating. He'd shown me the book I couldn't read and confirmed that I couldn't read it. He'd had me handle dozens of crystals and amulets and charms, watching for something ... what, I couldn't tell. He'd demonstrated how to cast a handful of bones across the tabletop, but while his seemed to form interesting shapes and patterns, mine simply scattered.

I felt more as if I were being tested than taught.

"Are you going to show me how to light the fire or not?" I snapped.

"I'm looking for your affinities. You won't be good at everything. You won't be good at most things. Magic is a lesson in frustration."

If that was true, then I must be learning a lot, because I was hot with aggravation.

My face was burning, my skin, too. Sweat ran down the side of my face. I could almost feel the heat on my breath like a dragon, yet it was all trapped inside of me, the crumbling sprigs entirely untouched. They sprawled on the tabletop, dry as tinder, mocking me.

I got close to the sprigs. I leaned over them. Then I exhaled, my breath fluttering the papery blossoms.

My breath is fire. I am fire. I'm burning up ...

A tiny curl of smoke twisted upward from the withered edge of one bloom. The edge glowed, and all in an instant the sprigs ignited.

"I DID IT!" I shrieked, leaping up from the cushion. "I SET IT ON FIRE!"

"You made a spark," Rasputin said. "The oil caught flame."

I didn't care if it was the tiniest spark in existence. I made it.

"I'm a pyromancer. Like Dimitri."

Rasputin gave a low laugh. "Don't get ahead of yourself. That was a weak affinity. Not one of your best."

"What's my best?"

Rasputin shrugged. "Too soon to say. Some will come easier than others. Most won't come at all."

"How many powers do you have?"

He smiled. "I've never counted."

Liar.

"How come there's so many pyromancers in Japan?"

"I've seen tribes where everyone has the same ability."

"It's inherited?"

"Perhaps. Or perhaps they simply expect to be pyromancers."

"What does that mean?"

"Magic and faith are not as different as you might think."

"Is that why you're a monk?"

"I'm a monk because I swore a sacred vow."

"But why did you swear the vow?"

I didn't believe Rasputin was actually religious, or at least not in the way I was used to. He wasn't pious like a priest, and priests weren't sorcerers. Before Rasputin took over the Sunday ceremonies, the bishop would remind us again and again that our powers were nothing compared to those of the gods. Priests believed in prayer over magic.

Rasputin consulted the clock on the wall, which included the phases of the moon as well as the hours of the day.

"You'd better get back."

I hated that our lessons were always so short. I could only steal away for so long.

"Give me another book," I begged.

Rasputin's collection was infinitely better than ours because every single book was on the topic of magic. Ancient and battered, the books appeared to have passed through many sets of hands before his. Some were missing their covers, some were even torn in half. Some were stained with horrid substances, dark and sticky, or rusty like blood.

Rasputin hadn't let me visit the library on the top floor. I hoped one day he would.

For now, he selected a book off the storeroom shelves and handed it to me.

"This should help."

The title was *Elemental Magic,* embossed on the cover in flaking gold script.

"Don't let anyone see it," he warned.

"I won't."

We both had much to lose if my parents discovered what I'd been doing.

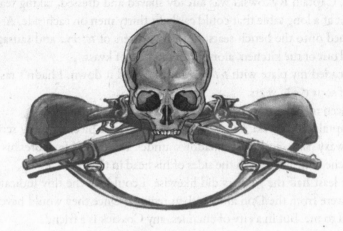

chapter 15

IN THE NAME OF THE KING

DAMIEN

I heard Nikolasha's snores rumbling through the main floor of his house as I slipped out the front door with everything I owned stuffed in a kit bag. I knew he'd be angry that I left without waking him, but we'd said our goodbyes the day before. And anyway, I was only going as far as the fortress on the north bank of the Neva. He could come to see me whenever he liked, and probably would, if only to drink with the officers.

I walked through the silent streets, the sun not yet up over the spires of the Peter and Paul Cathedral.

I wondered if Anastasia was still sleeping. And who she had danced with the night before.

Then I shoved that thought aside because it was weak and pathetic. I was getting soft like the aristocrats at the academy. I never would have given a damn about some freckled girl if I'd stayed with my people.

I'd be myself again now that I was joining a proper regiment. It wasn't like going home, but it was the next closest thing.

The moment I stepped inside the crowded barracks, I could smell the achingly familiar scent of the linseed Cossacks use to oil the hooves of their horses. Captain Rykowski was already shaved and dressed, taking tea as dark as paint at a long table that could easily fit thirty men on each side. As soldiers crammed onto the bench seats, heaping platters of *teterya* and sausages were carried out of the kitchen, along with pitchers of kvass.

I loaded my plate with *teterya* and shoveled it down. I hadn't tasted that tang of sour rye in years.

"Been missing proper food, have you?" Rykowski laughed.

Captain Rykowski was as lean and tough as a piece of ivory scrimshaw, with waxy skin and dark shadows under his eyes. He wore his blonde mustache long and shaved the sides of his head in the Cossack way.

At least half the soldiers did likewise. I could see the tiny indicators that some were from the Don and Greben regions. Once they would have seemed foreign to me. But in a city of enemies, any Cossack is a friend.

The men made space for me at the table, clapping me on the shoulder, heaping my plate with more sausage than I could possibly eat.

"Fresh blood," said one of the younger soldiers with a shock of flaming red hair. "It's about time, Captain."

"That's right," Rykowski agreed, forking up a mouthful of grilled kipper. "Because we're all damn sick of your jokes, Krudener."

Krudener pressed his hand against his chest in mock offense. "How can that be, Captain? Are you sure you understand them?"

"Krudener, a punch-drunk toddler would get your jokes and he still wouldn't laugh."

"Oh, he would," Krudener said, making a menacing fist. "That cocky little bastard would laugh till I told him to stop."

"What the hell are you talking about?" said a man with a haystack of wild dark hair and half his shirt still unbuttoned.

"He's threatening toddlers," the captain replied.

"By the gods, they'll take anyone these days, won't they?" the disheveled man said, with a glance between Krudener and me.

"Including you, Bachinsky," Krudener laughed.

"Those idiots. What were they thinking?"

"It was me that hired you," Captain Rykowski said, no longer smiling.

"Then you must have shown your usual canny intuition, Captain," Bachinsky said, straightening up with a smart salute. "I'm sure it will pay off any day now ..."

This was a far cry from the academy where the teachers would beat you with an iron bar for infractions as petty as forgetting to make your bed in the morning.

I had no doubt the captain kept his own punishments at the ready if his men disobeyed him, but the general atmosphere was infinitely more relaxed.

It reminded me of my father's host. The more intensely we trained and fought, the more we needed the reprieve of drinking and laughter and games afterward. My father knew that. He ordered that we celebrate after every battle, whether we won or lost. We heaped the men we lost on a pyre, and drank and feasted as we sent their souls to rise with the smoke to the stars.

I was only a boy, but I fought like a man with my uncles, my cousins, and my father at my side. I felt invincible even while death stalked the battlefield, men cut down all around me.

I wondered if I'd ever trust this motley mix of soldiers in the same way.

"Thank the gods for extra hands." Krudener gulped down his tea. "We'll need it today."

"You stick by me, Kaledin," Captain said, with a sharp look in my direction.

"Yes, sir."

"Gods, I love when they're fresh out of the academy," Bachinsky said, shoving back his plate and burping appreciatively. "They're so shiny and new. Look, he even polished his boots."

"You'll be polishing my boots with your tongue if you keep it up," the captain said, out of patience. "Show Kaledin where to leave his bag."

Bachinsky led me up to the tiny quarters I'd be sharing with three other men.

"No liquor in your room and no women, either," he said. "Captain's strict about it. We do our drinking at Bruthause and visit the girls at the Pink Canary."

"No problem," I said.

Women had never been my vice and never would be, as long as touching them led to nosebleeds, vomiting, and passing out. I hadn't so much as kissed a girl, though I'd never admit it to Bachinsky.

I should have become a monk, but I didn't believe in anything I couldn't see with my own eyes, and wouldn't lie about it, either. There were plenty of monks with no faith, but no honest ones.

I pushed my kit bag under an empty bunk and followed Bachinsky back down to the stables.

Hercules was already waiting for me—Nikolasha sent him over the day before. I was pleased to see the grooms had taken good care of him, and more pleased to do the job myself. I checked his hooves, curried his coat, and brushed his mane and tail.

"They already did that this morning," Bachinsky said, saddling his own bay mare.

"I'm doing it better."

Hercules was black and glossy, with a splendid broad chest and tufts of hair around his hooves. Nikolasha got him cheap because he'd bitten the duke who used to own him.

He'd tried the same on me. I ripped off my glove and seized him by the throat, hissing, "*Behave yourself,*" in his ear. The touch was not quite as effective on animals as on humans, but after a minute, even the great stallion was reeling on his legs, head drooping until I let go of him.

After that, we had a level of mutual respect.

Krudener whistled when he saw the stallion.

"Where'd a raggedy recruit like you get an animal like that?"

"Kaledin is the ward of Grand Duke Nikolaevich," the captain said.

"Not anymore," I corrected him.

Captain Rykowski raised an eyebrow.

"Sir," I added.

"Good," the captain said. "Means you'll be scrubbing the barracks floors with the rest of 'em if you don't keep that beast in order."

"He's perfectly behaved," I lied.

I wished I could talk to Hercules like Anastasia could to Artemis, if only to remind him that our fates were entwined. I'd have to trust that he understood no apples would be provided if he kicked someone in the face halfway through my shift.

By the time our regiment filed out through the gates of the fortress, I could hear chanting resuming in the factory district. The garment workers had joined the strike, and the dock hands as well. They were beating drums to keep time with their chant, and playing some kind of horn that howled like an animal.

I knew the sound of an army gearing up for war.

As we filed through the narrow streets on horseback, we saw people streaming from their tenements, heading in the direction of the strikers.

"Get back in your houses!" the captain shouted. "There's a curfew in place. All protestors are to disperse!"

The workers stopped and stared at us, faces sullen and pale in the early light. Others skirted around the corners of buildings and darted down alleyways, still heading toward the factories.

All the shops were boarded up, the storefronts dark and eerily quiet while the streets became a seething mass of people. Some only stood on the sidewalks, clutching their children's hands, watching with worried eyes as we rode past. Others huddled in knots, whispering.

The bulk joined the strikers. The trickle of workers became a flood.

Long before we reached the steel plant, we could no longer ride freely down the cobblestone streets. We had to shout and threaten to make any headway at all, our progress agonizingly slow.

The chanting of the strikers swelled, gathering like a storm, bursting out, drawing briefly back, then howling louder than ever.

I could see the strain on Captain Rykowski's face. He paused at the intersection of two roads, wheeling his horse, facing a mass of human bodies any way he turned. I saw burly ironmongers wielding pipes and gap-toothed fishermen carrying bricks in their hands.

"Put down your weapons!" the captain bellowed. "Anyone armed will be cut down!"

Slowly, the ironmongers lowered their pipes, eyes fixed on our guns, faces dark and furious. The fishermen only slipped the bricks into their pockets.

"The Tsar will hear us!" one of the ironmongers bellowed. "He will hear us today!"

"If you have a petition, you must submit it to the ministers at—"

"NO PETITIONS!" a woman shouted. "He will answer us, face to face!"

Before the captain could respond, a soldier from the 198th galloped up, reining his horse sharply as the crowd pressed in.

"They're marching on the Winter Palace!" he gasped.

The captain bared his teeth at the soldier's idiocy, shouting it out for all the crowd to hear.

"STOP!" he bellowed. "STOP!"

Too late—the crowd turned as one, making for the palace instead.

Their numbers swelled beyond all believing, a river that became a torrent.

"Beat them back!" the captain cried, drawing his whip.

The Cossack regiments were known for their horsewhips, usually more than sufficient to disperse an unruly crowd. All it took was a sharp cut down the cheek of a ringleader and revolutionaries became cowards.

Not today. There was no ringleader, at least not where we stood. The whole mass of bakers, teachers, matchstick-makers, and beggars seemed to move as one mind, unified in their mad resolve.

The captain whipped in all directions, cutting open the arm of the ironmonger, catching a woman across her back. The violence only inflamed the crowd. They flung bricks and stones at us, howling. A rock the size of a fist knocked Krudener's cap off his head. Roaring, he drew his pistol, but the captain shouted, "No guns!"

Yanking the reins to sheer his horse down an alleyway, he yelled for us to follow.

The workers had to scramble out of the way or be trampled as the captain charged ahead. He was abandoning the crossroads, heading for the Winter Palace instead.

We only made it as far as Narva Triumphal Arch. There we collided with the 198th in full-out war with the protesters.

The rebels had built a barricade as tall as a two-story building and were smashing all the windows along Prospekt Stachek, looting the shops of their wares, carrying barrels of beer out of the pubs.

I recognized the commander of the 198th. Gleb Saltykov had been a student at the academy and a friend of Vasta Vyachevslav. He used to electrocute me for Vasta's amusement.

He wasn't looking nearly as smug. A long cut down his cheek was bleeding onto his collar, his glasses were broken, and his uniform singed.

The protestors were chucking flaming bottles of liquor over the barricade. Those who knew pyromancy set alight the beer in the gutters, the broken furniture chucked down from upper windows, and even chunks of concrete torn up from the sidewalks.

"You'll burn down the whole city, you fools!" Captain Rykowski shouted.

"Let it burn!" a woman screamed back. "They feast and dance while we starve!"

"Kill them all," Saltykov said.

He pointed his rifle at the woman.

"NO!" Rykowski bellowed. "WHIPS ONLY!"

But he wasn't in charge of Saltykov's regiment. The men of the 198th raised their guns, only a few even hesitating. They fired indiscriminately into the crowd. I saw a man hit on the shoulder, then a child struck in the face. The girl was small and blonde. Her left eye disappeared, a dark wet hole where it had been. She slumped limp against her mother, who for long moments, didn't understand what had happened. She tapped her child on the back, trying to wake her. Then she began to scream.

I charged the soldier who fired, striking down his gun with the butt of my whip. Only to be clubbed across the back of my skull by the captain.

"*Control the crowd,*" he hissed through his teeth.

He was right—by charging among the strikers and beating them back, we prevented the soldiers from firing.

I brought my whip down left and right, telling myself it was better than shooting. I could save their lives with a slash instead of a bullet. But I couldn't close my eyes to the women and children in the crowd, the elderly, the unarmed. I saw a girl with her arm hanging broken, a man with his teeth smashed in by the butt of a rifle, a child trampled by a horse.

It was chaos and I could do nothing but bellow at them to get back in their houses, while the violence raged.

Not all in the crowd were so helpless—they carried pistols and clubs, and whatever powers they had, they used. One of the men from my regiment whose name I hadn't even learned was engulfed in flames and fell from his horse, screaming. Bachinsky turned to me and opened his mouth to say something, only for a black sludge to erupt from his nose and eyes. The left flank of horses went mad, rearing and kicking, trampling soldiers and protesters alike.

"GET BACK!" Captain Rykowski roared. "GET BACK!!!"

His whip cut through the air again and again.

One street over we heard the thunder of guns.

The other regiments were firing on the crowd.

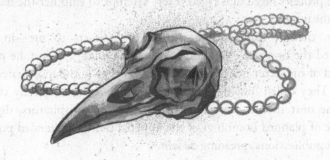

chapter 16

A STOLEN MEMORY

ANASTASIA

They called it Bloody Sunday.

Led by a priest named Father Gapon, the strikers tried to march on the Winter Palace to present a petition to my father, begging for their workdays to be cut from eleven and a half to eight hours. They didn't know Papa wasn't even there.

The strikers never made it, cut down on the banks of the Neva.

The secret police reported one hundred and thirty-three dead. The illegal newspapers swore it was ten times that number. They said the victims were buried secretly at night, a train of wagons trundling the bodies to mass graves outside the city.

The next day, bombing and looting erupted all over the city. Protests broke out in Moscow, Warsaw, Riga, and Baku. My father cracked down harder than ever, arresting thousands.

Tatiana fled upstairs to her room. When I checked on her, she had a pillow over her head, her face gray and sweating.

"I can hear them screaming," she gasped. "In the basement."

It took me a minute to understand that she thought she could hear the arrested ringleaders being interrogated in the basement of the police head-quarters. That seemed impossible, even for Tatiana. Dr. Atticus gave her a sedative that put her to sleep.

The protests raged and raged. Every attempt to smother the flames only fanned the inferno.

Even though Papa hadn't ordered the soldiers to fire—in fact, he instructed the opposite—he didn't arrest the captains. Worse, he promoted the head of his secret police. Von Plehve was already the most hated man in Rusya. They called him the Headsman, a nickname he actively cultivated. Over the next month, he arrested thousands of conspirators, digging up evidence of planned bombings of the imperial train, of intended poisonings, of secret publications spreading dissent.

Papa was furious. Some of the conspirators were members of his own guard, former ministers, even a few low-level aristocrats. Some were hanged, some shot, and many more sent into exile or sentenced to hard labor in Siberia.

We were surrounded on all sides by enemies, even within our own court.

My heart ached for the people shot down in the street, but to hear what was written in the letters opened by the Okhrana made my blood run cold:

The whole dynasty must die. The Romanovs are a stain on Rusya's honor. We'll never be free until every one of them is wiped from the earth.

They hated us.

The rule of the Tsars in Rusya had always been more than political—it was religious. I'd been taught from birth that we had a sacred compact with the people, a bond forged by the gods. It was our duty to lead and protect. And our divine right to rule.

The people had a saying:

Good tsar, bad boyars.

The Tsar was supposed to be father of the nation, protector of the people. That's why Father Gapon had been so intent on presenting the petition to Papa and Papa alone.

Now that trust had been broken. I could feel the difference in the way the people looked at our carriage as we drove through the city streets. They didn't cheer anymore. Sometimes, they even hissed.

The worst part was when I saw Damien again. He'd been serving in the city guard for over a month by that point—starting the morning of Bloody Sunday.

I happened to see him while riding through the Summer Garden. He was dressed in his uniform, guarding the Sadovyy Bridge.

Damien was mounted on Hercules and I was on one of Papa's horses, Artemis on my arm. It was the first time in a month I'd been allowed outside the palace grounds. Four guards trailed me on horseback.

"*Utro dobroye*," I said, riding up to him. "I wondered when I'd see you at work."

He hardly looked at me, standing at attention like he was one of the ridiculously stern Queensguard outside Buckingham Palace.

"You're allowed to talk to me, you know."

"Actually," he said, turning to face me, unsmiling, "I'm not."

Hot in the face, I said, "I could order you to speak to me."

"Yes, you could," Damien replied, with frosty politeness. "*Princess.*"

"Don't call me that."

"Is that an order, too? *Princess.*"

Now he was really pissing me off.

"I only came to see how you were liking the Third Brigade."

He turned to face me fully, pulling his stallion's head around.

"How I *like it?*" he hissed. "Do you think I *like* beating women and children? Watching them shot down around me?"

I drew back, my stomach sick.

"I didn't mean—"

"I don't know who I despise more," Damien said. "Your father for giving the orders, or me for carrying them out."

What he was saying was treason. If anyone heard him, if the other guards on the bridge or the ones lurking behind me breathed a word to Von Plehve—

I grabbed Hercules' bridle, leaning in close.

"I *hate* what happened," I said, low and fierce.

"It didn't just *happen,*" he hissed back at me.

Would we ever have a conversation that didn't end in argument?

I let go of Hercules. With a sharp sound through my teeth and a kick of my heels against my mount, I galloped away, leaving Damien alone on the bridge.

That was the one and only time I was allowed to ride out of the park. As the protests increased, whipped into a frenzy by the hangings and exiles, my father tightened the noose around all of us. We weren't allowed off the palace grounds, and barely anyone was permitted to come see us.

I escaped by visiting Rasputin in the White Tower.

In the tower, there were no barriers.

He was teaching me magic I'd never even heard of, let alone imagined I could do myself.

Plenty of things he showed me, I couldn't do at all, but occasionally his demonstrations would stir something inside me. He'd show me the trick, and sometimes, I could see how it was done.

I was learning the trick behind the illusion. If I could see it, I could replicate it.

Only there was no illusion. If he turned water to wine, it really was wine. It tasted of grapes and it would get you drunk. The hangover was real, too.

I had never realized reality was so flexible. The rules weren't rules at all—only guidelines.

It made my head spin. Sometimes the whole world seemed to lurch and warp around me, and I wondered if what we were doing was wrong, if we were damaging the fabric of existence.

But it didn't feel wrong. It felt good.

Power surged through me, like when I stood next to Damien. It was heady. Intoxicating.

Rasputin and I discussed much more than magic. We talked about the politics of the protests—whether my father should agree to a formal constitution, and what it should say. We gossiped about the courtiers and the ministers, who Rasputin was coming to know just as intimately as me—perhaps even more so. And of course, we talked about my family.

Rasputin was clever, with hints of wicked humor when discussing people we both disliked. We were interested in all the same things. We sought the same kind of knowledge.

Yet I never bonded to him in quite the same way as Damien. I never felt that I could see inside his mind.

There was always a barrier between us—perhaps because of the game we played.

We'd sit across the low table on our respective cushions, hands on our knees, not touching each other.

Then he'd close his eyes and I'd close mine, and Rasputin stormed my mind like a fortress.

It took everything I had to keep him at bay.

I built defenses he tore down with ease; I tried to distract him.

He would dig up the most humiliating memories: the time I got my period while sitting on Grandma Minnie's favorite hand-embroidered chair, or when I went fox hunting with my cousins and the dogs brought down a vixen, and I cried to see such a beautiful creature torn apart.

I couldn't stop him as he rampaged through my mind. But I never allowed him a clear glimpse of Damien.

I kept the secret of the Cossack soldier locked away tight in the most precious, the most private part of my brain. Hidden so deep that Rasputin would have to tear his way through everything else to find him.

The secret of Damien's identity was the only leverage I had. It was a maddening mystery that teased Rasputin, tantalizingly close. He knew I knew Damien personally, that he mattered to me. It was impossible to hide the little glints and flashes of our encounters with each other.

After our meeting on the bridge, Rasputin almost unearthed it all. I couldn't keep the image of Damien's angry face from rising in my mind like a phantom, chastising me:

I don't know who I despise more ...

I had to distract Rasputin with a vision of a thousand bats that rose in a swarm, flying at his face. It made Bat chatter and screech in his cage as if he felt it, too.

When it was my turn to attack Rasputin, I never got far.

His mind was as dark and cold as the wastelands of Siberia. Deliberately so, to keep me stranded in the snow and ice, never able to find my way to the secret shelters of his memory.

I knew they existed. I caught a glimpse now and then, like a light in the distance. Sometimes I even heard voices or laughter. Once or twice, strains of melancholy music.

One day I heard the music and I stopped trying to follow the light through the snow. Eyes closed, I followed the sound instead.

The wind howled in my face, freezing my lips, searing the inside of my lungs.

All of this was imaginary, but it was real, too. My fingers were stiff, gripping my knees as I knelt on the cushion, their tips blue with cold.

I followed the music, each step through the snow heavier and heavier as if ice were building up on my legs.

Then at last I saw it up ahead: not some illusory light that bobbed and danced and vanished before I could get close, but a house, steady and real, small and neat in the snow. Warm light pouring through the cracks in the shutters and the gap under the door.

I peered through the shutters, shivering with cold.

There he was, seated on a shaggy fur-covered chair next to the fire. Rasputin—perhaps a few years younger, but almost the same. The difference wasn't in his features, but his expression. His eyes were softer. His smile, too.

He held a child on his lap, barely more than a toddler. The child's face was turned toward him, but I thought it was a little girl. Her black hair was as thick as Rasputin's, with more curl. He rested his palm along the curve of her skull.

A woman stepped into view. I gave a little gasp because she was so beautiful—skin as clear as the snow on the windowsill, eyes as dark as the damp wood beneath.

The gasp alerted Rasputin to my presence. I was whirled away in an icy maelstrom, a wind so ferocious I thought it would tear me apart. Instead, I found myself back in Rasputin's parlor.

He glowered at me, angrier than I'd ever seen him.

"How did you find that?"

"Was that your family?" I said without thinking. "You looked so happy."

As soon as the words were out, I wished them back again. There was a blankness in his face that told me how insensitive I'd been.

"I'm so sorry ..."

"It doesn't matter." Rasputin made a motion with his hand like he'd sweep the vision from our minds.

I knew I should let it go but couldn't help myself.

"You had a daughter?"

He'd never mentioned her. Never mentioned his family at all. I didn't know he'd been married—probably before he became a monk. Perhaps the reason he became one at all.

Rasputin looked at me, seeming to weigh two options in his mind.

At last he sighed.

"Yes. I had a daughter."

He reached into the front of his robes, pulling out the silver raven's skull. He used the beak as a knife; it was wickedly sharp. But I'd always guessed it had another purpose. He wore it every day.

"Do you know what this is?"

I shook my head.

Rasputin pressed his thumb against the stone embedded in the bird's left eye, and the skull began to glow.

Light shot out from all sides, filling the room.

"Oh!" I gasped. "It's a memory-keeper."

In the gloom of the storeroom, it was easy to see the images projected all around. Now I could see the whole of that tiny house in Rasputin's memory: the fireplace, the stove, the table with its three chairs, two adult sized and one made small. I saw a bookshelf, and even little drawings propped up against the books: a fishing boat and a whale big enough to swallow it whole.

Then I saw the girl herself, dressed in a sarafan, her hair in plaits. She was a little older now, maybe five or six. She was like a doll in miniature, as beautiful as her mother, pink cheeked, dark eyes glinting.

She babbled to herself, drawing before the fire. It was too early to see what the sketch was meant to be. She used a bit of charcoal, no crayons or colored pencils.

Rasputin appeared in the doorway, watching. His wife slipped in beside him, wiping her hands on a towel.

"Did you tell her yet?"

"Not yet." His wife smiled. *"I wanted to surprise her with the cake."*

Their voices whispered like wind.

"I made her this..."

The Rasputin of memory held a toy in his hands, carved from wood. I thought it was a whale as well, or maybe a dolphin.

"She's going to love it..."

The woman's voice faded like she was rushing away from us at top speed. All the images melted away, those last words echoing over and over around the room:

She's going to love it...

She's going to love it...

She's going to love it...

The real Rasputin tucked the memory-keeper back in his robes as the vision disappeared.

The storeroom seemed dark and jumbled after the neatness of the tiny house.

"It was her birthday," I said.

"Yes."

"What happened to them?"

"They're gone." Rasputin's tone was the closing of a book.

I didn't dare ask more questions.

"I have a memory-keeper, too. Grandma Minnie gave it to me."

"Have you used it yet?"

"No."

I was almost afraid to after seeing what Rasputin and Grandma Minnie saved. It was beginning to feel like an ill omen. Like memory-keepers were doomed to store the last words of loved ones about to die.

The Rasputin in the memory was only a little younger. He must have lost his family shortly after. The wound was fresh.

It explained many things, like why he left Siberia and why his warmth and humor only ran so deep. Beneath was a river of sorrow, dark and cold.

"I'm sorry," I said again. "Your wife was so beautiful. Your daughter, too."

"They were to me," Rasputin said.

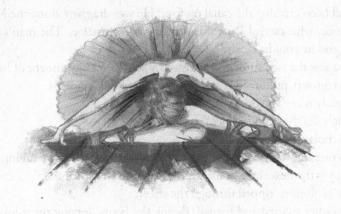

chapter 17

THE DYING SWAN

The protests raged without end. Everything we did to crush them only inflamed the people's anger.

Half my father's ministers argued conciliation, the other half greater harshness.

"You can't let them see that it's working," General Danilov said. "A god is only a god until he bleeds."

In November, as Papa returned from his monthly inspection of the city garrison, a woman standing outside a cheese shop waved her handkerchief, signaling to a watching sentry which of the two routes to the palace the royal cavalcade would take. As Papa's caravan traversed the Catherine Canal, the woman's accomplices moved into position. With a shout of "May the Gods save Rusya!" two students in suits chucked a bomb under the wheels of Papa's carriage.

That particular carriage had been a gift from Napoleon III, who knew something about artillery. The explosion blasted upward into the steel-enforced undercarriage. The horses were wrenched free of the traces, the coachman obliterated, but both my father and the minister inside the carriage were shielded from the worst of the blast.

Papa crawled out of the wreckage amongst the remains of five or six members of his personal guard and the blown-apart bodies of several passerby who had been crossing the canal on foot. He was dragging along the Minister of Finance, who carried Papa's scepter at his coronation. The man's leg was broken and he couldn't stand.

Papa saw the two students swarmed by soldiers. The remnant of his guard tried to regroup, pulling him away from the gathering crowds.

Already more voices were crying out:

"Nicholas the Bloodstained!"

"Nicholas Backbreaker!"

No one knew who among the watching crowd lining the railings of the canal threw the next three bombs at his feet, one after the other.

The explosions ripped through the street.

My father twisted and turned, fleeing the blasts, leaving the minister and the captain of his private guard behind.

He collapsed a few blocks away, burned down his back, blood running from his ears. His guards bundled him into an open cart and raced back to the palace.

The reprisal on the streets was swift and immediate. The interrogations ran all night long, one hundred and twenty-eight conspirators renounced before dawn. We knew it was only one head of the hydra. One cell of terrorists out of dozens. Hundreds, maybe. The Nihilists, the People's Will, the Narodniks, the Zemlya i Volya ... they all wanted us dead.

"They hunt me like a wolf!" Papa cried in his delirium.

It wasn't the first time someone had tried to kill him, but it was the closest anyone had gotten to success.

The god had bled, and everyone had seen it.

It wasn't just us. Over the stretch of that awful summer, 2649 ministers were assassinated, from Moscow to St. Petersburg. They were shot or bombed or hit with blasts of murderous magic in the streets, outside their homes, even on crowded streets.

Still, Papa refused to break. He called in Nikolasha and tried to announce a state of martial law.

"You'll take over as general-dictator until the revolt is repressed."

But for the first time I'd ever seen, Nikolasha didn't bend to my father.

He'd come in full uniform, already knowing what Papa would ask.

Nikolasha sunk to one knee, taking his service pistol from his belt.

"If the Emperor commands me to become military dictator, then I will shoot myself in this moment rather than disobey my Emperor. But I beg you to reconsider."

An awful silence followed.

I was clustered on the sofa with all my sisters. Papa's office had become war room and hospital as he convalesced. He was still covered in bandages, limping from whatever the blast had done to his back. He'd fled just ahead of the fire, running at a speed he could no longer manage as he had in his youth.

He stood over Nikolasha, bent and bandaged, a shell of himself. Begging his cousin to be his iron fist.

But Nikolasha, who would wage war on anyone, could not stand gunfire in the streets of St. Petersburg.

He begged Papa to make concessions instead.

After hours locked alone in his study, Papa allowed what I never thought he would allow:

He gave the people a Duma. Rusya's first parliament.

Papa appointed his laziest bureaucrat as its head, hoping that Ivan Goremykin would do nothing at all. The rest of the ministers were elected by the people.

Papa retained the right to veto any laws they made. Still, it was a concession the autocracy had never allowed. A symbol to the people that our rule was not absolute.

Papa always taught me, *To show weakness is to invite teeth at your throat.*

I could see what it cost him.

He was silent at dinner as he'd never been before. Mama had always asked that when we dined together as a family, we pretended nothing in the world existed but us.

For the first time, Papa couldn't smile or laugh. He couldn't tease Maria about which soldier she fancied that week, or quiz Alexei in his lessons.

He lingered at the table after we'd all gone, not allowing the servants to clear out the mess. Then he went through the adjoining room to his study, where he'd been staying late each night, reviewing the new structure of government.

"The Tsar doesn't want to be disturbed," his guard told me, an hour after I was supposed to be in bed.

I could have made a fuss at the door, but it was so much easier to go into the Mountain Hall and shove aside the cabinet that covered the passageway to Papa's office.

I was getting much too big to fit through the tunnel. I had to hunch down to squeeze through turns that felt sharper, swiping my arms through cobwebs that never would have been allowed to stand in the days when my siblings and I chased each other through the walls of the palace.

I came out through the back of the fireplace, into the study that so reminded me of a naval ship with its polished mahogany and brass fittings. A bust of my mother stood on the mantlepiece, as well as one of the studies for her formal portrait. The cues for the billiards table had all been put away. Papa used to play daily with Dimitri when he lived with us, but I doubted he'd touched the game since. He no longer had time to plant tulip bulbs in the palace garden beds or find new species of the iridescent butterflies he hung framed on his wall.

Once we'd been a family who also ruled. Now duty seemed to overwhelm everything else.

Papa raised his head from his papers. "It's been a long time since you visited me that way."

"I used to hide under your desk and listen to everything your ministers said."

"Alexei has been doing that all day long. Though not from under the desk," Papa nodded toward the chair next to his, a little throne in miniature. That was where Alexei sat. I preferred to perch on the edge of Papa's desk.

"What's all this?"

I wasn't looking at the papers from the ministers; I couldn't give a shit about that.

It was the map Papa had laid out of Rusya and its borders, marked in a hundred places with tiny flags. Not the marks of nations, but of factions within nations.

And then the markers of Albion and Germany, Prussia, Rhineland, and Austria, Japan, China, and the Ottoman Empire, heavy like chess pieces, each one a fulcrum of some corner of the map, the other markers scattering outward from their center like satellites.

Papa said, "A nation is a living thing. It grows or it dies. And it must eat to grow."

He showed me the borders that had been redrawn so many times already in the years of his reign—territories won and lost, trade routes defended and destroyed.

The great nations of Europe would take a mouthful of any country they saw as weak. When a country like Poland fell vulnerable because of a succession crisis or a revolt at home, the stronger nations descended and ripped the carcass apart while its people were still reeling. The bounty of Poland was parceled out amongst the Hapsburg monarchy, Prussia, and Rusya. But then the growing power of Austria or Prussia had to be balanced by a new alliance with Albion or France.

The rivalries between nations were bitter and personal, carried out in letters and whispers, by information passed secretly from foreign courts where Romanovs had married. We made alliances and then broke them, agreements that were bribes or promises to each turn the other way as another act of political violence occurred.

We were related to every royal house in one way or another, but also bitterest enemies. Once my great-grandfather had been so in love with Queen Victoria that the two wrote scandalous letters to each other still preserved in the national archives. But by the time Albion and Rusya faced each other in the Crimean war, Great-Grandfather said she was "nothing but an old madwoman," and she wrote that he was a despot with blood on his hands.

I knew war was brewing in Europe. Everyone knew it.

Each skirmish between nations seemed more brutal than the last. We'd made alliances that contradicted other alliances, trying to protect ourselves from a hundred different threats.

"The Duma just voted to limit conscription," Papa said.

I could see the flags of the nations all around us. I knew what their positions meant.

"I could strike down their first ruling. Perhaps I should, to show that the Duma doesn't control the Tsar. But then why did I allow it to form?"

He looked at the pieces without moving them. I knew he was playing out the game, many years into the future. What would happen if Austria took control of Serbia, if Finland were allowed an independent government, if the Ottomans tried to retake the Black Sea ports yet again ...

He touched the flag that represented St. Petersburg, so small and insignificant-seeming in a country that dwarfed our city a thousand times over. A nation of a hundred languages and cultures that all yanked in opposite directions, never wishing to be one.

"The students want to tear me apart from the inside, while every nation of the world attacks from without. Who will protect them when the German armies storm St. Petersburg? What good will their newspapers and their plays do them when the Kaiser has control?"

He looked up at me, deep lines in his face.

"What can I do?"

His hands were open. He waited for me to respond.

"I ... I don't know, Papa."

"Yet a ruler has to know. He has to be sure."

Papa faced the map once more.

I realized the impossibility of making everyone in a nation believe in your vision ... especially if you weren't sure of it yourself.

I thought that was why Papa had brought Rasputin into his study before agreeing to the Duma. Papa had been meeting with Rasputin more and more frequently. He said it was only because he liked to debate the Black Monk, who was far more liberal in his ideas and brave enough to argue with my father. I thought that Papa had come to rely on Rasputin's predictions for the future. In all the madness, even a cynic could find comfort in the assurances of a sorcerer who had yet to be proven wrong.

My parents' trust in Rasputin only grew with every month that Alexei continued in health and strength. My brother was taller than me now, catching up on all the growth he missed. He was fair haired, blue eyed, shoulders broadening, the bloom of health in his cheeks. When he wore his dress uniform, all the maids giggled over the handsomeness of the Tsarevich.

Of course I was thrilled to see Alexei galloping around on horseback and roughhousing with our cousins. But there was a difference in him now. He was quieter than he had been, sometimes even dull, staring out the window with a blank expression on his face. Between treatments from Rasputin, he grew pale and listless.

Papa said it was good that Alexei had become responsible.

I couldn't explain that there was a barrier between us that had never been there before. Like a glass pane you could only see when you got close, when you pressed against it and found you could go no further.

"Boys don't stay close to their sisters as they get older," Mama said. "He's a young man now."

But often he was the same brother as ever. It was only sometimes that I looked into his eyes and he stared back at me, cold and distant as a stranger.

Sylvie Buxhoeveden noticed it, too.

She'd never warmed to Rasputin. Several times she'd cautioned Mama that the rumors of the Black Monk's behavior only became more shocking and depraved.

"He shouldn't have free reign of the palace. He shouldn't be alone with the Grand Duchesses or the Tsarevich."

"The rumors are nonsense," Mama said. "Rasputin was sent to us by the gods to heal Alexei. I trust the gods."

"Trust the gods with all your heart. Rasputin is a man with a man's weakness."

I thought it was probably true that Rasputin cavorted with prostitutes and visited the opium dens in the seedier parts of the city. But that was hardly uncommon. How the courtiers behaved around my highly religious mother and how they acted in private had never aligned.

Sylvie had never cared before who kept a mistress or who flirted with an officer at a ball.

Her antipathy to Rasputin seemed to stem from their very first meeting when he read her future in the smoke. Sylvie never liked to talk about that night, and when Liza Taneeva invited her to a seance, she shuddered and said she'd had enough of communing with the other side.

"What do you think Rasputin meant when he said '*I alone must take the first step in my journey*'?" Sylvie asked me out of nowhere, when we'd only been sitting quietly, reading, in the largest library of the palace.

"I don't know."

"He told me I'd visit Japan, and I did, last fall. It gave me such a turn when Baroness Dietrich asked me to go with her. She knew nothing about the prediction—her sister invited her, and she invited me."

"I thought you always wanted to visit Asia?"

"I did. And the trip was lovely."

Yet she fretted on the sofa, anxious and disturbed.

"Did I have to go to Japan? What would have happened if I'd stayed home? Would everything else have changed, too?"

"I'm sure you could have stayed if you'd wanted to," I said. "But then you would have missed all the wonderful things you saw."

"They *were* wonderful." Sylvie looked like she wanted to say more, but lapsed into silence instead.

"How's the book?" I asked her.

She'd been reading *Anna Karenina*.

"Beautifully written." She looked a little happier. "I'll lend it to you when I'm done."

"I'll have to hide it from Papa."

Papa had been a fan of Tolstoy until the author started writing critical essays about the role of monarchy. Tolstoy was so respected that people called him "Rusya's other Tsar"—something the actual Tsar did not enjoy.

"I caught your father reading an English romantic novel," Sylvie laughed, "so don't you believe him the next time he says he only reads biographies of famous generals."

"Oh, trust me. I never did."

I COULDN'T RESIST VISITING Damien to see if he'd finally approve of something my father had done.

I cornered him outside the Peter and Paul Fortress, having told my body-guards that I wanted to visit the cathedral.

"There!" I said, triumphantly. "An actual parliament. Are you happy now?"

Damien looked at me somberly.

"Do you know who's heading the Duma?"

"Goremykin."

"No." Damien shook his head. "I mean, who's *actually* heading it."

I frowned.

"Yaro Vyachevslav," Damien said.

It took me a second to realize he meant Vasta's father—the brutal-looking minister in the extremely expensive suit. I licked my lips.

"So what?"

"He's not your friend. Not a friend to any of you."

"It doesn't matter. The Duma is powerless." I admitted what we both already knew.

"For now," Damien said.

"You're never going to be happy!" I snapped. "You hate us when we're despots, and now you're saying we're too permissive."

"All I'm saying ...," Damien rested his gloved hand on my arm, "is be careful."

He saw the guards watching and pulled his hand away.

PERHAPS THE RIOTS would have stilled on their own as winter came. Nobody wanted to march in the streets in the biting cold. A festive spirit reigned as colored lights were strung up all along Nevsky Prospect. The shops hung paper snowflakes from their ceilings, holiday displays in their windows.

Papa relaxed the ban on balls but still wouldn't let us attend the theater. At the height of the riots, the city governor was stabbed to death in the front row at the Mariinsky.

When Ollie and Tatiana's complaints of boredom were too much to bear, Papa ordered a private ballet for our own Chinese Theater.

He invited only our closest friends and family, who all accepted because they were wild to see Anna Pavlova.

Anna was the most famous ballerina in Rusya, though everything about her was wrong. In an era of dancers as compact and springy as gymnasts, the frail Anna, with her long legs and spindly ankles, was known as "the Broom." She had bent knees and bad turnout, and if she couldn't perform a certain leap or turn, she'd simply change it. Yet she danced like a demon, so passionate that she once leaped into the orchestra by accident.

I only knew what I'd read in the papers and couldn't wait to judge for myself.

That morning, Ollie said, "You ought to save the performance in your memory-keeper."

I'd shown her the gift Grandma Minnie gave me, and even played the memory for her. It wouldn't erase until I recorded a new day.

"I want to save it for the right day. What if the performance is so gorgeous I want to keep it forever, but the rest of today is shit?"

I had the strangest presentiment that I might only ever record one memory. I sensed how hard it might be to give up what you'd already captured.

"That's stupid," Ollie said. "How will you ever know when you're going to have a perfect day?"

Damien was coming to the ballet. Nikolasha invited him. He'd seemed gloomier since Damien moved to the barracks, though he wouldn't admit to missing him.

Damien had to stay at his post until 8:00. I was saving him a seat in the back row, next to Nikolasha and Alexei. Nikolasha said he liked to see the whole stage at once, and Alexei felt exposed in the imperial box, everybody staring at him.

Liza Taneeva gladly took his place, smug as a pussycat seated between Mama and Rasputin. She'd been much more cheerful since her husband was packed off to an asylum in Switzerland.

It'd been the talk of St. Petersburg for months—the servants found Alexander Vasilievich Vyrubov in his study, muttering and drooling. He'd attended work as usual only the day before.

"His uncle went mad," Liza said to Mama. "Alexander was acting strangely all year. Talking to himself. Keeping a notebook of voices he heard, people he thought were following him."

Vyrubov had been sober as a judge when last I saw him. It was hard to imagine anyone so stiff and proper going mad. I'd never heard Liza complain of her husband hearing voices—only that he kept her on a pitiful allowance and wouldn't allow her to throw any more parties in their lemon-yellow house.

Now Liza threw parties once a week. Rasputin deigned to attend when the guest list interested him. He'd confided to me that he found Liza almost as irritating as Ollie and I did, but couldn't entirely reject her.

"She introduced me in St. Petersburg. And besides, it's natural for a woman to seek a close relationship with the gods through her priest."

"Yes," I'd smirked. "She's very devoted to ... the gods."

Rasputin smiled in return. He said what he had to because he knew how to play the game.

Now he chatted with Liza as if nothing could be more interesting, paying her every ounce of the attention she so desperately craved.

I watched from above, able to see down into the box as easily as the stage. If Rasputin turned around, he'd see me as well. More to the point, he'd see Damien once he arrived.

I knew that both had been invited, but there was no way in hell I'd ask Damien not to come. Every time I thought of the costume ball and the way I'd pulled him aside like I wanted to hide him, as if I were embarrassed of him, I wanted to slap myself.

If Rasputin saw Damien, it would be the end of our game.

I knew it couldn't last forever.

Still, I relished the fact that Rasputin never managed to pry the information from my mind. It infuriated him that no matter how much stronger he might be, I'd managed to defeat him in that one thing.

I hoped he'd keep teaching me anyway.

The lights dimmed in the theater, only the golden lanterns along the walls remaining.

The Chinese Theater was like a lantern itself, glowing from afar in thick-falling snow. It was made of rich red lacquer carved into oriental shapes: swallows and scrolls, dragons and deer. The lustrous layers of lacquer reflected light off every surface, glimmering on the embroidered silk screens, bouncing off the porcelain chandeliers. Even the seats inside the theater were upholstered in scarlet silk. It was the most beautiful building in all of St. Petersburg.

The curtain rose. The haunting call of a violin sounded like a swan, and Anna Pavlova stepped onstage.

She was dressed all in white feathers, the straps of her costume slipping down off her thin shoulders. Her feet made rapid steps on pointe while her arms fluttered like wings. She looked as if she'd lift off any moment. Her head lolled, the music carrying her along as if she were helpless.

Damien slipped in beside me, his wool coat full of chill, snow on his shoulders and in his hair.

"You saved me a seat."

"Of course."

The theater was packed with cousins and courtiers. My sisters sat up front with my parents. Alexei was right next to me, on the opposite side as Damien. He pressed his fingers against his temple, only watching the stage sometimes. He'd complained of a headache before we came.

A dozen ballerinas joined Anna onstage. They danced as a corps, their tutus resembling flowers that opened as they twirled. They looked like lotuses floating down a river of dark water, swirling in the current.

A male dancer appeared, pulling Anna away from the others. The corps pirouetted offstage. Only Anna and the man remained to dance a pas de deux.

He held her hands outstretched on either side, balancing her while her legs made intricate movements beneath the hem of her skirt. She wore sheer tights that might as well have been skin. Likewise, the male dancer wore a pair of breeches so tight and transparent that I learned a few things about male anatomy.

I blushed as their legs brushed against each other, as Anna dipped and extended her foot up by his ear, her nose by his knee.

My eyes dropped to Damien's gloved hand gripping his thigh. I snuck a look at his face next and saw a muscle jump in his jaw.

The male dancer's hands encircled Anna's waist, bare without any gloves. He lifted her overhead with one hand as if she weighed nothing

Anna ran across the stage, fleeing him. Then she turned back, hesitating.

He held out his arms to her. She ran and leaped, soaring an impossible distance before he caught her and spun her around, her body posed like a figurehead on the prow of a ship.

"How can she jump so high?" I gasped.

Damien shook his head in wonder, keeping his mouth shut because he had better manners than to talk in a theater.

I couldn't take my eyes off Anna. She was magnetic, ethereal. So frail, and yet so powerful. Her spindly legs flexed and leaped, her dark eyes brimmed with pleasure and pain.

When it came time for the last act, the whole theater fell silent, not a rustle or whisper. We'd all been waiting for this.

Damien's gloved hand slipped into mine, concealed by the lowered lights. Our fingers entwined.

Even with his leather glove and my thin cotton one between us, energy throbbed through our bodies like a circuit finally linked up. Each beat of my heart seemed to send another pulse of power down my arm, with an answering surge in return—Damien's heart beating in time with mine. We synched up like two clocks, our heartbeats the ticking of the hands.

The soft strains of Anna's most famous ballet rose from the orchestra pit.

She crossed the stage alone. The swooning had become reeling, she was weakening by the moment. Still she danced like she'd burn up the last moments of her life floating on the points of her toes.

She drooped and forced herself to rise, again and again. She gazed at something we couldn't see, face anguished, arms bleached as white as the snowy feathers of her dress by the brilliant lights beating down. Her fingers reached upward, beseeching.

The light faded on the stage. Anna faded, too. She sank to the ground, neck bent.

Damien's hand was locked around mine, squeezing tightly.

Only a faint blue glow illuminated Anna's dress. The stage was so dark that it was impossible to see the wooden boards, the walls behind, or even the curtains on either side. All we could see was Anna.

She rose one last time, lighter this time, almost floating. There seemed to be no floor beneath her feet, only a black void all around. She fluttered on her toes, the beating motions of her arms like wings as she soared up, up, into the dark.

Then she was gone.

Tears ran down my face. The solo spanned the space of four minutes, yet I felt I'd watched an entire life bloom and die on the stage.

Damien turned. His face was wet, too. We looked at each other, unembarrassed.

On my other side, Alexei sat silent, staring at the stage. His face was blank like he felt nothing at all.

The rest of the crowd surged to their feet, applauding as hard as they could. Though the Chinese Theater was small, the shouts and cheers made it full to overflowing. I could see Rasputin below me, clapping as vigorously as anyone else, the heavy sleeves of his robe falling back. If he turned around, he'd be looking right at us.

"I've got to get back," Damien said. "We're supposed to be cleaning the rifles in the armory. I snuck away."

"I'm glad you did."

"So am I."

He grabbed both my hands in his and pressed them hard. His fingers shook with some feeling unexpressed.

I leaned forward and kissed him on the cheek, quickly, before anyone could see. My mouth only brushed his skin for a moment, but it made me reel like the floor had dropped out from under my feet. I drew back, lips throbbing like they'd been stung.

Damien looked at me, the expression on his face like Anna Pavlova's: anguished, pained.

Without speaking, he turned and left.

Rasputin clapped, still facing the stage as the dancers reemerged to take their bows.

If he'd turned around, he would have seen Damien.

But he never turned.

AFTER THE BALLET, Mama held a champagne reception to meet all the dancers.

I couldn't believe how tiny Anna Pavlova was up close. She'd dominated the stage amongst a throng of dancers despite being barely more than child sized.

So it was in conversation, too. She had a fierceness that made you pay attention to every word, and made you believe it, too.

Nikolasha seized her hand, gushing, "You're the flower of Rusya. Never have the gods bestowed so much talent in one person."

Anna lifted her chin.

"The gods give talent. Work transforms talent into genius."

I'd never heard a woman call herself a genius before, proudly, without apology.

I asked her, "How did you know that one day you'd be great?"

Anna gave me a level look. "No one thought I should dance. I was thin and sickly. The Imperial Ballet School rejected me three times. After they finally accepted me, I broke my ankles over and over trying to master the jumps. I saw a doctor and he told me my bones were hollow like a bird, they'd always be fragile. He said my dream was dead."

I remembered how the male dancer had lifted her like she weighed nothing, and how far she jumped, as if she'd truly taken flight. But also, how her legs bowed when she hit the stage, how the impact had rippled through her delicate frame. It must hurt, every single time.

"I told that doctor I would break every bone in my body a thousand times over before I stopped dancing. No one told me I'd be great—I decided for myself."

She made me burn with admiration. And with envy.

"I'd love to see you perform at the Mariinsky Theater."

"Come visit me backstage if you do," Anna said.

I did see her again.

But not under the circumstances I would have wished.

chapter 18

END-OVER-NOSE

Ollie was furious with Papa because he said it was long past time for her to marry. He said if she didn't choose a suitor by the end of the year, he'd choose one himself.

Ollie had engaged in several flirtations with friends of Dimitri Pavlovich, but none endured beyond a few weeks. It was lucky they hadn't, because none had born the title of Prince or Grand Duke, and Ollie wouldn't be permitted to marry anyone lower.

Ollie rebelled by sneaking away with Irina, pretending to visit the tea shops in St. Petersburg or some of Irina's female cousins on the Mikhailovich side, but actually meeting Felix Yusupov.

Nina Ivanova had been promoted to lady's maid and was now assigned to Ollie full-time. Since Nina was only a couple of years older than Ollie herself, it wasn't too difficult to convince her to participate in the subterfuge, even at the risk of her job. Nina enjoyed the skating parties and sledding adventures with Felix's friends almost as much as Ollie and Irina. She was so pretty that even the most snobbish aristocrats had to flirt with her, though she only laughed at them, saving her heart for her soldier.

"We'll be married in another year," she told me, showing me the silver charm bracelet he sent for her birthday. "We almost have enough money saved."

I admired the charms Armand had selected: a tiny love knot, a rearing horse, the double-headed Rusyan eagle, a silver moon, a plum, the icon of Nina's favorite saint, and a seashell to represent the coastal town in which she'd grown up.

Nina longed to be married just as much as Irina.

She seemed likely to beat Irina to the altar, even at the glacial pace she saved her servant's wages.

It had been almost six years and still Xenia wouldn't relent. She loathed Felix Yusupov more than ever.

Unfortunately for Xenia, Felix had no profession to occupy his time and unlimited resources to devote to the pursuit of her daughter. He kept a servant stationed on the corner outside the Mikhailovich mansion solely to inform him of occasions when Xenia and Sandro exited the house, leaving Irina unguarded.

We jockeyed for her as best we could, because we all loved Felix's lively humor and generous nature. Only Tatiana resisted his charms, annoyed by the chaos that inevitably followed any of Felix's plans.

"I don't know what you see in him," she said to Irina.

"Well he worships the ground she walks on," Ollie remarked. "That's a good start."

"He makes me laugh and he's honest with me," Irina said calmly. "I don't want a husband who loves me for a year, then takes a mistress behind my back."

I laughed. "Felix is so blunt he'd probably tell you straight to your face if he wanted a mistress."

"He tells me everything he does," said Irina, serenely. "And I love him exactly as he is."

"I want that," Maria said, pressing her hand against her heart.

"You know he can see through anything, don't you Maria?" Tatiana warned her. "He can see right through your clothes!"

"You think I want to?" Felix cried, sneaking up on us as he liked to do. "You think I like seeing what Liza Taneeva looks like under her dress?" He made a disgusted face.

The rest of us laughed, even Tatiana.

"Though it is useful once in a while," Felix admitted. "I've seen notes in people's pockets, I know when someone's armed, and it's easy to find books when I lose them. As long as they're only under the sofa."

He grabbed Irina around the waist and pulled her close, pitching his voice low.

"And it may have had *something* to do with why I was so enraptured by Irina the first time I saw her in the park ..."

She smacked his shoulder, red as a rose.

"You're terrible."

But she was pleased and smiling.

"Come on!" Felix said. "Everyone's waiting for us."

"Who's everyone?" Tatiana demanded.

"Dimitri, of course." He and Felix almost never went anywhere without each other. "Also Kolya Derevenko, Prince Ilya, Dario Dolgoruky. Oh, and ... that Cossack." He gave me a saucy grin.

Felix knew very well what Damien's name was but wanted to tease me.

"That's a lot of people," Maria said.

"We're going to get caught," Tatiana agreed.

"Nonsense." Felix hustled us along. "All my friends are completely respectable and utterly discreet."

An hour later, we were racing sleds down High Street, hollering at top volume and pelting each other with snowballs.

The sleds were pulled by a motley assortment of pigs, dogs, goats, and twin white reindeer, scrounged up from gods know where by Felix's friends.

Damien was driving the sleigh in which I resided, handling the reins so I could throw snowballs at the back of Felix's head.

We'd won most of our races, except when our reindeer became interested in Ollie's goat in a way that didn't seem quite appropriate between species.

We were about to beat Felix and Irina in the last and most important of our arbitrary races, pelting twice around the church in Foster Field, then crossing the frozen stream that was our finish line—until we hit a rock the size of a dinner plate concealed in the snow. Our sleigh went back-over-nose, catapulting Damien and me into a snowbank.

Damien dug frantically, yanking me out of the snow before the others had even reached us.

He cleaned the slush off my face with his mittened hands, his own face hilariously distraught. He looked like he'd set an orphanage on fire.

"Are you alright? Are you hurt? Gods, answer me!"

"Of course I'm alright," I laughed, spitting slush out of my mouth.

Then I noticed my arm hanging at a brand-new angle.

As my brain tried to puzzle out how that could be possible, the pain rushed in.

"Oh, shit."

I reeled back on my heels.

Damien caught me, scooping me up in his arms and sprinting off across the snow.

The drifts were thick. I was surprised he could run at all, let alone with all my weight. I wasn't a slip of a willow like Irina.

"You're strong," I murmured, turning my face against his chest.

His heart thundered against my ear.

When he set me down on the sidewalk, the fire in my arm brought me 'round.

"That doesn't feel good ..."

"I'll get you a doctor." Damien looked frantically about.

Before I could tell him that under no circumstances should we call a doctor anywhere but to the Dolgoruky sisters' house, where we were supposed to be enjoying an afternoon of card games and crustless sandwiches, I looked up and saw something much worse:

My Aunt Xenia.

She stood on the opposite side of the street, arm-in-arm with Uncle Sandro. From the stunned expression on both their faces, I had to assume they had not ambled over expecting to see their beloved daughter whipping the reins of a sled pulled by three black hogs and a pair of galloping spaniels.

Felix and Irina leaped out of their sleigh and ran up behind us, red faced and panting, covered in snow spray.

"What happened?"

"Did you hit something? I saw the sleigh turn over, gods Anastasia, you must have flown twenty f—"

"Irina!" I hissed.

She followed my gaze to her mother, going still as a mouse on the lawn when Artemis soars overhead.

"That's less than ideal," Felix said.

THE BELLOWING we got from Papa was one of the all-time worst. He shouted for the better part of an hour while us four girls sat on the sofa in the Mauve Boudoir, shame faced and staring down at the carpet.

In theory, Mama should have been on the hollering side, but some combination of sympathy and guilt for not supervising us better had her sitting in the chair next to ours, looking just as miserable as her daughters.

"And *you*, Tatiana! I didn't think you'd be a part of something like this. Lying to your aunt. Lying to *us*! Contributing to the ruin of your own cousin. Making a spectacle of yourselves in front of all of St. Petersburg! And Anastasia—you could have been killed! That could have been your neck instead of your arm!"

Papa turned on Ollie, his eyes full of fire.

"This is what comes of allowing you to run around like a child when you're a grown woman. It's time for you to make yourself useful. Your Aunt Olga will be taking you to the Danish court where you can shore up our interests with our allies."

Ollie's jaw went rigid. She knew very well that Crown Prince Christian also resided at the Danish court—a marriage prospect long cultivated by Aunt Xenia.

The fact that Aunt Olga would be her chaperone was only a light salve to the fact that Ollie was effectively being exiled, packed around the courts of Europe like a bride-in-a-box until someone took possession of her.

It was bad timing for us to upset Papa. Austria had just declared war on Serbia. War was a certainty.

I'd just had my arm splinted by Dr. Atticus. My head was reeling from the milky tincture he'd forced me to drink, the pain fading to a dull throb.

"At least it's your left arm," Maria said kindly.

"She's left-handed," Tatiana reminded her.

"Oh, right." Maria grimaced.

Alexei was nearly as angry as Papa, but only because he'd been left out of the fun.

"You've been sneaking off to see Felix and not inviting me?" he demanded once we were alone in my room.

I sank down on the bed, which felt like it was rocking beneath me.

Alexei sat beside me, denting the edge of the mattress, making the rolling sensation even worse.

"I'm sorry. It's a lot harder to bundle the Tsarevich out of the palace."

Alexei scowled. In some ways he was much less restricted than us girls, but his days were becoming packed with tedious meetings with ministers and appointments with diplomats.

I no longer envied his position. Training to be Papa did not look like fun.

Alexei had been listless all winter. Gray smudges lay like thumbprints under both eyes.

"Are you alright?" I cried, seeing the edge of a dark bruise poking up from his collar.

It'd been a long time since I'd seen a bruise so dark on Alexei's fair skin. It took me back to the old days, to the dread we felt when Alexei received the slightest bump on his body.

"What?" Alexei said. Then, pulling open his shirt collar and glancing down, "Oh, that. I'm fine, I don't even know where I got it."

"You should see Dr. Atticus," I said automatically, forgetting that Alexei was exclusively under the care of Rasputin these days.

"Rasputin will fix me up. He's gone back to Siberia to visit family—did you know that?"

"Yes, I heard."

Before he left he told me that we'd have to take a break from our lessons. He'd be gone over a month, even taking the Trans-Siberian railway most of the distance.

"He shouldn't leave you so long. What if you get sick again?"

"Don't be silly. I'm practically healed."

He wasn't, though. The disease always came back.

We were dependent on Rasputin, as he very well knew.

A thought came to my mind that might be brilliant, or the worst possible idea.

Rasputin would never show me how to heal Alexei myself, because then we wouldn't need him.

Unless ... I traded him something valuable in return.

Not Damien—I would never do that. I'd never trusted Rasputin's curiosity on the subject. He was fixated on what he'd seen in my vision for reasons I couldn't understand.

I couldn't keep them apart forever, but I wasn't about to hand over Damien as a bargaining chip, no matter how stupidly I'd phrased it at the costume ball.

No, I had something else Rasputin wanted even more.

I could show him how to time-walk.

My stomach lurched at the idea.

Papa would be furious.

It was a magic so rare, I doubted Rasputin could ever master it. But it was supposed to belong to the Romanovs alone, our greatest weapon, especially when coupled with Charoite. Together, those two gifts made us practically invincible.

No, I couldn't show Rasputin. Papa's shouts still rang in my ears. If I crossed that particular line, he'd string me from the city walls.

For now, Alexei was safe in Rasputin's care.

"You need a nap?" Alexei asked.

"Yes, if you bring me some water first."

Alexei went to fetch it.

He brought me water with ice made by our cook, not broken off from the icicles in the yard. I could tell from the shape, perfectly spherical and clear as glass.

He put a damp cloth across my forehead.

"You're a good nurse." I smiled.

"You learn a few things being sick all the time."

I was already drifting off.

Before he left, Alexei bent and brushed a quick kiss against the top of my head.

I thought I'd gotten off lightly, even after Papa put us girls in a lockdown that made the height of the riots look like a Sunday picnic.

Then the axe fell.

Papa was no fool. When he heard I'd been racing around in a sleigh driven by Damien Kaledin, he didn't even bother forbidding me seeing him. He had Damien transferred to the Rusyan 1st Army, where he'd be shipped off to a training camp in Gumbinnen and would be among the first sent into conflict.

It was Damien himself who told me.

He tried to visit to see how my arm was healing, but the guards turned him away at the gate.

He smuggled in a note instead, passed to Nina Ivanova.

She brought it straight to me, despite the fact that she'd already been demoted as punishment for taking us to see Felix. The only reason she wasn't sacked was because we begged and pleaded with our parents, swearing that we forced her to do it.

"Do me a favor and burn the letter," she said. "Margaretta's looking for a reason to get rid of me."

The note was only a few sentences, written in a rapid, slanting script I'd never seen before that spoke of Damien all the same. He'd pressed so hard that the pen practically went through the paper in places.

I'm being transferred to the 1st army. I leave tomorrow. I wanted to say goodbye in person, but this will have to do.

Don't feel bad about it. It would've happened eventually, especially if the troops are moving out like they say.

When I stop in Riga, my father's coming to see me. Do you think I got an accent living in the city so long?

You have one, but I always liked it.

—D

I held the scrap of paper in both hands, heart beating hard.

He was leaving.

Maybe forever.

I thought I'd accepted that nothing could ever happen between Damien and me. Even if you removed all the other obstacles, even if he was the crown prince of our closest ally, Damien's ability meant we could never kiss, let alone perpetuate a dynasty together.

I'd known that from the beginning.

But the sick feeling in my stomach told me that I'd never truly believed that it was best for us to go our separate ways.

Even though we fought all the time and agreed on nothing, he was my best friend. Every time I saw him, I lit up inside.

Without the bright threads of our meetings to look forward to, the stretch of years ahead looked dull and cold.

I didn't want to burn the note.

You have one ... but I always liked it ...

I burned it anyway, because we'd already gotten Nina in enough trouble.

Then I marched down to Papa's office and hammered on the door. The guard tried to stop me but didn't want to seize hold of me with my arm in a sling.

Papa opened the door himself, tall and terrible.

He hadn't forgiven me in the three days since Xenia heard shrieks and shouts on High Street and strolled over on the arm of Uncle Sandro.

"Are you pounding on my door?" Papa glowered down at me.

I felt myself shrinking.

"You had Damien transferred." My voice came out weaker than I wanted.

Papa didn't try to deny it.

"Yes, I did."

"You can't punish him for my mistake," I pleaded. "He didn't want to come, he didn't know I'd be there—"

Papa pulled me inside his office and shut the door, but only so the guards outside wouldn't hear.

"Your relationship with the Ataman's son is inappropriate."

"We're just friends, it's not like Irina and—"

"You can't be *friends*!" Papa shouted, color rising above his beard. "I'm training him to take control of the Cossack host. To lead his people under my command. He's not a friend or an ally, he's a subject! He shouldn't even know your name. I never should have let Nikolasha bring him near you."

"I'm allowed to have friends; I'm allowed to have opinions! I'm not one of your butterflies pinned to the wall!"

My shouts seemed to ring around the room in the silence that followed.

The anger in Papa's face drained away, his shoulders slumping.

"I don't want to be your jailor, Anastasia. But I have to protect you—even from yourself."

He laid his heavy hand on my shoulder, pushing me down on the chaise.

When he sat beside me, his weight pulled the cushion down far more than Alexei's had done.

"I only sent Damien a few weeks early. His whole unit is shipping out. The Germans are amassing at the border."

My stomach rolled over. It was real. The Great War was beginning.

I looked at the pieces on Papa's map, now arranged for battle.

Germany, Prussia, Austria, Albion, France ... all coming to fight.

"What will happen?" I asked my father.

"I don't know. No one does."

I VISITED ARTEMIS FOR COMFORT, while knowing that looking for comfort from a raptor is like searching for a swimming pool in the desert.

Even if she didn't care about Damien, I hoped she'd at least have some sympathy for my arm.

"Do you remember when Nikolasha first brought you to me? Your wing was wrapped up just like this."

Someone shot me. Artemis lifted her beak. *You did that to yourself.*

Still, she flew to my good arm and inspected the bandages carefully, making sure all was in order.

It will heal, she said, with some relief.

"Papa's sending Damien away," I told her. "Because of me."

Artemis cocked her head, her eyes black and liquid, without pupils or all pupil, it was hard to tell.

The horse boy is not a city creature. This is better.

I sighed. It was true—Damien never liked St. Petersburg. He'd probably be happier in the outlands. Assuming he didn't get shot to pieces.

"You're not a city creature, either," I reminded Artemis.

Yes. But I can fly.

Artemis could never be captive because she could fly away wherever she liked.

But she stayed with me.

I ruffled my thumb gently through the feathers at the back of her head, where she liked it best.

"You're the best gift I ever got," I told her.

She preened the feathers on her shoulder.

Of course I am.

PART FOUR

chapter 19
SO IT BEGINS

Alexander Palace was much quieter once Ollie and Tatiana were gone. It was only Ollie who'd been banished to Denmark, but Tatiana wanted to go along and Papa allowed it, probably thinking he could kill two hares with one arrow.

Ollie was twenty-three, Tatiana twenty-one. It was time for both to be married.

The difference in our family group seemed to work changes on all of us.

At first Ollie's letters home to me and Maria were furious pages of complaints: bitterness at being separated from Irina, boredom with the social events she was expected to attend, frustration with the frivolous fashion requirements of the Danish court.

After only a few weeks, her notes grew shorter and more cheerful as she made friends with our lesser-known cousins and began to attend skating parties and indoor tennis matches.

Tatiana had been taken under the wing of a woman named Juliana Jorgensen, who served as the Minister of Education. According to Tatiana, she could quote aloud any passage of any book she'd ever read.

Obviously, nothing could impress Tatiana more. She wrote gushing letters about her new friend, not neglecting to mention that, *"She's the most elegant creature imaginable. She often lends me her gowns, as we're exactly the same size."*

At home, we likewise fell into new routines.

Now Maria was the eldest Grand Duchess. When Mama wasn't around she had to serve the tea, walk first into every room, and head the dances.

Maria had always preferred to let her sisters take the lead, even me when I was very young. Now she had no choice.

I was surprised to see how well she bore the pressure. She grew more talkative at parties and allowed Aunt Xenia to add a wider range of partners to her ball books.

She was so charming at Papa's birthday party that both the Count of Flanders and Prince George of Greece made advances through Aunt Xenia. Papa said if he'd known how easy it was to find suitors at home, he wouldn't have sent Ollie and Tatiana so far away.

Then Germany invaded Belgium and began to amass troops in Prussia, right along our eastern border.

The balls ceased. Most of the parties, too. The Count of Flanders was packed off to Albion for safekeeping, and Prince George hurried back to Greece.

Mama wanted Ollie and Tatiana to come home, but Papa said they were safer where they were. Denmark had no alliances in the war and planned to remain neutral.

We lost Nikolasha's company. Papa appointed him Commander-in-Chief of the Rusyan forces. He left St. Petersburg to lead the counter-offensive in Galicia.

Alexei wanted to go with him. A massive row commenced when Papa said it was impossible.

"Why not?"

"Because it isn't safe."

Alexei cried, "An Emperor doesn't send his men where he's afraid to go!"

"Nor does he treat himself as expendable!" Papa thundered. "You'd only put more soldiers at risk trying to protect you."

Alexei stormed off.

I found him later, chucking stones into the fishpond. I pulled him over to our swing on the old oak. Moss had grown all down the ropes.

Alexei said, "They'll never stop treating me as a child. Mama still calls me 'Tiny' and 'Baby'. I want to fight, not sit in a palace."

"I want to go, too."

Alexei scoffed. "Girls don't go to war."

"I have a right to defend Rusya as much as you do."

"Well, neither of us can. Because you're a girl and I'm the Tsarevich." Alexei twisted slowly back and forth on the swing, toes dragging in the grass. "I'm trapped here. It's like a fist. I can't breathe. Every day it closes tighter around me."

I looked at him, startled.

Alexei hadn't been looking well that spring. He hadn't gotten any color in his cheeks, maybe because he hadn't gone outside as much as usual. He was tired, sleeping ten hours each night but still taking naps some afternoons.

He was moody, too, and irritable, quick to snap if any of us annoyed him.

Once I surprised him in his bedroom, stripped to the waist and bathing at the basin by the window. Another bruise marked the base of his neck, a smaller one on the inside crook of his arm.

"You're sick again!" I cried.

He rounded on me, angrier than I expected.

"Get out! And don't come in my room!"

He stretched out his hand, pelting me with pillows until I ran out into the hall, the door slamming after me.

I was worried about him, but at least he had the energy to chuck half the objects in the room at my head. His telekinesis was stronger than Mama's. I'd seen him lift the whole back end of Papa's Mercedes, straining, hands trembling. Alexei fell to one knee and the car crashed down. Papa said not to do it again.

"It's the war," Mama said. "Your brother's finally seeing the burden that will fall on his shoulders someday."

The hospital wards were filling with soldiers sent home with burns all over their bodies, limbs blown off, faces horribly mangled. Maria went to the wards every day to help with the nursing. Mama went, too, when her health allowed it. She'd been ill all through the winter from an infection in her lungs.

I joined them occasionally, but the sight of the soldiers' injuries made me sick with panic. I had dreams that I pulled the sheet back off one of the many bodies stacked on stretchers and saw Damien's cold gray face staring up at me.

If he died because Papa sent him to war ... I'd be destroyed. I'd never forgive myself.

The Germans smashed our 1st and 2nd armies. Damien was in the 1st. I could hardly eat or sleep until I got a letter from him several weeks later, telling me he'd been shot in the arm. He only spent a few hours in the infirmary before they discharged him and sent him back to his division.

I had a perverse impulse to poke a hole through my own arm as punishment. My guilt at getting him sent away was all-consuming. It ate at me day and night.

My only outlet was visiting Rasputin.

Our lessons resumed when he returned from Siberia. His sister came with him. She took up residence in the city, and visited him at the White Tower.

Her name was Katya.

I knew they were related the moment I saw her. She had his cool complexion, slightly blue in the undertone like skimmed milk, and a heart-shaped face. The same black hair, but her eyes were darker, set deep in their sockets, which gave her a sly look. Her mouth was wide and bold and red.

She wore a simple sarafan in folk style, with earrings in her ears that looked handmade. Like Rasputin, her face was smooth and unlined.

"Who's older?" I asked.

"Me," Rasputin said. "But only by a little."

Katya smiled. "The gap lessens every year, doesn't it?"

I felt the same with my siblings. Alexei had been a baby once upon a time, and Ollie and Tatiana tried to lose me when I tagged along. Now we were all friends and equals, or close enough.

Perhaps that would change when my sisters got married.

I didn't relish being left behind as Ollie and Tatiana entered matrimony and motherhood, but neither did I want to follow them. Not anytime soon.

"How long are you staying in St. Petersburg?" I asked Katya.

"Perhaps permanently. There's little left for me in Siberia."

Conditions in Rusya's outposts had only grown worse with the war. Food and supplies were shunted off to our troops. Jobs opened up in munitions and manufacturing, but other industries folded.

"Do you have family there still?" I asked.

Katya shook her head. "Not anymore."

"What will you do here?"

"Katya's a poet," Rasputin said.

"A poet!"

She shot him a look that was both embarrassed and gratified.

"I like to write poetry. I've never made a ruble off it, so don't let my brother give you the wrong idea. In Siberia I worked at a print shop. Perhaps I can find something similar here."

"I'm sure you will," I said. "There must be ten times as many printers in St. Petersburg."

"That's my hope."

248

Katya's voice was low and thrilling. I hung on every word like a radio drama.

I could see she already had a hefty stack of books in front of her, pilfered from Rasputin's library. She carried them off under her arm when she left.

Rasputin and I proceeded upstairs to take our positions across from one another at the low, circular table.

We'd gone over at least a dozen kinds of magic at that point. All I'd managed to master was a little pyromancy (weak and inconsistent), and a very little ability to freeze water with my touch (even weaker than the pyromancy, though Rasputin said they were two sides of the same coin and if I could do one, I ought to be able to do the other just as well).

I'd also managed to see a few visions in Rasputin's scrying glass. The images were foggy and indistinct, but I thought I'd seen a village of tiny houses, and a cavern of ice. I had no idea what either vision meant.

"Reading the future is like painting a picture in tiny patches," Rasputin said. "You work on an inch at a time, nose against the canvas. Eventually, you may be able to step back and see the picture in its entirety. But you won't learn much in a single session."

I'd never managed to learn anything from tea leaves or scapulimancy.

Neither had I been able to imitate Rasputin's ability to read foreign languages or predict the weather, despite several demonstrations.

On that particular day, I thought Rasputin was going to take me out in the woods to pick herbs. He'd been showing me plants that grew wild in Alexander Park, how they could be hung and dried, then concentrated in tinctures to preserve their potency.

Instead, he took something small from a leather pouch in his pocket. He extended his hand across the table, uncurling his fingers around a tiny violet-colored gem.

"Do you know what this is?"

The stone was minuscule, the size of a mouse-dropping. Yet its glow cast a light down the life line on Rasputin's palm. The charge in the air lifted the tiny hairs on my arm.

"Yes, I know it."

Neither of us said its name. We both knew how illegal it was for Rasputin to possess even a single grain.

He said, "Are you familiar with talismans?"

"You mean like an amulet or a ring?"

"A talisman is any object that channels power. An amulet can be a talisman. So can the feather of a firebird or the carapace of a desert scarab. This ... what I have here ... is a powerful talisman."

The flesh at the base of my skull tightened, sending a prickling sensation all along my scalp.

The purple gem glowed like the last glint of twilight. It pulled me in.

"Can I touch it?"

Rasputin opened his fingers a little more. I touched the stone. It felt heavy as gold, cool as water. Its power throbbed, sending a jolt all the way through my body, all the way down to my toes. The sensation wasn't entirely unpleasant. My fingertips tingled. I tasted metal in my mouth.

"Have you ever seen it before?" Rasputin's voice sounded distant, but also right inside my head.

That little burst of Charoite was still swirling around inside me like a tiny fish. Making me throb and ache here and there and all over.

"Once. Papa showed me."

Rasputin took my hand, his fingers smooth and cool. He dropped the Charoite into my palm. "What did he show you?"

"It was right after the war with the Kingdom of the Rising Sun. Papa came home burned." I swallowed hard, remembering the shiny pink skin of his arm, raw and sensitive. His back had looked the same after the Anarchists threw the bombs at his feet. "He brought back all the Charoite he had left, a lump the size of a hen's egg. He let me see it but not hold it."

"So you've never actually used it."

I shook my head.

I could feel the stone pulsing in my hand. It *was* alive. Or the power inside it was alive.

That power wanted to go inside me. I could feel it, potent and waiting, a mouthful of wine I longed to swallow.

"How did you get this?"

Rasputin smiled thinly. "It wasn't cheap. But I had to test it. You know mineral magic is one of my strongest affinities."

His mineral collection took up one entire wall—crystals, geodes, and calcites, in the rich, deep shades of the earth: jade, amethyst, carnelian, and rose ...

Rasputin had shown me how to use a selenium tower to help channel my power, gripping it in both hands while I tried to light a candle across the room. It helped—the candle flared up like a torch. Even without using the Charoite, I could feel it was much more powerful than the selenium—a cannon compared to a peashooter.

I longed to try it, but handed it back to Rasputin instead. All the pocket money I'd ever saved probably wasn't enough to pay him back if I drained the stone.

I thought of the store in the vault beneath Alexander Palace. How much was under there?

What I wouldn't give to see it. To hold it in my hands. All that raw power ... enough to flatten the palace. The whole city, maybe.

I shivered.

Rasputin tucked the stone back in its pouch and put it away in his pocket.

He looked at me, his eyes a winter sky.

"You won't tell anyone I have it."

"Of course not."

He kept my secrets and I kept his. That was our agreement.

I wasn't the only one enthralled with Katya. Whenever Alexei spied her walking across the grounds of Alexander Park, he felt an urgent need to visit the White Tower, which was damned inconvenient.

I couldn't practice magic with Alexei mooning around Rasputin's kitchen, asking Katya if she'd read aloud to him or join him in visiting the baby elephant that had unexpectedly emerged after a decade of our two Asian elephants ignoring each other.

Though Alexei was sixteen and Katya closer to thirty, I wasn't surprised he'd fallen head over heels. She was nothing like the aristocratic daughters who simpered after him, throwing their gloves at his feet in the hopes he'd return them.

Katya was blunt and opinionated, already popular amongst the *intelligentsiya* of St. Petersburg. She gave readings at salons where poets, artists, and musicians mingled with liberal elites.

Sylvie Buxhoeveden told me Katya's poetry was like a riddle you thought you understood, until the final line reversed everything you knew.

I wished I could hear it. Alexei and I begged her to read us a poem. Katya said she only performed at midnight, and only when very drunk.

She took a position with the liberal magazine *Vestnik Evropy*. Her job was mostly typesetting, but she could submit articles for publication.

Sylvie said to me. "I've seen her drinking with the Narodniks. If she tries to publish some revolutionary nonsense, even being the sister of the Holy Devil won't save her."

Sylvie had reverted to using one of Rasputin's less-savory monikers.

As Rasputin's wealth and prestige increased, so did the backlash against him. The rumors of his late-night exploits grew ever more depraved. Illegal newspapers published caricatures of Rasputin as a puppet-master, manipulating the doll-sized avatars of my parents, cavorting in the nursery with my sisters and me in nightgowns.

They wrote that his penis was the size of a stallion's, that he used it to bewitch my mother.

Papa was angrier than I'd ever seen him. He had the student presses burned at the St. Petersburg university, believing the poorly-printed fliers had come from them.

I had a different theory.

Yaro Vyachevslav had taken over the Duma just as Damien warned, pushing out my father's appointee. Every law the parliament passed seemed specifically designed to undermine my father, to cut the legs out from the under the war effort while Yaro publicly criticized our failures on the battlefield.

The people hated the war, and they hated every ruble spent on it.

But they also hated when we lost.

The illegal papers parroted Yaro's criticisms of my father so closely that I suspected that he might have written the headlines himself.

Even if I could prove it, the Vyachevslavs had made themselves near-impossible to dislodge. Yaro pulled the strings of parliament, while Vasta took control of two of the largest munitions factories in St. Petersburg.

They were connected to all the merchant families, and were nearly as rich as the Yusupovs.

I made a prickly enemy the day of my exhibition. Who was clearly holding a grudge.

chapter 20
REMINDERS OF HOME

DAMIEN

I wondered if killing would feel strange, after eight years away.

It felt the same as always. Which is, incredibly momentous and shockingly trivial, both at the same time.

I didn't enjoy death and bloodshed. Didn't like causing pain.

Some warriors loved it. For some, it was the entire reason.

For me, it simply happened to be what I was good at.

Nursed in a Cossack horde, son of the Ataman, I was trained to kill, raised to do it.

But it went so much deeper than that. I killed my own mother while still in the womb. And not from any of the usual mishaps of pregnancy, the tearing of birth or placentas in the wrong places. No, I killed her just from the brush of my foot against her belly, over and over again. Pressed for longer and longer periods as I grew cramped and confined.

My father wanted to cut me out. She wouldn't let him.

You don't ask your father if he regrets a choice. You just spend every day trying to make him not regret it.

I'd done a pretty shit job of that.

So while I'd spent every single day for eight years wishing I could see my father again, hear his voice, ask him a question in person, feel his hand on my shoulder ... I was dreading it, too.

I couldn't hide how I'd changed.

It's impossible not to capture some of the manners, the speech of the people around you. It clings to you like dust. And I'd been deep in the desert.

My father was so himself that I saw him across a crowd of men, just from the shape of his shoulders.

When he turned, I saw his face had changed.

He was older.

I knew it would happen, yet it hit me like a punch.

Years in the steppes are hard. Each month that passes puts a mark on you.

I'd missed so many marks.

We would have worn them together.

That's what tore me apart, all at once, all in that moment. Realizing that we'd parted paths, I was no longer his mirror.

Now I reflected his enemy back at him.

My boots, my rifle, the fucking way I stood, had all been shaped by the academy. I knew it and couldn't do a damn thing about it.

I dreaded that awful moment when he stood apart from me, appraising me like a stranger.

But it never came.

He saw my face and he put his arms around me.

He felt what I felt, and I didn't have to hide my face from him when we pulled apart. He was my father still.

"Gods, they fed you at least, didn't they? I knew you'd be taller than me."

"It's that old Rusky stick up the ass, Papa. They make you stand so tall, it stretches you."

"Well, we know what they're like, don't we? That was never the surprise."

What was the surprise, then?

Maybe the surprise was us. We swore it was death or freedom. Then the Romanovs offered a third choice.

Ten years of military service. Each and every man. It wasn't death, but we gave away our life.

My father signed his own contract. Ten more years—because of me.

He was taking his division of Cossacks to Dubno to join the Rusyan 3rd Army. I was headed to Gumbinnen to join the 1st. We only had a few days together in Riga.

My mother's elder brothers were there, and also Jacov Orlov, who was one of my father's *starshyna,* his most senior officers.

We sat and shared a pot of *salamakha* while they caught me up on what I'd missed at home—who'd been married, who had children, who'd been elected judge or scribe at the last Cossack Circle, and who had gone to join our ancestors in the celestial plains.

I slept in their tent that smelled so painfully of home from the pitch we used to seal the canvas, and the deeply-impregnated scent of our horses, which breed with the wild horses of the steppes and can run faster and further than the highest-bred Arabian or even the mustangs of the American west.

We parted ways, clasping each other on the shoulder, knowing we'd meet again soon if our armies converged.

I arrived at Gumbinnen to find a friend waiting for me. Nikolasha had sent Hercules ahead. In fact, he gifted me the horse before I left.

Nikolasha had been generous to me. While acting as my captor and head indoctrinator of Romanov interests.

I wondered if traveling away from the heart of their power would weaken my pull to them.

Nikolasha, Dimitri, Felix ... I'd considered them friends.

And of course ... Anastasia.

I thought of her more than any of them. More than I wanted to. More than I dreaded I might ...

Was it fucked to like my captors? To care about them, even?

Or was it only evidence of how poisoned my mind had become, steeped in the beliefs of the enemy ...

I wasn't foolish enough to think that I remained rational at all times, iron-hard in my integrity and resolve. I was a boy, alone and far from home. I needed a friend so badly.

And yet, and yet, and yet ...

I wanted a letter from Anastasia as much as ever. I wanted to know what she'd been doing, thinking, planning in the weeks since I left.

I wanted it worse once the fighting started.

I'd been to war against neighboring tribes, and then against the Imperial Army.

This was nothing like that.

The battlefields I knew had been a melee of guns, sabres, cannons, and abilities. Fireballs hurled by pyromancers, electric bolts from those that could draw charge from the atmosphere, and sometimes your own horse going mad beneath you as some animal whisperer made a noise that told the chargers they all had beetles burrowing in their ears.

Technology was beginning to surpass magic.

Rusya had been trying to modernize after the disasters of the Japanese war. We soon learned how paltry our efforts had been compared to the day-and-night operation of the German war machine. We had cannons; the Germans had tanks.

We attacked the Germans in East Prussia from the south and east simultaneously. Underestimating how quickly the Tsar could send his troops, the Germans only sent a single army to the Rusyan border, mostly composed of reservists and garrison troops.

We had the superior numbers, moving both the 1st and 2nd armies into position. And at first, we brutalized the German 8th. Our units were disciplined and well-coordinated, orders passed almost instantly via radio. The Cossack cavalry rode like reapers through the German infantry.

The 3rd Brigade from St. Petersburg came to join the Rusyan 1st. Captain Rykowski was now Major Rykowski. Krudener and another guardsman by the name of Chornyl rode beside me. The way they wore their uniforms and sat their horses was so like my uncles and father that I felt at home on the field once more.

But then, the Germans began to anticipate our movements. They'd suddenly change course, right when we'd been about to encircle them. They knew when we were about to change the thrust of our attack and shored up their defenses before we could arrive. And they knew precisely where to split our forces.

Our soldiers babbled that the Germans had new kinds of seers who could predict our generals' movements as soon as an idea came into their heads.

It wasn't magic at all. They'd been intercepting our radio transmissions. Our commanders hadn't known that was possible and hadn't even bothered to encrypt the messages.

We didn't learn the truth until the German 8th smashed our armies and forced us into retreat. The losses in the 1st army were heavy. The 2nd was almost entirely decimated. Out of a hundred and fifty thousand men, less than ten thousand survived.

The commander of the 2nd, Samsonov, shot himself dead in apology to the Tsar. It didn't bring back his soldiers.

After nearly eradicating the 2nd army, the Germans turned on the 1st. They forced us back against the Masurian Lakes. Bodies piled up on the shore, the waves rolling the corpses against the back hooves of our horses.

I was shot in the arm. I felt it happen, but hardly had time to look before a fireball the size of a barrel soared past Hercules' nose. It landed on Krudener's back, wrapping around him like an amoeba. He screamed as his whole body flamed.

A bullet ripped off the edge of the epaulet on my left shoulder. Another nicked my ear.

I shot back, targeting German officers, noting the stars on their breasts and shooting an inch to the left. I got six before a German dragoon charged me. His horse's shoulder was aimed at Hercules' side, intending to bowl us both over so I'd be crushed beneath the stallion and drowned in the lake.

Hercules had been a battle horse as long as any on the field. He saw the flicker of motion and turned, already rearing. He checked the charge but left his own neck vulnerable. The dragoon tried to cut his head off with a sideways swipe. I slammed my saber upward into his. The German got his arm around my neck and we both went down between the churning hooves.

I never wore gloves in battle.

My bare hands closed around his throat. All the fight drained out of him. We hit the ground and rolled into the water, his dead face glaring down at me, gray as stone, bleeding from the eyes and nose. I threw him off me.

A froth of filthy lake water rushed over my shoulders, red and stinking of iron.

I heard a crack overhead so loud I thought it was another onslaught of artillery. A fork of lightning streaked down into the lake, jagged with greenish light. Another boom, defeating and immediate, no pause between, then the rain poured down.

We probably would have met the same fate as the 2nd army if the storm hadn't blown in. In the darkness, in the wind and howling rain, we broke through the German flank and retreated. Practically fled.

Major Rykowski made me go to the infirmary. The medic dug the ball out with a penknife and poured vodka in the hole, which I could have done myself. At least his bandages were cleaner than my linens.

When I returned to the tent I shared with Chornyl, I had to tell him what had happened to Krudener. Chornyl had a nasty cut down his back and was missing the end of his pinky finger. That was better than most of the men who staggered back.

That night, the Cossacks drank and sang together as we did after every battle.

We toasted Krudener and threw his coat on the fire so the cinders could rise up to the stars.

It should have been his body or at least a lock of his hair. Because of the retreat, we could retrieve neither.

I stumbled back to the tent low and drunk. When I'd killed the German with my hands, I'd felt his emotions flow into me, and some of his memories, too.

What he felt as he died was regret.

He thought of a girl he liked back home. I saw her face: blue eyes, dark hair, a gap in her teeth. I didn't know the story, only the feeling—longing, longing, for what had never happened between them. What could never happen now.

I saw what he saw as I drained the life from his body: my own face reflected back at me. Snarling, furious, scarred down the eye. The face of a devil.

Then I saw a hundred flashes of everyone I'd ever touched by accident, or even brushed their skin—the winces, pain, sickness, drawing back, pulling away—the look of anyone I loved when I got too close.

Success on the battlefield reminded me what I was good at, and what I'd never be able to do.

Animals in traps die of many things ... sometimes madness or despair.

I ducked inside the tent and saw a letter lying on my pillow.

It was dirty on one side with the stamp of a boot-mark. Someone had dropped it, trod on it, and picked it up again. Yet it arrived, by one of those ironies of fate where a scrap of paper can make it through a war-zone while men are cut down all around.

I knew Anastasia's writing, thin and fine as a lady's, messy as a man's, slanting forward.

The writing made me think of the way she ran, one hand crushing a hat against her head if she'd been forced to wear one, other yanking up her skirts, legs churning away beneath. She always ran flat out, looking as if she'd trip any moment. But she wasn't as clumsy as she looked.

Sometimes she was almost graceful—dancing or riding. Anytime she moved in tandem with Artemis, arms reaching upward like wings.

I saw her red hair against a blue sky, clear as I've ever seen anything. And my heart lifted.

I hadn't even opened the letter. That was all from the slant of the way she wrote my name.

I heard her voice in my head as I read:

I got your note. It was kind. You wanted to spare my feelings—while yours must have been a hundred times worse.

I hope they were high as the heavens when you saw your father.

I only met him once, if you can call that meeting. But everything good I know of him is everything good in you. I don't think he'll notice the accent—you still say lots of things the Cossack way.

I have once or twice myself. Rusyans don't have a word for "thirsty," but Cossacks do. Remember when you told me that? When you learn another language, you see what ideas have been captured and named that you never thought of at all.

It's funny. Sometimes it was weeks or even months between us meeting. But it's different when you know you can, you might. This feels heavier and also empty at the same time. What a riddle. Maybe you can explain it to me. I always love to hear what you think, even when it drives me crazy.

Stay alive, please.

I've never asked you for anything before. So I may as well start with the hardest and most important thing.

—A

It was her, completely her: warm, teasing, playful, and honest.

What it made me feel was real.

And as much as ever, I couldn't hate her. No matter what I had to do that day.

262

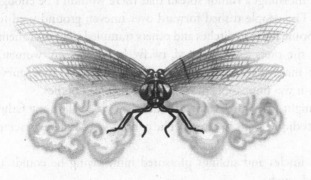

chapter 21
A THIEF IN THE MIND

ANASTASIA

After we lost the nearly the entirety of the 1st and 2nd armies, the mood in St. Petersburg turned dark.

The streets were quiet. The people were hungry and had no money for pubs or markets. They gathered together in houses, in basements. And talked.

The Germans had massed at our borders, but because we crossed into German lands to fight them, they pretended the war was forced upon them. That was what they trumpeted, and some of our own people believed them.

Illegal newspapers sprouted up faster than we could crush them. They wrote articles they never would have dared publish in the past: calling my father Nicholas the Bloodstained, blaming him for the failure of the crops and for the war.

That nickname came to him at his coronation.

The day started bright with promise. Mama and Papa planned to give every citizen that attended a commemorative cup stuffed with sausage and pretzel and candy and gold coins.

The people were so excited that they packed the Khodynka Field the night before, wanting to secure their place in line.

In the morning, a rumor spread that there wouldn't be enough cups for everyone. The people rushed forward over uneven ground used for military exercises. Some fell into ditches and others trampled right over them.

When the press finally cleared, twelve hundred men, women, and children were mashed into torn-up grass and earth. Or, they guessed twelve hundred—it was impossible to separate the mangled bodies.

That night, the ambassador of France threw a ball in my father's honor. My parents didn't want to attend. The corpses were still being scraped off the field.

Papa's uncles and siblings pressured him, saying he couldn't afford to offend the French.

My father was young. His father had died only weeks before. He'd been Tsar for a day.

He went to the ball. The rage of the people of St. Petersburg far surpassed anything the French might have felt. They adored Grandma Minnie, who built them schools and hospitals. They respected my Grandfather Alexander, though he was stern and conservative. An autocrat can be hard, as long as he's consistent.

They didn't trust my father.

What the people wanted above all was to feel safe. Papa let them down the first day of his rule. "Nicholas the Bloodstained"—stained with the blood of his own people.

The worst part of being a royal is when your best intentions end in ruin.

Now the papers printed that loathed name with impunity because they could. Too many of our soldiers had been rushed by train to defend the borders. Only a skeleton crew remained to police the city.

My parents had, at least, learned from the backlash to the costume ball. There were no more balls or parties held in St. Petersburg. Even our birthdays were celebrated with nothing more than cake and kisses.

Tatiana had returned from Denmark at last.

Ollie had not, because at last the impossible had occurred: she met someone she liked.

Not Crown Prince Christian, which Xenia would have loved, but his cousin Prince Axel. While Ollie hadn't fully admitted to romantic interest in Axel, her letters were so full of praise that Papa gladly agreed to extend her stay another few months.

Ollie wrote that Axel was splendidly athletic, and had even beaten her twice in tennis, which no one had ever managed before. He loved to race cars and was teaching Ollie to drive.

Tatiana came home taller and more beautiful than ever, so queenly that I hardly dared hug her. She hugged me back, harder than I expected.

"You'd love the Danish court, Anastasia. It's full of artists and philosophers. There's no stuffy rules about precedent like here, or at least, not nearly as much. People talk about whatever they like. They're all brilliant, not just there because their grandfather's grandfather kissed the top of the head of our grandfather's grandfather."

I laughed. I'd never heard Tatiana criticize the Rusyan court before.

"The Danes study magic so much more than we do. It's almost all they learn in school."

I looked at her, wondering if she suspected what I'd been up to with Rasputin.

While my parents were more distracted than ever, it was difficult to conceal from my siblings that I often disappeared for hours at a time. Nor could I hide the fact that my magic was improving. Drastically.

The last time Alexei chucked a slipper at my head, it was child's play to stop time long enough to pluck it out of the air an inch from my face.

Worse, I was fairly certain Tatiana had seen me practicing pyromancy out in the garden.

My sister's cool gray gaze gave nothing away. She was as skilled as Rasputin at sealing her mind when I most wanted to peek inside it.

"I'm jealous," I said. "Tell me everything."

As much as I enjoyed her stories, what made me feel that our hearts were aligned at last was when she grabbed my wrist and whispered, "What's happened to Alexei?"

He'd just passed us in the hallway, already wearing his pajamas. No one could miss how thin and pale he'd grown, and how deeply shadowed his face had become.

No one could miss it but my parents. I'd tried to talk to both my father and my mother. Each in their own way flatly denied that anything could be wrong.

"He hasn't had a bleed in six years and three months," Papa said, with a precision that pained me.

Mama said, "He never cries, he never tells me he's in pain."

"He never says anything he feels anymore," I retorted.

Mama rested her hand on my hair in a way that was sympathetic, but also made me feel like a puppy being patted on the head.

"He's a young man. It's supposed to be me who expects him to stay a boy forever."

Alexei barely nodded to us as he passed. His hug for Tatiana when she arrived home had been limp, like his arms touched nothing at all.

I said, "I don't know what's wrong with him. But something is."

Tatiana gazed after Alexei, her mouth a thin line.

"I agree."

THE ONE PERSON I hadn't asked about Alexei was Rasputin.

One afternoon, I abruptly said, "Would you ever teach me how to heal my brother?"

Rasputin had been showing me how to powder an herb that worked as an abortifacient.

He straightened, his eerie blue eyes looking into mine.

"I can't teach you. Only I can do what Alexei requires."

"How do you know? You haven't shown me the magic."

"This magic isn't like other magic. It exacts a heavy toll. You've probably noticed."

"From you?"

He shook his head slowly. "From Alexei."

I mashed my pestle into the herb. "What's happening to him? How can we stop it?"

Rasputin shook his head. "That's the result of the treatment. If I stop, his disease will come back. He must bear the price to be healed."

He turned back to his mortar, grinding the root into a powder finer than talc.

"It won't kill him," he added, almost as an afterthought.

It was killing part of him, though. I could see it.

The next time Rasputin and I battled mind to mind, I tried to steal the knowledge of how he treated Alexei. I tunneled through memories of my brother as Rasputin viewed him, from a slight bird's eye view as Rasputin was so much taller than me.

Memories of Alexei sitting across the kitchen table from Katya, refilling her glass. Memories of Alexei in his room, pale and sweating. Laying back against his pillow, stretching out his wrist to have his pulse taken …

I'd just snatched that image when Rasputin found me in his mind. I tried to race through his thoughts, zipping here and there like a dragonfly, too quick for him to follow.

Not fast enough.

When he found me, he grabbed me around the body with two gargantuan fingers and ripped the wings from my back with so much violence that I screamed as my eyes flew open, the shriek pulsing back at me, bouncing off the jars on the shelves and the mirrors on the walls and the untidy stacks of books.

Real pain had wrenched through my shoulder blades as the imaginary wings tore free. I'd felt it. I could feel it still, throbbing like a lash.

Rasputin smiled at me, cool satisfaction in his eyes.

"Be wary, as a thief in another's mind. Had I put one of those fingers though your eye, you might not find yourself so untouched in the real world. The mind is a powerful thing. If you believe you're blind ... you might be."

My lips were dry. I had to lick them before I could speak.

"How merciful of you."

"I *am* merciful." Rasputin's voice was low, his eyes fixed on mine. "Because I'm your friend. I'm warning you what another sorcerer might do if you encroach on his mind."

He said he was my friend, and he said he'd been merciful. But beneath the soft tone and smooth expression, I sensed an uglier emotion. Anger that I'd managed to snatch even that glimpse of Alexei's sickroom from his mind.

Rasputin didn't like when I surprised him.

The encounter bothered me. A few days later, I realized why.

I was down by the mews, training with Artemis. She didn't actually need training, she was the most lethal killer I'd ever beheld. I couldn't remember the last time she dove and rose with empty talons.

We trained anyway because she liked the exercise and I liked to visit her. I went most mornings, unless the weather so vile I knew she wouldn't want to come out. Then I brought her a hot toddy in the afternoon.

Farad also checked on her every day. He cleaned the mews and oiled her jesses and did anything for her that I hadn't already done, which was usually nothing but an extra scratch at the base of her neck. Farad was the only other person Artemis permitted to touch her, and very occasionally, his nephew Hamza.

Hamza had grown ridiculously tall, like a dog that was supposed to be a different breed. He towered over both Farad and me, though it never felt like he was towering. He was that rare sort of man that doesn't use his size to intimidate. His movements were slow and predictable, his touch gentle as he helped his uncle tend to our menagerie.

On that particular day, both Hamza and Farad looked exhausted. They'd been up all night helping a mare to foal. The mare was a favorite of my father's. She'd delivered some of the finest horses in his stable, and he'd had her bred once more at great expense. The foal was turned wrong in the womb, only one hoof proceeding outward, the other stuck inside.

Farad had tried again and again to reach inside and turn the foal, but the mare was in pain, the passage swollen, the foal wedged.

As he relayed the story to me, I could see his concern, his compassion for the horses that wouldn't have been any greater had there been two human lives in the balance.

"I thought it was impossible," He passed a hand over his face, shaking his head. "I thought we'd have to tear the foal apart to save the mare, or cut the mare open to spare the foal. But Hamza wouldn't let me."

He smiled at his nephew, who'd brought tea for all of us to ward off the autumn chill, small clay mugs with no handles that radiated heat into our bare hands. Hamza had barely touched his own tea because he'd half fallen asleep on one of Farad's chairs, his chin nodding forward toward his chest, the thin chair legs bowing out beneath his slumping weight.

Farad said, "He put a hand on my shoulder and pulled me aside like I was the student. Then he reached in and got the foal turned right. It was born less than ten minutes later. You can see it tottering around in the stable if you want to visit—a little black colt with a star on its forehead, perfect as you could hope."

I laughed at the look of Hamza's massive hands curled on his lap.

"He's more nimble than you, Farad—with those paws?"

"He's the better horseman all around."

"Better than you?"

"I'm his mentor," Farad said. "That's the point."

He meant it. He felt only pride in his nephew, no jealousy, no resentment.

That nagged at me, until I puzzled over the two occurrences long enough to see the divergence.

I was sitting in the window seat of the grand library, watching a white sleet rain break on the lawn. Off to the northwest stood Rasputin's tower like a skeletal finger pointing to the sky.

I thought of all the lessons I'd had within those walls. I'd never proceeded past the parlor. Never seen his bedroom or his library.

Each lesson was different, but in one respect, always the same: for all that

Rasputin had taught me, I didn't believe for a second that he'd ever want me to surpass him in magic.

I couldn't imagine him happy that I'd become more powerful or more talented than him. In anything.

And if that was truly a requirement of a mentor, as Farad had said ... then perhaps Rasputin wasn't actually my mentor.

And if he wasn't my mentor ... then what was he?

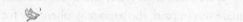

chapter 22

A THIEF IN THE TOWER

I t's a funny thing to finally become friends with your sister when you're adults.

I'd always loved Tatiana, but loving someone and feeling close to them aren't exactly the same thing.

Alexei was my partner in crime, Maria my roommate and confidante, Ollie a force of nature blazing new trails I sometimes liked to follow. Tatiana was our parents' favorite, the best behaved, the most beautiful, the most competitive.

I wasn't jealous of her exactly, but we felt like two different breeds: one perfect and precise, one messy, noisy, and barely domesticated. It was a bit like housing a prize Persian with an alley cat.

We'd never had anything in common before, shared only between the two of us.

Now we had two things.

The first was forced on me against my will.

Tatiana had been home less than a month when she ambushed me on my way out through the back garden door.

"Where are you off to?"

"Just ... thought I'd take a walk on the grounds."

"Perfect," she said. "I'll join you."

That was less than convenient, as I was supposed to be meeting Rasputin in the tower to continue our lesson on alchemy.

"Actually, I'm going to see Artemis first."

Tatiana had never enjoyed the elephant pavilion, Artemis' mews, or the stables, which were scrubbed and swept out regularly, but never entirely absent of droppings or animal smells.

"Even better. It's been forever since I visited Artemis."

Her cool gray gaze fixed on me in a way I knew only too well. She had her thumb on a tender spot and was going to keep pressing until I cried uncle.

"You hate coming to the mews."

"True … I thought you might take a detour on the way."

A frog seemed to be hopping around in my belly.

"What made you think that?"

"Oh … just something I heard this morning."

Damnit.

I'd passed Rasputin outside the Portrait Hall, and confirmed the time of our meeting in six quick words exchanged in an undertone. No doubt Tatiana caught every one of them.

"What are you seeing the monk for?"

I considered lying, but if I knew my sister at all, she already suspected the answer. And she was perfectly capable of reporting to my parents.

I decided to give as little of the truth as possible.

"He's been teaching me a few things. About astronomy and plants that grow locally, that sort of thing."

"And magic."

She might only have been guessing, with her usual obnoxious accuracy.

"A little magic," I admitted. Then, throwing all dignity aside I begged, "Please don't tell, it's the only thing I've ever been good at."

Tatiana bit down on her lower lip, drawing it into her mouth. If there was anything she could understand, it was the joy of doing something well.

She surprised me.

"I want to learn, too."

I was so unprepared that I made little fish-mouth movements, not sure how to respond.

"Our parents—"

"Won't know," Tatiana responded, smoothly.

"And Rasputin—"

"I want *you* to teach me. Whatever he shows you, I want you to show me after."

A reasonable request with far too much leverage for me to refuse.

"I'll try. But I don't know what I'll be able to teach you. Rasputin said I have a kind of ... affinity for magic. He's the same. If we see a demonstration, we can replicate it, sometimes. Honestly, I can't do most of what he shows me."

"Neither could I, in Denmark," said Tatiana. "I don't care. I want to learn, whether I can actually do the magic or not."

Her eyes burned, a faint pink flush coming into her cheeks.

I realized someone had already been teaching Tatiana, probably Juliana Jorgensen. Now she was hungry for more.

That's what bonded us at first—I would visit Rasputin in the tower, then repeat whatever I'd learned to Tatiana. Sometimes I'd even sneak her bits of the herbs or crystals we were studying so she could handle the materials herself.

Tatiana wasn't able to replicate any new kinds of magic. But she continued to develop the skills she already possessed, boosted at times by the supplies I stole for her. Once I smuggled away a turnip-like root that tasted of ginger that was supposed to amplify hearing. When I'd eaten a little, a chorus of birdsong swelled outside the window. I heard a tiny, trundling sound that turned out to be a minuscule beetle scaling the spine of one of Rasputin's books.

When Tatiana ate the root, her hearing became so vivid that she swore she could see strains of music floating through the air as I played records on our gramophone. It wasn't practical, but she said it was most beautiful thing she'd ever experienced.

More fearsome was how her accuracy improved as she continued to hone her marksmanship. She brought her arrows out when I trained with Artemis. I loosed the lures and Tatiana and Artemis competed to see who could bring down the targets the fastest.

It was the only time I saw either of them struggle to win against an equal opponent. Tatiana enjoyed it so much that she actually visited Artemis inside her mews on rainy days, and Artemis said Tatiana was *Pretty, for a human,* which she'd certainly never said about me.

The second point on which Tatiana and I bonded was our resolution to do something about Alexei. The agreement was reached within weeks of Tatiana arriving home. She observed our brother with fresh eyes, the eyes of someone who'd been away, who could see the changes clearly. What we could do to help him was less clear.

I'd relayed all that Rasputin told me, which was little and vague.

Tatiana had never liked Rasputin as much as Ollie and Maria. Or me, for that matter.

When she confessed the reason, I couldn't help laughing.

"I've never overheard him say anything he wouldn't want me to hear."

"How could that possibly make you dislike him?"

"Because," Tatiana said gravely, "no one's that careful. Unless they have something to hide."

Instead of pressing Rasputin for more information, Tatiana turned where she always turned: the library.

There were three in Alexander Palace, the largest of which contained one of the finest collections of leather-bound books in all of Rusya. Tatiana had already combed through the shelves of medical texts in the days when we still hoped to find something the endless procession of doctors that visited Alexei had missed.

Now we read through them all again, or at least Tatiana did. I threw aside *Maximow's Treatise on Hematopoiesis,* having only understood one word in ten.

"What if it's not a physical disease at all?" I said. "What if it's more of ... a curse?"

Tatiana looked up at me, colored pencils thrust in her hair so she could mark the textbooks in her own rainbow code.

"How could that be? The bleeding disease is heritable. You can see it running through the royal families."

"Well ... we've got a trail of enemies as long as our ancestors. If you wanted to curse a royal ... what better way to do it than to kill their male heirs for centuries to come?"

"Hm," Tatiana said.

I thought she'd shoot down my far-fetched idea. Instead, she tapped her index finger against the edge of her jaw.

"Where could we read about something like that?"

"In ... a guide to supernatural ailments?"

"Does that exist?"

I sighed. "Probably not here."

We scoured all three libraries top to bottom, lugging ladders over to the highest and deepest shelves, the oldest and dustiest books. They contained almost no information on magic.

I should have known better than to believe Mama would allow anything occult inside the palace. She'd even thrown away Papa's romantic novels before Maria could get her hands on them.

"It was stupid to think we might have a sorcerer's library tucked away," I said to Tatiana.

"*We* don't," she mused. "But you know someone who does."

BREAKING into Rasputin's tower posed several risks, the greatest being that if he caught me, I'd lose him as a teacher.

On the other hand, Alexei barely even spoke to us anymore. I'd even seen him refuse to pet his spaniel Joy when she thrust her nose into his palm, which was unheard of—Alexei had always loved dogs more than people.

What really shook me was when he told Mama that Andrei Derevneko might as well be assigned to a ship again.

"I'm too old for a nanny."

As if that's all Andrei ever was.

Andrei retired to a cottage by the docks instead, where he could visit his old friends easily.

No matter what Rasputin might say, no matter how Alexei's body walked around in health, his soul was dying inside him.

The only thing that seemed to spark interest anymore was Katya. His crush on her continued, a low fire on a bed of embers that otherwise sat cold.

He'd attended two musical salons and a literary party—something that in the past he'd have jumped out a two-story window to avoid—simply to see her.

It was ridiculous, of course. She was twice his age and a commoner to boot.

Perhaps Alexei hoped to take her as a mistress.

Papa had his little ballerina before he married Mama. We all knew that story because Ollie found the "anonymous" letters she sent to Mama after Papa sent her packing.

It was as expected of the males of royal houses to sow their oats prior to marriage as it was of the females to stay pure and virginal. Since it takes two to hoe a row, I wasn't sure how that was supposed to work.

I knew Irina had already been "romantic" with Felix, and I suspected Ollie had enjoyed a fling or two with her favorite dance partners.

Sometimes I woke sweating from dreams where Damien took off his gloves and slipped his bare hands under my clothes ...

But that was even more impossible. Just kissing him on the cheek had bruised my lips.

"What are you thinking about?" Tatiana demanded. "Your face is all red."

"Just ... hoping we don't get caught."

Liar, Artemis squawked from my arm.

She was coming along as lookout so Tatiana could go inside with me.

"And what did *she* say?" Tatiana cast a curious glance at Artemis.

"She said I'm her favorite person in the world and she never gets tired of spending time with me."

Liar, liar, liar!

Artemis spread her wings in fury, buffeting the side of my face. She soared ahead, circling around Rasputin's tower.

Tatiana laughed.

"Is she still going to help us?"

"Probably."

It was early evening. We'd watched Rasputin depart around dinnertime, his long black coat flowing behind him, head uncovered even though the clouds were heavy and low, threatening rain.

"We'd better hurry." Tatiana quickened her pace across the lawn. "If it starts to pour, we'll leave wet footprints inside."

Rasputin's front door with its lion's head knocker was bolted. Expecting that, we made for the back of the tower where ivy grew up a lattice leaning against the wall like a ladder. I stripped off my shoes and socks so I could poke my bare toes through the holes.

"Are you sure that's safe?" Tatiana gazed upward.

"I don't know any other way to get in."

The latch on the fourth-floor window had been broken since before I was born.

"You don't have to climb up," I assured her. "I'll let you in."

I gripped the lattice, shoving my fingers through the small, circular holes. The ivy leaves had turned the color of rust, the vines desiccating to twigs, stabbing at my knees as I began to climb.

The first ten or twenty feet weren't so bad. It was only once I passed the third row of windows, glanced down at Tatiana, and saw how small and distant her face had become, that my stomach gave a slow roll.

Artemis floated past me, the tips of her feathers brushing my arm.

You're so slow ...

"Because I don't have any wings," I grunted.

I feel sorry for you, Artemis said airily.

By the time I reached the fourth-floor window and tried to wedge it up while clinging to the lattice one-handed, I was feeling just as jealous of Artemis as she could have wished. She soared past me in lazy loops.

"Show off."

She gave the soft chirp that was her version of a laugh.

Careful ... I certainly can't catch you if you fall.

The window inched upward with an ugly screeching sound. Had Rasputin been home, he would have heard it.

I pushed my head in, bent double over the sill, and toppled inside.

I switched on a flashlight I'd pilfered from Alexei, which was temperamental and really did flicker and flash like the last gutters of a candle. Shadows jumped about like living things, making my heart spring up in my throat. Though I'd watched Rasputin leave myself, I still startled at each looming shape.

I'd entered through his dressing room. His clothes hung in the wardrobe, a row of black woolen robes that were so quintessentially Rasputin that it almost looked like he'd taken off his own skin and hung it up, limp and interchangeable.

I'd stood inside my mother's dressing room many times, and my father's. It was the closest thing to standing inside the circle of someone's arms, inhaling their scent. My mother's clothes smelled of her White Rose perfume, mixed with ambergris soap. Papa's clothes smelled of tobacco, ink, and—when he'd been visiting the troops—gunpowder.

Rasputin's dressing room had almost no scent at all.

I'd noticed that during our lessons—I could smell the pungent aromas of his herbs and powders, the dusty books on his shelves, and sometimes even the animal musk of Bat flapping around in his cage, but never Rasputin himself.

The double doors to the bedroom stood open. I'd longed to see these upper levels for months now, yet I hesitated in the doorway, remembering what happened the last time Rasputin caught me sneaking around where I didn't belong.

Be wary, as a thief in another's mind ...

I gave Alexei's flashlight a hard shake and stepped inside Rasputin's bedroom.

It was so cold that I almost expected my breath to rise in a frost before my face. The grate was empty, no fire burning, the ashes scattered and old. No rugs covered the floor. My bare feet padded across uneven boards that creaked and groaned. Heavy drapes covered the windows floor to ceiling, no ties to pull them back.

No pictures hung on the walls. When the court artist lived here, his room had been filled with colorful, half-finished canvases. I'd hoped Rasputin might at least have photographs in frames like my mother's wall of portraits of all her children at various ages.

The only item of decoration was the bed itself. The mattress sat within a stone frame, the headboard carved like a pair of outspread wings. The wings were beautifully detailed, each feather distinct in the dove-gray granite. Yet the thought of laying down on that bed gave me a chill.

Next to the bed stood a low night table with books stacked on top. On the books, a small leather folio containing a portrait.

I opened the folio. The portrait was painted, not a photograph. I recognized the long, slender neck, the ivory skin as smooth as her white satin gown, the rosebud mouth tilted up at the edges, and the large, sad eyes. This was Rasputin's wife.

Her hair was parted in the center, clusters of curls framing her face, the rest pinned up. In her hand she held a sprig of flowers, which the artist had painted entirely black.

She was so beautiful that I held the portrait a long time, forgetting about Tatiana downstairs. She held me fixed in her gaze, this woman who was dead, but seemed to be calling to me from another place.

I slipped the portrait out of its folio. On the back were a few lines written in copperplate. I couldn't read the language, only the signature—*Natalya*.

The flashlight flickered and weakened, casting a silvery glow like moonlight across the stone angel wings. I almost expected to see a name carved across the headboard. This wasn't a bedroom—it was a mausoleum.

Spine tingling, I returned the portrait and hurried downstairs to let Tatiana inside.

She was shivering on the porch, arms wrapped tight around herself.

"What took you so long?" Tatiana stopped to lock the front door behind us.

"What are you doing that for?"

"In case he comes home early. If he finds the door unlocked, he'll know we're inside."

I led Tatiana through the kitchen, which was untidy with dirty stoneware stacked in the sink and several stained wine glasses scattered across the tabletop. A stamp of dark red lipstick marked one of the rims.

Tatiana nodded at the glass. "You wouldn't believe how the women at court whisper about him. Princess Lina went to see him for hysterical fits ... she said he had her lay down on a sofa and take deep breaths while he chanted and put his hands on her body. It made her climax so hard she passed out."

I laughed. "Did it solve the fits?"

Tatiana snorted. "As long as her husband allows the treatments to continue, I'm sure she'll be *very* well behaved."

We dissolved in giggles.

"That lipstick looks like Katya's," I remarked. "Have you met her?"

"I went to one of her readings last week"

"How was it?"

"Illuminating. Half the powerful men in St. Petersburg have suddenly become patrons of poetry."

"Including our brother."

"He's got his competition cut out for him—the Minister of Justice and the captain of the city garrison were practically laying at her feet."

I wondered if Katya had come to make up with her brother. The last time I saw her, she came bursting out the door as I was coming in, shouting back over her shoulder, "And I *don't* need you checking up on me about it!"

She'd stopped abruptly, flushed in the face. Then pushed past me and stalked out.

Rasputin looked flustered, which was unusual for him. He swept his hair back with one hand, walking a little too fast across the entryway to close the door behind me.

As the door slammed shut, something flashed at me from Rasputin's mind: dark berries on white snow. The image leaped out like monster from a closet, garish and terrifying, then disappeared in an instant.

I didn't understand what it meant, but I felt the mix of emotions that escaped him—guilt, misery, and even a little fear.

"Don't worry," I said to him, quickly. "Alexei and I get into it all the time. We're friends again by lunch."

Rasputin let out a sound that was part anger, part sigh. "She thinks she has nothing to learn from me."

I thought of the color in Katya's face, how high and tight her voice had gotten. "She probably just wants to impress you."

The lesson that followed was one of the best we ever had.

Rasputin sat next to me at the low table and set a stone plinth before us, heaped with kindling.

"Where does power come from, Anastasia?"

"Well ... " I said, slowly. "The nobles say power comes by birth. The priests say by prayer."

"And what does a sorcerer say?"

"Maybe ... by practice?"

Rasputin eyes locked on mine. "The sorcerer says ... power comes by any means necessary."

He was sitting so close that his breath stirred the hairs at the nape of my neck.

"Humans don't just *have* magic, Anastasia. We *are* magic, as much as a domovoi or a rusalka." He moved his fingers above the dry sticks, drawing shapes in the sudden curls of smoke. "It's our passions that power us ... our curiosity ... our ambition ... even our hate."

Flames shot up from the kindling, so high they almost burned his hand. Rasputin snuffed them with a flick of his fingers.

"There are no apathetic sorcerers." He smiled with those bloodless lips.

I thought I understood.

Rasputin piled fresh kindling on the plinth.

I looked at the sweet-smelling pile of cedar sticks. Instead of trying to channel the warmth of heat, the brightness of flame, the sting of smoke in the throat ... I thought of my rage when I realized Damien was being sent off to war. My anger at my father as I hammered at his door.

Flame swept across the sticks. It was easy. Almost frighteningly so.

My heart thudded in my chest.

"You're a natural," Rasputin said.

It was one of the only compliments he'd ever given me.

"Come *on!*" Tatiana tugged on my arm, pulling me toward the stairs.

We headed up to Rasputin's storeroom.

Tatiana gazed around, open-mouthed. "He's got everything in here ... ten times more than Juliana had."

She walked around, examining the books, the crystals, the various instruments. She put out her hand to touch an hourglass that contained no sand inside, only a pale, swirling fog distributed equally in the upper and lower bells.

"*Don't!*" I said sharply.

Tatiana drew back her hand.

"Why not? What does it do?"

"I have no idea. But I guarantee you, some of the things in here are dangerous."

Bat was asleep in his cage. Rasputin had never given any indication that he could talk to the tiny creature, but I was suspicious. Like Artemis, Bat seemed too clever for a normal animal.

"We'd better hurry up," Tatiana said.

"Right."

It was so easy to lose myself in this forbidden place. Rasputin didn't even let the maids in to clean. Snooping around in the tower felt very much like wandering around inside his head.

"You look down here, I'll check in the upstairs library," I said to Tatiana.

We only had one flashlight, so I left it with her after stealing a candle from Rasputin's kitchen. The candle was stubby and gave off a queer greenish glow. It seemed to cast a circle of light directly around me, while illuminating nothing beyond.

The topmost floor of the tower was the library. I hoped that's where Rasputin might store his most secret books.

I scaled the stairs to the highest floor, the peaked roof open to the rafters, shelves of books lining every wall. A padded seat filled the base of the single window, providing a stunning view of Alexander Park.

Most of the books on the shelves were those that had always been there through generations of Romanovs. Finding Rasputin's additions was easy—his books were older and in much worse condition, cracked along the spines, stained with smoke, swollen with moisture, speckled with mold. Some were missing their covers entirely, and others were bound in strange materials—exotic embroidered fabrics, embossed metals, and stretched, scaly skin.

Some bore only symbols on the covers, others no titles at all. A few were in Old Rusyan, others in languages I didn't recognize.

Even those I could read, I couldn't always understand. I flipped through the pages trying to decipher complicated diagrams, old-fashioned verbiage, and magical terms I'd never heard:

A Charme F'r Recov'ry Of Yond Which Wast Lost

Taketh the fing'r bone of the coystrill
Powd'r and lie on a sleeping byre of liquid m'rcury ...

I knew that "coystrill" was an old word for "thief" but the rest baffled me.

The more of Rasputin's books I searched through, the more discouraged I became. How could I know if any of the spells even worked, or if I could perform them?

Artemis rapped sharply on the window, startling me so badly I dropped an armful of books.

When I forced open the sash, the wind gusted so hard it almost knocked her off the sill.

Someone's coming!

"Rasputin?"

A woman.

I thought it must be Katya, but when I looked out the window, I saw the short, plump figure and pretty blonde head of Sylvie Buxhoeveden wrapped in a cloak, bent forward in battle against the wind.

I yanked down the sash and hurried downstairs to warn Tatiana.

"We've got to get out! Sylvie's coming."

Tatiana set down the books she was holding.

"What's she coming here for?"

"How should I know?"

"Well, she won't be able to get in," Tatiana said reasonably. "We should just wait for her to go away."

I hadn't finished going through the upstairs library any more than Tatiana had completed her search.

"Fine. We'll wait."

I crept halfway down the stairs, wondering if Sylvie would knock or call out. Knowing how she detested Rasputin, I couldn't imagine what she'd come to discuss. Ever since he read her future, she'd hardly managed to be civil to him, and only because she knew it would upset Mama to criticize him openly. Liza Taneeva was constantly singing Rasputin's praises in Sylvie's presence, amused by her rival's struggle to hold her tongue.

Sylvie's light rap sounded on the door. A moment later, a key scraped in the lock.

I sprinted upstairs.

"She's got a key!" I gasped to Tatiana.

"How in the hell did she get a key?"

"*Will you stop asking me questions I can't possibly know the answer to?*"

I was already shoving Tatiana into the storage cupboard. It reeked of dried mushrooms and herbs, and some nastier things that Rasputin kept in jars.

We were long past the time we could easily fit in a cabinet together. If it'd been Ollie instead of Tatiana, I wouldn't have gotten the doors closed at all. As it was, a substantial gap remained that Sylvie would surely notice if she looked in our direction.

The steps creaked beneath her feet.

A moment later, she entered the storeroom.

She looked around, curious and a little repulsed.

When Rasputin led the Sunday services, he gave a good approximation of a holy man. When you entered his tower, you were in the house of a sorcerer. Everything he owned was occult or arcane, not a single icon of a saint to be seen.

Like Tatiana, Sylvie was drawn to the wall of complicated instruments—solar models and astrological sextants, chemistry sets and clocks. Her eyes fell on the swirling smoke within the hourglass. She stepped forward, finger outstretched like Sleeping Beauty about to touch the spindle of a spinning wheel.

There was no one to warn her. She touched the lower bell. Where her finger met the glass, the smoke turned scarlet. The tinted swirls diffused throughout the top and bottom of the hourglass until all the smoke had turned an angry red.

Bat woke on his perch. He flapped his leathery wings, chattering angrily with all his tiny teeth on display.

Sylvie jolted, drawing back her hand.

"You nasty little thing!" she hissed at the bat, before hurrying out of the room.

"What's she here for?" Tatiana whispered to me.

I could hear Sylvie climbing higher on the spiraling staircase. We could hurry down and leave right now, but like Tatiana, I was consumed by this new mystery.

I slipped out of the cupboard, padding along quietly in my bare feet, placing my steps on the outside edges of the stairs so they wouldn't groan as loud.

Sylvie wouldn't have heard me anyway. She was rummaging around in Rasputin's bedroom, not being nearly as careful as me. I'd tried to set down the portrait of Rasputin's wife exactly as I'd found it. Sylvie rifled through Rasputin's desk and drawers, searching for something.

An interminable ten minutes later, she came rushing back down the stairs, clutching something in her hand. She reappeared so abruptly that I scarcely had time to duck back inside the storeroom. She hurried by, holding what I thought was a packet of letters.

The door closed downstairs.

Tatiana said, "Looks like she got what she came for."

"What do you think it was?"

She shrugged. "I'm sure we'll find out soon enough. Come on—we better finish up."

I'd barely made it back upstairs before thunder crashed like a cannon outside the window. A torrent of rain lashed the glass, so thick that I could no longer see the open lawn. Artemis whipped past, flung about by erratic gusts of wind.

I hoped she'd find shelter. Rasputin would likely stay out until the early hours of the morning, especially with the awful weather.

I spent another forty minutes scouring the shelves, pulling out any book I could decipher that looked the least bit helpful.

Eventually I had a collection with titles like:

> *Curses, Imprecations, and Maledictions*
> *Evil Eyes and Evil Spirits*
> *Hexes and Jinxes*
> *Demons, Succubi, and Creatures Most Foul*
> *Black Arts and F'rbidden Spells*
> *Maladies of Evil*

This time it was Tatiana who came bursting in.

"He's here!"

"What do you—"

"He just came in the front door, we've got to get out!"

She was already dragging me back downstairs to the fourth-floor. If Rasputin was already inside, there was only one way out.

I stuffed the books down the front of my dress, hoping that would protect them from the rain.

"Did you—"

"Yes, I've got mine," Tatiana gasped.

She was struggling with the window in the dressing room. We could hear Rasputin coming up the stairs, his thundering steps so rapid it was obvious he'd hurried home on purpose.

If he'd run right into the dressing room he would have caught us, but he stopped on the third floor where Bat was screeching, where the hourglass stood scarlet ...

The sash wailed as Tatiana shoved it up. I prayed Bat's noise, or the rattling of the rain against the windows, would drown it out.

Tatiana went gray in the face gazing down at the drop, but she hoisted her leg over the sill and began to climb down.

I followed after her.

The rain drenched me in seconds, the wind whipping leaves and twigs and bits of my own hair against my face. Tatiana couldn't get a good grip with her feet, the toes of her boots too large to fit through the holes in the trellis. Her feet slid out from under her and she was left clinging by her fingers until she could get purchase again.

I had to hold on one-handed to get the window down. I lost my grip and fell backward, grasping at the ivy, catching hold of one twisted vine that ripped away from the trellis and dropped me half a story before catching with a yank that felt like it would pull my arm out of its socket. I clung to the soaked wood, heart pounding, knees shaking.

"*Hurry!*" Tatiana hissed up at me.

Half-climbing, half-sliding, I made it to the ground. We sprinted off across the grass, clutching our hands against the books stuffed down the front of our dresses.

It was only when I was halfway back to the palace that I realized I was running in bare feet, my shoes and socks still abandoned at the base of the trellis.

"I've got to go back! If he finds my shoes, he'll recognize them."

"If you go back, he'll see you." Tatiana's hair was plastered against her face. "He might have already seen us running away if he looked out the right window."

At that moment, one of my shoes dropped on my head and bounced away across the grass. Artemis dropped the other and swooped down onto my arm.

Idiot.

"Thank you!" I snatched up the shoes.

I couldn't see him in the rain, she screeched, angry with herself.

"It's not your fault. And anyway, I thought you went back to the mews."

I wouldn't leave you.

"He knew we were there," Tatiana said.

"He knew *someone* was there."

"Was it the bat?"

"I think it was the hourglass."

We looked at each other, sick with the realization that in the world of magic, we understood nothing at all. How could we ever hope to help Alexei when we could hardly master party tricks?

As I ran back home through the rain, heart still wild inside me and throat burning, I pondered something else:

Why was I so terrified of being caught by Rasputin?

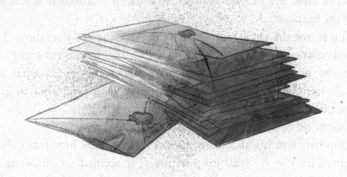

chapter 23

AN ACCUSATION

We didn't have to wait long to learn what Sylvie had stolen from Rasputin. She denounced him almost immediately.

She brought the letters to my parents, who called Rasputin into my father's study to answer the charges.

Tatiana and I were not invited to this meeting. We snuck into the passageway leading from the Mountain Room to Papa's fireplace, close enough that I didn't even need Tatiana's powers of hearing to follow all that passed.

We brought Maria with us, after giving her a twenty-second recap of our adventure in the White Tower. Maria had just returned from a shift with the Red Cross and was still wearing her nursing uniform. Her apron was stained with blood and pus, her stockings too.

"Couldn't you change clothes first?" Tatiana complained, wrinkling her nose in the cramped tunnel.

"I don't want to miss anything," Maria whispered back. "And hush or they'll hear us."

We'd missed the first part of the conversation, but it was clear Sylvie was accusing Rasputin of writing letters to foreign agents in some kind of secret code.

"It's not Romanian! It's not Hungarian! I took it to a translator and he says it's no language he recognizes at all."

I could only catch brief glimpses of the people in the room as they passed my field of view, eye pressed against the crack in the door that was also the back of the fireplace.

"This is not the usual rumors of sexual deviancy or liberalism. This is a serious accusation." I could hear in Papa's voice that he was frowning.

He was warning Sylvie. Asking her if she really meant what she was saying. It was one thing to smear a rival in the court, another to get them exiled or killed, which were the punishments for sedition.

Sylvie stood firm.

"Rasputin and his sister are spies. I didn't trust him from the day I met him. The way he read my fortune ... it seemed so innocent. But it ate at me. I knew he was lying to me when he said the words. You know that's my gift—I always know. But it seemed to fit so well with what I was seeing. With what I knew about myself. But I knew, I knew, he was deceiving me in some way. And I felt it, I heard it so often when he would speak to the rest of you. Nothing he said was wrong— in fact, what he predicted always came to pass. Even the most outrageous claims about Alexei. Believe me, I understand why you protect him ..."

She trailed off like she'd confused herself.

I expected to see spite on her face as she passed the fireplace. What I actually saw was fear.

Sylvie's ability was to know when someone was lying. She was an invaluable resource to my parents—her gift had been tested many times.

"But you never actually *caught* him in a lie," Papa said.

"No!" She paced past the crack, eyes downcast in frustration. "Everything he said was true. Yet there was deceit in every word!"

I could picture the silent communication passing between my parents: *She's not making any sense.*

"I broke into his tower. I admit that. And I found these letters. I knew they would be there, look at the stamps—look how many countries he writes to. In code! You can't believe there's an innocent explanation—*any* explanation but the obvious!"

Mama ventured, "He writes to neighboring countries, not specifically to our enemies. Some of these are our closest allies."

"Every court has its spies," Sylvie said. "Whether its government is friendly to us or not."

"I'm only saying that in the midst of this war, it would be much more serious if he were writing to the Germans or the Austrians."

Mama was already trying to minimize. How hard they worked to protect Rasputin, because of Alexei. What power he had, over us all of us ...

"There *are* letters to Germany in there."

"Not to anyone important," Papa said, rifling through the envelopes. I heard the rustling. "I don't know any of these people. Oh, here's one ... Emile Durkheim. But isn't he just some academic?"

I could hear Sylvie's anger mounting at their determination to deny.

"You have no idea what's in those letters. Because we can't read them."

"Then there's only one person we can ask," Papa said.

Sylvie paused directly in front of the crack, face blanching.

"I don't want him near me."

"The accused has the right to face his accuser and answer the charges leveled against him."

Papa spoke like a judge because in our system the Tsar was judge, jury, and executioner, especially for nobility. Once you reached a certain rank, *only* the Tsar could judge you.

He summoned Rasputin.

Tatiana, Maria, and I waited in the passageway, silent and cramped because Papa, Mama, and Sylvie stayed in the room. If we moved they'd hear us, especially with how quiet they'd all become. It was like they took a vow not to speak until Rasputin was part of the conversation.

The way he entered the room chilled me.

He knew someone had broken into his tower. Surely he'd searched his drawers and realized his letters were missing. So he couldn't possibly be ignorant of why he'd been called to Papa's office. Even an innocent man feels dread when he's escorted to a conversation by an armed guard.

Rasputin walked into the study like a man who knew none of those things. He was so calm, so confident, that for a moment *I* almost believed nothing could be wrong.

"Grigory Rasputin," my father said. "The charge of sedition has been leveled against you by Sylvie Buxhoeveden."

"Indeed?" Rasputin showed the level of surprise one might exhibit if you'd just informed them that you'd replanted all your garden beds. "On what evidence?"

He knew what the evidence was, he must know about the letters. I was beginning to see why Sylvie sensed deception in every word.

Papa produced the letters.

"With whom are you corresponding and why are you writing in code?"
Being asked these questions in Papa's study, by Papa himself, instead of in the basement of the Okhrana, was already a mark of favor.

Calmly, Rasputin replied, "I'm writing to my relatives. And I'm not writing in code, it's a dialect of Yeniseian, which is what we speak."

"These are *all* your relatives?" Sylvie sneered. "They *all* speak this ridiculously obscure language and prefer it over the common languages we all speak? All these relatives, whose names are *not* Rasputin."

I expected Rasputin to respond to her jeers, her accusations, and the breaking into his house, with some level of aggression. He showed not a particle of anger as he replied, "Some of their names are Rasputin."

That was unnerving to me, because I *had* seen Rasputin angry—when I managed to do something he didn't think I could do. When I bested him, even in something small. When things didn't go as he anticipated.

I could only take it to mean that Sylvie wasn't doing anything unexpected, not in his eyes. He didn't care what she said, and he didn't fear the outcome. His confidence wasn't an act.

"Have it translated," Rasputin said carelessly. "Or I can write out what it says."

"He's LYING!" Sylvie shrieked.

But she'd already tipped her hand when she admitted that the lies weren't tangible. Now my parents didn't believe her. Because they didn't want to.

I couldn't see Sylvie; she'd passed out of my view. Rasputin stood before me, calm, patient ... perhaps even the tiniest bit amused. Because Sylvie was so furious and so powerless.

She had one last arrow in her quiver.

"His sister's a spy, too. I see who she flirts with, who she *dallies* with. Uvarov, Baron Razumovsky, the captain of the city guard! They're conspiring against you, together, the pair of them!"

"The captain has a dozen mistresses," Papa said wearily. "And as for Razumovsky, whatever else you can say about him, my police say he's the one man in St. Petersburg who's loyal to his wife. Besides me, of course."

He threw that aside to my mother, not that she needed it. Everyone remarked that Papa was the first Emperor in memory not to install several mistresses in expensive houses close to the palace. My great-grandfather had allowed his mistress to move into the Winter Palace itself. As his wife lay dying, she listened to his illegitimate children playing in the apartments below her.

Perhaps that's why fidelity mattered to Papa. He had to kiss the hand of his new twenty-three-year-old grandmother a week after the death of his actual grandmother.

Papa was the exception, other men the rule. Flirting with the pretty poetess, or even sleeping with her, was not presumed to mean anything from a political standpoint. She was too beautiful, and artists always harbored liberal views. If that was sedition, every man fucking a ballerina, a singer, or an actress was guilty. And that was every powerful man in St. Petersburg.

I could almost hear my parents' justifications rattling through their brains.

There's a hundred spies in the court, everyone sends information to their relatives, their friends ...

There's no evidence here. Nothing harmful.

She's jealous of him, he scared her with the smoke-reading, she's never liked him.

She's been unstable lately, barely sleeping ... look at her.

I'd noticed it, too. Sylvie's golden waves of hair, her greatest vanity and loveliest trait, disarrayed as if she hadn't seen the hairdresser in a week. Too much powder on her face to hide the circles under her eyes. She'd lost weight in the way of someone who's been sick. She was wild-eyed, shrieking, while Rasputin's confidence was overpowering.

If he would have said, "I've done nothing wrong," perhaps we all would have heard the lie.

Maybe, maybe, perhaps ...

Even in hindsight, the past is unclear.

In the end, only one letter got Rasputin in trouble: a letter not yet sent, written in French, the language of the court, addressed to a minister in St. Petersburg. In it, Rasputin flaunted his relationship with our family, particularly with Mama. He implied that she'd do anything for him. The slight sexual tone was what *actually* offended Papa enough to reprimand Rasputin sharply.

We couldn't punish him because we needed him.

I needed him to teach me still.

He was the only one who could do more than me. The only one who could show me.

I thought the letters were suspicious—it was a code, of course it was, even if it was also a language. But was that so wrong? When I wrote to my siblings, we used secret codes. We had nicknames for everyone, including ourselves. We called us sisters OTMA, and Ollie signed her letters "Your disobedient Cossack" long before we ever met Damien.

The court was a sieve. Unless Rasputin was sending direct military knowledge to foreign adversaries ... did it really matter?

I swept the whole incident under the rug along with my parents. And when something much worse came along ... I swept that, too. Because I had so much practice.

WHEN THE MEETING was over and we crept back into the Mountain Hall, shoving the obnoxious cabinet back into place, our reactions spanned the spectrum.

Tatiana was ready to denounce Rasputin all over again. She'd been away for months; she had less of a personal relationship with him.

Maria, if anything, had only softened.

"I believe him. It's just letters to friends. Sylvie never liked him because he was a friend of Liza's. And you know those two have always despised each other."

"Don't talk about court intrigues like you understand them," Tatiana snapped.

She was right, but mean.

"I don't think that has anything to do with why Sylvie doesn't like Rasputin," I said to Maria, as gently as I could. "His smoke-reading upset her."

"But he didn't *say* anything!" Maria cried plaintively. She'd watched the reading. We all had.

I'd seen images the others hadn't. But they were only images of travel, which Sylvie loved ...

None of it made sense.

I inhabited the murky middle ground between my two sisters. I didn't trust Rasputin, but I still intended to visit him the very next day.

chapter 24

THIS MONSTER MOST LIKE MAN

"Can I tell you something?" Maria said, coming into my room in her nightdress.

"Always. Secrets are my favorite thing."

She smiled. "This one's probably exactly what you're expecting."

Actually, I'd been so busy practicing magic and writing to Damien and trying to solve the mystery of Alexei's illness that I hadn't been paying any attention to Maria.

She'd been volunteering every day, returning home so filthy that there was no question where she'd been or what she'd been doing. That was a part of myself I didn't entirely like: I was most interested in people when they were intriguing.

I pulled her down beside me on the bed, taking her hand, trying to show her how interested I could be all in a moment.

"Tell me everything! What's been going on?"

Maybe that was guilt, too. I hadn't told Maria or Alexei that I was meeting with Rasputin, because the only way to keep a secret is to tell no one.

Tatiana had pried it out of me because she was the cleverest, much as I hated to admit it.

Now I wanted from Maria what I wasn't giving to her: her confidence.

Maria took a breath, looking prettier than ever from all the pink in her cheeks. I was reminded of Irina, who always looked loveliest when Felix was around. And I could have guessed her secret then, but didn't want to spoil her moment.

"I'm in love," Maria said. "Not like before. It's real this time."

She certainly looked more bewildered than I'd seen in all her former crushes. She took quick breaths, giddy at telling someone at last.

"His name is Daniel. He was injured at Tannenbery. He lost a leg, but you wouldn't believe how strong he is, how brave. He never sulks about it, never complains, just says he has another and there's much worse parts of him he could have lost ..." Maria giggled and blushed, repeating the silly joke.

I could already see how bad it was. And I was certain how the story would end.

"Maria ..."

"Sometimes he even says he never would have met me at all if not for the leg, and it's true, the others get better and are sent back to fight but he's been here nearly two months. I don't know if they'll send him back at all."

"Maria," I murmured. "His name doesn't happen to be Baron Daniel or Lord Daniel, does it?"

Her smile faded.

"No ... his father is a ... baker, actually. But he's already been promoted twice! He's so clever Stassie, you'll see when you meet him—"

I opened my mouth to tell her it was madness, then shut it again. I'd be the damndest hypocrite in the world.

"He sounds incredible. I'd love to meet him."

My agreement scared Maria more than sense would have done.

"You want to tell me Papa and Mama will never allow it."

"Who cares!" I said fiercely. "If you have a chance of a beautiful day ... take it."

A few more days with Daniel might be all she had before someone found out or he got shipped away.

I wouldn't spoil any of them.

I DON'T WANT to say what happened next. Of all the mistakes I've made, and there are many, that's the one that tortures me. Because I wonder if there's any version of me that would have chosen differently.

I was reading through the books Tatiana and I had stolen from

Rasputin's tower. I didn't know if he knew they were missing—they'd be harder to notice than his letters.

It was slow going, like reading a treatise on shipbuilding—inherently interesting, but barely comprehensible to a layman. There was no glossary of terms and some of the books were so ancient that they were written in script, not even printed, the spidery scrawls flaking away.

My search began to feel pointless. I fell asleep most nights trying to puzzle through lists of ingredients I didn't recognize and magic I hardly understood.

Clever as Tatiana was, she was having no better success. She took endless pages of notes, none of them pertaining to Alexei.

Then, one evening in December, about eleven o'clock at night, when I'd long since eaten all the honey toast I'd brought up from the kitchens, and the last of my tea had gone cold, I opened *Demons, Succubi, and Creatures Most Foul*.

This was the opening line:

Rusya belonged to monsters once. The towns of men were tiny, scattered along waterways. In the endless acres of forest so dense and dark they never saw sunlight, that is where the monsters dwelled. That is where they bred. A thousand demons spawned in the wilds of Rusya, and spread ...

I was awake in an instant. I was reminded of old fairytales, and my favorite book of Romanov history that described how the first Tsar won his crown clearing the wilds.

That was a dry, old historical tome, and still Tatiana and I had pored over the wood-cut illustrations of Mikhail spearing a werewolf as large as the charger on which he rode.

Creatures Most Foul contained all the details I'd ever desired with full-color illustrations.

I devoured the descriptions of succubi and sirins, werewolves and basilisks, goblins and giants, rusalka and strzyga.

Some of these creatures I'd heard of before—the sailors on our yacht were always telling tall-tales of rusalka, the painfully beautiful redheads that lurked around waterways, hoping to drag sailors down to their deadly grottos.

"That's why I eat so much garlic," Andrei Derevenko told me. "To keep 'em at bay."

"Doesn't the mustache accomplish that all on its own?" I teased him.

Other monsters I'd never heard of even in rumor.

Apparently, herds of something called a todorat used to gallop around the Balkans, trampling humans to death with their hooves.

The sirin looked like a bird, but when people heard her call, they lost their minds and chased her voice until they fell into canyons or drowned in lakes.

In Serbia, a creature called the psoglav had the hind legs of a horse and the head of a dog, with one single eye in the middle of its face and teeth made of iron. It lived in caves and dug up human graves to feast on fresh corpses.

Some of the monsters were disturbingly human—mostly in the form of beautiful women.

There was the rusalkas, of course, and also the gamayun, birds with female breasts and faces. I paged through a dozen illustrations of disturbingly seductive bird-women who seemed to be painted by artists who wouldn't mind meeting one, even if it might rip out their throats.

Then I came to the second-last chapter:

Few creatures are as brutal or as cunning as the vampyr. This monster most like man may walk among us by night. Sunlight is deadly to its pallid skin.

The vampyr can be recognized by its pallor, its eyes black as stone, or its fangs. It sleeps as the dead, cold as a corpse, but if dug up, one will find fresh blood in its mouth.

The vampyr must feed on blood from the vein, or perish. No other food can satisfy its depraved hunger.

Those killed by vampyr are recognizable from the frenzy with which it feeds. The throat is savaged to such a degree that the head may be nearly decapitated.

To kill a vampyr is no easy task—swift and strong, their wicked guile is unmatched. Yet even their fangs are less deadly than their voice. When a vampyr speaks, it twists the minds of men. To look in its eyes is to obey. You must never meet a vampyr's gaze, or listen to its persuasion.

Resistant to injury, the vampyr may recover from wounds most deadly. This power is in their blood, and those who feed on vampyrs may in turn experience healing. Like many a dark gift, this promise is a lie. The effects are fleeting.

I felt like I'd fallen down a dark shaft and was still falling.

In all my time with Rasputin, what I learned most is that magic leaves a mark, like a black-and-white photograph with just one element in color. If you can see the edges of the magic, if you can follow the thread ... and then you can understand it.

I was able to slow time when I began to feel the flow of time. When I could see it, like clear water all around me. You can't see water, not exactly, but you can see the way the light bends and reflects when it hits it.

I'd been examining the marks of Rasputin's magic on Alexei for five years now. I saw it in the shadows under his eyes, his pallor, his exhaustion. And most of all, in the dark bruises that sprouted at the base of his neck, on his wrists, and in the crooks of his arms.

Alexei had always bruised easily. But only when he was sick. And only where he'd been hit.

Those who feed on vampyrs may in turn experience healing ... the effects are fleeting.

It wasn't a supernatural disease—it was a supernatural cure. And it wasn't really a cure at all. It only lasted as long as Rasputin was feeding on Alexei. If he ever stopped ... my brother would be right back where he started in a matter of months. I'd seen it happen whenever Rasputin went away.

I read over the description three more times.

It felt right in a way no other explanation ever had.

Yet some parts didn't fit at all. While Rasputin preferred to sleep away the day, I'd seen him outside in sunlight. Also, his eyes weren't dark—they were pale as winter sky. And there'd been no rumors of corpses found scattered around St. Petersburg with their throats torn out. Rasputin was known to frequent bordellos and bathhouses, but as far as I knew, his favorite whores lived to entertain him another day.

I tapped my fingers on the illustration of a tall, pale figure, its mouth dark with blood, its features distorted with rage as it savaged the throat of a buxom young woman.

Could the book be partially right and partially wrong? The author could hardly have observed all these creatures in person.

And if the description was flawed ... was it possible vampyrs weren't so monstrous after all?

Much as I distrusted him, Rasputin didn't seem like a monster. He seemed like a man.

He could do magic like a man.

The vampyr's power was supposed to be its persuasion and its physical resiliency.

Only humans had individual powers, no two exactly the same.

So was he ... or wasn't he?

I agonized for hours, until I no longer needed the lamp by the bed, the cool light of morning seeping through the blinds.

Still the puzzle twisted in my mind, complex, three-dimensional, never quite snapping into place.

I thought of telling Tatiana or my parents, then rejected the idea almost as swiftly.

I had no evidence, less even than Sylvie Buxhoeveden. If Papa hauled Rasputin in to hear my accusations, all it would do is put him on his guard.

There was only one way to be absolutely certain.

I had to catch him in the act.

I WAITED until the next time I knew Rasputin was treating Alexei.

This involved a certain amount of skulking around, since Rasputin often visited Alexei just to check on him. If I could have involved Tatiana it would have been much easier, but I couldn't risk it. While we'd grown closer in the months since she'd been home, Tatiana was still a rigid thinker, likely to run to my parents the moment she thought we'd crossed a line.

I crouched in the tunnel connecting the playroom nobody used anymore with Alexei's room. This was the second time in a month I'd hidden in these dusty passageways to spy on my own family members. When you're as cramped and filthy as a bridge troll, realizing you've got to pee quite badly, you start to reevaluate certain life decisions.

Even though I'd long suspected that the necessity for absolute privacy during the treatments was only a ruse for Rasputin to protect the secret of his cure, I still feared that interrupting Alexei might harm him somehow.

I was torn between the anxiety of causing some horrible accident and the dread of Alexei continuing to wither away if I did nothing.

I wouldn't have dared without a strong suspicion of what Rasputin was actually hiding.

Still, I was far from secure in my choice. As the minutes dragged by, the tension mounting along with the stuffy heat of the tunnel, I almost turned and scuttled back the way I came.

Then I heard the snick of Alexei's door opening and Rasputin's low, smooth voice.

"I saw you've been drilling with the palace guard."

"Drilling's all they let me do," Alexei said, dully. "I want to go to the front. I want to fight."

"You'd be a fool to throw your life away in that war. A bunch of callous despots squabbling over land none of them own."

Alexei didn't sound offended by the rebuke, despite the fact that he himself was the next "despot" in line in Rusya.

"I don't care. I want to get out of here. It feels like the old days when I'd bleed and bleed. Only now it's on the inside."

"Don't worry," Rasputin soothed him. "The wind is shifting. The stars realign. The way forward will soon be clear."

It sounded like mystical babble, and yet my dread swelled. I did feel some vast and looming change on the horizon.

I thought it was the war, the awful war that grew more bloody and confused by the day. The armies dug down in trenches against which the combatants battered themselves in waves, breaking and scattering with no progress.

The French invaded the Ottoman Empire. The Albions brought hundreds of ships to attack the Germans off the coast of Denmark. The bay filled with floating bodies until the boats had to cut a path through the carnage like a punt through a carpet of lily pads.

I followed every bit of news, especially when it pertained to the Rusyan 1st. If the intervals between Damien's letters stretched longer than a couple of weeks, I grew sick and irritable, snapping at Maria, quarreling with Tatiana, barely able to eat.

Sometimes two or three letters would arrive at once, streaked with mud. I'd run to my room and tear them open, shaking with relief when I saw that familiar script, dark from how hard he pressed the pen against the page. If I turned the letter over I could feel his words in reverse, raised beneath my fingertips.

Damien told me the silly jokes circulating among the soldiers, the things they did to entertain themselves in the long, cold nights. He tried to spare me. But when he described the conditions, even in dry terms, it was impossible to hide the frigid cold, lack of food, the infections and diseases that raced through the trenches.

It's like no war I've seen before. I'd give anything to be on an open field again. We're like rabbits in a warren, trapped, while they pour poison gas down the trenches, liquid fire, and the shells that scream and blast for hours at a time, shaking the ground, exploding in our ears.

Tell me about all the beautiful cakes you had at tea, and tell me how you took a warm bath and walked around the park. Tell me all the books you're reading, the records you play. Let me feel alive again.

I wrote him pages and pages of the most frivolous things—how the holiday lights reflected all down the Neva River, how I took Artemis hunting in the Frost Forest and she caught three white hares that I had made into a pair of soft fur boots. How Aunt Xenia had a huge row with Irina because she tried to force her into an engagement with Boris of Bulgaria, and Irina told her parents once and for all that she would never accept a proposal from anyone but Felix, even if it meant she was a withered old lady before they were wed.

> *But here's one piece of news that will make you horribly smug: Stana Lutchen-berg has run away from her husband. By all reports, she's fled to Galicia. Do you know anybody she might be meeting there?*

Nikolasha had been stationed in Galicia for months. Damien was headed there himself. I felt the strangest sense of envy for Stana, who might soon see both.

Damien had been gone for over a year.

He burned in my mind brighter than ever.

Even at this crucial moment, with Alexei and Rasputin only feet away, I couldn't stop thinking about him.

I dragged my attention back to my brother, to the muted rustle of buttons and cloth as he stripped to the waist. I couldn't see what they were doing, but from their murmured voices and the few quiet sounds, it seemed that Rasputin was examining Alexei, testing his joints, feeling the nodes beneath his jaw, tapping on his back, listening to his breathing, his heartbeat.

"You'll be taller than your father soon."

Alexei had indeed grown tall, but thin and reedy like a plant without enough light.

"I don't care," was all he replied.

Rasputin chuckled at his rudeness. "You're in a fine mood."

"Everywhere else I've got to grin like a painted dummy. Don't make me smile around you, too."

I wondered if I was one of those people who forced Alexei to smile, to seem happier than he was so I wouldn't have to worry about him.

I could hear Rasputin tapping lightly on Alexei's chest, perhaps pressing his ear against warm flesh to listen to the beating of his heart before pulling back and saying, "You didn't seem to have any trouble smiling last night."

Now at last Alexei made a sound of amusement. "Will Katya be at Madame Lessinger's party?"

"Yes."

"Good."

I heard the compressed sound of Alexei leaning back against the pillows.

"Go on, then."

"Close your eyes."

I leaned forward, straining my ears, holding my breath.

A long silence passed. Then Rasputin began to chant.

His voice was low and droning, like the Znamenny prayer chant of the Orthodox priests.

This was no prayer. The language was strange, foreign tones with harsh consonants rasping in the throat. The chant built and swelled with a swirling energy I could feel all the way in the tunnel.

The air was thick with vibration. The dark around me seemed to grow darker. Only three people were present: me, Rasputin, and Alexei. But it seemed as if there were many more.

I crouched in the tunnel, wondering if it were only my imagination, or if a chorus of voices joined to Rasputin's—low, whispering, swirling like wind. All of a sudden I didn't want to look, I didn't want to see.

But I put my palm against the hidden panel in Alexei's wall and pushed, ever so softly, ever so quietly, the minute creek of the hinges drowned by Rasputin's voice.

I peeked through.

At first all I could see was Rasputin's back, smooth as a crow's wing from the long swoop of his robes. His pale hands seemed to float in the gloom as they passed over Alexei's body, head to toe, without touching him.

Alexei lay back against the pillow, eyes closed. His eyelids were purplish, his lips gray. I remembered the night I thought he would die and my heart twisted like it would tear.

Rasputin saved him. He was our dark angel, though he hovered over Alexei like a demon.

Alexei's chest rose slower and slower. Rasputin placed his palm on Alexei's forehead and he relaxed completely, sinking into deep sleep.

Rasputin picked up Alexei's hand as if he intended to check his pulse. Then he raised the hand as if he would kiss it instead.

His body turned, blocking my view. I pushed the panel open a little further and even leaned my head into the room, but still couldn't see.

Rasputin wasn't chanting anymore. All I heard was a low, guttural sound that might have been gulping.

I slipped out of the tunnel, softly closing the panel behind me. Then crossed the carpet, feet sinking into the thick pile.

I was afraid. So afraid. But I had to know. I had to see for myself.

I was only an arm's length away when he heard me. He turned, swift and eerily smooth. His face was paler than ever, the only color to be seen the pinpricks of glittering blue beneath his lowered brows and the slash of scarlet smeared across his mouth.

Blood ran down his chin. He caught it with his thumb. Almost absently, he put his thumb to his mouth to clean it. When his mouth opened I saw his incisors, long and sharp, like the fangs a viper extends when it bites.

I thought I was prepared.

Still, I stumbled back, hands flying up in front of my face like that would protect me.

He could have leaped on me and torn out my throat. Instead he stood there looking mildly annoyed, like I'd interrupted him at tea.

"You can never leave well enough alone, can you, Anastasia?"

He sounded disappointed in me. This monster dripping my brother's blood.

I had an ash stake in my pocket. I'd put it there as insurance, if the absolute worst were true. Now the worst stood in front of me, calm and composed, looking like the man I'd always known.

"You're a vampyr."

"Of sorts." He clasped his hands loosely in front of him, only his fingertips peeking out from the long sleeves of his robe, white and curled, like grubs.

"How?" I whispered. "I thought they were all dead."

"All but one, perhaps."

"You?"

"My father."

He spat the word, lips twisting, still stained a garish red.

"That's impossible."

A human couldn't mate with a monster any more than they could mate with a horse or a dog.

"Evidently not," Rasputin said.

My head was spinning. Everything he said sounded like madness, like more lies. And yet, there was sense in it, in a situation that had never made sense.

I felt as if I were holding a sphere made of a thousand fragments. If I couldn't keep it contained, it would shatter apart.

My brother still slumbered on the bed, thin and languid, a dark bruise blooming on his wrist where Rasputin had fed.

"You're killing him."

"Don't be ridiculous," Rasputin snapped. "He'd have been dead years ago if not for me."

"Then why are you feeding on him?"

"Because I must. I drain the spoiled blood and fill him with mine instead."

My stomach lurched, as if he'd told me he was stuffing Alexei with rotted meat and motor oil. The thought of that demonic blood coursing through my brother's veins ...

"It's hurting him."

"His body's rejecting the treatment. I'm doing all I can."

I didn't believe him. I didn't believe him, but I had no other healer to turn to, no other sorcerer.

"You lied to us."

"Of course I did. Take a look in the mirror, look at the expression on your face. I've been hated and hunted all my life. Called a monster, a demon, a freak of nature."

"You *are* a monster," I breathed.

"Why?" Rasputin demanded. "What have I ever done that was monstrous?"

"Why don't *you* look in the mirror?"

Rasputin touched his bloodstained mouth.

"You eat meat. What's the difference?"

"Only animal versus human, I suppose."

His lip curled.

"I hoped in time you might understand. But you're the same as the rest of them."

A rush of heat ran up my neck. "If I was the same as the rest of them I'd call the guards to cut you to pieces."

His eyes went cool. "Do as you wish."

I thought, *I should call the guards. I should scream for my father.*

But I stood there, fractured, everything falling apart. I didn't know which pieces to hold onto.

"What are you waiting for?" Rasputin said, that edge of mockery back in his voice.

I hesitated because I knew what would happen if I told my parents. It was why I'd come here alone, without even Tatiana.

My mother had smothered her dislike of magic for Alexei's sake, but not even for him would she allow the black arts to be practiced in her home. She cared for our eternal souls more than our human lives.

Rasputin knew it just as well. He'd come to know my parents intimately. "Your brother needs me."

"What will happen if you stop treating him?"

I already knew the answer, but I had to hear him say it.

"He'll be dead in months."

My hands fell limp at my sides. I walked past Rasputin and sunk to my knees by my brother's bed. I picked up his hand, cold as a fish, and pressed it against my cheek.

"Does he know?" I asked.

Rasputin shook his head. "I put him to sleep so his body can heal. When he wakes, all he knows is that he can walk without pain. He needn't fear every razor and pair of scissors. He can live his life."

I heard the reproach, the reminder of my ingratitude.

We'd prayed for a miracle. No one had provided it but Rasputin.

"Do you feed on other people?"

"Mostly on whores. I pay them. They'd probably do it for free—it's quite pleasurable."

Without meaning to, I looked at his mouth, at the points of his fangs still visible over the full lower lip. I imagined hot breath against my neck, the warmth of tongue, and then the momentary flash of pain subsiding in a deep undercurrent of pleasure ...

Ripping my eyes away, I tried to fixate on a point somewhere near his ear. I could feel those pale eyes yanking at me, ordering me to look at him directly.

Through my teeth I said, "Explain to me how a human can mate with a vampyr."

"I was hardly there to see it, was I?"

I blushed and felt that insistent human need to meet his eyes, to check his face, to read his expression. But this wasn't a human—I couldn't use his face to check the truth of his words. It would only deceive me further.

That's what I told myself, while looking him full in the face again.

"He attacked my mother. Savaged her. Left her for dead. It took her months to recover, her belly already swelling. She prayed it was her husband's child—they'd been married a year. But she couldn't sleep at night, and she sweat all through the day, suffering the strangest cravings."

I pictured this poor woman in her cottage, going through all the normal struggles of daily life, milking the cows, sewing the clothes, washing the dishes, scrubbing the floors, praying, praying that the awful night she'd suffered was far behind her, that the baby in her belly was her husband's child, not some unknown creature that turned and kicked.

"When I was born, I looked normal enough. They pretended I was normal, that I belonged to my mother and her husband, and not the stranger in the night. They had more children together, my brothers and sisters. We were like each other ... but never entirely alike. I saw the differences."

I thought of the days before I manifested, when all my siblings had powers but me. Even Alexei, younger by three years, had powers.

I knew what it was to belong to your family while not feeling quite the same as them. The loneliness, surrounded by everyone you love.

"I never knew until I was twelve or thirteen ... and the hunger started. As a child she'd put blood in my milk, in my wine ... sheep's blood, hen's blood, whatever animals we ate. She cut their throats and drained them. It wasn't odd in the north—the Mongols did the same with their horses. But when I started to become a man ... I needed more. Then she confessed to me what she'd always known."

His teeth had returned to normal. He wiped his mouth clean on the sleeve of his robe.

"She told me the truth, while promising it didn't matter. I had the hunger, but I also had magic. I was sensitive to the sun, but I could live like anyone else. She said she'd give me the blood I needed, and she did, every week for years. I met Natalya, married her, we had our daughter. My wife knew. She let me feed from her as my mother used to do. She didn't care what I was. She loved me, all of me. We were happy ..."

He trailed off, falling silent like a toy that's wound down.

I'd never asked. Now I had to.

"What happened to them?"

His face was gripped by a spasm that was more awful when it fell away, leaving nothing but blankness.

"Men in the village discovered what I was. They came to the house in the night with guns, knives, clubs, torches. They nailed the doors shut and set the roof aflame."

Silence, in which I heard the faint tick of a clock. I was still kneeling on the carpet before him, holding Alexei's hand. Rasputin sunk into a chair himself, as if all the bones had gone out of him. For the first time, he looked old.

"I couldn't save them. I nearly died myself." He laughed bitterly. "But half of me is hard to kill."

"I'm so sorry."

He looked at me, lips pale and stiff, head jerking in a sharp negative.

"It was my fault. I should never have tried to have a family, knowing what I was."

He couldn't hold the state of anger. It ebbed away, until all I saw was sadness.

"I'm not a monster. I'm a man who was touched by the monstrous."

I felt sympathy for him, of course I did. While knowing that he still held something back from me.

To withhold this information from my family would be crossing a line I'd never crossed: keeping a secret for an outsider, even against them.

To tell them would risk losing everything, including, and most especially, Alexei himself.

Everything was falling apart. I grabbed for the one thing I knew I could save:

"I won't tell. For now. But if Alexei gets worse, I'll burn it all down."

chapter 25

THROUGH THE FLAMES

I barely slept that night. I wrestled with the blankets, sweating through confused dreams of trains rushing through tunnels that became snakes with their mouths open wide, trying to swallow me whole. I saw Liza Taneeva with a basket over her arm. She held the basket out to my mother, full to the brim with poisoned mushrooms. Then, just as abruptly, I was in a ballroom with all my sisters whirling around me in beautiful pastel gowns. I called out to them, but they couldn't seem to hear me. They danced faster and faster, until a cold wind whipped through the room, blowing them all away.

All that was left was the sound of sobbing, distant and forlorn. I followed the noise until I saw a tiny figure in a white sailor suit—Alexei, a small boy once more. He turned to me, blue eyes huge in his pinched face.

Will it hurt when I'm dead, Stassie?

Tears ran down both sides of his face, dark as blood.

I woke in a rush, strangling in the sheets, breathing hard like I'd been running.

Throwing an old robe around my shoulders, I sat at the window and began to write. I filled four pages on both sides, the longest letter I'd ever written to Damien. When I was finished, I sealed it up, feeling release. It would be weeks before I'd get anything back from him, but I already felt less alone.

That done, I went down to the breakfast table, surprised to see the rest of my family but Ollie already assembled there, dressed and eating in hushed somber.

"Papa's going to see Uncle Nikolasha," Tatiana informed me as soon as I sat down.

That explained why my mother was so tense and tearful. Uncle Nikolasha was leading the armies on the eastern front.

"When do you leave?" I asked Papa.

"In a few hours."

"I still don't see why you have to go yourself!" Mama burst out. "You could send Danilov or—"

"No, I can't," Papa cut her off.

"But you—"

"I don't want to argue about this anymore!"

It appeared they'd been running through the same conversation all night long. Mama looked peaky and Papa was clearly exhausted, despite his freshly trimmed hair and well-pressed uniform.

"I can't trust anyone else to carry it."

Papa must be bringing Charoite to Nikolasha. Probably a large volume, which is why he wouldn't entrust it to anyone else.

"I thought Nikolasha said he wouldn't use it again," Tatiana said quietly, from the end of the table.

Nikolasha had consumed large quantities of Charoite during the war with the Kingdom of the Rising Sun. He said he could feel it for years afterward—this thing inside of him that was a part of him and not quite a part of him. Usually sleeping but sometimes coming awake.

I'd been young when Nikolasha returned from Japan. But I remembered how he held out his arms to sweep me into a hug, grinning like always, and how I hesitated, seeing something in his face I didn't recognize—something that flickered behind his eyes, peeking out but never fully coming into view.

"We're losing," Papa said flatly to Tatiana. "Nikolasha will do what he must."

"Are you staying to fight?" Alexei asked him.

"No!" Mama said sharply, before Papa could reply. "Rusya needs its Emperor, not another soldier on the field."

Papa had fought in wars before. I suspected the real reason was the injuries he'd received in the bombing. He still limped, his back not quite straight, streaks of gray at his temples. Mama must fear that even with Charoite, Papa was not as invincible as before.

"Peter the Great fought his own wars," Alexei said.

He looked at Papa, unsmiling. Almost taunting him.

Papa turned his head slowly, regarding Alexei.

"Someday you'll learn to put duty above your own selfish desires for glory."

"Not glory," Alexei said. "Victory. We're losing because the strongest of us aren't fighting. We ought to take every last grain of Charoite and I should go with you. Together we could—"

"ENOUGH!" Papa bellowed.

It was unlike him to lose his temper. We all fell silent, even Alexei who looked as if he had plenty more to say.

"I spend all day with ministers nattering in my ears, giving me opposite advice. I won't sit at the breakfast table with my own family having my decisions second-guessed!"

"I'm sorry, Father." Alexei's tone was repentant but his lips were a stiff white line, barely containing what he actually wanted to say.

Trying to break the tension, Maria peeked up from under the crisp white cap of her nurse's uniform. "Papa's bringing Ollie back with him when he comes home."

"Ollie's coming home?" I cried.

"Yes," Mama confirmed, equally pleased. "Nicky will fetch her after he sees Nikolasha."

The thought of us all being home again together seemed like the first step toward everything being good again—everything being as it was.

Emboldened by this news, I caught Tatiana's eye across the table and mouthed, *Ask him!*

She knew what I meant, and she knew as well as I did that our best chance of getting our parents to do anything was for her to make the request.

She turned toward Papa, voice sweet as honey. "Father, you once told me that when you visited the vault next you'd take me with you. Do you have time today?"

"I don't have a minute of the day not already scheduled out." Then, his mouth softening beneath his beard, he said, "But I can make time."

"I want to go, too!" I jumped in. "Please, Papa!"

Alexei looked up from his picked-over breakfast, equally interested.

Smiling slightly, Papa said, "What about you, Maria? Do you want to visit the only room in the palace you've never seen?"

"Well…" Maria paused. She was probably thinking of whatever time she'd told Daniel to expect her. "Yes, actually."

"Will you come, Mama?" Tatiana asked.

Mama shook her head, pushing back from the table. "I hate that place."

Papa caught her hand as she passed, raising it to his mouth and kissing her fingers.

"I'll come see you before I go."

She pressed her lips together, blinking hard. "You'd better."

THE DOOR to the vault looked like any other door in the palace, except that it was guarded by six armed soldiers at all times and was located at the end of the last corridor in the lowest level of the basement. Well … the lowest level save one.

Today one of the guards was Kolya Derevenko, Andrei's eldest son and a favorite friend of Alexei's. Kolya saluted Papa smartly, grinning at Alexei and winking at Maria and me once Papa passed.

Papa took a key as long as his index finger from his pocket, turning the lock with a hollow clunking sound.

I could hardly breathe as I followed him through the door. I'd never been inside the vault before and had no idea what to expect.

At first, all I saw was darkness. We descended a staircase even deeper into the earth. The walls pressed close on both sides, rough and unplastered, cut directly into the stone.

No torches or lanterns hung from brackets, yet a strange purplish glow lit the stairwell from some source up ahead. Maria's white apron looked mauve, the red cross on her breast blazing like a brand.

Papa strode ahead with all the confidence of someone who'd been here many times before. Tatiana followed close behind him. I was in the middle with Maria, trying to name the scent in the air that singed my nose with some chemical tang. Alexei brought up the rear, resting his palm against the cold stone wall, then rubbing his fingers together as if he expected to find them wet.

The tunnel had been frigid at first. As we descended the steps, the heat increased. The violet light grew brighter and harsher, and I heard a crackling sound, not like logs on a fire, but like electricity dancing between two points.

We rounded a turn, meeting a wall of purple fire. The fire extended twenty feet from floor to ceiling, a solid, unbroken flow of flickering lilac flame. It seemed to burn from nothing but stone, yet the heat was intense, I could feel it on my face.

"Where's the Charoite?" Tatiana asked, confused.

Papa gestured to the fire. "Through there."

"How do we turn it off?" Maria said.

"We don't."

Papa strode forward, his long legs closing the gap in three steps. I still thought he'd pause before the flames—the heat was so intense I wanted to step back myself. Instead, he walked right through, the fire surging upward like a waterfall in reverse, streaming all around him like water would have done, flickering across his face, his hands his beard, but setting nothing alight.

He disappeared on the other side, the fire closing in a solid mass once more. We heard his voice calling us:

"You can come through."

Alexei and Tatiana looked at each other, faces stained purple by the flickering light.

"I'll go." I stepped forward, the heat increasing just as it would the closer you got to a bonfire. It was difficult to believe it wouldn't burn me. I stretched out my hand. My palm screamed at me to pull back, the skin tightening, the heat right on the edge of tolerable pain.

I closed my eyes and stepped through.

The fire closed around me like I'd jumped into a frozen lake in the middle of winter. It was intensely hot for an instant, the way a deep cold can feel like a thousand burning needles stabbing at you from all sides. Then I was through, skin tingling, but nothing burned, not even my clothes.

Papa looked mildly surprised to see me step through first. Perhaps he thought it would be Alexei.

Alexei followed next. He looked down at his clothes, checking them as I had. He hardly seemed to feel the heat. I was sweating while Alexei remained colorless and still.

We could hear Tatiana arguing with Maria on the other side of the fire. Maria stumbled through like she'd been pushed. Tatiana stepped through after her, eyes closed, teeth gritted.

"See?" she said to Maria. She threw Papa half a smile. "Glad to know we're all your children?"

Papa chuckled. "Apparently so."

"What does that mean?" I asked. "What would happen if we weren't?"

"Then you'd burn," Papa said, calmly. "Like you'd jumped in a volcano. Only a full-blooded Romanov can walk through the fire."

That was the real security—not the guards outside the door.

Now that we were past, we found ourselves in a plain stone chamber without windows or doors. I'd thought the space would be larger and much more grand. In truth, the only thing inside the vault was a single chest set on a stone plinth. The chest was stained and battered, latched with iron hinges.

"This belonged to Mikhail Fyodorovich," Papa said. "He brought it back from the Lorne Mountain, filled with Charoite."

Papa opened the chest, which had no lock. We all peered in, expecting to see it filled to the brim with purple stones.

It was less than a quarter full.

"Where's the rest of it?" Tatiana asked.

"That's it," Papa said. "That's all we have. The mountain's almost run dry."

Tatiana's mouth fell open. Even Alexei looked surprised.

Papa plucked up a crystal the size of a coin. "The miners haven't found a stone this large in months. Years, maybe. They break up the rock and sift through for grains ..." he stirred the crystal with his fingers, the bits of gem hardly larger than coarse salt. "But small pieces aren't as powerful."

"What are we going to do?" Maria cried.

"It doesn't matter. There's more here than we'll ever use."

Papa bent to look us in the face, one by one.

"You must never use too much. The power it bestows is never yours alone."

Papa grimaced, giving his head a rough shake as if to flick off a fly that had landed on him.

He gathered a handful of stones and dropped them in a leather pouch, holding it aloft.

"This is all I'm taking to Nikolasha and I'd be surprised if he uses it all. It should last him months of battles."

I frowned. "You think there will be months more of battles?"

"I hope not," Papa said. "Not once Nikolasha has this."

Tatiana was peering into the chest, the faint violet light of the stones tinting her face as the flames had done.

She reached in a hand.

"Tatiana!" Papa said sharply.

She looked up at him, her gray eyes turned purple in a way that made her look both beautiful and terrible.

"Can I touch it?"

He hesitated.

"For a moment."

Tatiana lifted the largest stone of all from the chest, thrice the size of any of the others. It rested in her palms like some unholy fruit, pulsing with light, a little slower than a heartbeat.

"When did we find this?"

"The Setos had a temple inside the mountain," Papa said. "That was on the altar. They called it the Heart of the Earth."

Tatiana gazed into the brilliant center of the stone. Its color reflected in her eyes, her pupils flaring bright with every pulse as if the light had already gone inside her.

"Put it back," I said suddenly.

Sluggishly, Tatiana looked up at me.

"I am putting it back."

Yet she held it still.

Papa took it from her hands, gently, and laid it back inside the chest.

For a moment I wanted to hold it myself, to feel the weight of all that compressed power pulsing in my hands. Then I remembered the tiny crystal Rasputin had shown me, and how it had seemed to squirm against my skin like an insect trapped. And I had no desire to touch it again.

chapter 26

ACCIDENTAL ALCHEMY

Papa left for the eastern front, accompanied by a fresh regiment of soldiers and carrying the bag of Charoite for Nikolasha. Since he planned to be gone for some months, he formally appointed my mother as regent to act in his absence.

It was a sensible decision, but it made me anxious all the same—as if some part of my father thought he wouldn't return.

Mama had already been taking on more of his duties to help with the overwhelming volume of foreign correspondence, news, and reports that flooded in every day.

Now she had to do everything in his stead. She leaned heavily on my father's ministers and also on Rasputin.

At first Rasputin joined the morning meetings with General Danilov and Ivan Goremykin, but he disliked getting up early and constantly quarreled with Danilov, who had always despised him. Soon he began visiting my mother in her Mauve Boudoir after the others had left, chaperoned only by Liza Taneeva or another of my mother's ladies-in-waiting.

Never by Sylvie Buxhoeveden. I'd hardly seen her around the palace since she accused Rasputin of treason. I didn't know if she was avoiding Rasputin, my mother, or both.

I'd heard a rumor that she'd been spotted wandering around Vitebsky Station in a nightdress. That seemed impossible for Sylvie, who never stepped outside her door without her gown perfectly pressed, hair coiffed, and shoes polished—at least, up until recently.

"Maybe she was drunk," Tatiana said.

"Or sleepwalking," Maria added, more charitably.

"I want to go see her. Will you come with me?" I asked my sisters.

We planned to visit her house in St. Petersburg the next day, when Maria was not expected at the hospital and Tatiana had the morning free.

That evening I'd been invited to a salon at Madame Lessinger's house, where I'd finally see Katya perform. Alexei was coming as well, though he'd declined my offer to share a carriage. He planned to dine with Dimitri and Felix Yusupov beforehand at Felix's supper club.

I hadn't seen Felix in over a year, since that fateful sledding incident that parted both Damien and me and Felix and Irina. Irina was under house arrest with Xenia as full-time jailor. Any servant suspected of passing messages to Felix had been sacked. Even her notes to Tatiana and me and were read by Aunt Xenia.

I was re-reading some of my own letters from Damien as I dressed for the evening ahead.

I hadn't received a response about Rasputin yet. It took almost six weeks for me to write to Damien and receive his reply. Sometimes our letters didn't arrive at all.

His last letter told me he'd been promoted to lieutenant.

We're all being promoted practically every week when the man above us catches a bullet. Orders come in and are contradicted an hour later.

But we're out of the trenches, thank the gods. I've got Hercules back and we're riding to Galicia. Well, riding and walking—he was shot in the flank. I don't want to work him too hard until it's entirely healed.

Do you know, I'd never left Rusya before this?

The food is different, and the shape of the buildings, and the way they say their prayers. And the magic is different, too. That's what you'd notice first ... how the Spaniards charm their animals, especially their horses. And how their fisherman can dive for mussels without any air.

A knock sounded at the door. I tucked the letters away.

Annette Bailey bustled in to arrange my hair. I wished Nina Ivanova could do it. She was a better stylist and I missed talking to her. Mama had banished her to the opposite side of the palace and wouldn't let her attend any of us girls anymore.

Annette suffered some sort of breathing difficulty that caused her to whistle out of her left nostril. It sounded like a tea kettle was circling round behind me, jabbing pins into my scalp nearly as hard as Margaretta used to do, though not intentionally. Annette was just clumsy.

She liked to talk in an unbroken stream about anything that happened to pop into her head. I was still thinking of what Damien had written, only paying attention to a small percentage of what passed through her lips.

"And cook was in a horrible mood, because we haven't been able to get pure white sugar in weeks and we're running low, and the Empress said she wanted cream cakes for tea, which used up a goodly portion of what was left. So cook sent me to buy some in town whatever the price, and as I was leaving I saw General Danilov walking down the lane ..."

I was immersed in a fantasy of Damien stripping off his gloves to write his letter. His bare hands uncovered, flattening his paper across his knee, scribbling, bent close over the page, then signing just his initial as he always did, folding the letter, slipping it into the envelope, addressing it with my name ...

Because I saw his bare hands so rarely, there was something unspeakably intimate in their shape and color, not a deep walnut like the rest of his skin but lighter like ashwood, moving in that firm and capable way ...

"He offered me to share his umbrella because it hadn't looked like rain when I left, and I was terribly grateful of course, though I hardly knew if I should take it. I said, 'I don't know if I ought to take the arm of a minister, 'specially not in my work clothes,' and he said, 'If that's all that's stopping you, you needn't worry—I'm not a minister anymore.' And I said, 'Lor, not a minister! Whatever are you talking about?' and he said it was true, the Empress let him go that morning, after forty-two years and three Tsars, he really wasn't minister of anything anymore."

"Wait, what?" I jerked up my head so that the curl Annette had been arranging ripped free of its pin, minus a few hairs.

"I was surprised, too." Annette caught the curl and twisting it up once more with her deft, plump hands. "Nobody else has ever offered me an umbrella on that lane, I can tell you that, but General Danilov is such a kind man, no airs about him. That's the mark of a real gentleman if you ask—"

"He's not minister anymore?" I interrupted.

"Not according to him!" Annette said cheerily.

I was shocked. Mama had never particularly liked Danilov, who was cantankerous and conservative, but he'd been a trusted adviser since my great-grandfather's reign.

"There!" Annette said, standing back to admire my head in the mirror. "You'll never be as lovely as Tatiana, or Maria even, but some of the maids think you're quite as pretty as Miss Olga was at your age. Lor, who knows what she'll look like by the time she gets home, it's been so long!"

"I don't care about being prettiest," I said, still frowning over what Annette had just relayed.

"That's lucky," she said.

It was no credit to me—my vanity simply lay in another direction.

I stood up from the dressing table, shoving back the chair.

"Thank you, Annette," I said distractedly.

"You're very welcome. I'm sure you'll have a lovely time at Madame Lessinger's house. She's got a new cook. I don't think much of French cooking in general, but they say she trained in the best school in Paris ..."

Her chatter followed me out the door.

My sisters were already waiting in the Marble Hall. Tatiana wore a smoke-colored frock with a black velvet sash, her hair pinned under a smart little cap of the same material. Maria's dress of juniper brocade was embroidered all over with peach and lilac blooms, with leaves in lighter green.

"You look like Mama," I said to Tatiana. And to Maria, "And you look like a walking garden."

"I want it to be spring." Maria smiled.

As she passed a row of ornamental trees in ceramic pots, the branches shivered. Clusters of white blooms burst into being like popcorn, tiny oranges swelling and growing in a matter of moments.

"Maria!" Tatiana cried, impressed. "You didn't even touch them."

"I'm just so happy!" Maria's arms spread wide. "You should see the plants in my room. It's a jungle almost."

"Because of your soldier?" Tatiana asked slyly.

"Anastasia! You said you wouldn't tell!"

"I haven't whispered a word."

"It wasn't Stasia," Tatiana said. "Your soldier's got a sister whose best friend works in the scullery."

"Can anybody keep a secret from you?" Maria shook her head at Tatiana. "Not for long."

Though we were all horribly worried about Papa heading into a war zone, our attendance at the party that night depended on Mama's softer heart. We'd cajoled her into letting us attend several social events since Papa had left, despite the fact that the mood in St. Petersburg was worse than ever.

It'd been a wet year, half the wheat rotting in the fields before it could be harvested. German blockades of shipping lanes and the bombing of bridges and train lines had caused more food to molder in train cars or at the bottom of rivers while merchants went bankrupt and peasants starved.

The empty city streets were eerie and depressing, the parties barely any better with half the men missing, some enlisted and some attending to uprisings on their rural estates.

Still, Tatiana and I were intent on attending, for reasons of our own.

Tatiana wanted to keep an eye on Alexei, who'd been out carousing almost every night since Papa left. I, too, felt the need to watch Alexei in the company of other people. What he'd said to Rasputin had lodged in my head:

I've got to grin like a painted dummy ...

At home, Alexei was behaving as the Tsarevich. I wanted to see him amongst his friends.

Mama was allowing us to visit Madame Lessinger's house because she didn't know how the parties had changed since she'd last attended. When St. Petersburg was at the height of its grandeur a few seasons before, the guest list would have included only the most celebrated artists and the usual contingent of aristocrats and courtiers. White-gloved waiters would have passed around trays of canapés and guests would have been announced at the door.

Now the parties started later, with mixed company. Painters, poets, authors, actresses, and ballerinas mingled with the members of high society who still lingered in the city. Women whose husbands were away flirted openly with men who never would have been invited in years past, but were now needed to balance the numbers.

General Lessinger was leading the Rusyan third army, so had wielded no black pen against the guest list. Even the footman who opened the door to us appeared visibly tipsy as he took our coats.

"Welcome, welcome! Is that the Trepova sisters?" He squinted at us blearily. Tatiana didn't bother to correct him.

"Is the Tsarevich here?"

"Not yet," he hiccupped. "But I have it on very good authority that he's coming, and guess who else ..." He leaned in close, swaying slightly. "The Black Monk himself."

It was clear which one the servant was more excited to see.

"Does Rasputin visit often?" Tatiana asked.

"Oh yes. He and the madame are ..." the footman smirked. "Very close."

Once the servant departed, Tatiana muttered, "Is there anybody with tits he's not fucking?"

"Just Mama."

Tatiana looked at me, unsmiling. We both knew that wasn't what everyone else believed. The papers continued to publish grotesque cartoons implying that Rasputin had much more than a friendly relationship with our mother and all four of us girls.

Sexual alliances had ever been a part of court life. Rasputin's harem of female admirers dwarfed any I'd seen and included more than the usual contingent of flirts and floozies. Even the most upright women giggled when he kissed their hands and defended him against his detractors.

I saw many of his supporters at Madame Lessinger's house. Perhaps that's what I would have seen at any party these days. So many of his enemies had departed the city. All that were left were friends.

"Let's split up," I said to Tatiana.

"Good idea." She was always happy to slip away so she could participate in her favorite activity of overhearing conversations not intended for her ears. Maria and I would only distract her.

"Don't leave me!" Maria grabbed my arm.

"Only for a minute," I promised.

I had my own reasons for shedding my sisters. They were too recognizable, especially Maria in her garden gown. I'd dressed simply on purpose. Because the war happened so soon after my coming out, I'd never attended parties and balls on the scale of my sisters. My photograph hadn't been published weekly in the society papers. And as Annette and everybody else liked to remind me, I'd never quite managed that Grand Duchess elegance. With my snub nose and freckles, I could have been just another of Katya's student friends.

A remarkable number of students circulated in their rough clothing, with their unkempt hair and beards and deliberately unpolished shoes.

I would never have guessed that I'd see the Minister of Culture discussing the writings of Karl Marx with anything less than a saber in his hands, even if the student in question was uncommonly beautiful, with sloe-dark eyes and hands that clearly had only a theoretical relationship with hard labor.

How the city had altered, and how would it look in a few more years?

Time was a river, ever-changing, eroding even its own banks.

The court shared no clock anymore, no ceremonies at precise intervals. The party started late and dragged on and on with no change of room or indication of when the performances would begin.

Though an Italian cellist and a popular soprano would also be performing, Katya was the guest of honor. Madame Lessinger brought her a cup of punch, which sat untouched on the mantle in favor of Katya's own hand-rolled cigarettes. She smoked them with the use of a unique little holder which was also a ring. It twined around her index finger like a tiny snake with plated silver scales, gripping the cigarette in its jaws.

The smoke from the cigarette's smoldering tip made elegant patterns around Katya's hand as she gestured, her long nails painted the same deep red as her lips.

She wore no gloves. Plenty of the students did not, and some of the girls wore trousers. Katya had dressed in what looked like a pair of silk pajamas, embroidered with moons and stars in silver thread. Even her slippers were hand embroidered.

I wondered if Rasputin paid for those, or one of her many male admirers. Her hair had been cut in a sleek black cap with bangs high above her finely penciled brows. She was the first girl I'd ever seen with bobbed hair.

She sat back on the sofa like a radiant celestial body, the other guests at the party satellites drawn in by her pull. They orbited around her while she remained unmoved in the middle, smiling slightly, and occasionally saying something in her low voice that drew laughs or murmurs of agreement.

When she saw me watching, she raised her glass to me. I raised my own in return, then went to check on Maria.

She'd been sitting awkwardly until a young priest in a cowl struck up a conversation, correctly intuiting that Maria wouldn't climb on his lap like the female students were doing to male guests. While Maria herself wasn't flirting, I saw that even true love hadn't made her blind to the appeal of black hair and smooth cheeks on a man of the gods. She'd accepted a second glass of champagne and seemed to be enjoying herself.

The party had grown hot and crowded, smoke drifting from a dozen cigarettes and twice as many cigars. The artists hand-rolled their own stubby cigarettes and smoked them continuously, lighting the next off the tip of the last.

Alexei didn't appear. It might be an issue if he never arrived at all—we'd led Mama to believe he'd be escorting us to and from the party. Such flimsy subterfuge never would have passed in the old days. Now she was too tired to check on us. She might not wait up at all.

In chaos, so many things slip through the cracks. We'd lost half the male guards at the palace and plenty of female staff as well. Everything was a little dirtier, everyone a little more distracted. Nobody was checking up ... on anything.

Rasputin arrived an hour later. There was no fuss. One minute he wasn't in the room and the next he was. I noticed the difference from the sudden hush.

I was used to excitement around my father, and to a lesser degree Alexei.

The stir around Rasputin contained a note of awe. I was surprised how many people dipped their heads respectfully when he caught their eye.

"You know him?" I asked one of the young women who had smiled at Rasputin. She might have been a down-on-her-heels aristocrat or a well-kept working woman. Her dress was well-made in a cheap material.

"He's the holiest man in Rusya," she said fervently. "He can see the future. He predicted this awful war."

"Did he?"

"Many times."

I was reminded of the night I met Rasputin, how his first admirers had been equally worshipful. These people saw him as holy, blessed by the gods. His rivals at the palace saw a savvy political operator whose Achilles heel was his sexual debauchery.

I'd viewed him as a teacher and friend. A little jealous, a little competitive, but a fellow traveler of unknown roads.

I wondered which of those faces were real ... or if they all were.

Rasputin came to speak to me, gliding across the carpet with that eerie smoothness that had once prompted Alexei to accuse him of taking rapid mincing steps beneath the hem of his robe like the female Beryozka dancers that seem to float across the stage. Rasputin only laughed and said if he were that talented a dancer, he'd never have become a priest.

Smoke swirled around the loose sleeves of his robes as he bought his hands together in front of him.

"Come to see Katya recite at last?"

"Even Sylvie said she's never seen better."

It was the first time I'd mentioned Sylvie Buxhoeveden to him since the incident with the letters. We'd never talked about it, though he must have assumed I'd heard. Or perhaps he knew more than I thought, if I'd accidentally left some sign of myself in his tower.

In our lessons since, I sensed a new tension between us. I wondered if he caught flashes of his own bedroom in my mind, of his wife's portrait, her sad eyes and thin, clever hands clasped in front of her. Or of the image I'd seen of Sylvie herself, fleeing across the lawn with Rasputin's letters clutched in her hand.

"A brother must be biased," Rasputin said softly. "Let us trust the witness of Sylvie Buxhoeveden."

Was he baiting me? Was I baiting him?

I never knew the rules of our games—only that we sat on opposite sides of the table.

A pack of young men came bursting into the house—one of them my brother, the next my cousin Dimitri, and the last a very drunk and highly boisterous Felix Yusupov.

With their stamps and laughter came a gust of winter wind, blowing bits of ice across the baroness' rug and giving me a cold slap in the face.

Alexei could stand up a little better than Felix, but not much. When he saw Rasputin, he threw his arms around the monk and kissed him on both cheeks.

"You should have come to dinner with us. That Finnish serving girl was carrying 'round the beer. I said to her—oh, Stasia, where'd you come from?"

I'd been standing there all the while.

"I saw you before we got through the door," Felix said, throwing an arm around my shoulders. He was thin but leaned heavier than I expected. His blue eyes were bloodshot and he had a dirt mark on the knee of his trousers. The tang of beer on his breath was not entirely unpleasant. "I never see you anymore, Anastasia. I never see anybody."

"Neither do I. Ollie comes home soon at least ..."

I said it like it would bring us all back together again.

"That's the only good news I've had in ages." Felix sighed. He turned his bleary gaze on Rasputin—up until that moment, he'd been pointedly ignoring him. "Did you hear we lost half our ministry this week? Probably you were the first to know. You're so close to the Empress."

"Those who pay attention are rarely surprised." The shrug of Rasputin's shoulders was a liquid movement, here and gone like a wave.

"*Half* the ministry?" I said sharply. "Who else left besides Danilov?"

"Arsenev, Chislov, and Goremykin." Felix ticked the names off his fingers. "All sacked this week. By your mother."

He was speaking to me but looking at Rasputin.

"Are you questioning the decisions of the Empress?" Rasputin posed his question to the open air. To everyone watching.

"Not at all," Felix stared right back at him. "I question the advice she's given."

Rasputin smiled.

His confidence had a way of making anyone else seem wrong. I'd watched it with Sylvie Buxhoeveden and now Felix. Rasputin was sleek and sanguine, unbothered by Felix's aggression to a degree that made Felix seem unnecessarily hostile.

Felix's hair flopped down over his eyes, greasy or sweaty or both. The outrageous cut of his trousers and tilt of his hat that had previously given him such an air of panache now looked slightly unhinged.

Felix Yusupov was popular in St. Petersburg—few people but Aunt Xenia disliked him. Yet the mood in the room wasn't with him.

The students cast suspicious glances at his heavy wristwatch, one of them muttering *"oil baron,"* to a friend. Even the Minister of Culture, a conservative nearly as old as General Danilov himself, said, with the pretty young woman nibbling his ear, "Danilov's time was long past. He's a relic."

Felix's gaze flicked to the minister and the girl hanging on his shoulders. His upper lip curled. "That relic was the only person keeping bread on the shelves."

"Not well enough!" a man with ink-stained fingers cried out. "The people wait in line for hours and return home with nothing."

"And who will replace him?" Felix swayed slightly on his heels. *"Him?"* He pointed an unsteady finger at Rasputin, his voice pitched high at the ridiculousness of the idea.

No one else seemed to find it ridiculous. Not even Felix's drunken friends joined in as Felix forced a laugh. They shuffled and blinked, while cold silence and angry stares radiated from this room full of strangers.

"Nobody's here to talk about politics." Alexei tried to put a hand on Felix's arm.

Felix shook him off.

"Go on." He squared off with Rasputin while Alexei and Dimitri tugged at him. "Who do you think should replace Danilov?"

"I'm no politician," Rasputin said.

"Then what are you?" Felix sneered.

"Only the most powerful seer in Rusya!" a dark-haired ballerina cried. She might have been one of the corps that danced with Anna Pavlova at the Chinese theater—she looked familiar.

Felix stepped in so close to Rasputin that they were almost nose to nose.

"The most powerful seer in Rusya ..." he scoffed. "Make a prediction for me, then."

"Felix—"

Nothing short of dragging him away was going to make him back down.

Alexei and Dimitri hardly seemed to exist as they pulled at him like impatient children.

"Go on!" he demanded. "Read my future."

"I'd be glad to."

Rasputin's sudden agreement made Felix falter, but only for a moment.

"Do it then." He thrust out his hand.

I remembered how Irina had wanted to have her future read, but Felix wouldn't let her.

The same impulse came over me, to grab his hand and yank it back.

Rasputin had already drawn the silver raven's skull from the breast of his robes. It dangled from its chain, rotating slightly. I felt a chill on the back of my neck, between my hair and the collar of my gown. Over the howl of wind outside the windows, I heard the distant sound of piano music drifting across the snow.

Felix held up his middle finger. Rasputin pricked it with the raven's beak. Blood welled up, sudden and dark. Rasputin lifted Felix's finger and touched it to his tongue.

Everyone in the room held their breath. I saw Tatiana by the fireplace, light and shadow flickering across her face. Madame Lessinger stood in the doorway, hands at her mouth, as feverish as anyone to hear what Rasputin would say.

He had no pipe this time, and yet the smoke of the room swirled around him, carrying a sickly greenish hue. Felix looked almost as pale as Rasputin, all his color draining away.

The images that flickered in the smoke were clearer than I'd ever seen them. I saw how they danced and swirled together, sometimes flirting like birds in spring, sometimes colliding and creating an entirely new image, then breaking to pieces and falling apart.

I saw a boy with copper-colored hair snatching a pie off a table. He twisted to avoid the outraged swipe of a wooden spoon and leaped out the kitchen window, laughing madly as he sprinted away, pie held aloft. A smaller boy pelted after him, rewarded with an equal share of the booty once they reached freedom. The little boy grinned the delighted grin I'd seen so often on Felix's face, his mouth stained with berry juice.

The two boys seemed to age in an instant, growing taller by two heads, the eldest sprouting a mustache. Now the younger wasn't smiling; he looked distinctly stressed, pulling desperately on his brother's arm.

"You don't have to go, Nikky—it doesn't matter what he said!"

His brother looked down at him, face rigid and set. "Of course it

329

matters." Then, with a hint of the old insouciance. "What are you worried for? You know I always come out on top."

A gunshot sounded. The real Felix jerked as if he'd been hit, though no one else in the room seemed to have heard it.

I saw rain falling into a hole in the ground and heard an echoing voice that said, *You're the heir now. Everyone's depending on you* ...

A weight descended on my shoulders so heavy I thought it would break me. Felix seemed to sink an inch or two before Rasputin until they were no longer the same height.

The smoke pressed black around them, thick and dark and smothering. Until a pair of blue eyes emerged, above a shy smile breaking over a face as beautiful as the dawn.

"Irina ..." Felix breathed.

I saw Irina at a party, Irina at a ball, Irina on Nevsky Prospect with a parasol over her shoulder. Irina turning, Irina laughing, Irina laying back on a bed of summer daisies, her hair a dark cloud ...

"You want to know your future?" Rasputin asked softly.

Felix nodded, face blank, eyes full of nothing but images of his beloved.

"This is what I predict ... you'll finally have what you desire."

"When?" Felix's hand floated in the air, reaching for what only he and I could see. Us, and Rasputin.

Rasputin smiled.

"Sooner than you think."

The smoke faded away. Felix blinked, no longer drunk but not even close to sober.

Madame Lessinger's laugh cut through the silence.

"I wish you had such happy news for *me*, Rasputin! Your last reading was so dreary."

"If only I could change the future as easily as I perceive it," Rasputin said, holding out his hand to her. When she offered her own, he lifted it to his lips and kissed it.

Tatiana slipped in beside me.

"That doesn't make sense."

"What?"

The line of puzzlement between her eyebrows only made her prettier. "If you can see the future, you can change it."

"Can you?"

"Of course."

"How do you know?"

For once, Tatiana had no answer.

"Maybe it's like Cassandra and the battle of Troy," I said, watching Rasputin. "Maybe a glimpse the future only makes it more painful when it comes to pass."

Rasputin couldn't save his wife and daughter.

But perhaps when they died, he hadn't yet learned to read the smoke.

"Is everyone ready for a little entertainment?" Madame Lessinger clapped her hands.

No seats had been laid out in formal rows. Everyone stood or sat where they wished. The drinking and conversation continued throughout the performances, though at lower tones.

The cellist performed first, then the soprano.

When Katya stood, the room quieted at last. Everyone turned to hear her.

No one was more entranced than Alexei, who'd been perched on the arm of her sofa, hanging off her every word.

"I was going to read *Winter's Voice*," Katya said, naming one of her more famous poems, the one Sylvie heard her perform. "But I thought I'd do something new tonight."

I saw a glance pass between her and Rasputin. Their eyes only met for a moment, but there was something repressive in the movement of Rasputin's head.

Katya ignored him. She smiled at Alexei, announcing, "This is for my Tsarevich."

Alexei beamed.

Katya took out a battered notebook in which I could see lines of verse scribbled and crossed out, marked and annotated so densely that I would never have been able to read it even if it were written in a language I understood. The strangeness of the verses gave credence to Rasputin's claim that his letters were simply a Siberian dialect.

Katya held her notebook open in front of her. Once she began to speak, she never glanced at the page. She recited her poem as all great performers do —speaking directly to her audience. Her voice grabbed hold of me. She seized me from the very first line and wouldn't let go.

> *Children are born in a shadow*
> *A shape they're meant to fill*
> *An idea*
> *A trait*
> *A need*

A tool
Flesh combines, spirit is summoned
Even the poorest magician
Can create this alchemy
Sometimes by accident
A permanent spell
Ingredients that can never be unmixed
Why summon a demon?
If you only wanted a dog

Alexei laughed at the last line. Rasputin did not.

I couldn't understand his look of fury or the impudent toss of Katya's head. Why would Rasputin care if Katya wrote a poem for Alexei?

Maybe he thought my parents would be angry at the veiled critique. But this was hardly a room of Tsarists.

Alexei applauded until his hands were red.

"Bravo! Bravo!"

It was the most excited I'd seen him in months.

Tatiana clapped with less enthusiasm. Her head cocked in that way I knew so well—like a dog, though she'd be furious to hear me say it.

"There's a messenger at the door."

I glanced at the clock on the mantle. It was well past midnight—too late for post.

Maria joined us. Her priest obviously didn't believe in witching hours, because he was gaily toasting Katya and Alexei with no apparent plans to leave.

"She's so talented! If she were a man, she could have been a priest like Rasputin—can you imagine that voice over a pulpit?"

"Quiet!" Tatiana snapped at her.

"Sorry," Maria clapped a gloved hand to her mouth. "What are you—"

"*Shh!*" Tatiana hissed again.

We stood in in the babble of conversation, the clinking of glasses, the jangle of Felix morosely picking out notes on the keys of Madame Lessinger's grand piano.

Tatiana let out an irritated huff.

"What was it?" asked Maria.

"I didn't hear. You were jabbering."

"She didn't know." I gave Maria a friendly bump with my hip. "And everybody else was making noise."

"Especially Felix." Tatiana turned her glare on the piano.

"He's a mess," Maria said, with nothing but pity. "He says this war is the end of everything. Says the whole country's falling apart."

"He's just being dramatic because of Irina." Tatiana rolled her eyes.

"I hope so." Maria shivered. "It does feel like everything's changing. I hardly recognize anyone here."

I said, "Ollie will be back soon. Papa, too."

In my mind, that was the thing that would put everything right.

Though I knew it was impossible, I imagined Nikolasha and Damien coming home at the same time. Everyone together again.

"She's not coming back alone, though," Tatiana said. "*He'll* be with her."

"Prince Axel's coming here?"

No one told me.

"I got a letter from Ollie this morning."

Tatiana looked at me, her somberness mirroring exactly what I felt.

That meant it was settled. Ollie and Axel must be all but engaged.

"I thought you liked him?" Maria said.

"I do ..." Tatiana made a face. "But he tries to be *funny.*"

Maria and I glanced away from Tatiana and ended up facing each other, which made it impossible to hold in our laugh.

"*What?*"

She glared as we sniggered through our fingers.

"Nothing," Maria snorted.

I shook my head, trying not to look at Tatiana, but feeling her scowl on every inch of my skin. Giggles squeaked out of me like a leaky balloon.

There wasn't an equation or conjugation that could baffle my sister, but some jokes flew right over her head.

The drunken footman bent over Madame Lessinger, whispering in her ear.

I saw his lips moving and watched the color fade from Madame Lessinger's face, blanching top to bottom like water running down a drain. Her mouth went slack and she gave a convulsive shake of her head.

I stopped laughing.

"Was is it?" Maria asked.

Tatiana answered, her voice weaker than I'd ever heard it:

"It's Sylvie. She jumped in front of a train."

334

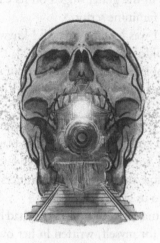

chapter 27

RUSHING DOWN THE TRACK

I visited Sylvie's house a week later than planned, all alone except for Kolya Deverenko, who waited outside the door.

Sylvie lived in an upscale neighborhood north of the city, in a robin's egg house with white sashes and garden beds full of irises, now blanketed in snow.

Despite attending her funeral in St. Isaac's Cathedral and watching her coffin slide into her family mausoleum, I was unprepared for the awful silence of her house. The ticking of her grandfather clock had never sounded so hollow, the scent of her perfume fading like flowers forgotten between the pages of a book.

I walked through the familiar rooms, realizing how long it had been since I'd visited. There was a time when Sylvie practically lived at the palace, spending more time in her suite of private rooms than she did here.

I was only now realizing how much less I'd seen her in recent years.

Thanks to Sylvie's highly efficient housekeeper, Madame Aubert, the house was as tidy as ever, with the exception of a few items oddly out of place. Several books had been shelved upside down, spines facing the wrong way, and one of the mirrors in the drawing room had been lifted off its hook and turned to face the wall. Though the fireplace was swept clean, a fragment of paper remained trapped in the grate, singed on its edges and bearing the tail end of a word written in feminine script.

I didn't know what I was looking for. All I knew was that Sylvie's death made no sense, and I couldn't accept it.

I was aware that people killed themselves, and it often came as a surprise to loved ones. I had a great-uncle who shot himself with a hunting rifle. No one ever knew the reason.

But I didn't believe Sylvie was one of those people. She loved good food and fine wine, jokes, and gossip. She kept a list of places she wanted to travel, monuments she longed to see. She had nieces and nephews she adored, dozens of friends, and more than a few male admirers. She was devoted to my mother, and I thought, to us girls.

Maybe none of that mattered to a mind that had begun to slide into darkness. But I had to see it for myself, written in her own words: *I can't take it anymore. It's all too much.* Then maybe I'd believe it.

I searched her house looking for a diary or letter. Because I'd wanted to visit Sylvie the day she died, I had some silly notion that she might have been thinking of me as well. Might have written me a note and left it on her writing desk.

I checked her room, searching her dresser, her drawers, even under her pillow and mattress. I knew how pointless it was long before I stopped, knew I was only paining myself with the scent of her soap, the familiar swoop of the SB monogram on her sheets, her pillows in the shade of rose she loved best.

One blonde hair still curled around the bristles of the brush on her vanity. I pulled the hair free and wrapped it around my finger where it gleamed gold like a wedding band.

Her writing desk was empty. Suspiciously so. If it had contained any private correspondence, the discreet and loyal Madame Aubert must have cleared it away—which would account for the fragments in the fireplace.

I spied the edge of something peeking out beneath the drapes and jumped up to investigate. It was Sylvie's copy of *Anna Karenina*, splayed open as if she'd tossed it aside in disgust, perhaps annoyed at the ending. She'd underlined a passage and made a note in the margin.

The passage read:

She hardly knew at times what it was she feared, and what she hoped for. Whether she feared or desired what had happened or what was going to happen and exactly what she longed for, she could not have said.

The note Sylvie made said only this:

Desire + fear = blindness

Flicking through, I found the book full of notes and tiny illustrations.

I tucked it under my arm. It wasn't stealing, not really. Sylvie had offered to lend it to me once. I'd read it now with all her notes, and it would be like reading a book together one last time, sharing our thoughts.

Besides, that's the excuse I gave my mother: I said Sylvie had some books of mine I wanted to retrieve before the house was commandeered by whatever relative had inherited.

Mama, who hadn't stopped crying all week, barely paid attention to my lie. She just nodded and covered her face with her hands, while Liza Taneeva put a consoling arm around her shoulders.

"Don't worry." Liza smiled up at me. "I'll take care of the Empress."

I could have slapped her for that smile. I could have slapped her for every time Sylvie's name crossed her lips with her enraging mixture of piety and false regret.

"Poor, dear Sylvie. May the gods keep and protect her. And I hope that they will even if the manner of her death ... well, we won't speak of that."

But she had spoken of it, again and again, in whisper and insinuation, making sure every single person in the court knew exactly how "poor, dear" Sylvie died.

"I don't believe she jumped," Tatiana said, right to our mother.

Mama shook her head, slow and miserable.

"The night watchman saw her. So did the conductor of the train. She was all alone on the platform. She walked right to the end where ..."

Mama didn't finish the sentence but I heard the words in my head: *where the train comes in fastest.*

I thought of that rush of metal, two hundred tons of iron and steam, barreling through Sylvie's body faster than a horse could run.

I prayed she felt nothing, but I feared she must have been in terrible pain for a long time before.

I fled her house, book tucked under my arm.

"Did you find what you were looking for, Highness?" Kolya asked me.

"I'm afraid not."

"I'm sorry to hear it. I'm just ... very sorry."

He was helping me into the carriage. His hand clenched around mine, once quickly, before he let go.

My eyes were hot. I blinked hard, the book clutched tight on my lap.

I didn't cry, not even after he closed the carriage door. Because I still wasn't sure exactly what I'd be crying for.

CHAOS GRIPPED the palace in anticipation of the return of the Tsar. Papa had successfully rendezvoused with Nikolasha in Galicia, then traveled on to Denmark where he spent five days with our friends and relatives. Now he was escorting Ollie home in the company of Prince Axel, who had officially become her fiancé after the successful negotiations that took place at Copenhagen palace.

Mama wanted our palace cleaned top to bottom, the guards in new uniforms, fresh flowers brought in for every room. But she'd fallen ill shortly after the news of Sylvie's suicide and had no will to supervise any of it.

Liza Taneeva had taken charge, much to Margaretta's annoyance. She bustled around barking orders at the servants, contradicting Margaretta's instructions and undoing half of what had already been done.

Margaretta had to vent her annoyance on the housemaids since she couldn't shout at Liza. I saw Annette sobbing while she dusted, and another maid hiding behind the mirror in the Marble Hall while Margaretta swept past like a ship at full steam.

Liza, by contrast, had never looked happier. Her main rival at court was vanquished, Mama needed her more than ever, and she had just been granted a formal divorce on account of her husband's insanity.

Papa had signed the documents himself, as well as the papers for Stana Leuchtenberg.

With Stana, there were no ameliorating circumstances. Being slapped around by your husband wasn't grounds for divorce. Papa signed the papers because Nikolasha forced him to do it. He flatly refused to accept the Charoite from Papa or to continue leading the armies as Commander-in-Chief without the reward of Stana, free and unencumbered.

Papa left Galicia furious at what he viewed as rank blackmail.

Even Mama thought Nikolasha had gone too far.

"Divorce is a mortal sin."

"But he loves Stana and her husband doesn't," I argued.

Mama gave me a wary look, folding the letter in which Papa vented about Nikolasha for the better part of three pages.

"It concerns me, Anastasia, that you think love matters more than the

sacrament of marriage. I worry what you girls are learning from these novels."
She gave a pointed glance at the copy of *Anna Karenina* tucked under my
arm. "Isn't that about a married woman who conducts an affair?"

My mother had all the compassion in the world ... except for scarlet
women.

"Yes," I said. "Because she was miserable in her marriage. I don't know
how it benefits the gods for a woman to suffer humiliation and loneliness all
the days of her life."

"That's why we choose carefully before we marry."

"And what if I make a mistake?"

"Not all mistakes can be fixed."

I'd left my mother's boudoir annoyed and no less on the side of Anna
Karenina and Stana Leuchtenberg. I knew exactly what "choosing carefully"
was going to look like when it was my turn. I'd be paraded through the courts
of suitable suitors, and if I was lucky, meet my husband perhaps a handful of
times before we were wed.

I felt nothing but happiness for Nikolasha and hurried off to write him a
note to tell him so.

I wrote to Damien as well, even though I still hadn't received a response
from my last. Our letters often overlapped, if they arrived at all.

I'm glad two people are happy at least, in all this mess.
   Do you know, are they waiting to be married or will they do it right away?
   I wish I could go but I doubt Mama and Papa would let me, even if it were
   right here in St. Petersburg.
   Papa says you'll be storming Lemberg.
   Please, please, please ... be careful.

Papa had only written what the army would be doing in general—he
wouldn't tell me news of Damien, even if he'd seen him face to face.

I was a rat scavenging every piece of information I could find. Even
though it tortured me.

The idea of Damien launching an offensive against those steep city walls
was unbearable. One of his friends had been gelded by a cannonball and his
favorite captain had been killed at the Battle of Krasnik a month after being
promoted to major. Now Damien was taking his place.

I tried to distract myself with the novel, spending hours every day sunk in
Tolstoy's dense, descriptive prose.

Sylvie's annotations grew increasingly deranged the further I ventured into the book. I was watching her mind deteriorate, the passages she marked becoming odd and obscure, her notes barely connected to the story. The illustrations were most disturbing of all. She filled the margins with inked symbols, sometimes drawing over the paragraphs themselves: hearts and vines, numbers and glyphs, tiny devils with horns ...

The book was the proof I'd sought that Sylvie had lost her mind.

But why?

She'd accused Rasputin. A month later she was dead.

He didn't push her in front of that train. He was at Madame Lessinger's party when Sylvie died, in full view of me and everyone else.

But what if there was more than one way to push someone?

What if you could do it a mile away, or a week in advance?

I'd read the book I'd stolen from Rasputin so many times that I had the relevant passage memorized:

When a vampyr speaks, it twists the minds of men ... You must never meet a vampyr's gaze, or listen to its persuasion.

Sylvie went mad, and so did Alexander Vasilievich Vyrubov—after they met Rasputin.

It sounded ridiculous, far-fetched in the extreme.

Yet I found myself turning the remaining pages in *Anna Karenina* faster and faster. I wanted to finish the story before Aunt Xenia arrived for dinner.

I'd been holed up in the library the better part of the day, the smaller one on the upper floor. Rain was pouring down again, monotonously drilling against the glass. It had been a long and miserable winter, broken by a cold, wet spring. The rain would wash away the last of the snow, but gods I missed blue sky.

I read and read, not noticing the chiming of the hour or how dim the light had grown.

I read through the tragic conclusion of Anna's romance with Count Vronsky, the loss of her child, her friends, her family as everyone she loved rejected her, even the faithless Count himself.

Then I turned to a page that Sylvie had covered on both sides with strokes of thick black ink. I strained to read the printed words through her drawing:

A feeling seized her, similar to what she experienced when preparing to go into the water for a swim ... life rose before her momentarily with all her bright past joys ... yet she did not take her eyes from the wheels ...

The drawing of a train spanned both pages, rushing down the tracks, its headlamp a glaring eye.

I slammed the book shut as if the train would rush straight at me, as if it would barrel right out of the pages. I gasped for breath, hands shaking.

I didn't know that Anna Karenina threw herself beneath the wheels of a train. Just like Sylvie ...

I recognized the image of the train because I'd seen it before: in the smoke, when Rasputin read Sylvie's future.

He knew. He knew all along.

Or ... he saw his chance and took it.

I sprang up from the window seat, the book tumbling to the ground, sprawling open as it had done when Sylvie tossed it aside.

Did she fling it away from her because she felt the story worming into her mind, the words on the page twining in her own memories, her own visions, her own dreams for the future?

You alone must take the first step on your journey ...

Sylvie took a journey to the most distant place, from which no traveler can return.

And who set her on that road?

My feet carried me through the palace without any actual plan. All I knew was that I was going to confront Rasputin. I was going to look him in the eye and ask if he killed Sylvie, and this time I'd know if he lied. I knew right where to look in his head ...

Maria tried to intercept me by the back garden door.

"Anastasia, where have you been? You're not dressed for dinner—Aunt Xenia will be here any minute!"

Maria's cheeks bore the blotchy strawberries-and-cream color that came over her when she'd been crying. That was hardly uncommon for her, but I feared it had something to do with her soldier.

"What happ—never mind," I said. "I'll be right back."

I ran across the lawn in the rain, not giving a damn that I was soaked to the skin long before I reached the tower.

I hammered on the door. When it swung open, Katya leaned against the doorframe, hands stuffed in the pockets of her trousers. She had on a man's shirt, rolled up at the sleeves, and the sort of cloth cap a delivery boy would wear. She took a pull off her rolled-up cigarette, pinching it between her thumb and index finger, exhaling slowly out of the side of her mouth.

"Where's Rasputin?"

"Not close enough to hear you no matter how hard you pound," she said, slightly amused.

I wasn't entertained in the slightest.

"*Where is he?*"

She tapped the ash off the end of her cigarette. I had the distinct impression that she was taking her time on purpose, enjoying my agitation.

"Some lord invited him to dinner," she said at last.

"Who?"

"One of the ones from the party." She waved her cigarette carelessly.

I knew she could have named the lord if she wanted to.

Katya cast a lazy glance down my soaking-wet dress.

"You're dripping."

She didn't invite me inside.

I liked Katya when I met her because she was clever and beautiful. Now I wondered if I was always that stupid, seeing only what people wanted me to see.

Coldly, I said, "Stay away from my brother,"

She smiled without showing any teeth.

"As you wish, Highness. But I can't promise he'll stay away from me."

She closed the door in my face.

I wanted to kick the door down and drag her out of the tower that *we* owned, that wasn't hers at all. But Aunt Xenia was waiting.

I trudged back to the palace through the rain.

Margaretta started shouting the moment I walked through the door.

"*There* you are! We've been looking everywhere, your aunt is waiting, you're not even dressed! And look at the floor, you're worse than Alexei and the dog put together."

She pointed at the mud I'd tracked onto the marble tile that had been washed and polished in anticipation of my aunt's arrival.

I wanted to scream. The only things that seemed to matter around here were the things that didn't matter at all.

I stalked upstairs to change clothes and towel off my hair as best I could, joining Xenia, Irina, Mama, Tatiana, Maria, and Liza Taneeva in the formal dining room just in time for the second course.

"Sorry I'm late."

I was even more sorry when I saw the only remaining seat was next to Liza Taneeva.

She gave me a thin smile, her eyes flicking over my wet hair and rumpled gown. "Fresh out of the bath?"

Irina waved excitedly from the end of the table, mouthing *How are you?* We hadn't seen each other in months.

Tatiana sat across from me, looking utterly furious. I thought she was pretty tetchy for someone who hadn't even had to wait for her soup, until I realized she was glowering slightly to the right of me at Liza Taneeva.

A strange tension gripped the room, Mama twittering like a bird as she often did when nervous, Liza looking everywhere but at Tatiana. Maria sat tearful and silent, staring down at the napkin draped across her lap. Even Irina was wan as a faded photograph. Only Xenia sat serene and imperious at the head of the table.

With forced cheerfulness, Liza said to Xenia, "And where is the Grand Duke?"

Aunt Xenia took a prim spoonful of soup, scooping it away from herself as I'd been taught by my governess, saying, "Sandro's dining with his brothers tonight."

Uncle Sandro had five brothers, all large-boned, dark-haired and clever, and ferociously loyal to each other when they weren't getting in brawls. He also had a sister, but we weren't allowed to visit her because she unapologetically bore the bastard son of a servant after her husband died.

"I heard his planes are having great success," Liza said, still sucking up. She was always trying to get in Aunt Xenia's good graces, though Xenia barely tolerated her.

Uncle Sandro had been adamant that Rusya needed an air fleet like France and Albion. Papa hadn't seen the use of the flimsy planes, but he agreed, putting Sandro in charge of the newly built aviation school at Sevastopol. Now my uncle was chief of the Air Service, and the planes that at first had only been used for reconnaissance were being fitted with machine guns and bombs.

I remembered the thrill I'd felt when I visited the airfield at Sevastopol and saw one of the fragile-looking biplanes soar up into the sky like a stiff-winged bird.

It had seemed so miraculous—a human technology more powerful than magic.

Even Artemis had been mildly impressed. She'd flown up next to the plane to see how it worked, returning a few minutes later.

I'm faster.

"Yes, but I can ride in a plane, and you can't carry me."

You're getting in that? The biplane gave an alarming wobble up in the sky.

I wanted to, desperately, but Uncle Sandro wouldn't let me. I found out later that while Uncle Sandro had successfully built us the largest air fleet of any nation, production had been rushed to such a degree that one in three planes had engine issues.

Now these planes were going to start dropping bombs on hapless soldiers. Soldiers like Damien.

I was sick to death of the war that dragged on and on. We made planes and they made planes. We sent more soldiers and so did they. We captured a piece of territory, they stole a piece of ours. Nobody was winning, and the bodies piled up.

Everyone was sick of the war. Not only the students at Madame Lessinger's party, but also the politicians and aristocrats. Everyone wanted it over, but no one agreed how that should be accomplished.

"Where's Alexei?" I interrupted Aunt Xenia in the middle of her description of the newest planes.

Mama answered. "He's dining with friends."

"Which friends?"

She looked embarrassed. "I'm not sure ... I was lying down when he left."

I wondered if Alexei was with Rasputin.

I had the most awful sense of time ticking past. I didn't know where I was supposed to be going or what I should be doing, but I was less than useless trapped at the dinner table.

"Migraines again?" Xenia asked Mama, with minimal sympathy. She was outrageously healthy and had little patience for illness.

"A painful malady," Liza said dramatically. "I'm often similarly afflicted. Though it never stops me waiting on the Empress."

Xenia ignored this as she ignored most statements spoken by Liza Taneeva.

"Pity he went out—I hardly see Alexei these days."

She hadn't seen Tatiana, Maria, or me in just as long, but that didn't seem to bother her.

It was Xenia who'd been keeping away from our corrupting influence. Or I should say, keeping Irina away.

Irina was paying no attention at all to the conversation at the table, fidgeting in her seat and checking the time on the grandfather clock in the corner.

Though still painfully lovely, Irina was looking only a little better than Felix. She'd lost weight she couldn't afford to lose. Her eyes were too big in her face, her hair dry and brittle.

"Has Irina been sick?" Tatiana asked aloud.

"No," Xenia said sharply, looking at her daughter. "She's in the bloom of health."

"Yes," Irina said faintly. "I'm quite well."

She didn't look well. She was tense as a rabbit.

"You got a letter today," Mama said to me, changing the subject.

"I did? Where is it?"

"Right here." Liza Taneeva pulled the letter from her pocket and handed it to me.

The paper was limp and worn. She'd obviously been carrying it for hours. Probably holding it up to the light, trying to see the words on the first page.

I tried to hide how angry I was.

"The servants bring my letters to my room."

"I was saving them a trip. They're quite busy at the moment, if you haven't noticed. Too busy to ferry notes from ... was it Galicia? But that's not Nikolasha's writing on the envelope ..."

Aunt Xenia snapped at the bait.

"Are you writing to that *Cossack?*"

She could hardly have said a curse word with more disdain.

Mama watched me, waiting for the answer.

I lifted my chin.

"Yes. I'm writing to Damien."

"*Anastasia,*" Mama breathed.

"I don't care! He's my friend. And he'll be Ataman of the Cossacks someday."

I threw that at Xenia, to remind her that Damien wasn't as insignificant as she thought.

The letter burned in my hand. I wanted to open it and read it, but wouldn't dare within grabbing distance of Liza or Aunt Xenia. Instead, I tucked it in my pocket.

"And I'll get my own mail, *thank you,*" I hissed at Liza.

"Good." She sniffed. "I've got better things to do with my time."

That was too much for Tatiana.

"Oh, yes!" she cried. "You've been *very* busy today."

Liza's cheeks flushed a dull brick color. She sputtered, "I only did what the Empress asked. I was perfectly in the right—"

"She didn't ask you to do anything! It was you who—"

"Tatiana!" Mama cried.

"She's always had it out for Nina! She's a nasty, jealous, sneaking—"

"TATIANA!"

Mama's face was as mottled as Maria's, but with anger, not sadness.

Xenia and Irina looked as confused as I felt. Maria was crying silently, shoulders shaking, head drooping down.

"What are you all talking about?" Xenia demanded. "What's going on?"

Tatiana turned her cold stare on Mama, who shrank in her seat.

"Mama sacked Nina Ivanova today."

"*What*?"

"As well she should!" Liza cried, rushing to Mama's defense. "The girl came bursting in with some cockamamie tale. Said she woke up in the barn with hay in her hair and her dress done up wrong. Started making wild accusations, said someone had interfered with her."

Liza cast a quick glance at Xenia, to make sure this wasn't too graphic for Irina's ears.

Xenia's dark eyes narrowed.

"Who did she say interfered with her?"

"That's why it was so ridiculous!" Liza snorted. "She said she couldn't remember anything that happened. She wanted to pin it on Rasputin, simply by proximity to the cathedral."

"Not *just* by proximity!" Tatiana cried. "He was watching her beforehand. He's been watching her for months!"

"He was lighting the lamps. As is his *duty*."

"That's not all!"

"No, it certainly isn't," Liza sneered. "I went to the girl's room to check on her, and what do you think I found?"

Xenia gave an impatient shrug.

"She'd snuck some officer into her room! I think it's quite clear who's been doing her dress up wrong ..."

"That's her fiancé!" Tatiana shouted.

"And that's as good as married these days, is it?" Mama's low voice cut through Tatiana's outrage and Liza's smug satisfaction.

Tatiana glanced involuntarily at Irina, who blushed to the roots of her hair.

Aunt Xenia seemed torn. She'd never liked Rasputin, but her grudge against Nina Ivanova was personal.

"That maid should have been sacked a year ago," she said coldly. "Good riddance to bad rubbish."

"Nina isn't rubbish!" Maria cried out. "She's kind and she works harder than any other maid in this palace!"

Xenia seemed shocked that the bashful Maria dared shout at her.

346

I wanted to defend Nina too, but I was afraid if I opened my mouth, I might vomit. I had the most awful feeling that this was only the tip of the iceberg.

"Where's Rasputin now?" I croaked out.

"He's dining in the city," Mama said primly. "He left an hour ago."

"Did you question him about this maid?" Xenia asked.

"Yes." Mama's hand was unsteady as she took a large draught of wine. "He said it was nonsense. He's barely passed two words with the girl."

"THAT'S NOT TRUE!" Tatiana bellowed.

Mama turned on her, stiff and white-lipped. "Leave the table and go to your room."

Tatiana's mouth fell open in outrage. None of us had been sent away from the table since we were in knee-socks. She pushed back her chair and stalked from the room. An enormous crashing sound in the hallway made me think she'd kicked over something expensive on her way out the door.

"*Well!*" Xenia said, eyebrows up to her hairline. "I don't know what sort of manners they teach at the Danish court ..."

"Mama ..." Irina said, in soft reproach.

"More wine?" Mama didn't wait for an answer, sloshing the remnants of the bottle into Xenia's glass and then her own.

"Thank you. I'm sure it's less than Sandro will be drinking tonight. His brothers are a terrible influence."

"All brothers are. Every stupid thing Nikky has ever done has been because of—some bad influence," Mama finished, remembering at the last minute that Papa's brothers were also Xenia's.

I was hardly listening to either of them. All I wanted was for this dinner to be over so I could escape and figure out what in the hell was going on. Where was Rasputin? Why had he attacked Nina? And where in the seven hells was Alexei?

"Maybe I should check on Tatiana ..." I ventured.

"You'll stay right where you are," Mama snapped.

She was wound up tighter than a spring, maybe because Aunt Xenia was witnessing our family drama, but more likely because she felt guilty about Nina Ivanova. The maid had once been a favorite of us all.

Four more interminable courses limped by before we proceeded into the drawing room.

"I'd like some music," Xenia announced.

Tatiana and Ollie were the most skilled pianists, but Ollie was still in Denmark and Tatiana had been banished to her room. Maria's eyes were too swollen to read the sheet music. She took her place at the piano anyway because anything was better than me plunking away at the keys.

That suited me fine—I planned to concoct a stomach ache so I could sneak away and read Damien's letter.

Irina slipped her hand in the crook of my elbow and pulled me away from our mothers.

"Rasputin's with Felix," she whispered.

"What?"

"*Shh.* He's with Felix right now. Dining at his house."

That didn't make sense. Felix loathed Rasputin.

"What's going on?"

"I—I'm not sure ..." Irina bit at the edge of her thumb. Her nails had been bitten so short that no white remained, only truncated beds with edges of raw skin on which she continued to gnaw.

"*Tell me.*"

"I—I think—"

I wanted to grab her by the shoulders and shake her.

"I think he's planning to kill him," she whispered, so quietly that I read the words off her lips more than actually heard them.

The floor seemed to drop several feet.

"That's a very bad idea. He's dangerous, Irina ... you have no idea how dangerous."

"That's what Felix thinks, too," Irina said miserably. "He says Rasputin is turning the people against us, that he's creating chaos, manipulating your parents. He says he has to be stopped."

"What's he going to do?"

"I'm not sure. He's been ... he's not in a good place. He thinks we'll never be married. He's given up hope."

I felt the sickest sense of impotence, like watching two carriages about to collide. I didn't know if I had time to stop it, but I had to try.

"Make an excuse for me," I said to Irina.

"What—"

"Say anything."

I was already running from the room. I heard Mama call my name, but didn't so much as turn, dashing through the remnants of the smashed crystal vase that Tatiana had toppled and Annette was now attempting to sweep.

I sprinted to the stables, throwing a saddle over the broad back of Barley, my favorite mare. As I led her out, I spied something glittering on the ground.

I stooped and scraped away the bits of hay, digging my fingers down between the floorboards.

I lifted a tiny silver charm, its bale twisted and bent. It was a Celtic love knot, the one Armand had sent Nina for her birthday.

Stomach heaving, I tucked the charm in my pocket and vaulted on Barley's back.

"ARTEMIS!" I bellowed.

She came swooping out of the mews as I galloped past.

No need to shout.

"Come with me. I'm going to Felix's house."

What for?

"Just come!"

I had no breath to talk and ride, galloping toward the gates as fast as Barley could carry me.

The guards stood at attention as I approached, giving me a smart salute.

"Your Highness! What can I—"

Without slacking pace, I barreled right through, the guards shouting after me.

Artemis gave her chirping laugh.

They're going to be in trouble. You, too, by the looks of it ... want to tell me what's going on?

"It's Rasputin," I puffed, bent forward over Barley's mane, clinging to the reins. "I think he's about to do something awful."

What that might be, I had no idea. The sense of foreboding that had gripped me from the moment I saw Sylvie's drawing of the train had steadily increased until I was filled with unnamed terror. Something was about to happen, I could feel it.

I galloped all the way to Felix Yusupov's mansion in the city, pausing only to bribe a paperboy to point me to the exact house.

If I'd ridden a little further down the street, I would have found it on my own. The front door hung open, several carriages waiting out front. Ominously, so was the personal car of the head of the Okhrana, Von Plehve.

He was the first person I ran into as I dashed into the house.

"Grand Duchess! What are you—"

"Where's Felix?" I gasped.

Von Plehve's thick gray brows dropped so low they covered half his eyes.

"What do you know?" he demanded.

I pushed past him. He made a grab for my arm and Artemis bit him so sharply that he yelped and stumbled backward, clutching his bloodied hand. Artemis clung to my forearm, body tense, talons digging in. She could feel the darkness in the house as well as I could. The servants clustered together, some crying, some murmuring. From the back of the house came a desperate wail.

"*My son!*"

I ran toward the screaming.

Princess Zinaida Nikolayevna slumped in the arms of a policeman, sobbing wildly. Her still-beautiful face was distorted with agony, broken glassware scattered all around her feet.

"What happened?" I cried.

She looked right through me, hardly seeming to recognize me though I'd met Felix's mother many times.

"*My son! My poor, sweet son!*"

I turned to the policeman instead, snapping, "Tell me what happened! I'm the Grand Duchess Anastasia Nikolaevna, Prince Felix is my friend!"

The policeman appeared torn between the imperative to bow and the need to support the reeling Princess Zinaida with both hands.

"It appears he was poisoned."

"*Oh gods! Oh gods!*" Princess Zinaida wailed.

"By who?" I said, though I already knew.

"By Grigory Rasputin," one of the servants rasped.

The servant was young and clean-shaven. His eyes darted from me to the policeman, and down to the broken glassware scattered across the rug. I saw an overturned tray, a few smashed cakes, and something dark spattered across the hearth that could have been vomit or blood.

The servant looked more than upset—he was distinctly nervous. With a brief, "I'll get water for Princess Zinaida," he hurried from the room.

I chased after him, corning him outside the kitchens.

"Tell me what you know."

"I know nothing!"

I pressed money into his palm and forced him to take it, pinning him against the wall. Or I should say, Artemis pinned him, rustling her wings, clicking her beak, which was still streaked with Von Plehve's blood.

"Felix invited Rasputin to the house, didn't he? Was he planning to kill him? Tell me what happened, where did they go?"

"I—I—" He cast a terrified glance at Artemis, who made a menacing sound in her throat.

"*Tell me!*"

"It's true," he whispered, his eyes unable to rest on my face, jerking to look over my shoulder, then over his own as he swiveled, shaking, face pale as whey. It was like he thought Rasputin might reappear behind him any

351

moment. "Rasputin came to the house. Master Felix ... there was arsenic in one of the glasses. It had been painted on the glass itself, invisible. But somehow ... Master Felix took the wrong glass. I don't know how it happened. They toasted and drank. A minute later he fell to the floor, choking, vomiting blood."

I could guess how it happened. It was no accident—Rasputin looked in Felix's mind and saw what he planned. He must have switched the glasses.

"Where are they now?"

"They've taken Master Felix to the hospital. But I'm afraid ... I don't think he'll ..."

The servant's face crumpled. He covered it with his hands.

I yanked them down and forced him to look at me.

"*Where's Rasputin?*"

"Gone," the servant said miserably. "Fled."

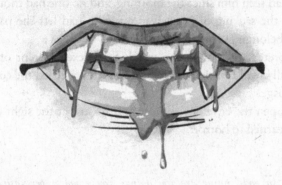

chapter 28

DAMIEN'S LETTER

V on Plehve insisted on driving me back to Alexander Palace, Barley remaining at Felix's mansion to be returned by one of his grooms. Artemis flew back on her own because she hated riding in cars.

Von Plehve tried to interrogate me as to exactly why I had galloped over to Felix Yusupov's house. I refused to answer his questions and he couldn't force me. I was one of the few people in St. Petersburg who couldn't be dragged down to his basement.

We arrived at a palace in worse chaos than Felix's house. Mama had sent out half the palace guard in pursuit of me. When a rider galloped up to the gates a half hour later, instead of news of her missing daughter, she was handed a note addressed to Princess Irina, informing her that Felix Yusupov had been carried to the Mariinskaya Hospital at the brink of death. When Xenia refused to allow her daughter to join him there, Irina collapsed in hysterics and had to be sedated by Dr. Atticus.

Even after I relayed what Felix's servant had said (omitting the part about Felix being the one who had laced the glass with arsenic in the first place), Mama refused to admit that Rasputin could have poisoned him and fled.

She kept saying, "There must be some explanation, some accident. He ran because he was afraid of being prosecuted. And *where* is Alexei?"

Now that I was back, the guards were hunting for my brother instead. The servants searched every room of the palace, the guards, the grounds, and St. Petersburg itself.

No one had seen him since the morning, and no one had thought to look, distracted by the sacking of Nina Ivanova, who had left the palace in tears with her few belongings stuffed in a carpetbag.

On the pretext of joining the search for Alexei, I crept off to a quiet corner to finally read Damien's letter. I desperately needed the comfort of his voice on the page.

I ripped open the envelope, almost in tears just at the sight of his script. But comfort turned to horror:

Anya,

What in gods' name are you doing? You've got a persuasive fucking vampire living in your house.

Maybe you're so "civilized" that your people aren't familiar with vampires. We hunt them like wolves.

They infest your life. They take over your whole village. The people you thought you knew, you thought were your friends, fall under their spell. You can't trust anything anymore.

You visit your cousins' village. You break bread. You think everything is fine, but you don't know they have a vampire in their midst. Then you go to battle, and your cousin isn't there. His host isn't there. You come back to his house and they're all dead, the vampire has flown.

You never know who it was at the table, eating and smiling with the rest of you.

You're on a razor's edge. How can you know what you actually know? How can you know how he's affected you?

Your brother be damned. His fate is set.

If I could leave, I'd ride to you and kill Rasputin myself.

Get him out of there.

—D

Too late.

It was like Damien knocked my hand off the scale. The balance swung, and I realized the full weight of the risk I'd taken.

It was this line that slapped me in the face:

How can you know how he's affected you?

You can never see what you don't know. That's the point—you don't fucking know it.

I could never be sure how much I'd fallen under Rasputin's spell, and how I might have behaved otherwise.

All I knew was what I'd done.

I'd kept his most crucial secret—the only certain piece of information anyone ever learned about him. Just like he wanted me to.

As I sunk to the carpet, the letter clutched in my hand, an awful wailing sound ripped through the air. The alarm screeched unceasingly, screaming through the palace.

I ran out into the hall, almost colliding with Tatiana who was fleeing the noise, her face a rictus of pain.

Kolya Deverenko sprinted past us in the opposite direction.

"What is it?" I shouted.

"Get back in your rooms!" he bellowed. "Someone's breaking into the vault!"

ACTUALLY, someone had already broken into the vault hours before. The six guards lay dead in the hallway, their heads almost ripped from their shoulders.

It was Alexei himself who had hit the alarm. He stumbled up from the vault, pale and delirious.

After Dr. Atticus stabilized Alexei and gave him a tincture that helped him to talk, it took the better part of an hour for Mama and Kolya Deverenko to extract a garbled account of what had happened.

Mama met Xenia, Tatiana, and me in the Mauve Boudoir, so weak with shock that Kolya practically had to carry her into the room.

"What's happening?" shouted Xenia. "Where's the Charoite?"

"Gone." Mama reeled against Kolya's arm. "It's all gone."

Xenia's face went the color of cheese. She stiffened, then slumped down on the nearest sofa.

"*How?*"

"Rasputin," Mama admitted, her voice barely more than a whisper. "He stole it all."

"How is that possible?" Xenia shrieked, recovering a little of her fire. "He's not a FUCKING ROMANOV!"

Mama swallowed drily, her throat clicking.

"Alexei gave it to him."

Xenia fell silent, horror-struck.

I shrank back against the wall, panic fluttering in my chest, my ears, my guts. I clamped my hand over my mouth, trying to swallow the rush of bile rising in my throat.

Alexei did it because he had to. He was under Rasputin's power.

I could have told my parents months before. I could have warned then.

It was my fault, not Alexei's. Entirely my fault.

Never stupefied for long, Xenia hissed, "Get his sister."

But Katya had fled as well. The White Tower was ransacked, already cleared of the most crucial of Rasputin's magical instruments and books. Even Bat was gone.

chapter 29

THE ARRIVAL OF PRINCE AXEL

The weeks that followed were some of the darkest I'd ever experienced. When Papa brought Ollie home in the company of her new fiancé, we struggled to greet them with anything like the enthusiasm we'd planned. We tried to paste smiles on our faces, while concealing from Prince Axel what a blow we'd suffered.

It was Xenia who insisted that no one could know we'd lost the Charoite. Rusya was already a powder keg. If the people knew we'd lost our most powerful weapon ... who knows what fresh hell would ensue.

Only Kolya Deverenko and two other soldiers knew the truth. They were threatened and bribed into silence, Kolya permitted to stay at the palace, but the other two soldiers packed off to distant outposts.

Everyone else was told that a theft had been attempted, but was unsuccessful.

I doubted the servants believed us. Rumors swirled, particularly about the poisoning of Felix Yusupov and the sudden disappearance of Rasputin.

The secret police hunted for any trace of where he'd gone. They found nothing. Rasputin had boarded a train at Vitebsky Station, the very platform where Sylvie Buxhoeveden had flung herself onto the track, and then evaporated somewhere between St. Petersburg and Siberia.

There were reports that Katya had been spotted in student quarters close to the university, but no sign of her since. She'd either gone to ground or followed after Rasputin.

I confessed everything to my parents the day Papa came home: the visits to Rasputin's tower, the magic lessons, and finally, and most damning of all, my discovery that he was half-vampyr.

"I swear to you," I sobbed, "I only kept his secret because I was afraid what would happen to Alexei if anyone found out."

That was true, but it wasn't the whole truth. I had my own selfish reasons for wanting to trust Rasputin, and that's why I was drowning in guilt.

So were my parents.

Papa put a heavy hand on my shoulder.

"You're not the only one who closed their eyes to Rasputin's flaws for Alexei's sake."

Mama sent a letter of apology to Nina Ivanova, offering her back her position as lady's maid. Nina declined. She thanked us for our patronage over her seven years of service, but said she had been hired as a seamstress in the city and was happy at her new position.

The truth was we'd hurt her, and she had no intention of coming back for more. I couldn't blame her for that, not one bit.

Sick with dread, I asked my father, "What's going to happen with the Charoite?"

His eyes were hollow. He'd lost weight on his long journey, and more since coming home.

"I can only assume Rasputin intends to sell it to another government. It's worth a hundred times its weight in gold. Our spies are listening for any news. Pray to the gods that he sells it to Albion or France, not Germany."

If Rasputin sold it to our enemies instead of our allies, they'd wipe us from the field.

We were losing Alexei even faster.

He came down to breakfast with a shaving nick on his chin. It continued to bleed through his consumption of tea and toast. He dabbed his chin with his napkin, trying to stem the flow. By the end of the meal, the napkin was spotted all over with blood while the cut still seeped bloody tears.

The only bright spot in all this misery was the return of Ollie and Prince Axel. While he had arrived in less than ideal circumstances, Axel was polite enough to pretend not to notice the melancholy around the palace. He himself possessed such a bounty of high spirits that he was soon coaxing

Alexei outside to join him for a tennis match, and asking Papa if he could take his Delaunay-Belleville for a spin.

Prince Axel radiated health and energy. He had a long, narrow face with a prominent chin and high hairline. His eyes were wide apart, mouth thin and straight. He was fit and sun-kissed, with a grin that could blind you.

He was phenomenally athletic. Ollie was always challenging him to tennis or badminton matches, to billiards or even races across the lawn. He beat her handily nine out of ten times—and I suspected he let her win on the tenth.

His gift was precision. He could fling a dart dead-center on the bullseye every single time. He could land a tennis ball at the exact corner of the back court. When he drove Ollie and me in Papa's car, it felt like we were flying. He soared around corners at a speed that would have flung anyone else into the nearest ditch, his touch on the wheel light and easy, his other arm slung around the back of Ollie's seat, resting on her shoulders.

My parents adored him. Mama's only complaint was that, "He and Ollie are so infatuated, they can hardly be left alone in a furnished room."

It was bizarre seeing Ollie in love at last. She collapsed in giggles at Axel's jokes, which were admittedly better than Tatiana had implied, and continued to fawn over him despite all the thrashings she was taking in tennis.

Prince Axel was not nearly as spoiled as most of the royals I'd met. He'd served in the Danish navy and risen all the way to lieutenant commander. Once his ship had been hit by a storm and he'd been thrown overboard. He managed to grab a piece of flotsam and clung to it for two long days and nights as the storm washed him miles from his ship.

When he was discovered off the coast of Norway by a boatful of fisherman, the Danish papers hailed him as "the Resurrected Prince."

Axel told the tale in such a humorous way that we all laughed at his peril, until I stopped cold in the middle of his story.

I'd just remembered Rasputin's predictions for Ollie's future:

You must find the one who can best you where you thought you would never be beaten ... the one who was lost and then found ...

No one had ever beaten Ollie at sports before Axel. And now I was learning that he had also been lost and found.

I tried to remember what else I'd seen in Ollie's smoke. A sleigh, a red flag, and something else ... a bowl? With fruit in it?

A sleigh ride had been the catalyst for Ollie's banishment to Denmark. The Danish flag was a white cross on a crimson field. And the fruit ...

"Did you ever see a huge bowl of fruit in Denmark?" I whispered to Ollie, when Axel inished his tale. "A golden bowl, with carvings on the side ..."

Ollie stared at me. "There was a bowl just like that in my room when I arrived. Full of pomegranates. How did you know? Did I write home about it?"

"I saw it in Rasputin's vision."

Ollie's eyes went wide. "Oh gods, you're right. He told me I'd meet someone. He said I'd be happy ... and I am."

I understood the confusion on her face. Rasputin had betrayed us all. It was not entirely comfortable to know that he'd correctly perceived our futures.

What else had he understood that we hadn't?

I tried to remember everything else I'd seen in the smoke, but it was difficult to recall the images that had seemed so random at the time.

I thought there'd been flowers in Ollie's vision ... and clouds? Was that supposed to mean something?

I tried to remember my own vision. Butterflies, like the ones on the frieze on my old bedroom wall. A mountain ... black and stark, like the Lorne Mountain. Perhaps the very same one.

My stomach sunk as I realized that might have been a warning. Whatever spirits controlled visions of the future might have been trying to show me that Rasputin planned to steal our Charoite.

I hadn't understood. I hadn't seen clearly.

What else, what else?

I racked my brain.

A snake, I thought ... and silver charms.

Nina's silver charms.

She hadn't even received the gift when I saw her bracelet in the smoke. I'd seen it, but it was meaningless at the time.

What I wouldn't give to watch that vision over again now that I understood a little more. I *had* to remember what else was coming ...

I saw people dancing. Perhaps that meant the end of the war?

And I saw Damien. Images of Damien as a boy, an adolescent, and a man.

Rasputin had been terrified by the specter of Damien, by his black, dripping hands. But why? What did that mean?

My only comfort was knowing that of all the things I cocked up, at least I kept Damien safe. As far as I knew, Rasputin had never discovered so much as his name.

"How long was he planning it?" Ollie said, her face somber.

"I think all along."

I'd have liked to believe differently. Would have preferred to think that

Rasputin had once been a friend, but was tempted by the unspeakable riches Charoite could buy.

But I couldn't lie to myself any longer. Looking back, I could see that he'd been manipulating us from the very beginning. Especially me.

What an idiot I'd been. A selfish fucking idiot. Blinded by curiosity and a hunger for magic.

Some things I'd done for Alexei ... but some things I'd done for myself.

I couldn't even blame Liza Taneeva for bringing Rasputin into our circle. I'd been just as eager to meet him as everyone else.

Liza took his betrayal hardest of all. She holed herself up in her little yellow house, "sick in bed," not even visiting the palace.

We were all glad of the reprieve, even Mama. We couldn't tolerate another round of moaning over the faithlessness of the man Liza had promoted for years.

I still suspected that Rasputin had driven Liza's husband mad at her request. In fact, now that I thought about it, Rasputin possessed the ability to put people to sleep, just like Alexander Vasilievich Vyrubov—I'd seen him do it to Alexei. I wondered if the power had been acquired through observation, or some darker method. Perhaps its extraction had driven Vyrubov mad.

There was nothing I'd put past Rasputin now. Even the story of his wife and child might have been a lie. I did believe they existed, because I'd seen the memory myself, but as to the details ... I no longer trusted anything he'd said.

It was a gloomy summer for Alexei and me, even with the cheerful presence of Prince Axel and the distraction of wedding planning. Alexei had sunk into a deep depression.

I thought he was afraid of dying, until he confessed, "I liked Rasputin ... but I loved Katya. I thought ... I thought she loved me, too."

His face contorted and he turned away, embarrassed.

I touched his arm.

"I'm sorry, Alexei. I should have told you what I knew."

He shook his head.

"I knew something was wrong. I could feel the grip he had on me, what it was doing to me. I didn't like the things I used to like. There was no pleasure in food or women ... I could hardly feel anything at all ... except when I was with Katya. I said nothing, I pretended I was fine. Because I didn't want to be sick again."

"It wasn't your fault. He had you under his power."

Alexei gave me a thousand-yard stare.

"What if I'd become Tsar while he had his hooks in me?"

We were silent, contemplating an outcome that might have been worse than the loss of the Charoite.

I said, "Maybe it's lucky he's gone."

"I don't know. I don't know what's going to happen."

None of us did. We waited in a state of awful anticipation, expecting every day to hear news of some great weapon acquired by a foreign court, or a horrific loss on the battlefield.

But we heard nothing, nothing at all. Not a whisper of Rasputin or the stones.

chapter 30
THE MEMORY-KEEPER

The strange thing about fear is that it has no stamina. You can't live in a constant state of vigilance and paranoia. Without tangible reminders of the danger hanging over your head, life intrudes with all its daily demands, its pleasures, its interests. It was inevitable that after months of silence, we no longer thought about Rasputin and our missing Charoite every single hour of the day.

We were pulled back into the endless flow of tasks required to run an empire and manage a war. Plus, we were planning the grandest wedding Rusya had seen in a hundred years.

A double wedding.

Felix Yusupov, after wavering between life and death for weeks, was finally recovering.

Irina had spent every day at his bedside, wiping his face with cool cloths, reading to him, bringing him water.

Miracle of miracles, this was all done with Aunt Xenia's consent. It might have been because she saw the steel in her daughter's resolve and realized that if she tried to ban Irina from seeing Felix on his deathbed, she'd lose her forever.

Or perhaps it was the fact that out of all of us, only Felix perceived

Rasputin clearly from the very beginning. He must have looked right inside Rasputin's chest and seen the blackness of his heart.

Irina came home one day with a ring on her finger, announcing to her parents, "I'm marrying Felix as soon as he's well enough to stand up at the altar."

After some discussion with Ollie, it was decided that the two cousins would share a wedding day. Both wished to be married as soon as possible, and collaboration would hasten the date.

This benefitted Ollie the most because it meant she could push much of the tedious decision-making onto Irina, who actually enjoyed choosing between fabric, flowers, and cakes. Ollie's only request was that her dress be light enough that she could dance in it.

The upcoming wedding reinvigorated the aristocrats of St. Petersburg, who hadn't attended any truly lavish events in far too long for their liking. Out of the many ornate invitations hand-delivered across the city, almost none returned with regrets.

The Danish royals would all be in attendance. Our Albion cousins couldn't come because of the difficulty of crossing the war zones in between.

I was happy for Ollie, but couldn't lift my sense of dread. Until I received a piece of news that made me almost as happy as the would-be brides:

Damien was coming back to St. Petersburg.

Not only was he returning just in time for the wedding, but he'd be received with a hero's welcome.

Damien had accomplished the impossible. After near-disaster at Lemberg, when the Rusyan forces were falling to pieces, Damien and his regiment of Cossacks breached the walls and captured the city.

It was our first major victory. Papa ordered all the papers to print the story and called Damien back to St. Petersburg for a triumphal parade.

Knowing I was about to see him in the flesh wiped every other care from my mind. It was all I could think about, day and night.

He wrote that he was traveling back to St. Petersburg with the remains of his regiment, which was now stuffed with men from his original Cossack host.

This is probably the last letter you'll get from me because I hope to travel faster than the mail.

I'm bringing some of my uncles and cousin, a few old friends ... They want to meet my favorite princess. Do you think you could visit our camp outside the city?

I was determined to make that happen, whether I was "allowed" or not.

The weeks until Damien arrived seemed to stretch out forever, each day passing slower than the last.

But then, all at once, we heard news that the Cossack cavalry was only three days away. They'd arrive the afternoon of Ollie and Irina's wedding.

I sent a note to Damien by messenger:

I hope you've got a clean coat stuffed away somewhere. I'm saving the first dance for you.

Actually, wear whatever you like. Or wear nothing at all. The girls will be lining up to dance with the Savior of Lemberg no matter what—especially if you pick the latter option ...

I planned to save every dance for Damien, etiquette be damned. But I felt a strange shyness admitting it to him. He'd been away so long.

I thought we'd grown closer than ever through the encyclopedic volume of letters we'd sent to each other, but the thought of seeing him again face to face put me in such turmoil that I hardly knew what was real and what was my own fevered fantasies.

The last three days flew by in an instant, stuffed with last-minute tasks for the wedding that had every single person in the palace pitching in, from the cook's six-year-old daughter to the Empress herself.

Mama was a high-strung mixture of nerves and elation. While terrified to be responsible for an imperial wedding, she was thrilled to have made a match for at least one daughter. Prince Axel was only fourth in line to the Danish throne, but he was the prime contender to be king of Finland. He was also fabulously rich. His father had already gifted Axel and Ollie a villa near Bernstorff Palace in Copenhagen.

"We're going to miss you so much!" Maria sobbed, the night before the wedding. We'd decided to lug out our old camp beds and sleep in Ollie's room one last time. "I love Axel, but I hate how far away you'll be!"

"Don't be silly." Ollie hugged her. "I'll visit all the time. And you'll come stay with me next summer, promise you will."

"I promise." Maria sniffed.

Maria was in the lowest spirits I'd ever seen her. She'd asked Mama if Daniel could come to the wedding. Not only had she been denied, but the request had alerted our parents to how far her infatuation with the injured soldier had progressed. There was rumblings that she might not be allowed to continue in her nursing duties, and plans were being made to send Daniel back to his mother's cottage in Staraya now that he'd been fitted with a prosthesis for his missing leg.

I'd visited Daniel at the hospital several weeks earlier. He had a plain, round face, untidy brown hair, and a small gap between his front teeth. Though his time in the hospital bed had shrunk his frame, I could tell he'd once been a strapping country boy, and likely would be again once he was on his feet.

We'd talked for over an hour, pleasant conversation mostly centered around the books he'd been reading with Maria. His opinions were intelligent and nuanced, much more than I would have expected from someone educated in a one-room schoolhouse. He obviously adored Maria, without taking any liberties with a girl he knew was a thousand times above his social station.

He could have been the most brilliant man in St. Petersburg and it would mean nothing to my parents. His relationship with Maria was even more doomed than mine with Damien.

Maria wasn't the only one watching Ollie's happiness with a touch of envy.

Aunt Olga had been in a low mood since returning to St. Petersburg. She hadn't traveled back from Denmark with Papa and Ollie, but instead had taken a circuitous route through Finland and Estonia. I suspected she'd been avoiding her husband as long as possible.

She all but confirmed it during a private tea together at her house.

I asked if Peter was happy to have her home.

She sat quiet for a moment, until tears welled in her eyes, surprising us both.

"He's so cold. When he passes me in the hall, I might as well be a lamp for all the attention he pays me."

That made me furious, because Aunt Olga was one of the loveliest women in Rusya, and funny and kind besides. Countless men would have given all they owned to possess her.

All I could say was, "I'm so sorry. That's awful."

She stared blankly at the cup of tea on her lap.

"I wanted children. I wanted affection. I wanted love. All my life is passing me by, faster and faster, and soon I'll be too old for any of it."

"You're not old!"

She looked at me, eyes red and swollen. "I'm thirty-seven. The time for children may already have passed."

She sighed, setting her tea on the side table, untouched.

"I'm happy for Ollie. But I'm so damned lonely. What I wouldn't give for someone to look at me like Axel looks at her ... just once."

"Maybe Papa would grant you a divorce," I said in a low voice. "He did for Nikolasha."

"Nikolasha had something he needed." Olga shook her head bitterly. "I'm just his sister."

I was beginning to wonder if love was the worst trick of the gods. It seemed to exist mainly to torture us. Unhappy marriages were so much more common than blissful ones. And marriages that could never occur seemed most painful of all.

THE MORNING OF THE WEDDING, I woke with the sunrise. I went to the window seat in my nightdress and looked out over the lawn, toward the dark expanse of trees to the south. Somewhere beyond those trees, beyond Alexander Park, Damien was riding toward me with his Cossacks.

Grandma Minnie's memory-keeper rested in my palm, heavier than it looked. With a deep breath that was part nerves and part hope, I depressed the crescent-moon button on the side.

For a moment, nothing happened. Then the memory-keeper whirred to life. It made a faint and steady ticking sound, like an old pocket watch. I could only assume that meant it was working.

I tucked the memory-keeper in the pocket of my robe, wondering which bits of the day it would save, and how it knew what to choose. The little box felt alive, the ticking like a heart, the whirring like a mind.

Grandma Minnie told me all magic was alive. Holding the crystal of Charoite confirmed it—I'd felt the power inside, squirming, longing to be free.

Grandma's memory-keeper lacked the malevolence of the Charoite. It felt warm and comforting in my pocket, a friendly companion.

After breakfast, I washed and dressed with unusual care, telling myself I needed to look my best for the wedding, while knowing all my efforts were for someone else. I put on my new riding habit and tied back the front bits of my hair, letting the rest hang loose.

Mama caught me trying to sneak out the back garden door.

"Where do you think you're going?"

Trying to avoid an all-out lie, I said, "Please, Mama, we've been working like mad, I haven't been riding in ages."

I'd spent the entire day previous filling hundreds of padded boxes with the delicate spun-glass ornaments that were to be Ollie's wedding favors, Maria closing the boxes and tying the silk bows.

The servants were so overrun with their own tasks that we'd all been slaving away, even Alexei, who'd volunteered to ferry guests from the train station to the palace. Axel's sister Princess Margaret arrived so disheveled that I knew what a lie it had been when Alexei promised to "drive safe as a nun in an abbey."

Mama folded her arms in front of her, taking in the suspicious neatness of my hair and clothes. She must have suspected where I wanted to ride.

All she said was, "Go ahead, then—but take the guards with you."

I took one guard, Kolya Deverenko, because I could trust him to keep his mouth shut. And to ride fast enough to keep up.

I got Barley ready at a feverish pace, hands shaking because Damien was finally going to see me using the gift he sent for my nineteenth birthday: an actual Cossack saddle.

I crossed the Alexander woods at a gallop, Artemis flying in lazy loops above the treetops.

Kolya was looking forward to seeing Damien himself. They'd become friendly Damien's last year in St. Petersburg, when Kolya and Alexei had occasionally joined in outings with Damien, Felix Yusupov, and Dimitri Pavlovich.

Kolya grinned at me as we rode, knowing exactly why I was riding so fast.

"Slow down! We're just going to have to turn around and ride back the other way with them."

"I don't know what you're talking about," I yelled over my shoulder as I urged Barley on. "I'm barely cantering."

I'd expected to meet Damien somewhere around Gatchina. Instead, I saw a cloud of dust rising in the air much sooner than I dared hope, then the glitter of sun on steel. The Cossacks must have risen early to finish their march.

I pressed my heels against Barley's flanks, surging forward once more.

At the head of the column, a lone rider broke into a gallop.

Damien was coming to meet me.

chapter 31

A HERO'S WELCOME

DAMIEN

I've never felt more divided than I did leaving Galicia. We'd captured Lemberg, but the war wasn't over.

I itched to see Anastasia like it would drive me mad. The Tsar's call to come back to St. Petersburg was like an invitation to Olympus—until I realized it meant leaving my father and half my men behind.

I knew exactly why the Tsar called me back. The war wasn't going well. This was the first clear victory he could celebrate. He wanted to parade us through the center of the city so everyone could see the heroes of the hour.

I didn't feel like a hero. I felt like a man who'd gotten very, very lucky.

When the Austrian army surrounded us from behind, we were pinned between their guns and the thirty-foot high city walls. Baron Zaltsa fell, then General Brusilov. Half the captains, too. Our armies panicked, no leadership or orders. Half the men would have bolted if there was anywhere to go.

My father had joined us with his Cossacks—my uncles, cousins, old friends. After Rykowski was killed, their regiment combined with mine. I was promoted to captain, which was starting to sound like Next Man in Line to Get His Head Blown Off.

I wouldn't have lasted an hour if all I had were Rusyans to work with, but by that point, half my men came from my old host. That was the lucky part.

My father led a rush against the Austrian's weak left flank, forcing them back across the river.

My men moved into the shadow of the city, the sun sinking on the west horizon, the city walls casting a long umbra to the east.

My cousin Yan dove into the river that ran directly through the city itself. His people came from a fishing village and he could hold his breath ten minutes or more. His feet were paddles, practically.

He stayed under, searching the murky water. His seal-like head popped up several times before he hauled himself up on the bank, looking doubtful.

"It's all full of gravel, don't know if we can squeeze through. And there's an iron grate."

"How thick?" my uncle Symon asked.

"About ..." Yan held up his index finger to indicate the size of the iron bars.

"A finger?" Symon chuffed. "Don't insult me."

My uncle was built like a barrel on top with bandy little legs. He'd once beaten a circus strongman in a lifting match.

He also couldn't swim for shit. He chunked down in the water like a cannonball and half drowned himself just getting to the grate. Yan helped him along.

Symon dove down once, twice, three times, coming up the third time gasping, hands bloodied, but grinning.

"Made a hole. It's a tight squeeze—won't be going through with you."

The six of us most likely to fit took the deepest breath we could manage and dove.

I swam till I thought my lungs would burst, through water thick with blood, garbage, and human sewage. Without Yan to guide us, it would have been impossible to find the gap Symon had made in the grate. We swam hand to ankle, forced to remove our rifles to squirm through.

I doubted the rifles would fire anyway, filled with sludgy river water. We came up through a sewer grate in the old marketplace.

We inched along the interior of the city wall, dripping filthy water and stinking in the late sun. I crept up on the sentries like a malignant shadow, wrapping my bare hands around their noses and mouths, sealing their faces like a mask and smothering them silently as their life drained away.

I preferred to kill with a rifle or sword. When I killed with my hands, energy flowed into me. Thoughts and memories, too. It was like I siphoned the life from my victims and it lived inside me until I burned it up.

I was a hypocrite writing to Anastasia about Rasputin. I said he should die for what he was, but I wasn't so far off a vampire myself.

We stripped the weapons off the sentries and arrived at the postern gate fully armed.

Our best scout found the concealed door. Petro could spot an ant in the dirt at midnight—he had no trouble finding the near-invisible seams in the mortar.

Locating the door from the inside was much easier. Most of the garrison was up on the wall—only four soldiers stood guard. We cut them down and opened a hole in the wall to the fifty Cossacks waiting on the other side.

My regiment poured through, fighting their way to the south gate. In less than ten minutes from the time we emerged from the sewer, we'd opened the main gate and the whole Rusyan army was pouring into the city.

My father clapped me on both shoulders, red faced with pride.

"An Ataman knows how to use the talent under his command." His fingers dug into my upper arms. "And he always leads the charge."

"I remember."

I looked into his face, sun-blasted as my own. The deep white cracks at the edges of his eyes showed a map of his expressions.

He grabbed the back of my neck and pressed his forehead against mine.

"Gods, it's good to fight together again."

"Keep honor, build glory."

We carved those words on our saddles. It meant that glory should never cost your honor.

I'd have liked to stay to celebrate with my father. Instead, I rode back to St. Petersburg to heap all that glory onto the Tsar's head.

The word for "tsar" comes from the Latin Caesar. It's why the Tsars call themselves emperor and use the eagle as their sigil. Nicholas wanted me to kneel and pay homage like Marc Antony at the feet of Augustus.

Papa gave me a warning as I readied to leave.

"Our contract's almost up. Try not kill him this time."

Actually, I looked forward to the Tsar placing that crown of laurels on my head with perverse anticipation. He had to give me the highest honor in the nation in front of Anastasia and everyone else.

I imagined looking over at Anya and seeing the glow of admiration in her face ...

It was a stupid fantasy, but it occupied me most of the way back to St. Petersburg.

Symon must have guessed some of it. He rode his bay alongside me.

"Is your princess going to be there to toss flowers on your head?"

"They're going to drown us in flowers," I said, ignoring the real question.

"They'll drown us in something," Symon smirked, chivvying his horse.

I wondered how Anastasia would be when I saw her. I'd thought about this moment so many times it seemed impossible that it could be anything as good as the fantasies I'd used to get me through the worst parts of the war.

Time and space create distance, in the heart and in the mind. Anastasia couldn't possibly be where I was anymore.

I tried not to think how many hours I had to get through before I'd see her, how many miles I still had to travel.

Time passed slow and then fast and then slow, until we crossed the border into Rusya and at long last made camp less than a day's ride from Tsarskoe Selo.

I would have ridden right through the forest to the palace gates if I thought the guards would admit me in the middle of the night.

Instead, I told my men we'd be back on the road early in the morning.

I STAYED AWAKE a long time by the fire.

I was thinking of the wedding the next day. I'd been invited not only by Nikolasha but by the Tsar himself.

Nikolasha had traveled back by train instead of horse, accompanied by his new bride.

Stana had been staying at the military camp with Nikolasha since she'd fled her husband's house. This would actually be my second royal wedding, as Nikolasha had invited me to their small, private ceremony.

I'd never seen him happier than when he stood beneath an arch of pine boughs in the winter snow, saying his vows to his beloved under the cathedral of the forest sky.

Stana wore a cloak of black sable, her eyes golden with the reflected flame of the bonfire.

After the ceremony, she pulled me aside and asked me again if I'd like her to read my future.

I tried to decline as politely as possible. She put her hand on my arm, looking me right in the eye because she was nearly as tall as I was.

"You cannot hide from fate."

There was something deeply eerie about her, especially at night. The flames seemed to flicker on her skin and in the depths of her pupils, like they were a part of her, as if she were composed of fire.

I said, "I don't want to hide from fate. Nor do I want to run to meet it."

She only smiled.

"I'll scry for you someday. I've seen that, too."

THE NEXT MORNING I dressed for our procession through the city. I had indeed acquired a clean coat, and new boots as well. I'd even managed to shave with a proper razor and have my hair cut.

Hercules was getting the grooming of the year, all the burrs brushed out of his tail and his coat curried till it shone. He was only two years old when Nikolasha bought him and still seemed to be growing. He was already the largest charger I'd seen—it was getting hard to reach the top of his head.

"You're going to have to have to bend down," I told him. "Because I'm not fetching a ladder."

Though Hercules couldn't speak like Artemis, he understood more than he let on.

He might even have guessed how anxious I was to get going. He was unusually cooperative, especially considering how early I'd woken him.

Symon was less pleased to be on the road shortly after sunrise.

"What's the hurry?" He yawned. "They can't start the parade without us."

I didn't give a damn about the parade or the wedding. All I could think of was Anastasia. I wondered if she'd look the same or different, if she'd be warm or reserved.

"Should we stop for lunch?" Symon asked after several hours' ride.

"No. It's not far now."

Symon grimaced but didn't argue.

A silver bird broke from the trees to the west of the road. I recognized her at once—I would have recognized her if we were still back in Galicia.

I kicked my heels against Hercules, knowing Artemis wouldn't have come alone.

A moment later, Anastasia galloped out of the woods, bent low over the back of her favorite brown mare, some poor soldier chasing after her.

She was pure joy, the sun gleaming on her skin, her thick banner of hair streaming behind her.

I urged Hercules up the embankment, leaving the road and riding toward her.

Anastasia pelted across a field of purple sage, her mare's hooves churning up a mist of lavender that floated in the air behind her. She leapt down and began to run. I did the same.

We met in the middle of the field, in an ocean of purple with papery white butterflies fluttering all around us. She ran to me, her whole face illuminated with a wild happiness that caught me like a whirlwind, so I swept her up in my arms and swung her around.

I forgot about my men and the guard right behind her. I even forgot who she was and what I could do. All I knew was that I'd never been happier to see someone, and there was no way to show her that but to kiss her like I'd never let her go.

Our mouths met, her lips warm from the sun. I tasted her, and all the world stopped around us.

Her mare froze mid-step in a cloud of violet specks that hung suspended in the air. Artemis paused as she swooped downward, her body long and straight and bullet-like. The guard, who I now recognized as Kolya Deverenko, had just caught up to Anastasia, his mouth petrified in a comic position of slow-motion surprise.

All the world stopped except us. We were bound together in its center, still spinning like two figures in a music box, locked in each other's arms.

Bits of golden light burned in her hair like embers, her freckles sparks on her skin. Her eyes looked into mine, blue-green as a warm summer sea.

I kissed her and our mouths opened, her tongue passing over mine. Her breath went into my lungs and our souls overlaid like two transparent images. She was me and I was her and we were one together, something that held all the world in its grip, stealing this moment for us alone.

Then I realized I'd been holding her, kissing her, pressing her against me for longer than I'd touched anyone before, and I let go, afraid that I'd hurt her.

"Are you alright?" I held her face steady in my gloved hands, looking at her closely.

"Of course, I'm fine," she said, but she was unsteady on her feet and I could see she'd lost color.

"I shouldn't have—"

"Oh shut up!"

She tried to kiss me again, but she had hardly pressed her lips against mine before she pulled back, wincing. Blood dripped from her nose. She swiped it with the back of her hand, dismayed.

"It's okay," I said.

But it wasn't okay. That wild, infinite happiness was sinking once more under the weight of reality. Kolya Deverenko stood over us on horseback, the imperial crest blazoned across his breast. If he didn't report this to the Tsar, he'd be risking his job and maybe his neck. I couldn't kiss Anastasia for a thousand reasons, starting with the fact that I could kill her with my lips.

She recovered quicker than I expected, mopping the blood off her upper lip with a handkerchief and grinning at me while she was still peaky and pale.

"You look so different! You got another scar ..."

Her fingertips brushed the one on my cheek, a souvenir from Lemberg. Just that light touch made my whole body swell, like my flesh and blood couldn't fit in my skin. I wanted to grab her hand and pull her close again, but I couldn't. Not with Kolya watching.

"You're different, too."

She looked like an autumn goddess bringing fall to the forest. Her hair was a riot of red and gold all around her shoulders, her riding dress the deep green of the Volga River when it reflects the winter pines. Most of all, she radiated magic. She'd stopped time without even trying and pulled me right in with her.

"You've gotten stronger," I said.

Her smile yanked at my heart.

"It's because I'm so happy to see you."

"Your Highness ..." Kolya said in a low tone.

The rest of my regiment had caught up and was waiting in the road, watching.

"Are you going to ride back to the city with us?"

"Of course!" Anastasia put her foot in the stirrup and swung back onto Barley before I could offer to help her up. She rode eagerly toward the line of soldiers asking, "Where's your father?"

"He stayed with the rest of the host. The Tsar only called back my division."

"Oh." She was slightly disappointed. "Well, I hope the rest will be back soon. Papa said the end is in sight—though you'd know better than I would."

"I doubt it." I shrugged. "A soldier only sees his square on the chessboard."

"You're not just a soldier anymore." She gave me a saucy look. "Captain Kaledin, very dashing."

"It's Major Kaledin now," Petro piped up as we approached. "The Commander-in-Chief pinned the stars on his collar himself."

"Even better." Anastasia grinned at me.

"Aren't you going to introduce us properly?" Symon maneuvered his horse to slip in next to us.

"I was trying not to. This is my uncle Symon. Symon, this is the Grand Duchess Anastasia Nikolaevna."

"I see why Damien made us get up so early." Symon looked her up and down. "You ride well. On a Cossack saddle no less..."

Anastasia beamed. Seeing her on that saddle was like seeing the moon and the stars together at last. I was so happy I hardly knew how to sit, how to look.

I wished my father *was* here to meet her properly.

"How early did you get up?" The smile she turned on me made me warm all over.

"Only a little," I lied.

"The sun wasn't up!" Symon cried.

"Damien must be excited for the parade." Anastasia rode so close her leg brushed against mine. "Every girl in St. Petersburg will be there to cheer for him."

"Every girl?" I searched her face.

"Every single one," she promised.

Knowing I'd see her at the parade and again at the wedding made me feel like I was vibrating. The day seemed brighter, the air sweet with the scent of wild sage and lavender.

I'd forgotten how good it felt just to be close to her. I was seeped in all the death I'd dealt, while Anastasia was overflowing with life, pure and bright and vivid, bursting out of her with every look, every laugh, every movement.

She was asking Symon if we were related on my mother's side or my father's.

"Damien's mother was my baby sister."

"What was she like?" Anastasia asked, with a quick glance in my direction to make sure I didn't mind this line of questioning.

"Wild as they come," Symon laughed. "More trouble than all the boys put together. There were five older brothers, myself included, and she was the youngest."

I hadn't heard my uncle talk that way before.

"It's true," Symon said, catching the look on my face. "When she was six she stole my horse and rode off across the steppes. We spent the whole night looking for her, only for her to ride back in the morning, calm as you please."

"Where did she go?" Anastasia laughed.

"Wherever she wanted! That was how she was, nothing could stop her when she got an idea in her head."

"Papa always says she was an angel on earth," I commented.

Symon snorted. "Taras had stars in his eyes when he looked at her, and she was the same for him. Nothing could keep them apart, though the gods know we tried."

"Why?" Anastasia cried.

"Taras wasn't Ataman yet. He didn't have a pot to piss in and she was too young. The five of us brothers ran him off with a horsewhip the first time he came 'round. Should've saved our sweat—she ran off and married him a week later."

This was a very different version of events than what my father had relayed—and probably a more accurate one. He'd always been vague on details.

"Good thing they did," Symon said, his smile fading beneath his walrus mustache. "They stole all the time they could, and it still wasn't nearly long enough."

Anastasia caught my eye. We looked at each other, something painful passing unspoken between us.

We rode on toward St. Petersburg.

chapter 32

RED SKY IN THE MORNING

ANASTASIA

Kolya and I rode all the way back to Alexander Park with Damien, then parted ways so I could hurry to change clothes before the parade.

I spurred Barley along nearly as quickly as I had on the way out, knowing I was an hour past when I was supposed to be ready to head over to the Winter Palace.

"Grand Duchess!" Kolya called after me. "Mercy on my horse!"

I slowed Barley to a trot, letting him catch up.

"I thought you said we were late," I teased him.

"We'll be later if Kiki breaks a leg."

"Can't let that happen." I leaned over to give Kiki a light pat on the crest of her mane.

Kolya was quiet for a moment, then said, "Don't worry, Grand Duchess. I won't say anything about how ... overcome with joy you were to see your friend."

I flushed, but not with embarrassment—with pleasure, thinking how

Damien swept me up in his arms and kissed me as all the world froze in place around us.

I hadn't even tried to do it. It happened automatically, effortlessly.

And I pulled Damien in along with me.

I hadn't even known that was possible. Damien wasn't a time-walker; he should have been a lead weight dragging me back. It was like I created a bubble in time, enclosing us both.

And inside that bubble, everything was different—the light, the sound, and especially Damien himself. Either it damped his power or my resistance was boosted. Though I kissed him for what felt like full minutes, it only affected me as if a moment had passed. It hurt, but it didn't kill me.

I touched the memory-keeper inside my pocket, praying it captured every bit of that kiss. It still whirred and ticked like a tiny clock. I'd play the memory over again right now if Kolya wasn't riding beside me.

Could I make it happen again?

Could I touch Damien even longer?

The thought made my face burn. I forced myself to think of something else.

"You're a good friend, Kolya. To me and to Alexei."

Kolya gave a sigh that rumbled in his chest. He heaved his heavy shoulders in an unhappy shrug.

"I should have seen something. That ... *monk*."

He managed to imbue the title with all the disgust of a much dirtier word.

"He's no monk."

Kolya looked at me with hollow eyes. "I know."

The throats of the six guards outside the vault had been torn out so forcefully that they were nearly decapitated.

I wondered if they'd been Kolya's friends.

What relief Rasputin must have felt, finally giving in to the impulse that must have tormented him all his time in St. Petersburg. I'd often thought of his eyes as a rim of pale blue ice with something lurking underneath. Maybe it was the constant desire to sink his teeth in my throat every time we were alone together.

Gods, I was so blind.

My parents tried to hush up the killing of the guards and the theft of the Charoite. Rasputin had damaged our reputations enough without anyone knowing we'd appointed a vampyr Archpriest of St. Fyodor's Cathedral.

It didn't work. The rumors still raged: Rasputin was a demon, Rasputin was a werewolf, Rasputin murdered the Tsarevich and fled. We'd have to parade Alexei around the wedding just to prove he was still alive ... for now.

"I'm worried about him," Kolya said.

Kolya was two years older than my brother. Andrei Derevenko had charged him with protecting Alexei, and he had, all his life.

He could see how fast Alexei was fading now that Rasputin was gone.

Alexei watched Rasputin slaughter those guards. He'd been standing so close that when he stumbled up from the vault hours later, the front of his shirt was soaked in their blood. Annette Bailey fainted when she saw him, thinking the Tsarevich had been stabbed.

He walked through the wall of flame, picked up the Charoite, and carried it back out to Rasputin.

Was he in a trance? Did he try to fight? Did he remember it at all?

Alexei had refused to talk about any of it. He'd hardly left his room in the weeks since, drinking Papa's wine and sleeping away the day. I knocked on his door several times. He pretended not to hear me.

"We need to hunt down Rasputin," Kolya said. "Force him to treat Alexei again."

"Every Okhrana in the country is looking for him. I don't think he's in Rusya at all."

Darkly, Kolya said, "I don't believe he ever left."

I looked at him, startled. "What makes you say that?"

Kolya's wide, friendly face contorted as he struggled to articulate something outside his usual realm of expression.

"There was a feeling when the Mad Monk was around. Like when the Tsar enters a room, but different. That feeling isn't gone."

Kolya wasn't a seer, but he did have a kind of second sight: he always knew what the weather would be. He could look at the sky in the morning, take a deep breath of the air, and tell you for certain if it would be sun, snow, or rain.

I thought I knew what he meant. Rasputin put a charge in the air. And that charge hadn't departed—it had only grown stronger. A storm gathering. Lightning about to touch down.

"He can't be in Rusya," I said, without fully believing it. "We would have found him ..."

"As you say, Highness."

Neither of us were convinced.

Lucky for me, neither Mama nor Margaretta had time to bawl me out for how late I'd returned to the palace. Mama was already dressed in her gown, Margaretta distracted by a shipment of lobster tails.

"You'll have to meet us at the Winter Palace," Mama said, already climbing into her carriage.

"I'll hurry." I didn't want to miss a minute of Damien's parade.

As a second stroke of luck, our newest maid Oksana came to help me dress instead of the aggressively inept Annette.

Oksana was elegant and neat, soft in her movements and even softer in her voice. She had a complexion like a petal, translucent, slightly bruised under the eyes, and a faint rural accent.

She was a wizard at arranging hair. My sisters and I had already begun to fight over her, especially when we particularly wanted to impress.

That's what I desperately wanted today, though I wouldn't admit it to anyone. I'd only just seen Damien and already ached to see him again.

When Oksana stepped back to reveal my reflection in the mirror, I let out a groan of delight.

"You're an artist."

She'd piled up my curls like a Grecian goddess, pinning them with combs shaped like golden oak leaves. The gown she'd chosen was light and flowing, draped in the front and gathered over one shoulder with a corsage of fresh white flowers. Maybe it was the flush in my cheeks or the swelling that lingered on my lips, but I'd never looked prettier.

Anxious as I was to see the parade, I stopped and rapped on Alexei's door once more.

When he didn't answer, I went round to the playroom and barged in through the passage in the wall.

His room stank, clothes and empty wine bottles scattered everywhere. He hadn't been letting the maids in to clean.

"I'm going to nail that passage shut," he growled.

Irritated that I'd gotten dust on my knees and cobwebs in my hair, I snapped back, "Answer the damn door, then!"

This wasn't exactly how I'd planned to go about the process of cheering him up.

Trying for a better tone, I said, "You've got to get dressed. Aren't you coming to the parade?"

"No."

"You have to."

"Why'd you ask, then?"

He was slouched on his bed, shirtless and rumple-haired, but it didn't look as if he'd been sleeping. In fact, it didn't look as if he'd slept in a long time. His face sagged as if gravity had been pulling relentlessly downward, his eyes staring through me and past me.

There were no books around him, no papers. Nothing that could have entertained him through the long hours of the day.

"What've you been doing in here?"

Alexei passed a hand over his face. "Absolutely nothing."

I sat down beside him on the bed. My eyes were adjusting to the gloom, the shutters closed, drapes drawn. It wasn't just messy in here—Alexei had turned over his nightstand and shattered his water glass flinging it against the wall.

"It wasn't your fault," I said.

He turned and looked at me, silent a long time.

"You don't know that."

"He had you mesmerized."

"Is that what he did to you?"

I stopped, mouth partly open. My eyes slid away.

"No," I admitted. "He just ... fooled me. I thought he was my friend. I was learning from him. And I wanted to protect you. I'm sorry, Alexei—I should have told you."

"*Don't apologize,*" Alexei hissed, real anger in his face. "All of this is because of me. Everyone wanting to protect me, to keep me alive ... especially *me*. That's all I cared about, staying alive. And it was all for nothing. He left me to die. So did *she*."

His voice broke on the last word, pain flashing across his face before he could smother it.

He burst out, "I thought she cared about me! She said she'd never met anyone like me. She said ... gods, she said all kinds of things. I was such a fucking idiot."

"You weren't! You're not!"

He shook me off, wanting no comfort.

"It'd be better if you all still had the stones and I died a long time ago."

"What are you talking about?" I grabbed him, forced him to accept my arm around his shoulders. He was bigger than me now, but painfully thin. When I put my hand in his hair it felt dry as a reed. He rested his head against my shoulder, his skull heavy, skin burning hot. "You're the best brother in the world and I adore you! So Rasputin lied to us and stole from us—he can go to hell. There's got to be another way!"

I was already thinking how I'd scour the bookshops of St. Petersburg. I'd find more books on magic, books like Rasputin had. There had to be some sort of spell, some kind of charm ...

"You never give up," Alexei said dully.

"No, I don't."

I clung to him with all my might.

Alexei looked at me, no light in his eyes.

"Well, you should. You *should* give up. Because sometimes no matter how hard you try, no matter what you do ... you just fail."

I squeezed his hand hard. "Not this time."

Standing, I said, "Get up! We're going to this parade and we'll cheer for Damien till our lungs burst. If we won this battle, we can win another one. We can win the whole damn war. We'll find something that helps you, or we'll capture Rasputin, or we'll find a different vampyr who's less of a dick. We're going to cure you!" I almost yelled it at him. "We're Romanovs—we're unbeatable together."

Alexei looked at me, slowly shaking his head.

"You're relentless."

"Yes."

"Obnoxious."

"Absolutely."

"And you're out of your mind. Completely delusional." He sighed. "But you make me believe."

"You *can* believe. I bet you ..." I looked around wildly for something precious Alexei wouldn't want to bet. It was a game we'd played since we were little to test each other's resolve. "I bet you Grandpa's sword we'll find some way to save you."

"Done," Alexei said, unflinching. "And you bet Artemis."

"I can't—but not because I think I'll lose! Because even if I won, she'd kill me."

Alexei smiled faintly. "Shave your head, then. If you lose, at least I'll have a laugh at my funeral."

I grinned right back at him. "That does sound pretty funny."

MY ENTIRE FAMILY took a position on the steps of the Winter Palace. Damien's regiment would be making a long procession up Nevsky Avenue, crossing over the Anichkov Bridge, the same route our army took after we beat Napoleon.

Uncle Sandro and Xenia stood a little to my right. Though I'd known to expect it, I still got a nasty jolt when Felix joined his future in-laws. If I hadn't already visited him several times, I would have thought the bent figure leaning on Irina's arm must be her grandfather.

His hair had all fallen out from the arsenic, his muscles atrophied from long weeks in a hospital bed. His skin hung loose on the skull-like bones of his face, an effect exacerbated by the stubble beginning to grow back on his head, not copper-colored anymore, but bone white.

His bow looked painful.

"It's so good to see you out again," I told him, hoping my face showed none of what I felt. "It's going to be the most beautiful wedding anyone's ever seen. Are you glad the waiting's over?"

Felix's smile was garish, his gums dark as liver. But there was a hint of the old roguishness when he said, "I think we're *all* getting something we've been waiting for today ..."

I was saved from answering by the sudden swell of noise all down the length of Nevsky Avenue. The roar washed over us, Mama looking startled at the ferocity of the cheers. Girls hanging out of windows on both sides of the street began to throw handfuls of blossoms in the air long before the column of soldiers appeared.

Damien's regiment rode up the avenue on their beautiful horses, their tooled leather saddles glistening with oil, the horses' manes braided with beads. They'd all donned the dark coats of the Rusyan cavalry but wore them open Cossack style, their rifles slung across their chests.

Loose blossoms drifted down on their heads, a riot of peach, marigold, scarlet, lilac, and sapphire. The crowd threw garlands, colored confetti, silk scarves. They banged on makeshift drums and played horns and pipes.

Dancers leaped and twirled ahead of the procession while acrobats flipped and dived under the hooves of the horses. Pyromancers blew huge breaths of fire that took the shape of rearing chargers and the Rusyan double-headed eagle.

Papa cast a glance at Axel's parents, Prince Valdemar of Denmark and Princess Marie of Orleans, to check if they were suitably dazzled.

Princess Marie looked intrigued by the extravagant display, but not necessarily impressed. She was known to be shockingly liberal even by Danish standards, tramping around Copenhagen without even a lady-in-waiting as a companion, joining her local fire brigade, and tattooing a large anchor on her upper arm.

Her husband, spectacled and mustached, had the look of a proper naval officer and might have enjoyed a military parade, had he not been so tired from the journey that he appeared to be falling asleep in the midst of all the commotion, his head nodding forward and then snapping up with each fresh surge of noise.

Girls screamed for the handsome officers. More than one threw her handkerchief directly in the path of the major on the massive gray charger. A few even reached up to touch the heel of Damien's boot as he rode past. Some of the girls were very pretty. Heat crept up the back of my neck.

The soldiers grinned and waved at the cheering crowd. Damien stared straight ahead at the Winter Palace, stern and unsmiling. It was only when he drew closer that he looked up to where I sat at the head of the steps, his expression softening a fraction.

I lifted my hand and gave him a salute. A slow smile pulled at his lips.

Then my father stood and the smile fell away.

"Welcome to the Heroes of Lemberg!" Papa shouted.

The answering roar made my eardrums flutter. Tatiana clapped her hands over her ears.

"They've retaken the city because Rusya is unbeatable!"

A howl of agreement.

"And Rusya is unbreakable!"

Another roar.

"Welcome them home in the name of your gods, your country, and your Tsar!"

The bellowing cheers were amplified by so much stamping and clapping and blowing of horns that the soldiers' horses shifted in place, agitated but too well-trained to bolt.

Papa lifted a crown of gilded laurel leaves from a cushion proffered by his minister Shuvalov.

"Step forward Damien Kaledin, son of Taras Kaledin, future Ataman of the Cossacks, Major of the 122nd regiment and Savior of Lemberg!"

Damien swung down from his horse, landing lightly on the cobblestones. He swept off his cap and tucked it under his arm, climbing the steps of the Winter Palace.

The hail of flowers was so thick that he trod a carpet of blooms. Where the blossoms touched the bare skin of his face and neck, they darkened and fell dead to the ground.

Damien paused before my father. I saw that they were equal height now, Damien slimmer but just as broad in the shoulders. Damien's scars, the weathering he suffered from a year out of doors, and most of all the sense of recent violence that radiated from his person declared him a warrior fresh from battle.

He stood before us in a kind of dark halo that made us all fall silent, as if the grim reaper himself had scaled the stairs.

When Damien was at his most powerful, even I was afraid of him.

He looked at Papa and Papa looked at him.

Then slowly, ever so slowly, Damien sank to his knees. Papa set the crown of golden laurels on his head. The crowd roared, flowers pelting down on us. Through the storm of petals, Damien's eyes met mine.

He stood and faced the crowd. Papa seized Damien's fist and hoisted it in the air. The cheers pressed against me like a wall.

"FOR RUSYA!" Damien shouted.

"FOR RUSYA!" the people cried in response.

"FOR FREEDOM!" he bellowed.

"FOR FREEDOM!" they howled.

Papa let Damien's arm drop.

He stepped slightly in front of Damien, saying, "Tonight we also celebrate the union of my eldest daughter the Grand Duchess Olga Nikolaevna to Prince Axel of Denmark. May the glory of our two nations grow together!"

The responding cheer was not quite as loud as for the soldiers, but still robust. Ollie was the firstborn and had always been popular. When she waved to the crowd, her hand linked with Prince Axel's, a fresh wave of flowers fell at their feet.

"This will be double wedding as Princess Irina Alexandrovna and Prince Felix Yusupov are likewise joined in holy matrimony!"

Fewer cheers, perhaps because the skeletal Felix lifting the hand of his beautiful bride confused the crowd. He looked closer to the grave than the altar.

"Raise a glass to their good health, courtesy of your Tsar!"

The doors below the grand staircase swung open. Dozens of burly footmen rolled out casks of beer and wine. Serving girls in Rusyan folk costumes bore trays of frothing tankards already poured. The crowd surged forward.

"How much did you send out?" Mama murmured nervously.

"Don't worry," Papa assured her. "There's enough for each and every wedding guest to get falling-down drunk and take a bath in what's left."

"That's not what I meant."

Damien had descended the steps to save Hercules from the press of the crowd. He swung back onto his saddle, his soldiers gathering around him. I crept forward from my seat.

As Damien turned to leave, I plucked one of the white flowers pinned at my shoulder and threw it down to him.

He caught it in his gloved hand and raised it to his lips without quite touching it. Then he tucked it away inside his coat.

chapter 33

WHAT DAMIEN MISSED MOST

DAMIEN

Olga Nikolaevna was married in the Grand Church of the Winter Palace, wearing a cloth-of-gold gown with a train so long it stretched almost the entire length of the aisle. Her face had been painted, her hair so elaborately arranged that when her fiancé lifted her veil he jokingly mouthed, *Who are you? Where's Ollie?* The bride laughed aloud, shocking the old biddies in the pews.

Her cousin Irina followed her up the aisle in a silver gown embroidered with flowers and birds. Felix Yusupov beamed so brightly at the sight of his beloved that he almost looked like himself again. He still needed Dimitri Pavlovich to stand at his elbow through the ceremony, helping to support his frail frame.

I paid zero attention to the long and droning ceremony, occupied by the much more interesting pastime of staring at Anastasia.

She'd changed from her Grecian gown into something made of transparent layers of powder blue gauze. Tiny bluebells wove through her hair, the freckles on her cheeks reminding me of a speckled egg.

In a church stuffed with every aristocrat in Rusya glittering with gold and brocade and pounds of gems, Anastasia was a breath of spring, light and airy.

I knew she hated changing clothes, but selfishly I loved when she did. She was like a gem with a thousand facets, her beauty hitting me fresh each time.

Much as she hated to admit it, she *was* beautiful, glowing with so much life that even the stained-glass windows dulled by comparison.

When she felt my eyes on her, she bit the edge of her lip, trying to smother the smile that lit her up so brightly that several male heads turned in her direction, including the one belonging to Prince Axel's younger brother Viggo.

A sudden and unwelcome image arose of Anastasia herself standing at the altar in this same church, across from some pompous prince like Viggo. I knew there must be a hundred highborn suitors at the wedding alone. She could be married within the year.

The thought made me so instantly furious that I spent the next twenty minutes scowling at Viggo's back, wondering how I'd prevent myself from throttling him if he asked Anastasia to dance.

Of all the things I'd imagined during our long months apart—and there had been many fantasies to keep me going during the most brutal battles and coldest nights—what I pictured most was dancing with Anastasia again.

I'd never forgotten what it felt like the first time I held her in my arms —squabbling and pulling in opposite directions, but falling into a rhythm all the same, until we were sweeping around the ballroom faster and wilder than anyone else, our bodies in motion together, even our breathing aligned.

I'd never felt so connected to another person.

That is, until I kissed her.

That I couldn't think about at all without risking a reaction that might be visible to the wedding guests stuffed in the pew on either side of me.

Instead, I turned my attention back to the ancient and tedious priest, the perfect antithesis to the overly-stimulating Anya.

It worked for a minute. Until my eyes were pulled back to her once more.

MOST OF MY regiment had returned to our camp outside the city, a few lingering in St. Petersburg to partake of the Tsar's free booze. Nicholas had apparently resorted to buying the people's favor, flooding the city with so much liquor that half the citizens were drunk before the ceremony even started.

The only other soldier who'd been invited to the wedding was Petro, a distant relation of the Romanovs.

Nikolasha asked us both to sit at his banquet table during dinner, a friendly gesture that also spared the newly remarried Stana the coldness of the Rusyan aristocrats who had never warmed to the Montenegrin princess in the first place. They called her and her sister Melitza "the Crows" and "the Black Peril" long before Stana divorced her husband.

Melitza happened to be married to Nikolasha's younger brother Peter. While Peter Nikolaevich was a gentler version of Nikolasha, Melitza was even more imposing than Stana and just as interested in the dark arts. When she shook my hand, she tried to strip off my glove to check the lines on my palm.

"He won't let you," Stana said with a small smile. "Damien prefers to be surprised."

I said, "I've never heard a fortune told that didn't make me more confused."

"That's because you're ignorant." Melitza gave me a cool look. "Magic is a science like any other."

"Melitza's an alchemist," Stana explained. "She got her doctorate degree in Paris."

Stana pressed her gloved fingers briefly against the bridge of her nose.

"What's wrong, my love?" Nikolasha jumped to attend her.

"Oh, it's nothing. I've had a headache all day."

"It's the weather shifting," Peter Nikolaevich said, so softly that I had to lean in to hear him clearly. "The air pressure changes."

"There isn't a cloud in the sky," Petro protested around a mouthful of the first of many dishes sure to pour out of the kitchens. I doubted the Romanovs would be satisfied with less than ten courses at the wedding of their eldest daughter.

"It's still changing. Summer's over, fall's begun."

"Don't say that," Stana laughed. "I'm not ready for another winter. I was never made for snow."

"You'll like this winter," Nikolasha said, close to her ear. "I'll take you on sleigh rides every night and wrap you in furs and put a hot brick at your feet. I'll take you skating down the Volga. At winter solstice, we'll fill the forest with candles and make love in the snow."

"Niko!" She laughed quietly, throwing a sideways glance at Petro and me. "Not in front of the children ..."

Melitza ignored her sister and brother-in-law, turning her dark eyes in my direction.

"Have you never had your future read at home, among your own people?"

"Once," I admitted. "My Baba had the second sight."

"What did she tell you?"

My grandmother burned a lock of my hair and read my future in the smoke. Or at least, that's what she intended. Instead, she stared into the flames for a long time, silent and grave.

I asked her, *What is it, Baba? Will I be a great warrior? Will I be Ataman someday?*

Her eyes flicked back and forth like a pendulum. *I see two futures for you, Damien, one laid over the other. I cannot tell which will come to pass.*

She wouldn't explain any further. I could only intuit from the expression on her face that one of those futures looked very dark indeed.

To Melitza I said, "She wouldn't tell me anything, and I've since come round to her point of view."

"Hm." Melitza sniffed. "We'll see about that. Stana says she'll read for you eventually, and she's never wrong."

"I'm wrong all the time!" Stana contradicted. "I married George, didn't I?"

"Yes, but if you hadn't, you'd never have met *me*," said Nikolasha.

"Well, if that's how you're going to judge it ..." Stana smiled. "Then yes, I'm very clever."

Our plates were whisked away, the next course carried out by an army of liveried servants. Most were well trained, but a few seemed hardly to know which tables they were supposed to be serving. I supposed the Romanovs had been forced to bring in extra staff for the wedding.

I wished they'd hurry up. I wanted dinner to be over so the dancing could begin.

I could see Anastasia, just two tables away but distant as the moon. She was sitting between Tatiana and that damned Prince Viggo, laughing at something her sister had said. Her head was thrown back, exposing the long white column of her throat and the lovely lines of her collarbones. Viggo was staring exactly where I was staring. I decided that I despised all Danish people, especially the men.

The only person who seemed to be having more fun than Anastasia was her sister Ollie. Every time the guests rapped their spoons against their glasses she was supposed to allow her husband a kiss on the cheek. Instead, the moment she heard a clink, she leaped upon him and kissed him so aggressively that even Axel blushed.

Irina and Felix sat close together, their heads nearly touching, talking quietly. The groom lifted his new bride's hand to his mouth and kissed each of her fingertips in turn.

I envied them with an intensity that felt like a thousand pinpricks all over my skin. I couldn't stop looking between the happy couples and the girl I could never have.

At last it was time to dance. The guests moved to the formal ballroom of the Winter Palace, the musicians already in place. Anastasia ran to me, smiling brighter than the sun. All my jealousy melted like frost. As she held out her hands to me, I wouldn't have traded places with anybody in the world.

♪♪ *Dreams—The Cranberries*

The dancers lined up, Ollie and Axel at the head of the set, Irina and Felix taking their place beside them for a moment, but moving to the side once the music began so they could sway together at a gentler pace.

I took Anastasia's hands in mine. The last of the sunset pouring in through the double bank of windows set her hair aflame and turned her skin to gold.

"Are you going to let me lead?" I teased her.

"If you can keep up," she said with that mischievous smile that seemed never to entirely leave her face, lurking under cover when it had to, but always bursting out again.

The music started slowly, then increased in speed. Anastasia's back felt tight as a whip beneath my gloved palm, her hand gripped in mine. She looked up into my face, her light scent of grass and sunshine and fresh linen laced with something head-spinning.

The other dancers around us hardly seemed real. They were a hall of ghosts compared to the vivid color of Anastasia's brilliant hair, her laughing mouth, and her eyes as bright and clear as the summer sky over the steppes.

"You've been practicing!" she cried.

I didn't want to admit to her that I'd asked Petro to show me the steps of the most popular dances. I found myself blurting it out anyway, because somehow it was harder *not* to tell her whatever came into my head.

"Don't picture how stupid I looked waltzing with a three-hundred-pound soldier with a mustache thicker than your hand."

"I won't," she promised solemnly. Then, with snorting little laughs, "No, I'm sorry, I have to. Were you the man or the woman in the waltz?"

"Everyone's a woman compared to Petro."

Her peal of laughter sounded like it would carry her away. It was impossible not to join in.

"Gods, I missed you," I said before I could stop myself.

She stopped laughing and looked up at me.

"I've never been more afraid than when you went away. Or more happy than when I saw you this morning."

"I felt exactly the same." My fingers tightened around hers. "When I ... when we ... it was the best moment of my life. Pure magic."

"The things I can do when I'm with you ..." Anastasia said, in wonder. "From the moment we met. Do you remember? I didn't even know your name, and it was like the whole world stopped when I saw you."

"I could never forget."

My soul left my body, like it was yanked toward hers.

"What do you think it means?" she asked me.

I knew what it meant. I knew it all the way down to my bones.

But I couldn't say it. Couldn't admit it even to myself.

Instead I swept her around like I could carry her away from here, like I could scoop her up in my arms and ride off on Hercules, never to return. I danced with her like we were the only people in the room, the only people in the world.

We stayed together song after song, ignoring every rule of etiquette, every dirty look from her aunt, every princeling to whom Anastasia had already been promised.

The sky outside the windows darkened, speckled with stars. Anya's skin turned from gold to silver, glowing like the moon. I could see her body through the transparent dress. She wasn't wearing a corset, which was why her flesh felt so warm and alive. In the strange half-light, the shape of her breasts became visible, and her well-formed legs.

My heart rate doubled, and not from exercise.

I put my hands around her waist, swinging her through the air, making her gasp. I pulled her tight against me, her body pressed against mine. We were both breathing hard.

She hadn't tired, though other dancers were dropping all around us, exhausted or drunk. Only Ollie and Axel were still going full steam, and Anastasia's Aunt Olga, who'd been asked to dance by a handsome young officer. At first she'd declined, but he was so persistent that she was now floating around the ballroom in his arms, as graceful as her nieces.

The Tsar called for more candles to be lit. The ballroom grew hotter and brighter, light sparkling off the golden colonnades, the chandeliers, the gleaming parquet floor.

"Should we get a drink?" I said to Anastasia.

The Montenegrin sisters were standing by the punch bowl, Melitza speaking to Stana in low tones.

"What's wrong?" I asked.

"She's ill," Melitza said in an accusing tone.

"I'm not!" Stana protested. "It's this headache ... it feels like someone's pounding a drum in head."

"You should lie down." Her sister scowled, but with her arm put tenderly round her Stana's waist.

"I don't want to make Nikolasha leave early."

"It's past eleven! And anyway, he doesn't have to leave; I'll take you home myself. Peter's been wanting to be gone since dinner. You know he never dances and he hates cards."

Stana looked at me, slightly ashen and swaying on her feet.

"Would you tell Nikolasha for me?"

"Of course."

The sisters departed with Peter Nikolaevich, Melitza's arm still wrapped protectively around her sister and her cloak thrown over Stana's shoulders.

"I was at their wedding," I said to Anastasia. "Nikolasha and Stana's."

"Were you?" she said enviously. "I wish I could have come!"

"They were married outdoors in the snow."

She sighed.

"That's what I'd want—all the stars as your witness."

I wondered who she imagined standing across from her.

She looked at me, her lips parting as if she had something to say. Before she could speak, her sister Tatiana grabbed her elbow.

Low and urgent, she said, "I have to talk to you."

"Right now?"

"Yes."

"Do you mind waiting?" Anya asked me.

The way she was looking at me, I would have given her the heart out of my chest.

I meant to wait patiently by the dance floor, but I couldn't help watching as Tatiana pulled her over by the windows, speaking rapidly, making short, jerky movements with her hands.

Anastasia threw a quick glance at the Tsar and the Empress, who had likewise drawn together and were speaking in low tones to several of their ministers.

Coldness crept over me.

Tatiana said something else, and Anastasia went pale. It happened all in an instant, the color bleaching from her skin until her freckles stood out twice as dark against the canvas of white. Her lower lip trembled and she turned and looked at me, agony in her face.

I wanted to run to her but felt frozen in place.

She was already returning, stiff and awkward, all her grace vanished. I knew she had something awful to tell me. I knew it before she even opened her mouth.

"Damien ..." she croaked. "A telegram came from Galicia. Tatiana overheard. Lemberg has been retaken. And ... and ..."

Tears were running down her face, her lips shaking as she tried to force out the words.

I grabbed her by the shoulders, too hard.

"*Tell me.*"

The tears magnified her eyes until they were all I could see.

"Your father's been killed. I'm so, so sorry."

My hands dropped to my sides. All the world seemed to crash down around me. I heard nothing, saw nothing, felt nothing because it was all gone.

I walked away from Anastasia and found Petro at the card tables.

"Get my horse. Round up the men. We're leaving."

Petro took one look at my face and jumped to obey, leaving his winnings on the table.

Anastasia followed me across the ballroom, trying to put her hand on my arm.

"Damien, I—"

I pulled away like she'd burned me. I didn't want her to touch me. I didn't want anyone to touch me.

The ballroom seemed stuffed with people, the heat overwhelming, the air suffocating. My collar strangled my neck.

"Damien ..." Anastasia said again, reaching for me.

"DON'T!" I barked, ripping away my arm.

She looked up at me, her eyes huge in her face, glinting with tears.

That only made me angrier. She had no right to cry for him.

I shouted, "*I wouldn't be here if it wasn't for you!*"

She went still, her hand fixed in the act of reaching for me.

"I didn't give a damn about the laurels, I only came back to see you. If I hadn't, I would have been there with him!"

Tears dripped down on the front of her dress, dark patches blooming on the thin material.

She didn't try to defend herself. That made me angrier, too, because everything around me—the candles, the musicians, the rich food, the glittering gowns, even Anastasia herself—was all fuel for the rage I had to direct outward or it would burn me alive from the inside.

"I'm so sorry," she whispered.

"If only *tears* could bring him back."

I turned on my heel, desperate to be free of the music, the laughter, and all these fucking Romanovs. I shoved my way through the crowd, passing the Tsar and his wife, who were toasting their new in-laws, already over the loss of Lemberg, not giving a damn how many men had died because they hadn't properly secured the city. To them, it was just another telegram out of the hundred they received every day.

They took everything from me, and the only thing I'd ever wanted, they'd never let me have.

I left the ballroom, the palace, the whole lot of them.

Petro was waiting at the foot of the stairs with Hercules and his own horse, and the half-dozen of our men he'd hauled out of the pubs and brothels around the palace.

I swung onto Hercules' back, hardly feeling his bulk beneath me.

"Damien, wait!" Anastasia cried.

She was running after me, slowed by her gown and the press of the crowd.

I didn't even look back at her—just kicked my heels and rode away.

Gods, what I'd give to go back to that moment and make a different choice.

chapter 34

ICE STORM

ANASTASIA

As I stood on the steps of the Winter Palace watching Damien ride away, the great clock under the eaves began to chime. It rang twelve times, deep and booming like a gong. Midnight.

The memory-keeper in my pocket stopped its whirring and fell silent. The day was at an end.

I let out a sob.

I'd hoped to capture a perfect day. And I had ... until it all went wrong.

I was so happy. From the moment I saw Damien and we kissed, it had been a steady rise where every second in his company lifted me higher and higher until it hardly felt like my feet touched the ground. We'd laughed and danced until I was thrumming with energy, until I felt like I was made of pure, electric light.

Then it all came crashing down.

His father ... oh gods, his father ...

Damien looked like he'd been stabbed. He stiffened and all the color drained from his face until his lips were gray and his eyes black pits. When I touched his arm, he looked at me like he hated me.

And maybe he should.

You could draw a direct line from the day we met to this moment.

Slowly, I walked back to the ballroom.

The space that had seemed so warm and golden only moments before now felt jarring and loud. The screech of bow against string was harsh and unmusical, the laughter of guests like the cackle of crows.

I wanted water, but all I could find was champagne. I swallowed it down, tasting nothing but bitterness.

"What's wrong?" Maria asked me.

She hadn't been dancing. In fact, she was the only person who'd been melancholy all through the wedding. Not because she wasn't happy for Ollie, but because her affection for Daniel persisted enough to cause her to flatly refuse to dance with anyone else even in the face of Xenia's bullying.

"I ... Damien left."

I didn't want to tell her what had happened. Didn't want to say it aloud, because I was hardly holding back the tears that made my head feel like it was stuffed with cotton wool.

"Where did he go?" Maria said, puzzled.

"Away."

I could feel the energy ebbing out of me, the further Damien rode out of the city. If he rode far enough, I wouldn't feel him at all anymore.

He'd never forgive me for this. I'd lost him forever.

All of a sudden I felt so weak that I slumped against Maria, my bones like butter.

"Stassie!" she cried.

Tatiana ran to my other side. My sisters half carried me to the closest table. Tatiana made me sit down. Maria brought me more champagne and held it to my lips, though I'd never wanted anything less. I set the glass down still half full.

"I'm sorry," Tatiana said. "I shouldn't have told you."

"Whether he learned it today, tomorrow, or the next day, it would have been the same."

The noise of the party shrilled against my ears. Most of the guests were drunk, even Axel's parents. His brother Viggo had unbuttoned his shirt to the waist, taken off his bowtie, and tied it around his head. Dimitri Pavlovich had his hand up the skirt of a Danish princess, only partly concealed by the drapes behind which they were hiding. Ollie and Axel were still dancing, but no longer following the proper steps, just swaying with their arms around each other's necks.

I was surprised Mama hadn't put a stop to the revelry. She'd had a few glasses of wine herself and had been roped into a game of Whist with Axel's mother.

She and Papa had received the telegram but they'd ignored it. Hadn't even spared a glance for Damien. They had more important things to do like entertain our guests and ring for more champagne.

For the first time I saw us as Damien must see us—spoiled, selfish, callous. Moving men around like pieces on a chessboard, caring no more than one would care when sacrificing a pawn.

But it wasn't a pawn. It was the person Damien loved most in the world. The person with whom he'd only just been reunited, after we took him away.

I'd never felt so dark. Even the candlelight seemed to fade around me, the room growing cold.

The musicians began to play a song that was not really a song—just one long, steady tone like the ringing of a gong. Only it didn't fade away as a gong would have done. It swelled and vibrated in the air, creating a muffling sensation against my ears.

"What are they doing?" Tatiana frowned, pressing a finger into her ear.

I looked at the remnants of the champagne at my elbow. A light frost spread across the surface of the liquid, the crystals forming like tiny shards of glass.

"What's happening?" A plume of condensation rose from Maria's lips.

The whole ballroom had gone cold.

The candles dimmed. The starlight outside the windows disappeared, blocked by a mass of black clouds.

The guests reacted slowly, confused by drink and the strangeness of the dark wrapping around us. The air grew thick and frigid, stiffening my muscles, turning my hands and feet to ice.

Nikolasha rose from the card table, reaching for his sword. But he had no sword. No one wore swords while dancing.

"GUARDS!" Papa bellowed.

No guards came. Maybe they'd been sampling the free champagne, or maybe they'd all disappeared.

Half the servants seemed to be missing, too. I hadn't noticed before how the empty glasses were piling up, or how long it had been since anyone refreshed the food.

The remaining servants set down their trays.

In one swift motion, they turned on the guests.

A dark-haired waiter leaped on Princess Margaret and tore out her throat. In the gloom, his bloodstained mouth looked like a gaping hole.

Screams erupted everywhere.

Dark-clothed figures streamed in through every door, some human and some like nothing I'd seen.

There was nowhere to turn, nowhere to run. Enemies swarmed us, and in the dark I couldn't tell friend from foe.

Our new maid Oksana appeared beside us. Tatiana tried to grab her hand, planning to pull her along with us as we ran, not asking herself why our maid was here when she should have been back at Alexander Palace.

Oksana grasped Tatiana's hand and ripped off her arm. She did it effortlessly, like pulling the head off a dandelion. Tatiana stared in shock at the empty space where her limb had been, then fell sideways, blood pumping.

Maria let out one long scream that seemed it would shatter the windows, until the point of a spear erupted from her chest. She'd been run through from behind by the musician who'd been playing the balalaika all night.

All of this happened in seconds. I stood frozen in place from the cold, the shock, and the darkness that gripped me like a hand.

Then a voice in my head shrieked, *Use your magic!*, and I tried to turn into the time-stream, to slow the carnage happening all around me.

I turned but the air was freezing, I was sluggish, confused. Time slowed but didn't stop.

I snatched up the closest thing at hand, which was my glass of frozen champagne, and flung it in the face of the musician who'd stabbed Maria. The glass shattered against his forehead, but hardly seemed to register. He leaped on me and we crashed into the table, his teeth snapping at my throat.

The table collapsed beneath us, smashing down on the chairs. We rolled through the wreckage while I desperately fumbled for whatever I could grab. I seized the leg of a chair, the musician lunging for my neck. His own weight drove him onto the splintered wood, the point sinking a foot into his chest. Dark liquid spurted from his mouth, burning my eyes.

I shoved him off and ran to Maria, who was closest. She'd fallen backward, the point of the spear still protruding from her chest. Her blue eyes stared blankly upward, face fixed in her final scream.

I grabbed for Tatiana next, crawling across the sludge of spilled drinks already beginning to freeze on the floor. She lay on her side, blood spreading around her like a cape.

When I touched her, she was horribly cold. Her eyelids fluttered and my heart leaped. I tried to lift her.

She turned to me, lips barely moving as she whispered, "*Stassie ... run ...*"

Then she was dead, too. I scrambled to my feet, mad with grief and terror.

It was a living nightmare, the faces of people I thought I knew transforming into something monstrous. The soft-spoken Oksana seized Irina and sunk her teeth into her throat, her eyes black and pupilless, her pretty face contorted. The waiter who'd refilled my glass three times at dinner grabbed Felix by the head and twisted until his neck snapped.

Nikolasha was trying to slow time just as I was, with moderate success. He wrestled a sword away from one of his attackers, stabbing and slashing at the dark-clothed figures who swarmed him, faster than any human could move.

But these creatures weren't human. They were swift as shadows and horrifically strong. They leaped on him like a pack of wolves, biting his arms, his neck, his face, his shoulders. Nikolasha flung them off, seizing one by the throat and legs, and breaking its spine over his knee. Six more leaped on him from all sides, taking down the one man I thought could never be overpowered.

The wedding guests tried to fight back with bursts of power that fizzled and died in the smothering darkness. They'd been drinking all night and the cold was like nothing I'd felt, even in deepest winter. All the windows had frosted over, a slick of ice forming on the floor. My feet slipped out from under me and I went crashing down again.

Dimitri Pavlovich managed to set three of the creatures on fire, their bodies flaming up like torches, before some monstrous animal, half-man and half-beast, ran at him on all fours and slammed him into the wall.

Ollie and Axel stood back-to-back, their wedding clothes torn to ribbons, a nasty gash on Ollie's cheek. Axel hadn't come unarmed—he had a pistol in each hand and was shooting the creatures dead through the eye with a precision that stacked their bodies up before him like cordwood.

Ollie was electrocuting anyone who got close, but her power required physical contact. A ghoulish being with greenish skin and long, bony fingers got its hands round her throat. Before she could jolt it off, it sunk its nails deep into her neck. Ollie shrieked and Axel spun around, firing wildly into its emaciated body. One of the waiters leaped on his back and bore him to the ground.

Mama was flinging every object in the room at the attackers. As two rushed for Alexei, she raised her hands high and brought a crystal chandelier crashing down on their heads. She had never moved anything so massive. Blood burst from her nose. She fell face down on the floor.

The beasts ripped apart Axel's parents, they leaped on Aunt Xenia, biting

411

and clawing, until her face was a mass of blood, her head nearly torn off. Uncle Sandro was next, then Aunt Olga, then Grandma Minnie. I saw them fall one after another, and there was nothing I could do to save them.

Four vampyrs swarmed Papa, their snarling mouths showing fangs like wolves. I recognized one as the beautiful student who'd been sitting on the lap of the Minister of Culture at Madame Lessinger's party, another as the priest who tried to flirt with Maria.

Papa had a steak knife in each hand and better control of his magic than anyone else in the room. He made short work of the student and the priest, then buried a knife in the chest of a supposed waiter.

Something enveloped me—pressure on every inch of my skin like I'd plunged underwater. I turned, knowing who else must be here.

I felt him like magnetism, like gravity. A force a hundred times more powerful than anything else in the room.

Rasputin entered the ballroom, his long dark robes flowing behind him.

Nikolasha staggered up, blood streaming from a hundred gashes all over his face, his neck, his chest, his arms. He was missing an eye and several fingers, but still he grasped the stolen sword. He rushed at Rasputin, howling like an animal.

Rasputin raised one slim white hand and blasted Nikolasha backward. My uncle was dead before he hit the floor, his body crumpled and twisted.

I tried to slow time but I was weak and empty, filled with so much horror that I could hardly remember how I'd done it before.

Rasputin glided toward Alexei with that eerie smoothness that wasn't human, that had never been human.

Alexei was the only person in the room not covered in blood and shattered glass. His white suit was pristine, his face blank as paper as he watched Rasputin approach.

"STAY AWAY FROM MY SON!" Papa ran at Rasputin, his last knife clutched in his hand.

Rasputin grabbed him by the wrist and twisted, the snap of bone like cracking ice. His pale eyes blazed with violet fire, his body so saturated with stolen Charoite that it seeped from his skin in a mist. He was so overwhelmingly powerful that I knew he must have consumed everything he stole from us.

We'd never prepared for that, never even imagined it. We thought it would kill him.

He grabbed Papa by the hair and wrenched back his head, exposing his throat.

With every last ounce of energy inside me, I ripped Papa's other knife from the chest of the fallen waiter and ran at Rasputin.

His back was turned. I hoped to sink the blade into his spine.

I looked at my father and remembered what it felt like when I'd saved his life before. At last I felt that transition where all the world spun slower while I ran as fast as I'd ever run.

I raised the knife, its wicked point plunging down like a fang to the nape of Rasputin's neck.

He turned and seized me by the throat.

I lifted off the ground, his fingers a steel vice beneath my chin. I couldn't breathe, couldn't speak. The steak knife tumbled from my fingers.

His eyes blazed into mine, a smile on his lips.

"There you are, little one."

Then Rasputin snarled, all his teeth exposed, as Papa sunk his knife hilt-deep into his shoulder. Rasputin dropped me and my father shoved me as hard as he could, shouting "ANASTASIA, RUN!"

With a howl of rage, Rasputin sunk his teeth in my father's throat. Alexei stood by watching, unmoving and unfeeling, as Rasputin drained our father dry.

Papa's shove was a boost of acceleration, the last of his magic. He transferred it all to me, leaving nothing for himself.

I used it to run.

It was so cold that snow had begun to fall inside the Winter Palace. The thin white flakes hung suspended in the air as time froze. I slipped and skidded over a floor soaked in the icy blood of everyone I loved.

Snarling faces loomed all around me, not entirely paused but slowed enough that I slipped past, twisting and turning through a gauntlet of fangs and claws that slashed through my clothes and ripped at my skin but never quite caught hold of me.

As I neared the back door of the ballroom, a wolf leaped at me, half-transformed, fur all over its body and face, its gaping maw filled with torn flesh.

The flesh of someone I'd loved. I screamed with rage, blasting fire in its face.

Choking and skidding, I scrambled up again, sprinting down a pitch-black hallway not nearly as familiar as the passageways at home.

Snow swirled in my face. I was back in normal time. I couldn't sustain my magic; I was too weak, too broken down. My breath came out in frozen clouds, panting, erratic. I was crying and I couldn't stop—they'd hear me.

My feet were stiff and numb, I couldn't feel them at all. Still I ran, stumbling, blinded by tears.

I'd reached the kitchens, as dark and silent as the hallway. I tripped over something heavy and soft, sprawling over the body of a murdered cook. The floor was slick with the blood of all the servants who hadn't been vampyrs in disguise, the scent of iron thick in my throat.

I heard the snap of a lighter as a flame burst into being. Katya leaned against the butcher block, lighting the tip of one of her hand-rolled cigarettes, blocking the exit to the stairs.

Through the bank of windows to my left, I saw it was snowing outside too, thick flurries of flakes swirling down from the clouds that blew in. Below us, the Neva River had frozen over.

Rasputin's power was unimaginable. My heart failed at the magnitude of what I'd allowed to happen.

Still, I closed my fingers around the handle of a butcher's knife abandoned on the countertop.

"Get out of my way."

Katya laughed softly, the tips of her incisors glinting in the orange glow of her cigarette.

"Poor little princess. All your family's dead. Who's going to save you now?"

I lifted the knife, gripping it tightly, the blade silver in the half light.

"I guess it's gonna have to be me."

She straightened, flicking aside the cigarette, her hands loose at her sides. Smiling in anticipation.

I'd only taken a single step toward her when a voice spoke in my head: *ANASTASIA.*

I felt my body turning.

♪♪ *Retrograde—James Blake*

I had no control. Everything that was me was locked in one corner of my mind, watching helplessly while I turned and gazed into the cold and depthless eyes of Rasputin.

All the kitchen faded around me until it felt as if I was floating in space. It was like facing him across the table again, only he was a thousand times stronger and I'd used up every bit of my magic.

"Why?" I whispered. "We welcomed you into our home. We trusted you."

Rasputin made a sharp hissing sound through his teeth. "I had something you needed."

I thought of all the hours I'd spent in his tower, not just practicing magic but talking and laughing. I'd shared things with him, he'd shared things with me. He showed me the memory of his wife and daughter. He didn't have to do that.

"No," I said, managing the tiniest shake of my head. "It was more than that. We were friends."

Katya's expression was part derision, part annoyance. I saw the points of her fangs against her full lower lip, and something clicked into place.

"You lied to me about your family."

Rasputin tilted his head. "I told you a mirror of the truth."

The story flipped in my mind.

Rasputin's story could be true ... but all reversed.

I imaged it from the opposite angle: his mother, her husband, his sister Katya ... all vampyrs. The attacker who'd forced himself on Rasputin's mother ... *that* was the human. And what had begun to manifest in his teen years wasn't thirst ... but magic.

A vampyr who could do magic. The very first one. And not just a little magic ... a powerful affinity.

No wonder they followed him—all the way from Siberia to St. Petersburg.

I wondered who his father had been ... a human strong enough to overpower a vampyr. It made me shiver.

"Your wife wasn't human."

I was trying to keep him talking because it was distracting him. I could feel his hold on my body loosening. I had the butcher's knife in my hand. If I could get closer ... if I could surprise him ...

"She was vampire," said Rasputin. "A powerful vampire. Stronger than me."

Now he was the one lost in memory, his eyes slipping away from mine, seeing the images of a door nailed shut, of fire and smoke. I could see it too, clearer than the kitchen around us. I smelled burning fabric and heard the screams of a little girl. Katya shivered.

"She forced me to take our daughter and flee while she stayed behind. They cut my wife to pieces and nailed the pieces to crosses all along the road. The last cross bore her head on a spike with her heart stuffed in her mouth."

His face was white as bone, the dark stain of my father's blood all around his mouth. Katya stood beside him, slipping her hand in his.

And I understood one thing more.

"Katya's your daughter."

Gods, I was so stupid. The little girl in the memory ... all grown up, but never aging, like Rasputin himself.

"How old are you?"

"Older than you can imagine," he said.

All the pieces danced before me, everything I'd noticed but never understood: the painted portrait of Rasputin's wife, the old-fashioned style of her dress, the toy Rasputin had carved by hand, and the ancient language of his letters that even the interpreter had never seen ...

"But why? What did we ever do to you?"

"*Everything,*" he hissed.

And he showed me one last image:

A horde of men on horseback, Cossacks and Rusyans in sable hats and embroidered cloaks, with swords and spears and flaming torches. At their head, a bearded man with a face I recognized from the Portrait Hall: Mikhail Fyodorovich, the first Romanov Tsar.

"You're a cancer on this country. Every one of you. Three hundred years of bloodshed and oppression—it ends tonight."

The knife shook in my hand. "I'll stop you."

Rasputin laughed.

"You can't even control yourself. You're reckless, selfish. It was never for your brother, that's just what you told yourself. You made it so easy, little one."

Before I could rush forward, before I could even raise the knife, he took full control of my body once more. I was shoved back in that cramped corner of my mind, watching helplessly as my own limp hand raised the knife and brought the blade slashing across my wrist. The skin parted, opening a gaping mouth on my arm. Blood pulsed out with each frantic beat of my heart.

I couldn't even scream at the sight of raw flesh and tendon. My lips were slack, my tongue as numb as the rest of me.

"No more games," Rasputin stepped closer, pale eyes drilling into mine. "No more lessons."

The knife slashed down again and again. I felt the pain, I tried to scream, a gurgle in my frozen throat.

"Speak his name," Rasputin whispered. "Who is the man in the vision? Where is he now?"

His voice compelled me to answer.

An image of Damien swam up in my mind: his face bright with happiness as he ran to me across a field of purple sage.

The thought was a burst of hope, because at least he had gotten away.

Damien was safe and always would be, as long as I could keep this one last secret.

Instead of using that spark to drop the knife, I locked Damien's name away in my mind, so deep that Rasputin would have to rip me apart to reach it.

He saw the door bolting in my mind, and his face darkened until he no longer looked human at all.

"Your choice."

He gripped me with his mind, my body bound in the serpent's coils. I watched helpless as my own hand brought the knife slashing down on my thigh.

Katya laughed.

"Make her cut herself to pieces."

Instead, Rasputin gave a jerk of his head and the blade turned directly at my face, its point lined up with my eye.

I screamed, but it was only in my head. My mouth was sealed shut, as unresponsive as the rest of me.

Then the windows to my left exploded as a silver bullet burst into the room.

Artemis dove at Rasputin's eyes, talons outstretched. Katya thrust her father aside, taking the brunt of the blow across the side of her face. Three long gashes raked down her cheek. She grabbed Artemis by the wing and wrenched.

Artemis gave a shriek of pain that echoed in my head. It jolted me so hard that I broke free of Rasputin's grip. Katya flung Artemis aside and I snatched her out of the air, cradling her against my chest as I sprinted for the windows.

Rasputin roared, snatching for me, too late …

I dove through the glass, jagged edges cutting all over as I plunged down toward the frozen river.

I broke through, sinking into the rushing water beneath. The river bore me along, black and cold beneath a thick rim of ice. I beat against the ice with my fist, trying desperately to hold Artemis against my chest with my injured arm.

I was bleeding heavily and the water was frigid. The last of my warmth seeped away, the ice above growing ever more distant.

Blackness took hold. I lost my grip on Artemis as the river swept me away.

PART FIVE

chapter 35
IN THE GRIP OF ENDLESS WINTER

1 Year Later

When I woke, it was dark outside my window. It was always dark in the morning now.

I was freezing, though I'd slept in all the clothes I owned, bundled in so many layers of tattered wool that I looked twice as big as I actually was. A thick rim of ice covered the tiny window—all the condensation from my breath that had frozen in the night.

I could hear Varvara downstairs, trying to stoke the iron stove. We'd saved our last lumps of coal to boil water for tea. There'd been no new shipments of coal to the city for over a month, and every bit of wood, fabric, paper, straw—anything that could burn—had long since been scavenged.

I broke the ice over the water in my wash basin and splashed a little on my face.

The girl who gazed back at me from the cloudy mirror was a stranger. Face pale and thin with a few faint scars crisscrossing here and there like white pencil marks, hair dark and straggling, cut off at the shoulders. I'd been dying it with boiled walnuts.

I brushed my teeth and pulled on my boots, stuffing newspaper in the toes to make them fit and to keep the snow from coming in through the holes in the decomposing leather.

The boots had once belonged to Varvara's husband. My long wool overcoat, too. They still smelled of his favorite cigars and of the old gray parrot Seymour who'd been his pet.

I clomped down the stairs from the attic room to the pet shop itself. It was still crowded with cages and tanks, all empty now. The monkeys had died from the cold, the reptiles from the lack of fresh fruit and insects. Varvara had kept the animals going as long as she could, often at the expense of her own meals. She'd cried at the loss of each one, until only Seymour remained.

And Artemis, of course. She had the advantage of being able to hunt for herself. She even brought back the occasional rabbit or pheasant for Varvara and me, though she was having to fly further and further from the city to find game. She hunted in the dead of night so no one would see her flying, too recognizable to go out in the day.

She was not quite so accurate anymore, either. Varvara had used all her considerable skill to heal Artemis' wing, which was the only reason she could fly at all. The damage was too severe to fix entirely. The wing hung crooked, and sometimes Artemis wobbled.

As soon as I came down from the attic, she flapped off the perch next to Seymour's and landed on my arm. I couldn't feel her talons through the many layers of wool.

Cold today.

"It's cold every day. Are you warm enough down here? You can sleep up in the attic, you know. Heat rises, doesn't it?"

Only if there's heat in the first place.

The winter before had been the longest and coldest on record, the summer short and wet. Snow had blown in by the second week of September and had remained ever since, the skies an impenetrable blanket of low, gray cloud.

It was dark when we rose in the morning and dark when we returned at night. The meager hours of gloomy daylight were lost to us as we labored in the windowless factory where Varvara and I now worked.

Varvara had gotten the fire lit at last. She shook out the match, saying, "There you are, you cantankerous old bastard."

She was talking to the iron stove, which seemed to delight in tormenting us.

"You should let me do that."

"Not a chance." She shook her head stubbornly. "Nina wasn't a pyromancer."

I'd been impersonating Nina Ivanova for the better part of a year. Nina had survived the October Revolution, only to die a month later when Spanish Flu ripped through the city.

Varvara was one of the most gifted healers I'd ever seen, but she couldn't save her daughter. I thought that was who she was actually crying for every time one of the animals died. She was mourning the loss of Nina again and again.

I was only partially aware when it happened, still in a delirium of fever from an infection in my arm.

I'd washed up on the riverbank beneath the Blagoveshchenskivy Bridge, right where the fish monger threw the guts and tails and scales from the day's catch. I was covered in mud and filth, lungs full of water, tangled in an old fishing net.

Varvara was crossing the bridge in the early morning when she saw Artemis trying to hop up the slippery bank, dragging the broken wing that had been half ripped from her body.

She hadn't recognized her at first, her feathers so caked in mud that she could have been almost any kind of bird. It was only when Varvara descended the riverbank that she saw the full size of Artemis and the glint of silver feathers beneath the mud.

Then she saw something stir in the snarl of net.

"I thought you were a rusalka. All that red hair ..."

She'd had to cut some of my hair just to get me out of the net. Then she'd flung her coat over me and begged and bribed the fishmonger to help carry me up the embankment. She'd kept the coat over my face all the while, telling him I'd been one of the victims of the riots the night before.

Her shop was only a hundred yards further down the road. She'd taken me inside, washed me, and sewn up the deep gashes on my arm and thigh, and the smaller cuts from the window I'd crashed through. She'd hidden me in the tiny attic space while the new secret police hunted all through St. Petersburg.

They didn't say who they were looking for, but the whispers, threats, and bribes centered around a missing girl with red hair.

Varvara started dying my hair before I'd even recovered. She didn't tell a soul that she'd found me, not even her own daughter. When Nina was carried away by the flu that infected half the city, killing the young and the healthy even more than the elderly, Varvara saved her newly printed identity card for me.

"I can't take this," I told her.

I'd only just come out of a month of fevered nightmares where I watched my family being ripped apart over and over again by a host of monsters with fangs and claws and fur and the faces of friends. The only thing that kept me from drinking the entirety of the opium tincture Varvara had given me was the sight of Artemis, alive and keeping constant vigil by my bed. That, and my need to know if Damien had made it out of the city safely.

Many had not.

They were calling it the October Revolution. Really it had been an invasion, a coup. Rasputin and his coven of vampyrs had been infiltrating the city for months ... years, maybe. They'd taken positions in government, in the newly formed Duma. They got jobs at the palace and joined the city guard.

Then they bewitched and beguiled everyone they met.

I had no idea of their actual numbers—maybe only a hundred total, but the vampyrs' influence was a thousand times stronger. They infiltrated the newspapers and the student groups. They became the lovers of powerful men and women and fed on them, increasing their control over their victims with every bite.

They joined with the Anarchists, the workers, the disgruntled aristocrats, fanning the flames of discontent until the city was ready to explode.

Then they lit the match by slaughtering my family, taking over the government in a single night.

They called it a revolution. They said it was the will of the people. But when the dust settled, only one man was in charge: Rasputin.

Many died that first night. It wasn't just my family and the wedding guests—any of the servants and guards loyal to us were killed. All across the city riots and bloodshed reigned. Fires raged with no one to put them out. A brewery exploded, then an ironworks.

Over the next several days, the new city guard and the new secret police regained order, mostly by instigating a total lockdown. All citizens were required to remain in their houses on penalty of instant execution.

The real purpose of the lockdown was to allow the police to perform a sweep of the city. They said they were looking for the assassins who had killed the Tsar. Really, they were hunting for me.

Had I been conscious at the time, I would have heard them stomping through the main floor of Varvara's shop. She showed them the little apartment where she lived and the cellar below, but made no mention of the attic space so narrow and low I couldn't stand up inside it. Not that I could stand at all back then.

It took a month for me to recover enough to descend the ladder to the main floor, and another month before I could walk around without coughing. I'd gotten pneumonia in my lungs, besides the infection in my arm so putrescent that Varvara had been within a day of removing the limb.

She used up her entire store of herbs and medicines, some of which Rasputin had shown me once upon a time, and others I'd never seen. The one that seemed to work best was a fever-reducer she'd only ever tried on horses.

"I thought it might kill you, but by that point ... it felt like a race to the grim reaper either way."

I recovered enough to walk, a shell of myself. A pathetic, broken-down wreck.

Varvara was barely any better. Nina was her only child, the miracle baby she'd longed for all her life. Nina should have been married in the spring. Instead, she was buried in one of the mass graves for the victims of the flu, not even buried under her own name because Varvara had to save her identification card for me.

The guilt I felt at surviving when everyone I loved had died was already overwhelming. I couldn't add on guilt for Nina, who was perhaps the most tragic victim of all. She'd been attacked, disbelieved, sacked, and tossed out of the palace after years of service. I didn't deserve to be saved by her mother. I didn't deserve to take her place and use her card.

"Oh, shut up," Varvara said when I tried to refuse it. "You're all I've got now, and I'm all you've got. What good does it do you to be snapped up by the Okhrana? How does that help Nina?"

When I still couldn't take it, she shoved it in my hand, saying, "Nina loved you. She loved all you girls. She didn't blame you for what happened."

I clutched the card, swollen-eyed and miserable. "Maybe she should have."

"No," Varvara said fiercely. "The one she hated was that monk. You're not giving him *anything* he wants."

I did need the identity card. It was part of the new order. Everyone had to keep their card on them at all times, and everyone had to report daily to the job they'd been assigned.

Varvara and I were assigned to a cotton mill. We worked eleven hours a day, six days a week, for the good of the new Rusya.

As payment for our labor, we were given chits for food, for fuel, for boots, but there wasn't enough food or anything else. We waited in line for hours, only to be told to go home and try again the next day.

Varvara made tea using the same soggy leaves we'd been using all week. The tea was hot, and that was what mattered. I cupped the mug between my hands, holding it out to Artemis so she could sip a little too if she liked.

You drink it, she said.

Artemis had become touchingly protective while I was recovering. I supposed it had something to do with the fact that she was now well into her adulthood, while in her eyes, I was a chick forced to leave the nest too soon. She stayed close to me whenever she could and fretted if I was late coming home from work.

Varvara poured the rest of the tea into a thermos, wrapping up the hunk of bread and the slightly moldy cheese that would be our lunch and dinner.

She'd cut off the worst of the mold using a butcher's knife that hung over the sink. Varvara washed the knife after every use. She ran cold water over the blade, wiped it with a sponge. I couldn't stop watching how the water broke on the blade, how the droplets looked like liquid and then like metal, swapping as the angle changed, reality bending back and forth.

Knives were a hole in my mind that couldn't seem to be stitched. Every time I saw one, impulses squirmed through.

"Ready?" Varvara asked.

I blinked hard.

"Yes. I'm ready."

I carried Artemis back to her favorite perch next to Seymour.

"Varvara's got some carrots," I said. "If you find a rabbit tonight, we can make stew."

You shouldn't eat things that grow in the dirt, Artemis said, making a disgusted clicking sound with her beak.

"Seymour loves carrots."

"Bird girl!" Seymour squawked, as if he were agreeing. Then added, as he often did, "Horse boy!"

The horse boy is gone, Artemis said, without any malice. She liked Seymour very much, even if she considered herself the superior being.

And where had the horse boy gone?

Back to the steppes, I supposed.

Damien must think I was dead. That's what everyone had been told. The war was over and the Cossacks' agreement had died with my father. Damien's father was gone, too—I wondered if he'd been voted Ataman in his place. I wondered if he still thought of me sometimes ... or if he hated me for what he'd lost.

How the Cossacks were faring with Rasputin, I had no idea.

Working in a factory in St. Petersburg did not provide access to nearly the same level of information I'd received living in Alexander Palace. Most of the local radio broadcasts had been shut down, and the only permitted newspaper was *The People's Voice,* edited by none other than Katya. Illegal papers still popped up like mushrooms, but the new Okhrana crushed them even more ruthlessly than the old one had done.

We heard when the war ended—that was announced triumphantly in fliers and banners and headlines, and a public broadcast. It was only months later we learned the terms of surrender, for surrender it had been. Rasputin handed vast swaths of territory over to the Germans, including most of Ukraine, and all of Poland, Lithuania, Latvia, and Estonia.

The treaty was practically as unpopular as the war had been, but no one dared say so. Rasputin's Black Coats patrolled the streets day and night. Assemblies of more than five people were forbidden. Anyone who dared oppose the new measures was shot in the street or sent to the labor camps in Siberia, or worst of all, to the mine.

The streets were silent as we walked to the mill. Other workers plodded along beside us in the dark of morning. No one spoke, staring down at the icy pavement.

It was fear that kept the workers silent. Nearly a third of the city's population had been murdered or hauled away to labor camps during the Red Terror. Friends and neighbors had turned on each other in the wave of denouncements that seemed never ending.

Now it was worth more than your life to engage in conversation that might be used against you. Better to do everything you could to stay invisible.

This winter seemed colder than the last. Already, icicles hung from the eaves all the way to the ground. Snow was packed a foot deep on the streets and the Neva had frozen solid by the first of October.

Though we were now midway through December, no holiday lights hung along Nevsky Prospect. Rasputin obviously did not care to provide them, and the shopkeepers couldn't afford it. In years past, the street would have been jammed with vendors selling candied apples and roasted nuts, knitted mittens and sable muffs, birds that could sing, and tiny kittens specially bred so they never grew too large to fit in a teacup.

Nobody could afford those luxuries anymore. We got our chits and our salary, which was the same for everyone—thirty-five rubles a month. The price of even the simplest items had skyrocketed. The cost of wheat, barley, and sugar had doubled in the last six months. Butter was three times higher, and salt as dear as gold. The only meat Varvara and I could afford was what Artemis brought us.

Stray dogs had disappeared from the city streets, along with cats, pigeons, and squirrels. Anything edible ended up in a cooking pot. There were whispers that a human foot had been seen in a stewpot by the docks.

"Did you bring your card with you?" Varvara asked me as we neared the gates of the mill. "The Okhrana checked every single worker at the bronze works yesterday."

"What for?" I said, feeling the constant paranoia that they might have received a hint, a tip. I knew Rasputin would never believe I was dead, not without a body.

Maybe he didn't care—what could I do, anyway? I couldn't even escape the city, let alone the country. There were guards everywhere and I could never afford the falsified papers for a travel pass. Black market papers were going for thousands of rubles. It would take me lifetimes to save up, assuming I could save a portion of my salary without starving.

But I didn't really believe he'd forgotten me. He was hunting for me and he wasn't going to stop.

You're a cancer on this country. Every single one of you ...

He wanted all of us dead.

Except, I supposed, for Alexei.

Alexei was the new Tsar, while Rasputin ruled as regent.

I wondered if my brother was actually even alive. He'd only been seen in public a few times and never by me. If he'd wasted away under Rasputin's "treatment," Rasputin wouldn't admit it.

Varvara said, "They've been taking trainloads of people out of the city."

"Well, I've got my card. I always do."

You could be imprisoned just for forgetting it at home.

Varvara nodded, but her frown stayed right where it was. We both knew my ID card wouldn't stand up to close scrutiny. I hardly resembled Nina at all.

We parted ways inside the mill, Varvara heading to the spinning workshop while I went to finishing. The chemical reek of the dyes burned in my nostrils long before I pushed through the double doors.

I stripped off most of my clothes and would take off more before the day was done. The mill was kept deliberately hot and humid so the threads wouldn't snap. We often worked in our underclothes, sweat streaming down our faces, mixing with the fumes and burning our eyes.

The unfinished cotton needed many treatments with harsh chemicals before it was actually useable. It was singed to remove the hairs on the yarn, then steeped in dilute acid and rinsed, then "scoured" by boiling the fabric in a harsh alkali. After that, it still needed to be bleached white and then mercerized with a caustic soda solution, and finally dyed.

None of these processes were gentle on the skin. My hands were continually cracked and swollen, rashes running up both arms.

The conditions were harsh for me but worse for the children. A fifth of the millworkers hadn't reached their sixteenth birthday. It was thought that children, with their small hands and speed, were perfect for jobs like switching bobbins and cleaning the machinery. The machines operated day and night, crammed together in tight rows with little room to pass. The moving parts were uncovered and were never turned off even during cleaning.

My first week at the mill, a girl's arm had been caught by the moving belt of a carding machine. The tiny six year-old was pulled in and crushed before anyone could help her.

I'd cried all the way home and all through the evening, unable to shake the image of her mangled body from my mind.

When I said to Varvara, outraged, "Who sends their child to work in a mill?" she only replied, "Families do what they have to to survive. Children have always worked in cotton mills."

I stared at her.

"Are you saying the mill was always like this?"

I'd thought the conditions were worse under Rasputin, as so many things were worse.

I was forced to recall my very first conversation with Damien, when I'd defended the mine in the Lorne Mountain.

The miners are paid for their work ...

Damien replied,

What price do you pay to smother on dirt? To break your back? To be crushed under a mountain of fallen rock? What price would I have to pay you to do it?

I burned with embarrassment, thinking how arrogant I'd been, how naive.

I wished I could tell Damien that I understood a little better now.

I worked all through the morning, in a haze of shimmering vapor that made my lungs burn. My hands swelled until they looked like two red gloves stuffed with oatmeal. They itched and ached, and still I worked, not even half the day gone by.

The work was repetitive, mindless. I began to feel like a piece of machinery myself, metal and gears. My mind floated away from my body and I stopped feeling anything good, or anything at all.

At lunchtime, I became human again when I sat with Varvara to share our cheese and bread. She gave me the rest of the tea, still lukewarm in its thermos.

We were joined by Katinka, a small and sturdy woman of about forty who had once been a cellist in the St. Petersburg orchestra. There was no need for cellists anymore, or bakers of confectionary, or hairdressers, or ballerinas, or any of the other "frivolous and unnecessary" professions that existed before the new order.

That was perhaps lucky for me, who could hardly have hoped to continue as a seamstress in Nina's place, but miserable for the thousands of people forced to work manufacturing jobs instead of the professions they'd loved.

Katinka had a remarkable ability to shrug off the awful things that had happened to her, remaining cheerful in the most depressing circumstances. She brought a much-needed light to our days when Varvara and I struggled to rise above the depression threatening to crush us both.

Today she was telling us about her neighbor who'd bought a pair of rabbits, planning to breed them for food. He'd become attached to the litter of tiny kits, and now his apartment was full of rabbits he couldn't bear to eat.

"If he starves this winter surrounded by food, at least he'll die happy." Katinka laughed.

Varvara and I chuckled, too. What humor survived the revolution was darker than it had been before, but it still brought warmth to my chest.

I passed Katinka a bit of our cheese. She shared the coffee she'd brought. This year of endless winter had brought out the worst in people—I'd seen men and women behave like savage beasts. But also I'd seen acts of bravery, selflessness, and incredible compassion in the darkest of circumstances.

Take Katinka's neighbor—he never would have given a damn about a rabbit before. Suffering changes you. Either you become cold and bitter, divorced from human feeling. Or the opposite occurs, and you can't bear to inflict the pain you've felt on anyone else.

"Damn this cold," Katinka said. "Makes it hard to practice when my fingers are stiff."

Going from the heat of the mill back out into the chill with sweat-soaked underclothes was always much worse than the walk to work in the morning.

"What are you practicing for?" Varvara said. "You think the orchestra is starting up next week?

"Because I like it," Katinka said simply. "But yes, if it ever does come back, I want to be ready. That's what bothers me most—I was so close to getting first chair. I would have had it in another six months!"

I could tell from Varvara's expression that she thought Katinka had a better chance of flying around the room than of the orchestra resuming, but she surprised me by staying silent.

"Back I go." Katinka folded up her empty lunch bag, tucking it in her pocket to be used again the next day.

Once she was gone, I teased Varvara just a little saying, "I thought you loved bursting bubbles."

Varvara sighed, putting away the remnants of our own lunch, which was just the dregs of the tea and the cloth that had been wrapped around the cheese. "There's too little hope left to take any away."

She turned away from me, shoulders slumped.

So low I could hardly hear her, she said, "I use to tell Nina I'd turn my store into her own dressmaker's shop once we saved a little more money. She made a wedding dress for her best friend that was prettier than anything I've ever seen from Madame Bulbenkova. Even if it could never happen ... I'm glad we had the dream."

The bell shrilled, the twenty minutes of our lunch break elapsed. Varvara and I returned to our respective rooms.

I was working with an assistant called Maritza who was fourteen but looked much younger. She was skinny as a whip, missing several teeth, and had a yellowish cast to her skin from some unknown ailment.

The children tended to be undersized for their age, with sores all over their bodies, swollen bellies, and patches of hair falling out. They looked like the dogs that used to roam the city streets. Many were lacking at least one parent, and those who had them weren't always better off. Children's wages went directly to their guardians, often evaporating the next day as black-market vodka.

I was grateful I'd been assigned the quick and clever Maritza. Without her, I could hardly have reached the quotas that increased weekly. If we missed our numbers or accidentally damaged a bolt of fabric, the fines came out of our earnings.

Maritza was struggling to work, coughing persistently every time a fresh wave of fumes hit her. Since we were working on the starching drum, that was about every five minutes.

As we were feeding fabric into the drum, her eyes were watering so much her hand went within millimeters of the press. I lunged across the machinery and ripped back her hand. All I could see was the mangled body of the six-year-old, all of her crushed, even her head. The image wouldn't disappear, and though Maritza tried to tell me she was fine, nothing had happened, I sank down in the corner, head between my knees.

My heart was beating so fast I thought it would burst in my chest. I felt a horrible sensation like I was falling and falling with nothing beneath me, like I was dying and I was never going to stop dying. Perhaps that's what death was, an endless fall through nothingness.

I saw the little girl and then I saw Maria again, face frozen in a scream, staring forever upward at nothing. Tatiana, blood spreading out around her like a banner. Then Irina and Felix, Ollie, Axel, Dimitri, Aunt Olga, Aunt Xenia, Grandma Minnie, Nikolasha, Mama, Papa, and Alexei himself, all the ghosts of everyone I'd failed standing pale before me, turning their dark and empty eyes toward me.

"Get back to work!" Ostap snapped. He was our overseer, eighteen years old, scrawny, with boils on his face and neck. He was only kind to the girls who let him put his hand in their blouses.

"She's sick!" Maritza barked back at him. She was rubbing my back with her bony little hand, trying to soothe me. I could hardly feel her touch or hear a word being spoken. It all seemed to be happening in a separate room to someone else.

"Then send her home. But I'm docking her three days' pay."

"She's not going home. She'll be fine in a minute," Maritza said fiercely.

She really was like one of those wild dogs—protective and always ready to fight.

"And anyway," Maritza added, smart enough to know what Ostap cared about most, "Nina's the only one strong enough to work the drum. You don't want to miss your own quota."

Oddly, it was the use of Nina's name that brought me back to myself. It rang in my head like a bell.

I forced myself up again, leaning against the wall. "I'm fine, I can work."

I wasn't close to fine, but I was going to pretend until Ostap moved along.

Before I could so much as touch the handle of the drum, the bell rang again, the one that usually announced lunch and end of shift. But it was far too early for the end of the day.

Ostap looked like he already knew what this was about.

"Get out to the main room," he said, giving Maritza a shove to hurry her along.

I followed her out, feeling faint. My heart rate, nowhere near back to normal, tripled when I saw the row of Black Coats blocking the exit door. I dropped my eyes to the floor, trying to position myself among the largest concentration of women. I hoped we'd all look like one featureless mass of pallid faces and untrimmed hair.

The temptation to scan the faces of the Black Coats was almost irresistible. I wanted to check if any of them were the vampyrs I'd seen the night of Ollie's wedding. Most of Rasputin's Black Coats were just rank-and-file soldiers, but the ones in charge were his own.

I'd learned to recognize them whether their teeth were down or not. They were pale in a particular way, with a blue undertone to their skin. Most had black hair, and all seemed to move with a boneless fluidity that made me think of snakes.

I watched them when I could, from as far away as possible. They looked like humans most of the time. But certain moments—when they smiled at each other, when something irritated them, when they moved a little too quickly—then the mask slipped, and I glimpsed the monster beneath.

Papa once showed me a counterfeit Faberge egg made of tin and painted plaster. When I first saw the two eggs sitting side by side on his desk, the fake and genuine, I wasn't sure which was which. But as soon as I lifted the false egg, I felt its flimsiness. Once my mind knew the truth, my eyes could see the gaudy shine of tin next to the mellow gold of the genuine egg. I couldn't be fooled anymore.

That's how it was with the vampyrs. Once I knew them, I recognized them.

And very lucky I could—the closest I came to being caught was when I almost walked right into Katya three blocks from my house.

She was facing the other way amongst a group of people. Something in the way she moved, the liquid flick of her hand as she tapped her cigarette, raised the hair on the back of my neck. I ducked back inside the grocer's just in time—her head turned sharply, nose lifted like she scented something. I crouched in the doorway until she moved on.

Now I had at least one vampyr right in front of me: the tall, lean officer with the hollow cheeks and the long, aquiline nose. His lips were thin and bloodless, his fingers long and shapely in his leather gloves.

He was clad head to toe in the sleek black uniform of Rasputin's enforcers, the coats high and severe at the collar, the hats made of black mink, boots gleaming like oil.

I kept my gaze fixed firmly on the floor, as did everyone else. The fear in the room had a noticeable scent, sharp and metallic, a cold sweat that every one of us experienced, whether we'd done anything wrong or not.

Varvara took a position a little further down the line. We didn't resemble each other, so claiming kinship was unlikely to help me.

"Straight line," the captain said in his silky voice, pointing a gloved finger at the portion of workers not perfectly flush against the wall.

"Present your identity cards," one of his minions ordered.

We dutifully pulled our cards from our pockets. I put an inky thumb on mine, hoping the smear would distract from the photograph of Nina.

The lieutenant went down the line, examining each worker's card. When he got to a burly man named Igor who worked the spinner, the officer paused a long time.

"The printing on this card is not correct."

"That's what it looked like when I got it," Igor said, trying to keep his tone calm. "The 'g' was always smudged."

"It's against the mandate to have an improperly printed card."

"I requested another." Igor's voice sped up and rose a little higher in pitch, though he struggled to control it. "They said I couldn't have one, this was fine."

"It's not fine," the lieutenant said. "You're in violation."

He nodded to the two Black Coats behind him. They seized Igor by his arms and began to pull him away.

"No, wait!" he cried, but the lieutenant didn't even turn his head. The captain smiled slightly with those thin, gray lips.

"Next!"

I held my breath while the lieutenant examined Varvara's card, then passed along without incident. Same with the next several women and children.

When the officer came to a strapping boy wearing no shirt at all because he'd been called away from the broiling hot dyeing room, his eyes flicked over the strong chest and arms. He barely glanced at the card before snapping, "This one is also incorrect."

"What?" The boy blinked, confused. He too was seized and hauled away.

Now I could see what they were doing. They pulled out a dozen of the largest and strongest men, leaving anyone weak or sickly behind.

Soon they reached my block of women, some of the last in the line.

The lieutenant passed over a few of the smaller girls, including Maritza. Then he reached me.

I was only wearing a sweat-soaked undershirt and trousers. Modesty was never the primary concern in the mill.

I was skinny as I'd ever been, scars and rashes all over my arms. Still, there was ropey muscle on my frame from long hours of lugging soaking cloth and turning the heavy drum.

The lieutenant glanced at his captain. The captain gave a small jerk of his chin.

"This card is incorrect," the Black Coat said, without even glancing at it.

"No!" Varvara cried.

I shook my head at her, hard. She quieted, eyes wide and terrified, hand at her mouth.

A sick, sinking sensation made the floor feel like goo. I was doing everything I could to stand straight, keep my face impassive, walk toward the men who'd been pulled out of the line without showing my galloping fear. I didn't want to draw attention to myself.

The Black Coats grabbed Katinka next.

"What are you talking about?" she cried, ripping an arm out of their grip. "There's nothing wrong with my card! How dare you!"

The lieutenant looked at his captain again, and this time the vampyr jerked his head slightly to the left.

"Take her out," the lieutenant said.

The Black Coats dragged Katinka toward the side door.

"Wait. What are you doing? Where are you taking me?" she cried, struggling against them. They had her pulled back on her heels, she couldn't get any purchase. "Wait. WAIT!"

We all stared, silent as fence posts.

After everything I'd seen over the last year, I knew what was about to happen, and yet I told myself it wouldn't. Denial was the first mechanism of the mind. It froze you in place, telling you there was a limit to how awful things could get. But there was no limit. It just got worse.

Katinka's shrieks grew louder as they dragged her through the door. A moment later we heard two shots. The screams cut off short.

I felt another drop—my mind sinking one more level into darkness. It had already fallen so far, sometimes I wondered if I'd ever be able to climb up to the light again.

The remaining women reeled in place, one half-fainting.

The lieutenant went down the line, taking two more of the strongest until he had twenty workers total.

We clustered together by the door, Black Coats all around us.

Varvara stood in the line that now had twenty gaps down its length. She looked tense and huddled, as if she might bolt at me.

I raised one hand to tell her to stay, or maybe just to say goodbye.

I knew where we were going. And I knew we weren't coming back.

Nobody ever did.

chapter 36

THE HEART OF THE EARTH

T he Black Coats loaded us into a wagon where we all huddled down on the wooden slats. They brought us our coats but didn't allow us to take anything else from our lockers.

They'd taken my ID card, so the only thing I had with me was the memory-keeper, which I'd carried in my pocket every single day since Ollie's wedding. Now I tucked it down the front of my undershirt, hoping that whatever might happen, I could keep it with me.

It had survived its long bath in the freezing river. I tried to use it once I'd recovered, having no idea if it would actually work.

Late at night, I'd crouched in Varvara's attic, the candle blown out, only a little starlight leaking through the tiny window the size of my hand.

I cupped the memory-keeper in my palms and held it up to my mouth, exhaling through the cuts in the metal shaped like moons and stars and pine trees.

I almost sobbed as it whirred to life, its mechanism ticking. Light poured out, projecting a whirl of golden stars on the low, sloped roof and rough wooden boards of the attic.

Then the stars disappeared and I saw a projection of myself dressing quickly in the green riding habit. I looked so much younger, my hair long and thick and flaming red, my steps light and bouncing.

I saw my mother stop me by the door and heard a snatch of our conversation, our voices distant and echoing:

Please, Mama, I haven't been riding in ages...

Go ahead, then ...

The sight of my mother—her gentle eyes, her soft voice, her slight smile as she let me go—broke me all over again. I sat down on the floor, back against the bed, tears running down my face.

I saw a glimpse of Kolya and me racing through the woods on horseback, and then I was surrounded on all sides by waves of misty purple, translucent enough that I could still see the grain of the wooden floorboards through the field of sage. Then I saw Damien and I forgot it was a vision at all.

He stood there large as life and twice as bright, his arms open, face blazing. I saw myself leap into his arms. He swung me around and around before kissing me full on the mouth.

Our happiness was like the slash of a sword. I slammed the music box shut. The vision disappeared, the attic room plunging into darkness. The mechanism wound down and went quiet.

I was crying, face mashed against my knees.

I couldn't bear to watch the rest of that day—couldn't stand to see myself dancing with Damien, my sisters laughing, Ollie smiling at Axel, when I knew the fate that would befall us all.

Most of all, I couldn't bear to see Damien's face when I was forced to tell him what I would have given anything not to say.

I hadn't used the memory-keeper since, but carried it with me everywhere I went, as if it contained the souls of everyone I loved trapped inside.

Now I huddled against the hard lump of metal down the front of my shirt, desperate to keep it hidden and safe. It was all I had left of them.

Igor asked where we were being taken. One of the guards pointed a rifle in his face and told him to shut his mouth. No one asked questions after that. We'd all seen Katinka's body abandoned in the snow on the side the building.

The wagon trundled over to the next factory, which was a glassworks. We huddled for about thirty minutes while half the guards filed inside and presumably reenacted the same charade we'd endured.

Soon the wagon was jammed with twenty more workers with "improperly printed" ID cards.

The Black Coats were taking the biggest and strongest, mostly men. That's what told me where we were headed.

440

During the Red Terror, tens of thousands were rounded up and shot in the streets or sent to the labor camps. They started with the aristocrats, then moved to bourgeoisie. The "revolutionaries" weren't shy about their intentions. The *People's Voice* printed a list of "enemies of the state" which included all Tsarists, priests, liberals, any socialists who didn't call themselves Bolsheviks, wealthy businessmen, wealthy peasants, foreigners, and political dissidents of any type.

Rasputin had allied himself with the Bolsheviks, who now headed the Duma. Somehow Yaro Vyachevslav had managed to maintain his position in the legislature, despite being one of the wealthiest bourgeois of all.

Their stated intention was to destroy the wealthier classes. Vyachevslav wrote, "Let there be a flood of bourgeois blood. As much as possible."

And the streets ran red.

That was months ago. Those who'd been hauled off to the labor camps had probably perished. Rasputin needed more workers—especially for the mine.

He must have used up a great deal of his stolen Charoite taking over the city. Maybe all of it.

Now he was in control of whatever was dug out of the Lorne Mountain. But Papa told me the mountain was running dry. If Rasputin was hauling out some of the best and strongest from his factories, he must be getting desperate.

I felt a bitter satisfaction, even as I knew I was about to be fed into the machinery of the mine.

It was the most dreaded place you could be sent. No letters came out. No survivors, either.

We visited three more factories until the wagons overflowed with terrified workers, some covered in plaster dust, some still wearing the heavy leather gloves of the ironworks.

"Where do you think they're taking us?" one of the girls whispered.

"*Shh,*" someone else hushed her.

At each stop, I considered running. The guards weren't particularly attentive. If I chose the right moment and slowed time even a little, I might be able to escape.

The problem was, it had been months since I'd practiced magic. I'd been weakened by the infection, the pneumonia, the gashes all over my body. By the time I recovered, I was assigned the job at the cotton mill and came home tired to the bone. Magic required energy. I had none to spare.

Crouched in the wagon, I already felt exhausted. I might jump into the time-stream and sputter out after a few steps. I'd stumble to the ground while a dozen bullets ripped into my back.

Besides, where would I go? I couldn't return to Varvara's house. Couldn't leave the city or travel the roads without papers. Even beggars were hauled off to labor camps.

So I stayed in the wagon as we lumbered from stop to stop. It was full dark by the time we turned toward the train station.

The large, grand Vitebsky Station looked nothing like it used to. Once it had been an opulent art nouveau structure with spacious hallways, elegant stained glass, and delicate wrought-iron railings. Papa had his own private pavilion that contained a marble statue of his grandfather.

Now the statue had been pulled down and all the lovely lounges destroyed. There was no traveling for pleasure anymore—you could only ride the railway with permission from the state.

The cathedral-like station was packed with military equipment, shipping palettes, and machinery. It was a warehouse now, and we were packages being shipped to our next destination. They packed us into train cars with no seats, no food, no water, no toilets. There wasn't space to sit or lie down.

The women huddled together in one corner. It hadn't taken us long to learn we were safest as a group, especially in situations where men became desperate.

Still, we were outnumbered, and any time the men grew irritable or shifted around, it sent a flutter of nerves through the women.

I was close to the window, which provided a little more air, but also cold wind and a dusting of dry, powdery snow that kissed my face and melted down my neck.

Several people groaned as the train lurched to life. That was denial again —as if until that moment they had hoped the Black Coats might open the doors and let us all out again.

Once we were speeding down the track, people stared dazedly at the pines flashing by outside the window. Most of us hadn't left the city in a year.

I saw a flicker of silver and craned my neck, staring out through the darkness. I thought I'd seen something swooping through the treetops.

I dozed fitfully, my head on the shoulder of the woman next to me, hers bumping against the wall.

By the next morning, the car stank of urine and unwashed bodies. Still the train clattered on. I knew how long it took to get where we were going, so I knew exactly how long I'd have to keep standing on aching legs.

Though I was headed to the worst possible place, I couldn't help feeling a thrill knowing that if Damien had returned to the steppes, I was closer to him than I'd been in a very long time.

Of course, "close" was a relative term.

The train stopped at the final station. The stark black pyramid of the Lorne Mountain jutted up into the thick mat of clouds.

I was about to descend further than I'd ever been.

WE WERE LOADED BACK into the same wagons, pulled along by heavy draft horses with wide backs and short, muscular necks. Even those huge beasts strained to haul us up the steep cutbacks to the mine.

It took the better part of an hour to ascend just to the base. By then, we were well above the tree line, nothing but naked black stone and ice-tipped peaks above us.

Just below the clouds, keeping her distance, I saw a bird alight on the tip of lightning-blasted pine. As she touched down, her left wing gave a slight wobble and she had to catch her balance. My heart twisted in my chest.

I knew she could see me ten times better than I could see her. I lifted my hand just a few inches, bidding goodbye to Artemis. I hoped she would fly back where she'd come from, where snow hares were plentiful and she could hunt for silver fish over the arctic sea.

I could see down to the wide expanse of the Frost Forest, the trees dense and tangled, the pines more black than green. Beyond that, a brown smudge that had to be the steppes, flat and frozen in winter.

So close and yet so far.

My heart strained in that direction, a pull stronger than gravity, while I was marched inside the mine.

My last look at the sky was churning waves of gray and purple cloud. Then the dark enclosed us.

The inside of the mine was wet and cold, worm tunnels cut through rough black stone. Water dripped endlessly. Sometimes you could hear it running behind solid wall.

The ground sloped steeply downward. We followed a trail of greenish lanterns deep into the earth.

Every step downward was a step away from light and life. The prisoners moved haltingly, turning back again and again to see the mouth of the cave receding behind us until it was only a circlet of gray like a distant moon. Then the entrance disappeared entirely.

The guards prodded us along with the barrels of their rifles. The Black Coats had departed. Now we were in the possession of the overseers, which did not appear to be an improvement.

The overseers had to live in the mine just like we did, and it had not improved their tempers. They were pallid, eyes bloodshot, wiry frames only a little better fed than the prisoners.

And prisoners we were. This was no work camp. A good third of the workers were manacled at the ankles, a short chain between their feet. I learned later that was the punishment if you tried to escape—the next time, they simply shot you.

If I'd thought the children at the mill looked bad, it was nothing to the misery I saw here. Nearly every person was covered in bruises and sores, their bodies emaciated. It was hard to tell the women from the men. Everyone looked ancient, bent at the back, withered in the limbs.

The new miners were stripped naked, doused with de-lousing powder, and sprayed with cold water. Women and men were separated, but all the guards were men. They watched us with hungry eyes.

I tucked the memory-keeper under my arm and held it pressed against my body while the freezing hose blasted me. I'd seen the guards pocketing any bit of money or jewelry they spied. One woman managed to save her wedding ring by hiding it under her tongue.

We were provided with heavy canvas coveralls and new boots that were old boots that used to belong to someone else. The boots were handed out at random, mismatched in size. We tried to trade amongst ourselves, but I still ended up with a pair two sizes too big. That was better than too small—the tallest of the women had to slit the toes of her boots to jam her feet inside.

We were each given a tattered blanket, a tin bowl and cup, and a single fork.

"If you lose 'em, you won't get more," the cook snarled. He slopped a spoonful of soup into the bowl. A few limp pieces of cabbage floated in a greasy broth with a soapy sheen.

By that point, I was hungry enough to gobble it down. When I bit into the dry little bun that came with my soup, my tooth ground against something hard. I pulled out a black pebble that looked like the rock all around us.

"Dirt gets into everything around here," a soft voice said.

I'd been assigned to a cell with six other women, one who'd been picked up at the glassworks, and the rest prisoners who'd already been here when we arrived.

The woman speaking to me now occupied the bunk two down from mine. She was frail and dark haired with large, heavy-lidded eyes and a rosebud mouth. With horror, I recognized Anna Pavlova.

I considered turning away, but it was pointless. I couldn't hide from her if we were sharing a cell. All I could do was play dumb and pray I'd changed enough that she wouldn't recognize me. I'd watched her dance onstage for an hour, but she'd only spoken to me for a moment. The dyed hair and the weight I'd lost had altered me significantly—or so I hoped.

"How long have you been here?" I asked her.

"Six months." She laughed without any humor. "I'm one of the oldest."

"What did they send you for?"

"I danced in the Imperial Ballet. If your job had 'imperial' in the title ... well, that's reason enough." She held out a slim hand. "I'm Anna."

I took her hand, feeling bones as delicate as a bird's.

"Nina."

I saw no sign of suspicion as she squeezed my hand once and let go.

"You're lucky to be in here with us. Some of the blocks are much worse."

"Why?"

"The guards. They prey on the women. But Hilda over there"—Anna jerked her head toward a woman built like a young spring bull—"she can make the earth shake. She threatened to bring the whole mine down on their heads if the guards stepped foot in our cell."

My stomach lurched at the thought of all those tons of smothering rock suspended above my head.

"That's good ... I guess."

Anna gave a strange sort of smile. "You may wish she'd do it before long."

Our cell was cold as a refrigerator. The clang of the iron door closing and locking at night was the most chilling sound I'd ever heard. I ran to the bars, gripping them in my hands, immovable as the stone walls all around. I'd never been locked in before. My hands were shaking, my mind screaming at me to get out.

The weak green lanterns in the passageway cast hardly any light into the cell. The blackness was thick and smothering, like the enchanted darkness Rasputin used to attack my family at the wedding. Cold stiffened my body, chilling my heart.

I retreated to my bunk and curled up in a ball, blanket wrapped tightly around me, the blackness throbbing against my ears with every beat of my heart.

The stirs of the women around me, each rustle of a rat, sounded like the creeping of some creature sliding into the cell. Behind my closed lids I saw sharp teeth and the wet gaping mouths of the vampyrs.

They frightened me. Gods, how they frightened me.

I huddled in my cell like a coward, trying to hold back tears.

So many things frightened me now. Sometimes I thought of the girl I used to be—reckless, bursting with energy, laughing at anything—and I wanted to cry for that happiness like a thin, sparkling bridge stretched out over a chasm. When the bridge shattered, I plunged down.

The morning was worse. I thought I'd woken in darkness in the attic—that was nothing compared to the darkness of the mine. The guard bashed his club against the metal bars to wake us. I jolted upright, thinking they were rousing us at midnight.

We shuffled through the line for food again, using the tin bowls that hadn't been washed from the night before. Breakfast was the same watery soup, barely re-warmed. No bun this time.

The overseers loaded us down with buckets, pickaxes, shovels, drills, and marched us deeper into the bowels of the mountain.

We passed through passage after passage of pitted, scarred rock where the miners had already dug. The tunnels sloped ever downward through the winding warren of stone.

Some of the passageways were so cold I expected to feel ice instead of water when I touched the walls. Others were hot from vents in the rock that emitted sudden blasts of steam. The mountain was uneasy, sometimes rumbling or shifting beneath us. A few miners whispered that the spirit of the mountain was angry because we'd dug too much away.

"Pipe it if you want to keep your tongue in your head," one of the guards snapped. "That's the Old Beliefs. We keep the New Order now."

The Black Coats had cracked down on mysticism and sorcery along with all dissenting political opinions. I knew exactly what that old hypocrite was up to—Rasputin wanted no whispers of spirits, skinwalkers, or especially vampyrs. He didn't want the Bolsheviks to know who they'd actually aligned with.

Once we came to the end of the tunnels where the new digging was happening, we got to work. The fact that we had no training, no experience in mining mattered not at all. We had a daily quota to hit, just like at the mill. Only this quota was impossible.

I chipped and hacked at the stone walls with my axe, digging out chunks of black rock, breaking them apart, sifting through the pieces for crystals of Charoite. We were each supposed to produce five grams a day, but Papa had spoken truly: the mine was running dry.

I worked hunched over and sweating all through the day with no break for lunch. The water brought round was gritty with black dust.

My fingers were raw, palms blistered, and still I hadn't found any Charoite. I started to panic, striking the wall with all my strength, smashing the rocks against sharp edges to split them open, but finding nothing within.

When the whistle shrilled, I had only a few sparkling flecks to show for my day's work.

I joined the line, filthy and slump shouldered.

Anna slipped in behind me.

"What did you find?"

I showed her the few pitiful flecks.

"That's not enough."

"I know."

She took her own tiny lump of Charoite and chipped it in half with the tip of her axe.

She handed me half. "That ought to be five each."

"Are you sure?" I said, hardly believing.

"I got lucky today. Won't be able to help you tomorrow. If you ever find a good piece, try to hide half for the next day. But hide it where you found it— if they catch you sneaking any out, they'll cut your hands off and *then* they'll shoot you."

The guards had already threatened us several times with dire consequences if we dared steal even a single grain of Charoite.

I'd still considered it.

I was much too depleted to escape on my own—if I ever wanted to get out of this place, I'd need a boost. We were deep in the mountain and high on the cliff. I'd need to slow time for at least four or five minutes, which meant I'd need a lot more than what Anna had found.

Even if I could get it, I hated the thought of using it.

I'd felt it in my hand, throbbing like a malevolent heart.

I watched it seep through Rasputin's pores.

And I saw it hiding in my own father's eyes.

It wants to change you ... all of you ...

Now I was in the heart of the mountain, the birthplace of that cursed crystal. I was trapped where it lived. Even if it was mostly gone, I could feel its evil seeping through the rock like cold sweat.

I took the little lump from Anna all the same and thanked her. It seemed to squirm between my fingers like a beetle.

I dropped it on the overseer's scale, resisting the urge to wipe my hand on my trousers.

"Five point five," he said. "Barely made it."

Half the workers had not met their quota. They were marched back to their cells without any food. Those who missed two days in a row were whipped.

One of those women was dragged back to my cell, her back raw and bleeding. Hilda, the spring bull, gently cleaned the slashes with a damp rag and sat with her until the woman's sobs faded away and she fell asleep.

chapter 37

WHEN ALL LIGHT IS LOST

🎵 *Sunlight—Hozier*

I woke the second morning in the mine, and then the third. By the fifth or sixth, I was already starting to lose count. We never left the tunnels of rock, never saw sunrise or sunset. Never saw the sun at all.

I was so exhausted that each hour was the same as the last, a dull grind of endurance.

My nails ripped, blisters popped and formed again. I was away from the chemicals of the cotton mill, but now my lungs filled with black dust as I broke and shattered rock, sifting for sparkling grains of violet.

Miners were lost in accidents, in cave-ins, from injury, illness, or starvation. More took their place.

Anna told me most prisoners lasted a matter of months. Only a few had been here longer than a year.

We dug ever deeper, through newly blasted tunnels excavated by amateurs who didn't know how to properly shore the walls with timber. The work was rushed, desperate. Weekly we heard the rumble and rush of rock collapsing. Sometimes it was the mountain itself that shivered and brought a ton of solid stone crashing down, sealing the miners in their own private tomb. Sometimes we heard weak cries or the tapping of a pick on the other side of the fall, but the guards forbade us trying to dig out the survivors.

"You'll never shift it, they're already dead."

They had their own quotas to hit and they drove us ruthlessly.

The pressure was relentless, the work back-breaking. Fits of violence broke out amongst the men, sudden and usually over nothing at all—a place in line, or a fork supposed to belong to someone else. Two scrawny combatants would bite and claw at each other until the guards descended with whips and clubs.

Other times we heard the scream of a woman dragged into a tunnel by a pair of guards. That had not yet happened to me, but I lived in terror of it. I tried to stay as filthy as possible, smearing dirt on my face, wearing all my layers of clothes. I rubbed dirt in my hair too, trying to hide the red roots growing in.

I stayed close to Anna Pavlova and she stayed close to me. We dug in the same tunnels and tried never to walk anywhere alone.

She was frail, those hollow bones ill suited to hauling heavy buckets of rock. I tried to carry the worst of it for her, and she showed me the best places to dig, tracing faint veins of lilac to small deposits of crystal.

"You have to go deep to find anything," she told me, squeezing through narrow passageways and into tight crevices to find unexplored pockets within the mine.

Anna could fit where almost no one else could; that's how she'd stayed alive so long. She'd never been whipped. She was so thin now it would probably kill her.

As we worked, she told me her history. How her mother had been a laundress, her father a hospital orderly. She'd been a sickly child, raised by her grandmother most of the time.

One day her mother took her to see *Sleeping Beauty* at the same theater where Anna would one day perform.

"I'd never seen anything so beautiful." Her eyes glinted in her filthy face. "The way the women moved—like fairies flitting from place to place. I had a vision of myself in one of those gossamer tutus with a pair of wings on my back ..."

"Were you a natural?"

She laughed. "Not at all. I auditioned for the imperial school and they rejected me. But I was obsessed. I choreographed my own dances, I practiced and practiced. I made myself a pair of insect wings and wore them to my next audition. I performed my own creation, *The Dragonfly*. Then I was accepted."

I longed to tell her that I'd seen her perform, that I'd cried like a baby. But that would be suicide. The reward for turning me in to Rasputin would be too much for anyone to resist.

"What was the school like?"

"Brutal," she said bluntly. "And I was not a favorite. They called me the little boy, the twig, *La Petite Sauvage.*" She smiled. "Actually, I liked that last one."

"You didn't care what they said?"

"Of course I did. But I never let it stop me."

At night, she bent and stretched for an hour before bed, no matter how exhausted we all were. She contorted her feet into the most outrageous shapes and put her legs around behind her head.

It made me think of Katinka, who never stopped practicing the cello until she was shot in the snow.

"I saw you dance at the Mariinsky Theater," Hilda said to Anna, surprising us all.

Hilda had worked at a dairy until her father wrote an open letter in protest of the Red Terror that had her entire family shipped off to labor camps, from her youngest brother to her elderly grandmother.

She was brash and kind, phenomenally strong and skilled at the engineering required to brace the tunnels. But she did not seem like a patron of the arts. She'd once told us she didn't believe the earth was round. She'd never ridden in an automobile and refused to ever try.

"How come the swan had to die in the end?" she asked Anna.

"Because," Anna said, bending herself in half like a paperclip with no apparent discomfort, "the most beautiful things are fragile and can't last. That's what makes them precious while we have them."

I touched the memory-keeper tucked away in my pocket. It was my talisman, the thing that kept me grounded when I thought I might sink into the earth or simply fall apart.

My mind was not as stable as it had been. The horror of watching my family slaughtered, followed by Rasputin forcing himself into my brain like a man shoving himself into a too-small suit, had caused rips and holes, weakened seams, and parts that no longer connected as they had before, floating loose and untethered.

I forgot things, even important things like Mama's birthday or the color of Alexei's eyes. I got distracted and confused, and sometimes I cried without knowing why, without even knowing I was doing it until I felt the wetness on my face.

What Anna said made me shake like a leaf. Everything on this earth was fragile and impermanent, even the earth itself if we really were just a speck of rock whirling through the infinite heavens. Touching the memory-keeper caused a gentle whirr against my fingertips, warm and alive like the purring of a cat. It calmed me.

I felt Anna's dark eyes, watching.

Weeks passed, or maybe it was months. Some of the women tried to keep tally of the days by scratching on the wall, but even they tended to lose count.

Anna grew thinner, and I must have, too, though I never looked at my own body.

One of the women in our cell, the one who'd been whipped for missing her quota, missed it again and was whipped twice more. The second time the lashes were administered by Artyom, one of the cruelest guards.

Artyom didn't drag women into tunnels, but he seemed to delight in whipping the youngest and prettiest girls. There was an avid glint in his eye as he ripped open the back of Dasha's shirt and struck her again and again, the tip of his tongue protruding at the corner of his mouth. He whipped her until sweat beaded at his temples, until Dasha had ceased shrieking or even whimpering and Hilda bellowed at him to stop.

Too late. Dasha had died quietly on the stone floor. She was twenty-two years old and had been a teacher, once upon a time.

Hilda only lasted two weeks longer. She cut the palm of her hand and the wound became infected. She wrapped it in cloth and tried to keep it clean, but that was impossible in the damp. Soon she was burning with fever.

A healer in the adjoining cell tried to help her, but her power was depleted and she had none of her usual supplies. She laid her hand on Hilda's forehead and sang to her until the large blonde girl fell into a fitful sleep. She never woke.

I began to realize it was only a matter of time for all of us. Even I'd been in denial, believing that we only had to endure, to survive, and someday we'd all walk out of here.

The final blow was Anna Pavlova.

It was the end of the day and we were heading back to our cells, passing a group of men trying to heave a load of rock onto one of the mine carts. The cart was ancient, a lattice of rust eating through its side. As they levered the mass of loose rock inside, the cart broke apart, spilling its entire load outward.

There was nowhere to run. Trapped in the narrow tunnel, Anna was swept under the avalanche. I screamed for the men to help. Frantically we dug her out, but it was too late. Her fragile legs had broken in a dozen places.

We carried her back to the cell. I put a blanket over her legs. When the guards came, demanding to know what had happened, I said she'd bruised her foot but she'd be fine by morning. If they saw the injuries, they'd drag her away and shoot her.

I thought Anna was unconscious, but when the guards left her eyes opened. She was strangely calm, her breathing slow, face relaxed.

I whispered, "Doesn't it hurt?"

"It's only my body." Her eyes slid away from me. She looked at the black stone dome just a few feet above my head. "I used to go to the park to watch the swans swimming ... I had a pet swan ... his name was Jack ..."

The girl who had taken Hilda's bed came into the cell. I hissed at her, "Get the healer, find Lyuba."

I hoped Lyuba could at least help Anna go to sleep like she'd done for Hilda. I knew Anna was past much else.

Something gripped my wrist. Anna's fierce dark eyes stared up at me.

"Take off my boot. The left one."

"I ... I don't think I can."

Her legs were twisted and bent, the bones coming through the skin.

"*Do it.*"

As gently as I could, I lifted the blanket and unlaced her left boot. It was too large for her and slid easily off her foot. Still, she hissed with pain.

"Look in the toe."

I reached deep into the boot, still warm from her foot. My fingers encountered something hard. I pulled out a crystal of Charoite a little smaller than a pea.

"Hide it ..."

Swiftly, I tucked it down inside my sock.

I tried to look for Lyuba once more but Anna squeezed my wrist tighter, pulling me back to her. Her face was tiny and childlike, her eyes huge and burning.

"I know who you are."

I stared at her, mouth falling open.

"I never forget a face. I knew the moment I saw you."

I clutched her hand between mine, trying to hold her to the earth.

"Why didn't you tell? They would have let you out of here."

She smiled sadly. "I am getting out of here."

Her face contorted, fingernails biting into the back of my hand as pain gripped her.

"I'll get you water—"

She shook her head, clinging to me. When the wave passed, she spoke again, her voice all but faded away.

"Save up to escape ... but don't be a fool like me ... don't die with salvation in your hand ..."

She gazed up at the stone ceiling once more, her eyes moving here and there. Her smile grew brighter and her eyes filled with tears as she cried, ecstatic, "Michel! Get my swan costume ready."

She lifted her hands in that position I knew so well, light and delicate and reaching for the sky, fluttering like wings.

Then the swan was gone.

WITHOUT ANNA, I was truly alone.

There was no one to talk to anymore. No one to laugh with. No one to keep safe.

The other women in my cell were strangers. The ones I'd known were gone, and soon the new ones would be, too.

The Charoite Anna had given me was more precious than the finest pearl, but it wasn't enough to escape. I was too depleted. I'd need more.

I tried to save what bits and flecks I could salvage, while barely meeting my daily quota.

Sinking by the hour, I crept away to a quiet cavern and tried to use the memory-keeper. All I wanted was a moment's glimpse of Damien—of that field of purple sage, that golden sunshine, and Damien's face, bright with happiness as I ran to him.

I pressed the music box to my mouth. Nothing happened. I was so empty of magic I couldn't even power it anymore. It remained cold and dark in my hand.

Day and night blurred together. There was no way to judge time with no clocks and no rhythm of the sun rising and setting.

Sometimes it felt as if the hours digging and chipping and scrabbling in the cold, wet rock stretched on infinitely. It seemed as if I'd always been there and always would be.

Other days my head hardly seemed to hit my pillow before I heard the pounding of the guard's guns against the bars jolting me awake. The hours of labor were repetitive and blank. I only noted the clang of the bell for breakfast and dinner, and then I was back in my cell.

Days flipped by like cards in a deck, which terrified me more than anything. I dreamed that I glimpsed my face in a puddle of filthy water and realized I'd grown old without knowing it, my whole life passing by in the darkness. But of course, that was impossible—no one grew old in the mines.

The only change was that more and more prisoners were sent to the mountain. The cells became crowded, the soup even thinner, blankets scarce. When workers fell sick or injured, they disappeared from their cells in the night, never to be seen again—even if the injury was small and they might have healed.

No one asked anymore why the new arrivals had been sentenced. The reasons were too petty, too obscure—perhaps they'd once attended a party with a known enemy of the state, maybe they were a professor who departed from the approved educational material, or a jealous neighbor denounced them. Most had not even been told their crime.

Rasputin's regime grew more brutal and paranoid by the week. Even after all I'd seen, I could hardly believe the stories the newcomers told.

Our quotas increased and the punishments for missing them became harsher. I could taste Rasputin's panic in the pressure put on the overseers and their violence toward us. It all trickled down because the man at the top was running low on the fuel for his power.

I'd read the history of my ancestors; I knew their rises and falls. The more power a tsar got, the more enemies he made, and the more power he needed to hold them at bay.

Rasputin didn't care how soon we died in the mine. In fact, it seemed the guards had been given orders to get rid of us quicker. People began to vanish from their cells at night whether they'd been injured or not: anyone over forty. Anyone under twenty. Anyone who was slow. Anyone caught talking. Anyone who hadn't found Charoite in a week.

The terror was constant. But that level of fear was too much to maintain as I grew weaker with lack of food. It began to fade into something much worse—apathy. And eventually, the faint belief that perhaps it might be better to find some dark chamber of the earth and curl up inside it and simply let myself drift away.

I am leaving this place...

I no longer imagined the feeling of turning my face into the sun, closing my eyes as the wind kissed my skin. I forgot what warmth was like. I forgot the smell of lilacs, the feel of fresh grass under the soles of my feet. I knew nothing but rock and cold dripping water. Roughness, hardness, and the endless ache of my lungs as I tried to cough out the fine black grit that could never be dislodged.

I had to find enough crystal to keep me alive for another day, while trying to save a few tiny flecks for myself. Knowing that if I were caught, I'd be tortured and killed, slow and screaming, while the others watched in silence.

Every day I grew weaker. I could hardly rise from my bed in the morning, shuffling through the narrow corridors, my shoulders bumping against the walls. It had been so long since I felt the slightest spark of magic.

The more feeble I became, the more Charoite I'd need to boost my powers. I wondered if it would even work at all. I imagined a pilot light inside me, flickering and dying, never to be lit again.

We tunneled deeper into the mountain, searching for the crystal that grew ever scarcer. The quotas were impossible to reach. I was whipped when all I could turn in were a few pathetic scraps. Anna's stone stayed hidden in my boot, never to be handed over to Rasputin.

Our cells moved closer to where we dug, which meant I was further than ever from the entrance.

In the most silent hour of the night when I heard nothing from the other cells, not even the racking coughs of my fellow miners, I took out my stash and spread it across my palm. The pinch of flakes was pathetically sparse. I'd need ten times this much.

This tiny sprinkling had taken me months.

I didn't want to do the math, but my brain jumped ahead. At this rate, to get what I needed would take me … eight years.

My fingers closed around the flakes, shaking uncontrollably.

Eight years.

No one lasted eight years.

I was going to die down here. Alone. Without ever tasting clean air again. Without seeing the face of someone I loved. Without feeling arms wrapped around me.

I thought of Damien, of the taste of his mouth, the feel of his lips. My face twisted till it hurt. Everything I wished I'd said to him choked in my throat.

The silent weight of rock pressed down on me, heavy as if it lay directly on my back.

No one would ever know I'd been sent here, not even Rasputin.

This was my tomb. I'd already been buried. All that was left was to die.

The last spark of hope flickered out inside of me. Everything I'd gone through since I lost my family, all the running, all the hiding, was for nothing. I wished I'd died with them that day, because at least we'd be together.

I wanted it to be over.

The flakes of Charoite slipped through my fingers, scattering on the rough stone floor. The one Anna had given me was a little bigger than the others. It glinted in the dirt like a fleck of diamond, illuminated by its own interior light.

Save up to escape ... but don't be a fool like me ... don't die with salvation in your hand ...

I saw Anna's face, blanched white, her eyes impossibly large. Gazing at me with fire still burning in their depths.

She never gave up. Not even at the end.

I got down on my knees and picked up every last fleck of crystal. I found them in the dark because even the smallest contained a glimmer of light.

I couldn't waste Anna's gift.

I lay awake until the guards banged on the bars. Then I joined the queue of hunchbacked workers limping down the shaft, their cracked and swollen hands hanging at their sides.

Deliberately, I angled myself into the group being sent into the deepest and most distant shafts, those that had only just been opened. This was the most dangerous work. No warning came before a collapse.

I winnowed deeper and deeper through tunnels that had barely been touched, wedging myself through narrow gaps in the rock until I left the other miners behind.

I found an empty chamber, hollowed out by dripping water centuries before. It was small, only the size of a closet, and so distant that I could no longer hear chipping pickaxes or the rumble of carts.

I dropped to my knees, setting my lantern down on the rock. Slipping my hand in my pocket, I took out Anna's stone.

It was small. So small. When I snuffed the lantern, its violet light could only illuminate my palm.

Yet it had power enough for a single act of magic.

I took out my memory-keeper.

Through all this time and suffering, through everything I'd lost, I'd held onto the music box like my own beating heart.

I took the tiny nugget of Charoite and set it in the mechanical workings, then closed the lid, set it against my lips, and exhaled.

For a moment, nothing happened. I thought I'd broken it somehow, in a scuffle or a fall.

Then the soft, tinkling music began to play. I set the memory-keeper on the center of the floor, heart stirring in my chest.

Light projected, beaming out in all directions. The stars covered the roof, walls, and floor of the stone chamber, whirling slowly like a tiny galaxy.

The lid lifted, the figures within spinning on their axis. All around me I saw my bedroom once more. I saw the books, the records, the portrait of my sisters that Grandma Minnie had drawn, and one of Alexei. I saw myself, dressing with excitement.

Then I saw Mama, and Kolya, and my horse Barley, and sunshine and grass and pines, and Artemis with her wings straight and strong as she flew above me.

And then Damien, Damien, Damien. I saw his face, I saw his arms wide open, and I could almost feel them wrap around me. I was warm in my chest, really and truly warm for the first time in so long.

I saw us riding, laughing until we swayed together and my head rested a moment on his shoulder.

Then we parted, but in the vision it was only for a moment—in the blink of an eye I was on the steps of the Winter Palace with my family all around me, Papa and Mama, Alexei, Ollie, Tatiana, Maria ... I was watching Damien ride toward me in a storm of brilliant blossoms, the hero of the city, cheered by all but looking only at me.

I watched myself pass him the white bloom from my shoulder. He kissed it without actually touching it, putting it away fresh and alive inside his coat.

Then I was inside the cathedral at Ollie's wedding, and I saw Damien again, sitting a few rows back, not watching the ceremony, his eyes locked on mine with longing in his face.

The tinkling music swelled, and suddenly the whole cavern was full of ghosts, dancing and swirling around me. It was everyone I knew and loved in their last, brightest, happiest moments—Ollie gazing up at Axel, Mama and Papa waltzing together, Aunt Olga with the handsome soldier whose name I'd never learned ...

And Damien, spinning me around with perfect, flawless steps because he'd practiced, because he'd looked forward to dancing with me every day we were apart.

I saw his face, his eyes, his smile, and my heart was so full that warmth overflowed, running down to my freezing fingers and toes. It throbbed through every part of me like Damien's own blood pumping in my veins.

I wanted to close the lid, to stop what I knew I'd see next, but I couldn't tear my eyes away from his face.

The memory-keeper was kind. It didn't show Tatiana, or the moment when I had to tell Damien what had happened.

Instead, it showed me something I'd never seen at all:

When Damien rode away from me, when he'd passed beyond my view, he turned and looked back. The anger was gone from his face, the hatred too. All that was left was sadness ... and regret.

The last of the memories faded away, the stone chamber dark and empty once more.

It was still cold, still wet. It looked as if nothing had changed.

And yet ... it had.

Deep in my chest, warmth still burned.

Hope had come back to me. When I thought it was gone forever.

Though the memory-keeper was silent, I heard my mother's voice, as if she were whispering directly into my ear:

Even if you see how dark the world can be ... choose to believe it could be better.

Life had been beautiful once.

It could be beautiful again.

chapter 38

VIOLET VEINS

🎵 *I'm Ready—Niykee Heaton*

T he next morning I woke to the banging of the guards. My cell was dank and miserable. Yet that flame still burned in my chest.

It kept me warm even when we had to break the rim of ice on the buckets of water to fill our cups. It powered me through the long day of digging and hauling, dragging loads of rock I couldn't lift, stumbling along on feet numb, bruised, and half frozen.

I returned to the deepest shafts and dug with all my strength, holding nothing back. I found three flakes of Charoite and shared one with a girl in my cell named Valentina, who'd found nothing for days and would surely be punished again.

She cradled the crystal in her hand, silent tears running down her face.

Valentina had been a clerk at a shop on Nevsky Prospect where my sisters bought ribbons and lace. She'd curtsied to me once, because I'd been her princess then. Now she didn't recognize me. But I knew her.

Papa said it was our duty to protect the people. Whether I had a crown or not, these were still my people.

All this time my goal had been to survive. What good was survival, if it was only cringing, hiding, scraping out one more day while all of Rusya died around me, frozen and cold?

Coming to the mine was like a year of midnights. I snapped awake in the dark, and at last, I saw clearly.

I wasn't as different from Rasputin as I wanted to believe. The mill and the mine were worse than they'd ever been ... but they'd never been acceptable.

If we were both willing to subjugate the people to get what we wanted, what was the difference?

Rasputin was a parasite, feeding on Rusya just as he'd fed on Alexei. He'd suck the nation dry and leave it drained as my father's corpse. His lust for revenge would never be sated—especially as the Charoite drove him deeper into madness.

He had to be stopped.

He was a monster of our creation—and I was the only one left. It was my responsibility.

I knew things about Rasputin that no one else knew. While he wormed his way into my family, he'd been forced to expose parts of himself in return. He'd shown me things. Shared his secrets. Perhaps only to gain my trust and manipulate me, but for once in my life, I'd been a good student. I might have learned more than he knew.

I was bent on escape more than ever, but not to see sunshine. I was going to find Damien.

I saw his face in the memory. He looked back. The memory-keeper showed me that for a reason.

He didn't hate me forever—he couldn't. Because he felt something much deeper for me, just like I did for him. Our connection wasn't one-sided, it couldn't be. The power had to flow all the way around.

That's friendship, that's love—it's only as strong as its weakest link.

He was my best friend, the person I turned to for help, for advice, to know what he thought of my ideas. Through hundreds of letters, through every hour we'd stolen together ...

Rasputin was my dark mirror. He showed me what I'd become if I followed the worst impulses that lived inside us both.

Damien was my true mirror. He forced me to look at what I really was. But also ... what I could be.

I was going to find him. And I was going to ask him to help me kill Rasputin.

It was my best chance of success. Probably my only chance.

I was one person alone, and Rasputin had Charoite.

I needed someone to stand with me. I needed Damien.

In the meantime, I'd save as many of my people as I could.

I dug and dug, day after day, tunneling deep in the earth. I wedged myself into the heart of the mountain, through winding shafts so narrow I could never have reached them before I became so emaciated. I began to find little nuggets of Charoite, more than I'd seen before. Some I smuggled back to my cell, and some I shared with others to save them from culling.

I pushed myself ever deeper, driven by that wild hope that burned brighter inside me each day.

Months passed by. I began to cough blood—and still I dreamed with a fury stronger than the reality I saw around me. I had to believe that in the battle between dark and light, somebody somewhere was on my side.

The best lesson I ever had with Rasputin was the one where he showed me to channel my anger and frustration into pyromancy.

Annoyed at Katya, he finally taught me something real ... anger is powerful.

As I fled the Winter Palace, drained of magic, I blasted fire in that were-wolf's face, fueled by fury as my family died around me.

Anger is *exactly* like fire—but even the hottest fire burns low without fuel. You can stoke the flames, telling yourself how angry you are ... but from the day of the offense, rage is ebbing away.

I ran out of my anger at Rasputin.

I needed something else to fuel me.

Damien was that light. The music box gave me hope that he might forgive me. My memories did the rest.

I thought of my best and brightest moments and used them to power me. That's the best motivation, it always is—we'll do anything for the people we love. Nothing pushes us harder.

Anger fades. Love only grows.

I thought of all my happiest days, the ones I could have captured and stored. The one that shone brightest again and again was my nineteenth birthday.

It started out so dull. We couldn't do anything because of the riots. My parents were stressed and annoyed with me, in no mood to celebrate.

Alexei seemed to have forgotten at first, but partway through the day brought out a book of old fairytales we had when we were young. It was a favorite until we lost it. He'd seen a new copy months before, sitting on a table in a shop like it was left for him. He bought it and saved it all that time.

Maria grew me a new window-box garden, full of speckled purple mushrooms and shaggy purple moss.

Even Tatiana, who found gift giving "tedious and contrived", brought me a stack of records I was listening to all through the rainy afternoon, after cake with everyone else.

So I wasn't too unhappy until in the rainy gloom, alone, I began to think of Damien.

I was missing him. Feeling guilty and stressed that he was far away and in danger because of me.

Then Nina came in with a gift. It had arrived a week before. She'd hidden away for me.

It was wrapped up in the ugliest burlap sack, tied round with twine. But I knew already it had to be from Damien. My heart leaped up. I'd never been more excited to see inside a package. I knew, I knew, it was something special, I could feel it. He'd been missing me too.

I opened it carefully, the scent of leather already overpowering the musty burlap sack.

It was a Cossack saddle, handmade by Damien for me.

He'd told me the hours and hours Cossacks spent making their saddles. A skilled artisan might manage only two in a year.

Each was a work of art, unique, made for its rider.

On mine, Damien carved a gyrfalcon. Artemis, fierce in the sky. Free as the wind.

He knew I'd think of her whenever I saw it. I'd think how much I loved her, and how when we rode together, I felt as fast as her on my horse.

I thought of Damien, too. The countless hours he must have spent every night, any minute he had free. It takes months ... the saddle has to form and take shape. You wet it and bind it and let it dry. You carve in the design and shape it ...

You couldn't give a bigger gift of time than a custom-made saddle. He told me later he made a deal with the cook to ferry it around place to place on the supply wagon, carefully wrapped.

All those hours, all that trouble ... for me.

I remembered the joy I felt when I unwrapped it, the scent of the leather, layered and rich and evocative of everything I loved—horses and riding and Artemis and Damien. The outdoors and the feeling of freedom ...

Inside the pocket of the saddle he slipped a letter:

Happy birthday, princess. You don't ride horses like a Romanov. You ride them like a Cossack. So I made this for you, because that's what Cossacks do—we put carvings of our favorite things on our saddles to remind us of home when we're away. To remind us what we fight for.

That memory gave me life, it gave me strength when everything else was gone. All those hours he spent thinking of me, working for me ... I knew what it meant.

Damien wouldn't turn me away.

I just had to get to him.

I kept going, I kept trying ...And then one day, in a distant crevice of earth ... I found a purple vein.

My heart stopped in my chest.

The vein was only as thick as my pinky, but I could see the bright glow emanating. I chipped at the rock. A great hunk of stone came away, revealing much more within.

The cache pulsed with light.

I could feel the power radiating out of the wall. It was like standing next to the electrical generator in the basement of the Alexander Palace. Little hairs stood up on my arms. My chest felt tight.

I'd found a massive store of Charoite. Far more than I needed to escape.

I could easily gouge out enough to power my exit. But the rest was buried deep, I'd never get it out on my own. If I even attempted to dig it out the other miners would hear me, and so would the guards.

This was the largest cache I'd ever heard of. More than Rasputin had stolen from the vault.

My excitement turned to terror in an instant. If Rasputin found this, he'd be unstoppable.

Using my axe, I gouged out a lump the size of a hen's egg. That would be more than enough to help me escape.

I tried to fill the hole I'd made with rock, smearing oil and dirt over the pulsing vein. A faint glow still emanated through the makeshift paint, but it was less noticeable than before.

I wriggled my way back through the narrow cleft in the rock, back to the main passageways. No one else had seen what I'd found. It was possible the Charoite might stay hidden for weeks, maybe even months. It depended on which direction the miners dug, and also on how large the cache might actually be—for all I knew, it spread everywhere beyond these walls.

The idea of that limitless power in Rasputin's hands made my stomach heave.

I had to get out of here. Fast.

I SPENT two more days agonizing over exactly how I was going to escape, and whether I could take anyone with me.

I hated the thought of leaving behind Valentina and the other women in my cell—hated to leave a single prisoner. But I knew it was going to be damned impossible to get myself out, let alone anybody else.

The Charoite would boost my power, but it would be like eating an entire cake and then trying to sprint a marathon. Underneath the magic, I'd still be weak and emaciated and sick with half a dozen ailments.

On top of that, the only person I'd ever pulled into the time-stream with me was Damien. I highly doubted I could do it with anyone else, especially not in my current state.

Getting out of the mine was the first step. We were in the middle of nowhere, and unless it happened to be June outside, I was going to escape into a snowbound wilderness. If the temperature inside the mine was any indication, Rasputin's perpetual winter had only worsened.

The morning of the third day, I made my decision.

Getting rid of Rasputin had to come before anything else. We were all dead, every single one of us, if he continued to vent his rage on Rusya unchecked.

I swore to myself I'd come back for everyone. I wasn't going to forget what I'd experienced here, not ever.

All I'd managed to stockpile from my meals was half a bun, barely softer than the rock around me. That would have to tide me over until I found civilization.

I watched the movements of the guards, but it was difficult to plan my escape when I saw nothing beyond my own cell and the tunnels down to the digging. I had no idea of the situation closer to level.

I waited until late afternoon when the guards were most lethargic. They were supposed to monitor us while we worked but hated descending deep into the earth almost as much as we did. The quota system ensured that everyone was motivated to work with or without supervision, so the guards tended to cluster closer to the cells, playing dice or cards, only stirring if they heard a prisoner approaching.

I had my bun in my pocket, the memory-keeper too. And the lump of Charoite. I'd carried it with me for three days now. At night, it made a faint whispering sound, always awake in my pocket, never sleeping.

Today I'd tried to stay as close to the cells as possible. I'd offered to carry water to the miners, one of the jobs that got you out of digging for the day. Artyom laughed in my face.

"Carrying water's a privilege. What have *you* done that deserves rewarding?"

He'd smiled at me, revealing a row of teeth tiny as milk teeth, brown as tobacco.

The Charoite throbbed in my pocket. I had a vivid image of putting my fist through those teeth. He'd smiled just like that as he'd whipped Dasha to death.

Instead, I hoisted my pick, shovel, and bucket, and shuffled off down the tunnel.

Now I was creeping back up again, trying to get as close as I could before I made my move.

I closed my hand around the Charoite. No matter how long I carried it around or how long I held it, the crystal never warmed. It wasn't squirming now. As if it knew what was about to happen ...

Taking a deep breath, I clutched the crystal and exhaled, allowing its energy to flow into my hand.

It ran up my arm like cold water, flowing up my veins into my heart. From there, it pumped all through my body, diffusing with every beat.

When I opened my eyes, all the world had sharpened. The stone walls came clear in the gloom of the mine. The scents of raw mineral and lamp oil intensified. I stood taller, back straightening, knees tightening.

Power throbbed through my veins. I could feel it coiled in my muscles, taste it on my breath when I exhaled. If I could have looked in a mirror I would have seen it burning behind my eyes as I'd once seen in Rasputin.

Gripping my shovel in my hand, I twisted into the time-stream and began to run.

The air turned smooth and frictionless, the stone floor slick as marble beneath my feet. My joints became pistons, my muscles springs. I sprinted up the tunnel, the black rock a blur all around me.

Reaching the first junction point, I passed a pack of miners frozen in place. One was wiping his filthy brow with the back of an equally filthy arm, another drinking from a dipper of dirty water. The third paused mid-swing, his pickaxe raised overhead.

They didn't flinch as I whipped past them, my speed causing their hair to ruffle as if blown by wind.

I'd frozen time fully and completely, but I could already feel my muscles starting to tremble, struggling to maintain this level of effort.

As I neared the new cell block, I could already feel resistance, running into the wind instead of with it. My legs began to wobble like Artemis' injured wing.

I clutched the Charoite and felt another boost, an injection of gasoline directly into my veins. I surged past the guards huddled around their scattered cards and coins. While I thought one of their heads began to turn, I was already well past before he registered. I'd be further still before he could raise a shout or reach for his gun.

My thighs burned as I ran continuously upward, arms pumping, shovel clutched in one hand, the lump of Charoite in the other. I hazarded a glance at the stone and saw it glowing brightly—only half depleted at most.

This was going to work. I was going to make it.

Shadows flickered at the mouth of the next junction. I darted into a side tunnel, pressing tight against the rock, letting time unspool for a just a moment so the guards could pass and my racing heart could rest.

A cramp hit me, sudden and sharp. I clutched my side, teeth gritted, trying not to cry out. My legs trembled beneath me, thighs already stiffening.

The guards passed by achingly slow, their conversation muffled and distorted. I wasn't quite back in normal time, the air felt thick as honey. Clenching my fist around the crystal once more, I heaved myself upright and reached for that acceleration, that blast of power that would rocket me out of here once and for all.

I ran through the green-tinged gloom, gasping for breath. All at once I felt the caress of something cool against my cheek. I breathed deep, tasting air laced with snow and pine. The darkness changed, thinning, going gray at the edges. There, like a portal to another world, the mouth of the tunnel appeared.

I burst out into the open like a baby newly born. The light dazzled my eyes, the cold, clear air searing my lungs. The shock jolted me back to normal time and I stood there, exposed.

The color alone was too much to bear. I hadn't seen real green in a year. The bruised shades of purple and smoky blue within the ocean of cloud were lustrous as pearl to eyes trained only to dirt and rock. The glare off the pure white snow blinded me.

The world seemed wide open, an endless expanse of sky overhead, a dizzying drop down the mountain to a sea of pines beneath. I was barely tethered to the rock; I could fall up or down just as easily.

Maybe I would have stood there forever, petrified, until someone found me. The Charoite had other plans. It pulsed in my hand, shoving me forward like a hand to the back.

The shock broke. I stumbled down the steep cutback, hunched over, trying to move from cover to cover on the exposed slope. It helped that I was coated with rock dust the exact color of the mountain, not an inch of clean skin on me—just the whites of my eyes and the occasional flash of teeth.

The wind gusted and my molars slammed together. The mine had been perpetually cold and wet but now I was exposed to actual wind, actual snow. The road down the mountain was slick with ice, sharp stones jutting up. Gritty sleet blew in my face.

I heard the rumble of wheels and crouched behind a cracked boulder, shivering. A wagon inched up the hill, the horses' hooves slipping on the ice. Another load of prisoners for the mine.

When they rounded the corner, I ran once more.

I ebbed in and out of the time-stream, hardly aware of when the wind blew slow or fast. My head seemed to float above a body as stiff and awkward as a suit of armor. I needed a horse or somewhere to hide, because I wasn't going to last much longer on my feet.

At last I neared the base camp. A cluster of the oversized draft horses stood tied to a post, shuffling their feet to stay warm. Muscular and shaggy, their coats were dull shades of sand and stone.

I crept up on the horses, slipping between their hulking bodies, whispering to them quietly.

I was about to set down my shovel and set to work on the rope's knots when a voice said, "Stop where you are. Put your hands up."

The man sounded close, maybe only a step behind me. The click of his safety was no more than a foot from my ear.

I slipped my hand in my pocket.

"Put that shovel down and put your hands up!"

I closed my fingers around the Charoite.

Power leaped up my arm, eager, like it had only been waiting. I slowed time, gripped the shovel in both hands, and swung it at the man's face.

I bashed aside his pistol and hit him across the jaw. His head twisted and he went down, the horses stamping in alarm, heavy hooves coming down inches from his face.

I kicked his gun away from his limp hand. Then, thinking better of it, I picked up the pistol and tucked it in my belt.

As I bent, I saw the guard's face, his jaw at an ugly angle, his eyes wide open like Maria's. I hadn't meant to hit him so hard. I hadn't meant to actually kill him.

I couldn't stop staring. Blood leaked out of the corner of his dangling jaw. The blood dripped down, but he didn't move, his flesh already stiffening in the cold.

His coat was unbuttoned and his shirt pulled up when he fell, exposing the sharp edge of one hip. His hands were thin, his wrists bony. He was almost as starved as me, almost as dirty.

The crystal throbbed in my pocket, trying to push me into motion again.

Instead, I grabbed the lump of Charoite and flung it away from me. It was only half depleted but I didn't care. I hated the weight of it, hated its pulses and flares, hated it burning in my veins.

I hadn't even considered before I'd hit that guard with my shovel. I'd felt completely justified, completely right. Until I saw him lying dead on the ground.

Sickened, I fumbled with the ropes tying the draft horses to the post.

Two guards emerged from a raggedy tent, drawn by the stamping of the horses. I seized the mane of a rust-colored stallion and heaved onto his back, slapping the flank of the bay next to him and shouting to send the rest scattering.

The horses bolted in all directions. I galloped down the mountain on the stallion, bent low over his back, bullets whipping overhead.

I heard a sharp screech behind me, but couldn't turn my head—the draft horse had no saddle and the cutback was steep and slick. The stallion was so broad I could hardly cling to his back with my knees, my frozen fingers thrust deep in his mane. At each corner, he banked so close to the edge that I feared his hooves would slide out from under him and we'd both go tumbling down the mountain.

Soon we were down amongst the pines. At the first chance, I veered off into the Frost Forest, into trees so tall and dense that their canopy blocked out the sky, snow only blanketing the ground deeply in the clearings. Some of the trunks of the pines were so thick it would take several people linking hands to encircle them.

The draft horse didn't like the deep woods, but he must have hated the mountain more. He galloped on, leaping frozen streams and downed logs that blocked our path.

I had only a vague idea of the direction we should go. All I knew for certain was that the steppes lay to the southwest and I had to cross the Frost Forest to get to them.

Whether I would actually find Damien there was another question—or if he'd be happy to see me if I did. I hoped, I believed what the memory-keeper had shown me was real—that he'd forgiven me. But maybe I'd only seen what I wanted to see.

Something exploded through the treetops over my right shoulder, startling the stallion so it sheered hard to the left, mashing my thigh against the trunk of a spruce.

"ARTEMIS!" I shrieked.

She rocketed past my arm, so exuberant that she had to swoop upward, circle around, and fly back again before she could land. She alighted on my arm, steadier than when I'd last seen her, her wing crooked but stronger than it had been.

It's you! It's you!

She spread her wings, fluttered up, landed again, rubbed her head against my shoulder, talons digging in.

I knew you'd get out! What took you so long? I've been waiting!

Her agitation made her jump about on my arm. I could hardly see her, my eyes blurred and stinging.

"How long were you going to wait there?" I choked out.

How long has it been?

"I don't know," I admitted. "A year?"

The seasons are wrong.

"It's Rasputin. The weather's been fucked since he called down that ice storm on the palace."

You think a man could do this? Artemis jerked her beak at the mottled clouds.

"He's not just a man. And his power ..." I swallowed down the bile that rose in my throat as I remembered how he operated my body like a puppet. "He's a hundred times more powerful than anything I've ever seen."

Why is he keeping it cold? Everyone will starve.

"Maybe that's what he wants. Or maybe the vampyrs need it—they're from Siberia, aren't they? Or maybe he unleashed something he doesn't understand and he's not in control."

I stopped, horrified by that last possibility. If Rasputin couldn't fix it ... maybe no one could.

No, I wasn't going to think about that. I had a bigger and more immediate problem.

"I'm going to kill him," I said to Artemis.

She gave me a look that was probably the last thing a rabbit saw before she put her beak through its eye.

He'll kill you, *idiot.* And then, when she could see I'd already considered that, she moved her head stiffly and said, *I just found you again.*

"I know. But I have to. It's my fault, Artemis. Everything that happened is because of me. I have to fix it."

You can't fix it.

"I have to stop it, then."

She was silent for a time. Then, abruptly, *There is no fault.*

"What?"

When a hawk eats a dove. There is no fault.

"It's different with humans."

Yes, but you behave as if you're a human at fault for what the hawk does.

"I am, though. Rasputin said it himself—I didn't see what was happening because I didn't want to see. I blinded myself so I wouldn't have to feel guilty doing what I wanted to do."

He puts lies in your head.

"Well, that one's true."

Artemis went silent, already annoyed at me again. I had to smile that I'd only lasted about five minutes in her good graces after a whole year's absence.

The stallion lumbered along, Artemis rolling on my arm.

Who's this horse? she snapped.

"I don't know his name. He might not have one—they didn't treat them very well at the mine. Look at his poor back."

The draft horse bore the scars of many whip cuts across his flanks. Some even on his face.

Call him Clumsy.

"I'll call him Rusty."

Silly name.

"That's his color—same way I picked your name. You know Artemis was the goddess of the moon, not just the hunt."

She puffed her chest feathers, offended.

"Artemis is a good name!" I protested. "I don't think you've ever called me anything but 'idiot.'"

Names come from observation.

That made me laugh. The intractability of Artemis was the one constant in the universe. I was glad at least one thing could never change.

The stallion slowed as he tired. Artemis moved up my arm a little and I sat easy on Rusty's back, shaking out my cramped hands, looking around.

I'd never been so deep in the Frost Forest. It was named for the birch trees with silver leaves that looked dipped in frost. In the winter the leaves didn't fall, but hardened on the branch, glinting like metal.

Frozen streams wound like black snakes through the snow. A few flakes drifted down between pine boughs laden with a foot of white on each branch, speared through with dark green needles.

I smelled crisp sap and rich soil. Even the musky scent of the draft horse was pleasant because it was the smell of things alive and growing instead of dead stone. Artemis' feathers were best of all. When I nuzzled my nose against her, I swore a trace remained of her downy baby scent.

Did you go mad in the mine? she asked seriously.

"I don't think so. Well … I don't know. I probably wouldn't know if I had. Are you even here right now? I could be talking to myself."

She bit me on the shoulder, making me yelp.

I'm here.

"Then I guess I'm sane."

How will you beat the monk?

I loved her for asking, instead of telling me it was impossible.

"I don't know."

You'll get crystal.

"No!"

I startled her with my sharpness. She opened her wings, hopping backward on my arm.

"No," I repeated, gentler this time. "I'm not ever using that again."

Why not?

"Because it fucks with my head."

But you need it …

"No!" I felt a sense of panic, a desperate struggle against a tide trying to pull me in again. "That's what got me in this mess in the first place—making excuses, justifying what I *knew* was wrong. That stone is evil. It's a bad influence, it always has been."

Three hundred years of Romanov rule and we all knew its nature, but we used it anyway when we "had to." And who knows what it did to us? Maybe it made us just a little more callous, a little more cruel.

476

I didn't think twice before I killed that guard. Maybe I had to do it and maybe I didn't, but I was done giving control to anything outside myself.

chapter 39

KING WOLF

I filled my lungs with cold, clean air over and over. I could hardly believe I was outside again. And still alive.

I made the stallion walk along one of the frozen streams for a time, hoping it would disguise where we'd gone if anyone tried to follow us. My hands were thrust under his mane to stay warm, his massive body radiating heat into my legs. The overcoat that had once belonged to Varvara's husband was more holes than wool at this point, ripped and rotted away.

Rusty's broad body rolled back and forth like a ship. I leaned against his neck, hoping I could hold on even if I fell asleep.

I was exhausted, but strangely starting to feel better instead of worse. I took the bun out of my pocket and ate a few bites. Soon I was sitting up again, feeling warm and even a little excited. It couldn't be that much further to the steppes. If Damien was there, I might see him by the next day.

I hardly dared let myself hope because the disappointment would be too much if I couldn't find him. But I'd never been able to be reasonable where Damien was concerned—I was already hoping with all my heart, holding nothing back. And that made me warm down to my toes, filling me with more energy than I'd felt in a very long time.

Somewhere beyond the trees the sun was sinking, early twilight falling in the forest. The shadows deepened, a purplish cast tinting the snow. The birds quieted. The stallion's hooves thudded steadily over the loamy ground. Artemis flew ahead when she grew bored of our plodding pace.

Suddenly the horse stopped, ears turning.

A high, lonely howl cut through the evening air, followed by an answering call from our other side.

The stallion bolted so abruptly that I almost tumbled backward over his flank. I clung to his neck as he thundered ahead, dodging trees and leaping logs, no longer heeding how I tried to guide him, his eyes rolling in panic.

I lay belly down on his back, face against his surging neck, trying to avoid the branches that whipped at my face and dragged at my clothes. We were charging through tangled trees at a speed that would take my head off if I hit a low-hanging branch.

To my left, a sleek, dark shape raced through the underbrush. Two more closed in on my right—enormous Timberwolves with black coats thick as manes across their chests.

The draft horse was heavy and powerful, but not nearly as fast as a Thoroughbred or an Arabian. Three more wolves appeared behind us, one so close it snapped at the stallion's heels. The horse kicked backward, almost throwing me forward over his shoulder this time. His hoof caught the wolf across its snarling snout and sent it flipping into the bushes, only for two more to take its place.

I'd heard the woods were overrun with wolves now that no one was sending hunters to cull them. Starving wolves gathered in packs far larger than normal to raid villages or take down the ancient elk of the deep woods whose antlers spanned fourteen feet.

The swarm of black wolves massing around us was larger than any I'd ever heard of. There might be fifty or a hundred, snarling shadows darting through the underbrush, flowing like water, synchronized like starlings.

Artemis came pelting back, tucking her wings to avoid the branches I could barely see in the darkness.

More wolves ahead. They're herding you.

"Which way?" I panted, clinging to the horse.

Here.

She turned sharply left, winging off through the dark.

I tried to turn the stallion, digging my right knee into his side, pulling his mane to the left. The horse was too crazed to understand, the wolves leaping and snapping, one nearly grabbing hold of my boot.

Remembering the pistol, I yanked it out and fired twice. I heard a yelp and thought I might have hit at least one, but it made no difference to the mass closing in. The stallion veered away from the gunshots, closer to the route Artemis had taken. The wolves flanked us on the left, pushing us right again.

We were thundering downhill, toward the sound of water.

No, no! Artemis cried from overhead, but I couldn't follow her, couldn't force the horse to turn. The wolves were pressing in and all the stallion could do was run.

The rushing grew louder. A cold spray hit my face. We'd fetched up against the base of a waterfall, a deep pool behind us, snapping teeth all around.

I fired at the wolves twice more, driving them back, but only in a tight semi-circle. Artemis dove, raking one across the face. Its brother leaped at her as she twisted away, its teeth missing her tail feathers by an inch.

She soared upward, turning as if she'd dive again. Pausing high in the air, she banked abruptly, crossed the river, and flew away.

I stared after her, too confused to even shout. I cocked the gun, expecting the wolves to surge forward. Instead, an eerie calm fell over the pack. They hung back as if waiting.

Something moved in the trees, huge and dark and brindled. Branches snapped beneath its weight. Its low growl raised every hair on my arms and made the stallion shiver beneath me.

The wolves parted to let it through.

The beast that stepped out of the trees was twice the size of the largest wolf, heavy through the chest and shoulders like a bear. Its eyes gleamed in the darkness, fangs as long as my hand glinting in its mouth. Its shaggy coat was white, but not white like snow or cloud. White like things bleached and dead, things found in caves and under rocks.

The beast approached slowly, snout wrinkling as it scented the air.

I know that smell ... it stinks of the one that comes with guns and dogs ... the bearded giant ...

The words weren't words, only barks and snarls, and yet I understood them.

"Stay back!" I brandished the pistol.

The giant wolf paused, ears twitching.

It speaks.

Like Artemis, this was no ordinary animal. I took a deep breath, trying to steady the shaking of my hand.

"King Wolf," I tried to project politeness instead of terror. "Forgive my trespass. I only want to pass through the forest, and then I'll be on my way."

The great wolf made a low growling sound, hackles rising. His pack responded in kind, pressing in. The draft horse took a step backward, inches from the water.

What magic is this, witch?

"I am a witch!" I cried. "You don't want to see what'll happen if you come any closer!"

It wasn't completely a lie—I was feeling a rekindling of my magic, like static at my fingertips. I hadn't felt a charge like this since I went into the mine.

The wolves crept in on both sides. I thrust my hand toward the closest and his tail went up in flame. He leaped upward, spinning at snapping at the brush of tail blazing like a torch, then turned and ran off howling, a trail of smoke and singed hair in his wake.

Two more leaped at Rusty's forelegs. I swept my hand and flung them away, their bones cracking, bodies twisting and contorting in the air.

It was more magic than I'd done in months, and yet I only felt stronger by the minute. I couldn't understand where the surge of power was coming from.

The pack went into a rage, leaping and snapping, growling and slavering. The king wolf let out a roar that seemed to shake the woods. The stallion reared back, hooves wheeling. I was flung backward into the water, the horse tumbling in after me.

Frigid water closed over my head. The waterfall was runoff from the mountain, only a few degrees above freezing. The pool was dark and turgid, the horse's hooves churned all around me, hitting me in the shoulder, sending me tumbling head over heels. I couldn't tell which way was up until the soggy overcoat dragged me down.

My feet hit something hard. I pushed upward, head finally breaking water. Gasping for air, I heard several more splashes. Dark shapes cut through the water. The wolves could swim.

I stroked for the opposite shore, hearing barks and snarls and the scream of the horse as the wolves attacked in the water.

"Rusty, swim!" I cried, but the horse was floundering, maddened with pain and fear as the wolves bit from all sides.

I wasn't so sure I was going to make it myself. The river was dragging me down and away, and I was getting colder by the minute. I tried to kick off my boots but my feet were already too frozen to respond.

Worse, half a dozen wolves were swimming straight for me, faster than I could get away.

I swam for the shore but seemed to swim through mud. I could barely keep my head above the surface. I went under, bobbed up, then sank again.

An enormous splash and something heavy landed right beside me. Hands gripped me, lifting my body, flinging me upward onto the bank.

I landed on the bank and rolled, retching cold water out of my lungs.

When I could lift my head, I saw Damien in the river, swarmed with wolves. They bit savagely at his bare hands and arms. He seized the wolves by the throat, throttling until they twisted and withered, then flung aside the soaking carcass.

Artemis joined him, diving down at the wolves, clawing their eyes.

Damien scrambled up the riverbank. I grabbed his coat and helped pull him up.

The wolves were enraged, dozens more swimming across the river. For each we killed, five more took its place.

The poor draft horse was still alive, bleeding from countless bites and gashes. It struggled up the bank, wolves leaping on its back, biting and clawing at its flank.

Damien ripped his sword from its sheath, cutting a long arc across the horse's throat. Blood poured from the wound and the wolves went into a frenzy like sharks in the water, pulling the stallion down, tearing it apart.

Rusty was doomed either way, but still I let out a sob as Damien pulled me up on the back of his own black stallion. The draft horse saved my life.

That was all the time I had to mourn him. The king wolf leaped into the river, crossing at horrifying speed.

"GO, GO!" I cried to Damien.

He kicked his heels against Hercules, the stallion galloping off, Artemis flying ahead to lead us.

Hercules was faster than Rusty but he had two riders to carry. The king wolf was faster still. He charged through the woods, branches snapping, small trees breaking against his mass, his howls of rage echoing in our ears.

I wrapped my arm around Damien from behind and pressed my face against his back. I held him tight and breathed in his scent, until his warmth flowed into me and I felt that vivid, electric power crackling in my hands.

I turned and unleashed a sheet of flame directly behind us. I swept my hand across the woods and the trees went up in pillars, fire racing up their trunks, leaping from branch to branch. Even the damp underbrush ignited in the immense heat.

The silhouette of the king wolf reared up in the flames, his great white mane alight, paws wheeling in the smoke. I sent one last blast at his feet, a gust of liquid fire that reached up and closed around him like a fist, pulling him down.

Anastasia

Then I sagged against Damien, all my energy gone.

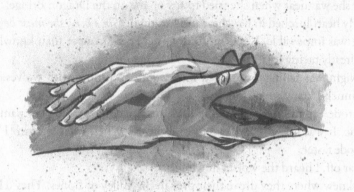

chapter 40

THE TOUCH OF A GHOST

DAMIEN

I rode back to the village as quickly as I could, Anastasia across my lap, Artemis flying overhead.

I slipped off my glove and touched her hair with my fingertips, careful not to brush her skin. I had to feel that bit of warmth. I had to know she was real.

At twilight, I felt a ghost.

I was riding along the edge of the Frost Forest when I felt something I hadn't felt in two years: a lifting of my spirits. The desire to look up at the first glinting stars in the lavender sky. Pleasure in the scent of pine.

Her face flashed into my mind: eyes that bright and velvety blue, tilted up at the corners so they always seemed laughing, especially when she looked up at me. The spatter of freckles across her cheeks and the bridge of her nose, usually a soft fawn color, but sometimes dark as chocolate from sun, disappearing by candlelight. And her mouth, wide, red, always quirked with some expression—curious, mocking, surprised, gleeful. She was a terrible liar, though she practiced enough.

I saw Anastasia in my mind clearer than I'd ever seen anything, and I knew, I fucking knew that I was feeling her. I'd felt that same sensation from the moment I first laid eyes her, and every time since. I felt it before I even knew she was near when she tried to spy on me on the Dragon Bridge.

My heart lurched in my chest and I thought, *She's here, she must be close.*

It was impossible, I knew it, but with a faith stronger than knowledge, I was already racing forward.

Night was falling. I galloped into woods swarming with wolves. That's how much I knew.

I rode left and right, doubling back, making loops, calling her name like a lunatic. It was like chasing a scent or a breeze. When I felt warmth I turned and rode faster.

Far off, I heard the wolves howling.

I knew where they drove their prey in the Valley of Bones. They'd hunted the woods bare this year, doubling in number, either because there were no imperial hunters anymore or simply because of the evil spreading everywhere.

I rode like a demon through the dark. If Anastasia really was alive in the forest, she wouldn't be for much longer.

Howls and snarls came echoing through the trees, bouncing off the water, from many directions at once. A distant flame burst into being, then darted off amidst more howling. I thought of following it, then turned to where it originated instead.

Then I saw that godsdamned beautiful bird.

Artemis came speeding across the pines, wheeling sharply above me. She called out, barely pausing to see if I would follow before turning and flying back.

From that moment, nothing could stop me. If Artemis was there, so was Anastasia.

I followed her down to the riverbank and leaped into the water, heaving Anastasia out soaking and filthy, feeling how frail she was inside her clothes.

The wolves bit at me and I felt nothing but hot liquid rage that they'd run her down. They died in my hands. Their fury flowed into me until I could have ripped their jaws open and torn their bodies to pieces with my fingers.

The more of them I killed, the more an animal I became.

I only came back to myself because Anastasia sat up on the bank, spitting water. Wolves surged into the river, too many to count. I sacrificed the draft horse and carried her away on Hercules.

As I lifted her, I felt that awful lightness again, her flesh cold as a corpse. She was so filthy I don't think I'd have recognized her if I'd only used my eyes.

But it was her, and she was alive, and that was all that mattered.

I'd never let myself believe she could be.

I'd ridden in blind and hadn't expected the largest wolf of all, the one Nikolasha called *Karol Volk*. It crossed the river, leaping more than swimming. It crashed through the woods like a locomotive, like it barely felt the trees in its path. Hercules could hardly keep ahead of it, weighed down by two riders, Anya's body frail but her coat heavy with water.

I urged the horse on, hand on my sword, thinking I'd have to jump down and face the monster.

Anastasia slumped against me, weak and sick. She wrapped her arm around my waist, squeezing me tight. And unleashed a sheet of fire.

I felt the surge of power blast through my body like a stick of dynamite.

I needed it when she keeled backward off the horse. I caught her in the crook of my arm and pulled her up, laying her across my lap.

I couldn't stop staring at her, at the little bit of her face I could see, so wan and thin.

She'd been alive this whole time.

I could have found her.

Fucking hell, I could have found her.

I RODE BACK to the village as fast as I could without jostling her too much, then shouted for Jacov and Petro to boil water. I wrapped her in a bearskin and put hot bricks at her feet.

Artemis perched on the carved gable of my father's house, hopping down to the windowsill to peer inside, then flapping back up again every few minutes. Symon said he'd bring her one of the rabbits we kept for food.

I sat Anastasia by the clay oven and brought her warm wine. It was hard to tell if she was getting any color back in her face because she was still coated in dirt despite the dunk in the river. The cuts beneath the dirt needed cleaning.

I made her drink the wine and watched her every minute.

Finally, she smiled at me over the rim of her mug. I saw her light was still there, even if her face was hollow.

"I found you."

I snorted. "Was that you finding me when I pulled you out of the river?"

"Well, I was practically on your doorstep ... I came more your way than you came mine."

"Anya." I passed a hand over my face. "I thought you were dead."

Her smile faltered.

"I'm sorry. They searched all the mail. We were prisoners in the city."

"No, I mean … I would have come. Wherever you were, I would have come. Every single day I've regretted riding away from you. When I heard what happened …"

For two years I agonized over that night. I thought of it over and over and over again. If I hadn't ridden away so angry, so bitter, I would have known she was in trouble, I would have felt it.

"It's not your fault," Anastasia said. "Your father—"

"That wasn't your fault, either."

"I was a part of it. I was a part of all of it. Damien, the things I've seen … I wish I could tell you I never knew, but I knew enough. I was arrogant and wrapped up in myself—"

"You're not—"

"It doesn't matter." She slipped out of the bearskin and came forward to put both her hands over mine. "It doesn't matter what I was. I'm telling you I'm different now."

I could see that. I could see the sadness in her eyes, the weight of everything she'd seen, everything she'd been through. The lesson was too hard, too cruel. I hated that she went through it alone. I should have been there with her.

I pulled her to my chest and pressed her against my heart.

"I'm never letting you out of my sight."

Jacov and Petro came into the little one-room house, lugging a copper tub between them. It was full of hot water. Symon followed with two more buckets and dumped them in.

"There's more coming," Jacov said. "Thought you might want to, uh, do an initial rinse and then fill it again."

He cast a glance at Anastasia, who resembled one of the soot-coated *domovoi* who haunted hearths and stoves.

"What?" She grinned. "Am I dirty or something?"

"Slightly." Jacov smiled.

"I've got dinner coming, too," Symon said. "Broth and fresh bread."

"Thank you." I clapped him on the shoulder.

Anastasia was so starved I hoped she could keep it down.

The men left us alone.

She tried to unbutton her coat, but the buttons seemed almost fused to the damp wool. She swayed on her feet.

"Let me."

♪ *Where's My Love—SYML*

Gently, I began to undress her. I stripped off the moldy overcoat, shocked by how thin she was beneath. Her ragged shirt hung on her body, her arms like sticks, nothing but skin over her collarbones.

When I pulled the remains of the shirt over her head, what I saw beneath was much worse. Her back was striped with whip marks, her forearms covered in deep, puckered scars that twisted like snakes, stippled on both sides with stitch-marks.

I put my gloved hand over her wrist. "Anya, who did this?"

"I did," she said, and her face crumpled as she covered it with her hands. "I tried to fight Rasputin. He was stronger than me, he took over my mind ..."

The room seemed to go dark around me. I put my arms around her because it was all I could do to calm the rage that rose inside me, black and electric.

I lifted her and put her in the tub. I took handfuls of the soft gray soap made of ash and lye and washed her gently, careful only to touch her with the cloth, never my bare skin. The dirt came off her in clouds, turning the water black.

She tipped her head back and I washed her hair several times. It started brown, then went a color something like burgundy. By the third scrubbing, the red was beginning to come through.

Symon brought more water. I wrapped Anastasia in a robe so I could dump the tub and fill it fresh.

When the tub was ready again, she hesitated, clutching the robe around herself. She looked downward at the rug, shoulders slumped.

"Maybe you should let me do it ... I don't want you to see what I look like." Tears slipped down her cheeks. "It's so ugly."

"Look at me, Anya. Look at my face so you know I'm telling you the truth."

I waited until her eyes turned up to mine, tears strung through her lashes.

"Every mark on you is something you survived to get back to me. You have *never* looked more beautiful."

She sobbed and I held her. I never wanted to stop holding her.

I set her back in the tub and washed her again, every part of her. I washed her toes and the soles of her feet. I washed her back and her hair one last time, so it was nearly back to the color it had been. When she saw it laying across her shoulder, red as the copper tub, she cried all over again.

I lifted her arm with the thick, twisting welts all across the wrist and brushed my lips against one of the scars.

"Does that hurt?"

She shook her head.

I kissed another scar.

"And that?"

"No. You're not hurting me."

I kissed each and every one so she would know there was nothing ugly about her to me, there never could be. Every part of her was precious, every part was perfect—her strengths and her flaws, her heart and her mind.

"I love you," I said. "When I thought I missed the chance to tell you that, I've never regretted anything more."

She leaned her head against my arm, clinging to me all curled up in the tub.

"I should have chosen you from the beginning," she sobbed. "I thought there were all these things keeping us apart. I should have believed in us first, over anything else."

"We're never going to be apart again. I'll die with you in my arms."

"Kiss me," she said.

"I don't want to hurt you."

"Look." She lifted her hand from the tub. The water hung suspended from her fingertips, the droplets glinting like gold in the glow of the clay stove. They fell slowly like honey, time stretching out between us. "I'm stronger already because I'm here with you."

She lifted up her mouth to me and I kissed her. I tasted her lips, her breath, and with my bare hand I touched her breast, soft and wet and slippery with soap. I ran my hand down her arm and twined my fingers through hers. All those things were things I'd never experienced before. I'd never been able to touch anyone like this, skin to skin, warmth to warmth. Nothing felt better than Anastasia, not silk or velvet or new spring grass.

When I pulled back, I saw how pale her lips had become and I knew it still drained her.

"Come here," I said.

She stood up in the tub. I wrapped a towel around her, carrying her to my bed to lay her down naked.

"Can I look at you? All of you?"

She nodded and lay back against the pillow, eyes closed.

I kept a novel next to the bed with a feather stuck between the pages as a bookmark. I lifted out the feather, soft and downy and clean. Sitting next to

Anastasia, I trailed it lightly down her cheek. She smiled, and I brushed it across her lips.

I wanted to memorize every inch of her.

I ran the tip of the feather down the side of her neck, then across her collarbones. I brushed it across her breasts, small and round and rosy in the firelight. Her nipples stiffened, pointing upward. I traced their shape, lightly, softly. Her lips parted and she let out a sigh.

I trailed the feather down her navel, along her ribs, across the winged bones of her hips. When I came to the little delta between her thighs, she parted her legs slightly. In between, she was soft and pink. I ran the feather up and down against the most delicate part of her.

Her skin was beginning to flush, pink tinting the white like cherry blossoms. I could smell her breath, her skin, that sweet musk between her thighs. She let out a groan that made my mouth water.

Leaning forward, I kissed her between her legs. I tasted her with my tongue and her whole body shivered. Her feet curled and her back arched. She grabbed the back of my head and pressed me against her, her hand shaking in my hair, her thighs trembling around me.

"I worship you, princess. I always have."

I lapped at her softly, gently, paying homage to her body with my mouth. I let my lips brush over her, each stroke of my tongue sending waves through her body. I ran the feather over her bare breasts and ran my tongue across her at just the same speed, linking the two sensations.

"You think you could ever be ugly to me? You *are* me. You're everything I love, everything I care about."

I kissed her, touched her, worshipped her, showed her instead of telling her how much I'd missed her, what a miracle it was to have her back.

"I love you ..." I whispered against her fire-warmed skin. "I love you, I love you, I love you ..."

She groaned softly, fingers twined in my hair.

"You're the reason I'm here, Damien. The only reason I made it ..."

I knelt between her legs and tried to touch her again, but I saw the wince, the way her knees drew back with pain, not just intensity.

I knew that look too well, from any time I'd accidentally touched someone I loved. My heart plunged down.

I drew back. "I'm so sorry ..."

"No, no ..." She grabbed my hand, showed me she could still touch me. "Don't stop. Just ... slow down."

Her face had whitened, especially around the mouth. She took a few breaths, got back her color again.

"Breathe," she said to me. "Take your time, focus on your magic. It *is* magic, Damien, not a curse. You can control it. I've learned to control things I never thought I could. We can do it together. Use the things that make you feel the strongest. When I want to do something impossible, I think of you. I think of riding my horse, with the saddle you made for me, coming to see you. I charge myself up ... off of you."

I closed my eyes. Tried to think of a single memory, one that made me feel strong.

Anastasia said, "If you've done something once, even by accident, you can do it again ..."

I thought of the first time we kissed. The first time I touched her, really touched her, without fear ...

I thought of riding to see her, and the moment when I saw Artemis in the sky and I knew that it meant Anastasia must be near. She came bursting over the hill, riding as fast as she could to see me ...

And I saw ... I knew ...

I knew she loved me.

I could see it on her face.

I was so happy, that's all I radiated when I kissed her. I kissed her because I believed I could. I took control of my body with my mind, and she used her magic, and together we made it happen.

If I did it for a moment, I could do it longer. She was doing her part ... I needed to do mine.

I bent and touched her gently in the place that made her shiver the most.

She whispered, "You gave me strength when I had nothing. I saw your face in the memory-keeper ... it showed me that you'd forgiven me, or you would eventually. I knew I had to get back to you. That's how I found the stone. Powered by you, when all my magic was gone."

Her love flushed through me and everything in me cried out that I could do anything for her.

I pressed my mouth against her where she smelled so good, where she was warm and soft and it felt like the inside of her. I was touching the most intimate, sensitive place. She trusted me enough to let me do it.

I licked her softly, gently, with no pain in my heart, only love for her.

"Don't speed up ... just like that. Just like that, Damien ... just a little bit more ..."

Her smell was so good, her taste made me hungry. The wolf woke up inside me and she gasped and said, "That's too much, slow down!"

But when I tried to draw away, she grabbed my head and pulled me back, saying, "Don't stop, Damien, I need you ... Just be soft, be light ... Like that. Just like that ..."

I let her guide me. I watched her face, followed her voice, her breath, her movements, finding just the right pressure and pace she could tolerate.

"Yes, yes ... right there ... don't stop ..."

She let out a moan that wrenched from her chest, hands grasping at me, thighs clenching.

Then she let go and fell back against the pillow, breathing heavily.

My heart was going a thousand miles. I couldn't believe it ... couldn't believe I'd given her pleasure like that instead of pain.

I licked the taste of her off my lips.

"What did you do to me?" she said, her eyes unfocused and dreamy.

I smiled to myself.

"I made you mine."

She closed her eyes, letting out a long sigh.

"I was yours all along."

496

chapter 41

TICKING CLOCK

I slept by her all night long, arm locked on her waist, body curled around her like a creature safe inside its shell. We had to wear clothes but our bodies radiated heat into each other until we throbbed with warmth like a furnace, and dreamed deep and senseless.

When I woke she was there beside me, the dream still real and alive. I had to touch her often. I never wanted her out of my sight in case she evaporated like magic if I failed to hold onto her.

I brought her food and we ate sitting up on the bed, the rugs and skins scattered all around us. She had on a shirt of mine that was near transparent in the morning light, all the natural shape and color of her body visible though the thin, clean linen. Her hair lay over her shoulder, flaming like filament when the sun chanced upon it.

She was like a pile of kindling catching fire, the color and light moving through her as it took hold, growing brighter and hotter by the minute.

I saw on her what I felt happening in me.

I'd been dead without knowing it. Then I saw her and I came alive again.

She ate the food, tasting each bite, flushed with pleasure. Already fullness was coming back to her cheeks.

If Anastasia was alive, if she could heal, anything seemed possible again.

"Tell me everything," she said, putting olives in her mouth with her bare fingers, licking them clean of oil and rosemary. "Tell me what I missed."

So I did. I told her everything from the moment we last saw each other—how I'd ridden back to the camp outside the city and got drunker than I'd ever been in my life, and how in the morning I woke to see pillars of smoke rising in the sky. I rode straight back to St. Petersburg, head pounding, only to find the city gates barred, the roads guarded by soldiers calling themselves the "Red Army."

They tried to capture my regiment, but they only sent twenty soldiers to inform us that we were now under the command of the "People's Government." We killed them and returned to the steppes instead.

Most of the other Cossack hosts did the same. A few joined the resistance, the so-called "White Army," but most rode back to their own territories and declared independence.

"It was chaos," I said. "Complete chaos. The Bolsheviks and the Anarchists were fighting, the Red Army and the White. There were rumors that some of your family might have survived, but the longer it went on, the more it seemed ..." I swallowed. "The more it seemed that was just a lie to cover up what they'd done to you."

I didn't tell her how they'd dragged her father's body naked through the streets, how they hung it upside down on the front steps of the Winter Palace and set it aflame.

Nor did I tell her of the darkness that settled over me once my father was gone and Anya, too. I hardly remembered those months that followed, faded as an old photograph in my mind, shades of dull gray, no color at all.

The country was falling apart. The new government pulled Rusya out of the war, but the soldiers brought influenza home, a strain that killed millions. One in ten died in my own host, including my cousin Yan who was only twenty-two.

I came back to the village, to my father's house. I lived there alone, every room full of regret.

"And when did you become Ataman?"

"A few months later. The host held a *Rada* and ... they chose me."

I remembered how the shouts had rung out around the circle, my name drowning the others. It had felt like a weight falling on my shoulders, like a sentence. All I could think was that I wished my father was there to show me how to do it. I'd watched him as a boy, but he never had a chance to teach me as a man.

"I knew they'd pick you." Anastasia smiled at me, bright and approving.

"I didn't," I admitted. "It's not a hereditary position. There were other contenders."

"But it always falls on you. It happened in the military, too."

"That was just circumstance. I'm not one of those people everyone likes. The opposite, actually."

"It doesn't matter if they like you. When something awful happens, they trust you to know what to do."

I looked at her, wondering if that was true.

"I don't always know. It's been hard here—the grass goes rotten before it's ripe, the horses have been sick, there's no supplies coming in, no trade."

The host moved around seasonally, letting our horses graze on the plains in the summer, sheltering in our village next to the forest in the winter. We needed the wood for fuel but this year the wolves slipped the bounds of the forest and stole our food, attacked our horses.

"You know why," Anastasia said.

"Because of Rasputin."

She nodded.

I'd seen the changes myself, but it still sounded impossible. No one could alter the weather over an entire nation.

"Is he really that powerful?"

"Yes," she said, with simple finality. "He called in the storm when he attacked us. The dark and cold went inside us, it made us sluggish, it made us weak. Our time-walking didn't work like it usually does. And the vampyrs were ... well, they were like those wolves last night. They tore us apart."

I closed my eyes, breathing hard.

"I hate that I left you there."

"You didn't know. It was my fault he got the Charoite in the first place. You tried to warn me—do you remember the first time we spoke on the train?"

"I remember every conversation I've had with you."

"I wish you didn't." She blushed.

I put my hand over hers. I was wearing my gloves again, but it still felt good to touch her.

"You can say anything to me, Anya."

She rubbed her thumb across the back of my hand, biting at the edge of her lip.

"Anything?"

"Yes," I said with a sinking feeling.

I already had a sense of what she was about to say, because I really did know Anastasia. I knew what she valued, what drove her.

"You know I was in the mine?"

I nodded, the skin tightening at the nape of my neck. I'd known it the minute I saw that black grit coating every inch of her skin.

"The mountain's been running dry of Charoite. Rasputin's been sending more and more people to dig, but we couldn't find enough. He was punishing us, the miners were dying."

It was impossible to hide the twitching of my hands, the flushes of stress and anger I felt when I thought of Anastasia locked away in those tunnels while I was only a few miles away. I didn't want her to see how it affected me, because I knew the thought of that place must affect her a hundred times worse.

She took a breath and spoke like she was jumping off a ledge: "I escaped because I found a cache of Charoite. A huge cache, Damien. More than we ever had before. More than he stole in the first place."

She jumped, but I was the one falling. Down, down, with nothing beneath me.

"Does he know about it?"

"Not yet. But he'll find it."

"When?"

"Could be days, weeks. Maybe months. But not years. Not with the way they're digging."

Chest tight, I said, "It'll kill him if he tries to take that much."

"That's what we thought the first time. He's not so easy to kill."

We were in unexplored territory. What a half-vampire could or couldn't do was beyond me.

I looked at her kneeling on my bed, lit up from behind by sunlight so she glowed all around her head and shoulders.

"Anya, tell me what you really want to say."

"He's powerful and he's evil and he's about to get worse. Unless we stop him."

"Stop him?"

"Kill him."

I needed her to say it out loud because if we were going to talk about this, we needed to really talk about it.

"Do you know where he is now?"

"He's in my house," Anastasia said, a shadow passing over her eyes.

The Winter Palace wasn't defensible, it never had been. That's why Anastasia's family moved to Alexander Palace, and why Rasputin waited for the wedding to attack.

"Who's there with him?"

"His coven. And maybe ... my brother."

"He's not your brother anymore." I said it because I had to. "Rasputin's been feeding on him too long."

"I know," she said, but I didn't trust it.

"What do you imagine us doing?"

"Someone needs to go to the mountain, free the miners, and collapse the mine."

"And dig the crystal out."

"No. The Charoite stays where it is. Forever."

I looked at her askance.

"You're not going to take any?"

She gave a quick shake of her head, steady and unsmiling.

"You took it to escape."

"And I'm not doing it again. It's a trick, a trap. It wants you to think you need it."

"You're talking about it like it's alive."

"It is—in its own way."

"But without it—"

"There has to be another way."

Her certainty scared me.

"How can you kill Rasputin without it? I don't even know if you could kill him *with* it. Anya, those things tore apart your father. Remember when *I* tried to kill your father, how that went? I have a death touch but I'm not superhuman. And Rasputin already beat you."

I hated to throw it in her face, but we had to speak plainly. This was too important to spare the truth.

She lifted her thin shoulders and let them drop. "I don't know if we can beat him. But I know nobody else is trying. And you know what, I *do* think we have an advantage. I know him. I've fought him before."

She leaned forward, her eyes bright and insistent. "Damien, you *know* how strong we are together. Don't you believe it means something? You can't tell me you think this thing between us is just chance, just magical chemistry. I think I love you because I was always meant to love you. We're made for each other—we're made for *this*."

It was hard to deny her anything when she looked at me like that.

But the one thing I couldn't do was lose her again.

I gripped her hands between mine.

"We're finally together again. We're safe here with my people. We don't have to kill Rasputin—we don't have to do anything."

"And what about the rest of Rusya?"

"Fuck Rusya. What has Rusya ever done for us besides try to keep us apart?"

She looked at me sadly, touching my cheek with her hand.

"The suffering is everywhere, Damien. It's everywhere. You can't imagine how much worse it's gotten in the city, in the mills, in the mines. Someone has to stop it."

"But why does it have to be you?"

"Because it's my responsibility. Because of what I did, because of what I didn't do ... because it's my country and my people. I'm still their princess and they still need me."

Gods, she was stubborn.

"I thought you were a Grand Duchess."

She laughed softly. And pressed on, relentless.

"Damien, you taught me this—you can't ignore what's happening right next to you. Rasputin's not just going to stay over there. There's no happiness for anyone anywhere if we let the worst and most awful things flourish."

I couldn't argue with her, but neither could I agree to ride with her to certain death. Because for all her ideals, all her hope, all her belief, there was almost no chance that we could kill Rasputin and leave together alive.

She saw the darkness in my face.

"I'm not going to make you do anything. I'm not even going to run off and make you chase me and try to save me, because that's still making you do it. I'm just telling you what I think is right—like you've always done for me."

She let it drop then, for the moment. I wasn't stupid enough to think she'd forget about it.

She was still weak and injured. I had time to convince her while she healed.

She was up and out of bed that very first morning.

"You won't rest even one day?"

"Not a chance. I've always wanted to see where you live."

I gave her some of my clean clothes, what I thought would fit her best, and a pair of boots from my cousin Ionna, soft untanned deer-hide that laced up the leg. She was the same height as Anastasia, and I hoped about the same size feet.

I could have borrowed a dress as well, but I thought Anastasia would be more comfortable in something of mine. Cossack women's smocks looked like what Tartars or Chechens wore, and besides, I liked her in my clothes. I liked how they hung on her, showing the difference in our shape. I liked how anyone who saw her would recognize my coat, my cap.

I'm making you mine…

"What?" Anya said, smiling at me. "Do I look funny?"

"You look like yourself again."

She stroked the red braid over her shoulder, the same way she touched Artemis. "I always feel like myself when I'm with you."

When we came out of my father's house onto the main street of the village—the only street, really—the sun had come out, turning all the icicles hanging from the gables to crystal. Smoke drifted from the chimneys, making low clouds that hung in the frigid air.

"What month is it?" Anastasia asked me.

"March."

"Gods," she murmured, "I was in the mine over a year."

She cast a dull look down the street. Brightening, she said, "Doesn't the snow on the roofs look like frosting?"

The small, uniform cottages, with their carved gables and thick caps of snow, did look like gingerbread houses.

My uncle Kristoff lived in the one next to ours. He called to us from his porch where he'd likely been waiting on purpose.

"I thought I heard you coming in late last night."

His eyes flicked over Anastasia wearing my clothes, over the red braid laying over her shoulder and the thinness of her frame.

"Anya," I said. "This is Kristoff, my mother's youngest brother."

"Welcome," he said, without remarking on the strangeness of the introduction, or asking how a girl of my acquaintance had materialized in the steppes. "Have you eaten yet?"

"At least twice since I came." Anastasia smiled.

"Only twice! What a poor host Damien is. Come over here, I have honey from my hives and clotted cream from my wife's cows."

Anastasia strode across the snowy lawn, stepping across the low fence that separated the houses.

"Olena!" called Kristoff. "Get some *chikhir* for us, will you?"

Olena was Kristoff's eldest daughter and one of my innumerable cousins. She was tall and broad shouldered, with pink cheeks and flax-colored braids. She came out of the house with a load of skins over one shoulder and a full bucket in the other hand, crossing the snow with long steps. Anastasia looked after her curiously.

"I have six girls," Kristoff said. "Olena's the strongest."

Anastasia opened her mouth. I thought she was about to say she had three sisters herself. She stopped, not because she was trying to hide who she was, but because she remembered that she had no sisters anymore.

"I—she's lovely," she said.

"I thought the dowries would ruin me, but my girls are so clever it seems everyone wants to take them away from me. Ah, here's another one."

Daryna came out onto the porch. She was the youngest, only eight. She had a kerchief over her head and a book under her arm.

"Mama wants to know if you're going hunting today."

"Does she want meat or want me out from underfoot?" Kristoff winked at us. "She doesn't like when I'm home too long."

"She wants pheasants," Daryna said. "And for you to stop smoking on the porch."

"Just as I thought," Kristoff said, unoffended. "Come in, come in!"

We went into the house, which was warm and slightly smoky, but from the clay stove, not Kristoff's pipe.

My aunt Bohdana was making barley cakes, my cousin Ionna embroidering large red roses onto a pair of deerskin boots like the ones I'd borrowed for Anastasia. Polina was working at the loom in the corner, and Lavra, who cropped her hair short and dressed as a boy, was braiding a fishing line. Kristoff's last daughter, Maryska, died of the flu the year before.

Kristoff's house was a little larger than mine, but not by much. All this activity was crammed into the one main room. The adjoining space was for storage, and the family slept up in the attic, with Daryna on a mat atop the stove.

I introduced Anastasia again, explaining that I'd known her in St. Petersburg.

"She escaped from the mine."

"A horrible place," Bohdana said, softening at once. She'd stiffened when she heard Anastasia's accent, which was obviously Rusyan and suspiciously posh. "Sit, eat."

She took fresh cakes from the oven, thick and crusty-warm, cracked them open, and spread butter, clotted cream, and blackberry preserves.

Olena had returned with a pitcher of *chikhir*, the red wine kept cool in clay jars in the barn. She also brought more wood for the stove.

We all ate together. Anastasia was ravenous, like she could never get enough food. She was trying to be polite, but Bohdana gruffly heaped more food on her plate saying, "Eat up, girl, it's painful to look at you."

My cousins were all talking at once, Ionna demanding to know what Daryna had done with her scissors, Daryna protesting her innocence and declaring that Lavra had them last, Bohdana rapping Lavra's knuckles when she reached for an oatcake with a hand that had clearly not been washed since touching the fishing lines, and Polina calmly ignoring all this to ask her father if he'd seen the new calf that had come early.

When Anastasia had eaten all she could stand, she sat back in her chair and let the babble wash over her, all the chatter and annoyance and laughter and affection of a family sitting around a table together.

Our eyes met. She smiled at me, both of us warm and safe and full of so much more than food.

When Anastasia tried to help clear the table, Bohdana shooed her away.

"I have too many helpers already. And *him*." She threw an unfriendly glance at Kristoff.

"Yes, yes, I'm going out, you won't see me all day." Kristoff hastily got his rifle down from the wall and his nets for the pheasants.

Anastasia had interested herself in Polina's weaving and was asking how the loom worked. Polina showed her, surprised when Anya was able to thread the next line with only a little correction.

"I worked at a cotton mill," Anastasia said. "I was in the dyeing room, but my friend, the woman I lived with, she was a weaver."

My cousins accepted this because Anastasia's hands were marked from the labor of the last two years. They never would have believed her when her hands were soft and white as an infant's.

Kristoff wasn't so easily fooled. He knew too much about my time in St. Petersburg, and there was something about Anastasia—a presence, a confidence—that was already returning to her. She didn't seem like a factory worker, whatever her hands might look like.

Once we were outside, he was in no hurry to tramp off into the woods.

He asked Anastasia, "D'you want a tour of the village?"

"I'd love it!"

Kristoff took her all around, showing her the high earth-banks and prickly bramble hedges that encircled the houses, and the large, shared gardens now containing only the remains of wilted pumpkin vines and blackened cornstalks poking up from the snow.

In the summertime, the orchards and vineyards bloomed, and fish practically leaped out of the river. The women ran everything in the village while the men served in the military or formed parties to raid neighboring territories.

The women weren't always pleased to have us back. Kristoff's wife wasn't the only one who liked to manage things her own way and preferred her husband to stay outdoors where he belonged.

Cossack women weren't like Rusyan women. They were fierce and independent, strong as men from lifting, chopping, and hauling all day long.

They weren't modest like Rusyan women, either. When they worked, they tied up their skirts, or used them as baskets for carrying, baring their scratched and tanned legs. They often took lovers, especially the unwed girls, but sometimes the married ones, too, if their husbands annoyed them or stayed away too long.

Anastasia was fascinated watching the women driving the cattle, chopping the wood, muscle standing out on their arms.

"They do everything themselves when you're gone?"

"And when I'm here," Kristoff chuckled. "That's Bohdana's house—she only needed me to help make all those fine daughters."

Kristoff was a favorite of mine. He'd always treated me as a son, having none of his own. He was warm and interested, and would ask the results of some endeavor you'd almost forgotten yourself. He liked to laugh and was impossible to offend. He was not at all handsome, short and broad with a wide face and gingery hair, but he was so charming that women loved him, with the exception of his wife.

He loved Anastasia hanging on his every word. I was free to follow behind them, watching Anya's bright eyes, hearing the quick peal of her laughter as she ran from place to place, touching everything, sampling what she could, asking questions faster than Kristoff could answer.

She stopped short when she saw our horses, the golden oriental Budyonny stallions, the smaller Basutos with a faint stripe on their coats, the gleaming chestnut Dons we bred ourselves, and the heavy chargers like Hercules with thick tufts of hair nearly covering their hooves.

"They're so beautiful ..." Anastasia sighed, hands at her mouth. Her eyes landed on Mercury and she gave a little gasp. "Your horse!"

"She's still here." I stroked her soot-black nose. "Though Hercules goes insane if he sees me riding her."

"What if I rode her?" Anastasia teased. "Would that make *you* jealous?"

"It would make me happier than anything."

Kristoff got a saddle. Anastasia cinched it with a sigh.

"What's wrong?"

She glanced at Kristoff, then murmured, "I was thinking I'd let them keep the whole damn palace if I could just get my saddle back."

"Never mind." I kissed her forehead. "I'll make you another. A better one."

"There's never been a better saddle."

"Then I guess I have my work cut out for me."

Kristoff mounted his own horse.

"You coming with us?" I asked him.

"Not if I want to sleep in my bed tonight." He winked, heaving the pheasant nets over his shoulder.

Anastasia hardly waited for me to mount before streaking off across the open steppes. Her hair came loose from its braid and streamed out behind her.

Mercury was no young filly anymore, but she was still swift as a swan swooping across the downs.

I galloped after Anastasia, sometimes side by side, sometimes crossing paths like two skaters making a chain of figure eights.

Whenever we locked eyes I wanted to laugh out loud, not because anything was funny but because of the happiness inside of me that I couldn't keep contained.

It was a miracle, a gift to have her back with me.

I couldn't risk losing her again. Not for anything.

chapter 42

TEN THOUSAND EMERALD POOLS

ANASTASIA

D amien told me there's a Cossack saying, *You can't understand a man unless you've lived inside his skin ...*

 I wasn't in Damien's skin, but in the Cossack village, I was closer than I'd ever been.

I was finally coming to know him the way he must have known me all along. He'd always lived with my people, my family—now I was living with his.

It was like a foreign country. So much of what the Cossacks did came from Chechens and Tartars more than Rusyans. Yet it was familiar to me because it had always flavored Damien.

Even when Damien wore Rusyan clothes in St. Petersburg, they never quite looked Rusyan on him. He'd worn them faded and loose, his weapons clean and polished—the opposite of aristocrats in their tailored coats who spilled brandy down their swords at cards.

Now I saw that was a trait of Cossacks in general—clothes loose and tucked into trousers and belts, hats worn at rakish angles, weapons on them always, bandoliers and guns and cutlasses, because these were warriors, their profession was battle and they called each other "braves." They reminded me of the plains warriors Alexei was always reading about in those books about America he loved so much.

The Cossacks had their own fashions and jokes, their own favorite foods and ways of living. I'd thought of them as subjects who refused to recognize their rulers. Now I saw why we were so alien to them.

The women's lives were nothing like mine. They were independent in ways I'd only ever dreamed of being. They lived alone most of the year, running their own houses, their own farms. They chose who they loved, who they married, and were fought over by men who wanted capable wives.

Not one of them wore a corset. They strode around in smocks that would have been too thin for a nightgown in Alexander Palace, and tied them up whenever they pleased as if they were bathing in their own garden. They wore their hair any sort of way, and spent all day long in the sunshine.

If Damien would've described his village to me when we first met, I think I might have run away to the steppes immediately.

I wasn't sure if I liked everything about the Cossack way—it was odd to see the women chopping wood in the yard while the men lay back smoking on the porch. But it upended certain ideas in my head to watch a copiously pregnant woman splitting kindling, barely out of breath. Most of the women I knew gestated flat on their backs.

You don't examine your own way of doing something until you see another option. I was starting to understand that Kipling quote, *What should they know of Albion who only Albion know?* It never made sense to me when all I knew was Rusya.

I was quite the libertine compared to the Rusyan Imperial Court, but when Damien explained that the girl his cousin fancied had moved on to another man, I said, "Oh!" in a stupid way and turned red, because I'd just seen them coming out of a shed all covered in hay the night before.

"I thought—I thought maybe they were going to get married," I muttered.

Those were the affairs I was used to—between people who longed to be married but couldn't.

"Not likely." Damien snorted. "I don't think Miya's ever thought about Marko that way. It's just a ... you know."

"What?"

"A physical thing."

That made me blush harder. But I had to ask because I was so damn curious.

"What if a baby came along?"

"Maybe she'd marry him then. Or someone else."

"Someone else!"

"Why not?" He shrugged. "A child's always welcome, especially a strong, healthy one. Daryna was born while Kristoff was two years away. He loves her just the same as his other girls."

When he saw the look on my face, he added, "That's not how my parents were. Their eyes only saw each other. And that's what I want, too."

I remembered when Damien rode into St. Petersburg, the parade in his honor, all the women throwing flowers at him. He never looked anywhere but at me.

And I had never longed for anyone but him.

Watching him among his own people made me ache for him more than ever.

I was seeing Damien the most *himself* he'd ever been, among the people he loved, who loved him in return. Here he was respected, admired. He was comfortable and confident.

Becoming Ataman had changed him, too. Some of his anger had worn away. He was quieter, he thought before speaking, because his decisions mattered now in a way they hadn't before—they affected people other than himself.

He seemed older, new lines of worry on his face. The burden of leadership was heavy on his shoulders. He knew his people, he knew what mattered to them. They listened when he gave a ruling because he was the one to volunteer to patrol the edge of the Frost Forest on the coldest nights, he was the first to help mend a fence or find a horse that had run away.

And the way the women looked at him ...

He'd caught plenty of eyes in St. Petersburg, even from good girls like my cousin Ella. Here, there wasn't a woman in the village who wouldn't sell all she possessed for a night with the handsome young Ataman.

The boldness of the splendid Cossack women made me so jealous I could barely breathe. I was sure they could all ride and shoot better than me, and what was worse, they were spectacular dancers.

On clear nights the Cossacks built roaring bonfires and brought their instruments out of doors, dancing in a ring around the fire.

I'd already learned that almost everything the Cossacks did was competitive. The women milked the cows or chopped the wood as quickly as they could, laughing and racing against their neighbors. The men made bets on how many trout they'd pull from the river or how many pheasants they'd bag.

They loved to play, and it seemed the men were drunk half the day when at home in the village. But when they worked, they sweated for hours, barely stopping for water, and they fought like demons—especially amongst themselves. Twice already I'd seen brawls that ended in bloody stabbings. The dancing was meant to channel those aggressive impulses between battles and raids.

The fire dance was wild and brutal. The point was to outlast every other opponent. The beat started slow, becoming faster and faster, the circle tightening as dancers were eliminated.

I competed every night, and every night I lost. First try I was eliminated after only a few steps. The second night, I beat an old woman and a very young boy. By the third night, I made an entire circuit around the fire and became completely obsessed.

The rhythm of the circle, the stamping of our feet, the clapping and spinning, seemed to possess my body. The deeper I sank into the dance, the faster I moved. Our faces were lit by the flames, our shadows thrown up like giants behind us. The wild music of the Cossack pipes and drums echoed over the steppes like wind and thunder. The sky was so deep it went down forever like a black ocean of stars.

I'd start facing Damien, our hands clasped together, mine bare, his gloved. We'd spin and face the opponent behind us, then our partner again, clapping hands, knocking knees, kicking our feet in complicated steps. As the speed increased, pace and stamina became ever more difficult. If your partner stepped right and you stepped wrong, you were knocked out of the circle.

The Cossacks chanted with the swells of the music. When I slipped into a rhythm with Damien, it was like we were connected every place we touched. I could feel the beat inside my chest, my feet knew how to move. Each stamp sent a pulse of pleasure up my legs, each breath of smoke made my head soar.

The sparks floated up to the sky and Artemis flew through the smoke, watching the pattern of dancers from above, shifting like a kaleidoscope.

The last man and woman standing were the winners. The man would bend his partner over his knee and kiss her to much shouting and hooting. Sometimes they'd disappear into the darkness together for a time.

Damien won often, but he only bowed to his partners.

I was wildly envious of the girls who outlasted me to steal my place next to him. I watched them dance, feverishly trying to memorize the steps for the next time.

It seemed impossible—no moment of the dance was the same as the next.

"You don't learn it," Damien told me. "You just feel it."

The days slipped by. Each was among the most precious and vivid of my life. Yet I felt a clock counting down with no idea how much time remained.

I didn't want to push Damien, didn't want to force him. But every day I thought of the people I'd left in the city and in the mine. I thought of Maritza, Varvara, Valentina, and I couldn't enjoy myself fully knowing things could only have gotten worse for them.

We heard stories from the few people who managed to escape the city, fleeing to Riga or Minsk through the steppes. Several groups had passed through since I arrived. A few asked to stay with the Cossacks. Damien allowed it, though I knew it made him nervous in case anyone recognized me.

His worry wasn't for nothing. Only a few weeks later, a caravan was spotted south of the village carrying someone I knew very well.

The Montenegrin sisters had been hiding in the Gothic-style Priory Palace on the shore of the Black Lake but had been flushed out by Bolsheviks. Most of their servants had been killed, and Melitza herself had been shot in the side. She was feverish when Kristoff and Petro found her, lying in the bottom of a sleigh pulled by starving reindeer.

Kristoff brought the whole party back to the village—the sisters, their old nanny, two footmen, and a toddler just beginning to walk. The little girl clung to Stana's skirt, her large, dark eyes like her mother's, a sheen of auburn in her hair when the sun hit it just right.

I knew she belonged to Nikolasha the moment I spotted her. I stood still in the snow watching her, this little miracle who was blood of my blood, one of the only ones who'd escaped that fateful night. She'd been carried away safely in her mother's belly an hour before the attack.

Stana felt me standing there. She turned slowly and looked at me with little surprise.

"I knew we'd meet again."

"Don't tell anyone." Damien stepped between us and put his hand on her arm. "If you want to stay—"

"I never told anyone before," Stana replied calmly. "And I've seen her in the scrying glass many times."

"What did you see?" I asked, instantly curious.

"Never mind that," Damien interrupted. "Call her Anya and don't say a word about knowing her, not even to your servants."

Melitza was carried away to Damien's grandmother's house. Esther was the village healer and midwife, possessed of the second sight.

"Where's Peter?" I asked Stana, not seeing Melitza's husband amongst the group.

"He died in the Red Terror. All of Nikolasha's family were killed, except for his littlest sister Galina—she was already living in London."

Entire families wiped from the earth. It was so common that neither of us became tearful—we only nodded, Stana touching her forehead to thank the gods that someone had been spared.

"And what's your name?" I asked, kneeling in the snow to look in the little girl's face. She hid behind her mother's skirt, peeking out at me. She was dressed in rabbit fur, already tall for her age.

"Celine," Stana said. "Nikolasha chose it."

"He knew?" I said with a strange mix of happiness and sorrow.

Stana nodded. "I told him it would be a girl."

I wondered if she'd sensed that Nikolasha would never meet his daughter. She couldn't have known what was going to happen that night or she'd have asked Nikolasha to escort her home along with her sister. I remembered her headache, how she'd been sick all evening. Perhaps her body had known, even if her mind hadn't.

"I miss him," I said to Stana. "I miss all of them."

She gave me a look I couldn't quite interpret.

"The ones we love aren't lost to us forever. Love endures past anything else. It's the strongest energy in the universe. It changes and flows, but can never be destroyed."

I wanted to believe that was true.

Damien gave Stana the use of the house of an old woman who had died of the flu. Kristoff's wife brought food and clean clothes for their party, and fresh milk for Celine.

Once they were situated, Damien asked me if I still wanted to go into the woods to do what we'd been doing every day since I arrived.

We saddled our horses, Damien taking Hercules, who had recovered from the bites on his legs and crashing through the wood with the two of us on his back. I saddled Mercury, who was quickly becoming one of my favorite horses I'd ever had the pleasure of riding.

She was so sensitive, it hardly seemed like I was guiding her. She almost seemed to read my mind. Her steps were light and swift and elegant.

She was still so fast, I couldn't imagine how Damien caught her in her youth. She loved to run and Hercules loved to chase her.

Artemis flew ahead of us, disappearing among the treetops. She disliked "magic tricks," which she found disruptive and unnatural, and she'd come to love hunting in the Frost Forest during the long months she waited for me outside the mine.

Damien and I followed her into the woods I was coming to know almost as well as a Cossack. The Frost Forest had been terrifying when I'd crossed it alone and starving. By daylight, with Damien at my side, it was a different place entirely.

The birch trunks gleamed as white as the snow, marked with wet black slashes. The pines were deeply green, untouched by winter. The streams had begun to flow again, alive and noisy, not silent ice anymore. Hercules ducked his head to drink from one and came up snorting, making mist in the air.

I liked to watch Damien on horseback. His seat was flawless, he and the horse like one creature. He held the reins lightly in one hand and kept the other free, guiding Hercules with nudges of his knees.

I could talk nonstop when my spirits were high. Damien was quieter. He rode a long time without speaking. I got excited when at last he had something to say.

"Look." He paused on the path to show me a crop of snowdrops at the base of an elm.

"Finally."

Spring had come late and wet and cold, but was arriving at last. A weak yellow sun shone from behind a thin screen of cloud, just bright enough that snowmelt dripped off the boughs with a gentle pattering all around us.

Damien and I rode deep into the forest, searching for a secluded place where we could practice magic together.

I'd been practicing every day as I used to do at home. My power was coming back stronger than ever—because I was with Damien.

He was a better teacher than Rasputin. Damien was used to drilling and training relentlessly, and he actually wanted me to improve.

He was fascinated by my ability to pick up new types of magic. Already I'd learned some basic alchemy from Bodhana. I couldn't yet turn grapes to wine like she could, but I could form butter from milk. And I was just getting the hang of chaos magic, which influenced probabilities. That I'd learned from Damien's cousin Adam, who could make dice fall as he wished or bring any card to the top of the deck, which was why he was banned from all games of chance within the village.

Mostly I focused on the manipulation of time. It was my most powerful weapon, the only way I stood a chance against Rasputin.

I had to practice pulling Damien through time with me. It would take both of us to kill the Black Monk, if it could be done at all.

Damien and I didn't explicitly discuss what we were doing, because he still hadn't agreed to help me. But he came into the woods with me every day and watched as I recovered, as I grew stronger. He was getting stronger, too.

Slowly he'd begun to achieve a measure of control over his death touch. He could never turn it off, not entirely, but he could contain it for short periods of time, like holding his breath. Then he'd release it like an exhale, twice as strong as before.

We sat next to each other on the damp ground, backs against a Siberian pine. I'd been practicing pausing time, making all the sparkling droplets of melting snow freeze in the air around us. I paused them and let them drop in a rhythm like a heartbeat, *freeze … fall, freeze … fall.*

Damien plucked a snowdrop and held it between his bare fingers, counting how long until it wilted black. He'd managed to extend the time by a second or two, but in the end, the flower always died.

He scowled, irritated with himself, throwing aside the withered bloom.

"I can't keep it in. It's just … the way I am."

"Don't be discouraged," I said. "You're already getting better."

He looked at me, anger and pain in his face.

Damien had never been able to hide what he felt, and neither had I. It made us vulnerable to the rest of the world, but when we were together, it was like we were speaking all the time without saying a word. I loved how his heart was bare like mine. For better or for worse, we kept nothing from each other.

He said, "My power isn't like yours. It's not a gift, it's a curse. Everything I touch, I hurt. Even you."

I leaned forward and kissed him softly on the mouth.

"You're not hurting me."

It wasn't completely true—my lips throbbed and my head pounded from that brief contact. But also my skin flushed, and my heart beat faster. I was coming to like that strange mixture of pleasure and pain. No sweet kiss could ever be so intense.

Damien looked at the pile of blackened snowdrops.

"I killed my mother before I was ever born. I killed my father, too."

"Damien …"

"It's true. If I hadn't attacked your father, Papa would have finished his contract years ago. I saw the Tsar and this rage came over me. There was no thought, no plan. No, that's not quite right … I did have one thought."

"What?"

"I thought, *Maybe this is why I'm the way that I am. To free my people.*" His eyes held mine, searching to see if I understood. "But I only enslaved them longer. That's why when you talk about our destiny together ... I want to believe you, but I've been wrong before."

I shook my head, stubborn as ever.

"You don't know that. You won't know if you were right or wrong until the end. Every step we've taken brought us to this moment—you may free your people yet."

"I don't know if I can do any good for them. Maybe I was born wrong."

"You do good every day!" I cried. "I've seen you."

"But I'm not good inside. I don't care about saving Rusya, not like you do. I'd let the whole country burn if I could just touch you the way I want to. Make you feel how I want to make you feel ..."

This time it was Damien who kissed me, roughly, deeply, both hands on my face. His fingers burned against my skin, hotter by the minute like an iron you can only tolerate so long.

Instead of pulling back, I put my hands under his shirt against the heat of his back and pulled him closer to me, tasting him, breathing him in, telling my body this was good and what I wanted and it shouldn't hurt me.

♪♪ *10,000 Emerald Pools —Børns*

The woods had gone silent around us. The birds sat motionless in the trees, even the wind had ceased. Snowmelt glittered in the air, transparent but reflecting the pines like so many tiny emeralds.

Damien's eyes were deeply green, shot through with flecks of black. His hair was thick and soft as fur—I ran my fingers through it and rubbed my palm against the part that was shaved, stippled like velvet.

Damien shivered. He was like a wild horse, not used to human touch.

"Try now." I plucked a snowdrop and laid it in his palm.

It rested against his skin for what felt to us like ten full seconds, and only then began to brown on the edges.

"See?" I said, bubbling with happiness.

Anything seemed possible when we were together.

Damien stared at the snowdrop, which was blackening, but slower than usual. He closed his fist around it, shaking his head.

"You make me believe, Anya."

"Good," I said, kissing him again. "Believe in us like I do."

He kissed me until I felt faint and had to sit back against the base of the pine. I let time relax around us. My head was pounding, but I wasn't drained

—quite the opposite. Blood rushed through my veins and magic sparked at my fingertips.

Damien said, "Can I show you something?"

"Of course."

He pulled a glove back onto his hand and reached inside the breast of his coat, pulling out a single white flower. The bloom was fresh and full, fragrant in the still air.

I stared.

"Do you remember this?"

He held it out to me.

"That's not the one I gave you ..."

"The very same."

I took the flower so I could feel for myself the slightly fuzzy stem, the single curling leaf, the delicate petals. It was real and alive two years later.

"I think you froze it in time when you handed it to me," Damien said. "I didn't notice anything when I put it away in my coat. But the next day, when I heard ... when I thought ... I took it out of my pocket and it was as fresh as before, still white, still glowing. That was the only part of the day where I felt the tiniest bit of happiness, remembering your face when you gave it to me. And the next day when it was still fresh, and the day after ... I wouldn't let myself believe. But it never wilted, and even though I couldn't believe ... deep down inside I still hoped. And that's how I felt you that day in the woods. Because the hope was still there, alive."

I let out a sound that wasn't quite a laugh or a sob.

"That's what happened to me, too. I lost my hope ... and found it again in you."

That was my fate with Damien: to be opposite sides of the same coin. Royal and common. Away and at home. Death and time.

Sometimes we swapped. Now Damien was the ruler and Damien was at home. Perhaps it was my turn to be death.

I asked him, "Do you really think I can freeze an object separate from myself?"

Damien took my hand, naked inside of his, linking his fingers through mine—something that had seemed impossible once upon a time.

"I think you can do anything. I really do."

I admired Damien more than anyone. To know he thought highly of me meant everything. It charged me up, it made me want to do crazy things to impress him. Last time I got that impulse, I smashed a whole cabinet of Faberge.

I jumped up anyway.

"Throw something!"

Amiably, Damien got to his feet.

"What should I throw?"

"Anything."

He hefted a rock about the size of an orange and tossed it in the air a little higher than our heads.

I tried to focus on just the rock, to fix it in place in its arc.

It thumped to the ground, rolling away from us.

"You might have slowed it a bit," Damien said, with more kindness than honesty.

"Try again," I begged.

He threw a slightly smaller rock into the air.

I imagined the stone separate from the air, the sky, the ground. I pictured myself holding it in my hands, carrying it into the time-stream like those Faberge eggs so long ago.

It still fell, but at half the speed as normal.

"*Yes!*" I shrieked. "Try something lighter!"

Maybe Damien thought I was being overly bossy. He stooped and cupped his fingers into the closest stream, flinging a handful of water right at my face. I threw up my hands automatically and the water hung in the air, gleaming and gelatinous, clear enough to see the treetops through it.

"That's just ... eerie," Damien said, walking around the silvery stream of water, staring up at it.

"Do it again!"

Damien stripped off his other glove and dunked both hands into the stream, throwing a cupful over my head. I followed its path with my hand and froze it in place, arced like a rainbow.

We looked at each other and laughed out loud, giddy with excitement. Damien swept me up in his arms and kissed me again. I was throbbing with energy, buzzing with the joy of how he looked at me, at the dimples on either side of his mouth that only appeared when he grinned his widest. I'd only ever seen them a few times.

Damien flung more water, more and more. It was easy to pause the water in time when I was charged up like this. I was bursting with magic; it poured out my fingertips anywhere I pointed. Anything seemed possible with Damien and that meant that reality became malleable, it became my friend.

All the colors became brighter and clearer. In that clean, fresh air, time itself became visible, flowing like the river all around us. It was no harder to encase an object in its own bubble of time than it would have been to blow an actual bubble with soap and a string.

The water hung in the air around us in transparent spheres and oblongs and streams, quivering in the sunshine, reflecting the green of the pines and the new spring leaves. It was like being inside a glass of soda pop, effervescent bubbles all around. Like we'd stepped into another world or made our own world together.

The air seemed warmer, the sun brighter. Whatever Rasputin had done to the weather, it held no sway here in the clearing, not when Damien and I were together.

"Can you pause something living?" he asked me.

I let out my breath and released my hold, letting all the water fall at once.

The splash was louder than I expected. It startled a robin from its branch. The bird winged upward, its soft orange breast turned toward us.

I reached out my hand and froze it in the air, just the robin, nothing else. It paused in place like a toy on a string, motionless in the sky.

The sight of a living thing stiff and trapped as a fly in amber was sobering. Damien and I stared upward, not laughing anymore.

He slipped his hand in mine, still ungloved.

"Let it go."

I released the robin. It flew away into a sky that for once was mostly blue.

Artemis hadn't returned. I supposed she was leaving us alone on purpose.

I was still throbbing with energy. When I held up my hand, I could almost see magic coming out of my skin like a fine golden mist.

"You're glowing," Damien said.

I looked at him and he was the same—face so bright he'd become luminescent in the sunshine.

I kissed him. This time the pain was distant, just an edge on the pleasure like salt sprinkled over sweet summer melon. I unbuttoned his shirt, letting my fingers graze the warm swell of his chest and down his stomach. His skin was brown as the earth, smooth and soft over muscle much harder than mine.

I'd imagined touching him like this a thousand times. My hands were almost shaking. Wanting something you can't ever have is a recipe for madness. Now I was finally tasting it ... even if I had to bend reality to make it happen.

Love is the strongest energy in the universe ...

I put my hand over Damien's heart and felt it beat against my palm. He put his own hand over mine and pressed it tight.

"When you walk in the room it beats faster. Every single time."

I kept my hand over his heart while I kissed him. It throbbed like it wanted to escape—like it would fly to me.

"Am I really not hurting you?" Damien asked.

"I don't care if you do." I kissed him harder.

He wrapped his hands up in my hair and pulled my head back, exposing my throat. He kissed all down my neck, with lips and teeth and tongue, nipping, biting at me. I was wearing one of his shirts. He ripped it open until my chest was as bare as his. He touched my breast, and I saw colors that have never been named.

My heart raced. I breathed like I was sprinting, blood thundering, every inch of me on fire.

I had wanted Damien, and only Damien, for as long as I could remember.

"Make me yours," I whispered. "Truly yours."

We sank down in the ferns, on the tangled roots and the soft, spongy moss of the deep forest where everything was alive and breathing, but slowly, at the pace of the trees that lived hundreds of years, that watched the seasons pass like days to us.

It was so easy to slow all of time, to cocoon Damien in that bubble that was just the two of us, because that's how it always felt when we were together. It felt like nothing could touch us, nothing could come between us.

The ferns stayed alive beneath his bare back because Damien was radiating nothing but happiness, and so was I. We were golden and beautiful. We felt nothing but pleasure in each other's touch.

Love is always magic. It's not rational, it doesn't follow any law. You can't make rules for it, you can't forbid it. You can't even make it disappear within yourself. It's alive like all magic, and it wants to change you.

"I get lost in you," Damien murmured against my mouth. "There's nothing but us."

I couldn't tell if time was passing or not, because I wanted the moment to last forever. I never wanted to be anywhere but there with Damien, doing exactly what we were doing.

He touched my breasts with both hands, he ran them down my sides. Each stroke of his palms sent the blood rushing through my body like I was the earth and he was the moon, strong enough to influence the tides.

I melted like the snow all around us, came alive like the new moss under our backs. Damien touched me with his hand between my thighs and I felt pleasure like I'd never imagined could exist. It transformed me.

I was transparent as glass, so light I could float. His heavy arm lay across my body, his hand cupped over my mound, fingers lightly stroking. Each flutter made me sigh, my breath coming out of my lungs in a silvery cloud. The water from my lungs, from the snow, from the river, floated in the air all around us. I floated, too, tethered to Damien and nothing else.

All the world was underwater. My hair rose in a cloud, dancing around my face, brushing against Damien's cheek.

My palm followed the curve of his ass, round and firm. I felt him pressed against my hip and took him in my hand. He let out a groan, turning his face against my neck, biting down on my shoulder. That part was as strong and alive as the rest of him. It might have killed me if we'd tried this before. But in that moment, I knew we were doing exactly what we were supposed to be doing. I was made for him and he was made for me.

I stroked him lightly in my hand. He touched me at the same time. We followed each other, sharing the sensation. When he touched me gently, I fluttered my fingers against the softest part of his skin. When I squeezed him harder, he pushed his fingers inside me. Electricity jolted up my spine. I pressed against him, our legs entwined, my calf hooked around his, our thighs locked together.

With each press, pleasure pulsed through my body. Each pulse was stronger than the last. Our mouths locked together, our breathing synced. His bare chest lay against mine, our hearts fast and then slow.

Damien rolled on top of me, arms on either side of my face. He was leaning on his elbows so our faces were close together, our noses almost touching.

"I love you," he said. "Only you, and always you."

"I think I loved you way before I knew it." I laughed. "Maybe the whole time."

I couldn't remember a moment when he hadn't been magnetic to me, the only color in a world of gray.

He kissed me, long and slow as if we had all the time in the world. And when he fit inside me, there was no telling if we were linked for minutes or hours. We were separate from time or gravity or any kind of magic that wasn't us.

We were finally linked the way that only two people in love can be—in heart and mind and body. I loved him more than anything, more than my own self.

I had no self outside of him. We were one and the same, not me and him, just *us*.

And when we were in that state, we were invincible.

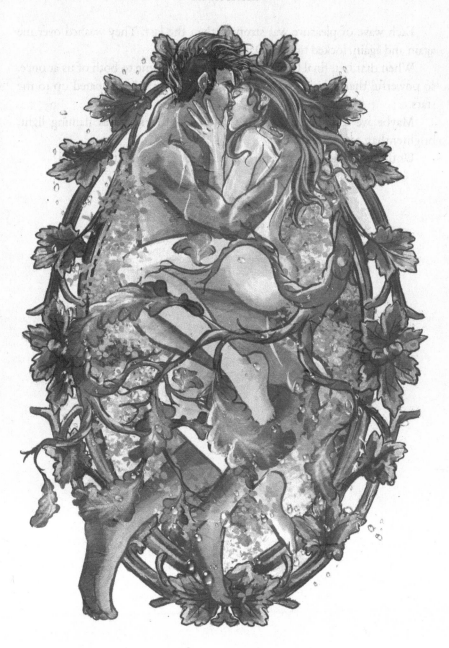

He moved inside me slowly, looking down into my face, stroking back my hair with his hand. He kissed me, his mouth warm and full against mine. His scent made me dizzy. I pressed my nose against his neck, breathing him in.

Each wave of pleasure was stronger than the last. They washed over me again and again, locked tight in Damien's arms.

When that last, final blast of pleasure came, it came to both of us at once, so powerful that if we'd let go of the earth, we could have floated up to the stars.

Maybe we did, because in that moment all I saw was flaming light, brighter than a thousand suns.

Until we opened our eyes and found ourselves back on the ground.

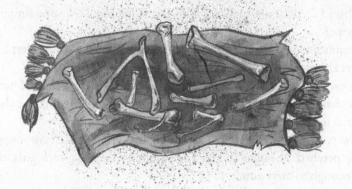

chapter 43
THE SCRYING BOWL

DAMIEN

We rode back to the village as the sun set. All the sky was red, a color so vivid and saturated it looked as if you could bite and suck it like a fruit.

Mercury turned rose gold and Anastasia seemed composed of fire. Her skin glowed and her hair burned. Her eyes were like the pale blue flame that dances over embers, burning hotter than all the rest.

I loved her so much it hurt.

I rode close to her and pulled her against me, kissing the hollow of her temple.

"I never could have done that with anyone else. I would have been alone all my life and never known what I missed."

The tragedy of not knowing seemed even worse to me than missing the experience itself.

"I would have been the same," Anastasia said. "Just a paper doll that thought it was real."

Artemis came flying in low like a bat, swooping upward onto Anya's arm.

She'd easily caught up with the horses, even with a bloodied hare dangling from her beak. The hare was such a pure white it would have been invisible to me on the snow, its ears and feet making up half its length.

"Thanks." Anastasia tucked it into her saddlebag. "Got one for yourself too, I hope?"

Artemis inclined her head and made a slight chirping sound that I could interpret almost as well as Anastasia. Something like, *Naturally.*

I knew Artemis well enough to know there wasn't a hare in the forest that stood a chance against her, and she'd eat her own dinner before she thought about making presents to anyone else.

"Are you still growing?" Anastasia lightly lifted the elbow on which Artemis perched. "I ought to give you to one of these Cossack girls; they're strong enough to carry you."

Anastasia would cut her arm off before she gave Artemis to anyone. I doubted she thought of herself as "owning" Artemis at all—or at least, not any more than you'd own a child.

Sometimes Artemis behaved more like the parent. Which made me happy, in a sad sort of way. None of us had any actual parents anymore.

Riding home in that vivid light, I was finally able to picture my father's face without pain. I thought of his smile, sharp white teeth under his black mustache. I asked him once why he never remarried. He told me, "I had my beloved and I have my boy. I'm as rich as a man can be, no need to be greedy."

We fought together before he died, that last battle where we retook Lemberg. All Cossack braves would choose to die victorious.

I looked at Anastasia riding beside me, not racing away across the steppes so I had to chase her. I thought of what she'd asked me to do.

She looked back at me, eyes blazing bright, all the sun on her face—the sun that came out for us. And finally, I believed. I believed I wouldn't lose her.

But my heart hesitated and I didn't tell her yet that I'd go with her, that I'd help her kill Rasputin.

As we neared the village, the sound of drums echoed across the dry grass. The day had been so fine, the hedges were strung with lights like for a festival. The scent of roasting nuts reminded us how hungry we were.

"Oi! They're back!" Jacov shouted from his position atop the gates. "Don't start yet!"

My cousin Adam took the horses, a favor I appreciated so much that I forgave him for all the knives of mine he'd ruined stuffing them half-cleaned into a sheath.

The fire blazed. I wanted to see Anastasia in front of it.

She stripped off her coat. All she had beneath was an undershirt because I'd ruined my own shirt ripping it off her. It didn't matter—the smocks the Cossack women wore were thin as a moth's wing, and they often dressed in men's clothes when they went out riding.

Anastasia had taken to wearing her hair loose like they did. Of all our customs, that was the one I'd have wished for her to adopt. The light moved on her hair like a living thing. Everything around her looked brighter by contrast. No one could help admiring her tonight—not even the Cossack maidens who considered themselves more beautiful than anyone.

She held up her hand, palm turned away from me, so I could lay the back of my hand against hers.

I'd put my gloves on before I mounted my horse so my knuckles wouldn't brush against Hercules as I held the reins. I wore those gloves religiously, never chancing that I might touch someone by accident.

Anastasia looked at me, firelight glowing on her face. "Take them off."

I wanted to. Now that my hands had tasted her skin, the thin leather gloves felt like a prison.

She said, "I'll do better if I can touch you ..."

Slowly, I stripped off the gloves and tucked them in my trouser pocket. All around the circle I felt eyes on us, and heard the rustle of whispers.

I laid my bare hand against the back of Anastasia's.

She winced, but breathed deep. The warmth of her hand against mine, and her peaceful calm, convinced me that I could touch her without hurting her.

♪♪ *NFWMB—Hozier*

My uncle Ivash sat on the large, flat rock that was his chair, his balalaika across his knee. His son Petro played a skin drum with his large, rough hands. My eldest uncle Myron spread his knees around the biggest drum, bell-shaped like his own body. His voice came out booming like the bass. He didn't sing words, just humming and thumping sounds. Petro's voice wavered over his, mournful like the wolves.

The dance began slow and steady, building like the layers of a pearl.

I could see Anastasia's determination to follow, to stay with me through the dance. She didn't want us to be parted, not tonight, not after what we'd done. She had something to prove to me.

I could see it all without her saying a word. I knew it from the way she bit the edge of her lip, how her eyes darted around, how flushed she was already, panting, grinning up at me.

You couldn't just be good to win the fire dance. You had to be perfect.

Anastasia watched the other girls, tried to imitate the shapes of their hands, the angles of their feet in their flat leather boots, embroidered all over with flowers and moons and stars. Olena, Polina, Lavra, all my cousins danced like deer, like they were made to do it. My cousin Nyura and I were the last two standing more often than anyone else.

Anastasia wanted to beat them all.

Leaning close, I said, "You'll never get it if you dance like a princess."

"What does that mean?" she puffed.

"It's raw, it's carnal, that's why it's fun, that's why we love it. It's why we dance around a campfire, not in a palace. There's plains all around you, forest, and wolves, the moon over your head. Stop watching everyone else. Be alive! It's instinct, it's feeling."

She pulled her eyes away from the circle and turned them only on me.

"Let me show you. Let go, be free ... but stay with me." I put my palm against hers, linking our fingers together.

Now our feet hit exactly in time. We followed the drums and pipes and my uncle's fingers dancing across the strings of the balalaika. The music told us when to jump, when to clap, when to spin. Lost in the sound, you could hear when Petro ran his fingers across the drum in a staccato pattern, the rhythm our feet had to follow laid out in the song.

I put my hands around Anastasia's waist and swung her high. I bent her backward until her hair swept the ground. Our legs entwined like they did in the forest, close and tight.

And just like in the forest, gravity eased its hold. Anya's hair swirled around her face, as free as the flames. Sparks danced across her fingertips, singeing me when we touched. Her lips brushed mine, tasting of smoke.

Dancers fell out of the circle all around. The circle contracted, pulling tighter, spinning faster.

The faster we moved, the stronger I felt. I wasn't tired, I could never get tired—not when Anastasia blazed in my arms. She fed me with every touch.

We were two swallows in the sky, connected by some invisible thread. She followed me so close it wasn't following at all—just together.

Ionna was knocked out of the circle, then Polina, then Olena. Of the women, only Lavra and Nyura remained.

Nyura's two long braids ran down almost to her heels. She was small and compact as a hare, made of a springier material than the rest of us. I thought she'd die before she'd let herself be beaten by a Rusyan.

She danced deliberately close to Anastasia, trying to jostle her, to knock her off the beat. That was fair game—anything short of strangulation was allowed.

When she stomped on Anastasia's foot I hissed at her, but Anya just smiled.

A moment later, Nyura froze for a half a second, her foot pausing before it stamped down. She missed the beat and was eliminated. I shot a look at Anastasia and caught the flash of glee that told me she'd pushed the edge of what she could do.

Watching Anastasia learn magic was like looking into two mirrors facing each other. It felt like you could fall in any direction forever.

I wanted to help her, to support her, but it worried me. She had that wild side of her, the part that wanted to run faster, leap further, just to see, just to try ...

The forces she was playing with were unimaginably powerful. Rasputin didn't care if he lost himself in Charoite or smothered Rusya in ice. What would Anastasia have to do to match him?

I couldn't plan for what might happen because this was no normal battle on a physical field. Anastasia and Rasputin had weapons I didn't understand, powers I'd never seen. There was no end to the awful things they could do to each other.

But to tell her not to use her magic was even more impossible.

It would be like telling her not to feel. This was her real state, how she was meant to be. When I saw her like this, glowing in the firelight, lit up with magic, it was impossible not to believe.

Only Jacov and Lavra remained now. Jacov looked tired, Lavra dogged.

We made one last circuit around the fire, following a beat that had grown as wild and unpredictable as the wind.

Anastasia grinned at me, her undershirt soaked through with sweat, her hand linked in mine.

Jacov fell, then Lavra. We didn't stop—we completed the whole last loop just the two of us, spinning so fast that sparks swirled around us in a whirlwind. When the music stopped, our feet landed firmly on the ground right on beat, the back of our hands touching once more.

The circle exploded with whoops and shouts. Even Lavra said, "Not bad for a Rusky."

Anastasia turned a look on me that made me feel like I'd grown a foot. Gods, how I loved to give her what she wanted. I knew then that I'd do whatever she asked of me. Whatever I even imagined she might want.

Without thinking, I lifted her in my arms and kissed her in front of every-one. The shouts of my uncles were as shocked as they were pleased.

"Finally found someone who can stand you, eh, Damien?" Myron chortled.

"Mind she's not made of rubber, that one," Ivash said.

I kissed her again to shut them all up.

When the dancing was done, the drinking began in earnest. The touch of spring in the air had whipped everyone into a frenzy. We were finishing the vodka made from winter wheat, anticipating the fresh wine we'd be brewing soon from the spring grapes.

Spring and summer were when the men went raiding and warring. I looked for Anastasia to tell her I'd go raiding with her to the mines, even to Alexander Palace if that was what she thought we needed to do.

She'd wandered over toward Stana, who had her daughter asleep in a straw basket beside her. A bowl of clear, cool water sat in front of her, its surface as reflective as a mirror. Stana knelt on the ground, peering into the shallow bowl as if it were much deeper.

She was scrying for anyone who wanted to know their future. My grand-mother sat beside her, laying out the bones.

I'd never let anyone read for me—not since Baba had done it the one and only time.

Stana looked up at me, her eyes so dark they appeared fully black.

"Damien Kaledin," she said softly. "Your color's changed."

It was obvious she didn't mean anything as pedestrian as a flush from dancing. What she might *actually* mean eluded me. My scalp prickled in the way it always did when I fetched up against one of the many faces of magic I'd never understand.

"Are you ready to let me read for you?" Stana asked, like she already knew the answer.

Anastasia's eyes flashed up at me, checking my face.

She said, "Will you read for us both?"

Baba watched, her eyes black as jet, her mouth a thin line with no lips left. She was bent and small, her hands twisted as driftwood. She'd forgotten more herbs and medicines than most healers would ever know, and saved many difficult pregnancies, though not the one that ended with me.

"Sit here," Stana said, gesturing to indicate the bare patch of earth oppo-site herself.

We knelt in front of her, peering down into her scrying bowl. All I saw was the reflection of the deep indigo sky and a few glimmering stars.

"I need a hair from each of you."

Anastasia wound one bright thread around her index finger and pulled. She dropped the hair in the bowl. It floated on the surface, curling in on itself in a loop before sinking under the water. When I dropped in my own hair, it sank straight to the bottom.

Stana lifted the bowl and swirled it, its surface rippling then falling still again when she set it flat upon the ground. Stana passed her large, long-fingered hands several times over the bowl. She wore silver rings below the joints and above. Her eyes looked darker than ever peering into the bowl, reflecting the silvery pinpricks of stars.

Though the water stayed still as glass, the stars began to shift and move, forming shapes like constellations.

My father taught me the stars—it was how we found our way on the steppes when the sun was down. I recognized Gemini first, the constellation like two figures linked at the hands. The figures split apart, forming Phoenix, Centaurus, and Lupus instead.

Lupus and Centaurus locked together and sank below the surface while Phoenix swirled like a galaxy and became the Horologium, the faint pendulum of a clock only visible in the darkest nights of December. Its brightest star swung in a circle around the bowl, making one entire circuit and returning where it began.

Stana watched the stars rearranging, her eyes blank and clouded. Baba watched, too, frowning slightly.

When all the stars had disappeared, the water grew cloudy like smoke. An image rose to the surface: my own face and hands. I wore no gloves, but my hands looked like they'd been dipped in black pitch. The inky darkness dripped down. My eyes were empty holes in a face as gray as the grave.

Anastasia slipped her hand in mine, squeezing hard.

"That's what I saw in my first vision with Rasputin. It scared him."

Softly, Stana said, "He knew he was looking upon the face of his own death."

Anastasia went stiff with excitement. "*I knew it ...*"

In the hollow tones of an oracle, Stana said, "Rasputin dies at Damien's hand."

Anya's fingers clenched in mine. "You see, Damien?"

"Yes," I said. "I see."

Almost to herself, she murmured, "We'll bring summer back again."

But I didn't see any summer in the bowl. Only darkness.

Stana blinked, her eyes clear and lovely once more. Her baby stirred in the basket, only half awake but making hungry sounds.

Anastasia got up to warm some milk. She stopped and kissed me first, her hands cradling my face. Stana followed after her carrying her daughter in the crook of her arm, the empty basked dangling down from her hand.

I stayed sitting next to Baba, who had watched all that passed.

"Will you read for me, too, Baba?" I asked quietly.

She took the bones in her claw-like hand but hesitated before shaking them out.

"Go on," I said.

The bones had three sides: white, black, and carved with an image. There were six bones in total. The combination of symbols made a language only Baba seemed to understand.

First shake, all six bones came out black. My grandmother's mouth went thinner than ever. She scooped them up and threw them down again. This time, all six landed white. That only made her scowl more. She threw again and some fell black, some white, some patterned.

"What does it mean, Baba?"

"I don't know. Your readings have never agreed."

"Then you don't believe what Stana said?"

"No, she's right." Baba shook her head bitterly. "You have a death bond with the wolf."

"Lupus is Rasputin."

Baba nodded.

"And I'm Centaurus."

That meant Anastasia was the Phoenix.

Lupus and Centaurus had sunk to the bottom of the bowl together.

Baba waited for me to understand.

I murmured, "A death bond goes both ways."

She nodded, just once. "If you follow that girl ... you'll never come back."

Maybe that was why I'd always felt dread at the prospect of my own future. Maybe I'd always known.

But ... the Phoenix survived.

I could kill Rasputin. And save Anastasia.

Anya came back out the door of Stana's house, carrying something cupped in her hand. She sat down next to me, opening a palmful of sunflower seeds. She cracked a few and held them out, smiling.

I smiled back at her, though my heart slowly tore in my chest.

THE START OF A PLAN

ANASTASIA

The next morning when I woke, I had bruises on me almost every place Damien had touched. Even my lips were swollen and slightly purplish. We'd slept in the same bed, wearing clothes but thin ones. The headache I'd gotten from all that contact mixed with the one I'd gotten from too much drinking.

I dressed while Damien was still sleeping so he wouldn't see the marks. The light coming in through the single window was gray as stone, the clouds the color of my bruises. It was like the sunshine of yesterday had never happened.

I buttoned the front of the shirt I'd stolen from Damien, the pale light shining through the sleeves, showing the raised and twisted scars snaking up my forearm. I remembered the look of the inside of my own arm, weeping red meat, open like a mouth.

The scars from the mine came over my shoulders and up the back of my neck. Sometimes I saw them peeking out from the collar of my clothes and I became cold and wet. The tips of my fingers ached and I drowned in hopelessness until the wave passed.

The memories tied to those scars were so miserable. I thought they must scream their ugliness to everyone else.

I rubbed my thumb over the scar that ran diagonal down my wrist. I could feel the seam, harder than the flesh around it, but brittle like it could split again.

When I turned around, Damien was sitting up in the bed watching me. He'd pulled off the rumpled shirt he'd been wearing. White scars cut across his tan from training, from fighting, from the academy, with fresher marks on his forearms where the wolves bit him, and the slash down his eyebrow from the day we met. The faint line went all the way down, still visible at his jaw. I'd only seen him the once without it, so to me it was as much a part of his face as his dimples or the tangled look of his eyelashes.

I don't know why we can love things on other people but not ourselves.

"Have you changed your mind yet?" I asked, half joking, half serious.

"No," Damien said, entirely serious. "I'm coming with you."

I got a burst of nerves that came out as laughter.

"Perfect. So all we need now is a plan."

"Do you have one?"

"I have the start of one. I know how to get into the palace. There's a tunnel that runs from the old horse graveyard."

"Does Rasputin know about it?"

"Probably not."

Damien thought for a minute.

"And you'll pull me into the time-stream with you?"

I nodded. "It's the one thing I can do that he can't."

"My power's weaker when you slow time."

"I know. Once you get hold of him, I'll have to drop us out."

"Then anyone can attack us."

"Yes," I said. "Especially Katya."

I hadn't actually seen Katya fight, but from what I'd observed, she was Rasputin's right hand. She was the one who made alliances with the students, the Bolsheviks, the Anarchists, and politicians. She made my brother fall in love with her. I didn't know the extent of her abilities, but at minimum she was highly persuasive.

I rubbed my thumb over the welts on my arm, seeing the knife flash again and again while I watched helpless and trapped in my own head. I thought of Sylvie leaping in front of the train and wondered if she'd felt just as powerless, just as terrified.

"We should attack in the day," Damien said.

"Rasputin can go out in the sun."

"They're still more likely to be sleeping in the daytime." Damien paused, eyebrows drawn together. "What do you plan to do about Alexei?"

I met his eye. "I don't know. But I promise you, I won't fuck this up again trying to save him."

Damien chewed the inside of his cheek.

At last he said, "Let's go talk to my uncles."

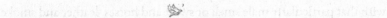

DAMIEN HAD six uncles still living—five that were the elder brothers of his mother, and one that was his father's youngest brother. I'd gotten to know Myron, Symon, Feo, Ivash, and Kristoff reasonably well over the last few weeks, but Evo Kaledin hadn't spoken a word to me. He was only ten years older than Damien and resembled him more than his own father, but with darker coloring. His hair was thick and black and shaggy, his build stocky. A few days' stubble shadowed his face.

He never joined the fire dance or the other games the Cossacks played in the evenings. He lived alone in a house at the edge of the village that fell into disrepair every time he was away, because there was no one to maintain it.

Even now, he sat a little away from everyone else, smoking his pipe next to the open window.

Myron looked mildly annoyed. This was his large, clean house and Cossacks disliked smoking indoors.

Out of all the men in the village, Myron was one of the only ones I'd seen actively participate in "women's work." Last time I'd visited, he'd had his sleeves rolled up and was floury to the elbows, helping his wife roll out dough on their long, scarred table.

He had thinning hair, an egg-shaped head, and sleepy-looking eyes. He could be a bit pompous, but hadn't held a grudge that his name was one of those that lost to Damien's in the vote for Ataman.

He set a warm, foaming mug of kvass in front of me, saying, "So our little Rusky won the fire dance already."

Damien's Uncle Ivash took his kvass and drank down half the mug in a draught. He was the one who played the balalaika for the dancing. He was thin with a long, mournful face and bloodshot eyes. His son Petro had come along with him and was rolling cigarettes, though he didn't light any indoors.

"Put Nyura's nose out of joint," Petro said, smiling as he licked the edge of his rolling paper and sealed it. Nyura was his sister.

"So what's this about, Damien?" Feo asked. He was the middle brother on Damien's mother's side, fair haired, blue eyed. His wife and infant son had died of the flu the year before. Melancholy followed him everywhere he went like a cloud over his head.

"It's about Rasputin," Damien said without preamble. "When Anya was in the mine, she found a cache of Charoite. Rasputin hasn't found it yet, but he will any day."

His uncles exchanged a complicated series of glances. The room was thick with that particularly male smell of sweat and horses, leather and smoke.

"What's it to us?" Evo said roughly. His large hands dwarfed his pipe and his pants bore rusty stains from whatever he'd killed last hunting. "New Tsar same as the last Tsar."

Technically, Alexei was Tsar, but everyone knew who ruled Rusya now.

"It's not the same," I said. "St. Petersburg's a prison and things are only going to get worse."

"That's the Ruskys' problem. Let 'em all kill each other so long as they leave us alone."

"They won't, though," Feo said quietly. "The Bolsheviks have already exterminated half the villages along the Don River. They're burning the houses, driving the women and children out into the snow, transporting the men to labor camps, and giving the farmland to Rusyan peasants. They're calling it 'decossackization.'"

"So we ride and help our brothers." Evo released a long exhale of smoke directly into the room.

"That's the tail of the snake," Damien said. "We need to cut off its head."

"And that's her idea, is it?" Evo's dark eyes watched me as he puffed on his pipe.

"Yes," I said. "It is."

"Over my rotted corpse will I be pulled into another fight for a Romanov," he spat.

Silence fell in the room.

Damien wasn't afraid to break it.

"It's true," he said. "Anya is Anastasia Nikolaevna. She was the Tsar's youngest daughter."

Kristoff said. "We're not blind and stupid. You didn't have that many friends in St. Petersburg Damien—'specially not gingers with a bit too much magic."

"Hiding her here's one thing," Ivash said. "Joining her little revenge mission's another."

"It's not about revenge," I said.

Evo snapped, "The hell it's not."

"We have to stop Rasputin from getting more Charoite."

"And who let him get his hands on it in the first place?" Evo pointed his pipe stem at the center of my face. "You want us to clean up your mess."

"Alright then, I do," I said, surprising him into momentary silence. "You're right—we never should have mined the Charoite. But now I've been in there and I've seen for myself what it's like, what it can do. I need your help to shut it down."

"Don't be a fool," Evo hissed at Damien. "She just wants control of it again."

"I wouldn't use one single grain," I said coldly. "We're going to blow it to bits. Collapse the whole damn mountain."

Now they all looked at me like I'd gone mad, except for Damien.

"You want to blow it all up?" Ivash said, not believing me for a second.

"You can't be in that mine and let the mine exist. It doesn't matter if it's better or worse conditions, or who's cracking the whip. It's not for humans to be in the ground. Especially not in that place. That stone will pull you into the depths of hell. It's corrupting."

Now Evo was looking at me like a fish in a net you thought was going to be one thing and turned out to be something else entirely.

"And what about Rasputin?" Myron said.

"Damien and I are going to kill him."

"Like it's so easy," Evo hissed.

"I've fought him before."

"And you didn't kill him then, did you?"

Damien answered before I could. "She escaped a whole palace of vampires, hid from Rasputin for a year, survived the mine and made it here. She has magic like you can't even imagine. She's going to take down Rasputin, and I'm going to help her."

Every chip in my confidence was restored a thousand-fold hearing Damien support me.

Petro twisted the ends on his last cigarette. "Well. Guess I'm coming, too."

"Not so fast," Evo snapped. "Let's say we help you. What do we get out of it?"

"How about the sun shining again for a start?"

"We want the steppes," he said bluntly. "All of it. And not on some bullshit agreement where you change the terms whenever it pleases you. *Ours.* Forever."

"She's not the Tsar," Damien cut in. "What do you expect her to do?"

"More than she has," Evo said bitterly.

He blamed me for his brother's death. And Damien blamed himself. And I blamed myself for Rasputin—and none of it helped anyone or fixed anything.

"I'll get you the land," I said recklessly. "Help me now and I'll do whatever I can to get what you want."

"That's not much of a promise."

"What d'you expect?" Feo said. He'd been looking out the window, hardly seeming to listen to what passed. "You saw her ride in here, muddy as a river bottom, holes in her boots. You want her to write up a contract, stamp it with her scepter? She hasn't got a bean."

"She's still a princess." Evo's lip curled.

"I give you my word," I said. "I've still got that."

"I've got Damien's, and that's good enough for me." Feo's dull voice seemed long since drained of any emotion.

"You really think you can beat him?" Myron was unconvinced.

"*Yes.*" I poured all my confidence and all my belief into that one word. "Because we have to. Rasputin is everything lying and conniving and leeching. There's evil, and there's good. It's not concentrated on sides, but it is concentrated in people. And if there's any justice in the universe, then it's on our side, because we want to defend the defenseless and he wants to drain them dry."

"Autocrat to crusader?" Evo mocked me.

"I learned a hard lesson. Gods forbid you have to learn it, too—what Rasputin can do and what he *will* do to everything you love."

Silence fell over the room, but a soft silence, malleable, listening.

Quietly I said, "The Charoite Rasputin stole from us would have fit in an apron. The cache in the mountain wouldn't fit in this house. There's never been a crusade that mattered like this."

Sensing that the tide had turned, Evo knocked his pipe out on the windowsill and brushed his palms off on his pants.

"Then what's the plan?"

SEVERAL HOURS LATER, we'd sketched out an arrangement for Myron, Ivash, Symon, and Kristoff to take a group of riders to the mine. They'd free the miners and collapse the mine on itself using whatever explosives we could lay our hands on.

I'd told them where the guards stored the dynamite for blasting out new tunnels, and where they used to patrol. The highest security had always been around the stones themselves, and the transport line.

Damien, Evo, Petro, and I would enter the palace via the tunnel. We were only taking the four of us, hoping it would be our best chance of entering undetected.

We meant to attack both places at once to avoid a warning being sent in either direction.

Rasputin still might have ways of knowing what we were doing. He'd known when Sylvie broke into his tower.

I was relieved Damien's uncles had agreed. Damien was Ataman, but the Cossacks followed him by choice. If his uncles stood against him, so would many of the host.

My spirits were high as we left Myron's house, Damien's less so. He walked slowly, his face as dark as I'd seen it.

"What's wrong? You worried that Evo's coming with us? Should we send him to the mine instead so we don't have to smell that pipe?"

His lips moved in the smallest of smiles. "I'm not worried about Evo. If he said he'll help us, then he will."

"What is it, then?"

He'd seemed so happy after we won the fire dance, but then Stana did her reading and his mood shifted. I didn't understand it—she'd said exactly what we wanted to hear.

"I just ... wish we didn't have to go so soon. When I first came back to the village, nothing felt right. I was Ataman instead of my father and I was all alone in his house. It finally feels like home again now that you're here."

I thought he was worried that if by some miracle we killed Rasputin and Alexei recovered, I'd stay with my brother in Alexander Palace, or go live with relatives in Denmark or Albion.

I took Damien's hands in mine and pulled off his gloves so we could link our fingers together like a chain. I loved the way they looked locked together like a basket woven in two shades of reeds.

"I'm coming back here with you, no matter what happens. Even if I could live in the palace again, I wouldn't want to. I've never been happier than I am here with you."

"I've never been happy at all until now. I'd trade all my life for this last month with you."

"There'll be more," I said, looking up into his face.

Usually I could tell what Damien was thinking. Today his eyes were dark as a midnight lake.

He touched my face, brushed his thumb over my lips. Heat burned in my stomach and I pressed against him. Nothing felt close enough. I wanted to step inside him.

"You know I'll always protect you," he said. "Nothing's going to hurt you while I'm with you."

"That's why I'm not afraid. Because we're doing this together."

"I'm not afraid either," Damien pulled me against his chest so I couldn't see his face. "I'm ready."

chapter 45

BOUND BY CHOICE

DAMIEN

I t took us a week to finalize our plans and gather everything we needed. Myron's eldest son Adam rode off the first day and returned on the last with twelve bombs bought off a watchmaker in Minsk.

"Almost shit myself every time my horse went over a bump."

Though I tried to cling to every moment remaining with Anastasia, those seven days flew by in an instant.

Time had never been my friend. The days we'd been apart had seemed like they'd never end, and now when I'd have given anything to slow the hours, they raced past.

And yet, every day I felt more certain that Anastasia was right about one thing: this was our destiny, mine and hers. Woven together before we were ever born.

A thread doesn't see the weaving, it doesn't know its own color and pattern. But it takes its place all the same.

I was what I was for a reason, and so was she.

I saw it every day in the village. I watched while Anastasia learned to bake bread with Ionna and took the cows out to the pasture with Daryna. I saw how she helped Stana with her baby and went into the woods to pick herbs with my grandmother. I saw her laughing with my cousins, riding with Nyura who liked to race across the downs as much as my beloved.

I saw how the Cossacks were drawn to her, how she brought smiles to their faces and lightened their loads, not just with her hands but with her laughter, her jokes, her unreasonable optimism. Her joy and her belief bound people together.

She had this unkillable spirit. This belief that she could do something, that change was in her power.

I thought how angry and defeated I was when I met her. I had no hope. I'd *never* had hope because I killed my own mother and I couldn't touch anyone and knew I never would. All I was good at was death.

Nothing could go right for me because it couldn't. I'd already failed when I tried to kill the Tsar and only made everything worse.

We were barely even friends, but she saw how low I was. She saw I needed something, anything, to lift my heart. And she got me a horse.

That moment when I rode Hercules across the field in the early morning fog and finally, finally felt happiness again ...

That was her real gift, over all her others. To find the smallest shred of hope and amplify it like a beacon.

I charged her up, but she illuminated everyone around her.

I loved my people. To her, everyone was her people.

She really was a princess, not because she'd lived in a palace or worn a crown, but because she took that mantle on her shoulders and never shook it off. She was the people's princess, my people and every Rusyan's. That hadn't changed, no matter what had happened to her.

Pain can poison people. It can twist and deform them. She suffered pain, but she never closed her heart.

I watched her practice her magic doggedly, obsessively, but not for power, not for revenge—to do what she believed in her heart her people needed her to do.

I believed as strongly as Anastasia that she couldn't do it without me.

I was death, but I was the battery for life.

Even if we couldn't shine together, she was going to shine after I was gone.

That's what kept me going, that's what let me smile back at her and kiss her and hold her without breaking down under the regret of all that could never be.

OUR LAST DAY in the village, I woke before the sun. If it was my last free day with Anastasia, I didn't want to waste a minute of it.

I lay on the bed, looking at her asleep on my pillow. Watching the steady rise and fall of her chest, the strands of hair stuck across her forehead, the sleep flush on her cheeks.

There was something childlike about her when she slept. It made me think of every age I'd known her. I remembered the first moment I saw her, a little redheaded demon whose eyes fixed on me with wild curiosity. The first thing I saw her do was an act of magic that changed my life forever. That might be the last thing I saw, too. It was all coming full circle.

When I thought of our first conversation on the train, I didn't think how we argued. I remembered how she forced the guards to let me have my last look at the steppes, even though I'd just tried to kill her father. I thought of how she tried to protect me from Vasta and Gleb, how she danced with me in front of everyone and convinced Dimitri Pavlovich to transfer me to the cavalry. She'd always defended me because she saw that I was alone and miserable.

We grew up together. We became stronger and wiser because we challenged each other, we believed that the best parts of each of us were the truest parts.

What would I have been if I'd never met her?

Less. Weaker and blinder.

She was my only touch, only kiss, only love.

She should have been my wife. I wished I'd had a child with her, grown old with her.

We were always interrupted, always ripped apart. We'd tried so hard to find each other again, but it was too late, we'd run out of time. The clock had run silently where neither of us could see.

I wanted to tell her so badly what I knew in my heart: that these were our last days together. But that was my burden to bear. I wanted her to have nothing but happiness in all the hours we had left. I couldn't destroy her hope when she needed it most.

Her eyes opened, blue against the pillow like a patch of sky in the clouds. She smiled when she saw me.

"I was dreaming about you."

"So was I," I said. "All night long."

"You don't look like you slept much."

"Waking up and feeling you in the bed was better."

"That's why my dreams were so good." She gave me the wickedest of smiles. "Every time I touched you it sent them in just the right direction ..."

"Then maybe you should close your eyes again ..."

I slipped down under the blanket and found her warm body. She was wearing my shirt and nothing else. I kissed my way up her thighs, soft and heated like bread out of the oven. I found the furnace between her thighs and inhaled my favorite scent.

She shivered, her thighs against my ears, fingers twining in my hair. I kissed her softly where she was warmest and wettest. Her nails scratched against my scalp.

I tasted her. I liked her best like this when she'd been walking or riding or sleeping, when she tasted of herself and the outdoors and her own wild energy that seeped from her even when she slept so all my sheets smelled of her. Her scent was in the air when I walked through the door.

The house felt empty and wrong before she got here. It couldn't be my father's house without him in it.

Now it lived again, with the herbs she dried in the windows, the crumbs she left on the tables, the echoes of her laughter in the air.

I wanted her in that house more than I wanted myself in it. I'd rather be her ghost than have her be mine again.

I plunged my face between her thighs because this was what made me live —the smell and taste of her. It did things to me. It changed me. An hour of this was worth a year of anything else.

I kissed and licked and tasted while she rolled her hips against me, making the soft, eager sounds that made an animal of me. I was on the hunt and I wasn't going to stop until she screamed.

She bucked her hips, squeezed her thighs around me, heels hooked over my back. She grabbed my head and pressed it against her, while squirming like she was trying to get away.

I devoured her until she panted like she was running full sprint, back arched, legs shaking. Her softness melted against my tongue. Her pleasure became my pleasure as I tasted every drop of it and swallowed it down.

I kept going until she collapsed, and then I cleaned her up with my tongue, softer now but no less thorough. Little aftershocks ran through her body. She was limp and dazed, her fingers sliding down my back.

When she could speak again, she laughed and said, "How did you know that's exactly what I was dreaming about?"

"You're not the only one who's got more than one kind of magic."

I did think I could read her mind. I was made to do everything for her.

I watched while she washed at the tin basin set under a cloudy mirror. She stripped off her clothes and made a game of it, teasing me, running the sponge slowly up her legs, squeezing the water out on her bare breasts.

Having her living here in my house, seeing her naked every day, touching her whenever I liked ... I finally had everything I'd ever dreamed of. But only for a brief moment in time.

Just like my father.

I'm the richest man in the world ... no need to be greedy.

He was right. It was enough.

Anastasia undid her braid and brushed out waves the color of strawberries late in the season. Her hair grew faster than horse tails; it was almost down to her waist again.

"Will you wear something for me today?" I asked her.

"Of course. What is it?"

"It belonged to my mother."

I knelt by the chest at the foot of the bed, throwing up the creaking latches, smelling fresh cedar as I lifted the lid. Inside were old letters, photographs, documents, mementos. Anastasia knelt naked beside me, poking in her head.

"Can I look?"

"Go ahead."

She leafed through the photographs, finding one of my parents on their wedding day. My mother wore a necklace strung with golden coins which were all her dowry, Papa a long coat with the tiny pockets across the breast that held bullets and powder. Mama was smiling like she had a secret. Papa stared at her like he couldn't believe his luck.

"Your mother ..." Anya breathed. "You look just like her."

I swallowed. "Papa always said how glad he was that he could still see her face in mine."

"What was her ability?" Anastasia held the picture close so she could look into my mother's eyes, a lighter green than mine. The sun was only just coming up and neither of us had lit a candle.

"She could charm animals. They'd come to her if she just held out her hand. Papa said she was the best rider he'd ever seen. She'd catch wild horses on the steppes and tame them."

"Is that how she caught your father?" Anya laughed.

"He said that, too. He said all the stray animals came to her doorstep, including him."

Anastasia shuffled through the rest of the photographs, finding one of my mother sitting on a swing hung from an elm, sunflowers drooping behind her.

"Is that you in this one?" She pointed to my mother's belly, rounded under her summer shift. The swelling wouldn't have been noticeable, except that she cupped her palm against it, the other hand wrapped around the rope of the swing. "Look how happy she is ..."

I'd seen that picture before but never noticed she was pregnant. It was seeing the two of us together, in a way.

She knew it would kill her to have me but kept going. She sacrificed herself for me.

I thought of the endless chain of people who had died for someone they loved. And felt closer to my mother than I ever had before.

"That dress ... it's the one I was hoping you'd wear for me. It was her favorite."

I took it from the chest. Opening its paper wrappings let loose the sweet and peppery scent of prairie roses.

Anastasia breathed in deep, tears in her eyes. "My mother loved roses, too."

I took her hand, lifted it to my mouth, kissed it.

"I thought of it the first time I saw you in that shade of blue. But I know you don't like dresses much—"

"I'd be honored," she said, taking it from my hands.

She pulled the dress over her head, soft and light as a sheet drying on the line. She touched the tiny roses on the shoulders embroidered by my mother's hand.

"What do you think?" She spun in a circle so the skirt flowed around her bare legs.

It was hard to speak. Impossible to explain.

Some moments burn in your mind and create a light you can look at forever. Memories that never fade, but only get brighter each time you visit them, like the place on a brass statue a thousand hands have touched.

All the brightest memories in my mind were Anastasia.

Here was another to guide me like a star:

Anastasia in my mother's dress, spinning barefoot on the wooden floor in that blue that meant water and sky and flowers in spring, that meant everything alive, everything I loved.

I said, "When you smile like that, it makes me happier than anything."

She touched the skirt, gently, like it could feel it. "This makes me feel connected to her. And to you."

My chest was so tight I could hardly speak. The way the skirt moved around her legs, the way she gave it human shape and made the fabric dance so the blue became liquid, light shimmering on the silken embroidery threads...

"I've had her dress all this time. But you brought it alive."

She wrapped her arms around me. Hugged me hard. My heart was aching, but she made me so happy, the two feelings mixing like paint, making a color that could never be matched exactly.

She stood in front of the cloudy mirror again. The dress was sleeveless but her eyes didn't flick to the scars on her arms. She smiled at herself, tucking the memory-keeper in her pocket.

"Does that still work?" I asked, remembering it had been doused in a river twice now.

"Let's see." She took it out again.

She knelt in the center of the room. This time it was me who joined her on the floor. I'd never actually seen the memory-keeper at work.

She pressed it to her mouth and exhaled, then set it on the ground. Music began to play, soft and slightly wistful. Golden moons and stars beamed out in all directions, rotating around the room. The lid lifted of its own accord and the light grew stronger, showing not singular images but an entire three-dimensional space all around us.

It was a room I'd never seen but knew must be Anastasia's. I knew her clothes scattered around, books we'd discussed. The projection was so detailed I could even see the rocks she'd gathered on Reval beach. I knew their shape and color. I never forgot anything when it came to her.

And there was Anastasia herself, kneeling at the window in a nightgown, hands pressed against the glass.

"Look how excited I was," the real Anastasia whispered. "Because I was going to see you that day ..."

I watched as she rode to me, as we met in the meadow of purple sage. I watched our first kiss, and felt a bolt of pure, electric happiness, unmixed with regret. I was swept up in it all over again. That moment could never be anything but bliss.

"Never erase that day," I said. "Promise me."

"I never would. I found you again because of that moment."

I watched the parade and saw Anastasia give me the white flower I'd carried with me every day like she did the memory-keeper. All our parallels were a thousand golden threads binding us together. We'd always been linked and always would be.

Anastasia's family stood behind her on the steps of the Winter Palace. It was strange to see them in all their grandeur. They looked so powerful, so invincible, just hours before their deaths.

Alexei sat by his father but he looked as if he sat by no one, staring at nothing.

Anya, the real Anya, watched the same part of the memory, the colored petals drifting down around Alexei while he sat still and cold as a snowman.

"That's what I dread the most," she said softly. "Seeing what Alexei's become."

I began to dread that I might have to kill her brother in front of her.

The parade melted into the wedding, filling my house with a projection of overblown peonies and the glimmering gold of the cathedral. It was so real that Anastasia's arms were bathed in slanting, multicolored light as if she were surrounded by stained-glass windows inside my tiny house.

Abruptly, I said, "We should be married."

She looked up at me, face lit with the glow of the music box.

"I want that more than anything. When can we do it?"

"Today."

She laughed. "Who would marry us?"

"I don't know ... usually the Ataman does it."

The vision of Ollie's wedding became dinner and then dancing. I saw Anastasia in the gown that must have cost more than everything I owned, that had looked so beautiful on her but no more lovely than how she looked in my mother's cotton dress.

The last moment the memory-keeper showed was when I lifted Anastasia in my arms, her body illuminated in the moonlight pouring through the windows, her face all aglow as she smiled down at me.

"That's funny," she said as the music box went dark. "It was a little different when I played it in the cave."

"Maybe it knows what we need to see."

"What did *you* need to see?"

"The two of us together. I spent two years regretting riding away from you. I want you to know, I'll never leave you again. Wherever you are, wherever you go, I'll be there too."

She looked at me and I thought I'd said too much.

Then she smiled and kissed me in answer, holding me as tightly as she could.

Before she rose, she slipped the memory-keeper back into her pocket.

WE HURRIED through the last of our preparations, determined to spend at least part of the day away from the bustle of the village.

Once we'd helped pack all the saddlebags and reshoe the horses, I asked Anastasia to go for a ride with me. It didn't take much convincing—since she'd come to the village, she hadn't let a single day pass without jumping on the back of a horse.

She whistled to Artemis. After a short delay that was probably deliberate, Artemis came winging over from the largest of the barns. She'd ousted the owl that used to live in the rafters and made it her home instead. My uncle Kristoff didn't mind because either way the mice stayed out of his wheat.

We rode across the downs first, Anastasia on Mercury and me on Hercules. Though I knew there wasn't a charger alive that could keep up with Mercury, I raced Anya anyway to make her happy.

That was want I wanted today: to give her all her favorite things. We'd had apple tarts for breakfast and trout for lunch, pulled straight out of the river. We'd ride and hunt and dance tonight, and Anastasia would light up like a lantern, chasing away every shadow of fear inside me.

Wind filled the skirt of my mother's dress as Anya rode. Her hair came alive, whipping around her face. Mercury was a silver arrow beneath her, shot straight from a bow.

I captured each image of her in my head and held it there like a miser.

At last we turned to the Frost Forest and rode into the wood with our rifles on our backs in case we saw anything worth catching. I'd been teaching Anastasia to shoot. She wasn't very good because she tended to shoot first and aim after.

Spring had retreated; it was colder today than a week ago. The animals seemed to be hiding—we saw a few old tracks from deer and hares, but nothing fresh.

Even Artemis failed to scrounge up any pheasants. She flew from treetop to Anastasia's arm and back again, clicking her beak irritably.

"What did she say?"

"She said she saw one rabbit, but it was too skinny to bother catching." Anastasia hid her smile.

A few minutes later, Artemis dove from the top of a pine and flushed something out of the underbrush. It reared up, squealing. Anya raised her rifle. I had already sighted the boar and pulled the trigger. The shot hit, but the enraged boar only barreled away through the trees.

We followed after it, the blood on the snow growing brighter.

The boar keeled over just before the cave it was trying to reach. It lay on its side, breathing weakly. I dismounted and cut its throat to put it out of its misery.

Anastasia slipped down from Mercury, to examine the mouth of the cave, not the boar. Overhung by trees, no sun shone here. Icicles lined the opening like teeth.

She hesitated, then walked inside. I saw how pale she'd gone and knew she was testing herself. She hadn't been inside anything more confined than a house since she escaped the mine.

I followed her in.

The interior of the cave was brighter than I expected, the light reflecting off a floor, ceiling, and walls all coated in ice. Pillars of ice had dripped and melted and frozen again, bluish over the white limestone. Every surface shimmered, clear as crystal.

The sounds of the forest had disappeared, the birdsong and creak of branches in the wind. All I could hear was the enclosed hush of the cave like the inside of a seashell. And within it, the beating of Anastasia's heart.

"It's like a cathedral," she said, looking around.

I needed to seal what should have been sealed a long time ago. I sank to my knees before her and took her hands in mine. My hands were naked around hers—I'd stopped wearing gloves when it was just the two of us.

"Marry me. I want you to be mine."

"I am yours. I always have been."

"Then say the words with me."

Anastasia knelt as if before an altar, our hands clasped together.

I spoke the Cossack vow, the same one my father said to my mother once upon a time.

"One heart, one mind, one soul. What is joined by choice can never be torn apart."

She looked up at me, her face my whole world.

"You're mine, and I'm yours. Yesterday, today, and forever."

I kissed her to seal our vow. We were alone, but that only made it more real.

As I kissed her she became my wife, bound to me forever through death and beyond. Warmth surged through me, through my hands into hers and back again. All the ice in the cave began to melt, dripping down on us like rain. Anastasia laughed, water sparkling in her lashes.

"I love you, I love you, I love you!"

I kissed her, hoping she would say it again.

She did, her eyes ten times a brighter blue than all the melting ice.

"I love you. I wouldn't want to be married any other way than here."

"I don't have any rings," I said, with sudden regret.

"It doesn't matter. This has always been between you and me."

When we came out of the cave hand-in-hand, Artemis was hopping around by the boar, highly agitated.

"What's wrong?"

"She doesn't want me to go under the ground."

Anastasia held out her arm. Artemis flew to her, digging her talons in enough to make her wince, but butting her head against her shoulder in a way that pulled at my heart.

"It's alright," Anastasia soothed her. "We're killing our fears today. We're taking back our happiness."

WE TIED the boar across Anastasia's horse. She rode back on mine, sitting on the front of my saddle with her back against my chest. My arms looped around her waist to hold the reins, and I put my face against the side of her neck so I could smell the clean and smoky scent of her hair. It brushed against my cheek, warm and soft, the ends lying across the back of my hand.

That night, the boar was our wedding feast. My uncles brought out the long tables from Kristoff's barn and we ate honey cakes and sweetmeats, stewed blackberries with fresh whipped cream, spiced carrots, and huge haunches of roasted boar, blackened on the outside and dripping within. My uncles and cousins, friends and braves, toasted us again and again until I was drunk on wine and the taste of Anya's lips.

When everyone was full we danced around the bonfire. There's no competition in the wedding dance—all the couples stay together, linked at the hand, the women's skirts swirling like seeds on the wind.

My cousins hung paper lanterns all through the trees. The golden lights were supposed to represent everyone we'd lost, present at the wedding in spirit if not in flesh.

As Anastasia and I spun together, time slowed as it always did when she was happy, when she wanted the moment to last. The lights floated around us, warm as the eyes of my father, my mother, her parents, her sisters, and everyone she'd loved.

Whatever they'd thought in life, they must be happy for us now. If the dead feel anything, it's the joy of the living. We must glow like lanterns to them, through the screen that separates us all.

chapter 46
BURN LIKE A STAR

The next morning, we left with the dawn. Myron, Simon, Ivash, Kristoff, and fifty braves rode with us through the Frost Forest, then we parted ways, my uncles taking their men toward the mine.

Before they left, I took three of the bombs we'd bought from the watchmaker. My uncles had cobbled together a motley mix of explosives—much more than they needed to collapse the mine. They weren't taking any chances.

Neither was I. If worse came to worst with Rasputin ... I couldn't let him walk away.

Evo, Petro, Anastasia and I headed to Zinberg where we'd board the train for St. Petersburg. We'd bought falsified papers, dressed in Rusyan clothing and even switched our saddles. Our goal was to attract as little attention as possible as we entered the city. Anastasia dressed as a boy, her hair tucked up under a cap.

"No sailor suit?" I teased her.

"I looked good in that suit."

"True," I said, with the feeling of another loop closing.

The journey into the city was longer than the ride to the mine. My uncles and the others would camp just inside the forest, waiting until we could all attack at the same time.

Artemis accompanied us most of the way to the terminus, then turned back to join the others. This was at Anastasia's insistence. I hadn't been sure Artemis would actually consent to part ways until I watched her winging away into the low-hanging clouds. I'd heard one half of Anastasia's hour-long debate with her the night before:

"They need you at the mine ... You know the area better than anyone ... They'll never get up there unseen without you ..."

Anastasia's arguments were interspersed with the sharp snap of wings and angry bird noises.

At last she'd cried, "You can't fly around inside a building. You'll get trapped in a room and they'll rip both your wings off this time!"

They both quieted down after that, murmurs and soft chirps indistinguishable. When Anastasia rejoined me in the house, she was swollen eyed and miserable.

"She's furious. But I can't lose her, too."

I held her until her heartbeat slowed and she could breathe without hitching.

WE ARRIVED at Zinberg just in time for dinner, sharing a meal at a run-down restaurant before we boarded the train.

The train was rusting and filthy, the carriages packed with miserable-looking workers who were being transferred from one factory to another. We had to bribe the porter to secure berth for the horses. He crammed them into a baggage car with several pieces of farm machinery and stacks of stinking suitcases.

There were no first-class carriages anymore, which allowed us all to be equally uncomfortable in worse conditions than the third-class passengers used to enjoy. The bureaucrats of the new People's Government rode in their own private trains. You can raze a civilization to the roots, but you'll never stop people from securing something better for themselves.

Evo cracked one of the windows in our carriage so he could smoke his pipe. A few passengers threw him dirty looks, but nobody dared complain to someone with a scowl as ugly as my uncle's.

Evo was never cheerful, but I was glad he was with us. I knew bigger men, but no one I'd want to fight less. Evo was a badger. You could never, never get him to back down, and if he got his teeth in your throat, you'd have to take his head off to get them out again.

He was the youngest of my father's brothers and the only one still alive. They'd been raised wilder than animals by a father who'd driven off several wives with his fists. One of his many children put a hatchet in his forehead. I suspected Evo but had never entirely ruled out Papa.

Petro filled the gaps in Evo's silence. He'd been with me at Lemberg, the scout who'd found the hidden postern gate. He'd be a useful pair of eyes if the palace was as dark as we expected.

His father Ivash hadn't tried to stop him coming, though we were headed into the viper's nest. Ivash had always been unconventional. He married the daughter of a Nogai Khan, oath-enemies of the Cossacks. Some of the braves mocked Petro and called him "Genghis." In response, he grew his hair long and wore sheepskin boots.

Maybe that's why he'd volunteered to come with us—he was a contrarian by nature.

He and Anastasia played a dice game that involved hiding your dice under your cup while bluffing your opponent. Anastasia kept losing because her face lit up when she got something good.

"Can you see through this cup?" she demanded, after her third or fourth loss.

Evo took his pipe out of his mouth long enough to say, "You've got no poker face."

"I win at cards all the time." She turned to me for support.

"Well ... not *all* the time."

"What?"

"Probably not even half."

"*What!?*"

The shock on her face made us all laugh.

"Did you think you were good at cards?" I teased her.

"It's better to know now that you're not," Petro said with mock sincerity. "So you can focus on other things."

"You can see through the cup!" she insisted.

"Sorry, love. I can see as well as your hawk, but I'm not one of those x-ray freaks."

"I knew someone like that ... someone who could see through anything."

Anastasia looked up at me. That was always the impulse when talking about someone we'd lost—to check if anyone remembered that they'd lived, they were real, you hadn't just imagined it all. Everything had changed so much, our old lives felt like a dream.

Rasputin played Felix like a fiddle. He accepted his dinner invitation and poisoned him just enough that Felix recovered in time for the Yusupovs to be slaughtered at the wedding along with everyone else.

Did Rasputin know it all before it ever happened? What else had he seen? Did he know we were coming right now?

"My sister could see in the dark," Anastasia said to Petro. "Dead creepy when she'd sneak up on you like a cat."

"My brother says he can see colors the rest of us can't. But I always thought he was making it up."

"What about you, Evo?" Anastasia was brave enough to ask. "What's your ability?"

It wasn't exactly a rude question but it was a personal one. Evo looked at her unsmiling for a long moment before knocking out his pipe and taking out his knife instead.

"Simple enough," he said.

He brought the blade down on the meat of his palm, making an inch-long slash in the flesh. It gaped open, a little blood running down his wrist. Anastasia's eyes went glassy and her lips blanched.

As we watched, the slit in the flesh sealed itself. In a few minutes it was only a thin line like a paper cut. I knew it would disappear entirely after an hour.

"Incredible," Anastasia said faintly.

"Are you alright?" I murmured in her ear.

She nodded, but she was pale and slightly sweaty. She didn't stop looking at the bloodied blade until Evo wiped his knife on his pant leg and put it away again.

"Bit like a vamp myself," Evo said. "Guess we'll see who's harder to kill."

He almost sounded like he was looking forward to it.

The closer we got, the more I felt the same. It was the waiting and dreading I hated.

Petro brought out his undersized chessboard. He'd carved the pieces himself, the knights like Cossack chargers.

Evo didn't look like he'd play, but after a moment, he moved a black pawn.

Anastasia watched the game in fits and starts, her head against my shoulder.

"You should get some sleep," I said to her. "We'll only have a few hours rest in the city."

"I'm too keyed-up to sleep."

The game moved swiftly. Chess is mother's milk in Rusya, for Cossacks, too. I was nearly as familiar with Evo and Petro's style of play as with their style of fighting. Petro looked five moves ahead, Evo came in aggressive and stayed that way until he lost or beat you.

Evo advanced. He neatly avoided several traps but when Petro seemed to leave his bishop unguarded, Evo took it. Four moves later he was in check.

"Ha," Anastasia said, softly.

We laughed together at her silly spite.

Ten minutes later, she was snoring softly with her head on my shoulder.

I stroked her hair with my hand, savoring every brush of my palm against the softest thing I'd ever known. If we would have had a child together, I would have prayed for a daughter with hair like hers.

Then I remembered that I wouldn't be able to hold my own baby, not without gloves. And I knew it was one more thing I was never meant to have.

I kissed Anastasia on the curve of her forehead, gently so I wouldn't wake her.

This was enough. This was enough.

WE ARRIVED IN ST. Petersburg at six o'clock in the morning. We'd slept fitfully on the train, Anastasia better than most of us, me hardly at all. The plan was to catch a few hours' sleep in a lodging house, then enter the palace in the heat of the day when we hoped the vampires would be sleeping. They'd have human servants keeping watch, but I'd take a human over a vampire any day.

"I hope *they* haven't got anyone like Tatiana," Anastasia murmured.

"We don't know what they have."

Anastasia had grown tense as the train pulled into St. Petersburg. She kept her head down as we walked to the lodging house, leading the horses through side streets and alleyways.

They still attracted glances, even though we'd left Hercules and Mercury at home and brought only our plainest mounts. Horses had become less common in the city. There were no aristocrats riding Thoroughbreds down Equestrian Row anymore. Half the carthorses had starved or been eaten during the long, cold winters.

The landlady led Evo and Petro to a room on the ground floor. Anastasia and I were given the attic space.

"All I've got left," she said.

"This is perfect." Anastasia crossed to the window.

It looked down over nothing more interesting than uneven rooftops. The room was tiny and dirty, dust motes swimming in the air. At least it smelled of the bare wooden beams of the ceiling and not the mutton stew cooking in the kitchen below.

I could smell Anastasia's skin, warm in the sunshine. Her hair picked up the scent of wherever she'd been so I knew if she'd built a fire or baked honey-cakes or been out riding.

Imprints and memories—everything leaves a trace.

Would a ghost of us stay in this room forever?

I hoped so.

We had only a few hours to rest.

Anastasia began to undress.

♫♪ *Infinity—Niykee Heaton*

She took off her cap and let her hair fall down, loose, bright, hiding a thousand shades in every shadow. She began to unbutton her shirt. Her fingertips revealed a line of bare flesh as they moved down, as if she were spinning herself into being.

The dust motes swirled around her, glinting gold like fireflies. Her eyes held mine, golden lights in the blue. The air glowed, tiny sparks danced across her skin.

She was lightning in a bottle, charged, ready for the storm.

I ached for her, throbbed all over my body, but it was my need for her that made me hesitate, because I knew how hard it would be to hold back if I put my hands on her.

"You're going to need all your energy. I don't know if we should."

She let the linen shirt slip off her shoulders and slide down her arms, dropping to the floor. She was naked beneath, her skin glowing, eyes alight.

"Does that drain you?" she said, low and teasing. "Or does it light you on fire?"

I seized her and kissed her. Her skin seared, her breath burned.

Lips to lips, she said, "You could never drain me. You make me burn like a star."

Magic flowed out of her, twining around us both. Could I really be the spark for all this?

I felt lucky. So godsdamn lucky.

When I touched Anastasia's skin, it was like every moment of denial, of disappointment, of shame, of longing, every day I'd been cursed had been to make this moment sing. It was to let me feel the full gift of bare hands on the person I loved.

I felt the pulse under her skin, the breath from her lips. Her body curved around mine, formed itself against me. All our parts seemed to line up perfectly, she was just the right amount smaller than me. Our hands linked up. Our legs looped. My chin rested on the top of her head, her face against my chest.

We lay together completely naked, all our skin touching, all of us entwined.

There was no rush. We had the power to make it last. Magic flowed around us, all across our skin. It pulsed between us like a circuit. Everywhere we linked up, we only got stronger.

I kissed her, my body wrapped around her, hands in her hair. We melted together, swirling like color.

It didn't matter if this was all the time we'd ever have, because the hours together stretched out infinitely. We lived a thousand lives in each other's arms, whispering the deepest wishes of our hearts.

"We don't have to hold anything back," Anastasia said. "Hope is believing in right now, not just the future."

As she kissed me, as I slipped inside her, I believed. I believed this moment was worth everything. Whatever I'd paid, whatever I'd still have to pay, I'd do it again and again and again. I'd choose her every single time.

I touched her face, looked into her eyes.

"I'm not a hero. But when I'm with you I believe I could be."

"We're exactly what we need to be. Look at us, Damien. Look what we can do."

She linked both her hands through mine, crossing my wrists over my head, letting her hands slide down my arms, down my body as she kissed me.

I loved looking up at her as she straddled me. I was a king with her on top of me. I grabbed her waist in my hands, feeling every part of her shaped so differently than me.

The sounds she made lit me on fire. Every gasp, every moan jolted my brain. I had to give her what she wanted. There was no choice about it.

I licked her, kissed her, touched her everywhere I knew she liked it best. I was holding in that destructive power that used to leak out of me like body heat. I was so charged up by her that I was holding it in almost entirely myself, it didn't even matter that she'd slowed time, that the dust motes hung frozen, the inn silent and still because everything around us had paused.

I could feel that darkness inside me like magnetism, but now it could flow either way, in or out, and I had hold of it.

I trailed my fingers over her breasts, touching her nipples lightly, teasing, pulling them into points. I squeezed, letting just a little of my power flow out.

She let out a deep groan.

Her nipple stiffened and swelled, hot and bruised under my fingertips. She was writhing on the bed, legs churning against the sheets.

I pinched her other nipple, tweaking it gently, tugging. I pulled on it, long and slow, and gave her another pulse.

Groans wrenched out of her. I went back to the first breast, touching her between her legs at the same time with my other hand.

Her moans were sobs. She wanted it, she needed it, but she could barely stand it. She pressed against my hand, slid back and forth against my fingers. I let a little more of the dark touch seep out of me. She shivered and twitched, thighs clamping together, body twisting. The cries yanked out of her, pleasure and then pain and then pleasure.

Letting it throb out like that gave me a sense of release that was mind-bending, head-rushing. Each jolt was its own small climax.

I rolled on top of her, looking down into her face. Our eyes were locked, faces flushed. We breathed together, groaning with each thrust. I dug deep inside her, pushing the edge of how far we could go. With each thrust, I let go a little more, watching her face. Her eyes rolled back. The pleasure lit her up and she could take the pain.

I let out more and more. The darkness in me went inside of her and burst out of her as light. The whole attic was a lighthouse beaming out through the windows. Anastasia was the beacon. Light was in her eyes, in her skin.

Each burst took us to a new place. I understood now why she was always pushing the limits of what she could do. Riding the edge of the overwhelming was a game that demanded to be taken too far.

Each wave was stronger than the last, more intense, more pleasurable. Pain and pleasure were two circles, perfectly overlapping. Pulling back felt like madness. Drowning was sanity.

Anastasia looked in my eyes, panting, urging me on. Her hips moved with mine, her legs hooked around me. I couldn't have pulled out if I wanted to.

Her hunger for me fed my hunger for her. The storm between us doubled and doubled and doubled.

The harder we went, the harder it was to tip all the way over. The pressure mounted and we were driving together, whipping each other on.

She rolled on top of me, cheeks flaming, hair on fire. Her eyes were blue flame, she was so bright I could barely look at her.

She sped up until light burst behind my eyes. I grabbed her hips, fingers digging in, and exploded.

She put her hands over mine and slooooooowed the movement of her hips, rolling her body in a wave that took minutes, hours, years. She was clamped around me, squeezing with all her might, but dragging out time so that each agonizing stroke, each endless, spiraling slide went on and on forever.

I could hear my own moan, slow-motion, distorted.

She was in charge; I had no control at all. She created the perfect torture, this agonizing peak of pleasure that didn't blast and dissipate but went on and on at maximum intensity.

She took me way past where I would have pushed it, and still we were locked in place, her hips moving infinitely slow through that epic stroke.

Finally she let go and I howled as it all rushed out of me, a cannon blast that left me panting, throbbing. She collapsed on top of me, her whole body shaking, smelling smoky and sweet, sugar and salt on her skin.

She lay there a long time while I stroked my hand through her hair. We both knew we'd have to get up in a minute. No time for a nap—we'd used it all.

"I wish I never wasted so many days," Anastasia said.

"What days?"

"The days I thought we were enemies."

I kissed her on the forehead. "You never really thought that."

chapter 47
COMING HOME

ANASTASIA

C lose to noon, we ate a quick lunch in the basement of the lodging house, retrieved the horses, and used our forged papers to travel the unpaved roads into the farmland south of the city. We'd gotten transfer papers for a farm in Tel'mana but turned off the road before Tsarskoe Selo.

We moved through Alexander Forest, through trees I knew like old friends. I'd ridden every inch of this wood, played in it with Alexei, built tree-houses, lost toys in here. I knew where the guards used to patrol, though maybe that had changed.

The forest was ill kept, undergrowth choking the trees, none of the dead brush burned away. The wood was darker, wilder, and smelled wet and moldering.

It was significantly colder the closer we got to the palace. We'd noticed it just coming into St. Petersburg, no hint of spring here yet.

Even four of us seemed too many as we neared the high stone wall encir-cling the grounds.

I wanted to tell Petro to turn back. He looked so young as he shimmied up the wall, fingers wedged in the smallest of cracks. Big as he was, he hardly made a sound. Damien told me it was a disgrace for a brave's weapons to jingle. A worse disgrace to turn away from battle—Petro volunteered before he even knew what we were doing.

He paused on top of the wall, spying everything he could as quick as he could before dropping down. He flung a rope over for the rest of us and we were on the other side in less than a minute.

I landed on grass grown long and weedy, untrimmed hedges all around us. The flowers had died in their beds. The imperial farm was abandoned, no chickens scratching in the yard, the stables silent. We passed the menagerie, the bleached bones of an elephant spilling through the bars of its cage.

Farad's little house was dark, several of the windows smashed. Artemis' mews stood empty.

Damien held out his hand, stopping us as we crept along.

Two guards were positioned on the Llama Bridge. They almost looked like scarecrows, uniforms faded and scruffy, figures strangely still. The one on the left scratched his nose, fingers fumbling at his face before his hand fell to his side again. A crow called from an elder tree. Neither man turned his head.

We backed up, skirting the stables instead. The park seemed so much emptier, the silence unnerving. The grass had browned. No rabbits hopped across the lawn. No birds either, besides the crow. The bees were gone. I doubted there were even worms left in the ground.

The whole park had become a graveyard, the palace its mausoleum. We saw it as we crested a rise, every window shuttered and dark as if it had gone to sleep.

That was my home for my entire life, but it didn't look like mine anymore. Ice had cracked the pavements and heaved the stairs. Vines grew up the pillars and stilled the bench swings. The stone facade had darkened and weathered as if snow had blown against it for a hundred years.

We slipped down the side of the hill into the horse graveyard. This place at least hadn't changed. My family's horses had been allowed to live to spoiled old age, grazing the meadows until they were buried here. I walked between the marble headstones, letting my fingers brush over their names—Ami, Flora, Cob ...

The memories came back so strong I almost expected to see Ollie leaning up against the mausoleum doors.

Finally got some guts, Stassie?

"What is it?" Damien murmured.

"Nothing."

The door was padlocked.

"It'll be loud busting that off," Petro said.

"I could set the door on fire," I offered doubtfully. The wood was rotted and damp.

"Someone will see the smoke," Damien pointed out.

"Don't make it so hard on yourselves." Evo jammed the point of his knife under the mechanism of the latch. He dug the screws out of the rotted wood and prised the whole thing off.

Cold gray light bounced off the blade. My face flashed at me but it wasn't my face—the eyes were too pale a blue. Something squirmed in the back of my head.

"Losing your nerve?" Evo said.

"I was just thinking ... that was smart."

"Glad to meet your approval, princess."

"Only I get to call her that," Damien said, voice low, hand on the small of my back.

"Technically we all have to," Petro said. "Unless they changed the law."

"You don't have to." I stepped up to the door. "We never did at home."

And this was still my home. Whatever it looked like now.

I touched the memory-keeper for luck, tucked deep in my pocket.

It brought us all home.

We entered the mausoleum, descending the steps of the tunnel within.

SOMEWHERE UNDER THE BACK GARDENS, a bat fluttered over our heads.

I stiffened, nails digging into Damien's arm.

"Rasputin has a bat."

"There's more than one bat in the world. Probably more than one down here."

"Where's this tunnel come out?" Petro said.

"She told you—the kitchens."

I heard rather than saw Damien's annoyance. Petro could have seen it plain as day if he turned his head. He was leading us, Evo in the rear. It was comforting to have Damien's uncle behind me, so long as he didn't decide to bury that knife of his between my shoulder blades.

I didn't actually think he'd do that. Honor was everything to the Cossacks. It was us who hadn't always kept our word.

"Won't there be a bunch of servants bustling around?"

"Not if all their masters are sleeping," Damien said quietly.

"The tunnel comes up in the potato cellar," I said. "So unless someone's about to make *pommes frites*..."

We came up in the scent of dust and earth and slumbering vegetables. Only a few withered apples and some sprouted onions sat in sacks. Either the vampyrs didn't eat much actual food, or things were hardly any better here in the palace.

It was like climbing up through the levels of hell. We went from frigid tunnel to musty cellar to the kitchen itself.

The kitchen was dim and quiet, but the first thing I saw when I popped up my head was a pair of eyes staring right at me.

Margaretta was sitting on a stool in the corner, hands in her lap. She wasn't sewing or mending—just sitting there.

She'd lost weight. Her skin hung on her pinched face, making her look ancient. Her hair had gone white, frizzled bits sticking out from her bun. Bruises marked her neck and wrists. One lens of her glasses had cracked.

Her dress was dirty. The kitchen was filthy. I could smell old grease, fetid meat. Some of the smell might have been coming from Margaretta herself.

When she saw me, her face came alive.

"Stassie?" she croaked. "Can it be?"

I clambered out of the cellar and ran to her. Her hands were cold as a corpse. The palace was like the inside of an icebox.

But I was more used to cold than before. I poured warmth from my hands into hers.

"I'm alive," I whispered. "Where's Rasputin?"

"Sleeping. They all sleep in the day now. They used to take turns, but they've gotten lazy. Eaten half the guards and most of the servants. They'll probably eat me too when I can't push a broom anymore."

They'd already half done the job. She staggered when she stood, clutching my arm.

I asked her, "Where does Rasputin sleep?"

"Your parents' room."

Anger flared in my guts, ugly and hot.

"I'll take you there," Margaretta rasped. "Through the servants' corridors."

We followed her. As we passed the hallway to the billiard's room, I jerked back, spying Yaro Vyachevslav and another minister inside.

"It won't matter," Margaretta muttered. "Keep your head down, they won't pay any attention to you."

Yaro's fine suit was nothing but tatters, hanging off his wasted frame. The two men mumbled together in low tones, eyes dull, billiards cues untouched on the wall.

They didn't raise their heads as we passed the doorway. The same was true of the few servants we encountered. Their glazed eyes slid over us as they dully went about their tasks. They'd been drained within an inch of their lives, pale and anemic, bruises like fingerprints all over their flesh.

The work they could do in that state wasn't near enough to keep the palace clean. Dust piled up everywhere, dirt on the floors, the carpets damp and muddy. The shutters had all been latched and heavy drapes hung so not a crack of light could leak in.

No candles for the servants, who fumbled along. Petro could see as well as the vampyrs.

"You one of them?" Margaretta asked suspiciously.

"No."

"Didn't think so, but you can't always tell."

We were making our way toward my parents' suite. The route felt strange because this was how the servants came. I only caught snatches of the hall-ways and the rooms I'd known, dingy, dark, rearranged. As we passed the Portrait Hall I saw the faces of my ancestors had all been clawed off.

The palace was in ruin, mirrors smashed, tables overturned, filth every-where. It smelled of rot, of caves, of basements. And beneath it all, the metallic scent of blood.

"Is that what he's done to everyone who helped him?" I asked Margaretta. "Is that what Liza Taneeva looks like?"

Margaretta gave an ugly laugh. "They ate Liza first."

As we entered the last hallway, she said, "Almost there."

I put my hand on her arm. "You stay here."

I didn't want her getting hurt.

If we could get Rasputin while he was still asleep, maybe none of us would get hurt. This could be over in minutes.

Margaretta slipped a key off the ring at her belt. She pressed it into my hand.

I hardly dared breathe as I unlocked the door to my parents' suite and turned the latch. The door cracked, the scent of white roses pouring out. My head spun. For a moment I forgot who I was about to see.

Petro drew his saber and entered the room first, the rest of us a few steps behind. I could sense the massive four-poster bed ahead of us, the one my parents had always slept in.

That's what tweaked my brain before Petro stiffened. Rasputin slept in a granite bed that was the headstone for his wife. He slept with her picture next to his face, probably dreaming that her cold body lay in his arms. He wouldn't sleep in the scent of roses.

"Go back," Petro said.

The door closed behind us.

I threw a ball of flame at the bed. The blankets ignited. There was no body beneath. Figures swarmed in from the next room: Rasputin, Katya, and a dozen vampyrs. Also the creature that had killed Dimitri, though now he was more man than wolf, with teeth and claws but hair growing only on the backs of his hands and the sides of his face. Behind them all, trailing Rasputin like a shadow, my brother Alexei.

I glimpsed him in the garish orange light of the fire, in the smoke and stink of burning cloth. He was a walking corpse. I thought Rasputin had killed him and brought him back again a ghoulish slave—until his eyes met mine and I saw the anguish of someone very much alive, though barely.

His face was a skull, skin stretched tight, his body bones under the rags of his suit. His hair was down to his shoulders, as white as Margaretta's. He might not have bathed since the last time I saw him.

I saw it all and then I turned away from my brother and into the time-stream.

The cold was nothing to me. I'd been practicing in the Frost Forest, stripping off my coat, standing in the snow. I'd learned to pump fire through my veins, to use pyromancy and time-walking simultaneously.

The vampyrs ran at us and to me, it was like they walked. Rasputin hung back, because of Alexei or to see what I could do.

I set the vampyrs on fire, one, two, three of them. The third was the beautiful ballerina from Madame Lessinger's party. I made her a dress of flame. I thought of Anna Pavlova and wings of fire shot from the vampyr's back, enveloping her until her milky skin cracked and bubbled and she shrieked like a demon.

Rasputin sent a blast of cold at me that was like a howling wind from the depths of December. It whirled around me, ripping, tearing, biting with ice. I let out a pulse of heat that blackened the wallpaper all around the room. The portraits of my sisters and me caught flame and burned on the walls.

"Careful!" Evo yelped, slapping at his face. The tips of his mustache smoked.

Petro had his saber, Evo two knives. Petro was fighting like a dancer, Evo like a brawler. Damien had his gloves off. The first vampyr that leaped at him was Oksana. He seized her by the throat, draining her life until her face went black and she withered like a crone.

I only saw them in a burst like a flashbulb because I faced Rasputin, and power poured out of him.

He hadn't aged, but he had changed. The Charoite had taken a toll on him. He was gaunt, rigid, every spare ounce burned away. What was left was hard as iron. His eyes blazed in his face with unholy purple light. I could see it under his skin, pulsing violet.

He blasted cold at me; he poured it on me like an avalanche. I staggered under the weight, quaked under the biting ice that tried to freeze my heart.

But my heart was burning, burning for Damien. He was right there with me in the room, only feet away, and nothing could crush me while he was there. Heat burst from me like a solar flare, so bright that even the flaming bed seemed dim.

Damien looked at me and I saw that same light in his eyes, bright and ferocious. The vampyrs swarmed him and he brought them down one after another, his bare hands empty holes that sucked out their souls and dragged them down to hell.

More vampyrs poured into the room, dozens of them. They knew we were coming; none were asleep.

Evo and Petro slashed and cut, but they were only human.

Petro was first to fall, bleeding heavily from a bite to the throat. He clamped his palm against his neck and fought one-handed, until he was born down by a vampyr as lean and dark as a wraith.

Evo fought like a devil, bleeding all over his face and arms. Some of the cuts were healing, sealing themselves, but the vampyrs were everywhere, teeth on all sides, biting, ripping at him. He gave a vicious cut to the wolfman, half gutting him. Then Katya leaped on him.

They grappled, Katya horribly strong but Evo composed of oak and grit and pure stubbornness. He had his hand around her throat, holding back her snapping teeth as he drove his knife toward her chest.

Then Katya said, "You have no bones in your hand."

Her voice seemed to cut through my ears. It echoed in my head, and when I looked at Evo's hand, it seemed to have gone floppy as a fish, the knife slipping from his fingers.

Katya turned the blade and drove it into his neck.

Evo scrabbled at the handle, eyes bulging. Both his hands worked again, they always had, but for a moment she'd convinced him that they didn't. That was all it took—Evo sunk to his knees.

Damien howled with fury, taking down two vampyrs at once, one with each hand. His eyes had gone completely black. When he looked at me, I felt like I was staring into a chasm.

Rasputin rushed at him, so horrifically fast that I realized he could time-walk. I realized it in the same instant that I used my power, sprinted at him, blasted fire in his face. He poured his cold into me from a foot away, so hard that my whole mind froze and all I could think is, *My gods, he can time-walk. He took it from my father as he killed him ...*

I'd only ever suspected that the way Rasputin learned magic wasn't quite the same as me, that it was tied to his vampyrism.

"TAKE HIM!" Rasputin bellowed at Katya.

He was locked in place, pouring as much cold as he could into the room to try to keep me frozen. I was trapped across from him, blazing out so much heat that we'd all be incinerated if he wasn't holding me in balance.

Katya panted, wiping her mouth with the back of her hand.

She looked at Damien and I saw a flicker of fear in her face. The scars from Artemis' talons had healed, but the one beneath her eye dragged down the lower lid, exposing a patch of the raw red flesh like a bloody tear.

She ground her teeth together, fangs flashing, and ran at Damien.

I tried to stop her, tried to pause her in place like I'd done to the robin. The moment I slackened my focus on Rasputin, his cold overwhelmed me. Frost formed on my skin.

Damien was a dark halo, the light of the fire stopping short of his body. The vampyrs rushed him and he brought them to the ground one after another almost as soon as his hands touched them.

Even Rasputin's face grayed as he watched. I heard Stana's voice in my head:

He was looking upon the face of his own death ...

And I knew, I knew we were going to win.

Until Katya leaped on Damien's back and wrapped her arm around his throat. He grabbed her face with his hand. She shrieked, she screamed, but still she held on, arm locked tight around his neck, throttling him with all her inhuman strength.

Damien began to sink, though he clutched her with his hands, though he poured his power into her.

"No!" I screamed.

His eyes rolled back, he crumpled beneath her. Katya bore him down, her face rigid, teeth bared.

Damien lay insensate on the carpet. Katya stumbled off him. She took a step toward her father, reeling.

"Are you proud of me now, Papa?"

Blood burst from her nose and eyes, dark as tar.

She fell to the ground.

Rasputin howled.

His shriek went on and on. The vampyrs cowered, the wolfman clutched his guts. Alexei stood in the doorway, still and expressionless. He hadn't looked at me once.

The howl reached a peak that seemed it would shatter glass, burst my ears, turn my brain to liquid until it ran out my ears. Damien was unconscious on the floor. Our bond was cut, my power flagging.

I tried to twist away from Rasputin, to find the flow of time.

He raised a hand and blasted me into the wall.

chapter 48
FIREWORKS

DAMIEN

I came to on the floor of a stone chamber.

An immense heat crackled behind me—a wall of purple fire.

In front of me stood a semi-circle of vampires, the core of Rasputin's coven. Their clothing was ornate, velvet and lace, but dirty and poorly pressed. Their fingernails were long and pale, hair lank and greasy. Some were still bleeding from the battle upstairs. All cringed with fear because Katya was not among them.

Rasputin's rage was electric—the air was thick with it, tiny hairs standing up on my arms.

He had Anastasia pinned to the wall.

She was pressed against the stone, feet hovering above the floor. Purple light enveloped her like an amniotic sac. It pulsed all around her, writhed inside her nostrils and poured out through her mouth, it wriggled across her skin. She choked on it, drowned in it. She gagged again and again while more squirmed down her throat.

Rasputin moved his long, pale fingers in the air, drawing invisible shapes.

Anastasia twitched and jerked with each movement, she heaved and thrashed, trying to fight him even as she drowned in his power.

Rasputin's teeth were bared, upper lip pulled back in snarl, furious that she still resisted him.

I tried to haul myself off the ground, but was bound hand and foot. There was something wrong with my back. Pain wrenched through me.

"The Cossack's awake," a rough voice rasped.

It was the werewolf, still clutching an arm across his stomach. His clothes were stiff with blood, his arm crusted with it. He'd survived his encounter with my uncle, but not for long.

"Shouldn't we just kill them, master?" one of the vampires hissed. He was the one who took down Petro, tall, thin, dark complected.

"She's here for a reason." Rasputin's voice wasn't as smooth as it used to be, or as controlled. "It's been two years—she didn't come back for nothing."

His eyes locked on Anastasia's. "*Tell me why you're here ... What do you know ... What have you seen ...*"

Anastasia's eyes rolled back. She shook like a seizure, trapped in the grip of that awful purple light, thick like sludge, forcing its way inside her. Still she wouldn't crack. He couldn't get what he wanted from her.

His hold on her broke and she crashed down to the stone floor, face smacking against the rock.

I thrashed against the ropes, pain ripping across my back. Something was very wrong with me. All I cared about was getting to Anastasia.

Rasputin turned on me instead, crossing the space between us. The wall of fire was behind me, all his followers blocking our access to the stairs. We were trapped deep under the palace, injured, halfway to dead.

I could feel the watchmaker's bombs still strapped to my body beneath my clothes. I twisted my wrists within the ropes but I was bound too tight, I couldn't get free.

Rasputin radiated a dark power so thick it seemed it would smother us all. He no longer looked any part human, his face harsh and angular, his pupils glowing, flickering, as the fire inside consumed him.

He had all the power, all the advantage, yet there was nothing but rage and misery in his face. He was a cyclone, feeding on his own fury. He'd tear us all apart. His followers cowered against the walls.

Alexei stood by the wall of flame, oblivious to the heat. He watched everything that passed, emotionless. In that moment I hated him, because Anastasia would do anything to save him and he wouldn't lift a finger for her.

She raised her head, eyes dazed, blood running from her nose.

Rasputin towered over me, hand outstretched.

"Tell me what I want to know," he said to Anastasia, "or I'll break his bones."

"NO!" she cried.

He gave a flick of his fingers and something snapped in my arm. The pain was hot, instant, overwhelming. I clenched my teeth but a cry wrenched out of me as I writhed on the ground, arms still bound behind me.

"Tell me why you're here ..."

"Don't tell him a fucking thing!" I bellowed.

Rasputin lifted his hand. It froze in the air in front of him. His body jerked, his fingers trembled, but he was locked in place. I saw Anastasia on the ground, straining, shaking, using everything she had to hold him, to stop him hurting me again.

He couldn't believe she was doing it. I saw the rage, the incomprehension in his face. He was full of Charoite and she was alone, battered, bloodied, but she wasn't actually alone—I was awake, and even if I was tied up on the ground, I was loving her with all my heart, believing in her with everything I had. It looked like the end, it seemed like we'd failed, but it wasn't the fucking end, we were still alive and that meant there was still hope.

"You can do it." I looked in her eyes. "You can beat him."

I said it to her, but it was Rasputin who faltered. His coven shifted and muttered. They were afraid.

"Get the Charoite!" he snapped at Alexei.

Dully, Alexei turned and walked through the wall of purple fire. Anastasia had explained to me how it worked, but I hadn't realized Rasputin was still storing his Charoite in the vault.

I saw the envious looks of the vampires, saw the way they whispered to each other. This was the fate of all despots. The more power Rasputin got, the more enemies he made, and the more he feared his own followers.

The vault was still the safest place in Rusya because only Alexei could enter it, and only Rasputin fed on Alexei. As long as he kept the puppet Tsar by his side like a pet on a leash, he could use Alexei's crown and hide the fuel for his power where no one else could reach it.

I worked my wrists back and forth in the rope. Each movement was agony, some bone broken in my forearm. I twisted and turned doggedly.

"You need it," Anastasia said to Rasputin.

"I don't need it, I want it," he snapped. "I enjoy it. I'm going to let it flow through me until I'm stronger than a god, and then I'm going to tear apart your mind, piece by piece, until I know everything you know."

He stood there tall and gaunt, hair blowing in some unseen wind, eyes blazing with a color never found in nature. Anastasia lay on the ground, small, frail, pitifully human.

But she wasn't broken. Not yet.

"You never figured it out," she said to Rasputin.

Bloodied and battered, she smiled as she taunted him.

"The hell I didn't!" He rounded on her, turning his back on me. "I knew you were coming. It was emptiness in the smoke—the hole in my visions. I'd felt it before. It was you clouding my mind, blocking what I could see, protecting him. I knew he must be coming here—and I knew you were still alive."

"But you never saw the truth. You never saw that you're going to lose."

He spat, "You're as delusional as ever."

But the werewolf had faded back against the wall, arm still clutched over his guts, and a few of the vampires had moved closer to the stairs.

The rest still encircled us.

Alexei stepped back through the fire, his hands full of Charoite. The purple stones throbbed with their own light. Rasputin looked on them with more than hunger—with desperate need.

"Give it to me."

Anastasia said. "Don't do it, Alexei."

For the first time, Alexei turned to his sister. I wasn't sure if he even recognized her. He stared at her unblinking, his face expressionless.

Anya looked back at him with nothing but love.

"You're stronger than him, Alexei. I can see you're still there."

"*Give me the stones.*" Rasputin's voice dropped low, gripping like a fist.

Alexei shivered. He was a dog being called by two masters.

"*Now,*" Rasputin snarled.

"Don't!" Anastasia cried.

With a jerking motion, Alexei thrust his hands back through the fire and dropped the Charoite on the other side.

"Pick it up," Rasputin ordered, but Alexei only stood there.

"Do it yourself," he said in that dull tone. "You can regrow a hand, can't you?"

"PICK IT UP!" Rasputin bellowed.

He pushed too hard.

Something burst behind Alexei's eye. The lights went out and he collapsed, used up at last.

Rasputin hadn't meant to do it. He stared at the crumpled body at his feet while Anastasia shrieked, unleashing a sheet of fire that whipped across the room. Rasputin batted it aside.

She wasn't aiming at him. The fire ran up the ropes on my arms, burning through. It burned my skin, too, and set my clothes alight, but it didn't matter. I ripped my hands free.

Before Rasputin could turn, before he could even look, I clamped my bare hands on his face and wrapped my arms around him, dragging him backward to the wall of fire.

"DAMIEN, NO!" Anastasia screamed. She struggled to her feet.

I shouted, "RUN!" knowing that if she used the last of her magic she could outrun anything, even this.

I pulled Rasputin into the flames, four bombs strapped to my chest.

As the liquid fire engulfed us, the last thing I saw was Anastasia sprinting toward us in a streak of stretched-out time ...

NOTHING
&
NOWHERE

PART SIX

chapter 49

OUROBOROS

ANASTASIA

I blasted through a tunnel of blackness. There was nothing at all: no ground beneath my feet, no feet to feel the ground, no eyes to see the nothingness around me.

How long the emptiness lasted I couldn't say—there was no time, no light, no Anastasia.

Then a hand gripped my ankle.

Five bony white fingers clutched at my leg, though the hand had been torn off at the wrist, ending in raw flesh with a knob of bone protruding. The fingers scrabbled as the hand tried to climb my body like a monstrous spider.

I kicked with all my might, spinning through space, the dead white hand scrambling up my leg.

There was an enormous jolt. I found myself in the window seat of my own bedroom in Alexander Palace.

A black wind whirled all around me, howling, screaming in my ears. The hand leaped for my throat and closed, squeezing. The wind tried to go inside me, tried to occupy my body. I knew it was Rasputin because I knew those pallid fingers and I knew the feeling of him forcing himself inside my mind.

I was weak and confused, my brain blasted open by the journey through nothingness.

He rifled through my mind, images flipping faster than pages in a book.

Before I could even begin to shut him out, he found the cache of Charoite, a sizzling vein of violet light, blazing bright.

He was ghost and I was flesh—I couldn't keep him out of my head. Like wind in a sieve, he whipped through my brain.

But the reverse was also true ... whatever barriers he'd built had disappeared with his body.

His mind was a maze with no walls. I walked straight through to the center.

There I found the memories he hid deepest of all—memories of his wife and daughter. They flashed through my head, one after another, bursting and gone in an instant, but still painting a picture ...

I saw Rasputin standing outside his little cottage deep in the woods, the one he lived in with his wife and daughter. In this memory, the house wasn't surrounded by snow—it stood in a grove of oleaster trees, their branches heavy with dark red berries.

His wife bid him farewell, kissing him as he buttoned his traveling cloak.

Be careful, my love. I don't like when you go into the city ...

I'll be back in a few days ...

But when the memory melted and shifted, the Rasputin of the past visited not a city but the house of a bent-backed old man, whose shelves of ancient books and fingertips stained with the materials of the arcane proclaimed him a sorcerer.

The older man's eyes were the color of pewter, clever and malevolent as he spied a dark red berry caught in the folds of Rasputin's cloak.

Do you ever gather those? His voice was distant and echoing, while his eyes glinted sharp. *Useful for potions. They only grow a few places ...*

The Rasputin of memory paled, noticeable even on his colorless face. He knew he'd made a mistake.

Rasputin wrenched out of me and smashed through the window, the disembodied hand and the whirlwind of his raging spirit, leaving me alone in my room.

It all happened in a matter of seconds.

I couldn't understand what just happened. How could an explosion blast me up to my room? Where was Damien? Where were the rest of the vampyrs?

I pushed up from the window seat. Broken glass fell from my lap and so did my memory-keeper, tumbling to the carpet. That was when I realized I was wearing a nightgown.

I stared around the room, so confused I couldn't process the simplest of facts.

My bedroom looked exactly as it had before. Empty teacups on the windowsills, stockings over the backs of the chairs, books stacked everywhere. Clutter aside, the space was warm, bright, and clean. It smelled of paper and ink, dried herbs, and fresh linen.

Outside the shattered window, the lawn was bright and green, the sky a cloudless blue.

I looked down at myself, barefooted, dressed in a rumpled nightgown, hair braided. And then I saw my arms, bare and completely unmarred.

The scars were gone.

I turned my hands over. They'd been calloused and damaged, the skin on the back permanently bleached from the chemicals of the mill. Now they were soft and healthy, the nails a pearly pink, the freckles returned to the backs of my hands.

The room seemed to spin.

I took one lurching step forward, still not understanding.

Maria walked through the door.

"What was that noise Stasia? I heard a crash—gods, what happened to your window? Did a bird fly in?"

She was standing right in front of me, dressed in her own nightgown, her fair hair in two fuzzy braids over each shoulder, her round blue eyes clear and innocent.

I stumbled toward her and grasped her by the shoulder. She was firm and real and warm. I threw my arms around her, squeezing as hard as I could, breathing in the scent of my sister. It was the same. She was the same.

"What's going on?" Maria was half laughing, half concerned. "Are you alright, Stassie?"

"You're alive," I sobbed.

"Of course I'm alive. Did you have a nightmare?"

Tatiana came into the room. She was wearing her favorite morning dress, the gray silk, hurrying because she'd heard me crying.

"What's got you worked up so early?" And then, seeing the window, "How'd you manage that? We better tell Margaretta, the guests will be able to see it from the back lawn—"

"What guests?" I croaked.

Tatiana stared at me like I'd lost my mind.

"The wedding guests, Axel's family—you know, everybody we want to impress? They'll be here in an hour."

All the blood drained from my head.

I sank to the carpet, not sure if I should laugh or cry or vomit. The world had gone mad, or I had.

"Ollie's getting married today?"

"Yes ..." Tatiana's eyebrows raised.

The pattern on the carpet seemed to pulse before my eyes. Vomiting might win.

"Where's Damien?" I choked out.

"He better be on his way here. Or our parade won't be very exciting."

It was Ollie's wedding day all over again. I'd come back—somehow I'd come back.

My eyes fell on the memory-keeper, laying on its side a few feet away.

"Careful!" Maria said, as I crawled through the broken glass to retrieve it.

I lifted it in my hand. It was silent and unlit, but warm as if it had been operating minutes earlier.

"What's going on with you?" Tatiana frowned. "You look ... sick or something."

In a voice that hardly seemed to belong to me, I said, "I've just traveled through time."

"You time-walked through the window? Better than into another cabinet, I guess."

"Not time-walking. I came back in time. Two years back."

My sisters looked at each other, Maria confused, Tatiana now genuinely concerned. She thought I'd lost my mind.

"That's impossible."

"I just did it." I clutched the memory-keeper in my hand.

"You really saw two years ahead?" Maria whispered. "What did you see?"

"I didn't see it. I lived it."

"Two whole years?" Tatiana was incredulous.

It felt like a hundred.

I couldn't stop staring at my sister's faces. They were exactly as they'd been, every mannerism, every movement. Even the things I'd forgotten were there: the small brown mole high on Tatiana's cheek, the way Maria twisted her toes against the carpet when she was barefoot.

This was real. I was really home again.

The three of us stood reflected in the full length mirror. We looked exactly as we did before.

I looked exactly as before. No scars on my back, my arms, my hands. No pain in my joints from the two years of heavy labor. It all vanished like it never happened at all.

But it *had* happened. It happened to me. The pain was real, the suffering, the sadness, the people we'd lost ...

Though I'd hated those scars, though I'd felt ashamed of them, they were my memory of everything. What I'd endured ... what I'd learned.

And then the heavier blow hit, the one that took the guts from me.

The Damien of the last two years, the one who saved me from the wolves, who took me home to his village, who danced with me, practiced with me, learned to harness our powers together ... the Damien who loved me, married me, and came with me to fight the most terrifying evil we'd ever known ... he was gone.

He'd been incinerated in the wall of fire. Only I, and some part of Rasputin, had blasted back here.

After everything I'd lost, that was what broke me.

It took the better part of two hours to explain to my parents and siblings what had happened.

At first, they didn't believe me. They thought I'd been hurt, hit my head, had some kind of magical vision. It wasn't until we sent a carriage for Grandma Minnie and she came to examine the memory-keeper that the tide began to turn.

I played them all the memory of Ollie's wedding day. They saw for themselves the parade, the ceremony, the dinner and dancing afterward. But that was all they saw, because the memory ended at midnight before Rasputin's attack.

"You're saying this really happened?" Mama was shocked and highly uncomfortable. She'd never liked magic. This affront to the fundamental rules of all she believed in was exactly the reason why.

"This and much more. I lived two years past this, Mama. I saw Rasputin take over all of Rusya. I saw what he did to the country, the people."

My parents still struggled to believe, but Grandma Minnie backed me up.

"It's a memory-keeper. It doesn't store visions, it stores the memories of a single day. Anastasia lived this."

I couldn't stop staring at my father, mother, sisters, brother, grandmother. To them, we'd never been separated, but I thought I'd never see them again. I clung to each of my loved ones, tearful, shaking. No wonder they thought I'd gone insane—I was a wreck.

"We have to cancel the wedding."

"Cancel the wedding?" Mama cried. "We have hundreds of guests coming, people have traveled from all over Europe!"

"You don't understand," I said, through gritted teeth. "Rasputin attacks tonight. All of you die. Every single one of you—except Alexei."

Alexei was hollowed eyed and gray. He'd barely spoken after hearing the horrific fate in store for him. I'd tried to lighten the blow, tried to tell him that in the end he'd saved me by refusing to give Rasputin the Charoite. But I knew that deep down *he* knew how much he'd already become Rasputin's puppet.

I said, "We need to arrest Oksana right now. She's one of them."

"Oksana?" Even Tatiana couldn't seem to grasp the reality of the situation. "She just dressed me this morning."

"And she's going to tear your arm off tonight!" I shouted. "They're everywhere, they're in the city, in the ballet, in the student organizations. You've hired them as waiters for the wedding! They've been planning this for months, years probably!"

But when Papa sent Kolya Derevenko and a half-dozen guards to capture Oksana, she was nowhere to be found. She'd disappeared from the palace.

So had the musicians and half the waitstaff. We hunted for them through St. Petersburg. All had vanished without a trace.

"This isn't right. This isn't what happened before ..." I bit at my nails, trying to understand.

It had to be Rasputin. His spirit came back with me. And maybe, maybe ... found the Rasputin of the past.

He knew. He knew everything I knew because he'd also seen the future.

And worse, he knew about the cache of Charoite. I was furious at myself for letting him rip from my mind what I'd kept hidden all the time he was torturing us down in the vault.

That's when it hit me.

Rasputin might not attack tonight at all. He knew he'd lost all the advantage of surprise.

He might be headed somewhere else entirely ... straight to the Lorne Mountain.

"Send a rider to Damien," I gasped. "Tell him the parade's cancelled, and the wedding. Tell him to stay exactly where he is."

"I'll find him," Kolya said.

Kolya left immediately, but Papa wasn't about to let me start barking orders at everybody else.

We'd all assembled in Papa's study, Nikolasha making the space feel particularly crowded as he loomed by the fireplace. The air was hot and stuffy, overly perfumed by the vase of white roses the florists had deposited that morning.

Papa had summoned Aunt Xenia and Sandro, and Aunt Olga as well. I wished he hadn't—all the conflicting opinions were putting us in deadlock. Time was slipping past.

"What do you mean it's not what happened before?" Papa demanded.

I explained to him about Rasputin, how we'd battled in my room and how he'd torn away the information before I even understood what was happening.

"There's a massive cache of Charoite in the mountain," I said. "And now he knows exactly where it is. He saw it in my mind."

"We've got guards on the mountain."

"Not nearly enough! I'm trying to tell you, the vampyrs are monstrous, and Rasputin is past anything you can imagine. He's already consumed the Charoite he stole before, we can't do anything to stop that. It's going to take everything we have to keep him from getting more. They slaughtered us at the wedding. It wasn't even a fight."

"Then we need to stay right where we are," Xenia said. "We need to fortify the palace."

"But is he coming here or not?" Sandro said.

"I ... I don't know."

I couldn't be sure anymore. But I could guess.

"I think he'll go to the mountain," I said firmly. "He's obsessed with the Charoite. If we load up the train with soldiers, we can beat him there."

"We're not going anywhere," Xenia said. "It's madness to leave our fortress and split our soldiers."

"It would take time to assemble an army to meet them on open ground," Papa said. "Weeks, months even. We'd have to call the soldiers back from the front. It would be disastrous."

"We have to go now! If he gets to that mountain before us and digs out the cache, he could give it to every single vampyr. They'd be ..."

"Invincible," Nikolasha said.

He'd been quieter than I expected, listening, taking it all in.

"I've got a small amount of Charoite left—"

"No!" I interrupted. "We're not using that. We never should have used it."

"It's not for *you* to tell us what we will and won't be doing," Xenia snapped. "They didn't crown you Tsar in your supposed future, did they?"

"That's not what she's saying," Aunt Olga tried to interject, but Xenia swept right past her. Xenia was full of hectic energy, pacing the room. Sandro sat behind Papa's desk, smoking. He'd also been quiet, probably because he was forming his own plans for what he'd do with his brothers once he was away from here. Sandro was a Mikhailovich first, everything else second.

My sisters clustered together on the sofa with Grandma Minnie, Mama, and Aunt Olga on the chaise. Alexei sat a little way off in the chair he always used when observing Papa at work.

My father stood, taller than everyone because Nikolasha was leaning. I faced him, feeling strangely like a witness with those seated as jurors.

"The city garrison isn't enough," Papa said. "Especially not if they've been infiltrated by vampyrs. And you don't even know if that's where he's going."

"We'll take Damien's unit. With them and us, a train-full of garrison soldiers and the palace guards ..."

It might be enough. We weren't going to be drunk and frozen by an ice storm this time.

"We ought to include Axel's family in this—Axel should be here right now," Ollie put in, indignant on the sofa. She should have been buttoning up her wedding dress at the moment, preparing for the ceremony.

Mama said, "This is a family matter."

"They can't know we lost the Charoite," Xenia asserted. "Or that Rasputin took it."

Ollie made a strange expression like she'd swallowed a coin. I guessed she'd already told Axel the truth.

"And what about Damien?" Grandma Minnie asked quietly. "Do you intend to tell him the full story?"

I turned to her. "What do you mean?"

"Are you going to tell him about his father?"

It felt like the floor plunged a hundred feet.

I hadn't put that part of the timeline together. Damien's father died yesterday, but he hadn't heard the news yet. He would have learned it at the ball tonight.

I was going to have to tell him. I was going to have to see his devastation all over again.

And after he found out, the last thing on the planet he was going to want to do was help my family fight Rasputin.

The treacherous thought occurred not to tell him until afterward. But then, just as quickly, I knew I could never do that. I couldn't keep something so important from him, not for a day, not for an hour. He'd see it in my face.

Besides, all our closeness depended on the honesty and realness of what was between us. If I deceived him, it would damage our bond. It would weaken us.

We'd need every bit of our connection to defeat Rasputin again.

What a devil's bargain I'd received ...

Damien had sacrificed himself to kill Rasputin, to destroy the mine, and now Rasputin was still alive, and the mine was back in full operation. I had my family back but I'd reset everything we'd accomplished.

And my family wasn't exactly cooperating.

They couldn't grasp the full weight of what had happened because they hadn't lived it, hadn't seen it. They wanted to believe me but they didn't trust me, not fully. Not enough to do what had to be done.

"I'm going to tell Damien everything," I said to Grandma Minnie.

"You said the Cossacks abandoned us and declared independence." The ruffled skirt of Xenia's gown jostled the table with its vase of roses. She wouldn't sit still for a second, her pacing making me all too aware of time marching by while we argued. "We can't trust them."

"Yes, we can!" Deciding it was best to lay it all on the table, I added, "They'll want their independence in return."

"Absolutely not," Xenia barked, without even considering.

Nikolasha said, "How many of these creatures does Rasputin have? Maybe we don't need the Cossacks."

"I watched you fight off seven of them. You were ripped to shreds. None of you can understand what happened. We were slaughtered in a *moment*."

"All the more reason not to engage." Papa had his arms crossed over his chest, which I knew from experience was a very bad sign.

I loved my father, but one of his worse traits was that when he was frightened, unsure, or angry, he became more and more stubborn. He'd fixate on the idea that felt safe and cling to it like a life raft.

"We have no choice. We need them."

That was a mistake. Papa also hated being told he *had* to do something.

"We're not carving off a piece of this country for rebels and traitors."

"They're not traitors! They never wanted to be Rusyan."

"But they are!" Papa bellowed. "And I'm still Tsar, here and now. They'll follow my orders or they'll hang. And so will you."

"I'll hang?" I said coldly.

"*You'll follow my orders,*" Papa seethed.

In his mind, I was still a child. I was still where I'd been two years ago—inexperienced, ignorant, a screwup.

I'd come a million miles from there. And I wasn't going to be shoved back in that box.

"We're staying here in the palace," Papa said. "We'll call in the soldiers from the city garrison, bar the gates, prepare for an attack. A king doesn't leave his castle."

"But he—"

"I'M IN CHARGE!" Papa towered over me.

"The man in charge doesn't have to tell people he's in charge."

Furious, I swept my arm against the vase of roses. They arced through the air, the flowers spilling out.

I put out my hand and froze them overhead, an immobile river of flowers, water, and vase.

Bitterly angry, I swept my hand back again, returning everything to its original position on the table.

The silence thudded in my ears.

I hadn't even known I could do that.

I'd only meant to show them how my magic had grown—how *I'd* grown. I wasn't the person they knew before.

Deathly cold, my father said, "You think you're in charge because you've become powerful? You think you're stronger than me?"

He stood very close, looking down with no hint of my father in his eyes. I was speaking to the Tsar.

"No, Papa," I said.

"Put her in Maria's room." He jerked his head at Nikolasha. "Lock the door."

Nikolasha took my arm. He didn't grab me hard, but getting away from him would be no easy thing.

I couldn't believe it had come to this.

As he escorted me upstairs I said, "You know he's wrong about this. And you know what will happen ... you're the general, not him."

When Nikolasha didn't answer, when he continued leading me inexorably up the stairs I said, "Ask Stana. She knows Damien and I are supposed to kill Rasputin. It has to be us."

He opened the door to Maria's room and waited for me to step inside.

"I'll talk to him." And then, when I tried to argue, "*I will talk to him.* Olga's with us. Xenia won't want to give the Cossacks anything. She thinks she's speaking for the old Tsar ..."

He paused. His eyes flashed at me, his beard particularly wild.

"You scared him with what you did with that vase ... he couldn't do that. I couldn't."

"I've learned a few things."

"Hm." He regarded me, eyes narrow.

The scars weren't there anymore. I was back in my old body. But after a moment he said, "You look different."

Then he closed the door in my face.

Gods, I'd fucked that up.

I was in such a frenzy when I saw my family, overflowing with love because I'd missed them so much. I'd forgotten how godsdamn stubborn they were.

Well, I was stubborn too.

I made for the window, only to see two guards stationed outside.

They were seriously going to lock me in here.

I could get out, but I might have to hurt the guards—or get shot in the process. And I didn't need to escape—I needed them all to come with me.

Rasputin had probably gathered his entire force by now. He didn't have control of the trains, not back in this time. If we left at once, we could still beat them to the mountain. Even though half the day was already gone.

I was furious at how much time had slipped past. It was afternoon already —maybe late afternoon. Maria's room had no clock.

I was sure Nikolasha was on my side. He was an actual warrior, more than Papa. He'd led the full Rusyan force many times. He knew what a disaster it would be if Rasputin got his hands on enough Charoite to spread it across his whole army.

It was almost funny, in a sick sort of way—I didn't think the Rasputin of the future would have shared the Charoite. He was too obsessed with it, too miserly. He hadn't even given it to Katya, which I'm sure pissed her off. Unless she'd realized what it was doing to him ...

The Rasputin of the past was a different beast. I had to remember that— he didn't know how to time-walk because he hadn't drained it from my father, but he was also younger and healthier, less deteriorated by years of Charoite use. He'd be saturated with the full power of all the stones he'd just consumed.

And I was going to have to face him with a different Damien. A Damien who hadn't lost me and found me again—who hadn't spent two years missing me, loving me, forgiving me, moving past the death of his father, enough to be able to see that for all my family's flaws, Rasputin's rule was worse.

This Damien hadn't practiced with me. He maybe didn't even love me yet—

No.

I crushed that thought in my mind. He loved me. And I loved him, a long time before Ollie's wedding night. We just hadn't said it yet.

I knew it when we kissed—time froze around us both because we *already* loved each other. That moment didn't create our love, it happened because of it. We were two pieces that connected perfectly, creating a circuit of limitless power.

That was real, and even if it hadn't happened yet in this time, it would the moment I saw him. In Damien's mind he'd just been away at war. He was missing me, too. Longing for me.

I just had to get to him.

I'd wait two hours, no more, and then I was breaking out of this room.

TIME HAD NEVER PASSED SLOWER.

Sitting in Maria's room was particularly strange because it used to be my room, too.

When I moved out, Mama took down the frieze of butterflies and had the whole room painted. Everyone thought Maria would want pink because that had always been her unofficial color when we wore dresses that matched— purple for Ollie, green for Tatiana, pink for Maria, and blue for me.

Maria surprised us all by requesting green. And really, Tatiana wore black or gray most days—she'd become more dramatic in Denmark.

The memories came pouring back, the way they had when I'd first seen the palace again.

I could see the real room before me, but also the ghost of our childhood bedroom. Where the four-poster stood used to be our two camp beds, side by side. Maria's prettily scrolled dresser had taken the place of our small book-shelf with Maria's copy of *Little Women,* which was her favorite book, and *Pushkin's Fairytales,* which was mine.

Childhood is a land you leave once and never return.

What if I'd used the memory-keeper when I was a kid and been blasted back then?

Gods, what a nightmare that would be. I already felt out of place in my own body. It didn't match who I was in my mind. It no longer showed what I'd lived.

The lawn outside the window was darkening, the sun sinking.

I thought of Rasputin racing toward the mountain.

Every minute I waited in here, he got closer to his goal.

What was Damien doing? What was he thinking?

I hadn't even sent a proper note to him yet, explaining what had happened.

I didn't send anything with Kolya because I wanted to explain in person. I couldn't write this in a letter; no one would believe it.

I thought I'd be there myself in an hour ... I hadn't expected to be locked in here.

I'd told Damien to wait because if he'd continued on to the city with his men, they'd only have to turn around again and go back the other way. I was trying to save time!

What a joke. The whole day was slipping away, this precious gift I'd been given squandered because my family couldn't get along.

Who knows what my father was doing—he might have already called Damien back to protect the palace.

Or not, if Xenia had her way.

Gods, this was infuriating!

They'd put blinders on me, while every second Rasputin was moving his pieces into position.

They didn't trust me. They wouldn't follow me.

Would Damien?

What about after I told him his father was dead?

The light was failing, and so was my confidence.

Maybe we were only destined to defeat Rasputin in our time. This was a new time. Everything was changing.

A key turned in the lock.

I'd been pacing worse than Xenia. I stood still on the carpet.

Nikolasha came into the room, Tatiana behind him.

"What happened?"

I could already tell from the stiff set of Nikolasha's shoulders that the news wasn't good.

"They're still arguing. Xenia's got her back up about the Cossacks. Sandro's brought his brothers here—they want to check the teeth of all the palace guards. You know how this will go."

What he meant was that nothing happened quickly in our family. Decisions were argued over, agonized over, for days, weeks. Whatever was decided upon would be a chimera of the worst four ideas.

"Then I'm going to Damien."

"I know," Nikolasha said. "You can take my train."

Warmth for him washed over me, and for Tatiana, who rushed forward and wrapped her arms around me.

"We're going to try to convince the others. But either way, we're coming to join you."

I grinned at her. "I always said you were the smartest one."

"She finally admits it."

Tatiana smiled back at me, calm and assured and truly brilliant. I couldn't wait to see what she'd do with all the years she might have ahead of her.

"I sent the guards away," Nikolasha said. "Go out through the window. Kolya's got Barley waiting."

Barley! All the things I'd lost brought back again—this *was* a gift. I just had to figure out how to keep it.

"I love you," I said to Tatiana, hugging her once more. To Nikolasha I said, "I've seen your daughter. She's beautiful."

"You've seen Celine?" His eyes shone.

I clapped him on the shoulder. "You will now, too."

I went out through the window, running across the dark lawn.

Kolya was waiting on his black destrier, Barley cropping the night-sweet clover on the lawn. I rubbed my nose against hers.

Damien's saddle was on her back. I touched the tooled leather, pressed my face against it and inhaled, tears in my eyes.

I wished I could have worn the same green riding habit I was supposed to wear today, but that was in my room all covered in glass.

It didn't matter. I was making a new memory—an even better one.

I'd kiss Damien and tell him everything, and we'd work through it together because we could do anything together.

I whistled as I passed the tall stone mews.

Through the window burst the most beautiful sight I'd ever seen: Artemis, flying as swift and straight, no crook to her wing.

Katya hadn't gotten her hands on her. And I was determined she never would.

Artemis kept pace with the horses. *Where have you been all day?*

"I haven't seen you in a lot longer than that."

chapter 50

chapter 50
ACORN TO OAK

Kolya said Damien's regiment was camped an hour south of
Alexander Park. Last he'd seen, Xenia was still fighting with my
father about bringing the Cossacks onto the palace grounds.

"She's never thought they should be part of the imperial guard. I heard
her arguing about it once with the Grand Duke."

"It's better this way." I leaned forward in the saddle. "They'll come with
us instead."

The closer we got, the faster I rode. Though I'd just held my family in my
arms, I could hardly believe Damien would be there too. I watched him die,
incinerated before my eyes. My longing to see him alive drove me to ride like
fury, like the hounds of hell were snapping at my heels.

Barley's heart thundered against my legs. Sweat streamed off us both as
the moon rose high overhead, full and golden—the exact moon I saw the
night of Ollie's wedding. A chill crept across my skin, cold breath on the back
of my neck.

Storm clouds gathered southwest of the city, far off in the distance, where
the mountains lay.

He was going to the Charoite—I knew it like I knew my own mind.

I was going to Damien.

Kolya had that look on his face I was coming to know all too well: the look of someone trying to work out the brain-bending implications of time travel.

"Was I 'sposed to die tonight?"

"I don't know. I never saw." But then, feeling the strange compulsion of the oracle to tell all they know, I added, "They took out most of the guards and servants first. I don't think you'd have let that happen to us if you were still alive."

We topped a ridge, a low valley spread out below us. From the hollow rose the distant beat of drums and the smoke from the campfires flickering between the pines.

Damien.

I felt him surging in my veins, that connection that fueled us both. It was still there, still alive.

It had always been, from the moment we met.

Time is an ocean, not a line. No matter where you sail, you're on the same ocean.

We rode down to the camp. The horses heard me first, raising their heads from cropping the grass. Two sentries barred our way, calling out, "Who's there?"

I recognized Feo. Like an idiot, I cried out, "It's me, Anya!"

"Who?" He squinted in the dark, saber drawn.

He didn't know me. Of course he didn't—in his mind, we'd never met.

"It's Anastasia Nikoloevna. I need to speak to Damien—immediately."

Feo exchanged glances with the other guard, who muttered, "I don't think that's a good idea."

"He's expecting me."

The dark looks on their faces confused me—a mood I didn't understand.

"Fine," Feo said at last. "But the guard waits here. The bird, too."

I passed Kolya Barley's reins and slipped down. Artemis perched up on a pine where she could see most of the camp.

Feo's hostility was a slap. I was a stranger to him. None of the Cossacks knew me—all the weeks I'd spent in their village were lost and gone.

That realization hit me again and again as Feo led me through the camp. Every face I recognized showed nothing but confusion and suspicion. Damien's uncles stared at me with stony eyes.

The drums pounded on and on. The Cossack braves clustered around the main bonfire, drinking and singing. Their revelry carried an eerie edge—celebrating because they'd won the battle, but also mourning.

Everywhere I turned I saw faces pulled down in anguish, even while they drank, even while they laughed.

Chilled, I said to Feo, "Has someone died?"

He looked at me, fire reflecting in his eyes. "Many died."

"But who are they mourning?"

He moved so I could see the fire.

Taras Kaledin's armor hung suspended over the flames. It had been positioned as he wore it, so the fire took the shape of his body inside the blackened steel. His saddle likewise burned.

My throat was too thick to speak.

"A rider came an hour ago," Feo said.

He must have ridden all through the night to bring news to Damien.

It wasn't the Cossack way to weep and wail. Wild cheers swelled like surf and tankards clashed together. The warriors chanted a eulogy to carry Taras' soul to the unknown realms.

The bowl of stars overhead yawned like a chasm into which I might fall if I lost my grip on the ground.

Bitterness filled my mouth. I'd arrived in time to save my family but not Damien's.

I felt his pain, fresh and raw, and turned because I didn't need Feo to lead me anymore.

Damien's tent was unmistakable: the grass had died in a circle all around it. It was pitched away from the others against an oak tree, the leafy canopy spreading sixty feet across, blocking out the stars overhead.

I ran to him.

All strategy, all sense fled my mind. All I wanted was to see him.

I burst into the tent, then stopped.

Damien sat amongst the sprawling roots of the oak tree, an empty vodka bottle toppled on its side by his boot, another well on its way in his hand. His eyes were bloodshot, his face unshaven, his clothes in disarray. The tent reeked of liquor and blood, and something else ...

Sharp like kerosene. Tight as wire. Hot enough to bring sweat to my skin. Anger. Radiating out of him in dark waves. Burning in his eyes, vibrating under his skin.

"Didn't you send me word not to come?" he hissed. "I'm summoned and I'm dismissed. The Romanov dog."

I'd planned to throw myself in his arms. But he looked like he'd rip my head off given half a chance.

"It's not like that," I stammered. "I—"

"It's always like that. Why should today be any different?"

His face contorted. He covered it with a gloved hand to hide it. I felt the pain like a stab in my side. I ached to run to him but was sure he'd shove me off.

Out of the thousand things I wished I could say, I chose the one most true:

"I'd give anything to bring your father back."

His hands dropped to his sides, fingers digging into his thighs. His face was dark in the gloom of the tent, only one candle lit. The shadows leaped around us every time we moved.

"Don't make me laugh. We both know where your loyalties lie."

"No, you don't."

Something in my tone made him look me fully in the face for the first time. Our eyes locked in the way they always had, where information passed between us whether we wanted it to or not.

I saw the pain he was feeling, clawing at him, gnawing everywhere like it would eat him alive.

I didn't know what he saw in my face. It confused him enough that he said, "Why are you here?"

"Something happened to me. To us, actually. It will sound impossible—like madness, or lies."

I wished he hadn't been drinking. I wished it was any day but this one.

I'd been given time, but only a little of it. I didn't have weeks to practice with Damien like before—I had hours at most before Rasputin reached the mountain.

It felt as if the ground was sinking beneath me, as if the whole world had become slippery and unstable. I'd never learned the silver tongue of a courtier —I didn't know how to convince him.

All I could tell him was the truth.

"I traveled back in time. For you it's today, but for me it's two years in the past."

Damien stared at me, face granite.

"Two years ago on this day, Rasputin brought an army of vampyrs and attacked my family. He killed them all except for Alexei. He almost killed me."

A line appeared between Damien's eyebrows but I pressed on, talking faster and faster, trying to get it all out.

"He took over all of Rusya, and it was ... worse than you could ever imagine. He fed off the politicians. Turned them to his will. They hunted down his enemies, slaughtered them in mass executions. Anyone who opposed him was hanged or sent to slave camps to be worked to death." I swallowed hard. "I was sent to the mines. For over a year."

A muscle twitched at the edge of Damien's eye. He remained silent while I babbled on.

"Everything got worse and worse—the whole country was in his grip. All of Rusya froze. The harvests failed, the people were starving—"

"Because he had the Charoite," Damien said coldly.

"Yes," I admitted. "He consumed everything he stole from us. You were right. You were right about all of it."

That didn't soften him, but it did confuse him.

"I'm *right?*"

"It happens once in a while."

A spark passed between us, what might have been a smile if Damien wasn't so deeply sad.

"People suffered and people died," I said. "And you and I—"

I stopped, chest hitching too hard to speak. I couldn't tell if he believed me, I couldn't tell if he believed any of it. This Damien was different—he was younger, harder, leaner. He radiated an anger so furious and violent that I was afraid of him. There was no green in his eyes—only darkness.

The Damien I knew spent two years regretting losing me. This Damien was only just beginning to learn the lesson of loss.

Still, I told him the truth. The whole truth.

"You thought I was dead, but you never gave up hope. I escaped and you found me, you saved my life. And then you went with me to kill Rasputin. Even though ... even though ..."

Only now, seeing the darkness in Damien's eyes, the shadow that lay over him ... only now did I realize why he'd carried the same shadow as we prepared to meet Rasputin. He'd known. Somehow he'd known.

"You came with me even though you knew you wouldn't make it," I choked out. "We killed him, but I was blown back here, and so was a part of Rasputin. So he knows everything I know. He's not attacking the palace anymore because there's a cache of Charoite in the mine and he knows exactly where it is, down to the passage. He's going there now."

"And you want me to help you," Damien said, low and rough.

"I *need* you to help me."

He lurched to his feet, the second vodka bottle dropping and rolling away, the remaining liquid glugging out.

He loomed over me in the cramped tent. Anger and sorrow radiated like dark poison, seeping into my skin.

"You want me to clean up your mess."

"Help me fix the problem."

"The problem *you* created."

"Help me fix it anyway."

He hissed, "Maybe you're the real problem."

That hurt me. I closed my eyes, took a breath.

He could say what he wanted in anger. I knew the truth because I'd seen it in the future with my own eyes: I saw what he'd do for me.

You loved me then, and you love me now.

I said, "It isn't fair, but it's still right. Because if Rasputin gets into that mine, *everyone* suffers. Your people will suffer. I know that matters to you."

His hair hung over his face. His shoulders shook with all the things he wanted to shout at me.

He lifted his head, eyes burning into mine.

"If you knew me at all, you wouldn't be here right now. You'd know this is how I was feeling and you'd know you shouldn't come anywhere near me."

He stripped off his gloves. His bare hands looked black in the shadows.

"I do know you," I said. "And that's exactly why I'm here. You do what you think is right—even if you don't want to."

I knew it was true and so did he. Still he shouted, "Why should I save your father when he killed MINE?"

He turned, laying his bare palm against the trunk of the tree.

Almost instantly, black rot spread from his hand all the way down through the roots and up into the branches. The great old oak, veteran of hundreds of winters, withered and died in moments, its leaves shriveling and falling, hissing down the roof of the canvas tent.

I laid my hand on top of Damien's.

The pain flowed into me, wrenching, smothering, drowning. It screamed in my ears, it tore me apart.

Damien wasn't holding back his power. He was letting it out so it didn't eat him alive.

I let him do it. I took it from him, because the only way to ease his pain was to share it with him.

"How are you doing that?" His face was blank with shock.

"It's because I'm so happy to see you alive," I sobbed out. "I watched you die, Damien ... you can't understand what this means to me. It's making me fucking invincible."

He tried to pull his hand away, but I pressed it tighter against the tree, locking my fingers through his.

"It's okay. You can't hurt me anymore. You can touch me as much as you want."

I lifted up on tiptoes and tilted my mouth to his. I kissed him like we'd been apart for much too long and I'd missed him with all my heart. I kissed him like we were never supposed to leave each other's arms and never would again.

Warmth surged through us both, warmth and light and all the happiness I'd ever felt when I was with him in the past, in the present, and in the future.

Time was no line. It was an ocean, and no matter where you dove down deep, I fucking loved Damien.

I looked into his eyes. "You gave everything for me and I gave everything for you. That doesn't disappear. Time and space can't destroy it."

He pulled me against his chest, turning his face against my neck, breathing me in.

"I believe you."

Under our hands, the tree came alive again, warm bark and fresh green leaves. Life spread through its branches and down through its roots. Clover bloomed beneath our feet.

"Come with me," I said. "I want to show you something."

We walked out of the tent hand in hand.

Damien's men turned and stared.

As we walked through them, I greeted everyone I knew. And as I passed Adam fleecing some poor soldier who didn't know any better, I passed my hand over his dice and ruined his roll using the magic he taught me.

That gave Damien a jolt.

"How did you do that?"

"You brought me to your village. I came home with you, lived with you, married you."

"We were married?" His voice broke.

"Yes, Damien, my love," I took both his hands. We'd reached the fire. The dancing had stopped, all the Cossacks arrested by the sight of Damien's bare hands in mine. "We *were* married and we *are* married because I'm yours, and you're mine, and that bond can't be broken."

I called to his uncle with the balalaika across his knee.

"Ivash—why aren't you dancing the fire dance?"

Ivash rested his fingers on the strings. "He told us not to play it."

"But he'll dance it with me."

I looked at Damien, pleading, teasing. Asking him to do me this favor, and then many more.

Damien knew a lot of things I didn't, but only *I* knew how to make him feel happiness.

"I can't take away what's hurting you. But you can lose yourself in me."

We took our place by the fire. I laid the back of my hand against his.

He said he believed me, but I had to show him, truly show him, our connection. We didn't have time to practice and train together. All we had was this.

"Play the one Taras loved," I called to Ivash. "The one he danced with Larysa."

Damien's head turned sharply. His eyes met mine and he saw across time to the night we danced this dance together in his village ... on our wedding night.

His fingers brushed against mine.

"Can you really do this?"

"Yeah." I grinned. "But I've only won once, so I'm going to need your help."

chapter 5/

FIRE DANCE

DAMIEN

♪♪ *The Chain—Fleetwood Mac*

The music started, Myron's low drum and Ivash's fingers plucking against the balalaika.

All the dancers around the fire were male except for Anastasia. The energy was dark, rough, aggressive.

They wanted to hit her. They wanted to knock her out of the circle.

She'd called them by name as if she knew them, she'd used Adam's own magic against him. While she'd done it in her playful way that almost always disarmed, tonight she was up against a bitter wall.

They were angry we'd lost Taras. And they knew she was the princess.

My father's armor stood on the wooden scaffold over the fire as if he floated in the smoke. When his helmet filled with flame it flickered like a face. We passed through his shadow.

I'd been so filled with rage I could have killed the world between my hands.

Then Anastasia touched me and I witnessed a miracle.

You can't feel hate in the face of a miracle.

When the hate was gone, she filled me with her love.

It flushed through every part of me. It changed me.

The story she told me was beyond the wildest fairytale. Yet she continued to work miracles before my eyes. She was doing it right now, dancing a flawless fucking fire dance.

She held my bare hands, she spun and whipped through the smoke and flame. Her hair threw sparks into the night in a whirlwind around her.

"How are you doing this, how are you touching me?"

"*We're* doing it," she said, all the fire in her eyes. "I *need* you to love me. I *need* you to charge me up."

She was tight like a spindle, her bright hair whirling around her like the shadow of her own soul. She was animal, spirit, human.

She glowed in the fire, she smiled so bright that while I still couldn't smile myself, for the first time I wanted to. I could feel the ice shifting inside me, the first cracking of the weight that crushed me from all sides.

I danced with her. The music went in my ears, that beat that was the heartbeat of some of the happiest memories of my life. My father played it when he was most triumphant. He played it for my mother—he thought she was somewhere smiling with him.

I felt a ghost of the way I'd always felt when he played it—happiness mixing with sadness like ink in water.

My father didn't fear death. He thought we'd always be connected.

Anastasia looked up at me. "I don't know where we go when we die, but love is a magnet and it brought me here to you."

She pulled me through the circle, swift like a river, clean like rain.

"Look how powerful we are together ..."

I couldn't deny the way I felt when our hands locked together. It was fucking electric. No pleasure I'd known in all my life compared to touching the bare skin of someone I loved.

The ice was cracking, I was coming back to myself.

Anastasia always reminded me who I was, because she really did know me. She knew what mattered to me most.

I hadn't lost my sorrow for my father but instead of a weight of rock that could crush me, it was turning to a hammer in my hand. I could use this anger.

Anastasia said, "Remember the first time we met. Remember that feeling we had, how we always knew when we were close. That's our connection, it's always been there. Remember how it felt. There's a bond between us and it's stronger than you can imagine."

I looked into her eyes and went from believing to knowing.

Just the easing of my anger against her was enacting a change in both of us. I could feel us reconnecting, I could feel us linking up.

Before she'd come, my body ached. Everything was misery, all the worst feelings screaming in my ears. I was trapped, drowning in despair, until she opened a door.

She whispered, "My magic appeared when I was about to meet you. There is no time—what we were to each other and what we'll ever be are one and the same to the universe. I loved you because I was always going to love you. That's what we were made to do."

We danced faster and harder than I could have dreamed of dancing with her, as perfectly as if we'd done it a hundred times.

My cousin Adam hit her hard from behind, but she shrugged it off like it was nothing, didn't miss a step. She slipped by Feo like an eel, her eyes locked on mine.

Her confidence was unshakable, it made her powerful. And it was infecting me, too.

But I was afraid—afraid of letting her down.

"I don't have time to learn how to do this with you. You've had two years ... I can't get there in time."

She smiled at me brighter than the sun, fingers locked in mine.

"You don't have to be strong enough—I just need you to trust me."

To prove it, she danced faster than ever. We whirled through the circle, her hair alive and her eyes made of flame. Everyone could see that she might be a princess, but she was also something more.

I didn't know if she was witch or goddess. All I knew was I wanted her, and I might finally have a chance of getting her.

"I'll help you," I said.

It would probably get me killed all over again. I didn't care.

She beamed at me so bright I was blinded.

"I can't wait to earn back all the love that I had from you."

"I do love you!" I said disgruntled.

She grinned. "Not as much as you will."

Dancers had fallen out all around us. The circle contracted, pulling us closer to the fire. Sweat streamed down our bodies. Anastasia's skin burned like copper, her arms streaked with soot.

The fire leaped so high it was more like a pillar than a bonfire. My father's armor was almost completely consumed, the steel beginning to bubble and crack.

The remaining braves danced with wild ferocity, howling, shouting. Those that had fallen out bellowed and beat at their drums. Their anger had a shape like the shadows.

Anastasia rode the dark wave. She was flawless; nothing could knock her from the pattern. And because she was flawless, so was I—all we had to do was stay in step.

There's more than one way to carry someone—and we all need it sometimes. That night, when my heart was broken and my mind was lost, Anastasia came to find me. She lifted me up and carried me with her until I felt like myself again.

As we finished our final circuit, the wooden scaffold finally burned through, my father's armor sinking down into the heart of the fire. The braves raised their rifles, pointed them at the night sky, and fired as one.

Anastasia and I stood still, watching the rush of flaming embers that soared upward, thrown up to the sky as the armor fell down.

COSSACKS ARE great believers in omens.

If your left hand itches, you'll have to pay someone money. Make a wish if you stand between two people of the same name. Never kiss over a threshold. Don't give an even number of flowers to a woman you love.

If you believe in that sort of thing, the arrival of a redheaded princess who wins the fire dance on the eve of the Firebird's death seems significant. Some of the soldiers even swore that when the armor dropped, the embers that rose formed the shape of a phoenix.

All I saw were a thousand sparks floating up into the sky, mixing with the stars until I couldn't tell one from another.

Anastasia's fingers linked through mine.

I was learning how comforting that could feel.

TWO HOURS PAST MIDNIGHT, my regiment was crammed on Nikolasha's train, speeding southwest to the final terminus.

Kolya slept against the window with his cap over his face. My uncle Evo played a game of chess against Petro. Anastasia watched them with more interest than the slow-moving match seemed to deserve.

Petro lost his bishop to Evo, and Evo smirked with triumph. A moment later Petro put him in check. He'd sacrificed the bishop to draw Evo in.

Anastasia frowned.

"What is it?"

"That's what happened last time, but the moves were different."

"What last time?"

"When we—never mind."

I saw her discomfort and realized this must have happened before, or some version of this. She'd had conversations with me I wasn't really a part of, experiences I didn't know.

She looked like herself but she was different, too. There was a sadness in her now. A seriousness. She still had her spirit, but she wasn't so careless. She'd grown up.

I took her hand. I couldn't get over how I could pull off my glove and lock my fingers in hers. Every single time, it charged me up.

"Tell me what's bothering you."

She touched the chess pieces, lined up in order of how they'd been lost. She turned the bishop in her fingers.

"In the fight at the palace, Rasputin lost Katya. He sent her against you, and you killed her."

"He sacrificed his queen."

"No," Anastasia said softly. "He already lost his queen a long time ago ... That's why he can't win."

"Then what's wrong?"

She looked up at me, tears slipping down her face. "I lost you, too."

She gripped the bishop in her hand. "I'm not sacrificing you, not again. And I *don't* want you to sacrifice yourself—what good is a life on the other side without you? It's all or nothing this time. Whatever happens, we have to stay together."

"We will."

"No, *promise me!*" She set the bishop down to take both my hands in hers. "We stay together no matter what."

"I promise you. I won't leave your side."

"Good." She let out her breath, shoulders sinking.

Artemis appeared outside the window, cutting through the slipstream of the train like a silver fish.

Anastasia pulled down the sash and the gyrfalcon darted inside, her feathers cold and smelling of pine.

Her clicks and cries meant nothing to the rest of us. Still, Petro, Evo, and I listened as eagerly as Anastasia.

"You brilliant bird." She nuzzled Artemis. "She found them."

"How many are there?" Evo said.

"More than us. And they're almost at the mountain."

chapter 52

THE TRUTH IS A BLADE

ANASTASIA

The Lorne Mountain jutted up in the sky, steep, black, and barren. All around its peak swirled swollen purplish clouds, jagged with lightning.

At its base, Rasputin's army had already overwhelmed the soldiers guarding the supply line. Howls and screams rose up in the darkness, lit by blossoms of fire.

The Cossack horses rode over the ridge with a thunder of hooves.

Damien and I rode the crest of the wave, Artemis overhead. Damien wore his father's wolfskin cloak, his head and hands bare. His rifle was strapped to his back, saber in hand. I had only my magic and a borrowed mare, because Barley was no warhorse.

We galloped down the hill, the Cossacks sending up an unholy din of whoops and shrieks, brandishing their swords and the long spears that jutted ahead of their horses like lances.

As we neared the battle, Evo sheared off along with Kristoff, Adam, and twenty other men. Their goal was the deepest tunnels of the mountain where they'd clear out any miners and set their charges—but all the fighting was in the way.

The rest of our army smashed into Rasputin's like two trains colliding. There was a great wrenching crash, then we were surrounded by the madness of the melee.

The fighting was illuminated in bursts by the balls of fire hurled by the pyromancers, by muzzle flashes and jolts of electricity. In the glare, I saw Rasputin's host—twice as large as before and twice as monstrous.

The creatures he'd spirited into St. Petersburg were those that looked mostly human. Here he'd brought beasts with the head of a bull and the body of a man, monsters with rows of teeth and leathery wings, and a woman who looked half snake. His werewolves were fully transformed, moonlight pouring down on their heads. His vampyrs mounted sleek black Andalusians.

The Cossacks were the fiercest fighters I'd ever seen—they reared on their horses, hacking, cutting, slashing on all sides. Horse and rider were one creature, their mounts kicking and trampling, charging with their shoulders and turning to shield their riders.

The Cossacks used their magic, their swords, and their guns interchangeably, an onslaught so vicious and unpredictable that Rasputin's monsters were cut down with horrible shrieks and gouts of stinking black blood.

The snake woman got her tail wrapped 'round Ivash's body, venom dripping from her teeth. Damien charged past, lopping off her head with a single stroke.

He wheeled his horse, staying close by my side. I threw a blast of fire in the face of a vampyr who swung his sword at Damien's back.

I flung fire with both hands, the reins of my borrowed horse wrapped around my arm. Artemis dove from the sky again and again, slashing and blinding with her talons.

No one could match the horsemanship of the Cossacks, but the vampyrs rode fast as wraiths and they had no care for their horses. They rode their mounts straight into the Cossacks and leaped from their saddles, bearing the braves to the ground and tearing out their throats.

The monsters could see in the dark. They were stronger than men, many times stronger. The Cossacks began to fall.

A high howl split the night, then many more.

Wolves came swarming out of the Frost Forest, hundreds of them, with the great pale king wolf at their head.

The werewolves in the battle sent up a wild baying. The Timberwolves howled in response. The king wolf let out a roar that seemed to shake the mountain.

The beasts leaped on the Cossack horses, ripping, tearing, dragging them down. The horses screamed in terror but didn't flee, the Cossacks slashing and hacking at the wolves that bit and snapped from all sides.

I saw Katya on the back of a black mare, head thrown back, laughing wildly as she cut down soldiers left and right. But I still hadn't found Rasputin.

"Where is he?" I shouted to Damien.

He jerked his head up the winding cutback to the mouth of the mountain cave.

Gods, I hoped he was wrong. We were too late if Rasputin was already inside.

The king wolf rampaged through the Cossacks, a terrier in a rat pit, seizing horses by the throat, dealing death with each swipe of his claws. His white mane was drenched in blood, his yellow eyes glowing in the blasts of fire.

Damien seized the shaft of a spear and wrenched it from the chest of a fallen vampyr. I grabbed his bare hand and squeezed it tight.

"Together," I said.

We galloped for the king wolf, the spear in Damien's right hand. Leaning forward on my borrowed horse, I touched Hercules' surging shoulder and poured my power into all of us, horses and riders.

The battle slowed, not completely, but to half the speed. The shouts and screams distorted, low and drawn out. A bullet whipped past my face, sluggish enough to see.

The king wolf leaped on a Cossack soldier, bringing horse and rider to the ground. He tore the man apart then turned, snarling.

Damien rose in his stirrups, spear in hand. As the wolf lunged, mouth agape, Damien thrust the spear down its throat. The king wolf rolled over and over on the ground, choking, thrashing, until finally it stilled.

Damien turned to me, face dark and eyes alight as the dry grass all across the battlefield began to burn.

"Do that again."

Side by side we fought, with fire and sword and magic. I warped the fabric of time, slowing it when monsters attacked, speeding it when Damien had his hands around their throats. We cut our way through the battle, making for the mountain path.

The Cossacks fought like demons, disciplined, trained, coordinated.

We were outnumbered and every one of the vampyrs had the strength of three men. Still, we might have beaten them.

Until Rasputin came down the mountain carrying a chunk of Charoite as large as a Faberge egg.

He cradled it in his hands, a single stone larger than any I'd seen. It pulsed like a heartbeat, swirls of violet light flickering and slithering inside.

When he reached the base of the mountain, he held the stone high overhead.

The clouds swirled faster around the mountain peak. Lightning crashed, blasting the rock. A great rumble shook the ground beneath our feet.

"STOP HIM!" Damien bellowed.

Too late.

Rasputin's body shook as the power of the Charoite flowed down his arms. The wind whipped his hair, the sleeves of his robe flapping like wings. His open eyes filled with purple fire.

Katya let out a wild laugh, cutting through the Cossacks like a reaper with a scythe, her hair streaming back, her eyes almost as mad as Rasputin's.

He sucked in every last drop until the crystal went dark. Then he tossed it aside.

He seemed to have grown. He loomed over the battlefield, throbbing with so much power that I could taste it in my mouth, feel it in the back of my teeth. No fire shone on him—he was composed of darkness, sucking in every bit of the light. Only his eyes blazed, and the silver raven's skull that hung 'round his neck, glinting like ice.

Damien's uncle Feo rushed at him, saber raised.

Rasputin stretched out his hand and blasted Feo and twenty other soldiers into bits. Everyone in front of him, Cossack, vampyr, werewolf, was flung backward, their bodies bent and broken.

I saw Petro look at Symon, their faces blanched with fear. Yet they gripped their swords and urged their horses forward.

"NO!" Damien shouted as Rasputin raised his hand.

Damien's uncle, cousin, and a dozen others were blasted into nothingness.

Rasputin's power was sickening, overwhelming. It throbbed in our ears, it gripped our hearts. The clouds swirled overhead, that bitter cold smothering the fire on the field as snow began to fall.

I looked at Damien. He was covered in blood and soot, ice catching in his hair.

I thought I'd see fear, I thought I'd see the hope fade from his eyes.

All I saw was his love for me as he grabbed me and kissed me hard.

"Thank you," he said. "For every minute I had with you."

Hand in hand, we turned to face our doom.

High on the hill came the sound of hooves once more.

Nikolasha galloped over the ridge with Dimitri Pavlovich, Alexei, and my father. The army poured down the hill, palace and city guards, and a small pack of soldiers wearing the Danish cross. Amongst them, I saw Prince Axel and my own sisters, Ollie on horseback with a saber in her hand, Tatiana with bow already strung. Even Sandro had come with four of his brothers.

My heart swelled. I shouted along with the Cossack soldiers, who resumed fighting as if the battle had only just begun. Nikolasha and my father surged forward, blazing through the bloodshed like twin comets.

Papa rode to meet Rasputin and Rasputin ran to meet him. Rasputin swept his hand and my father's horse crumpled beneath him, pitching forward. Papa leaped from its back, crashing to the ground, rolling over, up again in a moment. Rasputin slammed into him and they grappled.

It was a clash of giants, Rasputin swelled to enormous size, my father as terrible as I'd ever seen him. Papa twisted time, moving so fast I could hardly follow. His blows barely registered against the seething mass of power that was Rasputin.

Katya charged at Nikolasha, splitting him away from Papa, forcing him to turn and face her. She cut him across the face with her sword and Nikolasha swung a blow that would have taken her head off her shoulders had she not lain back on her horse and slipped beneath the blade.

I fought my way toward them. The battle was twice as chaotic as before, the press of soldiers and monsters so tight I would have been crushed without Damien next to me, cutting a path.

I could see my father just twenty feet away but couldn't get to him, blocked by cannon blasts and explosions of fire. I could only watch as Rasputin absorbed blow after blow that should have killed him.

Papa was using every ounce of his ability, but it wasn't enough. Rasputin swelled with Charoite like a blood-filled tick. It seeped from his skin, it crackled in the air.

Rasputin seized a handful of my father's hair and wrenched back his head.

Nikolasha wheeled his horse, abandoning his fight with Katya, racing for Papa. Rasputin flung him aside with a sweep of his hand, Nikolasha crashing down with his horse on top of him.

Rasputin sunk his teeth into Papa's neck. This time I could see that he was draining more than blood. Whatever was in my father flowed into Rasputin like wisps of silver smoke. He'd be able to time-walk like before—it was all happening again.

Papa withered in Rasputin's hands, his body shriveling, his hair turning white. He went limp and Rasputin flung him away, mouth dark with blood.

I jumped down from my horse and ran to my father, ducking through the churning gauntlet of swords and hooves, setting fire to some nameless slavering beast that leaped at me.

I fell on Papa's chest, grabbed his face, turned it to me.

His eyes were open, his face aged a hundred years. Blood ran from his mouth down his beard. I dabbed his lips with my sleeve, blind with tears.

"Anastasia ..." he croaked. I pressed my palm against the wound on his neck, thinking I could save him. I'd saved the flowers, saved the tree. "We should have come before ..."

I was trying to reverse what had happened, wind back time. But what I'd done with the flowers was a party trick, and saving the oak tree was fanning a flame still burning. My father's embers had already gone cold. Rasputin stole more than his blood—he took his magic.

"It doesn't matter, Papa," I choked. "You came to help in the end."

Something cold and hard pressed against my palm. Papa closed my hand around it.

"Take care of your mother ..."

His eyes were still open, still looking at me, but my father was gone.

I opened my hand.

On my palm sat his ring.

I stared at it, unable to make thoughts.

"Anastasia!"

Damien slashed at a vampyr that would have clawed my head off if he hadn't been standing guard behind me.

It wasn't the vampyr he was worried about. Rasputin strode across the field, blasting apart anyone who stood between us.

I slipped the ring on my finger. There was nowhere else to put it.

Katya heard Damien's shout and wheeled her horse. The fixation that came over her was electric. She rode at him like a spear, head down, fangs glinting.

"KATYA, NO!"

Rasputin blocked her way.

"The Charoite first!"

She pulled up, furious, the temptation to disobey burning in her face.

Doubtless Rasputin had told her not to fight Damien, but almost just as certain, she thought she could beat him. I could see it—the determination to prove what she could do. She gazed after Damien, pulling back so hard on her horse that her mare screamed and reared.

But the Charoite called to her, too. This Rasputin, whatever he was—some mix of present and future—was finally willing to share it with her.

Katya turned her horse, racing up the mountain path.

Damien watched her go. He stayed right where he was beside me.

The ground cleared around us. No one wanted to be in Rasputin's path, not even his own monsters.

His power was pressure on my chest, metal in my mouth, howling in my ears. I wondered if he would simply raise his hand and shred us to atoms.

I gripped Damien's hand, the only thing that gave me comfort, the only thing that kept me whole.

Wherever we were going, we were going there together.

He felt my father's ring pressed between his fingers.

We could drown in snarls and screams, the freezing chill, all the blood in the air. Every man that died around us was a stone that dragged me down. It was my fault ... my fault ...

Damien murmured, "You're their princess, Anastasia. They need you— save them."

I could hear in his voice he really believed I could. Even with Rasputin standing there in front of us, in all his power, in all his might, Damien still believed in me.

I said, "We'll do it together."

Rasputin laughed, low and mocking.

"What are you going to do now, little one? You have no wall of fire, no bombs, no surprises. There is no victory over me, it was an accident."

I shook my head.

"I don't believe in accidents."

That made him angry, because just as much as me, he had to believe fate was on his side, right was on his side.

"You and that Cossack *fell* into beating me, only at the cost of blowing yourselves up. I spent centuries preparing for this moment, you've been prac- ticing a few years. You're not ready to face me. You'll never be ready to face me. Destiny is with me—that's why I have another chance."

I linked my fingers tighter with my love.

"His name is Damien. And we could face you forward or backward in

631

time, an infinite number of times—you'll still never win. Because you'll make the same mistake you've always made."

He laughed, harsh and bitter.

"Your family were puppets dancing on my strings. *You* couldn't do what I wanted fast enough. The only mistakes were yours."

"Maybe. But despite all your grand schemes and your ideology and everything you claim to be, you'll always put yourself first. That's why you'll never be a leader. People only serve you in fear while your kingdom crumbles beneath you."

"Whose kingdom is crumbling now?" He put out his hand and blasted apart a whole flank of soldiers, Sandro and his brilliant and ferocious brothers amongst them. "Look at what you've done. Look at everyone you love falling around you." He thrust his hand to the right and slaughtered a dozen more. "I don't want to lead your people ... I want to destroy them."

He cut them down but he didn't kill Damien and me. I think in his heart, he wasn't certain he could.

Every man that fell was a weight on my soul. I couldn't save them ... I could only make sure their sacrifice wasn't wasted.

I said, "You've already done it again, and you don't even realize it."

The ground heaved beneath our feet, hard enough to knock us all off balance. This was not the usual groans and shifts of the mountain. This time, we were burying its heart.

The explosions rocketed through the caverns one after another in a chain. Those bitter, cold, backbreaking tunnels where men had sweat and died became the chink in the armor to deliver our killing blow.

The dynamite went off and the mountain collapsed, a million tons of rock crashing down. Rasputin turned, shock and fury blasting from his body like the force of the collapse itself, a wave of power that hit us like a blow, knocking us back. Still I held on to Damien's hand.

"You hear that?" Damien said to Rasputin, cold as a knife between the ribs. "That was you sacrificing your daughter again."

With a howl that wrenched his face into something unrecognizable, Rasputin leaped at us.

He had all his power, all his speed, all the force he'd drained from my father, but there was one of him and two of us. We locked together, Rasputin's hands around my throat, Damien's hands around his, our skulls slamming together like a cannon blast.

I fell down a tunnel a hundred miles long into the darkness of Rasputin's mind. There the real battle began.

It was him against me, in a space with no reality—only what each of us created from the darkest thoughts of our minds.

Tatiana floated up before my eyes, her arm a bloodied stump, her face cold as death. She whispered, "We all died because of you ..."

Maria appeared beside her, a spear through her chest. "We always die ... there's nothing you can do ..."

Ollie, with her throat torn out, blood all down her wedding dress, "You're not strong enough. Not smart enough. You were never supposed to lead, it should have been Alexei ..."

My father appeared before me, as dead and drained as he was here and now in the present, his throat a dark hole, his eyes empty ice. "You were never what I wanted. Someone stronger should have gotten my power ... You disappoint me."

The specters of my family surrounded me, authentic to the last detail.

But that wasn't what Papa said to me as he died.

He gave me his ring.

Rasputin's visions couldn't hurt me because they weren't real.

I'd already felt the guilt, the pain, the shame over my mistakes and what they cost my family. That's all I thought about in the cotton mill, in the mine. I suffered for my mistakes. I was baptized in fire.

I wasn't afraid of my worst memories. You don't forget what changes you—you shouldn't.

"Is that all you have?" I said into the emptiness of Rasputin's mind.

With a howl, he threw all my fears at me, everything I hated—insects, chaotic noise, my own teeth pulled out of my head ... it was nothing compared to what I'd already felt in the real world because of him. He broke my body but he made my mind strong.

I took it all, knowing it couldn't hurt me unless I let it.

Then I hit him again, relentless like a boxer, punching every place I knew he was weak.

I shouted it at him while he threw everything he had at me, fire and ice, broken glass and knives.

"The reason you lose is because you can only think like a power-hungry maniac. It never crossed your mind that we would possibly destroy the Charoite instead of using it for ourselves. In all your planning, all your strategy, you couldn't think like a decent person for one second."

After we'd journeyed through time, when our minds were blasted wide open, he stole the secret of the Charoite from me. But I saw his secrets, too.

"I saw inside your mind," I shouted. "I saw your memories. You realized you could do magic and you wanted to learn, no matter how dangerous it was for your wife and daughter. You visited the humans again and again and that's how they found you. You can blame the Romanovs for hundreds of years all you want, but if you hadn't lied to Natalya, you never would have lost her."

Rasputin shrieked at the sound of his wife's name, the very foundations of his mind shaking, pillars cracking, pieces falling down.

I hit him with the thing I knew would break him apart:

I played his memory-keeper.

All of it.

I showed Katya on her birthday, her joy at the cake Natalya made, the happiness of the little family as they sat down to eat it together.

Natalya was so beautiful it could break your heart. She sat on Rasputin's lap and ran her fingers through his hair. She murmured in his ear to never cut it because she loved it so much.

Katya had just turned six. Rasputin gave her the carved whale he'd made for her, and her face lit up like the fire in the hearth.

She brought out her own tiny carving, so rough and misshapen it was impossible to tell what she meant it to be.

She looked up into her father's face with all her love and trust.

Do you think I'll ever be as good as you?

And the Rasputin of memory, young, handsome, happy, looked back in her eyes and said, *You'll be better.*

I stood inside the memory, whispering in Rasputin's ear.

"During your rule I asked myself time and again, why would anyone want to be the emperor of desolation? ...Because they hate themself. That's what makes them hate everyone else ... I already knew you were weak before I met you here, because I saw what you did when you thought you'd won, when you could have done anything ... Your palace was a ruin because you're a ruin."

When Rasputin told me his lies, the twisted version of his own history, he told me a story that aligned with my own experiences. He made me think we were alike to manipulate me.

But the truth was, we *were* alike.

He was my own worst impulses, and I was his.

I whispered, "I know you. I know your strengths, I know your weaknesses. You were lying to me ... but we *were* friends. I've been in your mind. I know how to hurt you."

The truth is a blade that only cuts a liar.

And the most dangerous lies are the ones you tell yourself.

I ran through every part of his memories of his wife and daughter and his own fucking failures ... I tore through them and dragged them all up to the light. I dug and dug and dug where I knew it was painful, ripping it all up faster than he could bear, faster than he could pack it away, howling, only scattering it worse.

I blasted through the parts of him he couldn't fix because he didn't have control of those parts of his mind. He just stuffed them down and locked them away. I'd seen it in his head—the places he wouldn't discuss, the things he hid even from himself.

"You know my weaknesses," I said to him. "But so do I. Yours are going to surprise you."

I ripped apart every piece of his mind that was weakest: his arrogance, his ambition, his own selfish desires always dressed up as doing it for his wife, his child, his own fucking daughter who was with him the whole time, still alive, but sacrificed on the altar of revenge.

"Your quest for power *always* comes at the cost of the people you love the most. They die, and you continue to seek power because you don't love anybody more than you love yourself. You're here alone but I'm not."

There was nothing for him to say. Nothing for him to do. It was simply a mirror held up in front of his face ... and the truth broke him.

I ripped apart Rasputin's mind while Damien drained the life from him, bare hands locked around his face.

I saw Damien, his eyes completely black, a halo of darkness all around as he sucked in every bit of what kept Rasputin alive. Rasputin's body tried to heal again and again with all the tenacity of vampyr, his hair going white and black and white again, his face withering, regenerating, and shriveling away.

No vampyr could match the god of death. Damien had become the most powerful and extreme version of himself, and for the first time, I wasn't afraid. He was exactly what I needed him to be when I needed him most.

All the world went dark, a deeper midnight than any that had passed. The swirling storm that raged overhead gave no light at all, not even in its crashes of thunder. Lightning flared black as the pits of hell as Damien unleashed the full force of all his rage and sorrow.

I held time steady all around us, keeping the battle frozen in place so no bullets could hit us, no swords, no magic, nothing until Rasputin was dead.

Still, that purple light blazed in Rasputin's eyes, too furious to die. His withered corpse croaked at me, "We are the same. You want revenge."

The silver raven's skull rested on his breast. I thought of my own memory-keeper and what I should store in it as a talisman to myself.

"This isn't for me. I've seen the future ... my people will never know the suffering of your reign."

I stabbed him through the heart with the raven's beak.

Damien took the last of his life, Rasputin's empty body falling to the ground. I passed my hands over his corpse so it rotted away in an instant, leaving only his blackened bones.

He wasn't a monster—he was just a man after all.

chapter 53
SUNRISE

DAMIEN

Anastasia rose on the bloodied field and the first rays of the sunrise broke over the mountaintop behind her. The sun shone in her brilliant hair, setting her face ablaze.

The fur shriveled on the werewolves and the remaining vampyrs cringed before its brightness. Most of the Timberwolves fled when the king wolf fell —the few remaining ran back into the Frost Forest, and with them, several of the strangest of Rasputin's monstrous followers.

The battle died with Rasputin. The body of the Tsar lay on the ground. Everyone saw the dazzle of sunlight off his golden ring on Anastasia's hand.

Alexei was the first to come forward. His white suit was filthy with soot and blood, his face worse. Those bright blue eyes and a flash of teeth were all that showed when he smiled. The battle seemed to have enlivened him where nothing else could.

He laid down his sword to kneel and take his sister's hand, kissing her ring for all to see.

Nikolasha staggered up, bleeding from a hundred wounds, missing an eye, but still alive.

He came forward, too, and swore his oath.

Anastasia glowed in the rising sun, lit up like fire. It was a new dawn, and there was no question who should lead the day.

"Are you going back to St. Petersburg?" I asked her.

"Not until we burn the armor. Send their souls up to the stars."

I looked at her a long time without speaking.

"What?" She smiled. "Do I look strange?"

"You look like my best friend."

I linked my fingers through hers. She'd changed, and I'd missed some of it, but it didn't feel like two years. It felt like reconnecting after a very long day apart.

It wouldn't take forever for me to catch up with her. She was already there, pulling me along. Every step I took was a mile.

She rested her head on my shoulder, watching the sun come all the way up in the sky. The clouds burned away, streaked with red and gold.

I was the happiest I'd ever been. Underneath was sadness. But it wasn't too painful to bear.

Anastasia had given me the thing I'd longed for all my life. It was everything I'd hoped for, everything I'd wanted. Better than I'd ever let myself imagine.

I lost my father and she gave me that gift.

Nothing could replace him, but the only thing that could comfort me was her hand in mine.

Artemis flew across the sun, straight and silver.

"Look at her wings—still perfect," Anastasia said with a sigh.

"Why wouldn't they be?"

Her hand tightened in mine.

"Last time, she had to save me ... This time she could see I was doing okay."

"You did better than okay."

"So did you."

We stood there, connected, experiencing a moment of pure and perfect relief.

Fulfillment is equal to the difficulty of the job. Those who never face something that could break them will never know the satisfaction of finding yourself whole and triumphant on the other side.

She could have slowed time, stretched it out, made it last.
But the moment was perfect just as it was.

ALL RIVERS FLOW TO THE OCEAN

♪♪ *Once Upon a December—Emile Pandolfi*

I
n the months that followed, it was curious to see what changed and what stayed the same.

Ollie and Axel were married as before, Felix and Irina standing up beside them. The mood in the cathedral was much more solemn, all the white flowers dipped in black. Both the brides had lost their fathers.

Damien sat in the chair next to mine at the head table during the wedding feast. His uncle Evo joined us, a guest of honor. He was the one who brought down the mine.

There was no ball afterward, for which I was grateful. I couldn't have endured living through any version of those hours again.

Ollie left for Denmark a week after the wedding. It was still painful to let her go, but I finally felt ready. When you think you've lost someone forever, you can accept a little time spent apart.

Tatiana and Maria planned to make a long visit to her court the next spring. I didn't know if I'd be able to join them—I was already starting to come around to Prince Christo's point of view that nothing should ever have induced me to accept a crown. The number of things I was supposed to do piled up, a mountain with a mass greater than the world.

Not everyone supported my father's decision to give me his ring. It wasn't until a week before my coronation that Aunt Xenia finally visited the palace for a brief and awkward tea where she informed me that, "though she'd been hard on me, it was all for my good."

"Thank you, Aunt Xenia. You're nothing if not educational."

She gave me a beady look.

I smiled back at her, blandly.

I was learning from Grandma Minnie how to make my point in a quieter way.

I had no father or grandfather to show me how to be Tsar. Minnie had always been beloved by the people—and maybe that was the truest guide. The people are the mirror: what happens to them is a reflection of who you are. You're a king of nothing if your people are miserable.

And I had Damien. He'd always forced me to look at myself clearly. Gods, it pissed me off at times ... but where would I be without him? *What* would I be?

I told Damien every detail of our other life together. I told him how dark our world had become, how deep we'd sunk in sadness. But also how brave he'd been.

"You were the one who saved us all."

Everyone has a single life. You lay it down, and it's over. That's why it's the most precious gift, the one you can only give once.

Damien gave his life for a chance at a better world.

I was the only one who remembered that future, the only one who experienced it. That was my cross to bear, like Damien bore his when he walked to his death alone so I wouldn't lose hope. I bore the weight of what happened so it wouldn't happen again.

When I looked down at my arms, the scars had disappeared but the memories hadn't.

Late in December, I visited the Mariinsky theater to see Anna Pavlova perform the Sugarplum Fairy in the Nutcracker suite.

She wore a gown that seemed made of spun sugar, sparkling strands of pink and lavender woven through her hair. She skipped and leaped across the stage, playful, teasing, lighter than air.

The theater smelled of the gingerbread mansions in the bakery windows all down the street, fresh-dipped candy apples, and spiced roasted nuts.

We'd managed a decent harvest late in the fall, and this winter was no colder than normal. No Rusyan would want a year entirely without snow.

After the show, I visited Anna backstage, congratulating her on the enchanting performance. She remembered me from the night Damien and I saw her dance at the Chinese theater, but nothing more.

I would never forget what she'd done for me. I'd never forget what any of them had done—my survival depended on a chain of people who helped me, protected me, and fought with me until the end.

Damien and I did all we could to reward anyone who stood by us in another time.

Nina Ivanova was the first to receive an anonymous donation. We sent her enough money to set up a seamstress shop with Varvara anywhere they liked. She'd already been married quietly to Armand.

She was saved from the sweep of the Spanish Flu because it never happened. Some things changed on their own, but some things changed because I made them. Knowing what happened before, I quarantined the soldiers before they returned home from the front. The flu still spread through parts of southern Rusya, but at only a fraction the loss of life as before.

I found Maritza and sent her to school. Grandma Minnie was working with the Duma to raise the minimum age for laborers and to improve the conditions inside the factories.

I even sent Katinka a new cello, hoping it would help her make first chair.

Of all the gifts given after Rasputin fell, the one most miraculous came from Damien's uncle.

Evo had fought his way through the battle, cutting a route to the mountain path. Alexei joined him. Evo hadn't known the thin, pale youth riding at his side was the Tsarevich—all he saw was my brother's bravery in a hail of bullets and blades.

They set the charges together and brought the mine down, with no one inside but Katya.

Alexei's health failed quickly afterward. He didn't want to find another vampyr to heal him.

"If I die, I die master of myself."

On a cold night that winter, Evo came to the palace door.

He rode one of the shaggy plains horses. His traveling cloak and the hard frost on his mustache showed how far he'd come.

When I saw him on the step, I thought something awful had happened to Damien. He'd been back home in his village—the Cossacks hadn't yet chosen a new Ataman.

All that had happened was Damien showed Evo my letter where I wrote how ill Alexei had become.

Without speaking to anyone, his uncle rode to Tsarskoye Selo.

"I don't know if it'll do any good," Evo grunted, pushing his way inside in a swirl of snow, "but I'll try to help your brother."

There was no chanting, no secrecy about it. He put a rubber tube in his arm and ran it down into the crook of Alexei's elbow. After draining a pint of his blood into Alexei's arm, my brother's color turned better than it had in weeks.

The treatment lasted longer than Rasputin's, and Evo was willing to do it at intervals if it wasn't an inconvenience to him.

"I won't be riding up here again, that's for damn sure."

Alexei was thrilled at the idea of joining the Cossack host. He'd always wanted to be a soldier.

In all the irony of fate, I was jealous of him. Now that I was finally going to be Tsar, I wished I could take Alexei's place instead.

The burden of ruling terrified me. I planned to give power to the Duma and ministers; I wanted to spread the load. I'd still make mistakes. Things would go wrong, and it would be on my shoulders.

EARLY IN THE NEW YEAR, Stana gave birth to her daughter Celine. Nikolasha was there to see it—it happened at his country dacha, Melitza there as midwife.

We traveled to visit them, taking a sleigh through the snow pulled by a dozen white reindeer. Damien seemed leery to give me the reins, perhaps remembering my arm hanging at an awful angle. I let him drive, only so I could keep my hands warm inside his clothes.

Meeting an even smaller, younger version of Celine was an odd sensation. She was newly arrived in the world, and where she'd come from, who could say? I'd been there myself, and even I didn't know.

Damien didn't want to risk holding her, even with gloves, even with how far he'd come controlling his power.

He watched from a distance as Nikolasha cradled the infant dwarfed by the great slabs of his arms. Her hair stood up in a tuft, gingery eyelashes laying against dusky cheeks.

Stana looked calm and composed already. She was still water that nothing could disturb. Perhaps because she accepted the future, seen and unseen.

She wore a linen shift, her long hair parted in the center. With the baby at her breast, you could paint her on an altar as the Holy Mother.

Melitza sat before the fire wearing a velvet suit, smoking a pipe.

She took a light puff, careful to direct the smoke up the chimney and away from the baby.

I'd just set down all the gifts, the gilded rattles and silver spoons, and the great jeweled egg we'd brought all the way here in the foot of the sleigh, wrapped carefully in rabbit skins we'd leave for the baby.

"You saw her in another time?" Melitza pointed the stem of the pipe at the tufty egg that was the top of the baby's head over Nikolasha's freckled forearm.

I nodded.

"And Stana read for you." Melitza pointed at Damien.

"Hm," he grunted.

"So you believe now?" she crowed at him triumphantly.

Damien looked surly for a moment, but the baby was a magnetic presence in the room, so fragile and impossible seeming. He softened.

"If I did want a reading ... I'd take it from Stana, not some vampire. They can't seem to get their symbols straight."

Stana gave her beautiful, enigmatic smile.

"Would you like one now?"

I waited, unsure what Damien would say.

After a moment, he nodded.

"I want to see."

Stana plucked a hair from the crown of Damien's head. She took her sister's pipe, dropped the hair in the bowl, and puffed on the stem. When she exhaled, the smoke drifted in front of the fire, slow and delicate, luminescent with flame.

A vision kindled in the sparks—Damien's face, all aglow, looking down at the baby in his hands. An infant girl with a head of red hair.

Damien's arm slipped around my waist, his fingers gripping my hip.

"When?" he asked Stana, a little hoarse.

"When you're ready," she said.

On the sleigh ride home, I nervously asked Damien, "But you're not ... ready to be ready right now or anything, are you?"

He laughed, low in his chest. "No. She just gave me hope."

"That you could hold our baby?"

"That our baby would be like you."

I leaned against his shoulder. It was warm and strong in a way that soothed my soul. I loved him so hard it hurt.

"I want her to be everything good in you and me, and better than both of us. Later. In a while. When we're ready."

He laughed. It shook my whole body. I loved the way he held the reins, how large his hands were in his mittens. His jaw was widening already, his shoulders filling out. He was already becoming the Damien I'd known.

And we were both becoming something new together.

Something good, I hoped.

IT TAKES a long time to get a law passed in Rusya, even when you're Tsar.

After almost two years exactly, when time caught up at last, it was the eve of the Great Gift to the Cossacks. The ministers insisted on calling it that. They couldn't bear to lose face by anything less than pompously gifting the Cossacks their own land in recognition of services to the state.

I told no one until I told Damien himself. I showed him the document, stamped and sealed and signed with my full name and title, *Anastasia I, Tsarina of Astrakhan and all northern territories, ruler of Iveria, Lady of the Cherkess and Mountain Princes, and Empress of all Rusya.*

"The Duma put it through. I had to trade them—well, never mind what, we'll deal with that later. Just know it's all official and can't be taken back."

Damien stared blankly at the seal, the double-headed eagle in gold.

"You did it," I said to him. "You freed your people. And you didn't have to kill my dad."

He shook his head slowly at me.

"Anastasia ..."

"I'm a Tsar, not a saint."

He pulled me into his arms and hugged me so hard my ribs groaned.

"Thank you."

"You don't have to thank me," I murmured, lips against his. "Your queen is only here to serve you ..."

He pulled me tight against his body, hand on my back.

"You know ... I do like the sound of that."

The sweetest part of starting over was watching Damien experience human touch all over again. I could have lived those days a thousand times, and sometimes did when I used the memory-keeper.

On that particular day, we'd met and surpassed the expertise we'd been developing on our old timeline. We could really and truly take our time.

Pleasure had become so much more than a build and climax. It became a series of waves we could ride forever, fed on our feelings for each other.

When I looked into Damien's eyes and touched his bare skin, there were no limits, no edges. I thought of everything he'd done for me and what I'd do for him. It made anything less than that seem easy.

A Cossack's no gentleman. He's a warrior, an animal, a wild thing. That's what I wanted, because that's what I'd always been in my heart.

Sometimes we tore each other apart.

Sometimes we pushed to see what we could do.

The frenzy brought us back to life when the real world was hard, when our minds grew confused.

We escaped into each other. And when we came back, we were ready to try again.

I wanted to give Damien much more than a piece of paper ... I wanted to give him a perfect day.

I held the memory-keeper in my hands, clutching it tight. We were out in the steppes, in the high, browning grass, a blanket spread beneath us. The horses grazed a short way off.

"You know I'm making the official procession next week ..."

He smiled. "Yes, I remember."

"And everything's been decent enough so far, no major disasters ... I thought we should lock it in."

"Lock it in?"

"Capture a perfect day. One we could always return to if we ever ran off course."

Damien's eyes had become the most beautiful color to me. That deep moody green was the shade of all our conversations when I remembered them in my head.

"I don't know if that would ever work again ..."

"I don't mean literally. I mean ... Rasputin wasn't always so blind. You don't realize where you're going—you don't see what you've become."

"That's not going to happen to us." Damien kissed me firmly on the mouth. "You're my anchor and I'm yours. We're not drifting anywhere."

"Always tell me the truth," I begged him. "Even about myself."

"*Especially* about ourselves."

"We'll save today as a guide—a moment when we knew where we were pointed. When we knew what we wanted to be."

Damien tilted his head, examining me.

"And what are we?"

"People who can live with their mistakes."

"We've already made one ... we should have captured what we did earlier..."

I pressed the crescent moon, started the memory-keeper, set it whirring.

"That's a mistake we can fix."

He rolled me over off the blanket, pinning me in the sweet, dry grass. The earth was sun-warm beneath my back. Bits of golden chaff floated in the air and caught in his dark hair.

He touched the features of my face, tracing their lines.

I traced the scars on his jaw, his eyebrow, the bridge of his nose. He had many more on his shoulders, his chest, his back, pale against his tan skin, tiger stripes in reverse.

They always seemed so right on him.

The mind is a magician that doesn't follow its own rules.

I kissed Damien, breathing him in. I took off his clothes slowly, the ones he'd only just put on again. His body was so strong and so unlike mine, it was a bit like taking the saddle off a horse, everything beneath larger than you expected.

He was muscled like a horse, thick in the thighs. Sometimes I teased him he was jealous of my actual horse when I went riding too long. He gave me Mercury to keep, and I brought her with me everywhere I went.

Damien pinned me down on the earth, all his weight on top of me. He growled in my ear, "You think she can give you a better ride than me?"

He pulled me on top of him, the sun in my hair, the breeze in my lungs. I'd brought Damien out here because I knew his favorite place to be alone with me was in the wide open outdoors.

The breeze ran over our naked skin like a hundred extra hands. I rode on top of him in rhythm, his hips rolling beneath me. It really did feel like speed in my face, like the wind rushing by.

He was strong, breathing hard like an animal, thick like a brute, his hands on my hips, controlling each stroke.

I rolled my hips forward like I did when riding, arching my back, hands linked loosely behind me, bouncing upright. I closed my eyes, the two sensations overlapping, the real sun and real air bending fantasy and reality in my brain. All my favorite feelings blended together, sensual, sexual, recreational.

The waves broke over me, harder, faster, closer together, until I was dashed apart.

Damien rolled me over again, mounting me from behind. I was right about Cossacks—wild and uncivilized, bandits who take what they want ...

Of course, that's exactly what you need in a lover. Or the consort of a queen.

He pinned me down and rode me as I'd ridden him, mercilessly, until I panted like I'd run a race. We were both scratched and filthy before we finished, certain we'd started a perfect day.

EARLY IN THE AFTERNOON, we rode into the Cossack village. We visited all of Damien's family that remained, including Kristoff and his many daughters, and Myron and his cheerful wife. I wanted to spend the day where I knew Damien would be happiest. Most of all, I wanted to capture the memory of his face when he told everyone they'd finally be free. No more ten years of service—no more fealty to the Tsar.

I visited Alexei at the same time. He'd been happily staying with Evo for six months now, serving in the militia and raiding with the Cossacks. In the borderlands, no one knew he'd been the Tsarevich. He'd shaved his hair like a Cossack and tanned golden brown, his hair white as wheat.

How two such prickly people seemed to get along so well was a mystery. They both liked to drink and fight and live in a mess, so all the important things aligned.

Evo lost his brother and got mine instead. Damien was Nikolasha's ward, and now Alexei belonged with the Cossacks. Everything reversed, everything had its opposite.

Damien and I walked all around the village, seeing everyone he loved. He was giving up the chance to be Ataman to come to St. Petersburg with me. We'd visit often—even though the Cossacks wouldn't be my people anymore, they'd always be his.

Damien read the Declaration of the Great Gift aloud at the fire dance that night. The shouting and whooping went on until we were all hoarse.

I charged off Damien's smile, enough to last a hundred years.

The Cossacks had already selected Damien's uncle Ivash as their next Ataman. He seemed more annoyed than pleased about his new position. I got to watch Myron swallow down his disappointment and pretend to be happy for a second time.

Damien and I stayed at his old house, sleeping in a hammock on the open porch because the night was so fair. I swung in his arms, the hammock suspended above an ocean of stars.

The next day the Cossacks painted every door red on the houses of the men who'd given their lives in the fight that won their freedom.

DECREES CAN BE PASSED MUCH FASTER than laws. The first one I signed was for Aunt Olga, granting her a divorce from her husband.

Only a few weeks later, she happened to meet a handsome young officer at a ball in St. Petersburg. I had a feeling before I met him that he'd be the very same officer who pestered her to dance the night of Ollie's wedding.

Not only was Nikolai Kulikovsky the same man, but he'd grown no less persistent. In a matter of months, he persuaded Olga to give matrimony another try. This second pairing was far happier—Kulikovsky retired from the army and took Aunt Olga home to his estate in Kiev so he could devote all his time and attention to her. Their first son was born ten months later.

Olga's former husband, Peter of Oldenburg, hardly seemed to notice.

Maria didn't need permission from anyone to marry the man she loved— just the courage to do it. She'd be moving to the country with him, which to Maria felt as foreign and thrilling as trekking into the jungles of Africa.

"You always said you wanted to milk a cow," Mama said tearfully. She wasn't dealing well with everyone leaving, particularly Alexei, whose departure sent her bed-bound for a month. She'd aged a decade since losing my father.

Sylvie Buxhoevden was gone, Liza Taneeva permanently dismissed when I explained to my mother what Rasputin must have done to her husband to steal the power of sleep. I wished I had evidence but could only be satisfied with the fact that in another time, Liza had been eaten first.

Tatiana visited the Danish court to see Ollie and showed no signs of wanting to return. She'd resumed her studies with Juliana Jorgensen, and I suspected, rekindled a relationship more than professorial ...

In her loneliness, Mama finally reconciled with Grandma Minnie. If the two of them could agree on anything, it was how desperately they missed my father.

Grandma even moved back into Alexander Palace so it was the three of us together, three generations of women that formed the core of my new court, with Damien my right hand.

Irina came to visit often, less often once she fell pregnant with a little boy who soon proved to be more trouble than his father ever dreamed of being. Felix Yusupov mostly recovered from his poisoning. He was never quite as handsome as before, but the gold teeth that replaced the ones he'd lost were quite dashing when he smiled.

Ollie was the first of my siblings to have children—the first *and* the second when she presented Prince Axel with a set of twins. The Danes had invented little rucksacks with holes to stick your baby's legs through. Ollie and Axel strapped a baby each to their backs and happily hiked the Alps, sailed the straits, and even played tennis with the twins in tow.

Only Dimitri Pavlovich remained hopelessly single. Maria said it was because he never got over Ollie, while Tatiana said he'd been in love with Felix all along.

He'd come back to the palace to drink all that remained of Papa's best wine. Once that was gone, he turned out to be a useful assistant, introducing Damien to the complexities of the Rusyan Imperial Court.

We hoped to make them less complex in time, but that might be a miracle beyond anyone's ability.

Damien and I were married all over again in a ceremony a hundred times grander than our solitary cave of ice. I wore a dress almost as large as the carriage that carried us up to the cathedral. It was ridiculous and heavy and I hated it with all my heart, but I wore it and smiled and waved to the thousands of people who came out to cheer us. Not every battle was worth fighting.

We knelt before the altar and said our vows, to cherish and protect each other and the country in our hands. The priest set the crowns on our heads. We stood and kissed in the blizzard of blossoms that fluttered down. Damien glowed with so much happiness that not a single petal browned as it brushed his skin.

I changed into what I wanted to wear to dance, the blue cotton dress that had belonged to Damien's mother.

The look on his face when he saw it was the very best part of the day.

I spun in his arms, the ballroom of Alexander Palace filled with golden lanterns in the Cossack tradition. Some of Damien's family had come, and some of mine. I hoped everyone we loved was there in some way, on this side or the other.

As we danced together, his forehead pressed to mine, the barrier between us dissolved and we became as one for a moment in time. I saw our first wedding through his eyes, and he saw it through mine. We experienced it all over again, a memory we'd lost and found that had never truly disappeared.

I resented nothing anymore.

It all happened as it had to.

All we have are the days given to us. I was lucky enough to get a few more.

THE END

IF YOU'D LIKE TO GO INSIDE THE MIND OF RASPUTIN, CHECK OUT
HIS ORIGIN STORY ON MY PATREON:

AFTERWORD

If I'd known how difficult this book would be to write, I might not have started. I would have missed out on the most rewarding project of my life.

Most of what I knew about the Romanovs came from the animated film. As I started to dig into the research, I realized the story was much more complicated.

The Romanovs were proud autocrats. I was essentially writing about a dictator princess.

Since my story was set in a fantasy world, I could change anything I wanted. But it felt disingenuous to make the Romanovs heroes—and disrespectful to the people who'd been oppressed by them.

Imperial Russia was a brutal place. I chose to start my book with Anastasia as a child, because I felt it was crucial to feel what it's like to be indoctrinated in an environment where your parents are also the rulers of your nation.

I wanted Anastasia to represent the Romanovs, but also all of us. We're all raised in a certain culture with certain expectations. We're taught what's right and wrong by people with their own biases and agendas.

And we have our own selfish impulses. It's so easy to justify what we want, and what works for us. The Romanovs thought they were good people. They loved their family members. But they did horrible things when they felt justified.

The mirror on the cover of Anastasia is the key symbol of the book. It means looking at ourselves clearly. Taking responsibility for our real actions and motivations.

Rasputin is Anastasia's dark mirror—he shares her same temptations.

Damien is her true mirror. He forces her to be honest with herself.

As I was writing the book, Putin attacked Ukraine. It's a conflicts with roots going back hundreds of years, the same cruelty and oppression still happening today.

I asked myself, why are we so obsessed with Anastasia?

It's because of our dream of what we wish she could have been. What we wish Russia could have been.

Ultimately this story became a fantasy of what our world could be like if we had leaders who loved the people more than themselves.

That's what Anastasia has come to symbolize to people all over the world —a people's princess, someone who lived like everyone else and developed compassion.

Someone on team human.

–SOPHIE

ACKNOWLEDGMENTS

This book would not exist without all the people who carried me the last mile like Frodo and the ring.

I am so incredibly grateful to my alpha readers Janessa, Stephanie, and Arin. They gave me insightful and specific advice that tightened up the story and made it so much better.

Thank you to my editors Crystal, Elise, and Katie, whose mastery of the English language is humbling.

Thank you Emily and Nathan for creating a stunning cover for a very difficult book. Through several iterations, you worked tirelessly to perfect the final form. Emily you were there at the most unreasonable hours when we needed you, with your flawless eye and design wizardry.

More than anyone, I have to acknowledge Line's incredible contributions to this book. We worked collaboratively on this project, trading chapters and illustrations. She had a huge impact on character design, symbolism, and the emotion of the scenes, feeding me with her art and inspiring me every day.

Thank you to the rest of my incredible team Maya, Traven, Kika, and Kamrah. I would live in a garbage heap and nothing would get done without you.

For my boys Weston and Rhett, I'm the luckiest mom in the world. You two astonished me this year with your personal growth. Same for Paigey, my light and my love.

Much gratitude to my publicist Sarah Ferguson who took care of me at book signings and gave me so much good advice.

All the love and thanks to my mom and dad, who taught me all the best things I know, and for my little sister Angie who was my very first reader.

For BD who was such a huge part of this book. So many of the best ideas and funniest lines are from him.

And finally, thank you thank you thank you to all my friends in the book community. This was a rough year. When I was at my lowest, you wonderful people poured so much love on me. Every time I got discouraged, I thought how happy you'd be if I wrote you something beautiful and made your childhood Anastasia dreams come true. That's what kept me going.

Love you all,

SOPHIE

When I started writing, I wanted to create intelligent and powerful female characters who were allowed to be flawed. I've always loved dark and twisty storylines. I thought so many of my interests were strange until I found an online community of readers who love all the same things.

I write all kinds of stories including dark romance, fantasy, and suspense. I'm a sucker for anti-heroes and moral dilemmas.

My readers mean everything to me. I couldn't do what I love for a living without you, and I'd be lost without the outlet of writing.

The Love Lark Letter
Click here to join my newsletter

Merch & Signed Books → sophielark.com

Exclusive Content
Sophie Lark Patreon

Rowdy Reader Group
The Love Larks Reader Group